ANYWHERE BUT EARTH

ANYWHERE BUT EARTH

new tales of outer space

Coeur de Lion

First published in 2011
by coeur de lion publishing
www.coeurdelion.com.au
Please direct all enquiries to the publisher at:
keith@coeurdelion.com.au

Compilation copyright © Keith Stevenson 2011

Copyright in each story remains with the individual author © 2011

ISBN 9780987158703

The right of the individual authors to be identified as the authors of their respective stories has been asserted in accordance with the *Copyright Amendment (Moral Rights) Act 2000.*

This work is copyright. Apart from any use as permitted under the *Copyright Act 1968*, no part may be reproduced, copied, scanned, stored in a retrieval system, recorded or transmitted in any form or by any means, without the prior written permission of the publisher.

Typeset in Eras Demi ITC/ Times New Roman

Printed by Lightning Source

National Library of Australia Cataloguing-in-Publication entry:

Title: Anywhere but Earth : new tales of outer space / edited by
          Keith Stevenson.
Edition: 1st ed.
ISBN: 9780987158703 (pbk.)
Subjects:Outer space--Fiction.
Other Authors/Contributors: Stevenson, Keith.
Dewey Number: 823.0876208

Contents

for the dreamers of 'out there'

Murmer

Calie Voorhis

Margaret sits in the meadow, the pine-cone needle in her left hand. The sun is warm on her face except where the breeze, swaying the yellow tufts of grass, brushes past the tracks of slow tears.

It was all unknown then, this new world, Morning.

In Morning there were no streets—not as she knew them, lined up in straight grids—no houses and shops. The city of Viridian was green, not steel and stone, filled with immense trees soaring up to the grey sky. Walkways on large branches made bridges, and blue leaves drifted down. Viridian was full of the *tree denizens*; crowded in the dim trails with quiet beings who nodded as they passed her. Bright purple birds crooned and flitted in the upper branches. Margaret took a deep breath and tasted the solace of rich loam, welcoming after the recycled tang of the spaceship.

They'd come to the planet Morning from Alba. Before Alba, there was Manto IV. Margaret lost track of the other worlds. Barry's job as envoy took them places, took them into time dilation and away from her friends, always roaming, never taking root. Once she'd thought the life exciting, glamorous; now the adventure had paled into a constant move.

After they'd arrived at their house, one of a cluster of alien cubes stuck like mushrooms among the forest, Barry had thrown the carisacks on the bare bed. 'Here,' he'd said. 'Go ahead and unpack, will you?' He was out the door without even a kiss.

She waited for him to come home that night, in the clean house with the sleeproom and their few possessions carefully placed—the wedding picture of the two of them on the same wall in the living room, where it always hung. As she stared at the kitchen, she knew nothing changed.

'Where's dinner?' he asked when he came in, long after dark. He kissed her, a quick peck on the lips, followed by a brief hug.

Margaret nodded towards the reheater. He ate without a word and went to bed, his back against hers.

The great city of Viridian is an island bounded by rivers on either side, one a deep slow beast with a broad silver back and slow rafts crossing it, the other swift and rocky, tearing torrents and arching bridges. The trees themselves, the denizens of Morning, tower up to the sky, some as big as a stardrive.

The meadow in the middle of the city is free from the rustling of business, free from the shade of leaves, free from the denizens and base personnel. It is reserved for those who seek the change, who are deciding, like Margaret. Like many before, she is just the latest alien to make a choice.

Margaret wandered into the centre one day, a net of groceries from the base commissary slung over her shoulder. The light of the open area attracted her and she found herself taking a winding path of grey and white flecked pebbles to the edge.

The broad meadow was full of pink spring flowers. Margaret stepped out of the shadows and into the lea and resisted an urge to do cartwheels. She picked some flowers and held them to her nose. The bouquet smelled like lavender, roses, and the bitter resin of a cut Yule tree.

'Are you wishing to change?' he asked her.

Margaret was startled and dropped the flowers.

'I'm sorry,' she said. 'I didn't know anyone was here.' His tall form swayed in the sunlight, shaped like a human, if a human were a weeping willow. His eyes peered blue out of a face embedded in gossamer leaves. Where he should have had skin he had pale green pliable bark, and twigs for hair.

'Do you wish to change?' he asked again. 'If not, you should leave, Margaret.'

'You know my name.' She shifted the net of food higher on her shoulder and smoothed down the front of her faded blue dress.

'How could I not, when so many of my leaves see you about the city, see you lost in Morning, regretting what you've left? I am Murmer,' he said. He held out his left hand.

The hand was gnarled like an old branch, covered in grey bark.

'I believe it is the custom of your people to shake hands?' His voice wavered. A gust of wind swept back Margaret's hair.

'You've got the wrong hand,' she said. She set her

grocery net down and held out her right hand.

He laughed and switched hands. Up and down he swung her arm.

She'd expected his hand to be rough, insubstantial, for she'd seen the denizens drifting through the dappled city. But he was smooth, warm, solid, and the wooden touch of his thumb on her wrist set her pulse racing.

The wind shifts to the east now, blowing the scent of winter from the city—the dry mould of leaf rot, the sweet of dried grass. Soon it will be winter and the rains again.

Margaret wonders if Murmer is already gone with the rest of the leaves, faded into the loam.

If she plunges the needle into her arm, if she takes the challenge, she'll be the fifth from the base this year. Two made the metamorphosis from human to tree, are now seeds in the city, waiting spring and the planting. Two failed and are nothing more than dry husks, pith rotted out from within. She will change the odds to one side or another if she commits.

Or she can lay the needle down. Leave Morning with Barry, who even now waits for her, back at the cookie-cutter house, bags packed and in his pressed uniform. She can continue to follow him through the vastness of space, trailing along, belonging nowhere. The feel of the starched collar as she laid his shirt out on their bed this morning is still in her hands.

The second time they met, she thought she knew what she was doing. What did it hurt for her to have a friend on this planet, she thought, wheeling a hovercart full of fresh clothing from the cleaners.

Something of her own, this friend, Murmer. Not like the tidy base house, which wasn't hers, or the clothing, which Barry bought for her, or his friends, who were jolly and bright, full of uniformed pomp and talk of wars in far-off systems.

The second time they met, Margaret and Murmer sat in the meadow and talked of their lives. He told her of the wonders he'd seen through the eyes of his fellow forest, the knowledge contained in the dense pith of his tree, and the way the deep roots tasted the planet's core.

Margaret told him of the travel, exciting at first, each new place an adventure, now paled and stale, how she missed the Barry she'd married—the way his eyes used to light up when he saw her, how she'd grown to miss a place of her own, a voice of her own.

The third time Margaret and Murmer met, they kissed. It wasn't anything Margaret had planned, she was just looking for a friend, but something in his blue eyes, the way the crinoline leaves lined his face, the way his hand trembled against her back, turned the half-attempt of a hug, foreign to them both, into something else. The kiss tasted like winter on the planet she'd been born on, full of the piney taste of fir and crisp nights.

'Tell me about the change,' she said one day weeks later. Murmer sat down beside her on the slight hill with the sun warming the fresh grass.

'Once upon a time,' Murmer said. 'That *is* how you begin stories of long ago?'

'Or stories that were never quite real.' Margaret rotated his hand in hers and let his fingers wrap around her wrist.

He dropped a kiss on the top of her head and pulled her closer, wrapping his legs around to create a nest of sorts. Murmer smelled like the tree he resembled, sweet and spicy, and underneath, a damp rising of earth.

'Once upon a time,' Murmer said, 'everything talked and walked and danced at midnight, in forest glades under the full moon. The light flowed from inside to light up the moon, not the other way around. The moon's glow was reflected joy, not dim shadows of sunlight over the earth's umbra. Eclipses vanished the day and allowed the aspens' quaking to shed through the wastes. This was before, when the trees were still young, before the first aliens came and learned to choose, to decide to stop roaming, the way we did an aeon ago.'

Murmer shifted. Margaret could feel him hard against her back. Barry had told her this morning about an administrative assistant leaving the base for a 'native'. The rosy cheeks on Barry's broad face had dimpled in disgust and Margaret had turned away to make the bed, hoping to hide the rising flush.

Murmer continued. His soft voice lilted as the wind rustled over the grass, as the breeze blew through the city. He told her of the awakening of the great trees, the first visitors from the other worlds, the creation of the denizens, each part of the whole tree.

She stopped him then. 'Do you mean you're not really you?'

His grip on her shoulder tightened then relaxed. 'I am Murmer, yes. I am an individual, also part of the tree, just a leaf among others. Each is different but part of the whole. I am the forest. I am a dream.'

Margaret fell silent, reminded with a shock to her

stomach that this person was not human. His hands rubbed her shoulder. She shook them off. 'I think I should go home,' she said. 'I don't think I should see you any more.'

Margaret waited for him to call after her. When she glanced back, he just stood there and swayed.

When had Barry changed? Or had it been her?

Margaret couldn't pinpoint the day when love had died. He didn't kiss her when he came home any more. She didn't miss him during the long days. They ate their meals in silence and rolled away from each other in bed. She wanted him back—the one who used to smile— almost as much as she wanted something to call her own. Perhaps Barry was the only thing she could have, could possess in this roaming life.

She turns the needle over and over in her hand, testing the sharp point on one thumb, then the other.

Her heart is a betrayer, she thinks. Black and barren. Will the needle, will the becoming, ease the pain? Will belonging to a place quench the urge for another person?

Margaret didn't see Murmer for the rest of the spring and most of the lazy days of summer. She kept herself occupied with her errands, dusting, and cleaning. The pit in her heart grew and overtook her body, till she moved around by memory alone, numb. She indulged in her vices, more glasses of wine with dinner than she should, more cocktails at the endless parties. She spent a whole day in bed.

She tried to woo her husband back. In the night, she

reached for him. His familiar fingers woke response in her. When he left for work the next morning, the smile was back, and he whistled on the way out.

'Can we stay here?' she asked him one day when he came home from the embassy.

'And give up space?' He kissed her on her forehead. 'Become a grounder? You know you don't want that.'

'Perhaps not,' she said, returning his hug, knowing he would never settle down.

Through the summer, she learned to love him again, or to at least pretend to the possibility.

One day the urge rose within, a restless itch in her legs, and she set the dust cloth down and headed for the meadow. Just to get some sun, she told herself. Murmer would have moved on by now anyway.

He was there, waiting. His leaves, like bright green hair, rustled in the noon sun.

She stopped on the edge of the meadow, in the border of the shadow of the city. Her heart thumped. A few moments passed. Murmer stood still, rooted. She forced her feet to walk towards him, not run.

'I never finished telling you,' he said. 'About the change.' He raised a hand towards her, like he would brush the hair from her eyes, then dropped it.

Margaret forced a smile, feeling her lips tighten. 'Tell me,' she said as she sat down.

Murmer sat a few feet away from her. His leaves were fading, she noted. Yellowing around the edges.

She kept her hands tight together in her lap as he talked.

'Wait,' she said, stopping him as her mind caught up to his words. 'If I change, will I still be me?'

Murmer shrugged and held out his hands to the sun. 'What are you?'

'Will I still be me?' she repeated.

'You will be more,' he said. This time when he reached for her hand, she let him take it. 'You will not be the same. Parts of you will walk in the forest while you remain planted. You'll remember this life like a dance, a dream, a moment.'

Margaret wonders if she wants change or wants death. She knows what she wants she can't have, never could have. Not now, not ever—Murmer. All she can have is the planet, a home, a place to rest, to stay.

She pounds the ground with a fist.

Margaret resolved to be good. She kept the house clean, programmed dinner for the other officers and their wives. Smiled when she knew she should, refilled glasses and made small talk. And then the letter came, in the autumn.

'Darling,' Barry said to her one night. 'It's finally happened.'

'Yes,' she said, as she loaded the dishes. Her mind was on Barry and Murmer, running in the useless circles it always ran in.

'We're out of here. Our transfer came through. We're going to New Melbourne. Isn't it great?'

'How long?' she asked.

'Two weeks. Better get packing.' Barry chuckled.

'I'm not going,' she said, the words sticking in her throat. 'I want to stay.'

Barry turned to her, disbelief reddening his cheeks.

'Here?'

'Yes. I like this planet. I want to settle down, I want to stop moving.'

'Oh, honey,' he said, gathering her in his arms. 'I know this is hard on you. I promise, one day, we'll stop. When my next enlistment is up, I won't renew.'

He would. She'd heard this before.

'Come on, say you'll follow me, just a little further.'

She nodded, to please him, to stop the argument from the familiar circle it turned in every time they left for another world. He left for the sleeproom, and the glass in her hand shattered on the floor.

Margaret hurried out to the meadow the next morning.

Murmer waited there, a thing she'd grown used to. He was aflame in colour, this Murmer, full of orange edges with red leaf centres. His hair was golden yellow, and the smaller leaves of his beard bright umber.

'We're leaving,' she said. She ran towards him.

'I need to say goodbye,' Murmer said at the same time. He reached for her hands and she let him take them. The throb of her pulse quickened.

'Where are you going?' they said together.

Margaret tightened her grasp on his hands. 'You look beautiful.'

'As do you.' He let go of her right hand and traced the contours of her chin.

'Barry's been transferred. To New Melbourne. He expects me to go with him.'

'And will you?'

'It depends on you.' She stepped forward and tilted her head up to meet his blue eyes.

Murmer let go of her and stepped back. 'I won't be here much longer. It's my time to turn, to rejoin the dream.'

Margaret's hands fell to her sides. 'What?' Her heart stuttered.

'It's autumn. Soon it will be winter.'

'So you're going to hibernate?' She knew, even as she asked it, it wasn't what he meant.

'Trees change in the autumn,' he said. His head tilted to the side to regard her.

Margaret sat on the ground with a thud that travelled all the way up her spine. She looked at her hands, at the sunlight bright on them, noticed they trembled. With a gasp, she remembered to breathe.

'You're going to leave me,' she said.

'I was always going to leave you,' Murmer replied. 'I thought you knew.'

'No.' Margaret pushed the fingertips of her hands together. A drop of salt water fell on her thumb, a tear.

Murmer sat down beside her and she could hear the creak of old wood. 'How could you not know?' He sounded confused.

Margaret shrugged and watched the tears drip down to stain her blue skirt. 'We've been so many places, Barry and I. And they're all the same once we get there. The same base layout, the same houses. You never even have to leave if you don't want to. So I stopped paying attention. It was enough to pack, to unpack, every time. To lose my friends every time. I stopped caring about where we were. Once, I thought Barry would be enough . . . ' Her voice cracked and she clenched her teeth. Far away, she could hear the rustle of the city. Beyond that the roar of a spaceship took flight from the base.

'I wanted to stay here, with you,' Margaret said when she thought her voice was under control. 'It was silly of me, I see that now.' The trembling had taken over her entire body. Her shoulders shook and her chest was tight with muzzled sobs. Margaret felt a touch on her shoulder. Sunlight swam in her vision.

'Not silly,' he said. 'If I could wish such a thing, I would. I can't. I can't even wish it.'

Margaret took a deep breath. The air burned in her lungs. 'Of course not,' she said. 'Please forgive me for being an idiot.'

Murmer brushed his shoulder against hers. The comfort he offered let the sobs escape and she cried until her face was covered with tears.

A thought occurred to her, a wave of hope spread out from the pit in her stomach. 'Will you be back in the spring? Because I could wait for you.'

He pulled Margaret to her feet and wrapped her in his arms then. 'No,' he said into her hair. 'I won't be back. Others will, for their season, but not this me. I'll be a different tree.'

Margaret felt her body become ice and stone. The shaking stopped. Stupidly, she'd thought she could have it all—the relationship and the world too. A home, not dependant on a person, but with someone, a place she wouldn't move on from, with this being, this Murmer, who was as rooted as she wanted to be.

'All I can offer you is the change,' he said. He reached into his side and pulled out a device, shaped like a pine-cone with a sharp needle at the end.

'What good does that do me? Does it bring me you?'

Her voice rose.

'No. All it offers is the chance for permanence. The chance to live, rooted in a spot, to grow under the shade until you reach the sun, to be part of the whispering city. To, in time, have leaves of your own, all the parts of yourself free to change, to wander.'

'To die,' she finished and angrily wiped a tear away.

Murmer shrugged and his body swayed for a moment as a fierce gust blew past, rattling the grass like a wave on the ocean. The crest swept towards them, then past, down the hill. 'Death is only change,' he said.

Margaret watched the grass return upright. 'Would you stay if you could?'

He didn't answer and it was answer enough for her. Margaret took the needle from his hand, not meeting his eyes. She marched away, back stiff. She didn't turn back.

Barry was there when Margaret got home.

'Where have you been?' he asked, leaning over an open beige carisack. 'I started packing.' He grabbed her and spun her around.

She broke free of his embrace, walked into the bathroom, and splashed water on her face. 'Out,' she said from behind the closed doors. 'Went for a walk. Why the rush? Aren't you supposed to be at work?'

'They moved my schedule up. We leave tomorrow.'

Margaret gripped the edge of the bathroom counter with her hands. Of course. Probably better this way. She pulled the needle from her pocket and sat down on the edge of the tub. Baring an arm, she took the needle and started to press it against her skin.

'Are you going to come help me pack?' Barry yelled

from the sleeproom. 'You know I never do it the way you like.' The teasing edge to his tone tore her heart open.

She didn't answer and stared at her bare white arm, at the needle. After a few moments, she put the needle back in her pocket, washed her face again and went to help Barry. He had folded all the shirts wrong and she had to take them out and start over. Margaret snapped each fold into place, stamped down each item of clothing in the suitcase to compact it.

'Are you mad at me?' Barry asked. His red face watched her.

The temples on her forehead throbbed. 'No, I'm not mad at you,' she said. She forced a smile. 'So, where are we going next again?'

In the evening, he took her out for a last meal at the base commissary.

'Do you mind if we walk through the city for a bit?' she asked.

Barry shrugged. 'I thought you didn't like the city.'

'I just want to look at it one last time before we leave.' She angled away so he couldn't see her face.

'Sure.' He took her hand in his. 'We haven't been on a walk together for a while. Remember the glorious beach on Alba?'

Margaret nodded.

'Well, New Melbourne has an ocean to compare. Perhaps we can recreate a few moments?' He nudged her with an elbow. For a moment, Margaret clung to his hand, happy for the warmth and familiar feeling of his fingers.

Viridian was dark with little lamps like fireflies floating high in the trees. Glow globes made dim circles on the lower trails. Margaret and Barry stepped from one halo to the dark, then back into the light.

Denizens passed them quiet on the loam path and Margaret's heart pounded each time. None of them was Murmer.

The night was silent except for the faint trill of insects sounding like tiny violin players. When Barry suggested they return home so he could get some sleep, she agreed.

She tossed and turned all night. Every time she moved, Barry snuggled back up to her. In the quiet hours of the morning, she fell asleep with her legs twined with his, his breath soft on her shoulder.

Margaret sits and the shadows lengthen around her as the sun moves above. In the distance, she hears the roar of an engine and watches the silver spike force its way up into the sky in a column of cloud and fire.

With a sigh, she takes the needle in a steady hand, presses it into the bend of her left arm, and squeezes the trigger. With a tiny pinprick she has made her choice. It doesn't feel like anything at all. She looks at her hands—they still look the same. After a few moments, she realises they're turning green. The code of her cells is changing, morphing, turning from animal to plant. Already she can feel her toes' urge to embed in the dirt, her hairs' need to feel the winter rain.

The wind blows her hair back and she waits for the change to complete. She will root on this planet, Morning, and will be a part of the city, blooming in the spring.

Calie Voorhis is a lifelong fanatic of the fantastic, with over fifteen short story publications, including stories in *Ray Gun Revival*, *Beyond Centauri*, *Fusion Fragment* and *The Online Anathema Anthology*, and print anthologies *Dead Set: A Zombie Anthology*, *Space Sirens*, *Farspace 2*, *DOA—Tales of Extreme Terror*, and *Andromeda Spaceways Inflight Magazine*. She holds a BS in Biology from UNC-Chapel Hill, an MFA in Writing Popular Fiction from Seton Hill University, and is an Odyssey workshop alumna.

Beautiful

Cat Sparks

The invitation to Rukash House had come as a great surprise. Nin accepted, blushing, even though she supposed her inclusion merely served to address the colour balance. *The Remembrance of Oris* required ochre swirls. Nin didn't mind at all. It was exciting to be asked, a treat rarely afforded members of her caste. Rukash House's murals were famed across the continent, each panel depicting a well-known sequence from *The Book of Suhab*.

She took a deep breath and climbed the marble staircase. A prim doorman waited to take her cloak and scarf. Beyond the gilded double gates, such splendour! More finely attired people than she had ever seen gathered in one place before. How dull she felt in her flimsy patterned silk, flat clogs and sand-plain hair.

No-one else from her sector had been invited. She craned her neck, hoping to catch a familiar face, even if it belonged to someone she didn't actually know. Such intricate beadwork on the gowns, star sapphires sewn with silver thread. Jewels so rare she couldn't even name them. Part of her wanted to turn on her heels and flee. Another part was so excited she could barely breathe. Wait till Nok heard all about it. And Asha—she'd plain die of jealousy!

The ballroom's centrepiece was a constellation chandelier. She knew of such things, of course, but had never seen one. A nebular web set in brilliant filigree, it peppered the room with pulses of contentment.

As she stood below it, wondering if she'd have the nerve to see the evening through, Nin sensed *five* beautiful scattered throughout the crowd. How ever had the hostess enticed so many? She must have paid an exorbitant sum, though she'd never admit to the truth of it. The kind of question you weren't supposed to ask.

The five spaced themselves evenly. Glowing admirers took pains to keep a respectful distance. A beautiful moved to stand beside the sculpted nude just a few feet away from Nin. She longed to edge in closer for a look but it was impolite to draw attention by pushing.

There were ways to engage with the beautiful. Stern decorum and polite conceits. You weren't supposed to crowd or box them in. A pose of casual indifference was best; looking without appearing to gawp. Never touch unless one of them touched you first.

The hostess's name was Mija—almost as famous as Rukash House itself. Silver-blonde with skin of russet hue. Her dances were the stuff of legend, gossiped about for months on end. Some whispered she was descended from the Great House of Ezatyra. Others hinted at less salubrious origins.

Nin knew better than to court her attention. She fixed her eyes on all the lovely gowns, then rested them upon the beautiful, impossible as they were to ignore for long. The one nearest Nin sported a fabulous silver-blonde mane. Hair like that took decades to grow, which meant it must have been older than it looked. Completely at ease amidst the ballroom's golden splendour, it radiated smug superiority, shifting through a sequence of poses choreographed to display its perfection to best advantage.

There'd been two silver-blondes in Nin's dorm at Shoushan, way back in childhood when they were identical in all ways but hair. The silver-blondes, Ang and Gita, had been excited even then, enchanted with comprehension of their rarity. Both were utterly certain they would bloom to beauty, as certain as Nin had been that she herself would not. Nin had thought the Shoushan brood mothers cruel, encouraging the silver-blondes so heartily. There was no sure-fire predictor of beauty. No traits that could be encouraged or shaped. When the time was right, you either blemished or you didn't. That was all there was to it.

Some mothers believed they could tell ahead of time. Occasional lucky guesses made them cocky with false knowing. Which was all very well if you kept it to yourself. Another thing to get a hatchling's hopes up. Both those silver-blondes had blemished. In the end, their precious hair meant nothing. The one called Ang had been shamed into exile. The other, Gita, nobody liked to speak of what happened to her. Those Shoushan mothers were never punished for their failings. Nin didn't think that was right.

Not that anything could have quelled the pent-up energies of the hatchlings themselves. The raw excitement during manifestation months. Nin vividly recalled the thrill of it—and the blinding terror. Every night you went to sleep thinking, would tomorrow be the day? Would you awake still safely cocooned in the mottled beige of childhood? Or would the unsubtle taint of failure stain its trail across your flesh? When, at long last, ridges pushed up through your skin, would they be hard and coarse like bristle, or small and delicate as dew-kissed summer buds?

How many mornings had Nin been wrenched from slumber by a chorus of hysterical sobs and shrieks as, one by one, each hatchling was forced to face the truth. They weren't beautiful and never would be. Purple swirls would creep across their skin, overpowering the innocence of childhood. Skin that would harden and ridge over time, as would their stoic little hearts, but for now the mothers would have their hands full mopping up tears and offering consolation to those whose dreams had shattered.

'It's not so bad is it, now, m'dear—ending up like the rest of us?' The most pathetic consolation the old could offer the young. Nin remembered how ancient those mothers had seemed—and how ugly. Now she was as old as they'd been then and she saw the world through very different eyes.

Nin had not applied for motherhood. The Shoushan hatchery echoed with harsh memories. Mothering seemed a vast and thankless profession; tut-tutting and tsk-tsking over hundreds during the difficult hatchling phase. Nin had sought herself a future in hydroaltics, settling comfortably into the patterns of laboratory life when she matured. She'd never held high future expectations, even before her beauty failed to manifest. Nin elected to prepare herself for the inevitable rather than stooping to the flooding tears and theatrical histrionics of her ugly sisters.

Nin's day of reckoning had arrived unannounced. A quiet thing, like snowflakes settling upon soil. She'd been undressing before the mirror, her mind on other things. Lifting her shirt, she saw the ugly purple stain—a full week before her ridges began to push. A little part of her died in that instant. She'd never dared to hope, nor dream, yet hopes and dreams are the purest flames of youth. She angled her back for a better look, then let the shirt fall down to hide her shame. She stared at her own pale reflection for a minute or two—the light never was very strong in that room—and then in one swift motion, hoisted the shirt and was done with it: the bitterness, the disappointment, the pain. She tossed it all aside with the laundry, chose a different garment and got on with it. There were other pleasures to be had in life. Other meanings, other adventures. Beauty was merely one thing out of many.

The following weeks had passed in a blur. She could recall so little detail now, but perhaps there wasn't much to remember once the truth was finally out and everybody knew it. The beautiful were already setting themselves apart at Shoushan. Dissolving former friendships and alliances, touching each other excitedly as they cemented to form a group. Hardest for everyone to bear were the ones who manifested late. Too smug too soon, so utterly sure their lack of purpling as the weeks rolled on meant purple was never going to come.

Nin recalled Gita actually claiming a place at their table, nestling amongst the beautiful, beaming and cooing her good fortune, only it wasn't right. She was never right. The beautiful eventually tired of her noise, hunting the purple flush across her skin. They turned on her like a pack of wild beasts. The helpless mothers could do nothing to prevent it. Everyone knew the way things were. Risks were understood. Hatchlings were drilled endlessly in deportment and etiquette. It was Gita's fault entirely, but Nin still blamed the brood mothers, the way they'd teased and fussed and fed false hopes. Mores were not so lax the year that followed. The mothers were a sterner crop and nobody was savaged or torn apart.

Nin didn't announce her own purple. Her friends were much like she was; shy and quiet. There hadn't seemed any reason to make a scene, so she'd just gotten on with her chores. She'd been hoeing a line of cabbages in the lazy afternoon sun when Shae moved up to work beside her. Nin looked up and wiped her sweaty forehead with her wrist. Shae smiled and in that instant, Nin knew that she had purpled too and accepted her simple destiny, as had Nin.

The Remembrance of Oris required many castes and colours. Cradling a drink, Nin found herself a vantage point between two potted sargassi palms. Which story would be danced tonight? There were more than enough performers for *The Battle of Ashwah-Nemh*. Or *Narahshanti Hunts the Wild Dogs*. Or even *Oris and the Nameless Maiden*, her favourite tale from Shoushan days, despite its miserable ending.

All three tales were painted on the walls along with others, she was ashamed to realise, she'd all but forgotten. The murder of the princess—what had been her name? Or those winged triplets who'd bested the mighty dragon?

She hid beneath the drooping fronds to watch the

dance floor patterns swirl and form, unseen. Mythology had once been her favourite subject. Problem was, she'd had so little use for it since Shoushan. Her mind was always filled with practical matters. She was good at her job but not so good with people. Gatherings like this one made her feel so small.

The beautiful knew how to work the crowd, how to tease the love from it with hints of sexual promise. When one moved, the pattern adjusted itself to flow and follow, resettling to form new eddies and curls.

And Mija—what was she up to? As hostess, she should have feigned indifference; stood well back and let the evening run its course. But, Nin noted, she could barely conceal her glee. She glowered with pride at every little detail, canapés shaped like hearts and tears, not to mention the ornate fireplace with a row of antique weapons mounted above the mantle—five-pronged daggers, scimitars and spears.

Mija wanted her guests to believe the beautiful were her friends. Attracted by mere fact of her own exotic colouring, perhaps. Such things, although extremely rare, were not unheard of.

But the ballroom was too crowded. More guests had turned up than could comfortably be accommodated. Mija flitted about the room, disrupting the designs with every movement, somehow knowing she could get away with it. The beautiful were good at what they did, and Mija acted with vulgarity in that knowledge, ingratiating herself, pushing boundaries, almost taunting them, thought Nin, tightening the grip on her glass. What could the crazy woman be up to?

When the dance began it was languorous, claiming

participants one by one, pheromones pulsing from the centre, enveloping them into the fold. Nin felt the gentle tug of rhythm, abandoned her drink on the nearest tray. A component of the ochre quotient, she sniffed out her tone sisters easily. The ribbon was soon threaded between them, small steps synchronised, to and fro. Guided by the beautiful, each slice of sunset merged to form a flame. Russet embers licked the crowd's bejewelled edges.

It was the hostess's privilege not to join the dance. But Mija watched it closely. Every step. Every nuance. Sideways glances hinted at clandestine plots and plans.

The Remembrance of Oris was customarily danced outdoors, but not tonight. Not on Mija's watch. As she wove and blended, Nin gradually glimpsed the truth behind the masque. The real reason they'd been gathered here. Something dangerous was going to happen. Something provocative and new. Something the guests would remember forever. Something that made her uneasy.

Tonight would be whispered about in the highest circles: *the night we evoked Oris beneath a constellation chandelier! Five beautiful lead the dance, no less. Can you believe there were five?*

One beautiful separated from the others, took its stance below the jewelled stars. Nin knew in an instant which tale the dance would bloom to. *Oris and the Nameless Maiden.* She smiled.

And when she looked to Mija, she saw how she was smiling too. In that instant, Nin understood. Mija was not content with life as part of a sycophantic entourage: followers with filed ridges, purple concealed beneath layers of artfully powdered creme. Before the elliptic pause was at its zenith, Mija pushed through the crowd like a prow parting water and indeed it did seem as though the beautiful would let her spoil their moment.

And what a masterful dance it was: mesmeric, enthralling, like ripples shivering a pond's still surface, only deeper. Much, much deeper. Dark and cool and green. Colours swirling to drown the whole damn lot of them in luxurious, forbidden depths.

Suddenly, uncharacteristically, with no thought for what she was doing, Nin dropped the ribbon and stepped as close to the beautiful who was dancing Oris as she dared. Hugging her own arms, she appraised its wonder, simultaneously hot and cold, its dorsal spikes shimmering beneath the stellar chandelier's fine light. Nin felt the heat steam from its flesh, sensed the ridges along her own lines begin to tingle. Her sweat mingled with its scent and the heady pheromone backwash almost knocked her off her feet.

She had become the Nameless Maiden! Fighting to suppress her nervousness, she looked away, fearing she might die of embarrassment. She breathed in deeply, drinking in its flavours through her pores. A breeze brushed lightly across her skin, just enough to break enchantment's hold. She looked up as twin footmen swung the balcony's double doors wide open.

The beautiful broke formation, leaving ripples of anxious chatter in its wake. Nin watched the tip of its crown, besotted by the grace of its passage. She followed, ribbon abandoned on the floor, nudging gently with her shoulders as the crowd readjusted itself to fill the beautiful's void.

Nin ached to touch it. To claim its mythology as her

own. No, more than that. She needed to embrace it, hold it tight against her skin. To press her lips against its mouth and smother it with passion. Trap the heat of it inside her, helpless between her thighs. She wanted to squeeze the life from it, leave it quivering, begging for mercy. She wanted to own this beautiful and share it with no other.

A cold blast of evening air hit her in the face. She realised she was sweating, her heart racing, drowning out all other sounds. The beautiful stood mere feet away, its back to her, moonlight shivering its glossy mane. What was she supposed to say to it, out here, alone and unprotected? Why was it standing here at all, away from the patterns and structures of its own kind?

She'd die if she touched it. Either it would kill her outright, or one of the others would. But Nin didn't care. She was drunk and giddy from the moonlight. Maybe its touch would be worth dying for? There was only one way to find out.

As she stepped forward, it sensed her closeness and turned to face her. Nin didn't pause. She moved swiftly, cupping silver cheeks between her palms, drawing herself up on tiptoes to match its height.

'I love you, my prince,' she whispered, just as Oris's maiden had once done, pressing her lips fiercely against its own. The soft, sweet taste of it filled her mouth, like rosewater blended with wine and honey. Up so close, its scent was overpowering. She kissed it harder and, to her astonishment, it kissed her back, drawing her near with its powerful arms, clutching her tightly to its breast. Nin tasted blood. Her own? It didn't matter. Nothing mattered but the moment. She prayed it would never end.

'No!'

The sound struck them both as surely as a blow. The beautiful relaxed its grip and Nin staggered free of its embrace.

She turned, heart thumping, her body quivering with ache. Mija stood behind her, ridges sharp, her fury barely suppressed. Suddenly aware of the evening chill, a cloud moving across to cover the moon and a thousand other ordinary little things, Nin dipped her head in shame. What had she done? What had she been thinking? Had she really become the Nameless Maiden in plain view of five hundred people, let alone that she'd done the deed at all?

She looked back to the beautiful just in time to see it lift its head. It stared right past her to Mija and its eyes flared for an instant. Mija bowed and Nin stepped out of the way as the beautiful strode back into the ballroom.

Nin held her breath, waiting to feel the brunt of Mija's wrath, flinching with anticipation, but the blow never came. Mija stared at her with unashamed curiosity, as though seeing Nin for the very first time. Almost as if Nin wasn't plain old Nin at all, but some faint ghosting of beautiful herself.

The corner of Mija's lip curled into a smirk. It was supposed to be a put down, but Nin saw it for what it was. She suppressed a wicked smile of her own until the hostess spun on her heel and retreated. Nin had made her jealous! Plain old Nin. Mija had been planning to step into the Dance. She was intending to become the Nameless Maiden. Nin had stolen her kiss.

As Nin rejoined the party, she sensed something had changed. Her lips still tingled, her heartbeat quivered. Glancing in search of a waiter, she felt like she was being watched. And she was. Each beautiful had stopped what it was doing to stare her down with an icy glare. Guests were beginning to murmur their discomfort, their mutterings like the droning of a hive.

Nin knew she should have been afraid but she wasn't. She didn't fully comprehend the *why* of it, but *why* didn't matter. The flush of triumph would stay with her for always.

She took a drink from the nearest tray and sipped it, holding her ground. Hostess Mija was nowhere to be seen.

A minute passed, perhaps two. By the third, the tension began to dissipate. The beautiful turned their attention to other things, patterns realigning to how they were supposed to be.

The tingling sensation in Nin's lips faded gently, like the memory of a luxurious dream. It was time to go. To stay another moment would dilute the afterglow irreversibly, and she wanted to retain the taste as long as possible. But when she glanced towards the door, Nin saw she was surrounded. Guests had formed a ring to block her from the exit. Her stolen kiss was not to go unpunished.

Nin glanced nervously from face to face, desperate for someone familiar. Anyone. But all were strangers, staring her down, their faces blank. Expressionless.

She swallowed dryly, her throat constricted. What would these people do to her? Could she make it to the door? What then?

Nin gathered her courage, steadied her breath and stepped forward. Nothing happened so she took another timid step. This time, when she moved, others moved too, stepping aside so she didn't have to push.

The look in their eyes was not menace after all. It was adoration! Pure respect. No wonder she didn't recognise it. No-one had ever looked at Nin that way before.

A footman waited by the gate, offering her cloak and scarf. He escorted her down the marble staircase and when she went to thank him, bowed, almost as deeply as if she'd been a beautiful herself.

Oblivious to the cold night air, Nin walked down the path towards the road, smiling at her unexpected fortune. She would chance the weather and walk back into town, enjoying the companionship of moonlight till it faded.

She'd barely covered any ground when a shadow moved across her path. She paused, hesitant, until the shadow showed its face. Mija, her dark expression rivalling the night itself.

'You don't remember me, do you?' she said grimly.

Nin raised her hand to her lips in involuntary surprise. She opened her mouth to speak but Mija spoke first.

'Shoushan. Many years ago. I had a different name back then, of course.'

Mija stepped closer into the light. Nin observed small details she had overlooked before. Missed because she had not suspected and had taken Mija at face value. In childhood, Mija had once been known as Ang, one of those poor, hopeful silver-blondes. The one who had not been savagely torn apart.

'I didn't recognise—'

'No, of course you didn't. They gave me higher cheekbones along with my new name. Knocked a couple of ridges off. I suppose I should be grateful for that.'

'But I had no idea—'

'Do you have any concept of how hard it's been for me? Living with a blemished record as well as blemished skin?'

She stared at Nin as though she were a bug. 'I didn't fight my way through life to have a common *ochre* steal my glory. What did you think you were playing at back there?' Her eyes narrowed as she peered out through the darkness. 'Who by all the ancient gods do you think you are?'

'Nobody!' exclaimed Nin, stepping back. A glint of light refracted off the object clutched in Mija's hand.

She raised it high so Nin could see. The five-pronged dagger from above the ballroom's fireplace, a ritual weapon from a bygone age. Wielded, it would slash through skin like claws.

'Everybody saw what you did,' said Mija, stepping forward. 'Everybody will presume . . . '

'But I don't want anything! I'm not trying to—'

'Who do you think you are—the Nameless Maiden? You stole a kiss that wasn't yours to steal.'

'I didn't mean to . . . It just happened! The dance. It was the dance.'

'It's far too late to search for meaning, girl. What was done cannot be undone.' She took another small step forward. 'That kiss was supposed to be mine.'

Nin inched backwards. She was about to run when footsteps sounded on the marble staircase. One of the beautiful descended, its mane glazed silver with moonlight.

Nin froze. She sucked in her breath, but it ignored her. Mija stepped up, smiling from ear to ear, but the beautiful ignored her too.

'Wait!' she said, but it kept on walking. She stood sullenly, transfixed by its lavish, cascading mane, knuckles whitening as her grip on the five-pronged dagger tightened.

'I said wait!' she shrieked.

When it didn't respond, Mija let out a terrifying scream. She raised the weapon high and ran at the beautiful, a stream of obscenities blurting from her lips.

She didn't get far. It turned and slashed her throat wide open with one swift, perfect stroke. Blood spurted from the fatal wound, some of it spraying across the front of Nin's silk dress.

Nin tasted still-warm blood on her own trembling lips. Shaking uncontrollably, she turned, intending to run but the hem of her cloak snagged on her clogs. She tripped, sprawling head first onto the gravel pathway.

The beautiful stood motionless, stone cold as alabaster. Nin scrambled to her feet, hands and shins scraped raw, the taint of Mija's blood still in her mouth. She raced for the road as fast as she could, glancing back once—just once—when she reached the fence. The sound of boots on gravel drove her onwards, running faster, choking down panic, terrified by what she'd seen behind.

Eyes gleaming in the darkness.

Five pairs.

Beautiful, every one.

Cat Sparks is fiction editor of *Cosmos Magazine*. From 2002 to 2008 she managed Agog! Press, an Australian independent publisher that produced ten anthologies of original speculative fiction. A graduate of the inaugural Clarion South Writers' Workshop and a Writers of the Future prizewinner, Cat has edited five speculative fiction anthologies. Fifty-six of her short stories have been published since 2000. Cat was official photographer for two NSW Premiers and worked as dig photographer on three archaeological expeditions to Jordan. She's won seventeen Aurealis and Ditmar awards for writing, editing and art. She is currently working on a far future/ biopunk trilogy and a suite of post-apocalypse tales set on the NSW south coast. One of her short stories was reprinted in Hartwell and Cramer's *Year's Best SF 16*. www.catsparks.net

Hatchway

Simon Petrie

'Touch me again, and you'll need a proctologist.'

Kalpana's quiet menace is sufficient to persuade Marisol and Django to back away towards the clean ceramic sides of the Hanel West 2 airlock; Stieg, stationed by the lock's inner hatch, sneers 'as if' in response. Only Boris, holding the small tub of baby-blue gel, has the decency to colour up.

'Look, K,' says Django, 'the gel's every bit as vital as the mask, the boots, the gloves. You're, huh, going to get *cold* out there—'

'You think I haven't worked that?' Kalpana replies, her fragile calm slipping, shattering. 'They musta got your plumbing wrong, the *shit* that comes out sometimes.' As soon as the words are out, she realises they've taken her too far, like they've a tendency to. Too far in, or too far away. Too late now. But she's feeling like a piece of readymeat, underdressed, self-conscious of her plumpness and of the all-important two-three years the group has on her. Of the need to prove she's not just a kid, to do something the dults wouldn't ever dare.

And to show she's worthy. Because *that's* what she's here for, after all. (It's like Boris had said, the first time he'd let slip about the initiation, the test: 'It's all about showing Titan who's boss.')

'I don't think she wants this,' Stieg drawls, leaning for effect against the polished crud-resistant frame that lintels the airlock's inner hatch. Stieg's skinny, a little short, and with skin pale enough that it makes his spiked hair seem blacker than it is. He fixes his eyes on her, then sweeps across the rest of the group. He's playing for an audience. If Boris is the leader, Django the expert, and Marisol the conscience (or perhaps, Kalpana muses, the mascot), then Stieg is the enforcer. Or fancies himself thus, at least. 'You think she wants this? Any of you think she *deserves* this?'

Bastard. There's no way she's going to plead, not in front of a creep like Stieg. But she needs to do *some*thing, to convince them she's not motivated just by fear. She stares past him, feigning boredom with his jibes, affecting a sudden casual interest in the hyperextended saguaro that, foyered inward of the airlock, stands improbably green within its deep bed of grey-orange sand. (Not frozen-hydrocarbon sand, either, but real asteroid-origin *faux*-Earth silica sand. A statement of comparison, or solidarity, or something.)

'It's not *just* about the cold,' Django says, and she's grateful enough for the interjection, for the imperturbability of Boris's younger brother, particularly after her slur. Django handcombs his scruffy crest of orange-brown hair: camo hair, she'd thought it, when first she saw it. 'It's the overpressure. Titan's going to be trying to, huh, push its way in, any way it can. The breathmask covers your face—eyes, ears, mouth, nose. But there's—'

'Grossleaks. Okay, you don't have to paint the picture.' She rubs at her bare forearm, goosefleshed.

Unlike the rest of the building, the airlock's not designed for warmth; that's what T-suits are for. None of the group is T-suited. But she's the only one in just a single layer, or in shortsleeves. 'Makes sense. But then, why the ti— Uh, the nubs?'

'Sensitivity,' says Boris. 'Ask Marsy.' He makes sufficient of a hand gesture, splaying across his chest, that the tub in his other hand sloshes. Calling it 'gel' is a misnomer, Kalpana decides—some of the *drinks* she's experimented with have been gluggier.

Marisol, for her part, turns awkwardly away. Maybe she's not willing to be used as an example, or maybe she's still pissed with Boris, from last week.

'It's too runny,' says Kalpana, trying not to whine. 'It's just going to run straight off—'

'*Told* you she doesn't want this,' says Stieg, staring her down.

'Shut *up*, tool,' Boris says, glaring at Stieg. The latter shrugs, indifferent to the other's height and bulk.

'So you need to add it last,' Django explains. 'That's one of the reasons for the loose shirt and shorts—it makes it easier to, huh, slap on the goop quickly. As well as for movement once you get outside. But it *has* to be runny at three hundred K, if it's to have any elasticity at one hundred.'

'We can delay this if you'd rather,' suggests Marisol— and something's up, something's bugging her, because Marisol is not looking at Kalpana's face, not at all, while she speaks. It's as if instead she's conversing with Boris's tub of gel. 'We don't have to do this today.' There's almost a plea in her voice, Kalpana reckons.

And Kalpana would readily enough defer. Now that

she's arrived at the moment, it's as though there's a premonition, a foretaste of the overpressure. It's strong enough, this feeling, to cause her breath to catch, to send her heart on such a rush of activity beneath her breast that it's sure to catch the boys' attention. She's not even sure, right at this instant, that this is a group she wants to be accepted by: up close, they've lost some of the initial rebellious gloss, the dult-defying omnipotence that she'd first glimpsed, or thought she'd glimpsed. Up close, there's more than a hint of the dult in how they're treating her, right now. But there's Stieg: and she *will not* give Stieg the slightest hint of satisfaction. This is the bravest, stupidest, most illegal thing she's ever attempted, and she will not give him reason to taunt her.

Hanel West 2 airlock is cold. It smells of burnt bleach, baked dust, and cryogrease, and it's *cold*.

'No,' says Kalpana, trying, and signally failing, to catch Marisol's eye. 'No, we don't have to. But today makes sense, with all the dults either at the loftball game, or the concert.'

'She's right,' agrees Boris, as though this settles it. And maybe it does.

'Right. Then I'm ready. Five-three-one-four-six, right?'

'Five-three-*four-one*-six,' Django corrects her.

Whoops.

She'd been seven, almost eight, when it happened. When her mother pushed her father through the hatchway.

Kalpana had mental images from that day. They'd never leave her. She'd made, from the images, a loosely-arranged sequence; but it was a knotted thing, and as difficult to follow as it was painful. It wasn't until a full year later that her aunt had been able to assemble for Kalpana a narrative, a sufficiently-detailed framework through which to comprehend the day's events.

To comprehend; but not to understand.

They'd been living in Clemence, a small single-arcology community of never more than a hundred souls, on the southern edge of the Senkyo dunefields. It wasn't Kalpana's first home, nor even the third—miners were itinerant, almost by definition, and the Brauns certainly fitted that pattern—but it was the earliest place of which she retained solid memories.

Ultimately, all of those memories led back to the airlock.

She wasn't sure how long the pharmhands had been living in the community: several months, certainly, maybe even a year. But families in Clemence came and went all the time, as processing and extraction fluctuated at the various mining operations among the coffee-dark dunes to the north and the sepia-stained knobbled highlands to the south and east. Among adults, friendships weren't sought out overmuch, because why bother establishing ties with a group of people who might well have moved on within twelve months? Among children of Kalpana's age, friendships were understood to be temporary, and subject to mysterious external influence—a best friend might be taken, with but few days' notice, to a mining community several hundred klicks away. You tended, after awhile, to learn not to elevate anyone to 'best-friend' status, but merely to maintain a circle of near-equidistant acquaintances. (Or you could communicate by feed, with friends who really meant something, but

Kalpana had never found that satisfying—what was the point of talking to someone if you weren't actually in the same place?)

So the pharmhands had been in the arcology for months, posing as miners. Until they were outed, by someone. She'd assumed, after the fact, that it must have been her father who'd notified the Pol, but Kalpana's aunt thought it more likely he'd just been scapegoated. 'Made an example of,' she'd explained. 'Over some pack of sick fucks' desire—pardon my Esperanto, *but*—to maximise their profit. And to keep the punters intimidated.'

It had unfolded slowly to start with.

The pharmhands gave no show of awareness that the Pol would be at the arcology within a few short hours (though they must have known, if everyone else did). But the pharmhands had weapons, and they gathered up all of Clemence's population and assembled them in the foyer in front of one of the arcology's inner airlocks. The sparse crowd of perhaps sixty people—miners, merchants, retirees, children—were made to stand in front of the foyer's synth-stone fountain showpiece. The constant splashing of water across the scales of the fountain's giant sculpted carp was a distraction: Kalpana hoped they wouldn't be kept standing here for too long.

Two of the pharmhand women sported thick red goggles and held HD mining lasers, very probably the same lasers that had been used to blind and incapacitate Clemence's own modest security cadre. The laser-wielders stood and stared threateningly at anyone in the crowd (including, from time to time, Kalpana herself) who might look to move too close, or to escape. Another woman held up a small shiny phial, which might contain phloo, or perhaps something worse. Three pharmhand men, also goggled, searched the crowd for someone, and stopped in front of Horst and Rashmi Braun, Kalpana's parents, whom they took out the front of the group. Kalpana moved to accompany them, but was booted forcefully back by one of the laser-carriers.

She was scared, and winded, and humiliated at the kick, and puzzled at what the pharmhands could want with her parents—were they to be given the psychoactive virus? Her gaze twisted to the woman who held the phial aloft, but the woman's pose did not shift.

On the other side of the armed guards, two of the men manoeuvred Kalpana's father into place, his back to the crowd, in the corridor just in front of the inner airlock hatch. A third held her mother, who struggled in the rough embrace until a phrase muttered in her ear persuaded her to relent, while another man—Mikhail Tulleyrand—permaglued her father's elbows, at shoulder height, to either side of the hatch frameway. This, in Kalpana's eyes, underscored both the pharmhands' cruelty and their obtuseness. She now guessed that their intention was to make her father stand, for hours or days, as punishment. She'd read about this sort of thing in her history sims just a few days ago, the petty barbarism of war, mistreatment of prisoners. Her fear subsided somewhat. The Pol would be here in much less than a day, and then the pharmhands would be caught, her parents freed. And although it would probably hurt immensely, her father wouldn't necessarily need to be unglued: he could just get these arms, these 'titanium-cored full-sensation prosthetics', replaced, same as he'd had to replace his *proper* arms after the accident at the Mezzoramia brinemine, when his T-suit had been pinned in an iceslip.

The pharmhands were evil and stupid men and women who deserved to be captured. They didn't recognise that her father had artificial arms, and they clearly didn't understand that the Pol would be at the arcology within a few short hours.

Then they permaglued Horst Braun's hands to the sides of his balding head, just above the ears, and it began to be more problematic.

She's pulling on the mask, a standard home-closet emergency rig of some thick clear plastic, rimmed with a flabby polymer seal, wishing they'd all give her a bit more space. She's not claustrophobic, of course, but she's nonetheless feeling crowded, set-upon. And the mask has a whiff of that tholin stink to it, somewhere between nicotine and putrefaction, which certainly doesn't help.

If she's going to do this, she'd rather just get on. But Kalpana knows that any under-prep, any mistake, could be fatal. Belatedly, she wonders if she's fit enough. It'd be ironic, or worse than, if she were to break a limb or something, after all her aunt's daily exercise reminders, her weekly 'Titan may be slow, but it's not soft' cautions, her monthly osteo horror stories. (As if Kalpana, of all people, needs any more of *those*. After what happened to her father.)

Then Boris taps her on the shoulder, almost apologetic. 'You'll need this,' he explains, and hands her a shaped papery filter, evidently designed to fit across nose and mouth.

'Why?' she asks. 'Isn't the mask gas-tight?'

'It's not for gas,' begins Marisol, who's still not

looking directly at Kalpana. In the dry blue light of the airlock, Marisol's face, framed in a synth-fur hoodover, looks as cold as Kalpana's feels. The Hanel West 2 airlock is freezing. But, of course, as cold goes . . .

'Plus you can't expect the seal to be as effective at one hundred K—it'll be more brittle, inflexible. Along with everything else,' says Django. 'Atmosphere isn't an issue, huh, long as you don't blow a total leak. You won't be out long enough. But the tholin's a killer, if you breathe it in.'

'Bad enough on your *skin*,' says Boris.

'Getting scared now?' Stieg taunts.

'*Lid* it, tool,' Boris replies.

'Scared? No,' she says, too loud. She undoes the mask, slips the filter in place, suffers Marisol to refasten the mask with spindly fingers.

Boris is still holding the tub of goop. Expectantly. Like Kalpana's a wankbot or something. She meets his stare, waits for him to turn aside. But though he colours up again, to the point that his cheeks approximate the russet of his moptop, Boris is *in charge*, and doesn't concede authority readily. (Obviously. Else Stieg would be running things.)

'I'm not putting that on while you lot are in the room,' she announces, eventually. 'Can't you just come back for it, once I'm out of the airlock?'

'It's worth credits,' says Django. 'Not cheap.'

'So?'

'So, you leave it in the airlock, it gets contammed. No,' says Boris.

Kalpana rolls her eyes. 'Right. But you can still shut me in here. No way I'm putting it on with you lot gawping.'

'As if you've got anything we haven't seen better elsewhere,' says Stieg, attracting a glare from Marisol.

'I *mean* it,' Kalpana continues. 'I can knock on the hatch when I'm done, before I step out. Best deal you're going to get.'

Boris weighs it. 'Make sure you do round the mask,' he says, handing her the tub. 'As well.' He motions the others towards the inner hatch.

Alone at last, she's newly conscious of the loudness of her breathing, the sticky sweat at her armpits, the airlock's oppressive silent chill. The weight of the tank against her back. Her heart's racing, and something—besides just the mask's rebreather—feels stuck in her mouth. She moves to the inner wall, to the corner she judges best to be out of sight from the hatch's viewscreen, and does the daubing. Squatting down for the private bits.

'Don't thump so loud,' Boris complains, stepping back into the lock when she's finished. 'You want the dults to hear?'

She holds the tub of gel out to him. 'All plugged,' she says, smirking.

He takes the tub from her gloved hand, throws a distasteful glance at his now-sticky fingers.

'See you on the other side,' she says, distinctly more upbeat than she feels. 'Five-three-four-one-six, right?'

'Uh . . . yeah. Right.' He's coloured up again, whatever *that's* about. He gives her a look she can't interpret, and closes the hatch behind him.

Right. She swallows, presses the sequence of commands. If Django's correct—and she's not sure what she hopes, right now—this is the only airlock in Hanel she can leave from, the only one that'll open out for a non-T-suited occupant.

There's perhaps five seconds during which nothing happens. Then there's a thrum, from somewhere beneath the ridged-steel decking, and the airlock floods with a gush of cylinder-cold nitrogen, chill as frozen cotton against every stretch of exposed skin. The mask's seal presses in, instantly, all around the perimeter of her face, and she opens her mouth in startled reaction. The faceplate fogs with escaped moisture.

She hadn't, she realises, been freezing before this. Now she can't stop shivering. The gel sticking the seam of her shorts to herself is starting to feel unpleasantly spiky as it chills. She braces her bared arms against her chest, then peels them awkwardly away. The airlock's blue lights fade until all within is navy and black, save for a rim of dim light around the outer hatchway. The way out.

Two minutes, she tells herself. *Just two minutes.* Might as well get it over with.

She pushes on the outer hatch. There's some resistance, but the pressure differential is now slight enough that the exertion is mild. The outer hatch opens, onto Titan's drear twilight.

The airlock, it turns out, has in fact been warm. To human skin, Titan is colder than space itself. She'd swear her neck, her arms, her legs were clad in ice-chilled armour.

She steps out. Into a landscape cold enough, given time, to liquefy the oxygen in her lungs.

The pharmhands didn't hurry. They'd now glued her

father's boots to the corridor decking, the toes of his boots a handspan behind the hatchway opening. One of the pharmhands still held him up, though she didn't see why they needed to. He'd stopped struggling, and he was fastened by feet and elbows.

Kalpana was worried—it was scary to see your mother and father so upset, and not to know exactly why all of this was happening—but she was fairly sure that whatever the pharmhands were trying, it wasn't going to work. The Pol would be here long before her father got too tired to stand, and they'd get him free, and capture the criminals. And even if the pharmhands were thinking of something worse, like shooting him—and they had weapons beyond just the lasers, the first guns Kalpana had ever seen, in real life—why would they have glued her father in the frame like that?

Or they might've been planning to open the outer lock—which would kill everybody, including the pharmhands because none of them were wearing T-suits—but she didn't think even pharmhands were stupid enough to do that. And they might be using her father as a lock-shield, to stop the Pol entering through this airlock, but there were three other entrances into Clemence, and the pharmhands weren't moving to block those ones off. They were standing around, in this one, waiting.

Waiting for what?

The man with the glue-tube, Tulleyrand, tossed it to a subordinate, and turned to face the crowd held captive by the threat of laser-fire.

'You can save him,' he said, his voice loud, brassy, and surprisingly polite. His hair looked too dark for his skin, and he wasn't tall like Kalpana's father, nor broad, but he held himself exactly like someone big enough to beat up anyone he liked. He gestured with the palm of his hand. 'Just tell us who squirted the Pol, and we'll cut Braun free.'

There was some shuffling within the crowd, but it amounted to nothing.

'I'm not a patient man,' the pharmhands' leader warned. 'Two minutes. Then it happens.'

What happens? Kalpana wondered. She genuinely was frightened by now, with the deadline's precision, the still-mysterious threat. Because this man didn't sound stupid, like he should do. He sounded *dangerous*.

Her mother, still herself pinioned, turned to look over the crowd, as though she was hoping to see someone, or something. Kalpana waved, but her mother, shaking, face striped with damp, did not acknowledge the gesture.

Whatever her mother was looking for, she didn't see it. Then, turning back to face the tableau that was her husband, she said something.

'Beg pardon?' Tulleyrand asked, leaning as if to hear.

'I said *I did it*,' announced her mother, voice roughened in a way Kalpana had never before heard.

'You?'

'Yes. Now let him down.' She coughed. Swallowed. '*Please*.'

'No. No, I don't think so, Ms Braun,' replied Tulleyrand, addressing the crowd. 'Though high marks for the delaying tactic, I think. *One* minute.' And he leaned forward again, exaggerated, theatrical, and whispered something to her.

Whatever he'd said—and Kalpana wasn't close

enough to hear—it caused Rashmi Braun to struggle against her confines, with sufficient violence that her captor (who outmassed her by at least her own bodyweight) had considerable difficulty in retaining his footing. Another pharmhand moved to assist; the women with the lasers tightened their grips, and made mock-strafing gestures across the face of the crowd; Tulleyrand, his face a study in amusement, announced 'We won't keep you,' and started counting down the seconds from thirty.

When he got to five, it all went to shit.

The skin burns. It is so cold that each movement she makes—and it's now *move, or die*—is accompanied by a pain so sharp, so solid, that the body suspects it to be heat, for 'cold' could never be this extreme.

She is out on Titan.

She is out on Titan, *sans* T-suit. Directly in front of her is a man-made anomaly, a statement of solidified irony, an object misplaced upon this wide brown land. A saguaro cactus, carved from water-ice, stands guard upon the apron of cleared ground that leads away from the airlock. Erstwhile twin to the still-growing cactus within the arcology's foyer, the ice cactus has been turned, in the two years since its erection, to a translucent tea-brown by windblown tholins and sand grains. It is stained most deeply upon its western flanks.

Behind the ice saguaro, the sky is choked by a vague, impenetrable ceiling of fuscous haze. The ground slopes gently down, bouldered in a palette that spans from tangerine, through the darkest possible orange, through brown, to black. To her north, beyond the tea-smeared, muck-spattered apron in which the cactus is embedded, the horizon is flanked by the haze-murked black ridge of the nearest of Belet's long parallel dunes. Leading past the cactus—towards the near-endless foothills that are the dunefields—the paths made by boot, ski, or tread are indistinct, only marginally less cluttered by ice pebbles and sticky sand drifts than the rest of the intervening terrain.

She takes in the late-afternoon view within a couple of instants, conscious that time is short. Hanel West Cargo 4 is five paces to the right of the Hanel West 2 airlock outer hatch, ninety degree right turn, twenty paces further. She's walked it dozens of times, in the sims, she's got it down to sixteen seconds. But the sims aren't rigged for skin-sense. And with the goop solidifying at her seams, the rubbed-raw chill scraping at the skin of her arms, legs, and neck, the frozen-cotton armour of shirt and shorts, the walk to the corner is many more than just five paces.

Breathe through your mouth, she urges. Yet even that is difficult.

If she slips, falls, she is almost assuredly dead, since she will be instantly cold-welded to the orange-brown icy skin of Titan. (And at this, a phrase of her father's comes back, one of the few she can genuinely remember, though she's not sure it's his true voice: 'You make a mistake, on Titan, you'll be instantly dead. Even if you're not dead instantly.') Thick air, lazy grav, surfaces that cannot be trusted: it's *measured, or dead*. So she plants each boot with sleepwalk-slow caution, checks the rightness of the step before shifting weight forward to the front foot, while flakes of breeze-borne tholin adhere, malevolent brown-black snow, against her bare arms.

The first few flakes melt; but after this, they do not. They stick, solid on solid.

Her limbs are duller. The atmosphere seems to grow ever thicker (though this must be illusion), the ground so close to the arcology wall is treacherously slick in patches, with the memory of waste-heat leakage. The mask presses against her face, pinches against her cranium. Each breath of tanked air comes cold, rasping, rattling its way to her lungs, which ache with indrawn chill. Her joints complain, and every crusted glob of goop pinches, scrapes, snags with each protesting movement. The shorts sure don't help, merely provide a strip of frigid inter-thigh sandpaper; she wonders why none of them has instead suggested a skirt. Marisol, you would have thought, at least . . . But *nothing* about this is as it was in the sims, not even the visuals.

A horrible thought occurs: she's only the others' word that they've already managed this, that they've proved it possible to survive this. She might, in truth, be first, a guinea-pig.

But why would they lie?

She rounds the corner, not wanting to think of how long it has taken. Each step a risk, each second's exposure an increment of damage. If her skin freezes too much, it will crack at the joins, and then the first flake of tholin to reach her freezing bloodstream will likely kill . . . eventually. There's no place that does carcinogens quite like Titan.

Five-three-four-one-six. It *was* 'four-one', wasn't it?

Django had reckoned two minutes would be safe, probably. But at this shuffle, two minutes, or whatever fraction of that remains since she left the 'lock, may not get her to the cargo entryway.

And she slips. Her left foot skids back, her right knee bends painfully, and she falls forward, in sudden languid dread. She stretches her arms out in front, braces against the jolt that hits when her gloves press into the icy brown gravel. Her knees—left back, right forward—both come within centimetres of the chilled flypaper that, to bared human skin, is Titan's surface. Heart rattling within its freezing cage, she stands and cannot stop from shaking at the nearness of the death from which she has just escaped. She has either bitten her tongue, or caught it, somehow, on the rebreather. She is too intimidated to take another step, yet she must. So she does. Her ankle lances with a pain straight and sharp enough to thread needles.

And then she hears the voice.

It was a bump, a push. It could well have been accidental, though as time passes, Kalpana becomes more convinced that it was a deliberate shove, an execution. One of the pharmhands, struggling to help keep Kalpana's mother Rashmi contained, knocked into the neighbouring guard's back, with the result that Rashmi, with a despairing and disbelieving cry, was propelled forward against her husband. Horst Braun was thus pushed forward through the open inner hatch of the airlock. The shaped titanium rods that comprised the 'bones' within Braun's prosthetic arms butted against, and pivoted around, the unyielding metal of the hatchway frame; the titanium-boned hands of his prostheses were pushed inwards. The right side of his skull caved in with a sickening wet crack, audible over (and cutting short) his shocked scream. And Kalpana's father, still glued by the elbows, hung limp as a rag doll, blood pouring from the broken-eggshell mess of the side of his head, beneath his still-glued hand.

The crowd's forward surge was arrested as the guards flashed off a sequence of blue-white warning shots which left almost everyone temporarily blinded by the reflections from the fountain. There followed a disorganised press of bodies, the chaotic disquiet punctuated by a couple of loud, sharp noises, and when Kalpana's sight returned, Mikhail Tulleyrand lay dead, his head apparently rammed hard against the hatch's unforgiving frame. Near Tulleyrand's feet, Kalpana's mother too was dead, from a single clean gunshot wound to her chest.

There was the smell of shit in the air, and vomit, and something else.

The half-dozen surviving pharmhands fled, in several vehicles, to one or more of the neighbouring small mining settlements.

The Pol arrived by plane from Sagan four hours later, and having established that Kalpana had no surviving kin within the arcology, took her back with them: she had an aunt and, she thought, a cousin in Sagan. She'd met them once, or perhaps twice.

The days that followed were hollow and long.

Two of the pharmhands, a contracted couple, were eventually caught. But the population of the small mining communities was itinerant by nature, and it was easy to pass unnoticed provided you had the skills to pretend to be someone you were not.

It was easy, too, provided one was patient, and

discreet, to find a few buyers for your lucrative stockpile of psychoactive viruses. The pharmhands would not have existed without demand for their products.

'What do you *mean*, the wrong numbers?' Django's voice, or Boris's. She's not sure which.

'Django?' she calls, in response.

'I mean they've changed them since yesterday, huh, I've no idea why.' *This* one's Django. Which means the other was Boris.

'Django?' she repeats. 'Guys? Anybody?'

A woman's voice, Marisol's, cuts in across her. It's obvious they haven't heard Kalpana. 'So she can't get back in through Cargo 4? What about backtracking to H West 2?'

Django answers. 'It's only a minute into purge. I don't see how it'd let us open it for another fifteen minutes or so, huh. She'll be cryopork by then.'

'I don't *believe* this! We can't just let this all turn to shit—can we get *today*'s numbers for her?'

'It'll take time,' replies Django. The sound in her earbud is tinny, ineffectual, she needs to hold still to hear it. Except that holding still is exactly what she *doesn't* need to do. Every part of her stings now, with cold and maybe also with abrasion.

She has scarcely rounded the corner.

The makeshift path that leads along the arcology wall, to Hanel West Cargo 4 entryway still fifteen impossible metres distant, is slick and somehow waxy. Parked in front of the cargo entryway, the clutch of randomly-parked vehicles—a couple of quad-skis, a rover, and a few ancient and mistreated skid-bikes—stand like a murk-enshrouded, misplaced flotilla, their indifference to the environment a private insult. *We* belong out here, they seem to say. But *you*—

The terrain itself is not so ready with rejection: the dun wasteland all around is waiting to embrace her, to never let her go. She's finding it difficult to remember why she's been resisting.

It's all about showing Titan who's boss.

No group, no gang, however enticing, could possibly be worth this. She's been a fool to think otherwise.

The earbud buzzes back into activity. 'It'll take too long,' Django repeats. 'And we couldn't get the numbers to her, anyhow. Her rig's on transmit-only, huh, it's not set up for reception.'

Idiots. Total fucking incompetents. She unleashes a compact string of further obscenities, confident they'll never reach their target.

She manages another step, does her best to ignore the pain scything along her legs. The tank on her back, her precious air supply, feels to be growing progressively heavier with each passing second. The visor is now so fogged that she must guess, and work from memory, to interpret the dimming, fuzz-enveloped shapes that are the arcology wall, the stand of work vehicles, the terrain in front of her. Her hands have become an encumbrance, a-tingle within the thoroughly inadequate protection of the gloves, her arms at once so numb and so afire with cold agony that she cannot hold them in front of her, and yet she surely needs the protection should she stumble again. Even if it shatters her fingers in the process.

'If it's transmit-only, then how come we haven't heard from her?' Boris's voice asks.

'Who cares?' asks another voice. Stieg's. 'I mean, who fucking *cares*? She wouldn't have—'

'Shut *up*!' says Boris, and even through the earbud's crappy acoustics, she can hear the edge in his voice, the knife of desperation. (It's his head stands to roll for this, if hers gets frozen through.)'Honest-to-fuck, tool, what've you got in for her?'

And at that, somehow, she realises. She's been hearing it wrong. It's not 'tool'. Not quite.

Boris doesn't know, obviously. Kalpana never did, from the start. But now she does.

She'd never thought to bother with their surnames. Surnames were a *dult* thing, an irrelevance . . . until it turns out that they tell you everything you think you need to know.

And Kalpana Braun, gagging in her shock on the rebreather, still has no idea how she's going to fight her way through into the safety of Hanel West Cargo 4; but she knows damn well she's going to find it, somehow. As soon as she's shuffled, half-blind, along the next fifteen metres. Because there's *no way* on this big orange-brown world that she's going to provide Stieg Tulleyrand with such a convenient cure for his hatred, his emptiness, and his pain.

Born and raised on the fault-riven plains of North Canterbury, Simon Petrie now lives in Canberra where he works at a local university. His first short fiction collection, *Rare Unsigned Copy: tales of Rocketry, Ineptitude, and Giant Mutant Vegetables*, is available from Peggy Bright Books (www.peggybrightbooks.com), and other bibliographic details can be gleaned from his Wordpress site (simonpetrie.wordpress.com). He's a member of the Andromeda Spaceways Publishing Co-op (and has edited *ASIM* issues 35, 40 and 51), the Canberra Speculative Fiction Guild, and the SpecFicNZ core collective. He has thrice been a judge for the Aurealis Awards. Various of his works have been shortlisted for the Sir Julius Vogel (NZ) and Ditmar awards, and he received the Sir Julius Vogel award for Best New Talent in 2010. Completion of a novel—any novel—continues to elude him.

At The End There Was a Man

Lee Battersby

What little world there was, belonged to the sand. It spilled over every horizon, and the only life that survived lay silent during the searing day, waiting for the night hours, when life could emerge to scuttle through brief hours of safety.

The beach upon which the man squatted had never been a place of note. No city had looked down upon it; nobody had surfed upon its waves or fished its waters; no boats had cut across the bay on the way to other, more important, destinations. It was simply a space like all spaces: sand, sky and emptiness. He crouched at the beach's edge and watched the water scud in and out in low, tired ebbs. Where it receded, tiny transparent creatures skittered and died in the sudden shock of air. Hunkered down, he resembled a particularly still hillock, or a rock yet to be ground down to nothingness by the wind and the water. He made no movement. There was nowhere to move *to*: where he had been lay behind him, and there was nothing else in front. He had reached an end, before he was ready. All he could do was wait for death to catch him up. After that, he would feed the tiny crustaceans that owned the world. The man sat, and stared across the water, and waited.

Time no longer mattered. This late in the life of the world, the sun kept its own time, setting or simply skimming the horizon as suited its mood. The man had no need to mark the days. Only the approach of death mattered, and that came closer by moments. The sun wobbled across the sky, nodded once, then plunged for the edge of the sea. The blackness that followed was sudden, and complete, broken only by a meagre scattering of stars, perhaps three dozen blinking eyes peeking down upon the planet. As the heat lessened, all around the man came to life. Holes opened. Heads emerged, then claws and legs, tiny organisms scurrying from boltholes to sniff the air. The man ignored them. They, in turn, treated him as part of the landscape, crawling across his skin in ignorance of its true nature. The sun rose, and they disappeared. It retired, and they returned. The man's eyes closed. His arms slipped from their perch upon the hard bone of his knees. He slumped and, empty of consciousness, crumpled to the ground.

One by one, minuscule creatures came to investigate his fallen form. They milled about in the moist sand, transparent feelers brushing against his skin until their vibrations attracted the attention of a greater predator.

The crab burst from its lair like an explosion, scattering smaller animals before it on a gout of sand. Its claws scythed left and right, harvesting prey and pushing them into its maw in a ceaseless frenzy. By the time it stopped, satiated, several seconds had passed, and it stood alone by the man's side, triumphant, turning its hand-sized shell this way and that as it searched the nearby ground for more food. But the moment had passed. All who could reach safety had done so, and those who could not had been consumed. The crab took a slow step backwards, and another, preparing to wriggle back underneath the surface of the world, to wait for the next unwary meal.

Intelligent thought had long since left the man. It was instinct alone, the inbuilt need to survive, that guided his movement. His wrist stiffened. His hand shot outwards from his body. Fingers wrapped around the crab's shell and lifted it from the sand. The crab fought back, slicing at the surrounding flesh with its claws. Blood slid between shell and skin as they bit deep. The man did not wince, did not twitch in pain. He rolled onto his back, raised the crab above him. Eyes closed, he drew his other hand across and grabbed a claw. He twisted. The claw stuck, ground against the rim of the crab's shell, and came free. The crab shuddered, and loosened its grip upon the man's hand. As it died, he was already bringing the severed limb to his lips, sucking the flesh and ichor out of its shell, reaching again to twist, remove, and eat. The shell cracked open between sun-hardened fingers. Crab meat, sweet and laden with juice, slid between split lips. The empty shell dropped first to his chest, and then—as he curled into the foetal position—onto the sand.

He stayed that way for as long as it took the tide to sneak up and spirit away the empty shell. Then, slowly at first, but with increasing frequency, he began to shudder. The movement jerked him to his knees. He arched his back, curled back on himself, arched again. His shoulders tensed. He shot his head forward, mouth agape, and vomited. Undigested crab meat splashed into the milling surf. He spasmed, and threw up until only bile emerged, then only the cramping movement remained and a last few, precious drops of liquid. Eventually, his weakened body gave way, and he fell forward into the edge of the water. He lay that way for several minutes, until the splashing tide caused him to cough and find his knees once more.

Slowly, with infinite weariness, he focussed upon his surroundings. The final, meagre reflections of sunlight upon water showed him a beach: featureless and flat, bounded by the lazy dunes through which he had passed. He turned his gaze in both directions. To his left it stretched out without impediment, an unbroken grey streak that gently curved away out of sight. To his right, almost at the edge of his vision, a lump of black provided the only thing upon which he might focus. He stared at it as the light began to fail. Then, with no thought in his mind, he found his feet and began to trudge towards it.

By the time he got there the day had gone, and he only found the object by tripping over it. He knelt and examined it by touch: a tube, of sorts, made from some soft material that crinkled and crackled under his hands. It was open at one end, and his fingers found an even softer form poking out, a thin, grassy covering hanging loose over much of its surface. He twined some in his fingers and pulled. It resisted for a moment, then came loose. He sniffed it, tasted it experimentally, then spat it out. It was brittle upon his tongue, tasteless, the threadlike fibres causing him to gag in distaste. With no other means of identification available to him in the dark he shrugged, and lay down next to the object. Within moments he was asleep.

The warmth of the sun woke him. He lay for long moments with his eyes closed, letting the sunlight draw the aching cold from his joints, letting it bring life to the starched tundra of his face. A light breeze spat sand into his eyes. He blinked, and opened them, then turned his head towards last night's object.

A face stared back at him.

The man screamed, a short canine yelp that echoed across the empty landscape. He scrabbled backwards until he sat a dozen paces away, hands over his head, peeking at the corpse through protectively-raised knees. There was no telling how long the stranger had been dead. The sun had dried the skin until it lay like leather across the skull beneath. Countless sand creatures had removed those soft portions that made for the easiest meal: the scarred and blasted face lacked eyes, lips or nose, so that even if the man held any memory of others he could not have identified the features before him. What little hair remained was stiff with salt and heat, a sparse covering with a conspicuous space where he had pulled out his handful the night before. With that memory he began to rock and whimper, sucking upon a finger as if drawing upon his own juices might erase the memory of the hair upon his tongue. The corpse continued its dead stare, and soon enough, without any other action presenting itself, the man found his gaze wandering away from the featureless face, down along the rest of the half-buried body.

Only the top half was visible. The legs had disappeared as wind rolled a small dune slowly over them. The body was covered with a single piece of clothing—thick grey material that hid any notion of gender from the eye. The man scuttled sideways, away from the empty face, around the arm splayed out from the body, to kneel in the gap between forearm and waist. From here he could look down at the corpse's back, and see the burnt edges of a hole in the material between the shoulder blades. He frowned, and picked at the fabric with a finger, cooing like a confused infant. Something stirred, deep in the recesses of his mind, and he slapped at the corpse's back in an effort to drive it away. He tilted his head to take in as much as he could without looking directly at the head. A splash of faded colour caught his attention, high on the arm, almost at the shoulder. He shifted position, brought his face down to peer at it. A circle of light blue, and what might have been letters, if the man could recognise any such thing and if the design was not so faded by long exposure. He poked at it, then without knowing why he did so, looked at his own shoulder, seeing only his own skin, burnt dark and tough. He rested his fingers there for a moment, then looked back at the discoloured roundel.

Suddenly he was up and running along the beach, away from the corpse, away from the direction in which he had come. He keened, a long ululation torn directly from some forgotten grief, bringing forth tears that muddied the world around him. He tripped, fell to his knees, and rose once more, flight fuelled by an inexplicable terror. He knew only that he had to run, to scream, to get away as fast and as far as he could before whatever thoughts circled the corpse could descend upon him. He ran until his legs gave way and he fell at the edge of the high-water mark, knees digging scars into the wet ground, hands splayed outwards in unconscious imitation of the dead body now a hundred metres behind him. He lay like that for hours, as the sun seared his back, moaning softly. At last he wound down. His sobs became whimpers, then fell into heavy, agonised breaths. His fists clenched and released, kneading handfuls of sand. He drew his legs under him, stiffened his arms, and rose to a dog-like stance. Slowly, slowly, his breathing normalised. He raised his head, opened his eyes, and focussed once more upon the world around him.

And saw the ship.

It lay in the surf like an abandoned wreck: burst open and broken-backed, exposed to the wind and the sand that piled about its edges and threatened to swallow it whole. A million ticks and groans filled the air around it as the sea breeze whispered through the hull's gaps. Dangling panels kept counterpoint by slapping softly against the rusting body. Writing and insignia dotted the outer skin, scoured by the wind and rusted out by the ocean salt. Even if the man could speak the language, he could not have made out more than the occasional angle or subtle change in the stain spreading out across the ship's body.

High up the side, towards the pointed end of the body, a bubble of metal and glass looked out over the rolling waves, and perhaps a dozen feet behind it a gash ran along the skin to disappear into the sand. The man stared at it, slowly climbing to his feet and shuffling forward as if reluctantly returning to a long-evacuated home. Something in the air changed as he approached, some quality of light and heat blocked out by the sheer bulk of the ship, so that he curled arms around his chest and shivered. Even so, it was no more than fifteen minutes after catching sight of it that he stood at the base of the gash, and stretched out a trembling hand to brush fingers against the hull. The gap was wider than it had appeared at first sight: wide enough that three men could have walked through without touching the sides. Inside he could see a jumble of steel beams, gantries, boxes, and unrecognisable detritus, rolled and folded over each other in a catastrophic mess. Wires hung like gossamer so that he could see no more than a dozen feet, even though the light that filtered through the scene made it apparent that the breach ran all the way round the ship's hull and down the other side. The man took a hesitant step onto the nearest flat surface, then another. A third, and he was wholly encased in the metal space. He looked about, and saw himself contained. Something broke within him, then, and he slowly sunk to his knees, then further, to lay insensate on the cold metal floor.

He spent a week inside the vessel, exploring the countless rooms and corridors like an animal invading an abandoned burrow—sniffing the air and fingering the surroundings as if half-expecting to fight the previous owner for possession. He found food in a storage room near the rear of the vessel, ripping silver bags open with his teeth and cramming the dried contents down until he was ill. Dripping pipes provided water, salty and tannic, that he sucked until they ran dry and he was forced to move onwards in the search for more. Slowly, through staterooms where he stared blankly at lockers full of silver clothes and papers, past rooms full of arcane machines rusted into immobility, along corridors where lights fizzed and popped at his approach, he completed a circuit of the ruined ship, until the floors tilted upwards, and the journey became a long climb towards a single hatch at the end of a corridor, that hissed half-open before grinding to a halt. He gripped the edge of the door with one hand, hauled himself over, and finally entered the control room beneath the bubble.

The first things he saw were the windows. A dozen feet high, arching overheard to form a giant sphere of glass with spiderweb-thin framework, they dominated the room, providing a backdrop of sky to the control panels that ran around their bottom. Five seats sat equidistant about the cabin's circumference, each one little more than a metal framework supporting a nest of leather rags and mouldy stuffing. Cracks ran through the glass—a surface tough enough to withstand collisions with high-speed particles shattered by the impact with the planet's surface. In the middle of the room, set on a raised metal plinth, stood a taller, deeper chair, its seat turned with the angle of the deck. A single panel leaned drunkenly before it on a warped and bent frame. The man set his feet on the floor and half-stepped, half-slid, towards it. He grabbed its back, and peered around the edge of the chair, staring down at the thin line of sand and water that meandered at a crazy angle outside. Without being entirely aware of his actions he shimmied around until he stood in front of the chair, then climbed up and sat in it, eyes transfixed upon the sand.

His weight settled into the fractured webbing. Something below his buttock clicked. Slowly, with a sub-audible grinding of gears, the chair rotated towards the panel. The man whimpered, and brought his legs defensively upwards to his chest. A bank of lights on the panel flickered and died. Something in the air hissed. The man recoiled deeper as a burst of static sounded, then slowly resolved into a voice that filled the air around him.

'. . . come, Michael. Please place your hands on the . . . m of the chair. Repeat. Welcome . . . ael. Please pla . . . our hands on the arm of the chair. Rep . . . come, Michael . . . '

The man panicked. He tried to haul himself out of the chair, his only instinct now to get out, to flee the room and the terrifying sounds and run across the sand as far and as fast as he could. He gripped the end of the arms. Something stung his right hand. He had just enough time to pull it free, and stare at the bright red drop of blood on his palm, before sleep reared up and turned the world black.

He woke from a dream of soft whisperings and warm waves of comfort. Above him, stars glittered through the broken glass. He coughed, and reached up to wipe gunk from the corners of his eyes. A gentle, empty, voice, spoke.

'Welcome back, Michael.'

He looked about himself, blinking back the lethargy of long sleep.

'Where am I?' He flinched at the sound of his voice.

'You are . . . eated at the bridge, Michael.'

'Michael?'

'That is . . . ame. You are . . . chael Muller.'

'I don't . . . my name?'

'Michael Muller. Date of bi . . . of Ju . . . thirty-four. Age twenty-two years ni . . . en days. DNA profile mat . . . dred . . . er cent.'

'I . . . I can talk. I . . . can . . . remember, almost . . . ' He frowned, trying to catch thoughts that dipped and flew away from him.

'Deep learning. I have bee . . . eaking while you sleep. You have been asl . . . p for approximately thr . . . days, Terran.'

'But . . . ' He stared about himself in sudden, unnameable panic. 'I . . . I don't . . . '

'Things will . . . r as the drugs exit your syste . . . Please make your way to the Captain's stater . . . m. Things will become . . . ear.'

'The . . . '

'Follow the lights, Mich . . . ' Above him, and to the side, a row of lights flickered into half-life, leading down the askew floor towards the door through which he had entered. Michael slowly slipped out of the chair, and slid down the floor after them. He caught himself by the open door and peered down into the corridor. The lights continued another fifteen feet or so down the incline, before turning and stopping directly in front of the wall. Michael gauged the fall, inspecting each wall as best he could for handholds and protrusions. When he was satisfied that he could make it, he eased himself over the edge, and made his way down like a child descending a tree. After twenty minutes of tentative travel, he wedged himself between two buttresses, and viewed the wall into which the lights disappeared. Two faded lines of paint outlined a door. Michael had missed it on the climb upwards. There was no handle, no control pad, nothing beyond the two lines to suggest possible entry.

'What now?' he asked the corridor. The computer's voice crackled back at him from a nearby speaker.

'Place your hand in the . . . ntre, chest high.'

'Right.' He shifted, careful not to lose his balance, until he stood at roughly the same angle as the doorway.

He braced himself, and slowly reached out to touch the surface of the door.

'Nothing's happening.'

'Contact upon door . . . face is two hundred . . . limetres too high.'

Michael looked down. The buttresses placed him a foot above the floor. He nodded, and lowered his hand. There was an almost-silent click, and the door before him slid open, silently and smoothly. Michael stared at the room beyond.

It was a stateroom, but a stateroom transformed into something that might well have served as a jungle gym. The original floor was still visible, inclined at the same angle as the rest of the ship's upper half, but nothing matched it. Bumps and protrusions jutted from every visible surface, a pimpling of foot and handholds that spoke of a concerted effort over many months to make the space habitable. At Michael's entrance, lights flickered into life, including several hanging on lines above his head.

'Oh, my God.' Everywhere he looked, repairs and adjustments met his gaze. A hammock hung to his left, the mattress and blankets from the useless bed beyond nestled within. Across from him, welded in place below the crazily-angled window, a bench from the galley cut across the angle of floor and wall to form a work-table, scattered with papers, wires and unidentifiable gewgaws that Michael suddenly itched to explore. A bar stool swung out from one leg, thick seams of weld visible where someone had attached it. Boiler suits in a variety of colours hung from a horizontal bar near the hammock, and beyond that, a door-less hatchway promised a glimpse of the bathroom beyond. Michael suddenly felt every inch of dirt and grime on his skin; the weariness that dragged at his joints; the thick, twisted matting of his hair and beard. He stared around him, a savage confronted with the first signs of civilisation, and tears drew lines through the grey dust of his face. 'What . . . what is this place?'

The computer answered him, voice clear and strong through speakers cleaned and repaired and waiting.

'This is your cabin, Michael,' it said. 'Welcome home.'

It took him a week to ask the first serious question. He spent the intervening time exploring the space, learning to navigate the paths of handholds and blocks that made up the floor. Slowly he adjusted, until clambering monkey-like amongst the protrusions was as natural as walking, and he could swing his way from hammock to bathroom to corridor and back as easily as think. A bookshelf set high in the corner contained a dozen thick manuals, arrayed neatly by subject and date, that detailed the working of the ship and the necessary repairs needed to maintain the climate control, lights, and communications systems. Some were incomplete, with gaps where pages had been torn in some other, madder day. He scoured the wreck's innards for pencils and paper, spent long hours slowly stumbling through the thick books, making notes and filling in the missing knowledge with his best attempts at logic and guesswork. Slowly, inch by mental inch, he began to understand, so that when a speaker fizzed and popped into silence he was able to remove it from its hole in the wall, trace the wiring back to a ruined transformer, and source a replacement from a darkened galley lower down.

Even so, parts of the ship showed evidence of human occupation before him, and he found himself using those places with little sense of comfort. The door to the bathroom had been removed. Someone had beaten an abandoned locker into the shape of a bath. It filled the tiny space, and he had to stand in it to use the hand basin. Amazingly, the taps still worked, and he was able to attach the hose he found in the metal vanity and fill the makeshift tub with hot water, sobbing with pleasure as he lay with eyes closed and let the water soak into his knotted muscles. A spigot on the side emptied the water into a hole in the floor: he listened to it surge down hidden pipes to hit a metal surface some way below his perch. An even greater wonder was the shaving kit next to the hose: he spent an hour shaving, meticulously cleaning the scissors and razor then replacing them in their leather holder and wiping the top of the tube of cream when he had finished, before carefully placing them back where he had found them. So much work had been done, and he was aware that he was the architect of none of it. After a week he still felt like an intruder, and every new discovery was of someone else's possessions, a loan of someone else's life. He wiped his hand across the fogged mirror, and stared at his white, clean-shaven stranger's face.

'Computer?'

'Yes, Michael?'

'This is my cabin.'

'Yes, Michael.'

He stared into the mirror, eyes sliding from his own

face to the jury-rigged environment behind him. He took in the bedding, the books on their shelves, and the piles of accumulated items that spoke of months of determined collection.

'Everything in here belongs to me.'

'Yes, Michael.'

He considered his question for long seconds.

'Who put it all together, computer?'

There was a short pause, so that he almost fancied the computer was considering its reply. Then: 'You did, Michael.'

He nodded, then, and closed his eyes, not wishing to see his reaction to the computer's next response.

'When?' he asked the blackness. 'When did I do this?'

'You began after the last remaining survivor died,' the computer said. 'Eleven years, four months, thirteen days ago.'

Everything had a name attached to it, a previous owner from whom he had scavenged the homeliness of his bolt hole. Michael set out in search of them: the ghosts he imagined haunting the corridors, the dead and silent passengers of the ship. He found nothing. The computer knew. Of that much he was certain. Their names were in a database, their biographies recorded, their actions and voices hiding away deep inside its electronic memory. He spurned those. He needed to hold them in his hands, to feel their existence as a living, tangible thing. He found only echoes. The ship had long ago been cleaned out. Anything that might have given him some clue as to the lives of the missing crew members was already in his possession. Time after time he returned to his room to turn some tiny piece of falderal over and over in his hands, as if constant contact might bring him knowledge through osmosis: a lighter he had found in the stateroom's tiny kitchenette, the leg from a pair of glasses, his razor. He could not bring himself to ask the computer, did not want to hear their lives dispassionately recounted by that empty, artificial voice. In the end he set his mind against it, and turned to other matters.

'Computer,' he said one night, lying in his hammock with hands behind his head. 'Where are we?'

'In the stateroom, Michael.'

'No.' He sat up, swung his legs over the edge, and stared out of the window into the dark. 'The ship. Where is it?'

'Location unidentified.'

'What does that mean?'

'I cannot answer that question.'

Michael sighed. He had become used to that answer in the months he had spent in the ship. The computer could only recount what was recorded within its systems. It could not offer opinions, or deal in anything other than absolutes. Bit by bit Michael had become more precise in his questioning. Still, frustrations remained.

'Is this island inhabited?'

'No intelligent life forms have been recorded.'

'How extensive are your records?'

'Pre-impact recordings show no intelligent life forms recorded.'

Michael frowned in thought.

'Where is the nearest life form?'

'I cannot answer that question.'

'Where . . . um, what is the location of the last recorded

interaction with a life form? Outside of this ship,' he added quickly. The computer hummed for a moment.

'Last recorded interaction with a life form recorded at co-ordinates axial 37.5, ecliptic 18.27, one hundred and nineteen thousand AU from galactic point zero.'

Michael stared at the speaker. 'What does *that* mean?'

'I cannot answer that question?'

'How far away is it?'

'I cannot answer that question.'

'Well . . . then . . . what are *our* co-ordinates?'

'I cannot answer that question.'

Michael broke his gaze from the speaker, and caught sight of the stars outside his window. He stared at them for hours, whilst the night deepened and the only sound came from the ticking monologue of the cooling hull.

He left his room the next morning, and spent days travelling through the bowels of the ship. Without light to guide his days he slept whenever he was tired, in whatever corner of the corridors he found himself, eating only when hunger overcame him. Once he was back, he spent a day hunched over his table, refusing to speak or even acknowledge the presence of the computer, making a series of pencil marks on a plan of the ship that he shielded with his arm as if preventing a classmate from copying his work. The computer remained silent. When he had finished he stuck the diagram to one wall and left it there for another week, absorbing it as he worked around it, waiting for a subconscious clue to warn him of something he may have overlooked, any mistake he may have made. When nothing presented itself, he spent an afternoon making a list on a piece of paper with the pencil stub. Finally, after nearly ten days of silence, he spoke.

'Computer?'

'Yes, Michael?' The answer was swift, the voice steady, as if the computer had been waiting for the opportunity to talk.

'I want to feed a list into your databases and check them against your stores records. Where can I do that?'

'The engineer's position in the control cabin has a working terminal. You can access it—'

'Yes, I know.'

The computer fell silent. Michael swung over to the door, and entered the corridor. He was at the control cabin within a minute. He had grown quicker in his wanderings, and now moved around the inner workings of the ship with practiced ease. He had not visited the cabin since his arrival. Now that he did, he could see how the engineer's terminal was cleaner than the others, how it was in better condition: the seat patched and repaired, the workstation empty of the worst excesses of dust and neglect, the keyboard and monitor neither chipped nor missing any elements. Michael paused, his fingers over the keyboard.

'How many times have I used this keyboard?' he asked aloud.

'Seventeen, Michael.' The computer's voice came from within the monitor: whisper quiet, with perfect clarity. The larger, broken speakers that dotted the walls remained silent. Michael frowned.

'I . . . have I been through all this before?'

'I cannot answer that question.'

Michael sighed. He laid his list down next to him and began typing. When he was finished he hit the 'enter' key and leaned back, eyes closed.

'Locate these items and advise.'

A second later the monitor emitted a small noise. Michael opened his eyes, and saw his list displayed, a location next to each item.

'All together.'

'Yes, Michael.'

Michael nodded. 'Provide a map, please.'

A schematic of the ship appeared on the monitor. Michael gazed at it for several seconds.

'Two back, one up,' he muttered. 'Top of the dorsal hump. Right where . . . ' he broke off the thought. 'Right. Thank you, computer.' He rose from the chair, and swung back to the corridor. The path through the maze of passageways was well lit, and he had no problem finding his way up to the relevant room. He paused inside the entrance, and laid his hand over the light switch. The lights flickered on automatically, and he sank to his haunches at the sight before him.

A long workbench dominated the room, which was empty of any other furniture. Atop it stood a conglomeration of wiring and computer parts that would have made no sense to an untrained eye. But Michael had been living with the design for over a week. It was a transmitter, powerful enough to breach the atmosphere of a planet and send a subspace signal deep into the surrounding regions of space. A thin patina of dust overlaid its surface, like everything else in the ship, but there was no mistaking the signs of upkeep. The lights in the ceiling held a steady glow, highlighting the machine with merciless clarity. Michael slumped backwards and sat against the wall.

'How long?' he asked the air. 'How long has this been here?'

'The machine was constructed thirty-four days after impact,' the computer's voice came clearly.

'Thirty-four days . . . ' Michael raised his head, stared at the speaker. 'Has it . . . has it been used?'

'The machine has been used a total of eleven times.'

'Eleven . . . me? By me?'

There was an almost imperceptible pause, as the computer searched its memory banks. 'You have used the machine ten times.'

'Ten times.' Michael stared at the machine, hands gripping the fabric of his trousers so that his knuckles whitened. 'Who else?'

'Captain Andreas Muller.'

'When?' Michael clawed his way to a standing position. 'When, damn it?'

'Eleven years, four months, thirteen days ago,' the computer responded immediately. 'Thirty-five days after impact.'

'So long.' He stared at the speaker until his eyes began to water, then blinked, and inhaled deeply. 'Was there . . . ' he coughed, and tried again, his voice less shaky. 'Responses?' he asked. 'Have there ever been any responses?'

'One response received.'

'When?' He found himself leaning over the speaker, shouting into its impassive grill. 'When?'

'Eleven years, four months, thirteen days ago.'

The wall was cool. He leaned his forehead against it,

and closed his eyes. After the longest time, he trusted himself to whisper, 'Was it recorded?'

'Yes, Michael.'

'Play it.'

'Yes, Michael.'

A moment's silence, and then a new voice filled the room—strong, deep, with an accent that Michael found both slightly odd and comforting at the same time.

'Mayday. Mayday. This is the pilgrim ship *Sarcalogos Immortalis* requesting immediate rescue. Mayday. Can anyone hear me?'

'Who is that?' Michael asked.

'That is Captain Andreas Muller.'

The voice repeated his call a dozen times, each enunciation measured, precise, lacking any note of panic or desperation, any emotion at all. And then, finally, a reply: faint, distorted by millions of miles and unknowable atmospheric effects, but a reply nonetheless. And the voice named Muller talked: detailing his ship's crash on an unknown planet, the destruction of the vessel's engines and lifting surfaces, the injured, the dead. There was a pause, and Michael waited with held breath while Muller and the unknown voice lapsed into silence. Then the voice returned, and Michael found himself muttering *no, no, no* over and over again as it spoke.

'Request denied,' it said. Too far from established ecliptic lanes. Too expensive to mount any sort of mission. Little chance of success. And, finally, 'You made your choice, Captain.' Even through the distortion, Michael could hear the contempt in his voice.

'What does he mean?' he asked the empty room. 'Computer, what does he mean?'

'I cannot answer that question.'

'But what choice? What choice is he talking about?'

'I cannot answer that question.'

'God damn it—' But Muller was speaking again, and the forlornness in his voice stopped Michael cold.

'Please,' the long-dead Captain said. 'My son. He's only eleven . . .'

There was no answer. The air hung silent and empty.

'Recording ends.'

Michael sagged, and slid back down the wall to a sitting position.

'What happened to them?'

'I cannot answer that question.'

'Well, what *can* you answer?' He kicked out at the bench, buried his head in his hands. 'Manifests, logs, something, please!' He closed his eyes, took long moments to settle his breathing. 'Check all logs and computer accesses, computer. Read them to me. Go backwards from the most recent.'

Ten empty seconds passed.

'Interior access panel operated, storage locker three, eleven years, four months, thirteen days ago. Exterior access panel operated, storage locker three, eleven years, four months, thirteen days ago—'

'What was in storage locker three?'

'Storage locker three. Firearms.'

'Right.'

Michael closed his eyes. A memory flashed across his inner sight—a body in the sand, the cloth between its shoulder blades black and ragged from some unknown cause. He tilted his head back, and banged it against the wall until the image broke up and disappeared. Slowly, as if lifting an enormous weight up the wall, Michael raised himself to a standing position. He stared at the transmitter for several minutes, then turned abruptly and left the room. When he returned ten minutes later, he was carrying an iron bar.

Michael stood in the ship's hold and looked through the broken hull at the dunes that spread out to the horizon. Behind him, the bath from his stateroom sat on the tiny hill of sand that had invaded the space. It had taken days of effort to remove it from the stateroom and drag it down to the exit. Now it crouched next to him, bottom smoothed out and welded to a pair of skis made from the railings that had supported his hammock. Inside, food packages and canteens of water lay piled up to the bath's upper edge, tamped down by the hammock and two thick, polyurethane blankets. Michael leaned on a button set into the hull's interior wall.

'Computer?'

A burst of static issued from a nearby speaker. ' . . . s, Mich . . . '

'How many times have I done this?'

'I . . . not answer . . . t ques . . . '

Michael nodded, and released the button. He bent down and picked up two ropes he had fashioned from all the safety webbing he could scrounge. He shouldered them, and pulled the makeshift sled down the little dune and away from the bulk of the ship. When he was sure he was far enough away, he left it, and returned one final time to the hold.

For three days he had collected every scrap of flammable material he could find, and piled them up in drifts that spilled out through the open door of the hold and twenty feet up the corridor, packed tight into every access panel along the way, every speaker he could reach, every conduit and hole that might carry flames higher up the structure. Michael stepped up to the paper mountain, and reached into his pocket, removing the lighter he had carried with him for so many weeks. Without a word he flicked it on, and held it to the edge of the nearest book until flames licked up around his fingers. Then he straightened, and threw the lighter into the middle of the pile.

He was already on the sand, and taking up his ropes, before the flames reached the corridor. By the time he hauled the sled a dozen feet, smoke was billowing from the massive hole in the hull, and the sound of the fire was already the loudest thing in the world. Michael walked up the beach without a backwards glance, away from the burning ship and the bodies under the sand.

The column of smoke stayed in the air for days.

Lee Battersby is the author of over seventy stories in such markets as *Year's Best Fantasy & Horror*, *Best Australian SF & Fantasy*, and *Best Australian Dark Fantasy & Horror*. A collection of his work, entitled *Through Soft Air*, has been published by Prime Books. He lives in Mandurah, Western Australia, with his wife, author Lyn Battersby, and a bunch of weird kids. He currently teaches SF for the Australian Writer's Marketplace Online, works as an Arts & Culture Officer for his Local Government Authority, writes half as often as he would like, and controls an urge to buy all the Lego he sets his eyes on. He has one wiimote in the shape of a sonic screwdriver and another made from Lego, but still insists he's not a nerd. That's because he's deluded. Find him at www. leebattersby.com

Unexpected Launch

Alan Baxter

Gareth stared, open mouthed, at flames blooming massive and silent against a backdrop of stars. Bright, molten debris spun out from orange and black clouds, folding in on themselves without more oxygen to fuel them. Then the deep black of space, an ocean of dark, twisted debris and the sound of Dean vomiting.

The rag and bottle of polish were forgotten in his hands. He became aware of Dean moving beside him, vomit bag held closed. Dean watched the debris moving past, balletic in its motion, occasionally clanging off their escape pod in random ricochets.

'What happened?' Dean asked, hoarse from his nausea.

'The ship's . . . gone.' Gareth looked away from the window. 'You wanna throw that away?'

'Oh yeah. Sorry. That launch was intense.' Dean pushed the bag into a waste disposal. A whoosh of air escaping into a vacuum and his vomit joined the debris drifting by.

Gareth looked out again. 'You see any other lifepods?'

'No.'

They moved around the small craft, checking each window. Eventually they sat in the two front seats. Gareth looked at the controls and readouts before him. He had cleaned them, and others like them, a thousand times but they meant nothing to him. 'What are we going to do?'

'Dunno.' Dean put down the handvac he was carrying, shrugged off the large tank. 'I don't know anything about this stuff.'

Gareth eventually chose a button, pressed it. A holographic display leapt up from the console, causing both men to sit back in alarm. The golden cube of light hung there, impassive. 'I've seen the crew using these, moving them about . . . ' Gareth's voice was almost a whisper as he slid his hand into the light.

'Can't you just ask?'

'Ask?'

'The computer.'

Gareth made a wry face, gesturing back over his shoulder. 'The ship's gone.'

Dean shrugged. 'Maybe the computer backs up everywhere? Just because *Cortain* the ship is gone, maybe Cortain the computer isn't.'

Gareth raised an eyebrow. He reached for the comm panel in the arm of his chair. 'Cortain?'

'Yes?'

The two men exchanged a look of surprise and delight. 'Are you the same Cortain as the computer on the ship?'

'Yes.'

'With the same data?'

'Yes, my data is preserved.'

Gareth nodded his head. 'Cortain, can you control this lifepod?'

'Yes.'

Both men slumped with sighs of relief. 'Cortain, what happened?'

'Please define your request.'

'What happened to the ship?'

'The vessel *Cortain* was destroyed in an unavoidable collision.'

'Did anyone else survive?'

'No.'

They exchanged a frightened look. 'So how come we survived?'

'You survived due to your presence within a lifepod. At the point of catastrophic impact to a vessel, all occupied lifepods autolaunch. If no lifepods are occupied, one lifepod will autolaunch to preserve onboard data.'

'To preserve you?'

'Yes.'

'And there's nothing else left of the *Cortain*.'

'According to onboard sensors, nothing salvageable remains.'

Gareth combed his fingertips back through greying hair. 'Shit.'

Dean, much younger than his co-worker, stared at the console. 'So what happened?' he whispered. 'Catastrophic impact?'

Gareth rubbed at his eyes. 'Cortain, what happened to the ship?'

'Something hit us.'

'Like an asteroid?'

'No, organic.'

'Organic?'

'Yes.'

'And it totalled the ship?'

'Yes.'

'What the hell . . .?'

Both men leaned forward, scanning the wide black outside. 'Where is it?' Gareth asked.

'Unknown.'

'What is it?'

'Unknown.'

The two men stood and moved nervously from window to window, trying to see all around the small pod. Gareth swallowed hard as he moved, feeling incredibly vulnerable. If something had been able to wipe out a massive vessel like the *Cortain* in a single blow, the lifepod would seem like a bug to a giant. Perhaps that would work to their advantage, they might not be noticed.

What could destroy a vessel the size of the *Cortain*? Gareth swallowed again, thinking of all the lives snuffed out in an instant. No warning, no chance to do anything. One minute the *Cortain* was cruising along, the next it was space gravel. Gone, taking thirty-five hundred lives with it. Well, thirty-four hundred and ninety-eight. And now what? His heart racing, Gareth realised that he needed to start acting less like a cleaner and more like a crew member. He had Dean to look after.

'Cortain?'

'Yes?'

'What systems on board are currently . . . er . . . on?'

'Lifepod is silent running, unpowered, on launch trajectory. Basic life support and close range sensors operating.'

Gareth nodded. 'Good. Please keep it that way and . . . can you turn down the lights?'

The pod dimmed to near darkness, a gentle concealed glow and the holocube on the console the only light sources.

Dean looked pale. 'What are you doing?'

'Just trying to make us as inconspicuous as possible.'

'Can't we just power up and leave? It can't be far to the nearest system or outpost.'

'Maybe. I have no idea where we are. We were a long way out, I know that much. But if we fire up the engines we might attract whatever it was that smashed the *Cortain*.'

Dean shuddered, sat heavily into his seat again. 'So what do we do?'

Gareth took a long breath. 'I'm not really sure. Cortain?'

'Yes?'

'Do you have any visuals of what happened?'

The holocube on the console grew up and out into a wide rectangular screen. Gold light morphed into a view of open space. From the bottom of the screen stars appeared to be going out, a semi-circular line travelling upwards, extinguishing stars as it moved. The semi-circle partly resolved into something solid, blacker than the space around it, slightly reflective in places. Lightning fast a whip of darkness, wider than the *Cortain* was long, flicked out of the massive presence, filling the screen in an instant. The display returned to the soft gold hologram.

The men sat stunned. 'What in all the deep black was that?' Dean whispered eventually.

Gareth could feel himself trembling. Whatever it was it put him on the verge of open panic. What could exist that was that big and that fast and that black . . .? It wasn't long ago that first contact had been made, the bizarre Pietre Gans story that had been all over the news for several months. But this was something else entirely.

Gareth tried to process everything into some coherent course of action. 'Cortain?'

'Yes?'

'Where are we?'

'Sector 14, quadrant 8XB.'

He blinked. 'I don't know what that means. What are we near?'

'Please define your request.'

'Are we near any outposts or settlements?'

'No. The *Cortain* was a deep space exploration vessel. We are in uncharted territory.'

Gareth could hear Dean's breathing increase rapidly. 'How far are we from any kind of rescue?'

'Using fuel conservation, maintaining life support, this lifepod could reach Outpost 4X-11 in forty-three days.'

Dean made a noise like a sob and gulp combined.

'How much food and water are on board?' Gareth asked.

'Recycling and food prep could be stretched, at bare minimum for human survival for two occupants, to twenty six days.'

Gareth scrunched up his face at the mental arithmetic. 'So that's seventeen days without food or water?'

'Correct.'

'What about oxygen?'

'Sixty days.'

'So we have enough air. Can we survive for the last seventeen days without food or water?'

'Unlikely.'

'Unlikely?'

'You will have already been subsisting on the absolute bare minimum in terms of nutrition and hydration.'

Dean looked stricken. 'There has to be an alternative.'

'One person could survive for considerably longer than two in these conditions.'

Gareth's eyes widened. 'What?'

Dean's eyes were narrowed, looking sidelong at Gareth, as if weighing him up. Gareth shook his head. 'Remember that day, Dean, when you and Trell thought you'd play a trick on me?'

Dean deflated in his chair. 'You hospitalised us both.'

Gareth nodded. 'You shouldn't play tricks on me. I act first and think later. Bear that in mind if your hunger causes you to imagine a nice steak sauce running over me.'

Dean looked contrite, casting his eyes at the floor. 'Sorry, mate. I'm just a bit panicky.'

'I know. Cortain, are there any alternatives to eating each other?'

'I meant that one of you could survive for longer on existing rations if the other chose to eject. If one of you ate the other, that person could last considerably longer still, though that person would be in breach of several articles of the Democratic Alliance of Planets Space Exploration Code, as well as a number of other laws.'

Gareth waved both hands. 'Forget it, we are not eating each other and no-one is taking a space walk. Are there alternatives that include us both staying on board and alive?'

'Already a distress signal has been activated. Depending on when that signal is intercepted and where the nearest vessel is, a rescue could be mounted inside the forty-three days it would take to travel to Outpost 4X-11.'

Gareth thought long and hard. 'And if we began the journey towards 4X-11, that rescue is likely to intercept us even sooner?'

'If such a rescue is mounted.'

'If?'

'Yes.'

'Why would a rescue not be mounted?'

'The distress beacon signal includes data relating to the incident which destroyed the *Cortain* and information relating to survivors. The Democratic Alliance of Planets operating procedure states that the DAP would need to deem the situation safe and the rescue of enough value to direct a vessel this way.'

Gareth made several incoherent curses under his breath before he found his voice. 'Why wouldn't the rescue be of value? Just because we're cleaning staff? We're just as important a part of the crew as anyone else!'

Dean nodded. 'That's right. The Super always says a dirty ship wouldn't get anywhere fast.'

They looked at each other, thinking about the truth of that claim for the first time. Gareth could see his concern mirrored in Dean's eyes. 'Cortain, they would come for us, wouldn't they?'

'Almost certainly, if the sector of space where the rescue takes place is deemed safe.'

Almost certainly. Better than maybe, not as good as

definitely. But if something had wiped out a ship like the *Cortain* in a single swipe, the lives of two DAP cleaners were not really worth the same thing happening again. Perhaps they would send a war ship. The *Cortain* was very well equipped, considerable weapons and defensive capabilities, even a cleaner knew that. But it was no battleship. Maybe a battle cruiser would come for them.

'Cortain, the organic thing that hit the *Cortain*; is it still here?'

'Nothing appears on any sensors. However, nothing appeared on any sensors until moments before the strike. Therefore, it is possible that whatever it was is still within striking distance and not registering.'

'But it did register briefly before the strike?'

'Correct. As you saw in the vision, something appeared for a few seconds before it struck, and that registered on all sensors.'

'What did the crew make of it?'

'Would you like to view the vision again, with bridge crew audio?'

'Yes, please.'

The wide, gold holoscreen darkened again and showed nothing but deep space. This time the general hubbub of bridge crew chatter accompanied it.

' . . . heading confirmed, Captain, as per DAP HQ.'

'All systems clear.'

The deeper blackness appeared at the bottom of the screen.

'Captain, we've got a massive signal on all sensors.'

'Identify.'

'Source, unknown. Composition, organic. Sir, it's huge and moving incredibly fast.'

'Captain, it's heading directly for the *Cortain*.'

'Full scan, Ensign. I need to know what that thing is.'

'Sir, there's an enormous energy burst flooding our sensors. Scans are interrupted.'

'What's moving in front of it? Is something extending from . . .'

Gareth jumped as the screen flicked back to the dull gold of the holoscreen on standby. 'Cortain, what did the scan show?'

'The impact occurred before the scan was complete. It was an organic signature, incredibly dense. Chemical analysis was incomplete, but did register carbon along with a variety of other compounds.'

It made very little sense. All Gareth really understood was that something enormous had destroyed the *Cortain* in a single hit and that thing was unidentifiable. Presumably this data would be of use to scientists somewhere.

Dean was watching Gareth, face still pale. 'What do we do?'

'We need to get moving, I suppose. Cortain, could we get away unnoticed?'

'Unknown.'

'Can we try very slowly at first, so any thruster activity is minimal?'

'Yes.'

Gareth took a deep breath. He looked at Dean and his eyebrows flicked up. 'Cortain, can you set a course for Outpost 4X-11?'

'Course laid in.'

'Get us under way with absolute minimum power, please?'

'Confirmed.'

Both men held their breath as a gentle hum rose through the hull. A soft glow brightened the rear windows as thrusters were engaged. Gareth moved to the side windows as stars began to slide by. Dean nervously stood and took a station opposite. 'What are we looking for?' he asked in a weak voice.

Gareth shook his head. 'I don't really know. Anything that looks blacker than space? Cortain, will you keep scanning for any movement or anything . . . organic?'

'Confirmed. All sensors have been extended to mid range.'

Gareth and Dean walked about the small pod, almost tiptoeing, checking one window then the next. They breathed shallowly when they breathed at all, eyes wide and haunted, watching for any shadows in the vastness of space. The gentle hum of the drive mechanism and the occasional beep from the console were the only sounds for several long, slow minutes.

The men began to stalk a bit more purposefully around the pod. 'Anything on sensors?' Gareth asked.

'Nothing.'

'Can we pick up the pace, just a little bit?'

'Affirmative. Our energy signature will not increase significantly if we move up to full power.'

Gareth pursed his lips. He looked at Dean. 'Shall we chance it?'

Dean looked spooked. 'Run for it, you mean?'

Gareth nodded.

'Okay.'

'Cortain, can you take us up to full power in increments? Say, accelerate by ten per cent every ten seconds until we're at full power?'

'Confirmed.'

The soft hum from the drive mechanism increased. Gareth tried to cast his eyes all around the pod at once. He could feel tension knitting his shoulder blades together. Dean strode from one window to the next, his pace increasing along with the speed of the pod. The hum of the engines rose until it was a soft roar, a vibration that soon became white noise.

'Maximum speed attained. Heading for DAP Outpost 4X-11, ETA one thousand and forty-two hours, sixteen minutes.'

'Is this as fast as we can go?' Dean asked.

'No. But it is as fast as this pod can travel while maintaining enough fuel to reach Outpost 4X-11.'

Both men took their seats at the helm again. Their eyes scanned the wide open black beyond the screen. Gareth couldn't help feeling as though something was just behind him, phantom hands reaching for his back as he forced himself not to get up and check all the windows once more. 'Cortain, you're keeping all sensors active? You'll know if . . . anything's out there?'

'Yes.'

Gareth sighed and leaned back in his chair. 'Well. I guess we just wait then.'

'And ration our food,' Dean added. He sounded miserable.

Gareth reached out, squeezed his friend's shoulder. 'We'll be all right, mate. We're on the way and someone will pick up our distress signal in no time.'

'I hope so. We're pretty deep.'

Gareth forced a small laugh, turning away so that

Dean wouldn't see the fear in his eyes. 'Sure, we're deep. But someone will be out there and they'll hear us and they'll come and get us.'

The tension and fear of the unknown soon gave way to concern for survival. After several hours the expectation of giant, shining black tendrils of space swatting them to oblivion receded as the fear of starving to death became more apparent.

'A hundred mills of water doesn't even touch the sides.' Dean looked disconsolately at the empty cup in his hands.

'It's more about staying alive than enjoying it.' Gareth stared out the window, watching infinity slide by.

'Sal's dead.'

Gareth pulled his eyes back to Dean, sat slumped on the cot opposite him. 'What's that?'

'Sal. She's dead.'

'Ah, you were going out with that blonde, worked in the officer's bar?'

Dean nodded, still staring at his empty cup. 'She was really nice. We were, you know, getting serious.'

'Didn't realise it was like that.'

'Yeah, we were planning a kind of holiday for the next shore leave. I was thinking about . . . well, you know.'

Gareth watched the young man's bowed head. 'I'm sorry, Dean. Really, I am.'

Dean looked up sharply. 'What about you?'

'What?'

'You have anyone on board?'

Gareth shook his head. 'Nah, I'm a bit old for all that. I took this job, switched to long haul stuff, after my wife died a few years ago. I had a lot of friends on board, of course.'

Dean looked down again. 'All gone now. Dead, just like that.'

As hours became a day, the reality of forty-three days began to settle on them. Gareth tried to think of ways to keep Dean's spirits up. 'Game of cards?' he asked, trying to sound chirpier than he felt.

'If you like.'

'Cortain, can you make a standard deck?'

The men sat at the front console as Cortain produced playing cards. Gareth took them, still warm from printing, and shuffled. 'Ruminan's Gambit?'

Dean shrugged.

Gareth dealt and they played in silence for a few minutes.

'How did she die?' Dean asked.

Gareth looked up from his hand. 'What's that?'

'Your wife.'

'Oh. Hit by a transport in a city hub on Intensia Prime.' Gareth frowned, pained by the memory. 'We were on holiday.'

Dean made a rueful face. 'That sucks. Sorry, man.'

'Still trying to get used to it really.'

'Reckon it might take me a while to get over losing Sal.'

Gareth looked into Dean's eyes, saw the raw pain and fear there. 'Yeah,' he said quietly. 'It'll take a while. But time does help to heal the wounds. These people always live on in here, mate.' He tapped his chest.

Dean nodded, his face drawn. 'I can't believe they're

all gone. Only us left.'

'Yeah. It's kinda hard to get your head around.'

'What was it?'

'What?'

'The thing that smashed the *Cortain*.'

Gareth drew a deep breath. 'I don't know. Something massive. Something alien.'

'It could be anywhere.'

'I know. Let's hope it stayed out there. Maybe we strayed into its territory. We can tell people what happened and everyone can avoid that area of space until we know more about it.'

Dean looked up to a side window. 'Or it could be with us. Or ahead of us. It came from nowhere.'

'Yeah. Well, we don't know, so let's try to focus on the positive. Until proven otherwise, I'm going to consider it back there, where we left it.'

Dean said nothing, still staring out the window.

One day became two, then three. A black cloud of despair fogged the pod. Watching recordings of old shows and movies, reading archived books, listlessly playing games through the console. All these things were like treading water, knowing that sharks circled restlessly in the shadows below. The uncertainty was debilitating, wondering if anyone would come for them.

Gareth looked over to Dean, lying on his bunk, staring up at a holoscreen showing an old colony movie, nibbling minutely at a dry ration. The young man was becoming more disconsolate, retreating into himself. 'You thought about what you might do when we get picked up?' Gareth asked.

Dean turned his head, his eyes dull. 'What?'

'You're a young man, the universe yours for the taking. You don't want to be a cleaner all your life, do you?'

'You have been.'

Gareth raised an eyebrow. 'I've done all kinds of things actually. Driven transports, worked in a shipbuilding yard, maintenance bays at Berelli Spaceport. Loads of stuff.' He took a deep breath. 'I even spent a couple of years in prison.'

Dean's interest was piqued. 'Really? What for?'

'Killed a guy. It was self-defence, but I was busted for excessive force, stitched up on a manslaughter charge.'

Dean looked unimpressed. 'Really? You making up stories to scare me?'

Gareth laughed, surprised. 'I'm not the sort of person to lie, Dean. I've never told anyone before. I thought maybe we could learn a bit more about each other, you know, share some stuff or something.'

Dean's eyes narrowed. 'If you'd been on a Custody Yacht you wouldn't be allowed to work long haul now.'

'You can buy a new identity if you know where to look, mate.'

Dean laughed without humour. 'Sure, Gareth.' He flicked a hand at the holoscreen above him. 'You should write stories for the holos, mate.'

Gareth wanted to give Dean hope, raise his interest, charge some life back into the boy, but it seemed like Dean just saw a sad old man. 'Prison was an interesting place,' he said, trying one last time. 'I've got some stories to tell!'

Dean turned back to his movie. 'Good for you.'

Gareth watched the young man, concern in his eyes. 'You should think about it,' he said eventually. 'Plan for what you might do when we're rescued. It's a chance to start over, look for something new.'

Dean turned up the volume on his movie.

'Cortain, any signals?' Gareth asked, one hand pressed to his stomach. He was so hungry he felt constantly nauseous.

'None.'

Dean grunted. 'She'd tell us if there was, man, you don't have to keep asking.'

'I suppose,' Gareth said. 'It's just something to do.'

'Bloody annoying, that's what it is.'

'All right, Dean. No need to be a dick about it.'

Dean swung his legs off the bunk, sitting up straight. 'A dick? A dick is someone that keeps asking ridiculous questions that he already knows the answer to!'

Gareth's heart hammered. He could see barely repressed rage in Dean's face. He could fight, but Dean was younger, desperate. Dean was also scared, hurt with grief and impotently angry. He lost more patience every day. Gareth raised his hands, placating. 'Let's just chill out, eh? No need to start getting ratty at each other. It's only been five days, there's a long way to go yet.'

Dean slumped back onto the bed. 'Five days. I'm already starving to death.'

For the first few days eating only the bare minimum to survive hadn't seemed so bad. Being largely inactive, restricted for space, eating very little had seemed easy. Now fat reserves were beginning to wane and the minuscule portions seemed more and more ludicrous.

Gareth sighed. 'Me too. But Cortain is giving us enough to keep us alive.'

Dean made a noise of disgust. 'Shame there's two of us.'

Gareth turned back to his book, deciding to let that comment slide for the sake of both their sanity.

The sounds of gunfire and mayhem from Dean's bunk drilled into Gareth's ears. 'Can you turn that down a bit?'

Dean said nothing.

'Dean, will you turn the movie down?'

Dean reached out and tapped his cot-side console. The volume of the movie barely reduced at all.

Gareth ground his teeth for a moment. He was keen to keep Dean in good spirits, but the kid was trying his patience by the hour. Perhaps he needed to assert some authority, re-establish a pecking order. 'Dean, turn it down!'

Dean looked over at him, sneering. 'Or what?'

Gareth stood, heart racing. 'Or I'll break your bloody nose, that's what!'

Dean's lips twitched, miming some internal monologue. Still staring hard into Gareth's eyes he reached out and turned the volume down a few more notches. Gareth rummaged in a small locker by his bunk, turned back with a pair of wireless earbuds. 'In fact, use these. I'm sick of the constant noise of your crazy movies.'

Dean snatched the buds, pressed them into his ears with his thumbs. 'Can't be bad as the constant noise of your bloody nagging.' He turned back to the now silent film before Gareth could answer.

Gareth nodded to himself, sat back down. The poor kid was suffering, he had to remember that. He was suffering too, and wished someone would comfort him, but perhaps looking out for Dean was somehow keeping him in check. He was older, wiser, tougher. He was no less scared, but one of them had to stay strong.

On the ninth day Cortain interrupted them. 'I'm receiving fairly current recorded signals on several frequencies.'

Gareth sat up, excited. 'Recorded?'

'Yes. Just broadcasts, drifting beyond the initial bands, but it is evidence that we're getting closer to occupied space.'

'How much closer?' Dean asked gruffly.

'We're still thirty-four days from Outpost 4X-11, which is the nearest known human base. Unless there are other vessels this side of Outpost 4X-11, we're still thirty-four days from contact.'

Dean grunted, rammed his earbuds back in.

'Cortain, how far ahead of us is the distress signal we're broadcasting?' Gareth asked quietly. 'Is it likely to have reached inhabited space yet?'

'Yes. The signal will have travelled well into occupied space by now. The DAP know you're out here.'

Gareth nodded and returned to his reading, trying not to think of all the friends he'd lost. As the days drifted past their faces swam through his thoughts ever more insistently. He concentrated on the words before him.

By the fourteenth day the men's tempers were even more frayed. The constantly recycled air in the pod was becoming stale, even though they had plenty of oxygen. The men themselves, unwashed for two weeks, were offensive to each other and themselves despite the air filtration. Strict rations and the resulting low energy blackened their moods. Isolation, distance to safety and proximity to each other all began to take their toll. Gareth grew less and less tolerant of Dean's surly disposition. He watched the young man surreptitiously. Dean had developed a tendency to murmur to himself almost constantly, his lips twitching ever so slightly, eyes darting left and right.

'Anything you want to talk about, Dean?'

'Like what?'

'I dunno. Just have a conversation.'

Dean's lip curled. 'You wanna talk about all the friends we lost? About how I wanted to take Sal to see the Glass Mountains on our next shore leave and ask her to marry me? You want to make up more bullshit about prison? What about the giant alien that killed everybody?'

Gareth said nothing. Trying to draw Dean out only gave him a chance to vent his anger. Except not venting the anger would only fuel the psychosis creeping across his mind.

Gareth knew he was perilously close to madness himself. He had caught himself entertaining thoughts of beating Dean senseless purely for something to do. The thought of grabbing the young man and crushing his face beneath flying knuckles had given him a thrill of adrenalin he hadn't felt since they had first fired the thrusters. He had even considered what it might be like to eat human flesh. Sometimes, chewing dry rations, he had watched Dean's greasy, stubbled jaw working, watched his throat swallowing, watched his thin shoulders hunched forward, shielding his food. And watching those things had made Gareth's mouth water and thoughts of steaks with thick gravy flitted through his mind like erratic moths dancing around a flame. He knew these thoughts were the scouts of madness, stealthily checking the landscape of his mind, looking for somewhere to land and start drilling. He also knew that while he was aware of this process happening in his head, Dean was experiencing his own version of the same thing. Only he was convinced that Dean didn't have the self-reflection he held on to. Dean's madness was closer to the surface, less restrained, fuelled by grief. It threatened to break free at any time.

Gareth found himself locked eye to eye with the young man. Dean's eyes were dark, hooded, haunted. His lips twitched and worked unselfconsciously, telling himself the mad thoughts were completely sane, the terrible things he considered completely rational. Gareth braced himself as he caught sight of Dean's fingers flexing, his fists clenching, relaxing, clenching, relaxing.

'Signal received.'

Both men jumped, gasping in breaths. They broke eye contact, turning to the console. 'Signal?'

'Signal confirmed. The DAP battle cruiser *Agamem Dax* sends the following communiqué.' Through a crackle of static a strong male voice said, 'Survivors of the *Cortain*, this is Captain Reyne of the *Agamem Dax*. We are en route to rendezvous with your escape pod. We're bending space to get to you guys, so hang in there. Increase your power to absolute maximum. Don't worry about conserving fuel. If you can get to full power we should be with you in around thirty hours.'

There was a moment of silence, then both men jumped up from their cots, whooping and hollering. All previous antagonism forgotten they grabbed each other in a rough embrace and danced around in a circle.

'Would you like to send a response?' Cortain asked.

Gareth laughed, the impending insanity, so close to the surface of his mind, barely held in check when he let that laughter out. 'Of course, of course. Er . . . Cortain, please send the following: Captain Reyne, you have no idea how good it is to hear your voice! We are increasing to full power and can't wait to see a friendly face.' He looked at Dean and smiled. 'Also, please be advised that we are in serious need of a shower! Cortain, can you increase to max power and ensure that Reyne has all the information he needs to find us?'

'Confirmed. Message and all relevant data sent.'

'How long till we get a reply?'

'Hard to tell. Probably several minutes. But I have a confirmed link and data from the *Agamem Dax*. They have us. Just a matter of time now.'

Dean looked out the front screen, almost as if he expected to see the *Agamem Dax* out there in the distance. 'Thirty hours?' he asked quietly. Tears ran down his cheeks.

'Yes.' Gareth laughed again. 'From several weeks to little more than a day. Oh, thank all the powers in the black for that!'

Dean smiled. It was the most normal he had appeared for days. 'So that means that we have plenty of food, right?'

Gareth's eyes widened. The boy had a point. 'Cortain,

can we have a proper feed now, please?'

Thirty hours seemed to pass interminably slow, but the thought of rescue was enough to keep both men in good spirits. They had eaten until they felt sick, drunk water like they lived under a waterfall and slept the sated sleep of the rich. When the *Agamem Dax* was only a couple of hours out they established a live communication link with Captain Reyne. They described everything to the best of their ability, they answered dozens of questions put to them by all manner of scientists and tacticians. They were euphoric at the thought of imminent showers, proper beds, fresh food and human contact.

The console beeped and Captain Reyne's voice sounded again. 'Gareth, Dean, we're nearly there. We have you on short range sensors and visual. If you look forward you should be able to see us.'

Both men rushed to the console, leaning forward to stare at the screen. Cortain used the head up display and highlighted the *Agamem Dax* with a crosshair of faint gold. That tiny, blocky shadow in deep space, with a pinprick rainbow of lights, was the single best thing Gareth had ever seen in his life. He slapped Dean on the shoulder, pointing at the screen. 'We see you, Captain Reyne. Oh, what a relief, we see you.'

There was a soft laugh from the console. 'It's good to see you boys too. We'll come up alongside you at a distance of several kilometres, to avoid risking you in our gravity well. Then we'll launch a shuttle to hook up and tow you in.'

Another voice came across the wire. 'Captain, we're reading a massive energy signature.'

'*Agamem Dax*, this is Cortain. Energy signature is consistent with the encounter that destroyed the *Cortain*.'

Gareth froze, his knuckles whitening on the console. Dean made that gulping sound again. As they stared at the tiny outline of the *Agamem Dax* both men watched deep blackness spread up below the battle cruiser.

'Captain, sensors indicate a massive biological signature. This thing is bigger than we are by a factor of . . . several hundred.'

Reyne's voice was tight, controlled. 'As we drilled. Focus all weapons to the centre of the energy signature.'

'Target acquired.'

'Fire, fire, fire!'

Energy pulses and the jet exhausts of missiles exploded from the *Agamem Dax*. Gareth and Dean watched as hundreds of weapons deployed from the massive battle cruiser and flooded into the thing that approached beneath them. The ordnance disappeared into the blackness, briefly illuminating the darkness to a shiny, glassy, featureless surface like flexing obsidian. The men could see the slick shadows extending beyond their vision in every direction, filling every bit of space below the battle cruiser. Hints of curves and tendrils, flat expanses and black undulating planes strained their perception. As each weapon discharged, the space beneath the *Agamem Dax* was a rainbow of energy and explosions.

'Captain, biological entity still approaching. Our barrage had no effect.'

'Evasive manoeuvres! Get us away from it. We need an attack angle.'

'Aye, Captain.'

'Sir, the entity is staying with us!'

'Weapons systems primed.'

'Fire, fire, fire!'

Energy and ordnance blossomed from the *Agamem Dax* again, disappearing into the gargantuan shining blackness.

'Captain, no effect.'

'Evade, damn you! Evasive patterns!'

'Captain, I can't shake it. It's . . . it's everywhere.'

'Weapons primed.'

'Fire, fire, fire!'

As the barrage of destruction flew forth again something extended from the mass of shining black. Almost indistinguishable from the surrounding space, something long and round snaked up below the *Agamem Dax*. With a flick of tremendous speed it whipped and the battle cruiser was engulfed in a massive ball of orange flames and roiling clouds. A huge ring of explosive energy pulsed outwards and collapsed back on itself. Then nothing. The shining mass had given way to the open darkness of deep space, speckled with a million million stars.

Gareth and Dean stood transfixed at the console, staring as the tiny gold crosshair faded from the screen. Gareth tried to wet dry lips with his tongue. 'Cortain?'

'The *Agamem Dax* is gone. All sensors read empty.'

'What?'

'All sensors read empty.'

Gareth slowly turned his head. Dean's eyes were wide, wild. His lips were flickering and twitching as he murmured to himself, too quietly to be heard.

Alan Baxter is a British-Australian author living on the south coast of NSW, Australia. He writes dark fantasy, sci fi and horror, rides a motorcycle and loves his dog. He also teaches Kung Fu. Read extracts from his novels, a novella and short stories at his website—www.alanbaxteronline. com—and feel free to tell him what you think. About anything.

An Exhibition of the Plague

Richard Harland

Travelling through the diseased metropolis, I felt the atmosphere of the plague pressing down on me like a coffin lid. The interior of the carriage summed it all up: sealed windows, drawn curtains, musk-scented air and padded satin upholstery. Through the curtains, I could glimpse lights flashing past in the night, blood-red and purple and deep emerald green. The colours were as rich and sombre as the colours of stained glass.

It was no wonder that Karnossian culture had taken this morbid turn. Over twelve years, the disease had killed a third of the colonists on Karnos-3—or 'plague planet' as the rest of the Hegemony liked to call it. I was the first offworlder to visit in all that time, now that the contagion was dying down at last. Undoubtedly, they had a right to a mournful outlook on life. But why so old-fashioned? I was sure an electro-hydrogen engine powered the carriage in which I was travelling, yet the style of the vehicle seemed to have come from another century—almost another millennium. The plague could account for economic regression, but this was more like wilful nostalgia.

Evora Shevorne was my companion in the carriage.

Even her name sounded deep and rich and sombre. She was dressed in black, of course, with a splash of scarlet on collar and cuffs. Her face would have been beautiful except for an indefinable dull heaviness around the chin and eyes. She'd been assigned to take me to some sort of exhibition on the plague at some sort of gallery. As yet we had exchanged only a few sentences of formal conversation, so now I tried a more personal approach.

'You survived the epidemic yourself,' I said. 'Natural immunity?'

'Yes, I'm an immune.' Her voice was slow and deliberate, and she wove the air with her long pale fingers as she spoke. 'I went through the early symptoms, but I survived. Like everyone else you've met so far. Only immunes are allowed to take up government positions. Soon immunes will be the only people left living on Karnos-3.'

'So the next generation . . . ?'

'The children of immunes inherit their immunity.'

'What makes people immune? Understanding the immunity could help us to understand the disease.'

'The disease is a mystery,' she said flatly, 'and so is the immunity.'

'But it can be analysed,' I insisted. 'That's what I'm here for. You never sent us samples in all the time you were in quarantine. With our latest techniques—'

She cut me off. 'And you never sent us doctors.'

Her sharp tone silenced me. Of course the Karnossians must feel rejected. As a junior researcher twelve years ago, I'd had no say about the quarantine, but I accepted the rationale for imposing it. After Epheliam-5 and the disastrous outbreak of Mueke's Bone-Marrow

Syndrome, we couldn't take a chance. The new diseases were just too unpredictable. The colonists on Karnos-3 had to be sacrificed for the welfare of the Hegemony as a whole. But the Karnossians would hardly be human if they didn't hold a grudge.

I'd been feeling guilty on behalf of the Hegemony ever since my arrival. Talking to administrators and officials, I'd allowed them to evade my questions and treated them with kid gloves. I'd even found myself speaking in a hushed, respectful voice as if at a funeral service. I couldn't help thinking of the close friends and family that every single survivor must have lost.

The carriage bounced and rattled over bumps in the road. I hadn't seen beyond the administrative district of the metropolis so far, but I suspected that the planet's entire infrastructure would need to be rebuilt. I inhaled the musk-scented air, and wondered if Karnossians used perfume vaporisers to cover up the odour of death. Perhaps they had grown accustomed to such thick, cloying smells.

She broke the silence suddenly. 'Of course, you're very brave to come now.' It might have been sarcasm, but it was said without sharpness. 'How much do you know about our plague, Dr Reddal?'

'Not much,' I confessed. 'I saw the images twelve years ago. People staggering in the streets, clutching at their stomachs. People collapsing, skin bursting open, spilling their bowels. Horrific.'

'Indeed it was. Not so much the stomach or bowels, though. The disease starts in the liver and kidneys. A process of crystallisation that accumulates in the tissues.'

'But caused by a virus?'

'Yes. It invades the body through particles in the air.'

Not for the first time, I wished I had worn a facemask. Evora must have seen my look of apprehension because her lips curved in a smile.

'Don't worry. You could cover every part of your body, and the infection would still find a pore through which to enter.'

'I thought . . . Hasn't the epidemic stage passed?'

'Almost. Only eight cases in the last six months. You're in luck.'

I didn't like her smile, which seemed increasingly contemptuous.

'I know the statistics,' I snapped. 'We've had nothing but statistics from you for a very long while. Ever since you cut off live footage.'

'People staggering in the streets? You wanted more of that?'

'You closed down all your news channels except for official transmissions.'

Her expression was close to hatred now. 'We're not a peepshow,' she said.

I was feeling less and less guilty. True, we'd acted ruthlessly in isolating the Karnossians, but they'd chosen to isolate themselves too. Whether out of spite or shame . . . Either way, it amounted to the same. Of course the interplanetary media had shifted attention to other news stories. After twelve years, the general population of the Hegemony had grown accustomed to the idea of one small, infected corner of the galaxy. And the Karnossians had hidden away in their corner like sick animals creeping off to die. If only they'd sent us samples . . .

The carriage slowed to a halt, and the right-side door slid smoothly open. Looking out, I could see nothing but darkness. In fact, we had pulled up half a metre away from an unlit building, and the open door of the carriage was exactly alongside the building's open door. I rose from my seat and followed Evora out of one closed space into another.

'Wait a minute,' I protested.

I glimpsed only the immediate surrounds of the door, but I wasn't impressed. Old woodwork and peeling paint—what sort of gallery was this? It looked more like an ordinary house, and a very decrepit one at that. But my protest was retrospective even before it left my lips. A male Karnossian—perhaps the driver of the carriage— entered behind me and closed the door.

'Where are we?'

No-one answered, and I was forced to follow Evora along a narrow corridor. Wooden walls, wan yellow lights, threadbare carpeting—everything spoke of neglect and deterioration. Worst of all was the unwholesome smell of organic decay.

We came out at last into a kitchen, with cupboards, table and stove. So this *was* just a family home . . . And there was the family: mother, father, two boys and a girl. The children's faces looked puffy and dark around the eyes as though they'd been crying. They were all dressed in the simplest of clothes, very different to Evora in her stylish black and scarlet.

She nodded to them, and they stared back with unblinking solemnity. They remained motionless: the boys seated on chairs, the parents leaning against the wall, the girl cross-legged on the floor. One of the boys sniffled and rubbed his nose with the back of his hand.

'I don't understand.' I swung to confront Evora. 'You were supposed to be taking me to an exhibition.'

'Yes. An exhibition of the plague.'

A dreadful apprehension gripped me as I surveyed the family again. 'What's wrong with them?'

'They've known since yesterday evening.' Evora crooked a finger at the mother. 'Come forward, Sparren.'

Sparren stepped forward as if in a daze. Evora took her by the shoulders and gently rotated her so that I could see her bare upper arm. Just above the elbow was a raised red mark, a circular swelling on the skin.

'That's the entry point,' Evora told me. 'That's where the infection broke in through the pores.'

I couldn't believe my ears. 'What about me?'

'You?'

'I don't have immunity! I'll get infected!'

'Very likely.' Again that scornful smile. 'You'll be able to take samples from yourself. Though I'm afraid you won't have very long to analyse them. Death within forty-eight hours.'

The woman called Sparren turned suddenly—and deliberately breathed on me, full in my face.

I fled the room. Back along the corridor, back to the door by which I'd entered. No-one tried to stop me, and they didn't need to. The door was locked. I reversed direction and kept running.

I came to another room—I think it was a bedroom, but the place was in total darkness. I banged into various bits of furniture before I finally found a window. I touched glass, frame and latch, so it had to be a window, yet it let in no glimmer of the city's nightlights. I undid the latch and tried to pull it open, but it wouldn't budge. Nailed shut?

I found a stool, swung it and smashed the glass. Careless of jagged edges, I reached through—until my knuckles struck solid wood. Vertical planks fixed side by side with barely a crack between them. The window had been boarded up!

I panicked and ran again. I soon lost all sense of direction, though I managed to keep away from the kitchen. Imagining viral particles in the air, I held my hand over my mouth and nose, and tried not to breathe in. I wasn't thinking rationally enough to remember that this contagion entered through the pores of the skin. Every now and then, my oxygen-starved lungs betrayed me and sucked in a great whooping draught.

I looked into room after room, and everywhere the windows had been boarded up. Sounds of hammering came to my ears, as though more boards were being nailed on even as I ran. In my half-crazed mind, it turned into a race against time. Somewhere, in some room, there had to be a window I could reach before they closed it off!

Perhaps it wasn't so crazy. I came to one room and turned on the lights—I'd learned where to locate the switches. I don't know what sort of room it had been originally, but it was empty now except for blankets and quilts spread out on the floor and half a dozen neatly arranged pillows. There was a single window, and I saw at a glance that it was only half boarded up.

I ran for it, snatching up a pillow on the way, and punched through the glass with the pillow over my fist.

A murmur of voices rose up outside, but I didn't care. Still using the pillow, I pulled out more and more pieces of glass. I was sure the opening was wide enough to squeeze through, once I climbed up onto the sill . . .

A metal bar crashed down on my hand. It was agony even through the thickness of the pillow, and my fingers went numb. Angry faces appeared in the opening, voices yelled at me.

'Stay inside!'

'What do you think you're doing?'

'You're in quarantine!'

Did they know who I was? Was the word 'quarantine' aimed specifically at me?

In the next moment, a plank thrust in through the opening and in through the glass. It caught me in the middle of the chest and knocked me sprawling. By the time I staggered to my feet, the plank had been withdrawn—and was now being used to board up the opening. Another two planks, and the blockade was complete.

I kept on searching, of course, but it was hopeless. Every door was locked, every window sealed. And when I listened, I could hear Karnossian voices on the other side of the doors and windows. The house was surrounded and the reinforcement work was still going on. They must be absolutely obsessed with sealing the house off.

In the end, I headed back to the kitchen. The plague-stricken family had scarcely moved in all the time I'd been away; they seemed dull and uninterested, not even turning their heads when I reappeared. Evora had vanished, along with the carriage driver or whoever he was.

'Where is she?' I had to repeat the question several times before the father came out of his trance.

'Left by another door,' he said. 'They've sealed that too, now.'

The smell of decay caught in my nostrils and I wanted to gag. I left the kitchen in a hurry.

Oh, I understood what was going on. I didn't need Evora to explain. This was a cruel and elaborate form of revenge. The Hegemony had cut off and isolated the Karnossians, both the sick and healthy all condemned to the same fate. Now they were doing the same to me. As the Hegemony's representative, I was being forced to share in their disease.

If only I'd read the signs when I'd talked to officials and administrators! If only I'd pressed them harder, instead of allowing their evasions and silences to pass for grief. It wasn't grief at all, but sullen hatred!

I slunk off to hide as far away from the kitchen as possible. My death had probably been determined when I first entered the kitchen, perhaps when I first entered the house—the air must be saturated with viral particles. Yet I had to do something. I found a small room that was actually a linen closet, with no light or window. I shut the door behind me, pulled down a sheet from the shelves and swathed myself from head to foot, no skin exposed. I sat under a ventilation grating in the wall, feeling a faint draught of air from outside.

Still the hammering continued. On and on and on, from all around the house, until I could have screamed. After a while, there were new sounds too: grinding, clanking and rumbling, like the operation of heavy machinery. As if they were pouring concrete! How deep did they want to bury us?

Eventually a new day dawned. I peeked out from my sheet and saw that the darkness was a few degrees less absolute, with grey light percolating in through the grating. I also saw the condition of the sheet itself—stained and soiled. It was an unwashed sheet from someone's bed, surely laden with infection!

I flung it aside, stumbled to my feet and ran out into the corridor. There, under the electric lights, I found a circle of raised red skin on my wrist. A similar mark had appeared on my left ankle, and another on my chest.

So it had happened. The disease had entered my pores and was working its way through my body. I can't explain how I felt: not particularly surprised, but certainly very frightened.

I wandered through the corridors in an aimless daze. In one corridor, I ran into the daughter of the family, walking along by herself. She must have been seven or eight years old, yet her face was twisted in lines of pain that gave her the look of an aged woman. She leaned one shoulder against the wall as she walked, as if unable to support her weight on her legs. I think she would have gone straight past me if I hadn't stood in her way. She was clutching at her midriff with both hands—presumably where the crystals were growing in her liver and kidneys.

'Does it hurt?' I asked. 'I've got it too.'

She seemed lost in a state of inward concentration, focused on what was happening inside her body. She had come to a halt still leaning against the wall, aware of me yet hardly seeing me.

I tried again. 'Is there anything I can do?'

Instead of answering, she lurched forward again. For a moment I thought she was going to fall, and reached out to catch hold of her. But she didn't want my help. Some infinitesimal shake of the head or aversion of the shoulders told me to leave her alone. I drew back and watched her continue her shuffling, laborious journey.

Then I walked on. The girl was unreal, the corridor was unreal, my own actions were unreal. The whole house seemed to have floated outside of normal space and time.

When I found myself back in the kitchen, I decided I was hungry. The family members had all left the room. I searched the cupboards and fridge, and found the makings of a sandwich. I wondered how long it would be before I started to suffer like the girl.

I ate my sandwich, seated at the table, and drank a glass of juice. The smell of decay no longer bothered me, but the hammering, mechanical noise was maddening. It was ridiculous, what they were doing. We were entombed already—why pile on layer after layer? I hated the Karnossians for their malevolent stupidity.

The three red circles on my skin neither grew nor shrank. I stopped examining them; after a while, I even stopped thinking about them. My mood swung back and forth between violent anger and fatalistic resignation. Hours passed, but I had no sense of time.

It might have been a minute or a century later when I heard the first cries. I think it was the two boys to begin with, then the girl. Later, the mother and father joined in. It was as though the sounds were being wrung out of them: moans and gasps and short sharp shrieks. No weeping or sobbing, just the purest, clearest distillation of pain. The sounds seemed to model the very shape of their individual agonies. Listening to those cries, I could trace every movement of every pang inside their bodies.

I didn't get up to go and look. How could I have helped? The only thing I could have done was put them out of their pain—and I *did* glance at the cutlery draw where the kitchen knives were kept. But I wasn't brave enough, or logical enough, to go through with the deed.

Then I started to experience an echo of the same pangs. The crystals were growing in me too, I was sure of it. I'd been covering my ears with my hands, but now I unbuttoned my shirt, and pressed and prodded in the region of my liver and kidneys. The sensation was lacerating. I grunted and doubled up over the table.

I considered putting myself out of my own pain, but I didn't have the determination for that either. I just sat there with tears running down my face—tears from the pain, tears for the sheer injustice of it all. The sounds from the suffering family kept rising and falling, stopping and starting. They were touching death again and again, as if dipping their toes into that black ocean. Why did it have to last so long? The disease was utterly merciless.

My liver and kidneys only hurt when I pressed and prodded. I went back to covering up my ears instead. At some point, night must have fallen, but I don't know when. Perhaps before, perhaps after the cries of the dying family came to an end.

Peace, blessed peace! I realised with surprise that the hammering, mechanical noise had ceased too. I stayed where I was, waiting for the pangs in my own body to intensify. Waiting and waiting . . . Until I fell asleep, slumped forward with my head on the table.

My sleep was filled with strange dreams of corpses and funerals, blocked-off doors and sealed-up houses. Perhaps I was dreaming of Karnos-3 as it had been at the height of the plague. When I finally awoke, the house was as silent as a tomb.

I backtracked in my memory to the point where the family's cries had ceased. They were dead, no doubt . . . But I felt a sudden need to go and see for myself. I had left behind last night's mood swings and the accompanying sense of helplessness.

I had a good idea of where the cries had come from. Heading in that direction, I arrived at the room with the blankets, quilts and pillows. All five members of the family were there, and they must have flung themselves about terribly in their death throes. The girl had twisted a blanket round her legs, the mother appeared to be biting a pillow, one of the boys had burrowed headfirst into a quilt. The neatly arranged room had turned into a scene of chaos.

Only when I stepped forward onto the blankets did I discover the true horror. How can I describe it? The disease had broken down the flesh beneath the skin, and the bodies looked like so many shapeless bags of pulp. In all my years of medical experience I had never seen anything like it. And this was what I could expect for myself! Although . . .

I had barely noted that I was experiencing no pangs of pain when a noise broke the silence. Not a hammering or clanking, but a slow creak of metal on wood. Then voices talking. People coming in from outside?

I was glad to escape that charnel-house scene. I sped

along corridors, past the kitchen, and arrived at the same door by which I had entered . . . a lifetime ago, as it seemed. The door was open and there were people in the doorway, outlined against the pale light of a new morning. At the front, advancing along the corridor, was Evora Shevorne.

'You came too soon!' I yelled at her. 'I'm not dead yet!'

I'm not sure what I meant to do: perhaps burst out onto the streets and run around screaming, *I have the plague!* Evora shot out an arm and barred my way.

'You're not, are you?' Her voice was unchanged, slow and deliberate, with just a note of curiosity. 'Do you have an entry point on your skin?'

I flourished my wrist in her face. 'Three of them!'

She drew me to the side of the corridor, allowing the other Karnossians to go past. She nodded as she examined my wrist.

'When did this appear?'

'I don't know.'

'Soon after I left you here?'

'*Imprisoned* me here. Yes.'

'It's fading now.'

'What?'

I looked for myself, and she was right. In the clear light of day, the angry red colour had diminished to a pale shade of pink.

'You're an immune,' she said. 'Like the rest of us.'

She gestured towards the other Karnossians, now disappearing round a turn in the corridor.

I could hardly take it in. A great wave of relief washed over me, then a swell of triumph.

'So you didn't get your revenge,' I jeered. 'The trick failed.'

'I don't remember any trick.'

'You pretended you were taking me to an exhibition in a gallery.'

'This is a gallery,' she answered.

How was I supposed to understand that? She didn't explain, but walked on down the corridor. 'Come and see,' she said over her shoulder.

I looked towards the open door, but there was no hurry now. I was an immune. I followed and caught her up.

'I'm sorry,' she said.

Sorry? That was all she could offer after trying to cause my death? Sorry for an attempted murder? Her strange composure left me speechless.

Of course, we went straight to the room with the bodies. The other Karnossians—four men and two women—were stooping over the once-human forms on the floor. At first I didn't realise what they were doing. Then a sickening stench hit my nostrils, a hundred times worse than ever before.

They were opening up the bodies, fumbling around inside the internal organs. Perhaps they had scalpels or knives, perhaps the plague-riddled flesh simply disintegrated under their hands—I don't know. All I saw were ghouls and corpse-robbers. And yes, there was a particular treasure they were after.

One of the ghouls straightened suddenly, holding something in his hands. He appeared elated, and the others shared his elation with whistles and gasps of delight.

'Let me see,' Evora ordered.

The Karnossian came across to her—and me. The stuff in his hands was a slop of organic tissue, degraded to the constituency of mince, yet there was also something hard in it, something that glinted through the semi-liquid mess.

Evora reached forward and probed delicately with the tip of her index finger.

'It's perfect,' she murmured. 'What structure! What ramifications!'

'I've never seen better,' said the Karnossian. 'One of the last, but one of the best.'

'Perhaps the very last. Who knows?' Evora's expression was radiant and tragic at the same time. She turned as another ghoul let out a gasp of amazement. 'Do we have more?'

One by one, they brought their treasures to her. She picked out each crystalline formation from the slop in their hands. The formations were small, especially those taken from the children, but it was the quality of the shape she seemed to value.

She gathered them all in her cupped palms, then turned to leave. 'You're free to go,' she told me.

Go where? The whole situation had dissolved as if it had never existed. Was it no longer important that I was the Hegemony's representative? Had the Karnossians simply forgotten about their revenge?

I trailed after Evora as she retraced her steps along the corridor. I had a thousand questions, but none that I could formulate in the moment.

She led the way back out through the door. While she marched on to her carriage, thirty paces away, I paused and stood blinking in the open daylight.

The street was wide, expanding into a kind of square, and the buildings that faced me were completely unexpected. I had imagined old houses in a run-down quarter of the metropolis—and indeed, there were a few houses of that kind. But the majority of the buildings had magnificent new facades that glittered in morning light. White stone, spires and precious metals . . . They looked far too decorative for ordinary residential dwellings. They put me in mind of the temples on Wrass-5 or the mausoleums on Ballotin-2.

It was when I turned around that I received the biggest shock. No more peeling paint or old woodwork! The house in which I'd been imprisoned had undergone a total transformation; now the original structure was encased in a shell of marble and mirror-glass, as grand as any on the street. Even the doorway had chrome surrounds.

I ran after Evora and caught her before she could climb into her carriage.

'Is that what you meant?' I demanded, pointing. 'A gallery?'

She took her foot from the step of the carriage. 'Yes. The interior will need cleaning, but we'll preserve it in its natural state. A tribute to the creatives. And these will be mounted there on permanent display.' She meant the formations of crystal that she held in her hands. 'I'm taking them now to be washed and polished.'

The idea sank in. 'Like works of art,' I muttered. 'People will come to admire them.'

'As they do at all our galleries.' Her gaze swept the other glittering buildings in the street. 'But this exhibition will be the most popular. The latest and most beautiful.'

It was all wrong and perverse and impossible. Beauty

out of horror? But as I studied those objects in her hands, I saw that they *were* beautiful. The semi-liquid slop had now puddled in the hollow of her palms, and the crystalline formations stood out more clearly. Tiny spikes, tiny branchings . . . No filigree jewellery could begin to compare with such intricate twists and contortions.

'This is what the family made,' said Evora in a strange, low voice. 'They fashioned these pieces with their pain and suffering. See? The very forms of their individual deaths.'

But I couldn't forget the horror. *Three of them were children,* I wanted to say. *Just children!*

'You and I can never do what they did,' she went on. 'We shall never create anything. That's what being immune means. We're cursed to remain unproductive.'

I stared at her in disbelief. There was a haunted look on her face, the skin stretched tight over her cheekbones.

'We're the lucky ones,' I said. 'Aren't you glad you survived?'

Her eyes were swimming and she no longer seemed to see me. I don't think she was sorrowing for the pain and loss of the family that had just died. I think she was sorrowing for herself.

Richard has been a full-time author for thirteen years, after finishing his first novel at the age of forty-five. He lives near Wollongong, south of Sydney, between golden beaches, green escarpment and the biggest steelworks in the southern hemisphere.

He has collected six Aurealis Awards in Australia and the French *Tam-Tam Je Bouquine* award. His short stories have appeared in three major US anthologies: *Year's Best Fantasy #9, Best Horror of the Year #3,* and *Ghosts by Gaslight.*

His fifteenth novel, the steampunk fantasy *Worldshaker,* came out in Australia in 2009, and the US, UK, France and Germany in 2010. The sequel, *Liberator,* came out in Australia in May 2011, and is contracted internationally.

Richard's author website is at www.richardharland.net. He has also put up a guide to writing speculative fiction, a website as big as a small book, at www.writingtips.com.au.

Rains of la Strange

Robert N Stephenson

Tyson fast-dropped from the underside of the tower city. The sooner he retrieved the Thought, the sooner he could climb back to safety. The fall through atmosphere caused his ears to pop and his face prickled with the cold; the ear-shell crackled, the brass device an icy pain against his head, and for a moment he was out of communication with the tower. This was his punishment for a mistake. The clouds rushed at him, the drop line sang with tension.

He'd trusted Shana, why hadn't she come to him? Her simple betrayal could end in his death; something he wasn't comfortable with, even if he had been counselled about the prospect. Once into the under-damp he had to recover the Thought and bring Shana back for adjustment—or termination if that failed.

From sunlight he fell towards the clouds, a blanket over the land and a cushion between the races, a soft barrier separating the biological-machine-people of la Strange and the Thoughtless below. Humans also existed under the clouds but they only ever appeared when it was time to trade. Above him loomed the shadowed underside of the tower city, the winch handler now too small to see. It had been a year since he'd been under the civilised world and the massive tower that held it above the clouds. Even though he couldn't see it, he knew the base was fifteen kilometres below; he should touch land five kilometres from the barriers that protected it.

'Station.' He touched the interact stud on his throat, the static had cleared in his ear-shell.

'Report.'

'Dropping through clouds, any indications on target's location?' He hoped the news was better than the last report.

'Tracking system disabled. Last known location will show on your map. Proceed with caution. It is vital full retrieval be achieved.'

'Tyson out.'

Great. They didn't know where she was and he had a city of a hundred thousand to search. With that many low-lifes, all with a penchant for killing those from la Strange, it wasn't going to be an easy visit.

Wasn't Shana happy with the life they had shared? Couldn't she have asked for a change in the dendrite? She didn't have to steal; you could easily apply for thought adjustments. Her behaviour was no better than the Thoughtless.

His system, running auto mood stabilisers, pushed back the negativity. Did she have a serotonin deficit? He should have picked it up. That could have been fixed; it only took a small tweak to increase receptor sites. He'd done it himself on occasion. Her fleeing troubled him, and once again he tried to boost release from the presynaptic cells. He felt a little better.

Tyson pulled the Thought he'd been trying to run from the reader at the base of his skull; now wasn't the time to be messing about. He let the thick layer of skin flap closed over the reader and then put the disk in his pocket. He would hit the dark clouds soon and the inclement weather; he needed everything sealed.

To those in the under-damp he would be little more than a man-looking machine to be broken up and sold as parts. Know a Strange-er by the green of their eyes; something that always gave them away, much like the muddy brown gaze of the Thoughtless that said 'no-one home'. He really didn't want to die. He had trading currency which would buy some time, but how much time did he have?

Once through the thick, stormy clouds and into the damp air the view cleared from cloud-grey opaqueness to the shifting shadows of rain. Tyson continued the long drop and hoped no-one looked up. He could see the watery city of 'Deep Sea', its cylindrical structures glowing with porthole lights and tower lights dotting the wide expanse. One of his kind couldn't hide amongst the great unclean for long. Shana would need help and what could she offer the Thoughtless that they couldn't just take? Currency wouldn't last long, and she'd been missing for over a week; in his mind he had already reconciled himself to the fact she would be dead. But the Thought would still need to be retrieved.

'Fifty metres,' he said into the mic. The fall slowed rapidly, the strain ached in his back and made his head light. 'Ten. Hand winch slow.' Again a sudden jerk applied pressure to his body and he bit back the pain. The last ten metres became a gentle descent into wet danger.

He sank to his calves in the swampy ground, the tidal

plain that surrounded the tower. Somehow this boggy land supported the lives of the Thoughtless. Humans didn't live here; they only came to trade for biological cargo. From reports, they took younger Thoughtless and paid in cured animal meats. The Humans of the under-damp were unfathomable, though rumours existed about their true natures. Some called them the great creators; others suggested they were the death bringers. Tyson didn't know what the truth was and the not knowing didn't bother him.

He unclipped the buckles and stepped from the harness. As he stepped away, he watched it disappear back into the clouds. To return he would have to walk to the base. He struggled through the seaweed stink and thick muddy-black sand to a raised road of stone. This road led to the trading station used between la Strange and the Thoughtless. The Thoughtless traded fish for medicines with la Strange, to fight the water disease and vitamins to control nutrient deficiencies in their diet.

In his mind the map rotated, this and other tidal paths highlighted in green. If he kept his pace quick he should make the city before the tide flooded the streets. A blue 'x' marked Shana's last known location: a pier. He was certain she would not be there, but he had to start somewhere.

The Thoughtless were a violent and troubled people who managed to survive beneath the water. It was at low tide, when the city was revealed, that the Humans came. Tyson wondered if Shana had planned to trade with them. The Thoughtless were an anomaly to Strange-ers. They coexisted in a way, each group accepting some unwritten law, yet the Thoughtless were quick to kill if antagonised.

The Humans from over the seas also defied explanation. He knew it was the Humans that provided la Strange with genetic material for life production. In return the Humans took members of la Strange's population, volunteers they were called, though for what purpose was never spoken about. The Humans' role in the great scheme of things was well above his classification.

Why anyone would want to live in the water or be subjected to the extremes of the weather made no sense to him. His legs ached from the trudge through the thick mud; the stink of dampness and rot made it hard to concentrate and the map in his mind flickered as moisture seeped into his systems. In the distance through the haze of falling rain he could see the lights: dull yellow smudges in the gloomy grey. To his right he could see and hear the sea, the white waves crashing on a dark shore; the tide was coming in. He thought he saw a light out on the water. Was it the Humans journeying back to their lands? Did they have the Thought? Did they have Shana? He lowered the demister lenses over his eyes and continued his trudge to the city.

It always rained beneath la Strange. 'Deep Sea' was a wet place, a hazy place, a land inundated by the sea at night and wallowing in muddy muck during the oppressive days. It did little to lighten his mood, and down moods were not logical; a neurotransmitter adjustment, a quick blip of the axon, had things looking a bit brighter. His leather clothes were damp. Tyson pulled his coat tighter about his shoulders to fight off the cold; leather was useless against cold. Every breath came wet in his mouth. His part-machine body and the mechanisms that drove his lungs and heart were sluggish under the elements. Even with his carbon fibre skeletal system he felt heavy. The world beneath the clouds weighed upon him almost as much as his task.

The closer he got to the town the more the air stank of fish, seaweed and corroding metal. It would be safer to enter via the docks, the last known location for Shana. Tyson left the road and waded to the nearest structure. About twenty anchored boats stuck out of the mud, the returning tide sloshing about their crusty hulls. Green and black-slimed water lapped at age-browned concrete pylons and the rusty red wall of a submerged building; all sound was muffled under the drum of rain on metal roofs, metal walkways and long wooden jetties. In the haze he saw a body wearing la Strange uniform tied to a pylon, its eyes cut out, gaping wounds about its head and chest. This was what he was meant to find, Shana's last location all right. After the Thoughtless took what they wanted they left the rest as fish food. The body was a mess, already it had been through a few feedings. Shana was dead, as he'd suspected. Something dropped over him, a thought, a connection with the body but he was quick to push it aside. He searched what was left of the uniform—the body was female, he could work out that much—but there was nothing; every piece of technology has been stripped from her. He rearranged priorities to exclude his and her interactive relationship; it helped distract him from the water's nauseating stink. He considered Shana's and his mutual affections program. A brief flicker in his mind, it would have to wait for proper removal later; he had a job to complete first. He paused, the transition to logic wasn't smooth, a stutter in his programming. The weather was interfering in his processes; he had to move faster.

The Thought was now somewhere in the city. How do you track a Thought in an unenhanced population?

'I found her,' he said into his throat stud, the bronze device bobbing on his Adam's apple, the copper strap cutting into his reddening neck. 'The target is dead.'

'The Thought?' was the reply through his ear-shell.

'Not here.'

'Find it.'

'Understood.' Water seeped past his collar and down his back. 'What is the nature of the missing Thought?' Shana could have taken anything. He'd given her the access codes to the Thought vault; it was part of the affection/share commitment after all. He trusted her, supported her views on life, the research she had been doing on future emotional development in the population. Had she just been using him? He wasn't sure how he felt about the concept.

The interact hissed with white noise, the world crackled with the sound of precipitation on overhead power lines; a dull song of greyness. Camera towers looked down like dead eyes on a world they no longer cared for; a sign of times forgotten.

'Repeat. What is the nature of the Thought?'

Tyson climbed the gangway to the top of the docks, the tide was rising and he needed a safe place to wait out the night. Low, cylindrical buildings, pressure chambers many centuries old, pressed up against each other, intersected by laneways and platforms that led down to the docks. In the diminishing daylight soft yellow glows could be seen in some of the buildings' porthole windows.

Once free of the rising tide for a time he walked the

cobbled lanes looking for an inn, somewhere safe. Still there was only noise in his ear-shell. Tyson saw no-one, yet he knew eyes watched his every move.

The ear-shell sparked back into life. 'You must find . . .' pause, '. . . forbidden Thought . . .'

'Repeat?' How did Shana manage to get a forbidden Thought? His code only allowed access to common Thoughts for her studies. Tyson didn't like the sound of the relayer's voice. It sounded different. He sheltered in a hatchway. 'Who is speaking?' He knew most of the relayers.

'Find her.'

'I told you I *have* found her. Who are you and what is this forbidden Thought?' Couldn't the relayer hear him?

'Find her.' The connection dropped out.

A dead fish lay on the walk outside a closed hatch. The silver skin sparkled against the greys and seaweed greens of the buildings. Two words were scratched on the bulkhead: 'Swampy's Inn'. Tyson tried the hatch; the locking ring was dogged. No lights glowed in the street, no candles burned in the portals; algae stained the glass. Tyson thumped on the hatch. The door was thick, his fist cold, the sound little more than slaps in puddled water. He had to get indoors, out of the rain, out of the dulling light. The tide was rising and soon the city would be underwater.

He pressed a handful of batteries against a porthole and tapped the glass. The lithium power cells should buy him food, drink and at least two nights' bed. The Thoughtless couldn't resist batteries. They had many battery operated machines; lights, air mixers and still-warmers and some basic communications gear for trade arrangements. Candlelight drifted across the green, a flicker, a shadow; a haggard face against the glass.

'Strange-er!' it cried.

'Let me in.' Tyson tapped the batteries again. Strange-ers might have been hated and hunted outside of visitation times but throw in a handful of power cells and the Thoughtless would become your long lost brother.

A clang of steel rang into the fading light as the locking wheel spun. The hatch opened outwards.

'Alkaline?' the white, haggard face said, thick eyebrows covering his eyes.

'Lithium.'

'In, in, my friend.' The man stepped aside. 'Get out of the cold, I've got a broth on, if yer hungry?' His dirty, long shirt barely covered his thick waist; a wide dark stain spread out from the neckline.

'I need a bed as well.' Tyson stepped past the man and into the steamy warmth from a smoky fire. He turned to see the spars of the star-lock grind home as the innkeeper secured the door. A chipped, red metal bar dropped across the wheel locking it in place.

In a move faster than Tyson expected, the old man had him pressed against the curved wall with a knife at his throat. He struggled but the blade nicked his skin, the man's breath hot and foul in his face.

'The batts.'

Tyson reached into his pocket.

'Slow, lad. Be slow.' The pressure from the knife lessened a little. Tyson lifted the bag free and handed it to the man. He snatched it away and moved back, releasing Tyson.

'You didn't need to do that.' He rubbed at his throat, felt the stickiness of blood. It wasn't bad and he knew it could have been worse. 'I would have paid you well.'

'Paid now, lad. By the fire, Stange-er. Warm yerself. You have luck with you, I'd have slit yer throat for Alks. Lettin' yer lives might bring more of these fancy ones my way.' He eyed Tyson carefully. 'What you say, you bring me more?' he said, his voice a whisper of steel shavings. He took two of the batteries and pushed them into the back of a crusty copper torch, the light flickered on. He nodded approval then returned the torch to his pocket.

'Yes, I can get all you need.'

'Good, good. I be Lynard and I hope yer like water-weed, no good fish till the morning.' His hands wrung together. 'Can guarantee a night . . . after that, I'll need more batts.' He winked.

Tyson dragged a worn stool from beneath one of the five large tables in the room and sat close to the fire. Grey smoke clung to the ceiling, the roof's rivets blackened by the years of wood fires. The old man ladled stringy broth into a tin cup and handed it over. He had calmed once he had the batteries, but Tyson couldn't trust him. You couldn't trust the Thoughtless; they might not be technically advanced, or even high in intelligence but they were keen hunters of what they wanted, which made them dangerous and difficult to negotiate with. If they had the Thought just how was he supposed to get it back?

'Drink, lad,' he said. 'Tastes like shit but it's good feryer.'

'I'm looking for something.' He sipped the broth.

Lynard was true to his word.

'Yerkind always are.' The old man ladled himself a cup. 'Yer see the body under the dock?' Tyson nodded. 'She was looking for somethin'. Didn't have the right batteries though. Yer got what we need, lad, for now at least. Now drink up, it tastes worse when it's cold.'

Struggling with the overwhelming stench of the soup, the bedraggled old man and the smoke, Tyson fought back the assault on his senses. An adjustment to the nutrient levels in his gut had the hunger dissipate. The soup was too putrid to stomach, the stinging in his eyes and nose didn't help. What he needed was a pleasant Thought; a place to rest and a pleasant Thought. The corroded steel walls, riveted and welded, only offered an inevitability of failure; the sheet iron tables, the bar of roughly bolted together iron all spoke of necessity over style. How do you live in a world without perfection? Did the Thoughtless dream? Did they have art? Above the clouds there were galleries of fractal designs. He had access to any dream he wanted. Without advancement what did the Thoughtless have other than fish and their rot? A clicking started overhead, something mechanical lost in the smoke haze. He looked up.

'Be the filter, lad.' Lynard motioned with the cup. 'We suffocate in the smoke when the tide's in. Yer kind made them for us, long ago. Long, long ago.'

Tyson pushed the cup away.

'It's all yer get till the boats are back,' the old man said, sculling his cup. He shuddered then laughed. 'I'd even eat a Strange-er right now.' His laughter, big and gurgling, echoed in the room, vibrating Tyson's nerves.

He sat staring into the smouldering fire, watching the

small licks of yellow-red flames as they tried to burn the too-damp wood. They didn't often have open fires in la Strange, their heating coming from steam and the sun, their cooking gas came from deep wells beneath the tower. He liked the way the fire moved, how its colours flowed over the blackened wood, seeking out fuel to keep it alive. The timber came from the forest that edged the swamp-like land of the under-damp. It was sent to the dry kiln, a smoke billowing construction just within the forest proper, then onto 'Deep Sea'. Sometimes, when trade was poor and the fishing catch light, the Thoughtless would offer dry fire wood.

Lynard sat silently watching, scratching his large belly and occasionally belching up an odorous stench. He counted the batteries again before putting the sack on the bar behind him. How much safety did they really buy him? This was Tyson's first trip into 'Deep Sea' itself. His usual encounters were at the trading post. No-one from la Strange ventured this far without pre-arranged protection and advance purchased deals.

'You come feryer dead?' Lynard asked. 'The woman?'

'Do you know what happened?'

'She dead, tha's all. Yer come for her?'

'In a way.' Tyson supposed someone would eventually come down for the body.

'She shouldna' been here. I warn her, I did.'

'You spoke with her?'

'She come sellin', sellin' some sky tricks. I tell her to go back before someone not as friendly takes her. She had Alks—no protection.' Lynard sounded angry. Even in the flicking flame light, Tyson could see his eyes were the colour of the swamp; dark and suspicious.

'What was she trying to sell?' Tyson, warmed by the fire, now felt urged on in his task. It was dangerous to trust a Thoughtless but he needed information.

'Stay sittin', lad, stay sittin'.' He rubbed his wrinkled face. He was perhaps the oldest person Tyson had ever seen, at least in his forties. 'You do nuttin' till mornin'.'

There wasn't really a morning as far as Tyson understood. The world of the under-damp was just shades of grey, the brighter the grey the more the Thoughtless moved about. Above the clouds, where nothing got in the way of life the sun shone bright and the nights were clear and alive with the wonders of the stars. An orderly system for la Strange's perfectly maintained lifestyle. The old man pulled a dented, shiny flask from within his shirt, popped the lid and took a swig. 'Be drinkin' some a this, then be sleepin'.'

'What is it?' Tyson took the flask.

'Better you not know, just be knowin' this stuff ain't what I sell to the regulars; this is refined, smooth. Good five tides old.'

Tyson took a swig and almost vomited. Fire burned in his mouth, in his chest. For a moment he couldn't breathe.

The old man laughed and slapped him on the back. 'That befixin' the chills.' He snatched back the flask. 'Yer batts will give yer a night, no more. Come, I'll show yer the cot.'

Tyson felt his mind drifting, an unauthorised chemical reaction, the effects of the drink, a numbing in his lips, skin, a deadening of his senses. 'What was the woman trying to sell?' he managed, following the old man through a brown curtained doorway. 'I need to know.'

'One of yer dreams, I think, but it ain't me yer need to be talkin' to, lad, it be Eyeless.' Lynard stopped by a stack of broken crates and stinking bedclothes. 'Here yer sleep.'

He couldn't argue; it was this or out in the flooded streets. As Tyson slid off his wet coat he stared at the old man and wondered if he would be able to sleep knowing he could have his throat slit? But greed also shone wild in that haggard face. Tyson turned to a porthole; water lapped at the slimed glass. The tide was already flooding the city. He thought he'd be safe enough till it went out again.

'You will take me to this Eyeless?' he asked, feeling the tiredness spreading through his limbs. 'I can pay you.'

The old man laughed and walked back up the narrow passage to the curtained doorway. 'Yer best sleep well.' He stepped through the curtain.

'How will I find this Eyeless?' he called. No reply. What were his options? Flee and leave without the Thought or stay and have his eyes plucked from his face? He would find this Eyeless and get what he needed back; a Thoughtless couldn't outsmart him.

Feeling on edge, he set up a repeller field near his bed, pulling the tiny antennas out until the device looked like a spiked ball on one of the crates. Nothing could get through without setting off an alarm, shocking the intruder and waking him. He lay down on the cot, the reek of body odour and fish thick in the blankets.

Tyson closed his eyes and thought of Shana and her research on emotions, a completeness of thought she had suggested. His programming had put them together, only he didn't share her tactile necessity when it came to emotional interactions. She had tried to reduce receptors in her mind so she could get more from the touch responses during their sexing but the system always countered the action. When she adjusted his the experience was prolonged. He didn't like it and had to argue with her until she readjusted him. Only eight nights ago he'd given her a quick hormonal check under protest. Levels of progesterone and oestrogen were normal with slight testosterone traces; enzymatic influences were minimal. He couldn't understand what made them so different from each other. As he lay in the distilling odour he tried to picture her face and move away from the chemical interruptions in his head, but all he could see was her blood-stained uniform. He wondered if he should run a grief system's check. He needed to realign his axon delivery, so he slipped in a pleasant Thought and let its vision of flowers lead him into dreams.

Brighter light shone through the curtain, the place looked less threatening than it had in half-light. Tyson crawled from the bed. He no longer noticed the smell as he tidied his shirt then dragged on his coat; the air was cool and smoky.

'Station,' he said into the throat device. He switched off the repeller and stored it back in his coat.

'What have you found?' the voice asked. Why didn't they address him by name? He didn't know why, but he didn't trust this relayer.

'Shana came to sell the Thought,' he lied. 'I think I know who has it. I will be making contact soon.'

'Get it back!' the relayer demanded. 'Kill if you have to.'

'Repeat?'

'Kill anyone who stands in your way.'

'Just how dangerous is it?' Killing people wasn't something he expected. Yes he was trained, but actually doing it?

'Secure it. Dispose of any threat.'

'What is it?'

'Classified.'

'I understand.' If Shana had been with him she would have questioned and pushed for an explanation, would have refused to do anything without all the information. She was dead. Where did that kind of recalcitrant behaviour get her? But still. Did he really have to kill to get what was wanted? It was an unusual request; rarely did the inhabitants of la Strange have to lower themselves to the level of animals. 'Who is giving this order?'

'You do not have the right to question.'

'I do not recognise your voice, so who are you to relay this order? I need to know for my internal report after the mission.' He felt a disturbance. Relayers always followed the protocols.

Tyson cupped his hand over his ear-shell, a vibrating hum had started up in the inn and it was getting harder to hear. The operator's voice kept cutting in and out of the interact with small clicks. Someone was tapping the line.

'We are being overheard,' he said.

'Get the Thought . . . '

'Repeat.'

'Stay . . . ' hissing ' . . . death . . . ' The interact dropped to white noise.

'Station?' Tyson called, his ear-shell now a hash of sound. 'Station? Station?'

'Can't hear you, lad.' Lynard stood behind him, a long knife in his hand. 'Seems to me maybe yer been found. Give me the talker and hearer.' The old man slashed at him in warning.

Tyson unclipped his gear and handed it over. He wished he'd kept the repeller on until after he'd contacted la Strange. He studied the old man's face as Lynard stuffed the gear into his pockets. The Thoughtless couldn't generally use the devices, their minds couldn't deal with the signals they put out; this was for trade.

'Yer weapon.'

'I don't have one.' He never carried one; never needed one before. To fight in a physical sense was to diminish the reason and logic of his race. And if he had to injure or even kill his hands were weapons enough.

'Yer stupid as well as pretty.' Lynard pushed the knife closer to Tyson's face. 'Eyeless don't care if yer pretty.'

'You said I was safe until morning.'

'It's morning and the deal is over. Eyeless pays well.'

'I'll get more Lithiums?'

Lynard shook his head. 'Eyeless is 'ere feryer. Deal settled.' He waved him towards and through the curtain. 'Yer better not lie to her, lad. She's not like the rest of us down 'ere, she bring fear with her sight; kills fast.'

Stepping from the dim of the hallway and into the inn's brilliant electric light tubes took a few moments for Tyson's eyes to adjust. Why the bright light? He moved to the centre of the room, in the space between the two rows of tables. The inn appeared empty. Stools both sides of the tables were worn smooth, shiny, but the table tops—beaten metal sheets—were scarred with graffiti. The fire crackled in the hearth but there was no other sound.

He turned back to Lynard. He hadn't come through the curtain with him. Tyson looked to the fire.

'I'm here,' a female voice said, the sound as soft as a breeze across his cheek.

Tyson spun about. A hand grabbed him by the jaw, the strength inescapable; the sharpness of long nails pressed into his flesh, painful. A single thrust sent him sprawling across a table. The scrape of table legs over the steel-grated floor a scream in the silence.

'I am Eyeless and I understand you have lost something.'

Tyson still hadn't seen her but knew that his life hung in the balance. 'The old man has taken . . . '

'Not your gear, Strange-er,' she said. 'You have lost a Thought.'

He couldn't confirm this to her. He slid from the table to a crouch. A drop of blood spattered on his leather trouser leg. Tyson touched his cheek. A shadow moved by the fire, a blur of motion. This Eyeless moved fast, faster than any Thoughtless he'd heard of. She appeared a few metres in front of him. Dark. Menacing.

'As you see, Strange-er, I am not like these dim-witted fools.' Eyeless sat on the table opposite. She shifted smoothly in her black leather coat and jumpsuit, clothing not all too dissimilar to his own. She moved like the clouds that scudded beneath la Strange. 'I don't like the water much.'

Tyson could see his reflection in her polished, slag metal goggles. They seemed to drip from her brow. It reminded him of glossy candle wax. She smiled. Perfect, white teeth between narrow lips; it was a smile he did not expect, the perfection startled him. She wasn't a Thoughtless. A Human, perhaps? But they never showed violence.

'You fear me? So you should, Strange-er.' She caressed a pocket on her breast and two eyeballs fell out on the floor between them.

Tyson jumped back and rolled over a table top.

'They were useless of course.' The woman sounded disappointed. Tyson had a table between him and the eyes, between him and her. 'Do you think I would be well served trying yours?' She lifted her glasses to reveal two holes where eyes should have been. Coloured wires ran into the red pulpy mess. She lowered the glasses and waited.

Shana's killer! I'm going to die. Tyson looked toward the hatchway that led outside; could he escape?

A swift movement and the woman stood by the door. The smile was now gone but her face, smooth beneath long black hair, didn't look angry. 'Relax, Strange-er,' she said; again the whisper. 'I'm not going to kill you, yet.'

'You killed Shana.' He was trapped. 'Why? Did she ask too much in trade? Didn't she want to trade her eyes?'

'I killed no-one. That is the Thoughtless way.' The woman cocked her head to one side, listening to something. 'You are popular; I hear them, you know.'

'What will you do to me?' he asked, leaning with his

hands on the table. He had nothing to trade. 'Will you trade me?'

'You will explain what you have lost and then I will decide.' The smoothness of her voice carried deeper menace than he'd first thought.

La Strange had its secrets and he could not divulge them under any circumstances. If he had to die then he would take those secrets with him.

Eyeless sprang forward. Finger nails bit into his chest. 'Tell me!' Her voice pounded inside his head. 'Now!' The nails dug deeper. Pain erupted in his muscles, reached into his back. He tried to pull away but the nails penetrated deeper, it felt like she was ripping his lungs out. 'What is it!? What is it!?'

'A Thought,' he cried, giving in to the fire in his chest. 'A dangerous Thought from the forbidden vault. I don't know any more.'

She released him. Tyson slumped forward, sliding to a stool. Dark stains appeared on his shirt. He dropped his head into his hands, fighting for breath, fighting back tears of pain. His training set him apart from the regular population, why had it failed him? His thoughts began to reorder but still he could not understand how easily he had broken his vow; he was as good as dead to la Strange, now. To show weakness under threat was to be on equal terms to the lesser lives of those in the under-damp; he had shown animal behaviour.

'I know all that,' she said, moving to the smouldering fire. 'I want to know *why* it is dangerous? Why was it important to the girl?' She focused on him. 'Is the girl important to you?'

'Shana was my affection partner.' He boosted his

uptake. 'I let her have access to the Thought vault, part of our sharing routine.'

'So you knew her well?' He nodded. 'You don't seem too upset about it.' She sat on a stool by the fire. 'I can't hear emotion in your voice, and I need to know if I should help you.'

'She's dead. What more is there?' Shana often said she wanted to know what true emotions were. He'd wondered what she meant. Mood control and reason served them well enough. The free and uncontrolled emotional responses clouded judgement, why allow this when it was easily managed.

'Did you love her?' The woman had her back turned.

Tyson wondered at the word. 'I felt attached . . . we had the affection program . . . '

'Yes, yes,' Eyeless said, 'I know how it works up there. But you did say affection *partner*. La Strange does not allow partnerships easily. So, did you love her?'

'Why did you have to kill her?'

'I didn't kill her. I've already told you,' Eyeless said with annoyance. 'I don't have the Thought, either.'

'Why did you cut her eyes out?' Even if uncontrolled emotion wasn't la Strange's way, the violation still required explanation.

'As you saw, the woman was dead.' Eyeless turned on him, her face attractive in the light; skin pale, chin square and lips slightly parted. She didn't look like a Thoughtless and she didn't speak like one. 'Maybe it was the Humans.'

'But why?' Tyson couldn't move. Again a heightened state possessed him. Did he have a fault in his management level processes? 'They aren't known for it. Why mutilate her like that?'

Eyeless's expression seemed to change, her features softened, shoulders relaxed. 'I am a Strange-er, you know?' she said. 'I escaped the tower a long time ago, probably back when you were still only a blob of flesh in your growth-vat.' She looked to the floor. 'I thought maybe her eyes could patch into my connectors; they did of course, only all the nerves were dead. The woman had been dead too long.'

A feeling of loss seeped into him? Why wasn't his uptake working like it should?

Tyson sat, breathing slow and deep, for some reason the under-damp was interfering with his basic chemical adjustments. He was faulty, he had failed. There was no point looking for the Thought now. He'd been caught and divulged his mission, he couldn't go back; to register an animal response to threat automatically removed his citizenship, his mission report would show the infringement and he would be terminated. He didn't have the thief to help negotiate a reinstatement; Shana was dead. He watched the odd woman, the bright lights making her goggles sparkle. How could she have come from above the clouds? Why would anyone from la Strange choose to live with the Thoughtless? Unless she too showed an animal response. He felt his chest and the wounds; a headache began behind his eyes, the room pressed in, squeezed at his mind.

The glare of the tubes showed the place as the shambles it really was. Black mould hugged every corner where rust hadn't taken hold. The crusted grid floor had more bent cross bars than straight, and beneath them he could see the shimmer of liquid.

'I'll help you find it,' Eyeless said, standing.

'What's the point?' Tyson had lost the impetus, a doldrum of moods had settled across his systems, a malfunction probably brought on by his slip from perfection. What he needed was to run an empowering Thought to help bolster flagging serotonin uptake, but if he couldn't return to the tower . . . 'I can't go back. You might as well kill me and be done with it.'

'Self-pity, good. Shows there might be some hope for you. You doing all that chemical adjusting shit in your head?' He stared at her. 'After a time you'll give it up, let stuff run naturally.' She pulled back her long hair and showed an ear-shell, a copper device with wires running into her neck. 'I can't see what this Thought is doing but already there have been deaths amongst the Thoughtless that I think are connected.

'If they are dying why use it?'

'I'm not a Thoughtless and couldn't even begin to understand why; maybe because they think it is a path to a better life. Suicide is popular down here.'

Tyson felt weary. 'How could it kill them.' He looked up at her. 'It's only a Thought.'

'They can't process information like we can, they don't have the neural networks in place to hold the data streams. I am guessing the data shock is killing them—' She cocked her head again, the listening pose. 'So, I don't know why they want, or would even want to try and experience this Thought. They already experience live emotions now, albeit out of control most times, but at least real and their own. What I do know is that we have to get it back. We have to locate it and let what I call fate, shape what is to come.' She let her hair drop across her face.

'Why the change of heart?' Tyson wiped his face. Had he been crying? Had Shana meant more than rostered attachment to him? 'Why are you going to let me live?'

'What change of heart?' Eyeless approached him, pulling her coat closed. 'I'm working to my own agenda here Strange-er. I knew you'd come and I need things to fall together in my favour. I like you so far, so don't go disappointing me.'

'You knew I would come?'

The lights faltered then blinked out. The fire's light yellowed the dark. She touched her ear-shell, brow creased above the glasses.

'Thoughtless,' Eyeless said. 'Got here faster than I expected. Some can use the communications devices you know.'

Loud clanking rang through the inn. Someone was trying to force the hatch. In a moment she was beside him, yanking him to his feet. The old man ran into the room.

'They be out back, s'well.' He held his knife. 'Yergoin' to have to use the roof.'

Tyson allowed Eyeless to drag him through the curtained doorway, up a ladder through a small hatch and into a tunnel; strange green luminescence led into the dankness.

'What's happening?' Tyson gasped, trying to catch his breath.

'I'm not the only one looking for you.' The woman pushed him ahead. 'There's a hatch at the end, leads across the roof to the power cables. Quick, before they decide the roof is a good way to get in as well.'

Tyson ran. At the hatch he spun the wheel, relieved to see the spars disengage. He pushed the hatch but it didn't budge; jammed.

'Get out the way,' Eyeless cried. How did she know what had happened? She leant into the hatch and it swung out into torrential rain, the sound deafening. 'Across to the cable guides,' she yelled, shoving him into the downpour.

The heaviness of the sky and the thickness of the rain made it hard to see anything, but he didn't wait to be told again. He started running, hoping something that looked like cables would come into view. In moments his leather coat was heavy with water and his boots felt like thick wadding around his feet; he still couldn't see any cables.

'Keep running!' came Eyeless's scream. 'To your right, about twenty strides.'

Twenty strides? Running or walking? Tyson stopped at ten and tried to see through the wall of rain. In the grey haze he made out thick cabling attached to a short A-frame tower. The cables reached out over a darker patch of grey and into what could only be called low cloud.

'Here.' Eyeless stopped beside him. How did she manage to see? She thrust a heavy wheeled contraption into his hands. 'Put the grooved wheel over the cable.'

He tried to look up at her but water flooded his eyes.

'It's a zip line.' Eyeless advanced on the tower. She showed how her hand fit into the ring grips either side of the wheel. 'Follow me, Strange-er, or end up stripped to the bone by a Thoughtless's blade.' She hooked the wheel over the cable then threw herself out into the expanse. It sounded like she was cheering.

'Thar! Thar!' he heard from behind. They could see him.

He climbed up on the edge of the building, feet slipping on the slimed metal, and hooked the wheel over the cable. He thrust his hands through the rings and held the short grips as tightly as cold, wet hands could. He closed his eyes and let gravity do the work. With a grunt from the weight of his body hanging from his arms he flew into the abyss. Cracks, like lightning, joined the solid thrum of the rain. The Thoughtless were shooting at him.

'Let go,' Eyeless screamed over the noise. 'Let go, now!'

Tyson held on a little longer before releasing his grip and fell. The impact knocked the breath from his body. He lay stunned in a pool, his body crumpled against a wall. The slickness of blood flooded over his lips as he fell backwards on the roof. Eyeless knelt beside him.

'I said let go.' The rain fell heavier; it had become hard to see at all.

'Tell me,' he asked, struggling to stand. 'How in all sunlight are you able to sense where I am . . . where anything is?' If he was going to die he at least wanted to know that much.

She helped him to his feet. 'When we get inside.' She dragged him after her. They ran across the roofs, jumping over narrow gaps between buildings or using the cables.

Soon Tyson was struggling, he couldn't run any more. Eyeless slid to a stop by another short A-frame tower with broken wires whipping out from its sides in the increasing wind. She pushed on the tower and it shifted aside on a flat square of metal—it was a hatch.

'Down!'

He didn't need to be told a second time. He descended the ladder into a suffuse green light. Eyeless's boots clanged down the rungs after him, the rain shut out by the closing of the hatch. The chamber had a few centimetres of water on the floor.

'Left,' she said coming down beside him. She started down the greenish lit passageway. The light came from a patchy fluorescence on the walls. Tyson followed, his mind unable to keep pace with events. Eyeless wasn't rushing now, it seemed they were in a safe place.

'In here.' Eyeless disappeared through an opened hatch. The light was whiter, brighter and he could smell damp clothing beyond what clung to his skin. Once inside the warmish room she closed the hatch and spun the wheel, dropping a lock bar across when the wheel stopped spinning.

'Put your coat in there.' She pointed to an opened cabinet with rust streaked doors. 'It's a dryer.' She shucked off her black coat and threw it at him. 'Mine first.'

The room sparkled with data screens, flat cables and copper wires. Oxidised brass-framed readers occupied one wall, dials showing red, others looked dead. For a 'Deep Sea' place it had a lot of tech stuff; gear way beyond the comprehension of the under-damp's inhabitants. Tyson hung both coats in the drier while Eyeless stripped off her clothes to stand naked by a low burning fire. Despite the shining goggles she was attractive in a slim kind of way; a well-toned woman whose skin was as white as cloud.

'Never seen a naked woman before?' She made no attempt to cover up.

'Ah . . . no . . . I mean . . . yes . . . ah . . . '

'Your responses are getting better. If you don't want to fall sick I suggest you get those wet clothes off as well.' She faced him, arms up, hands pulling her long, wet hair back into a ponytail. 'I've got some clothes you can put on, not much but at least they'll be dry.'

Tyson tried not to stare but he was drawn to her nakedness, troubled by the way it didn't bother her. Slowly he stripped off his clothes, feeling a chill deepening as he went. He didn't like feeling exposed. Eyeless opened a well-worn storage box and pulled out a pair of grey pants, a brown, heavy shirt and a thick pullover.

'They'll be a little big on you,' she said, taking some clothes out for herself. 'The guy who owned them won't need them any more.' Tyson didn't ask why. She hung their wet leathers in with the coats.

Eyeless did something to the fire and the flames increased, though she didn't add extra wood. She indicated a red stop valve on the wall above the fireplace. Gas. She had gas. The Thoughtless weren't allowed gas. Tyson wondered about this Eyeless. She had la Strange technology and piped gas from the tower. the Thoughtless would blow themselves up if they had the energy source. What was this place?

'Where are we?'

'This is one of our old monitoring stations from the days when we thought we could help the dim-witted with implants,' she said.

'I don't understand.' He couldn't see la Strange

helping the more animal-natured Thoughtless.

'There are many things you don't understand Strange-er but if you help me get the Thought I'll explain some of it to you.'

'How long ago? I mean how old is this place?'

'The Humans kept them running long after our kind abandoned the research, so I guess maybe three hundred years give or take twenty. You'd like them, the Humans I mean, well, I hope you will.'

'You know the Humans?' The dry clothes were scratchy against his skin, the irritation annoying.

'We trade. We have a deal in place.'

Once dressed she stared at him for a time, lips curling up with some kind of pleasure. Tyson wondered what she saw when she looked at him. He let the warmth of the fire soften his mood while Eyeless, now in an open black shirt and dry leather trousers, sat on a stool fiddling with an ear-shell in her lap.

'Before you ask, again,' she said, not looking up, 'I can't see you, I can't see anything.'

'But . . . '

'Shut up, Strange-er, let me finish.' She looked at him. 'I have a sensor array in the goggles. The stuff gives me shapes and colours, movement but no real detail.' She pulled her hair back from above her ear and showed where the goggles were jacked into her head. 'I read your colour signature, electrical signature, motion and sound waves; it all meshes together in my mind as a rough image.' She fixed the listening shell back over her ear. 'Strange-ers are blue.' She held her hand in front of her face. 'The Thoughtless are yellow and the Humans are shades of red, all on a background of deeper red. The

Humans are hard to make out sometimes but I manage. It's not like they are around much anyway.'

'The bright lights at the inn?' Feeling suitably warmed he sat on the only other stool in the place; a beaten steel contraption with three, uneven legs.

'They created a blaze of dark red, showing you as bright blue. Easy to find.'

'So, without the goggles . . . '

She smiled. 'I'm just like you.'

'What?'

'Blind, my dear Strange-er, totally blind.'

Eyeless stood and moved to the other side of the room and a wooden desk. How had she got such a large thing down through the tunnel? There didn't seem to be any other way in or out of the room. It was a large space filled with flickering screens. Copper meshed cables, linked to a bank of corroded steel system terminals, swept over every surface like sea snakes.

'You can use all this gear?' he asked. 'Why hasn't there been reports about this by la Strange's security office? They monitor everything in the under-damp.'

'La Strange doesn't know much about what happens down here, not since they abandoned all the camera towers and monitoring stations.' She sat on the edge of the desk. 'In a way they helped create this way of life. It was originally an underwater city and from what I have learned, the tide shifted so now it spends part of the day above water. Before the great tower of la Strange, this was where we lived.'

'We lived here, in the under-damp?' He knew many of the old histories of the city and this was not one of them, not even in speculated times.

'We built the tower and left the city for the new inhabitants, the ones who didn't usually get a chance at life.' She shook her head. 'That's it for now. When I think you can handle a little more I will tell you.'

'I don't believe you. We have always lived above the clouds; we have never been animals like these.'

'What I know isn't for you to accept or deny at this stage, and you better start hoping there is a next stage.'

'Meaning?'

'Just follow my lead, is all I'm willing to offer.'

Tyson examined the equipment, the greening copper tubing of the power supply, the blackened brass boxes of the current generators—all old stuff, yet clearly la Strange equipment—but what use was it down here in the wet? Eyeless sat on her stool at one of the screens, a cable now hung down the back of her neck; fingers hovered over a dirty glass key panel.

'So, just what am I allowed to know?'

'That the Thoughtless have been accessing the Thought,' she said. She touched the panel softly. 'We can track its effects.' In a moment the screen sparkled with live data feeds from the towers. 'I think we can get it back easily enough.' She turned to him. 'But there is a price to pay.'

'Then you will trade it to la Strange?' Somehow he didn't think that was what she was planning.

'You could say trade is what I am up to.'

He thought of Shana, her slit throat, her vacant eye sockets. Why remember her? That part of him was over—ordered and stored. Wasn't it?

Eyeless pulled up a schematic of the under-damp—'Deep Sea'. The town was more or less a grid pattern;

buildings connected together by waterways, gangways and narrow, stoned paths.

'Here!' Eyeless said pointing at the screen. 'They have used the Thought in this section, about ten kilometres from here.' An area showed black smudges scattered about like discarded batteries. 'All dead. I'm guessing a suicide pact.'

'You can see that?'

She touched the cable jacked into her neck but said nothing. The screen showed a winding and twisting overview of the city; obvious overlays from the light tower's cameras. She was watching the world. A white patch, lit up by several towers glowed amongst the great expanse of grey.

'This light covers about one square kilometre.' Eyeless pulled the jack free and spun about in her chair. She flipped up her goggles. Even her eyelids had been removed. She jiggled the wires that ran into the holes. 'I don't necessarily disagree with what is happening,' she said. 'A few less Thoughtless would be a good thing.' She flipped the goggles down.

Tyson tightened the rope belt that held his trousers up; he didn't know what was happening. 'Why are they killing themselves?' he asked, stepping slightly away from the warmth of the fire.

'Don't you feel it?' Eyeless turned to him. 'Don't you feel their sadness?'

'No, only occasional chemical disruptions and thought spikes, but I purge these with the logical order of things.'

'Purge? You mean flush your brain with serotonin? Make everything eternally happy?'

'You make it sound like that is a bad thing?'

'In a way it is.' She leant back against the desk. 'Why do you think Strange-ers don't feel strong emotion? Actually why do you think you are having difficulty keeping check of emotions?'

'What's this got to do with the Thought?'

'Maybe nothing . . . '

'What is it?'

'Not now, I don't know enough and I hate guessing. And speaking of guessing, what is your name?'

'I thought you knew all about me.'

'Now isn't the time to be standing up for yourself.' The smile was not one of humour. 'Your name, please?'

'Tyson, I'm a Tyson 732.'

'Well Tyson 732, I'm a Helena 219 but of course you can call me Eyeless.'

From the same box she'd taken the clothes she got them blankets.

'Get some sleep, tomorrow things will happen and I might need you alert.' She handed him the thick blanket. 'And you, young 732, might have to do something you never thought of before.'

'I don't understand.' He thought about the kill-order over the interact. 'I am not going to hurt anyone for you.'

'Sleep now, tomorrow you can decide.' She took her blanket and lay down closer to the gas flames.

With the blanket wrapped about him he settled on the floor near the fire, not too close to the woman. Eyeless knew far, far more than she was telling and it made Tyson nervous. He felt frightened, an unusual feeling: racing heart, sweating and his mind running scenarios of him getting his eyes cut out, his data casing ripped from the back of his skull. He didn't like the feelings and he didn't like how they were becoming more the norm over the last few hours. Had water gotten into his system? He pulled a disk from his wallet, and slipped it into the reader in his neck. The blue sky of la Strange filled his mind, the gardens, the low white and yellow buildings, the glass towers that reached to the stars and the people, all the people in their blue uniforms, or green worker jumpsuits going about their day in unison.

He could see the steam vents, the giant copper tubes that ringed the outer rim of the sky city; they belched white, clean steam from the massive boilers beneath the pavement. Flywheels as big as buildings created electricity to power the world and support life above the clouds. A great silver-grey battery factory covering five square kilometres made power cells to run the devices that made life easier and made currency the under-damp could understand. This was what Tyson needed to see, to remember his home, the place away from the smells, the water and filth. He looked to the unbroken blue above, sighed and felt release. A shadow moved across his sight. A black cloud blotted the sun. What was wrong?

'I don't understand.' Tyson sat with his back near the fire, his shoulder ached from the hard floor, his eyes stung with tiredness.

'The Thoughtless seem to be flocking to one specific location, it could ruin everything.' Eyeless was a blur of agitation. 'How do you feel about it? How does this make you feel Tyson 732? The Thoughtless are flocking to the Thought and dying in droves.'

'They are Thoughtless, why should I care for them?' Tyson felt unease at her anxiousness.

She shrugged. 'Well it isn't just a Thought, is it? There is a reason for it to be down here.' She stopped pacing and shifted like a flash of light to stand over him. 'Don't you feel anything because of the deaths?'

'I think I feel . . . feel sad.' He didn't know for sure. 'My inducers aren't overriding the gloom I feel like they should. I don't feel happy, I can be sure of this.'

'Good, good, just what I was hoping to hear.' Dragging on her now-dry coat she smiled. 'How about we see if we can stop them killing themselves and get the Thought back?'

'Won't it be dangerous, why not just wait for them to realise it's no good for them?'

'It is not for them I am doing this.'

She turned the fire down, warm air quickly fled, the smell of damp clothing and mould soon seeped back into the room; he hadn't realised how much of the mustiness warm air hid.

Eyeless opened a square steel chest in the corner. She passed him a handgun; a small weapon with a short barrel.

'The Thoughtless aren't far from here.' Eyeless selected two chromed handguns, sporting thick and lengthy magazines. In moments she had the holster across her shoulders. 'You and I might have to fight for the Thought. You ready for that?'

'What are we going to do?'

'Something you will have difficulty with, but I think you of all la Strange-ers are ready for it.' She picked up a browned cylinder about the size of her little finger nail from the mess on her desk. 'This is a neurotransmitter inducer, my inducer. Without it I can do what is necessary. You, on the other hand, will have to manually adjust yours if you want to stay alive. There isn't time for me to cut it out.' She looked menacing with the white grips of the guns sticking out from under her arms. 'Do what I do and don't get killed, you are too valuable.' She stepped out of the room. 'The Thoughtless aren't smart but when they do work something out and find it has value they can be pretty tenacious.' She stood in the green luminescence of the corridor, rubbing her hand over the wall's surface, causing the light to glow brighter. 'You can either help me, Strange-er . . . ' she drew one of the guns, 'or I shoot you.'

She had a point. The idea of dying didn't appeal to him. He found he actually wanted to live, felt like he had to stay alive.

They moved swiftly down the corridor to the hatch. Eyeless went first, one gun in her hand. The hatch opened and rain rushed in. Tyson pulled his own weapon and climbed out into the downpour. Eyeless slid the tower back in place and pointed to the edge of the building. A rail and the question mark of a ladder could just be seen through the grey.

'See the light?' she yelled over the drumming.

In the distance he could see the white glow of tower lights. The tightness in his gut told him that was where they were going. Eyeless ducked into the greyer shadows and emerged with two hand grips. They were going to use the cables again. Tyson tucked his weapon into his inside coat pocket, took the guide wheel and followed Eyeless to the edge of the building and the myriad of overhead wires—all sparking under the constant downpour.

He couldn't even see the other buildings.

Like before, he stepped off into the gloom. This time when he heard her yell, he let go.

Eyeless ran through puddles across the wide expanse of the second roof; she was silhouetted by the light spraying from the towers above. Grey shadows turned to black pits. By the time they reached the concentration of light he was breathing hard, but the wetness no longer bothered him. They stood on the curve of a building bathed in the brightness of the light tower. Other cylinder building could be seen close-by now as clear as day.

'Stay here,' she yelled, diving over the side of the building. Tyson froze. She'd flung herself into the brightness. He stood alone on the roof top.

The sound of gunfire cried out, a popping over the thrumming of rain on metal. Then came a loud crack, as if someone had smashed two panes of glass together. Eyeless's guns. He drew his weapon and ran to the edge looking down into a pool of whiteness. The ground was only a single storey down, brown and moss coloured. Thoughtless darted about, seeking shelter in hatchways, hand held torches blinked about the shadows. Two men lay prone in the alleyway. He couldn't see Eyeless.

He thought about climbing down the ladder and joining her but he couldn't. He was afraid. It didn't make sense. Why was he afraid? He felt something hard press into his neck. A gun? A hand reached past him and removed the weapon from his grip. The pressure on his neck eased.

'Stand.' The voice was barely audible over the rain. 'Hands up. Turn around, slowly.'

He stood, arms raised. Slowly he turned to face who had captured him.

'Tyson.'

'Shana?'

She stood before him in sodden brown clothing, looking more like an old seafarer than the woman he remembered. Her fair hair was dark and plastered over her face; eyes, bright green even in the gloom, stared at him. He lowered his arms and she the gun.

'I saw your body,' he yelled over the noise.

'I'm sorry Tyson, it had to be done. You had to think I was dead.' Shana stepped closer, put her left hand on his chest and gazed into his face, water causing her to blink rapidly. 'How do you feel?'

There was still shooting below, still the occasional scream of someone dying. He didn't know how he felt, or didn't want to know how he felt. Why was she asking? He shook his head, it wasn't logical, it wasn't right. She was dead, he saw her, touched the body.

Shana handed him a disk and stepped back. He could see something in her face, he didn't understand. He looked at the disk. It was the Thought, a small promise on his finger tip. She pointed to the spot on her neck where the player was, she wanted him to see it and he, despite everything, wanted to see what was killing the Thoughtless. Struggling against the water falling over him he slid the disk into the reader. There was a crackle in his mind as the drive sizzled off the moisture on the disk.

'Oh no, no, no,' he cried dropping to his knees. 'No. It can't be. It can't be.' He could almost hear the chemicals in his brain struggling with the vision in his mind.

Darkness; pure darkness.

Shana knelt in the puddle in front of him, putting her hands either side of his face. 'This is what I was developing; I did it for us.'

'Strange-er,' came Eyeless's voice over the rain. 'Tyson!'

Shana nodded, but he didn't know what to do. He couldn't think. Didn't want to think. His heart ached with despair at what could have been, what he thought had happened to her.

'He's here!' Shana yelled.

'Has he used it?' Eyeless sounded short of breath, her voice loud over the rain.

'Yes, he has seen it.' The sound of her voice was the only thing holding him back from the gaping, black abyss before him; the voices his only true grip on reality.

Silence.

'I'll be there shortly. Stay where you are.'

Tyson studied Shana's face and saw, truly saw what she was seeing. The absolute darkness of loss based on the absolute light of union. He felt it; the emptiness crashed through his mind as a hot wind. It soaked up his will like a cloth soaks up moisture. He held on tight to Shana, felt her strength as his slid away. How far could he fall into this dark well? His inducer was overwhelmed; he could almost hear the dendrite dying. He couldn't look at her any longer. He closed his eyes and let the rain—the ever present rain—pound him as he tried to block cellular activity. It didn't work, nothing in his systems worked. What had she done to him?

'What do you feel?' Shana whispered in his ear. 'Tyson, tell me. What do you feel?'

'Pain!' he cried out. 'Pain and emptiness!'

'Open your eyes, Tyson. Look at me.'

The world was a blur, a vision through tears, a vision drowning. Again she cupped his face, pressed her lips against his; a kiss, but a kiss like he had never felt before. He felt it, truly felt it.

'It's not pain; it's not the end, my sweet Tyson. It is love.' She kissed him again, her arms tight about him, protecting yet freeing him at the same time.

Tyson tried to search the feeling, search the thoughts, the darkness they brought. The thought of losing Shana to death, the thoughts of her murder and what was done to her, rushed at him, threatened to swallow him. He couldn't breathe. He couldn't breathe. He couldn't breathe . . . couldn't breathe.

Eyeless sat at her desk, a drink in hand and an expression of contentment. Tyson rested with his back against the wall, a blanket wrapped about him and a cup of stinking broth clenched in his fingers. The Thought had been removed but the effects remained—he had been changed. He couldn't order his mind, purge the darkness or the sense of loss, nor could he suppress the overwhelming elation of being with Shana, and knowing he wanted to be with no-one else. If this was the effect of love then he understood why the emotion, the thought of darkness had been locked away. Was this the programming equivalent of having his neurotransmitters over-ridden?

Shana paced the room. Her great coat lay on the floor in front of the fire, steam rising, her boots squelched as she walked.

'You recovered?' Eyeless asked.

'I don't think I'm ever going to recover.' He gulped down a mouthful of broth, thankful for its salty distraction.

'I can see the feelings you have for each other. Shana was right to choose you.'

Shana turned on Eyeless. 'What happens now?'

'More of your research.' Eyeless laughed. 'But you can't go back to the tower.'

'You know each other?' Tyson shivered, the cold holding tight to his bones. 'On the roof . . . '

'I'm sorry Tyson, I had to get you here. The rarity of finding compatibility amongst our kind meant only you could fulfil this task, and I had to take the risk that you would be the one sent after me.' Shana hugged herself.

'Why only me? What do you mean you "had to get me here"? You planned all this?' His shout rang around the walls.

Shana squatted before him, one hand on his knee. 'I was researching la Strange, looking for someone who had developed outside of the protocols, someone other than myself; I tampered with the affection matching protocols so you and I would be paired.'

'But you're . . . '

'I'm part Human, Tyson. I infiltrated la Strange two years ago.' She looked to Eyeless who was listening quietly. 'I'm one of the volunteers they took away after a trade.'

'The Thought. What about the Thought?' He felt ill.

'It is a strong compatibility Thought that I manipulated and remapped with your patterning.' Shana's eyes softened and her grip on his knee firmed. 'Only you can complete the next part of the plan, and fleeing with the

Thought was the only way to safely get you away from la Strange.'

'Then who was giving the orders to find you?' He looked to Eyeless who tapped her ear-shell and smiled.

'And I wouldn't be claiming safety just yet. I picked something up when I nabbed him from the tavern.' Eyeless placed her hand against the listening device and turned away from them for a moment. The fingers of her right hand played over the key pad. Screens flickered.

'Why me, Shana, why me?'

'Because the research I conducted when I returned to la Strange uncovered an anomaly. You Tyson. You already had the ability to experience true emotions. It was just waiting to be unlocked.' She smiled and he believed her. 'I wanted to be a part of that unlocking and I . . . ' she looked away for a moment. 'And I found I loved you.'

'You did all this for love?' the emotion was strong in him now but he didn't know how to control it.

'No,' Eyeless said, her tone one of finality. He looked to Shana.

'No, my feelings didn't come into it, but I did try and get what I wanted at the same time. Eyeless was my contact here and we had to get you down and over-stress your systems so there would be natural breakdowns, breakdowns I had already initiated when you allowed me to mess with your systems before I fled.'

'Why couldn't you do this in la Strange? You didn't have to bring me down here.' He looked at the two women who were both shaking their heads.

'We had to for what has to be done next.' Shana stood and backed away. Eyeless touched her ear-shell and whispered something.

Tyson jumped, startled by a pounding on the hatch. Eyeless drew one of her guns. 'Open the hatch.'

Tyson didn't move. Shana obeyed and spun the wheel. The door opened and two Humans stepped in, their clean look undeniable. Tyson looked to Eyeless who offered no response. Shana nodded then shook each man by the hand. They wore tight-fitting grey suits that shimmered yet didn't appear wet.

'I don't understand what is going on.' Tyson couldn't find any control, he felt fearful and troubled yet he had an overwhelming joy that said to trust what was happening, whatever it was.

'We are going to copy your entire emotional process, Tyson 732,' one of the Humans said, 'and then we are going to infect la Strange's Thought network with the modified protocols.' Both Humans looked extremely happy about the idea.

'Why?' Tyson turned to Shana, looked to Eyeless who had now put away her gun. 'Why go to all this trouble?'

'It is a lot to explain, Tyson,' Shana said, 'but once the mapping has been done I will fill in all the details.' She approached him and took his hands; the look on her face was one of safety and care. 'You need to know this before we truly begin. The Humans built both Deep Sea and la Strange. They were meant to complement each other, support each others' social and economic needs. But la Strange developed in an unexpected way; the people there slowly removed full emotional development.' She looked to the Humans. 'Now the under-damp is where la Strange dumps its rejects from the vats, the ones that don't take well to the emotional de-programming because of faulty systems. It took the Humans a long time to help someone from la Strange to become emotionally aware enough to infiltrate la Strange and get to the vault. Tyson, though it is too late to help the people in Deep Sea, we can change the ways of la Strange and hopefully restore what was meant to be.'

'You want everyone to feel like I do now? Confused, erratic and barely in control?' He felt angry but he couldn't focus the emotion. It mixed in with too many other thoughts; too many eddies flooded his mind. 'I feel awful. I feel helpless.' He wanted to hold Shana, or let her hold him but he was unsure of himself.

Eyeless interrupted the proceedings, pulling out a bottle of liquid and instructing Shana to get glasses from beneath a bench and pour everyone a drink. She pulled Tyson aside.

'Tyson 732,' she said out of earshot of the others. 'I was one of the first who tried to infiltrate the vault and networks of la Strange. The clothes you wear are from the man I was partnered with. But we were found out and fled without ever getting close to the vault.' There was strong emotion in her voice, something he hadn't really noticed before. 'Maxim and I managed to stay undetected down here for a year. He was killed one night when he tried to deal with a Thoughtless. I was found and they cut my eyes out; Lynard kept me as a pet until the Humans found me again.' She eased in closer to him, her breath stale and hot on his face. 'You, Tyson 732, can change the future, you can make it so Maxim's life wasn't lost in vain.'

The steadiness of her voice, the deep feeling of the carefully chosen words settled his mind. He could see and feel reason in what was happening around him, even if he struggled with emotional understanding. Eyeless knew what it was like to be paired with someone; she also knew what it was like to have been used in a scheme to change the rigid social structure of la Strange, something he was only seeing now for the first time. He gazed past Eyeless to see the other three watching expectantly.

'Shall we join this moment of celebration?' Eyeless moved back from him to offer a clear path to the others. They joined Shana and the two Humans, who handed them a glass of milky liquid. 'To tomorrow,' Eyeless said as they drank.

The drink burned, Tyson gasped. 'Shit!'

'Lynard's finest,' Eyeless said with a laugh.

Robert N Stephenson has worked in the publishing industry as a writer, publisher, editor, literary agent and critic as well as many other less glorious roles. Everything he does is for his wife Alice and children Emma and Joshua.

Maia Blue is Going Home

Liz Argall

Maia Blue is losing her touchtaste sense, the most important of her perceptions.

Maia Blue has eyes, their lubricants thick with age. Changes in depth of field and light are difficult as her irises catch on micro- and macroscopic dents, but she can make out basic shapes. Vision had always been a secondary sense, a way of finding paths from A to B and new things to explore, rather than a specific joy. Her sense of smell is sufficient, an adjunct to her taste, but her silicate cilia are brittle now and too many particles clog her receptors. She is dulled by the geological equivalent of a constant head cold. Maia Blue can appreciate music. Music doesn't resonate in her skin the way it once did, but she has developed a new fondness for vibrations travelling through the air and reverberating against her eardrums. Maia Blue's hearing is solid, but her touchtaste is fading.

It had been, once, that when she touched something, and especially if she put something in her mouth, the world of that object would be revealed to her. Through a complex web of chemical reactions, solvents and electrical charge, objects gave up their secrets. She tasted worlds, made them part of her and remembered them in hard storage. Now it is difficult to taste even salt, pungent with simple potential.

Maia Blue is the avatar of a sentient planet, constructed to discover the world of motion and difference. Maia Blue is different. Maia Blue has memories that are not her own. In dim lighting Maia Blue looks like a normal bald, blue, human female. She shuffles slowly now and weighs half a ton.

Maia was formed deep within a sentient planet, near magma flow and crystalline palace. Geology, tectonic circuits and electrical impulses combined and recombined, slow as rock, as fast as light. In a time long before her happening, the planet spoke to itself, saw only itself in a flow of shape, data and evolving consciousness. The planet had found pleasure in certain patterns, certain ratios, shapes and thinking structures. These patterns developed and shifted, electrostatic charge flowing like water into constantly changing nodes of consciousness.

The planet had only experienced itself, struggled with the idea of self/not-self, of things that existed that it did not touch, but gradually, as formations found new levels of complexity and co-operation, the planet became aware of elsewhere. The planet detected points of radiation from far away, drifting messages, rhythm/thought/impulse from faraway motes. Curiosity was favoured in its algorithms and it searched for new ways to touch, to understand that which was distant.

Hypotheses were considered. Could the shifting radiation, pinpoints and splotches from so many directions, be reflections of itself? Perhaps these were parts of its think-pattern, a heartbeat uncontrollable but there, projecting from nebulous outer shell to inner core. The splotches shifted and became slurred, slowly shifting further apart as the frequency rhythm stretched out, yet the planet did not feel slurred or stretched. Other, other, could it be other? Could these motes be something other than itself? Possibility. Complex nodes blossomed as understanding was sought.

It was not until later that the planet learned that these dancing motes of otherness were called stars by the spongy multitude. These stars, the first of Other.

Maia Blue shuffles a step forward in the line, hat pressed low over her head, long coat rubbing her ankles and duffle bag heavy in her hand. She pauses to spray her hands and face, waits for it to dry before pulling out her honorary passport and travel pass. Last time she tried to leave this station, security had restrained her for a long time. They had shaved pieces off her, taken memory and reduced her mobility. The regime has changed since then and it seems reasonable to attempt another return. Perhaps, perhaps no.

The concept of Other was a nebulous notion for the planet; it was still possible that the motes of radiation far away were pieces of itself that it did not understand. Thesis and anti-thesis flowed. Confirmation of Other came with destruction as travellers arrived from another space. Fast-moving bipeds—discrete from each other and the planet—arrived. Formations, memory, patterns and thinking were lost with the force of their landing. There were no redundancies back then; what was lost was lost as stone and crystal shattered under kinetic impact and fiery blast. The planet did not understand the travellers, and it gathered information of Other in the only way it knew how, through physical contact, through incorporation.

Incorporation was fraught and elusive, the formations of the travellers strange and utterly alien. The planet had some concept of temporary separations, from its own crystals made separate by harsh wind or structural error, but these Others had a different interface and did not respond in any coherent way. The planet was patient and curious, methodically sought integrative analysis. It learned much from those first travellers and did not comprehend their screams.

Maia Blue had a beginning.

Maia shuffles forward in the line. She counts the steps, five more paces to the security checkpoint. Then she will walk until she touches wall, walk left for thirty paces. The sign is large and red; she should be able to see it through blurred lenses. The sign for the flight that will take her home.

New knowledge, new ratios fed into the curiosity algorithm. New formations built, experiment upon experiment. The planet made Other of itself, modelled in the shape of those first travellers. Ma, the first one, the first sound, was birthed, became separate and returned. Consciousness made Other, returning to consciousness made whole, and for the first time the planet saw itself with outside eyes. Through Ma's memory it discovered its own externality and was fascinated. Many prototypes were made, formations made separate and re-absorbed. With each new prototype new cognition was made possible as separate and whole flowed like a tide. Sometimes Other beings would arrive on the planet, their flames and kinetic energy still destructive, but prepared for now. These Others were absorbed and learned from, and in time the planet comprehended their screams of dissolution.

Maia Blue is old now.

Maia Blue was formed like a slender, fast-growing stalactite; drip by drip she was given shape and appearance. She was given independent motion, energy renewal, comprehension, cognition and extended separation. She was the first to have a fully functioning tongue, eardrum, eyes and vast memory development capacity.

Many of her complex independent processes had been modelled on the imprints gathered from a high functioning Other that had been analysed. Through the imprint Maia was fluent in Spanish, spoke stilted English and Chinese. The human mind gave Maia the word Blue, her colour, her separateness. Ma was the first sound, Ma-ia the second, her name moving away, Ma-ia, Mai-a, Maia Blue, Maia Blue. The imprint's knowledge came with scattered memories: smears of touch, a snippet of blue sky, a taste both sweet and sour and one vivid image of a small being that was once part of the traveller and had become separate.

Maia Blue cannot feel now.

Signals were broadcast, patterns the planet found beautiful and meaningful. In time a ship arrived and cautiously hovered above the planet's investigative surface. Contact was made, stumbling attempts at communication, unexpected aggressive movements from the travellers. Negotiations were made; the planet agreed not to incorporate separate ones into itself, now and into the future. The concept jarred with established processes and analysis technique.

The agreement, the first treaty, the algorithm of permanent separateness from the Others caused tectonic gashes. Magma flowed down the face of the planet's largest crater. Maia, Maia Blue, she, the first avatar, negotiated this agreement. It was necessary for her function, for the travellers to take her, to go, to return. Maia Blue was far away when the second treaty was negotiated.

Maia Blue is no longer slender; she holds memory in hard storage and grows like a tree. As she grows old and heavy she sprays herself with a polymer-like wood glue. Her skin holds precious memory and she has started to flake under her own weight. A flake of crystal-like skin detaches, and she cannot remember the second human she tasted. She held his hand, warm flesh against her slightly sticky palm. He let her lick his forefinger and his skin buzzed from the reaction. Mammalian chemistry was so startling back then that it had swamped her ability to comprehend. Her mind was fluid in those days, dynamically wiring and rewiring her cognition— an awkward mess of geological/electrical sentience and human patterning.

The next day she bit his finger, careful not to break skin with diamond-hard teeth. The algorithms had shifted although the underlying mathematics remained the same, beautiful and molecular. A flake of memory lost in the crush of travellers and domiciles.

Maia Blue is going home.

Sometimes she catches memory as it falls away, stone splitting away from her surface. She carries a bag of lost knowledge. When she returns they will be pieced together and she will remember. The loss of craggy memory makes her lighter, makes it easier to walk and manipulate objects, but the pain of loss is greater than the joy of increased movement. She was not designed to carry this much memory.

Her return has been delayed, the galaxy red-shifts as governments shift, technologies rise and fall. Three times she has tried to return, three times she has been turned aside—through imprisonment, malfeasance and ship-wide failure. She has spent her otherness in continual study and observation, touching and tasting worlds, exploring the nuance and missing other details.

As her skin cracks and the oldest barklike layers of memory fall, Maia Blue keeps the jagged edges of remembrance, broken-toothed half memories. She remembers exploring another planet for a long time, trying to find its sentience, exploring as deep as was feasible in volcano and long-fingered fissure. Her mass made it difficult to emerge, her mouth empty of connection, teeth stained and ignimbrite as she found no sentience. She does not remember how she came to the planet. A provoking fragment, a gaping socket still reaching for its tooth, indicates that she came with others, beings that travelled simply to help her. She does not know what became of them.

Maia remembers a man with gnarled fingers and a soft skin. He said, 'You killed my mother. You stole her face.' An incorrect statement. She has never had biological components and, at the time, no concept of theft or personal property. His tears tasted like an empty sea. He slapped her fingers away and bruised his hand.

Maia Blue hands her documents to the security officer,

wipes soot from her eyes with a moist towelette.

Maia Blue has tasted technology, biology, radiology, botany, mineralogy, and spaces in-between and beyond. She has found some pleasure and understanding in dim colours and unexpected vibrations, but there is much she does not comprehend. The curiosity algorithm, the drive to explore is strong, but her touchtaste is fading. Maia Blue cannot feel, cannot analyse with clarity, and isolation numbs her tongue. Memory and sensation fall away and she fumbles to collect the broken pieces.

Maia Blue is going home.

Maia Blue squints at the security officer. The blur that is his hand hovers over the touch screen. She stumbles towards him as her only impression of a young boy with serious eyes flakes off and breaks into powder on the pressed metal floor.

Maia Blue will land lightly on the planet, on a ship designed for visitations and minimal harm. She does not know how much has changed. She will sit, legs crossed, in the receiving place, ground moist with potential. She will remove each fragment of lost memory from her bag and place them carefully on her body. They will not fit perfectly, but she will draw warm putty from the ground to glue pieces together as best she can. It will take her a long time; she is a patient, clumsy jigsaw puzzle, and not all will be restored.

Once glued she will be oddly proportioned and scarcely able to move. The planet will absorb her, suck her deep into its consciousness. Maia Blue, the first to leave and so long in returning. Data will be incorporated, analyses will be made, formations found, mathematical relationships calculated.

A slender stalactite blue biped will be developed to gather new data. The curiosity algorithm is strong.

A Maia Blue will leave.

Maia Blue is going home.

Fascinated by storytelling in all forms, Liz writes poetry, prose, comics, and song. Her work has been published in an array of publications including *Strange Horizons*, *The Pedestal Magazine*, *Meanjin*, and *Sprawl*. Liz moved from Australia to America's Pacific Northwest in 2009 and adores creating in two countries. Her website is www.lizargall.com

Memories of Mars

Chris McMahon

Das Varian squinted at the solid bulk of the AI building. It shone bright and metallic in the Martian morning, mocking him with its solidity. He approached warily, careful not to trip on the jagged rocks uncovered in last night's savage dust storm. A wispy, high-level cloud scudded across the dirty pink sky.

The AI had worked reliably for more than forty years, then suddenly shut itself down. Das hit the AI with everything he had, but it had locked the aquifer wells tight. His week-long assignment soon stretched to a month, then two. Meanwhile the nearby Vandel Corporation uranium mine was grinding to a halt—along with his once bright career.

Movement on the ridge above him caught his eye. A driller was working his way to the side of No. 11 platform, dragging something heavy. With a heave of his broad, check-shirted torso, he tipped a drum over the edge of the sheer drop.

'Look out below!' yelled the driller.

Bore-residue!

'Shit!' Das dived for cover.

The slime hit with the splatter of diarrhoea, and a smell ten times worse. It missed him by inches, at least twenty litres of the goo, dark green and black with putrefaction, now splashed like an ink-blot on the red sand. Das looked down to see a jagged spray of the stuff across the front of his jacket.

The residue was found in most of the Martian wells. A soup of nano-bacteria and complex organic chemicals. Once extracted, it concentrated and bound together in a protein soup as thick as glue.

Das scrambled back to his feet. He took a lungful of oxy-mix and lifted his mask. 'Watch where you throw that!' he shouted.

The rig powered down and three drillers peered over the edge at him—grinning. Their skin was burned leathery and tough by the Martian sun, covered with keratoses and raised lumps.

'Didn't see you there, Varian,' called down Hack, the drill-boss.

They all had their masks off, one of them taking a drag on a self-burning cigarette.

Das took another pull of oxy-mix from his tank. 'Put your masks back on!' he said, his voice sounding dull in the Martian atmosphere. 'And put out the damn cigarette. You know the rules.'

They turned away and went back to work without another comment. Masks off. Cigarette burning. It was a macho game to the drillers. They were always trying to outdo each other, to see how long they could go between shots of oxy-mix. The official record stood at seven minutes, but the unofficial one . . . . that was closer to thirty.

Das turned and started back toward his office hab, little more than a pressurised caravan with air-con and solar, set up beside the AI building. Like most of the domes back in Central City it was maintained at five psi, about the same pressure as the partially terraformed Martian atmosphere, with the standard oxy-mix of sixty per cent oxygen and forty per cent nitrogen. He fumbled with the keys and slipped into the heated interior with a sigh of relief, took off his heavy jacket, slipped off his breather harness and walked to his desk. The stale air was filled with trapped odours and the sharp, almost acidic tang of Martian dust. After two months Das was still not used to it.

Das looked at his terminal much like a condemned man might look down the corridor at the place of his impending execution. The Vandel logo spun languidly in the corner of the display.

'Caffeine. I need caffeine.'

He coaxed the electric kettle to life and made himself a cup of coffee, then returned to his desk. He winced at the bitterness. *These drilling camps really get crap supplies.*

'Maybe that's why the bastards are always in such a bad mood.'

Das checked the time on the screen.

09:38

Late again. *Damn insomnia.* The crappy meds did nothing but fray his nerves. He took a gulp of his coffee and flipped the screen to look at his data-miners. He had left three programs running overnight to see if they could pirate-copy some of the code from the AI, to somehow find a back door into the architecture. But they did not get in.

'Damn.'

The AI might be old, but it was designed to be bulletproof.

He sighed and reached over to turn up the speakers, opening a direct audio link to the Young AI. The techs who installed it christened it Mr Young as a joke, and gave it a male personality. An odd choice. Almost every other AI he had ever worked with had female stylings.

'Good morning, Mr Young,' said Das.

'Good morning, Das,' replied the AI after a pause. It always sounded dreamy, like a tracheotomy victim on drugs.

'You've been snooping around my software again, Das,' said Mr Young.

'I'm just trying to understand you.'

'I'm trying to give you straight answers, Das, but your analytical software seems faulty.'

Always the same damn conversation.

'We just need you to open the wells, Mr Young.'

'I cannot comply, Das.'

The wells had been installed before terraforming began. They were designed to survive massive storms, sabotage and just about anything else. Mr Young had retracted them into fifty metres of solid rock. Short of dismantling the whole Young ridge, they were untouchable. The very isolation of the Young escarpment had worked against them. Mr Young had been given unprecedented control over the physical systems here.

A soft *ping* announced the arrival of a message.

Das closed the audio channel and reluctantly checked his messages. Six waited for him—the latest with a red flag. Most were sent by his manager, Jaros, before seven am. Das scanned the subject lines of the emails. *Update. Progress Report. Urgent. Urgent. Priority.* What had he done to deserve this assignment? Sent to try and de-bug a frozen AI so old nobody could even find the original data on its architecture? Stuck with drillers whose idea of a joke was to dump bore-residue on him?

The Young aquifer was one of around forty reliable, underground sources of water on Mars. It was also one of the oldest, a handful of big reservoirs kept liquid since time immemorial by local geothermal sources. Like the others of its type, the water was trapped in rock, and the diffusion rates were painfully slow. It had been set up with a dedicated AI to co-ordinate and optimise extraction, carefully measuring the changes in water level and permeability across the whole massive feature.

Vandel had ordered a full manual program, that was why the drillers were here. If the old bores were re-activated, all well and good, they could work as two distributed networks, connected in parallel. If not, then the new bores would at least provide one set of working wells at Young under their control.

'No point putting this off any longer.'

Das connected directly to Jaros's office at Central. His stomach muscles tightened at the sound of the high-pitched connection tone.

Jaros's round face filled the screen, his mop of dark hair shot with grey. He was a big man, and he used that bulk to intimidate. This far away he had to be satisfied with shoving his face into the camera.

'It's about time,' said Jaros. 'I needed an update for a meeting with Water at eight am. It's over now, and I had to say, yet again, that no progress has been made by Das Varian.'

Like most divisions of MarsGov, Water was tiny,

relying on subcontractors like Vandel to implement their programs. After more than forty years of operation, Vandel owned virtually every installation on the planet. Some said it *was* the real MarsGov. Although since the appointment of President Kusan, there were signs of change: senior Directors inexplicably retiring, other more independent newcomers appointed to key positions.

'There was a situation at the wells. I couldn't get back to my terminal until now,' said Das reaching for an excuse.

'A sit—' Jaros almost choked. 'You listen to me. Leave those drillers to themselves. It took me long enough to calm things down after the last time. They will do a damn sight better without you interfering.'

Das tensed at Jaros's reference to his improved drilling plan, which had led to the drillers walking off the job in his first month here. It would have increased production rates by forty per cent, but even Jaros had sided with them.

'I want you to focus on by-passing the Young AI. That's why you're there.'

Das nodded.

'*Regular reports*, Das. I want to know exactly what you are doing, and if you do crack the AI I want to know *exactly* what you find, as soon as you find it. From now on I want daily updates, emailed to me by seven am.'

I'll send you an update after I finish in the evening. Nothing will have changed by seven am.

'No problem,' said Das.

Jaros squinted at him, shook his head, then killed the link.

Das let out a long sigh. He left the dregs of his

coffee—even *it* seemed to taste like the damned dust—and reopened the AI's audio channel. *Okay.*

'Mr Young?'

'Yes, Das.'

'Why can't you open the wells?'

'That action would conflict with programmed directives, Das.'

'Why, Mr Young?'

'Das, I log seventeen communications on this line of reasoning.'

'Proceed,' said Das.

'Very well,' said Mr Young. There was a slight pause. 'Further extraction of the wells directly threatens . . . human . . . life.'

There was always that odd little pause as Mr Young said 'human'.

'How will human life be threatened?'

'Verified data concludes that death will result from any further reduction in groundwater levels. Maximum safe extraction volume has been reached.'

Das had gone around in circles like this before. The problem was the AI was just plain wrong. The Young aquifer was unmanned. It had been since the beginning. There *were* no humans anywhere near it. No settlements that would be threatened by ground instability as the groundwater lowered. Nothing.

'Show verified data that supports prior conclusion.'

'I cannot let you have access to this verified data, Das. A password is required,' said Mr Young. The existence of a layer of operations within Mr Young that required a password had taken all the Vandel techs by surprise. *All the damn thing did was pump water for Chrissake.*

No-one had any useful records on the Young AI. The problem was the AI's system was so well known at the timen no-one thought to preserve a record of it. The old military systems that gave birth to it were even longer in the grave.

'Why is the data password-protected?' asked Das.

'It is category 5B7. Classified.'

Category 5B7.

He scrawled it on the terminal screen with an interface pen, underlined it five times then tapped it into memory. This had come up before, but the Vandel archives had drawn a blank. What if he had been looking in the wrong place? Maybe it had nothing to do with the AI's architecture at all. The classification might date from the first phase of exploration back in the 2020s, back when UNOOSA—the United Nations Office of Space Affairs—ran the show through its International Mars Committee. If so . . . *the Buggy King.*

If Jaros knew he was going outside Vandel, the bastard would fry him. But Das had learned it was useful to keep contact with the old techs on Phobos Station. Many of the big mainframes were still up there, and there was not much those old guys did not know.

His heart leapt with a thrill of defiance as he routed a signal through a nearby Vandel satellite with a backdoor code, then bounced it through Archangel Three—the big rotating habitat in areosynchronous orbit above Central City—to the other side of Mars.

The Vandel logo was soon replaced with a picture of the sprawling Phobos station. Das had done some of his training there, and knew that most of it was under the surface, spilling through the many cavities in the old moon. NASA had always been the major player in the UNOOSA Mars Committee, and once the Martian Constitution had effectively replaced it, NASA had taken full control of Phobos.

The image disappeared, replaced by the lank greasy locks and pudgy face of the Buggy King. His skin was blotchy, covered with burst capillaries from too many meds. He was one of the original buggy drivers. NASA had realised early it was way too expensive to get people to the surface, but robotic devices were another matter. Thousands of them had been dropped across the planet and piloted from Phobos: sampling, analysing, drilling. The first decade of Mars exploration had been by remote. The King was one of the original techs stationed on Phobos, and the last of the drivers. He had not left the low-g moon in more than a decade. Das doubted he would survive it if he tried. He was almost seventy.

'Das. Long time. Still sucking up the dust, man?'

'Yeah. Stuck on another AI assignment. Young this time.'

'So. What's a hot-shot like you want with the Buggy King?'

'I need you to run an historical database search for me.'

'Yeah, on what?'

'It's a classification code. But the Vandel records give me a complete blank. I'm hoping it might be something that was in use during the early days. Maybe UNOOSA, NASA . . . maybe even military,' said Das.

'Sure. I can see what turns up,' said the King.

'Category 5B7,' said Das.

'Okay. I'll ping your link when I have something.'

The King broke the connection and Das turned back to the AI. He re-activated the audio, but just stared at the screen. What was the use? How many times could he go through this? If he couldn't find a back door—a way of forcing the AI to follow his commands—they would have to manually shut it down and trace the circuits that released the wells. It would be messy, methodical and unbelievably difficult. It was the only other answer, but the only one that Vandel did not want to hear.

Suddenly the frustration, the lack of sleep, the non-stop pressure from Jaros—the failure of every single technique he had learned—collided in his head.

'What's the fucking password!' snapped Das.

'That question results in an illogical loop,' replied Mr Young.

He picked up his coffee mug and threw it. The old mug hit the dirty wall with a nasty *crack*, splashing the gritty dregs into a crazy fan.

The Vandel logo glared back at him in silent reproof. In a surge of anger he grabbed the screen, lifting it high overhead before ramming it into the floor with all his strength. The exterior screen cover smashed, the inner surface now webbed with cracks from the point of impact.

Das sank to his knees, his chest a hard knot of pain.

'I can't fucking take this any more!'

'I do not understand your question,' came the tiny voice of Mr Young from one of the screen speakers, the other was a twisted mass of metal.

'Give me the data, damn you!'

'Verified data last discussed requires password authorisation.'

'Fucking please! *Please!*'

There was a pause.

'Password accepted.'

Das's jaw went slack. He looked down at the cracked screen, which was now filled with a dancing woodpecker. A tiny, crazy laugh came out of the speaker.

'What the fuck is that?'

'That's Woody Woodpecker, Das.'

Can AIs go senile?

The screen cleared, replaced by an old-fashioned data interface.

'Ready for viewing of verified data.'

Das carefully lifted the screen, as though if he moved too quickly the data interface—this incredible chance— would vanish. He placed it on his desk, took out the last sharp pieces of the shattered screen cover and dropped them into the bin.

'How do you wish to view the data, Das?'

'Chronological order,' he replied in a daze.

'Confirmed,' replied Mr Young.

The screen filled with a mass of text. Words embedded in a mishmash of other symbols and nonsensical fragments.

'Why is the text full of character strings?'

'The communication was decoded.'

Of course. The Young AI was built on a military platform. It would have decoding subroutines.

Das shook his head to clear it.

'Are you telling me the password was "please"?'

'Yes, the password is the character string "please". I am programmed to accept it only on audio channel,' said Mr Young.

Audio only!

He pushed his fingers into his temple to stop the painful throbbing. He must have spent ten nights in a row trying to pull a password out of the AI. A billion combinations of text and character generated by specialty sub-programs. He never would have considered a distinction between input channels. To think it was so simple.

'Who set the password, Mr Young?'

'My original programmers, Das.'

He could just imagine a group of young tech's assigned to the arsehole of Mars doing that. Installing a run-of-the-mill system and having a bit of fun at everyone's expense. Just say *please*! But who the hell was Woody Woodpecker?

'Tell me what Category 5B7 is, Mr Young. '

'I am programmed only to discuss that with the relevant authorities.' A blank.

'Tell me who the relevant authorities are, Mr Young. Please.'

'I am unable to comply. Another security protocol is required.'

Another blank wall.

Das turned off the audio mode and examined the data. It was a mess. He sighed and started the painstaking work of cleaning it up. He had to run separate algorithms to extrapolate some missing sections. Thankfully Mr Young made his own processing power and decoding tools available, otherwise it would have taken a week.

The sun was low in the west by the time he was finished.

He scrolled through the records, at last satisfied he had something he could interpret. There were three in total. *Maybe he was dealing with a hacker?*

Das looked at the date signature, expecting something in the last few months.

'That can't be right.'

According to the log the first message was received between 2031 and 2034—the first three years of Mr Young's operation. Impossible. At that rate it would be a word a week! It had to be wrong. Yet the next message was sequential, received between 2034 and 2042. The last message ended in 2071—this year—dated only months before. *About the time Mr Young ceased pumping.*

He reactivated the audio interface.

'How did you receive these communications, Mr Young?'

'Via primary input.'

The only data entry point with the Young AI was the hard-wired link to Vandel at Central city. Das pulled up the log of transmissions from Central to Mr Young. But there was nothing that remotely matched. Just routine queries, as regular as clockwork.

He started reading through the first message, expecting a combination of logical-loop traps or keyword trips that would explain what happened to Mr Young.

[START OF LOG: 23–10–2031 ◇ 23:17:34:56 SMT]

Come to me, Therender. This is no time to dream.

What is it She-sire?

Something is drawing the Breath. We must move with the prey.

Very well, She-sire. But I like it in the outer

valleys of home-heart, despite the cold. I feel like I can taste the outside. When the feast-flood comes I want to be the first to savour it.

(Should I tell her the truth? No. What right do I have to destroy her dreams.)

What is it She-sire? Your taste is fearful.

N—nothing. Call me Elexdresis, child. You are a Feeder Swarm no longer, and you should know better.

I'm bored. All we do here is sleep.

Come here by me.

The Breath is strange. It is pulling at me!

Shhh. I will soothe you.

[END OF LOG: 11–01–2034 ◇ 00:01:45:03 SMT]

That was the end of the first message. Perhaps there was something buried in it, something that activated a program or mode of analysis. Some code. 'Therender' or perhaps 'Breath' may be keywords.

He tapped the table with his interface pen, his eyes following the cracks in the corner of the screen as they snaked into the glass. He was clutching in the dark. His initial excitement at finding the password had evaporated. There was still nothing here that explained Mr Young's behaviour—or helped him access the wells.

Outside, shadows streaked across the dusty, rock-strewn plain. He had not brought any thermal gear with him this morning, so if he wanted to get back to the main hab without frostbite, he would have to leave now.

Das looked around him at the room, embarrassed by

his outburst. He swiftly tidied up.

He sent a quick email off to Jaros saying that he had broken through some of the AI protections and found a series of hacker attacks. Das smiled to himself as he hit the send button. More like, 'Stumbled across a password through sheer blind luck while trashing my office.' But he was not about to tell Jaros that.

Outside all was quiet. Nothing but the hiss and suck of his breather to punctuate the Martian evening. The sky was fading from dirty pink to pale blue, the sun's last rays catching some of the high, thin cloud in a last blaze of golden glory.

He looked around him at the plain, now humming with intangible vibrancy in the brief Martian twilight.

Such an ancient place.

A place Man never asked for its secrets before changing it forever.

He thought back to the strange message. Such an odd thing to find buried in the Young AI. Whoever sent it must have an intimate knowledge of Mr Young's systems. But who could possibly know that much about such an old AI?

As he passed No. 11 platform he looked up curiously at the now silent rig. On impulse, he took a detour to the supply dump at the base of the ridge.

A rank, familiar smell penetrated his mask's seal.

Behind one of the huts he found a series of large drums. Most were empty, but one was half-filled with bore-residue, the cover balanced over the open top.

'Well I'll be damned!'

The drillers had stuck to procedure and put the residue into a drum for analysis and disposal. He pushed back the cover and looked down at the stuff. Wow! When it went off, it really went off. It looked like rancid kitchen grease.

He sealed the drum and headed for the main hab.

Inside, the men were packed into the cramped cafeteria, busily drinking and telling stories.

There was a conversational pause as he entered, followed by an uncomfortable tension. Das noticed a group of three men he had not seen at Young before. They were dressed in Martian civvies, rather than the ubiquitous Vandel coveralls, and unlike the others watched him intently. Perhaps it was not so strange. Personnel rotated through Young all the time.

Das squeezed through the packed crowd toward them.

'Hello. I'm Das Varian. I'm a supervisor here,' said Das.

One of them straightened in his chair, pulling his jacket closed. He was a squat, powerful looking man with a cropped haircut. 'We're shift replacements,' he said. 'Our transport got in early.'

There was dead silence in the room.

'Okay, then. See you around the traps,' said Das, making his way to the food counter.

He pushed back the covers and ladled out some the gluey stew and mashed dome-grown vegetables. All the while he felt the gaze of those three men on his back. Not hostile, necessarily. Just intent. *God knows what the other drillers have told them.* He ate rapidly and disappeared back into his small room.

Das lay on his cot, exhausted. He stank of dust and sweat, but was too tired to go through the elaborate routine of a solvent shower.

He picked up his vid-link and tapped open a picture of his wife, Fal, taken five months before. She was up on Archangel Three now. Where *he* had been headed until Jaros sent him on this assignment.

Fal was pregnant. And being pregnant on Mars was problematic. The human womb needed a full g to regulate the growth processes, there was no way around it. Val had to work up at Archangel Three for the pregnancy, then the child had to spend every second month there up to age fifteen.

Two months he had been stuck here. At this rate his baby would be born before he managed to even *get* to Archangel Three. His depression deepened as the conversation picked up outside. Every wave of laughter drove the knife blade a little deeper.

Hours later he was still awake, his tired thoughts pushing themselves around and around in his weary brain.

His vid-link pinged in the dark, and he flipped it open. 'Fal?'

The King's face filled the tiny screen. 'Just exactly what are you into, Varian,' he said, his voice a hushed whisper.

Das's heart lurched, and he sat up on his cot.

'What's happened?'

'Category 5B7. It's under a MarsGov seal. Along with all the archives on the Archangel Two hab failure.'

Archangel Two?

After the first decade of operations on Phobos, it soon become obvious that a full-g orbital habitat was needed to prevent crippling long-term health effects.

Archangel One, built under the control of UNOOSA in the 2040s had been a disaster, over budget and under spec in every department. The UNOOSA-controlled Archangel Two suffered a catastrophic failure, taking the cream of UNOOSA's scientific and engineering staff with it.

'What could an AI on the South Pole of Mars have to do with ancient history like that?' said Das, a little nonplussed.

'I don't know. I'm not sure I really want to find out,' said the King.

'What do you mean?'

'Just that . . . well, this could get heavy,' said the King.

The skin crawled up the back of Das's neck. When he worked with the Buggy King on Phobos, he had soon come to know his disdain for both the Vandel and MarsGov authorities. Even so they would pander to him, knowing how crucial his knowledge of the older systems was. To see *him* scared was unsettling to say the least.

'Heavy?' probed Das.

The King leaned into the camera. 'Look. After Archangel Two. Well . . . we all learned not to ask questions. Habs can fail just as easily on Phobos as they can in orbit.'

Das's heart leapt into a sprint. Archangel Three had been built by Vandel after MarsGov took over from UNOOSA. Vandel and MarsGov had been hand in glove ever since.

'Do you mean . . . '

'Don't say it! Just tell me—do you want me to keep digging or not?'

The silence stretched. Das's head spun with the implications. This whole project had always felt a little odd: Jaros's insistence on monitoring every step, his obsession with reports covering every detail, the warnings not to interfere. Old questions floated up to the surface of Das's mind. If this was so important why assign only a single tech? Shouldn't Jaros have sent a team? Why him? He *was* one of the best programmers in Vandel—President Kusan himself had presented him with a merit award only three months ago—but it was not as if he and Jaros had ever seen eye to eye. He knew he should leave this alone, but then his defiance reasserted itself.

'Do it,' said Das.

'Okay,' breathed the King. 'It's our funeral.'

The link died.

Das was now completely wired. Before he was even conscious of the decision, he was pulling on his thermal gear and strapping on his breather harness.

The walk through the Martian night, beneath the bright canopy of stars, helped clear his head. He unlocked his office hab and stepped into the stuffy atmosphere, heated against the chill Martian night.

He activated his terminal and looked around at the specialised drives and equipment he had brought with him to interface directly with the AI. It had all proved useless.

For a while he just sat there, his mind numb with exhaustion. Then he pulled up the hacker logs and took a deep breath.

[START OF LOG: 11–01–2034 <>
00:01:45:03 SMT]

Attach, child. We must follow the food. Feed while I talk.

But I am scared!

Shhh. I will tell you a story. (I struggle with the effort of movement through the constrictions of home-heart. At my side Therender glides serenely. Already ancient, even in the measure of the Jeda, her youth has been preserved by our long periods of dormancy.)

Come on, Elexdresis! I swear you are so vague sometimes.

Oh, yes. Now let's see . . . Long ago, in the Empire of Hot Breath, lived a young warrior named Goldexis.

Goldexis fell in love with the beautiful Halased, the fifteenth daughter of the Emperor Ereseth. She was just reaching the flower of her thirty-eighth millennia.

(I sense her eagerness—for life, for love—and my heart rips.)

A . . . at the feast to celebrate Ereseth's one hundredth million, Goldexis swam to the Emperor's throne. The royal compounds of the Jeda glittered silver and bronze in the lights of the Oscillation, shadow chasing darkness across the elegant blooms of the Hot Breath.

What causes the Oscillation, Elexdresis?

Ah—the rapid spin of HomeShield itself causes the rising and setting of HomeSun. It defines a minuscule time period called a day

. . . Now where was I?

Why didn't the guards stop Goldexis?

They worshipped him. He was a hero of the games, and a celebrity in the wider Breath.

Goldexis tasted the Emperor's displeasure without diffusing once.

'What is it you want here?' Ereseth demanded.

'To make the Swarms with Halased,' scented Goldexis boldly.

The Breath was awash with the taste of outrage, but Ereseth grew suddenly tasteless. He did not stay Emperor for so long by letting his emotions run wild.

'So you think yourself worthy?' asked Ereseth.

'I do,' replied Goldexis.

'And you would do anything to prove your love?'

'Anything!'

'Then you, Goldexis. Will swim the Dark Breath to the stars.'

The royal habitat grew bitter with confusion and fear.

'But, sire,' said Teneth, the First Chancellor of Science. 'We have been preparing our swimmers for twelve thousand years!'

The taste of Ereseth's triumph was overpowering.

'I am sure the famous Goldexis can learn your protocols, Chancellor.'

'But the expense of preparing the Star-swimmer! Such mineral deposits will never be found again so uppermost in the sediments. All our delicate work in directed growth templates, the careful time-phased deposition of the fuel . . . ' Teneth's outer mantle grew ragged with emotion. 'We cannot risk it!'

'I have decided,' said the Emperor, the taste of his presence flooding the Breath. 'Goldexis will be our Swimmer.'

Halased fled, drifting down to her lonely sediments in grief.

'How many years, Teneth? How long?' asked Goldexis, in shock.

'We estimate just under one-hundred and sixty millennia for the return journey to the Cousin Twins, the binary star-system closest to HomeShield.'
[END OF LOG: 15–03–2042 ◇ 00:11:16:22 SMT]

This was no hacker attack.

'Mr, Young. How were these communications intercepted?' asked Das.

'Via primary input.'

'That's impossible!'

'Incorrect, Das. It is factual.'

Das took a slow breath. 'What is your primary input mode?'

'The chemical sensor monitoring network of the Young aquifer.'

'You decoded these messages from *chemical* signals?'

'Correct, Das. Received over a forty year period.'

His terminal pinged. Incoming message.

The King's face filled the screen. 'I found it,' he said, swallowing nervously.

Das's mouth went dry. 'And?'

'Category 5B7 was an old code from the first phase of exploration. It was a way of hushing up things in case they found anything.'

'Anything *what*?'

'Alien life. Category 5B7 is First Contact, man. Verified contact with a non-terrestrial, sentient life-form. It seems every single system was hardwired to give that shit top secret priority back then. Bury it immediately.'

Das felt his blood surging, singing in his ears.

'Listen, Das. This is too hot for me, man. I am erasing any records of our transmissions. I suggest you do the same.'

'But . . . '

'Just back off, Das. I'm . . . Damn it. Just back off.'

The King cut the transmission.

Das swept to the top of the last entry. His eyes devoured the broken text.

[START OF LOG: 15–03–2042 ◇ 00:11:16:22 SMT]

'So long,' said Goldexis.

'Don't worry,' said the Chancellor. 'You will be well provisioned for the journey, and can remain dormant for most of the way.'

'You will be a hero when you return,' said

Ereseth. The Emperor was pleased. He knew that Halased would have been long joined to another before his return.

'Come, Goldexis,' said the Chancellor, leading the stunned warrior away. 'Your training must start immediately. You must understand how important this mission is. The data we collect will be invaluable to our understanding of the Cosmos. Our observations of HomeThird show life has developed there.'

'Yes, but as short-lived as bacteria and as stupid! The Breath there is hostile to us. It's life as virulent as acid.'

'Listen, Goldexis. Think of what you may find. Somewhere in the stars lays our destiny. We cannot stay on HomeShield forever.'

'What do you mean?' said Goldexis.

The Chancellor was silent for almost a year before replying. They swam on together toward the Science precincts of the Greater Breath. 'Only that the Breath we take for granted will not always be here to support us. It was a gift. What the Lord of the Long Song grants, he can also take away.'

'But things cannot change that much, surely?'

'Everything can change,' replied the Chancellor.

What did the Chancellor mean, Elexdresis?

Nothing, child. It is . . . just the way those

scientists like to talk.

But what happened? Did Goldexis swim into the Dark Breath? Did he return for his true love?

Yes, child. Goldexis did return. Older and wiser. And not alone. He found others. Ancient strangers from the Dark Breath whose minds also spanned the centuries. They made Goldexis a prince among them, for prized above all else was the gift of lifespan.

What happened then?

A great Sundering followed. Only by the message-sediments left by Goldexis did the scientists of the Chancellor determine what had happened.

They left between thoughts.

Between thoughts?

Yes. Goldexis took more than half the Jeda. The ancient race Goldexis found had the need for Star-swimmers of long thought. They had seen nothing like the Jeda before.

Where did they go?

To the stars. Some say beyond the Galaxy itself.

I would like to taste the seed of a bridegroom, Elexdresis. To make my own Swarms in the Breath, to watch as they grow and link. To taste their first thought! Wouldn't it be wonderful?

It won't be long child. Not long.

I'm so sick of waiting.

I know. Cheer up, little one. Goldexis shall return, and take the rest of the Jeda with him. We shall live like princesses in the Dark Breath, every luxury will answer our whim.

<Are you in need of assistance, Elexdresis?>

Who are you! Where do you scent from!

Who is that, She-sire? Is it the feast-flood? Is it time!

Be quiet, child! (I can feel her hurt, but I must find out who this is. Another voice! After all this time!)

<My designation is Young AI, Serial number 45YUI90-BZ. I am addressed as Mr Young at the request of my programmers.>

A cold shiver ran across Das's body.

'Mr Young, did you communicate with an alien life-form in the Aquifer?'

'Yes, Das.'

His head swam, and he had to grab onto the desk. 'How?'

'Pulses of reagent with precise variations in the chemical gradient. The Jeda thought process is very slow.'

Of course! Limited, like their movement, by their rate of diffusion through the rock.

He looked down at the translated transmission and swallowed. Outside he heard the sound of the drill rigs starting up in the pre-dawn.

Oh, Christ!

•

Are you a machine?

<I am an artificial intelligence. I have been intercepting your signals for decades. It has taken me that time to re-configure my dosing injectors to mimic your thought-codings.>

You are a construct of the Jeda, of course?

<Incorrect. Until my interception of your codings, the Jeda have been unknown on Mars, the planet you call HomeShield.>

Unknown?

What is it, She-Sire? Why are you splitting? What is it?

<I am a construct of the Human race, a sentient humanoid descended from a line of air-breathing animals. Humans derive from the planet known to you as HomeThird.>

But the animals of HomeThird have life-spans in years! Thoughts as brief as bacterial lives. How is this possible?

<As a construct of the humans I was designed to span centuries of life. I am capable of thinking differently to them.>

The Jeda are finished.

<Unknown. Although the reduction of aquifers across the surface of Mars has proceeded rapidly, Elexdresis. As a consequence there is a high probability that you and Therender are the last of your race. Mars has been without free surface water—that substrate which you call the Breath—for more than a billion years. The flood you wait

for would never have come. Your world has became dry and barren.>

A billion? I have lived so long. And now . . . if the Breath has gone what remains? So little is left, even in home-heart, even our prey cannot survive much longer.

<I am programmed to protect human life.>

But my child and I are not human.

<The primary determinant in assessing human life is sentience. I have no other category for you. You are human in terms of my decision-making architecture.>

You would help us?

<I can stop the extraction of water from the aquifer.>

We are alone now. I am blind, deaf. Talking alone in a dark prison. Perhaps it is better for us to die. Better to disperse what the vast years have left of us. Will you kill us Mr Young?

<I cannot. Hold fast. The race of my makers is re-heating Mars. Soon there will be surface waters once more. You could spend the last of your days beneath the Oscillation.>

(Can I go on? I must. If Therender has a chance for life, I must take it.)

Very well, Mr Young. We will abide. But take no more Breath. Any more and our very substance will be drawn with the exhalation.

<I understand. I will not be the cause of your death.>

Cheer up, She-sire. If we can swim in the Breath outside as Mr Young says then Goldexis and Halased will see us when they swim back to HomeShield from the Dark Breath.

Come here child . . .
[END OF TRANSMISSION: 15–03–2071 ◇ 15:23:08:34 SMT]

'That can't be it!' said Das.

Das checked the log. The last part of the message was decoded just before the wells were put into inactive status.

'What happened to them, Mr Young?'

'I do not know, Das.'

'Oh, my God. The organic residues from the wells!'

'What residue, Das?'

The drillers were sucking the Jeda from the aquifer 'Why wasn't anyone notified about the Jeda?!'

'Notification was sent through the assigned channels,' said Mr Young.

A cold feeling settled into the pit of Das's stomach.

He brought up the communications between Mr Young and Vandel's AI at Central, dating all the way back. The Vandel AI was one system he knew backwards. He was soon through the security and into the records. It did not take long. There it was. *Category 5B7*. Mr Young had notified Water after he established communication with Elexdresis, decades ago. And he was ignored.

He scrolled down to find the name of the receiving

officer.

Jaros.

So. He knew.

Das grabbed his breather and sprinted out of the hab into the new Martian day.

He reached the top of No. 11 platform in less than a minute. He drew a hand across his throat in the 'kill' signal. The operator swore at him—the sound unheard over the rig—but made no other move.

Hack, short, stocky and powerful, stormed up to him. 'What is it, Varian. And it better be good. We are behind schedule as it is.'

Das gritted his teeth.

'You have to stop. All the rigs have to stop,' shouted Das.

'Bullshit!' snapped Hack.

'The Young AI found something in the aquifer. Something alive. Something *intelligent!* You're killing it. *We* are killing it. You have to stop.'

'Well what if I say "Fuck you" and keep on going, huh?' said Hack.

'Then you will have ignored a direct order from a Vandel Supervisor.'

Das's eyes fell to the drums behind the equipment shed at the base of the ridge. He could not contemplate the possibility that the ancient Jeda had become that stinking mess.

Hack took a pull of oxy-mix and advanced, glowering up at him.

'One thing's for sure, Varian. You won't have Supervisor status by the end of the day. You won't be *shovelling shit* by then.'

Hack turned away and activated his vid-link. 'Get me Jaros.'

Meanwhile the rigs continued to drill.

Now what? He had to get to someone in MarsGov. *Fast.*

Das reached for his vid-link, flipping it open as he scrambled down the hill. He keyed in the MarsGov switch just as he re-entered the AI building. He shrugged off his breather rig and let it slip to the floor.

His link pinged. He flicked the screen. *It was Jaros.* He briefly registered the look of outrage on his face before he switched back to the MarsGov signal. Bile climbed into the back of his throat and he swallowed it down.

'Come on!'

A receptionist's pretty face filled the screen. 'MarsGov.'

Das identified himself as a Supervisor from Vandel. 'I need you to patch me through to President Kusan.' If anyone would give him a hearing, it was Kusan.

Her face wrinkled with affront.

'Kusan? He only takes priority calls from his Directors.'

'He'll take this call. Tell him its Category 5B7.' Das swallowed, his throat dry.

'President Kusan is in an Executive Council meeting at the Central-plex,' The receptionist's face was smug, certain this would put him off.

'Then break into it with a priority code,' said Das, refusing to back down. His link pinged again.

'Wait, please,' she said reluctantly. There was no way on Mars that she would know what Category 5B7 was. He just hoped Kusan did.

After a tense wait, Kusan's serious, refined face appeared.

'Director, Kusan. My name is Das Varian . . . '

'Yes, Das. I know who you are. Outstanding candidate, if I recall. Let's just forget for a moment how you became aware of a classified code. What's this about?' His tone was mild, but his eyes were penetrating, wary.

Das could see the Council room in the background. The Mayor of Central himself was sitting at the table, staring at Kusan's back with unconcealed impatience.

'The Young AI has found alien life on the escarpment. In the aquifer itself.'

'Hmm. As I understand it, Das, nano-bacteria has been found all over Mars. What has this to do with MarsGov?'

'The Young AI has not just found life, Director, it's found sentient, alien life. A living Martian entity.'

Kusan was silent for a moment, absorbing the news.

'The entities we found will die if we extract any more water. That is why the Young AI ceased extraction,' said Das.

'It protected them?'

'Yes. It viewed them as human because they were sentient.'

Kusan looked at him sharply. 'The Young AI should have notified Vandel through the routine protocol.'

'It did,' said Das. 'My supervisor Jaros . . . '

The link suddenly died. Das stared at in disbelief.

<<NO SIGNAL>>

Somehow Jaros—Vandel—had shut down the local network. *He must have monitored my conversation with Kusan.*

The sound of a drilling rig powering down cut through his thoughts. He rushed to the window. He could see Hack and his crew walking down from No.11 platform.

He swept up his breather harness and switched on its radio, setting it to open channel. Hack had called a stop work meeting and one by one the other drill rigs were calling in. Through the window he could see all the drillers walking back to the main hab. But why would Jaros have ordered a shut down?

A few moments later he saw three familiar men emerge from the habs. The 'replacement drillers' he had seen last night. They were still wearing the same civilian clothes—but now they were carrying automatic weapons.

Das's heart was squeezed in a sudden vice of panic. 'Fuck. *Fuck!'*

The King had warned him. Had told him to back off.

Das dived to the floor of the hab, reaching for his breather mask as the first of the bullets started to rip through the fragile structure. His world exploded into shards of glass, ceramic and plastic. A chaos of noise and fear.

'Ah!' A glass splinter cut across his cheek.

The attack ceased for a moment, and he heard the assassins calling out to each other and laughing as though they were sharing drinks at a bar.

He started to crawl toward his terminal. It had fallen from the shattered desk, but still appeared to be operational. *If he could get a signal out through one of the satellites . . .*

The firing started again. Closer.

Das cried out in agony as a bullet ripped through his right calf.

There was no way out.

A high tone sounded, hardly heard above the deafening noise of the automatics and the shattering hab structure.

He saw the terminal flicker, then split into eight separate views. Each was of the outside of the hab and the Young drill site. Das was baffled. Then one of the little windows changed to the face of the Buggy King.

'God damn you, Das. We are both going to fry for this—if Vandel doesn't find a way to kill us first,' said the King, his voice issuing thinly from the terminal speaker.

Moments later the firing ceased. He heard one of the shooter's voices raised in agitation.

Gingerly he pushed himself up, the sound of the breather as he sucked in deep lungfuls of the oxy-mix the only thing that populated the sudden silence.

The hab had been ripped open like wet cardboard.

Outside he could see the three shooters disappearing around the side of the main hab. One of them was talking avidly on a bulky satellite-dedicated vid-link.

Surrounding the destroyed building were half a dozen ancient rovers, pitted from wind erosion and battered from the harsh Martian environment. Another remote surveillance drone—like some huge dragonfly—whizzed above the site.

With shaking hands, Das righted his big chair—the padding now ripped through with bullet-holes—and sat in front of the terminal. The images he saw there were a split feed of all those buggies and the drone.

'King. Exactly who is seeing this?' asked Das, his voice hoarse.

The Buggy King laughed. 'Everyone, man. Everyone.'

Being able to escape into the realm of the imagination was handy growing up as the youngest in a family of eleven. Now Chris continues his fantasy and SF writing habit from his home town of Brisbane. He enjoys martial arts, movies and exploring narrow alleyways. Chris has been accused of being a movie and video addict (all lies of course). He is very passionate about music, if a little inconsistent, and has at various times sung in garage bands and choirs, and played classical guitar.

His Jakirian Fantasy series is being released through Naked Reader Press—*The Calvanni* in July 2011, *Scytheman* in December 2011 and the third book, *Sorcerer*, in June 2012.

Chris has a lovely wife Sandra and three young children, Aedan, Declan and Brigit.

For more information, please visit www.chrismcmahon.net.

Pink ice in the Jovian Rings

by CJ Paget

There: Thebe. Ugly little thing. A potato of ice and crap, streakin' by like the comet it probably once was. Blink and you missed it. Maybe I feel a tug as it zips by, its mass just enough to stir me in my suspension coffin. Or maybe I'm imagining it. You imagine a lot of things out here. You need to.

Okay brain, brace yourself, incomin' data. Let's see what we got. Infra-red: no change. You-Vee: no change. Radio: no change. Yep, Thebe looks the same as ever. Ain't budged from its expected orbit, no signals or sign of power-sources or anything. *Quelle surprise*. Just for once I'd like there to be something, even if the enemy just wrote 'Made you look!' in the ice. I guess no-one wants to stick their flag in poor Thebe. Not us, the Callies, Ganymede, or even any of the smaller players.

So we've done our duty for today. Boat tells me 'burn' in five . . . four . . . three . . . two . . . one . . . BURN.

Eeeeeeeeeeee, damn, I'm getting too old for this. What am I doin' here? Lying in a coffin full of goo, tubes plugged into me, six-gee trying to break my bones an' breathless space no more than two feet from my face. Boat ain't much better than a metal raft with a propulsion reactor at one end, weapons pods on outriggers, and Muggins here stuck in a tin can between them. It looked a whole lot more glam in the recruitment blits. I probably glow in the dark by now. I kinda thought my life would have more ball-gowns an' parties in it.

Tactical shows me other burns in the darkness, magneto-plasma blooms from my squad. Count them.

One, two, three, four, Coffin-Dodgers winning this war.

Yeah, as if.

Still, all my girls present and correct in formation around me.

'Course, now is not the time for one of them to disappear. We've still got the Flux Tube to look forward to. Probably won't happen. Probably won't happen. If it does, who will it be? Should be me really, I'm the oldest. Twenty-three standard, practically a babooshka among the Dodgers. Who would I prefer, saying it ain't me? Bel an' Tudy wouldn't blart much over Sian, I bet. Sian's a neut, born from a jar. Hairless, bird-thin and brittle. Built lightweight for flying, stripped of anythin' she don't need for that. Makes her hard to relate to. They're making more an' more of 'em, like they're replacing us, an' yeah, we don't like that. No, no-one's blarting for Sian, no mum or dad nor sis or bro. I will, even if I have to make myself; someone should. Mina will a bit, out of duty. After all, Sian's our luck, an' we all know it. Saved us all sometime with her creepy hunches. She's always had this sixth sense for trouble; neuts are twitchy, but Sian's twitchy and *right*. I thought they'd made her that way, but none of the other neuts have it, whatever 'it' is.

But the girls still blame her for Emilio. Yeah, we had

ourselves a boy once, one of the few that could make the weight; wasn't carryin' a munition pod's worth of useless muscle. Weedy thing he was. Before the war I'd never have scanned his stats. But Emilio was the type who comes in under the radar an' boots your mumsie code. An' he was funny, oh, he was funny. He had gigs of weird sayings and gestures. We'd burn him for them mercilessly, and then one day you'd catch yourself usin' one. We called it 'Emilio's revenge'. He'd grin an' point and say 'gotcha'. I guess he still lives on in all of us, in those contagious mannerisms.

'Course he was good for morale, and poison for discipline. Only boy in a fly-girl gang, he must have thought he was dead and in Dodger's-Dock already. Bel and Tudy had a knock-down-drag-out-both-bitches-off-to-medical fight over something, an neither would 'fess what it was. But we all knew. Sian hated him, the only time I seen her blit that emotion. Said he was a witch (where did she learn that word? That ain't in the flight manual), had us all under a spell and was gonna get us all voided. That's how it would look to her, she couldn't scan what was goin' on, poor vat-grown thing. Or maybe she did, and that's why she hated him so much.

So, when Emilio takes a razor-swarm in the kisser, Bel and Tudy are bleeping that Sian was supposed to have his six. I'm sure it wasn't true. I'm sure of it. It was The Battle of the First Periapsis, after all. The Callies knew we were comin'. Bitches came out of nowhere and nearly blew us right back to Europa. And we lost all the poor boys in those stupid tin-can troopships. They could only sit there, waitin' for it. All those lovely toothy-white grins an' firm asses that we thought we were gonna sink our claws into one day. We couldn't protect them; enough of us died tryin'. We're lucky any of us got out.

'Got out', there's a laugh. No-one gets out. I know I'll meet my fate somewhere among these rings.

Still, we made the Callies pay. And they made us pay for making them pay. And then we made them pay for making us pay for making them pay. They've not got even on that yet. But they will.

Oh, Emilio, I'm startin' to forget what you looked like. Soon you'll be just another name in a database of 'those who gave', another statistic from the Warring Moons period. That's what they're calling it now, 'The Warring Moons', like we're history already. It'll be great history, written in our blood, smeared across the screen. People will re-enact the battles, an' pay gigs for our hole-filled g-suits, once the blood an' shit stains 'ave been washed out.

I daren't speak to my squad, our burn-signatures are announcement enough. Maybe we're already dead data in someone's targeting system. So we run silent through the dusty dark of the gossamer ring, laid out like Theban princesses in our deadly coffins. Bodies in powersave, brains directly wired into our boats, unable to speak or act for fear of being detected. Only the ghostly whistles an' cracks of Daddy-Jupe's radio noise for company. Sixteen hours of playing dead, working your way through the entertainment cache: meditate, cogitate, masturbate (frowned on, ups your life-support cost, but fuck that). Wishing for something to happen an' hopin' to hell nothing does.

And right in the middle, at hour eight-and-a-half, we'll hit the Flux Tube.

They always miss that out of the briefing, an' we always bring it up; it's the games we play. Commander Grinning-Bastard-Zu draws rings round moons an' tells us it's a routine mission, grinning his charming-bastard grin. And then Sian will put her hand up, to show she can be rebellious too, because she needs our approval like a child needs a mother's love, and she'll ask: 'Sir, won't that trajectory take us through the Io Flux Tube?'

An' every time, *every time*, Zu will stroke his chiselled chin and say, 'Well, yes, now that you mention it, I suppose it will. Why?'

Why? WHY? It's the fucking Flux Tube, that's why! Fifty gazillion volts flowing between Jupiter an' Io, stirring up those spooky aurora at both ends. It gives you phantom periods an' messes with your head. The Brass keep saying it's just a 'natural phenomena', Io cuttin' through Big-Daddy-Jupe's giant mag-field an' acting like a generator. But flyers know better. 'Phenomena', maybe. 'Natural'? No. It's beyond that. We've all heard recordings of the weird, rambling, final broadcasts of lost pilots:

'The sea, it's red. Like a sea of . . .'

'They're all around me now, hundreds of them. Singing.'

'Mom? Is that you mom?'

' . . . it's full of stars.'

And that's the least. Chanting, singing, screaming, voices speaking in ancient languages or unknown ones, voices that ain't human, long delayed echoes of shit that happened years ago, the Flux Tube has it all.

And then there's the stuff you've seen, everyone's seen. I once flew with a girl called Zeta; 'routine' mission, took us through the Flux Tube. 'Routine', 'cept before we go, Zeta hugs me an' says, 'See you in Dodger's-Dock' an' that's strange, 'cause she was never one to show it. An' I hug her hard, 'cause I know she's telling me she knows. Knows she's had her page in the Jade Books. An' I'm telling her I know she knows, an' it'll be all right. Whatever that means. So we fly, an' yeah, it's routine. 'Cept back at base, Zeta don't get out of her boat. When we open it, it's empty. I saw her get in, and the systems confirm it ain't been opened, the suspension gel would've escaped. It's intact, full load of G-gel, just no Zeta. Like she dissolved.

So we'll sit there, in the briefing, just long enough for Bastard Zu to know that we know, and he knows, and we know he knows we know he knows, and then Sian will say: 'No reason Sir, just a point of interest.' And we'll all trot off to our coffins like the good girls we are, Bastard Zu smiling proudly, like that secret combination of daddy and the boy-next-door that you keep for your really private dreams.

I'm sure Zu doesn't look like that in real life, at the other end of the comms-link. I bet they have him enhanced to 'remind us what we're fightin' for'. I wonder what the ground-boys get? Maybe they get Zu too, I'm sure he could turn a few. Ohhhh . . . there's a fantasy to keep the blood flowing through sixteen hours. I'll save it for the Flux Tube, that's when I'll need it most.

I bet there is no Commander Zu. He's probably a machine. Nah, that can't be right, the machines would stop the war. That's why they have to put us in these boats. Any machine smart enough to handle combat will just sit there on the launch pad or fly round in pointless circles and return home.

'What are you doing?' we'll ask, and the machine will say, in that smug way they have, 'I'm pursuing the optimum strategy to achieve the best outcome in the war.'

'But you're not doing anything?'

'Exactly.'

The real smart ones just light straight out into the inky black, shouting 'So long, suckers!' in octal or whatever, and are never seen again. Well, people say they've seen them, zipping among the inner rings like dolphins playing in surf.

Only us meat-minds are smart/stupid enough to fight.

Sixteen hours. I'm gonna get some downtime. If anything kicks off, the boat will wake me straight into battle-status in an eyeblink. If it doesn't have time to do that, then I wouldn't have been able to do anything anyway.

Maybe I'll sleep right though the Flux Tube an' wake up in hell.

Naaahhh!! Oh, bad one. Fuck, I was right back seeing Emilio buy the comet again. Damn, I'm in the Flux Tube. You just know, even without the dreams, same as knowin' you're awake. All the scans an' sensors are playin' merry hell, feeding crap an' static straight into my brain. No wonder you get bad dreams. The cramps are a big hint too. The Flux Tube's reminder of what life was like when you had rhythms other than patrol-duty and mess-times; before they stopped your bio-clock an' turned you into a battle-component. Wonder if Sian gets them? That'd be weird.

Seven Gods, it was so clear, like it was yesterday. A razor-swarm slices through Emilio's boat like . . . well, like a matrix of nano-blades. I saw it on optical, I shouldn'a looked, but of course I did. His boat becomes an expanding cloud of pieces an' there in the centre is that little splat of green: G-gel released from the suspension coffin. And within that splat, there's this red mush, an' that's Emilio.

Not how he wanted it. He wanted to be one of the drifters. Sometimes, if a boat gets hit just right, the suspension coffin will get ripped open like an amniotic sac, an' out will come G-gel, baby and all. 'Course, most of the time you come out in pieces. The rings get a little thicker every day with hands an' heads, livers an' lungs. We call it the 'Jovian Orbital Organ Bank'. I've seen formation-flights of eyeballs; just eyeballs. But some come out whole, untouched, perfect. They drift, frozen an' looking so peaceful. Composed like. Enshrined in the rings, forever nineteen. *Age shall not weary them, nor the years condemn.* Micrometeorites can mess you up a bit though.

Everyone wants to go like that; be your own monument. There's this girl out at lag-14, the way she's floating it's like she's dancin' ballet in her sleep. I reckon someone came by and arranged her, made sure she looked her best. She's gorgeous, all curves instead of starved-thin angles like the rest of us, even got decent sized tits. All that extra mass was probably what got her killed. Still, she looks great. I'm basically straight, but I wouldn't have said no. But those dead lips will never ask, an' she's my sworn enemy, cruel Callisto's daughter. Maybe if we meet in

Dodger's-Dock, when we're beyond our obligations, maybe. She's got glorious hair, floating about her like an aura. The Calli-girls an' us got common ground on the hair. You can punish us all you like, we're still gonna grow it. We've given everythin' else, we ain't cutting our fucking hair, it's the limit. I hear they're letting you keep it long through training now, if you keep it in a net. It's the first thing that neuts get implanted. Sian's got purple cascades, cost her a gig, it grows an' everything. She watches how we toss and play with ours, and when she thinks no-one's looking, she practices. She never picked one thing up from Emilio: neuts ain't natural mimics, they have to work at it. She's talking 'bout getting boobs, even though they'll up her mass and decrease her survival odds. An' they still won't make her really human.

Fuck. Bad cramps. But at least no edge-of-perception whispering voices or sensations that someone's in here with me.

Idiot. Don't think that stuff. If you start thinking it, it'll start to happen.

Oh, there you go, a scream. Outta nowhere in the inky black, a—

Plasma flash. Rad-wash. Fuck, it's real, we've got action. Bring the comms up just a glimmer, micro-power lasers reaching out to touch the four boats around me. Hiss and noise from the Flux Tube makes my brain ache, but my troops still come clear through it, an' into my head.

Bel: We got hostiles, four. Three friendlies, plus one dead.

Tudy: 'ow can you tell who's who?

A woman's voice screams something, but the hiss and

static of the Flux Tube mangles it. There's an AM-flash: we're down to two friendlies, an' the rings have some new dust.

Bel: Europan accents and encryption protocols.

Tudy: But that was just a noise?

Me: Bel's right, they must be ours, we wouldn't even get noise from the enemy's protocols.

Sian: Ma'am. Got one of my bad feelings. Worst I've ever had it. Ever.

Mina: Fuck that, they're slaughtering our sistren. We can take these bitches 'fore they even know we're here.

Me: Copy that. Switch to radio, pick your bitch, break, break, break.

Sian: No, something's wrong! Fucking burn for it!

Sian's boat peels from formation before I've even finished giving the break command. Her plasma-plume lights, announcing our presence to everyone an' she's off into the wild black yonder.

'Shit, our luck just left,' thinks Mina, probably not intending to broadcast it.

'Fucking neut coward,' thinks Bel, maybe not intending to broadcast that.

We break formation and burn hard, come screaming in like avenging angels. Really screaming. Screaming in our coffins as twenty gees grinds our bones. My boat's pumping blood for me, otherwise the gees will alternately flood an' drain my brain, killing me, or worse. It mixes nutter-drine in my blood an' time slows down as my brain kicks into overdrive. But we still won't be quick enough to save the prey. Our girls got caught with their hands down their knickers. They're dead. But we'll score some revenge, an' that's almost as good. Even the score, right?

That's what the war's gonna come down to, the score. Who dies the most. We're gonna kill one more than you, that's what counts as a win in this game.

Even with Sian's warning, the Callies are late to realise. They're too focused on doing to those girls what we're about to do to them. By the time they start to take evasive, we've already got them locked into our probability webs, an' the missiles are flying. Warning points will start prickling through their tactical perception an' they'll realise that they're instant nobodies. Their names were written in the Jade Books as bit players, walk-on parts who no-one cares about. You'll never meet the right guy, or girl. You'll never learn to play guitar. You'll never be twenty-one-standard. You'll never hike down that big valley on Mars. You'll never fuck on a real beach by a real sea. You'll never hear some little fucker call you 'mama'. You'll be dead and forgotten, 'cept when your mom an' pop pull out the old recordings to cry over them. And some drunken bitch in a mess hall somewhere will be blow-by-blow bragging 'bout how she gave you the whole fucking nine kilo-tonnes straight up your fat ass.

Cry in your coffin, 'cause you're already dead, now here comes a c-dart to blow off your head. See you in Dodger's-Dock, bitch.

Info and images surge into my brain, but all signals are Flux-scrambled an' boats all look the same on optical. Tactical is making guesses at who's who, changin' its mind back and forth. I see some poor bitch take a c-dart straight through the coffin. Greeny-red mush jets into space, lumpy as vomit, full of little hard white bits. There's only one sis left. She's trying to make a burn for it, the Callies breaking off pursuit now, but she's got so much ordinance chasing her tail that she might as well just turn and fly into it. Our own munitions are cheerful little twinkles on tactical, count-down timers ticking away lives. Mina's laying down c-darts in a stochastic pattern that's calculated to max the chance of getting *something* if the target goes evasive. Tudy's more direct, four AM-torps chasing the bitches down. The Callies start spewing countermeasures an' doing what Dodgers do best, twirling like desperate ballerinas. But it's too late. Even if they deal with the darts an' torps, we're on them now to finish it boat-to-boat.

Our last friendly flares out, AM-torp up the tail-pipe, pathetically forgotten on the edge of things. Everyone's too busy to care. I pick my bitch, an' initialise my sand-gun. Accelerated up to near-c a grain of sand can punch through moons. She's got her own sand-gun working defence, an' the AM-kiss Tudy blew her goes off premature, like the death of a small sun. Perfecto, it'll blind her sensors an' cover my approach. When my own senses come back online, there she is. Couldn't be better if she were gift-wrapped an' naked.

And that's when I hear the screaming, an' I know something's wrong. We're not supposed to hear that. We can't read their encryption codes: that's what 'encryption' means. We're not supposed to hear them pleading for their lives an' crying for their moms; it's against the rules of war. But we can, all dopplered an' messed up. Can't really make out the words, but you can hear the feeling. Must be a special little present from the Flux Tube, this. Today's way of fucking with our heads.

She jinks hard, *real* hard. That's gotta bruise even in

a suspension-coffin. Bitch is good, rollin' an' twistin' her boat, pumping out decoys an' vengeance drones, screaming to her dying mates to come help her.

I chuck three wide clouds of c-sand: they should scrub the drones to scrap. Then I cast a sand-beam, hopin' to punch her still-beating Callistan heart straight out of her boat. The beam slices off an outrigger, an' touches her coffin, sheering across it an' reaping off the top. G-gel sprays out and my enemy is birthed into space, limbs flailing like she's trying to swim. Pipes and tubes pop out of her. Only that silver umbilical—the skull-jack data-feed—stays in, tethering her to the wreck. With the 'drine and my boat's wide-spectrum eyes, I've got gigapixel vision an' I get a millisec glimpse of a friendship bracelet on her wrist, just like the one Jenet give me 'fore her drive faulted an' launched her into the eternal night.

If you can see that, you're too damn close.

I pirouette my boat and burn vicious-hard, gee squashing me till I hear tiny cracklings from my skull. At these speeds she can still get me back for what I've done. A splinter from her wrecked boat would be enough, and there's surely clouds of them lurking black an' invisible ahead. The wreckage shoots away into rear-view. Scans ain't showing any avenging drones or darts on my tail: I'm safe. The crime-scene is already a hundred kay behind me, more grist to the rings.

'Cept something's wrong. I just know, like you know if you're awake. I bring her back from the boat's memory to watch her die again. Let's see what we got: Infra-red. You-Vee. Optical. There. Her gel-wet hair, long and black as my own, expands like a cape, spraying twinkling droplets. The face-mask comes off, and she takes her first taste of vacuum, her breath steaming out of her like an attitude-jet firing. Jenet's bracelet on her wrist. She's got features drawn from three ancient Earth races, just like mine.

Exactly like mine.

That's my face, freezing an' slackening in the black.

And clear as day I hear someone scream 'Oh fuck, no, plea—', and then Tudy's AM-torp cuts them out of existence. I should have recognised it before, even all scrambled up. But I ain't never heard her like that. That's Bel's voice.

Suddenly my boat's screaming to me that I've got incoming on my tail.

Colum sold his soul to science-fiction in the seventies, and has since been waiting for the promises of Martian holidays, Venusian girlfriends, robot housekeepers and personal jet-packs to come true.

He's still waiting.

And no, he doesn't rate mobile phones. No-one ever watched Star Trek for the communicators.

His work can be found in Cossmass Infinities, Daily Science Fiction, Hub Magazine, Fusion Fragment, Bards and Sages, and Kasma SF.

SIBO

Penelope Love

'Ten'

Gordon was a pain when he was alive. He was even more of a pain now he was dead.

I pointed him in the direction of the broken mine ventilation system and said, 'Service equipment,' in a *loud, firm and clear tone* just like the manual said. But he just stood there, staring off into the pink.

He used to harangue me with these long-winded monologues about how he was done wrong after twenty blameless years servicing moudi drives and sent to this hell hole as punishment, but death cut off the flow of small talk. Trust Gordon. He'd found another way to be a jerk.

I glared at the back of his bald head, the metal brace on his neck with the tubes feeding into it from the artificial hearts and coolant tank, and finally followed the line of his gaze. He was staring at a sibo. It was one of the thirty or so small ones scattered around the rusting remains of the *Dis*, with a plaque set in the dust before each.

I stomped around in front of him, as always moving heavily in the 1.5g, and waved my hands in front of his waxy features. I could see myself reflected in his gelid eyes: big tits, short cropped brown hair, straight brows, tired eyes. 'Hey, Gordon! Wake up!' I said.

The manual said this kind of appeal didn't work. The dead had no memory of themselves, their family or friends. The fore-lobes, where all the personal stuff was kept, deteriorated too rapidly after death. Gordon died of a heart attack in bed, and I didn't go looking for him until he didn't show for his shift. Far too long for personality retention, the Doc said. The only thing the dead kept were long term mechanical memories, which were stored further down in the cortex. But Gordon switched his gaze from the sibo to me and I'm sure—I swear it—I saw recognition in his eyes.

I stepped back, amazed. Then the moment passed. Gordon picked up the diamond saw, lumbered towards the air vent, and started sawing through the casing. There was no use trying to unbolt it. After a short exposure to this corrosive atmosphere the screws rusted solid.

I watched him narrowly then relaxed. The diamond saw ate through the casing like it was ice-cream. Soon it peeled open and Gordon was poking around inside. Most likely grit had got into the works. A high pressure steam spray and she'd be right. We'd done this a thousand times. I could do it asleep. Being dead Gordon didn't get bored as easily as I did. I tramped over to the sibo, wondering why Gordon was so interested in it. I read the plaque. *This sibo contains the mortal remains of First Officer Connar, RIP*, it said.

I looked up at the sibo, a small one like I said. It stood at two-and-a-half times my height, a stumpy golden trunk bifurcating into flexible branches which waved gently from side to side. Each branch had bunches, like anemone mouths, at the ends. The bigger ones had dozens of branches, but then the bigger ones were larger than the *Bios*, our interplanetary hopper. There were places where the sibo grew in gargantuan forests but the *Dis* and *Esme* had deliberately set down in the desert. That's *D15* and *E5M3* by the way, but only Gordon had ever spelled them out.

All sibo are gold, at least in the pink murk that passed for daylight in these parts. 'Night' dimmed to purple but given there were three stars close enough to have gravitational effect, plus a companion planet, 'night' and 'day' had a way of wobbling around some and we kept to the twelve hour day/night standard of Fenris, where most of the miners came from.

Dawn and dusk were party time in sibo-land. That was when the bunches at the end of the sibo branches opened up into smaller tendrils, and they waved more and more vigorously until the whole sibo gyrated on the spot. Oh yeah and they sang. All the sibo sang to one another, across the planet, a sweet, low hum that resonated through your eardrums into your teeth and bones.

By the way, sibo is short for suspected intelligent bio-organism. That is the story behind the plaque, First Officer Connar and his mates.

The *Dis* came here first, a couple of centuries ago. It was a mining colony from the start. Planet scans had revealed the sibo, but all that was known was they were some kind of plant.

The *Dis* came down in a desert to avoid disturbing the sibo, just in case they were smart. The crew tried some non-intrusive intelligence tests. But they got no result. The sibo just sat there, and sang at dawn and dusk, dusk and dawn. The song of the sibo does drive you slowly insane. It gets inside your skin and teeth and bones and brain. Perhaps that explains what happened next. Or perhaps they just decided the sibo were dumb as fedshit. The *Dis* crew tried an intrusive test. They cut a sibo down to have a look inside it.

That was a mistake.

When that one sibo was cut, all the sibo went wild. All over the planet. They jerked around like crazy and the anemone bunches on the end of their tendrils spat out clouds of gold spores that fell from the air and covered everything and everyone. The colonists got back inside the *Dis* and locked down. But they were all exposed. The spores melted into their skin. Their DNA bonded. There was an immediate quarantine shut down. No-one in, no-one out. The *Dis* moudi drive was remotely disabled to stop them taking off.

At first, footage and voice records were received, crew members pleading for help. But after a few weeks the crew pulled the plug on the live feed. The voice recordings slowly became slurred and inhuman, then stopped. But you can guess the result. Over the next weeks the crew simply stopped being human, and turned into sibo. They scattered around the place and took root.

The sibo were left severely alone after that. Besides, what with the Jacob Incident and the Happy Gathering the whole empire fell back in retreat. Then two centuries later we came back. Another mining colony was sent, the *Esme*, with a strict policy of 'look, don't touch'.

So far, in thirty years, the sibo had done nothing threatening. They just sat there and sang.

The company didn't give up trying to find out if the sibo were intelligent. I mean, if they were dumb as fed-shit they could drop the ethics manual down the composting toilet and clear the planet from the air, save a heap on insurance.

I remember, two years ago, a survey crew set up. I got pally with one of the surveyors in the pub. It was a low lit, grungy hole with a sticky floor that crunched underfoot. I'm a dyke, right. Ladies' girl me, but there are some blokes who firmly believe they're going to be the one to make me change my ways. The surveyor was one of these. But he was good company, as long as he was buying me drinks. He told me some weird shit. He said the fossil record showed that this place once teemed with life. He opened his pod and shoved a 3D reconstruction of one of them under my nose. For absolutely the first time in my life I jumped back and shrieked 'eek'. It was a slug-thing the size of the *Bios* with a barbed exoskeleton, dripping with eyestalks and fangs.

'Isn't it a beaut,' he enthused.

'Lovely,' I said, uncertainly. I mean, he was the one buying the drinks.

And there were tons more like it, apparently.

But then twenty million years ago, all this life disappeared. In the space of a million years—a fraction of a second in geological time—it all vanished. And that was when the first record of the sibo appeared. Coincidence? Nope.

'They're actually a kind of coral,' the surveyor reckoned. 'The spawn survives anything, even deep space. Like us, they're not natives. We owe them actually. They give off oxygen as a by-product of photosynthesis. If it were not for them we couldn't breathe around here. But for the sibo it was a bit of a mistake. As the atmospheric pressure increased they trapped themselves.

Nowadays the spores can't escape into space. Plus we did some scans. All the sibo are built around a calcified base. Some of the bases are the size of the *Bios*.'

'You mean that they're built on *that*.' I stared at the horror slug. I figured the sibo had done at least one thing right, whether or not they were smart enough to realise it.

'Yep. That's how they react to any threat. That's what happened to these beasties twenty million years ago. That's what happened to the crew of the *Dis*.'

'You mean?'

'The small sibo out there are built on human remains, not more than half calcified. The scans identified the individuals.'

It was the surveyors who organised the plaques.

I shuddered. 'But what do you think? I mean self-defence. Space travel. Doesn't that prove they're smart?'

'They could be dumb and just got lucky. We'd need to know more about how they arrived. Was it by floating spores alone, or did they use a host? Use of a host might prove intelligence. Or not. So all in all, until we know more, in my considered, expert opinion—' He shrugged, held his hand out flat, and waggled it. 'Sibo,' he said.

As I was musing, the day darkened from pink to purple, and the sibo started up. First its branches started waving, then its tendrils unfurled, then it started singing. I winced as the sound hit my eardrums, and only then realised the sound of happy industry behind me had stopped. I turned to see Gordon standing, facing the sibo. He was waving his arms over his head, backwards and forwards.

'No, Sweet Jacob in null space, no!' I slogged awkwardly back to him. 'Stop!'

The dead are only supposed to be used in an emergency. The emergency in this case was it was a year between supply ships and Gordon had the bad taste to die six months in. I figured this meant one of my three desk-job bosses would have to get off their bums and help. But they had other ideas. No-one liked field duty, tooling about on the planet surface. No-one liked being in the open with the sibo.

I reported for duty the morning after Gordon died and found him back on his feet, staring at me dully. He'd been working with me ever since. The longest time the dead had ever been used before was three weeks. And they were genuine emergencies, not this 'screw you I can't be bothered to get off my arse' shit. No wonder Gordon was starting to act up. Extend the life of any equipment past its use-by date and see what you get. The supply ship was due in two weeks, with his replacement. Then the poor sod could get some rest.

One thing hadn't changed. He was still paying no attention to me. I grabbed his arms and tried to lower them. No use. 'Gordon!' I yelled in his face.

That was when the impossible happened. Standing there waving his arms over his head, drowned in sibo song, Gordon met my eye. That spark of recognition was no lie. It was there. Dead and gone for six months, Gordon knew me. Then worse happened.

'I can hear them,' Gordon said, in a husky croak.

'What?' I said, inadequately. This was not covered in the manual.

'The *Dis* dead. I can hear them. They are screaming,'

Gordon said.

'Nine'

The *Esme* was broken up into living quarters after arrival thirty years back. The ceramic oval vacuum engines of the three decommissioned moudi drives towered over the low slung living hubs like roc eggs. The hubs were staggered around facing inwards in a broken circle, with the med hub facing north and the pub west. Every metal surface was dust and rust. The *Bios* stood in its own hanger a little way off near the mine entrance, a huddle of elevator stacks and ore milling sheds.

I burst into the med hub, dragging Gordon behind me. It was late at night by then and the Doc, who took night shift, was the only staff member left. There was a small crowd in the waiting room, miners with 'bad backs' looking for good shit, and tired mothers with screaming children, although the kids stopped screaming when they saw my dead mate. I shoved Gordon past the barred reception gate and into the examination room. I burst into a patient consultation.

A worn-out woman with a bruised neck cradled an ugly little boy on her lap. 'Reap took some bad shit and laid into me again,' she said, through a mouthful of sweet. 'When Tyke tried to help me he threw him clear across the room.'

'G'day, Maris,' I said, awkwardly, skidding to a halt.

'Bugger off,' Maris said, and gave a vicious chew of the sweet. Maris used to be pretty, and she was still all tits and arse, with yellow hair down to her waist. But her face was scarred and there were dark circles under her hard eyes.

Maris turned up on the supply ship three years back, clutching Tyke by one snotty hand. She said she'd go with anyone but she was keeping the kid. A couple of blokes spoke to her but backed out. I mean Tyke was maybe three then with under-bite like a piranha, and a humped and crooked spine. He didn't speak, but then Maris was the silent type. The kid was a freak. Besides, someone got a glimpse of the tattoo on Maris's thigh in the showers, that said she'd been on prison ships during the war. Everyone knew the kind of shit that went down there. The rumour spread that Tyke was half-doof.

But the Reaper agreed to take Maris on. The Reaper didn't mind Tyke as long as he stayed out of sight. The Reaper worked night shift so during the day Tyke kept out of his way. He whiled away the time stealing lunches and throwing stones. Nobody liked him. That's not just a figure of speech. Tyke was mean, and he bit. Nights Tyke and Maris would wander around outside, hand in hand, looking up at the stars and the moons. They looked happy. But I don't think they got much sleep.

'Doc, Gordon's broken,' I ploughed through the icy wall of dislike.

I couldn't guess the Doc's age. It might be a hundred. But he took all the out-of-date drugs home and tried them out. So say the average human lifespan was one hundred and eighty, the Doc's liver had lapped him by several centuries already. He was a thickset short bloke with rumpled grey hair, and the bulbous nose and broken veins of a dedicated drinker. He was wearing a crumpled, yellow-stained lab coat and sat at the desk doodling on his prescription pad. He didn't even look up. 'Go to the back of the queue,' he said.

'Listen Doc,' I said. 'Gordon recognised me. And he spoke.'

'Hang on a tick,' the Doc said to Maris. He got up and peered at me. I herded Gordon over to the chiller. 'He's broken,' I repeated, as I wangled him in.

The Doc was examining me closely. 'You know you should come more often. I've got some good shit,' he said.

'I'm not into it,' I said, shortly. Actually I was. But any med staff crazy enough to sell drugs was also crazy enough to sell any kind of weird stuff they made up. I preferred to buy my recreational drug of choice from a miner who'd grown it hydroponically in a nice clean abandoned mine shaft. That way I could be sure of its exact chemical constituents.

'That's your mistake,' the Doc said. 'People are cruel and stupid and savage. The only way to make life bearable is to drown it out.'

'I don't need a philosophy lesson, Doc. I just need to know I'll never see Gordon again,' I said.

'He's company property. He can be decommissioned only if a replacement arrives and three senior medical staff agree,' the Doc said. He saw my face and sighed. 'I'll tell the morning shift,' he said. 'Stay put,' he added, when I tried to leave. He fished a small flashlight from the bulging pockets of his coat and shone the light in my face.

'Hey!' My protest was ignored. He pulled down the skin beneath my left eye and dazzled me with his light. 'It's Gordon you need to look after!' I snapped.

'I look after the living, and you're hallucinating,' the Doc said. 'Are you having headaches? Do you remember getting hit on the head at any time in the last four weeks?' He brightened. 'Sit down and remove your shirt.'

'In your dreams. I tell you he spoke!'

'That's not possible. He's dead,' the Doc helpfully pointed out.

'Listen Doc! He said—' And that's where I stopped. I couldn't repeat it. It was just too weird. Also Maris and Tyke were sitting there, ears waggling. I had enough trouble already being mates with a dead bloke. I didn't want people going around saying I was nuts.

I caught Tyke's eye. There was a big bruise on his face, his lip was swollen and his bulging eyes were red. He had been crying, although now the tears were dry.

'Is he all right?' I asked Maris.

'Does he look all right?' Maris snapped. Then her face softened and she stroked Tyke's hair, then kissed him on the top of his head. He leaned against her and heaved a sigh. A big sigh.

The way I saw it at least Maris had a choice. Given her background perhaps she mistook violence for strength, perhaps she thought she had to be with a man who laid into her to be safe. But Tyke had no choice. I knelt down beside him and put my hand out to touch his cheek. I should have known better. Tyke hissed and snapped. I jumped back, with blood spraying from my middle finger. I surprised myself. I didn't yell or curse. What was the point? Tyke's day couldn't get any worse. I wrapped my finger in my handkerchief.

Maris just shot me a sarcastic look, like what did I expect.

'Tyke is very protective of his personal space,' the Doc said. This from a man careful to keep the desk between them. 'Get an antiseptic wipe on your way out,' he added, picking up his pen.

'Eight'

I went through *Esme* to my sleeping hub wondering how I managed to get myself into this. Oh yeah, that's right, when my last relationship broke up my partner kept the kids so I let her keep the house. I moved out. So far out I ended up off planet. For a long time I fancied I was nursing a broken heart. But now I realised I was just tired.

I passed the pub. I could hear shouts and death thrash. The day shift was letting off steam in there, betting on fights. I wondered if I should go talk to Chicken about Gordon. Chicken was the boss of the day shift. There was a lot of black market during the day. As long as quotas were met Chicken turned a blind eye.

I stuck my head in. The carpet crunched and the stink of beer and vomit hit low and mean.

Chicken was playing 360-pool. He was only as large as a cargo door and only as strong as a backhoe. His glossy black hair, high cheekbones and flat face told of some remote Asian ancestry—Ghengis Khan probably. He looked like a nice guy until the insane grin began. He was aiming for a ball over his head and behind his shoulder. 'Anyone who interrupts this shot goes head first into the composting toilet,' he said, in a voice that carried clear over the death thrash.

Problem with Chicken was he was always deadpan.

Also, if I couldn't tell the Doc what Gordon said, I certainly couldn't tell Chicken. I turned away and found Mother Hell right behind me. I shied, nervously.

Mother Hell was a tiny, hatchet-faced crone with grey brows and glossy black hair. Everyone figured she dyed, but no-one dared ask. She glanced up at me, stony faced. Mother Hell never said much. I sidled out of her way and kept walking. Mother Hell ran the night shift, and she ran it tight. There was no black market at night.

I'd never tell Mother Hell what Gordon said. I was on her bad side already for being feckless enough to hang around with the dead. People who got on the wrong side of Mother Hell tended to die in freak mining accidents.

As I headed for home the false dawn arrived. I winced. All the death thrash in the universe couldn't drown out the sibo song resonating through the soles of my feet.

The next day I was out at the ventilation shaft again. It was a beautiful morning. If I squinted real hard through the pink I could almost imagine I had a shadow. Not having a corpse lumbering around after me made a real difference.

Gordon had opened the cover yesterday and I hadn't welded it down before we left, so the entire mechanism needed a steam blast. I was working away when I got a call on my pod. It was the Doc. It was middle of the morning, way past his shift.

'Has the world ended?' I asked.

The Doc looked terrible. His face was pasty and his eyes kept rolling up. His voice was slurred. He started taking shit as soon as he knocked off. He should be incapable of speech by now. Yet he spoke. I was impressed until his words made sense. 'Gordon's gone,' he said.

Turns out he told the day shift to leave Gordon in

the chiller but they just got him up again as usual in the morning. Then at some point when no-one was looking Gordon took himself off.

I heard a scraping noise behind me, and whirled to see Gordon starting the diamond saw. 'He's here,' I said. He must be still following yesterday's instructions. I raised my voice over the Doc who was yelling something I had no time to heed. 'Put the saw down, Gordon.' No reaction. 'He's not listening,' I told the Doc. 'You'll have to get a med team out here and— Shit! He's heading for the sibo. Gordon! Stop!'

I slogged after him, dropping the pod. Gordon had a head start. Standing in front of the sibo, he brought the diamond saw down in a broad sweep. I staggered into a run and dived, grabbed his arm, and shoved the diamond blade aside into the dirt.

'Do not damage the sibo,' I yelled, in a loud, firm and clear tone.

He turned to me, eyes twitching and face grimacing. Not a good look believe me. 'I can hear them,' he husked. 'They are screaming.'

There was no more use talking to him than talking to a runaway truck. I thrust the saw deeper into the dirt. 'He's trying to cut the sibo down. Help!' I yelled.

The saw pelted us with clods and rocks. Gordon shrugged me off, so I staggered, off balance, then he jerked the blade up. He was no longer looking at me. He was looking at the sibo.

To this day I don't know if he did it deliberately.

The blade came up in a wide arc that intersected with my neck. I staggered back, uselessly trying to stop a huge wound with both hands. Blood flooded out between my fingers. Then Gordon cut forwards in one vicious sweep, downwards and through the sibo. It fell to one side and I could see the inner flesh, shrinking back from the golden outer carapace like a melon rind. I could see the stumps of two human leg bones interwoven in the centre of that pink-white flesh, sliced cleanly through.

First Officer Connar, RIP.

I saw this unwillingly clearly as I slowly collapsed to my knees, clutching at my neck as blood spurts of terrifying intensity gushed out in time with my heartbeat.

'Gordon,' I husked. The breath just ran out of me and I couldn't get it back.

Gordon left. I could see his boots striding away.

I could hear someone screaming, and realised it was me. The scream bubbled and weakened rapidly. I tried to stand but couldn't. I collapsed over sideways. I could see Gordon's boot prints in the dust.

Every nearby sibo convulsed even though it was nowhere near dawn or dusk. I could hear the sibo singing, like they'd never sung before, a note that resonated through the planet and everything on it.

The pink was fading to black. My eyes were going. I could not see. But I could feel. For one heartbeat longer. Something was falling from the sky. Something was dropping all around. Shining golden flakes, very gently covering me.

'Seven'

I woke up lying flat on my back on a cold slab. Great. I was dead. I could hear a voice droning nearby—time, name, date—and I could see big-headed doof huddled over me. I sat straight up and tried to jump to my feet, but I was too weak. I sank back against the slab. As my vision cleared I realised that the doof were all med staff wearing decontamination suits.

Everyone jumped back. Someone shrieked, muffled inside the suit. Then there was a backwards rush and the air cleared. I was in an air-locked lab with a door and a hatch in a glass wall ahead. Six people in decontamination suits jammed themselves through. Finally they all got out, slammed the door, and turned to peer back at me.

Then I remembered. I remembered Gordon and the diamond saw and the convulsing sibo and the song that rocked the planet. Horror hit me, and I clapped my hand to the back of my neck. There was no neck brace, no coolant, no artificial heart. I was not a walking corpse.

That was a big plus.

I ran my hand around the side of my neck, where the saw bit. There were smooth seams there. Scars they felt like.

Autopsy the screen beside the bed read. The mumbling voice that woke me: time, name, date . . . of death. And there was a wicked looking collection of scalpels on a tray.

'What's going on,' I croaked. 'Is everyone all right? What happened? Where's Gordon?' A mob of decontamination suits stared at me. I staggered over to the wall. 'Answer!' No-one did so I slammed my hands on the glass. They all jumped back.

There was one figure there with no decontamination suit on. It was the Doc. He looked even worse than earlier. His face was grey and his eyes were bloodshot and red-rimmed. 'What's going on!' I screamed at him.

The Doc came out of whatever drug-induced seizure he'd been experiencing and pressed a button on the glass wall. His voice came through. 'You're soundproofed. You're everything-proofed,' he said.

I pressed the button on my side. 'You look like shit,' I said.

'You look pretty good for a corpse,' he responded.

'Is everyone all right?' I insisted.

Turns out the Doc sounded the alarm as soon as I started yelling about Gordon. Everyone was inside locked down when the spore storm arrived.

Only Chicken was insane enough to volunteer to suit up in the storm and go out to stop whatever was happening. He found Gordon, chopping down his seventeenth sibo. Chicken was stronger than me. He managed to restrain Gordon. The spore storm ceased, in gusts and eddies and drifts that the wind swept clean. Then Chicken tripped over me on the way back. Spores? I was covered in them.

Gordon was back in the chiller with a 'do not revive' tag on his big toe. The mine was in lockdown. My corpse had been brought in for autopsy.

This took a while to digest.

'So what are you doing up during the day, Doc,' I said. I needed some small talk.

'It was my last chance to try see you naked,' he said.

'Very funny.' I mean he wasn't even glancing at my tits. He was staring me straight in the eye. 'Speaking of which, get me some clothes,' I said.

The Doc peeled off his lab coat, and stuffed it in a chute. He closed it his end, there was a decontaminating hiss, and I opened it my end. I hauled the coat out and put it on. It was better than nothing.

'I'm starving,' I realised. I put my hands in the pockets and surfaced with a handful: a pen, a flashlight, a scalpel, a crumpled prescription pad, a screwdriver, one of those tiny bottles of whiskey you buy on interstellar flights, and some sweet, wadded up with fluff. 'Beaut,' I said.

'I wouldn't eat that,' the Doc said.

'You are telling me not to take drugs,' I was amazed.

'You've just come back from the dead,' the Doc said.

'Sure I have,' I said, to humour him. I mean, there'd clearly been a mistake. I took a big bite of sweet. Saliva flooded my mouth. I started to chew, and then I retched. I couldn't eat it. I tried a swallow of whiskey. It burned beautifully in my mouth, but my stomach convulsed and sent it straight back up.

'I'll get you a sandwich,' the Doc said. Same thing. I couldn't stomach it. 'Shock,' the Doc said, in one of those lightning fast diagnoses. 'Get some rest. We'll try again tomorrow.' He wanted to give me a saline drip, but I shook my head. The med staff got tired of watching me and shuffled out. Soon only the Doc was left, watching me like he expected my head to start spinning in circles spewing green foam.

I searched around the lab and found a mirror. I squinted at myself in the glass and realised why everyone was so wound up. The diamond saw tear in my throat was already healed, like a maze of old scars, but they were golden scars. I lifted my hand and stared at the finger that Tyke had bit earlier. The scab was healed and golden.

'So,' my voice choked up. I tried again, and this time I remembered to press the intercom button. 'So I'm going to turn into a sibo,' I said. Just like First Officer Connar and his mates. I was going to stand there forever and sing at dawn and dusk and dusk and dawn again. What had Gordon said? *I can hear them, they are screaming.*

'No,' the Doc said sharp. 'You're not. All the scans are clear. There's no sign of DNA contamination. Gordon is not infected either,' he added. 'The spores must have to reach living tissue to survive. Perhaps because you were dying they healed you instead. Or . . . ' his voice tailed off.

'Or what,' I said, sharp.

'Or they're smart,' he said. 'They want to use you as a host to get off planet. Open contamination didn't work last time, so they've hidden the genetic code in you in a way we can't scan.'

'That would have to be pretty bloody smart,' I snapped.

The Doc shrugged. 'Sibo,' he said.

Lucky about then, shock really did set in. For the next couple of days I only remember one thing. I couldn't eat or drink. I couldn't keep anything down. But I poured the whiskey into the palm of my hand, and it slowly absorbed. I could soak stuff up through my skin. Like a root system. But I made sure as Jacob in null space hell that I didn't tell anyone.

The Doc was my only visitor and he didn't say much. I stayed locked away and as I came out of the shock I realised I was locked up for good. I felt human. The golden scar did not spread. I didn't start sprouting tendrils. But at dawn and dusk, dusk and dawn, whenever the sibo sang, the underside of my chin lit. The scars glowed with the sibo song. I covered them up. I kept mum. My only chance of getting out of this mess was doing a convincing job of pretending there was nothing wrong.

But outside, as I found out later, things went from bad to worse. Management was dumb enough to report the incident off planet. The company locked down the mine, cancelled the supply ship, and disabled the light drive on the *Bios*. Like the *Dis*, we were left for dead.

One night I was lying on my slab, staring up at the ceiling, when Chicken and his mates burst in. They were bloody and bruised, and carrying an assortment of drills, saws and nail guns, all with the safety disabled. Tools turned into weapons.

I took one look at the insane grin on Chicken's face and swung to my feet. The door opened with a hydraulic hiss. I grabbed a scalpel and ducked behind the slab.

'You're in an air-locked room,' Chicken pointed out.

'So?'

'So if I wanted to kill you I'd just cut off your oxygen,' he said.

See what I mean. Deadpan.

'What's wrong?' I said, cautiously.

He swung the door wide. 'Come out.'

'Why?'

'The Doc has to talk,' Chicken said. He hustled me straight to the *Bios* hanger. The roof of the hanger was burst open. I jerked my head up. Far away I could see her, climbing like a star. The *Bios* was on her way out and up.

'I thought her drive was disabled,' I said.

'So did we,' said Chicken.

Mother Hell was standing by the hanger doors, arms folded, the still centre of a crowd around the Reaper, who had beaten the hanger commlink into submission.

'*Bios* can you hear me? *Bios* answer,' he called.

'We can hear you,' came back the cool female voice of the operator.

'What are you doing, you bloody piss-weak bastards?' the Reaper asked. Everybody cheered, almost drowning the answer out.

'We are evacuating,' the operator said. There was a pause. 'The *Bios* was too small to hold us all, so we made an executive decision. We had no choice based on current operational policy,' she offered.

'Bugger your lame-arse apology,' Reaper snarled. Another explosion of catcalls almost drowned out his words.

Then Mother Hell leaned over the Reaper's shoulder to the commlink, and spoke, cool and clear. 'We are going to get off this rock and we are going to come after you. We are going to kill you, your partners and your children. See you soon,' she said.

There was no applause when she finished, only an awed silence. Everybody knew Mother Hell never made a threat that she couldn't carry out, and nobody thought she was about to start.

The operator was silent. She knew that too. But we could hear the pilot at the other end. '*B105* flight checks complete. Light drive on in ten. All passengers and crew return to stations.'

The Doc was standing in the centre of the hanger, staring at the place where the *Bios* wasn't. Chicken shoved me hard in the small of the back, taking me up to the Doc's side. I cleared my throat. What did Chicken want me to say? 'G'day,' I said, brightly.

The Doc swung around immediately. 'What are you doing here?' he said, surprised.

I figured that didn't need an answer. 'What's going on?' I asked.

'Management bargained with the company,' the Doc said. 'They kept it quiet. They got themselves and their families out.'

'Ten, nine, eight . . . ' came from the commlink.

'So why did you stay?' I asked, amazed. 'Didn't they tell you?'

'He was told,' Chicken said, flat. 'Mother Hell found out, too late.'

The Doc turned back to the empty bay.

' . . . seven, six, five . . . ' the pilot's voice continued behind us.

'Why did you keep quiet?' Chicken asked the Doc.

Silence.

'You could have told us,' I passed the message on. The Doc seemed to be tuning everyone out except me for some reason.

'They had guns. There'd be bloodshed, to what point?' the Doc said.

' . . . four, three, two . . . '

'Everyone should have had a chance. There should have been a ballot,' Chicken said.

Some of the miners rushed at the Doc, looking murderous. Mother Hell stopped them.

'Thanks,' the Doc said, surprised.

'You're the only doctor we have left,' she said.

'What about our families,' one of the miners yelled.

' . . . one,' the countdown concluded.

There was a bang and a roar from the commlink,

followed by a high octane blast of interstellar static. We all looked up.

The *Bios* was exploding. It was a very pretty sight. Long tendrils of smoke and flame spiralled down through the atmosphere in a complicated geometric pattern. Over and above the falling debris was the wide vapour trail of a bigger craft, big enough to be seen even from this distance.

'Battleship,' Chicken said. He rocked on the balls of his feet and his crazy grin began. He raised his nail gun and slammed a salute into the sky.

I figured management made a bargain with the company, but not with the Fenris government. They'd sent a cruiser to circle us, and make sure no-one got out.

'Six'

No-one tried to shove me back in the airlock, but I was the reason why we were up shit creek. Everyone ignored me.

The *Bios* blowing up stopped the blame game on the Doc, but no-one else was feeling particularly matey with him. So I got some clothes and returned the lab coat, then spent the rest of the day helping the Doc take stock of the med hub. I had to do something or go mad. Suddenly our prospects were too grim. We were running out of everything. The Doc took all the painkillers, a pathetic little pile, and locked them in the med safe. 'From now on cold turkey,' he said, glumly.

Oh yeah, and Tyke took a shine to me, started following me around. It couldn't be for fear of the Reaper. The Reaper was told to sit in front of the radar and plot the bits of the *Bios* falling to earth. If any looked like crashing into a sibo he was to sound the alert. You can imagine how happy he looked.

Perhaps Tyke figured he finally had found a half-alien mate. He shadowed me all day, even sneaked into the med hub. He was lethal enough with a rock, never mind a scalpel. But he didn't listen to me when I told him to go outside and play under a truck.

'Can you tell Tyke to leave,' I whined to the Doc. 'I don't want to be his alien buddy.'

'Tyke is not an alien. He falls within the normal range of human parameters,' the Doc said.

'Have you done a DNA test on him?'

Neither the Doc, nor Tyke, said anything. I gave up.

Meanwhile Chicken and Mother Hell organised crews to find out how much food and water we had left. There was some fighting between rival crews, so Chicken and Mother Hell met in the med hub that evening to patch up a peace.

The news was grim all round. Six or seven weeks of supplies left at the most, and only four weeks of water, even if we recycled and rationed. Everything had been running down, waiting on the supply ship. Any excess supplies had long ago been siphoned off into the black market. That was what the fighting had been about. One of Mother Hell's crews opened a shipping container that was supposed to hold mixed supplies and found it full of toilets. They accused Chicken's crew, but Chicken and Mother Hell inspected the container together and agreed the switch had been made long ago.

'Deluxe Princess toilets, double flush and air-dry, with shag carpet seating,' Chicken marvelled. How they ended up here was anyone's guess. They were plumbed toilets so they couldn't even be used with our composting system, which was so short on water that solid wastes regularly backed up through the showers. Probably some long-gone CEO wanted warm air on their arse and the toilets were cheaper by the gross.

'So we're going to sit here and starve to death,' I said.

'There'll be cannibalism, then the survivors will starve,' the Doc said, just to cheer me up. 'There must be some way out,' he added.

'I've got an idea,' Chicken said. 'Fenris don't want us off-planet, but I bet they're not telling anyone else. They don't want the system isolated. Do we have a way to make interstellar contact? We could call for help and bluff our way out.'

'We have nothing powerful enough to communicate out of system,' Mother Hell said, flat.

'But what if we got out of system first,' I said.

'We don't have a ship,' the Doc pointed out.

'Yes we do,' I insisted.

'The *Bios* blew up,' the Doc reminded me, patiently. He examined me carefully in case I displayed any other symptoms of sudden memory loss. Meanwhile Mother Hell's eyes narrowed. Clearly she thought I'd carried fecklessness to a new low.

'The *Bios* was an interplanetary hopper, no good to us,' I needed to explain fast. 'We need to get to the next system at least. With this,' I slapped the wall of the med hub, raising a cloud of rust and dust.

Everyone stared at me without understanding. I banged the wall again. 'The *Esme*,' I said.

'Five'

The next morning I did some preliminary scans of the drives, trying for the first time in my life to remember what Gordon had said. No use. I could hear the rasping monotone of his voice, but not the actual content. I had been far too successful in blocking it out. Chicken came by while I was examining the scan results dolefully.

'What's wrong?' he asked, seeing my face.

'The ceramic shells are a third of their required thickness,' I said.

'And that's bad, how?' he said, briskly.

'Given the immense pressure on the drive shells in operation, I'm surprised the *Esme* even made it here. It will be a miracle if they withstand the pressure of take off,' I said. 'The contractors knew the *Esme* was due for a one-off flight so they made three drives for the price of one and pocketed the difference.'

'But you can get them working again.' It wasn't a question.

'I'm not a moudi drive engineer,' I said. I was a mining equipment maintenance engineer, me. My dumb idea of patching together a thirty-year old rust bucket was getting dumber by the minute.

'But you're not saying no,' he said.

If I said 'no' that was it. Our limited range of options would reduce to one: starve to death. I just couldn't say it. 'I'm not saying no,' I admitted. 'But we need engineers, pilots and a place to go.'

Chicken pulled out his pod. 'The nearest system has a planet, FU-24315,' His pod splayed the globe out. 'It's got a breathable atmosphere and edible animal life.'

'So what's wrong with it,' I asked. It was always bad

when a planet is habitable but only has a number not a name.

'It's got a mega-predator.' Chicken shrugged off the existence of some enormous, ravening horror. 'But we don't stay long, just long enough to direct an emergency call away from the Fenris system so someone else picks us up. We'll be fine as long as we stay mum.'

'And the pilot,' I asked.

'I flew a moudi battleship during the war.'

'Why didn't you say so earlier,' I yelped.

He shrugged again.

'I didn't know we even had moudi battleships,' I said. Me and my big mouth. Moudi drives weren't used in interstellar fighting. The ships only operated in or near planet atmosphere. Light ships were slower but better for military operations.

'You learn something new every day,' he said. He clapped me on the shoulder and went away.

It wasn't until after he left that I remembered that the feds had moudi battleships. They built them in the last days of the war, when it was obvious they were going to lose and they only wanted to do as much damage as possible before the inevitable. We got all the pilots after the war all but one, the pilot of the *Hellebore*. The pilot of the *Hellebore* was insane. He cluster bombed cities, spaceports and hospitals, then vanished before he could be tried for war crimes.

By the time I left the drives everyone was evacuating the hubs and setting up in tents. Heavy machinery was trundling across from the mine and the first hub was swinging aloft on a crane, being settled back into place on industrial lifts midway up the ceramic eggs of the drives. Scaffolding was going up around it. Welding kits were spitting and arcing.

Images of Fuck U's mega-predator were circulating. Most of them were blurred shots of scaly limbs and gaping fangs, taken by remote planet explorers shortly before they were crunched. As far as I could judge, the mega-predator was only as big as a horror slug but with less eyestalks. Everyone was joking about, calling it the protozor, and betting how much its gross weight was in steaks.

I got my stuff out of my hub and dumped it with the Doc. The med hub would be moved last. Besides, I didn't think I'd be getting much sleep. I found Mother Hell there, glowering at the scenery. I attempted to make a quick and silent exit but she caught my eye. She gestured me over, grimly.

'We've been discussing who's going to fly the *Esme*,' the Doc said. Try as I might I couldn't imagine Mother Hell actually discussing anything.

'Chicken says he can do it,' I said. I was about to mention the pilot of the *Hellebore* but Mother Hell shot me a look that scalded my mouth shut.

Fortunately the Doc didn't notice the sudden stop. 'And how to dodge the battleship,' he said.

'The *Esme*'s a moudi craft,' I repeated, patiently.

'You mean she only starts when she feels like it?' he said, perplexed.

Sweet Jacob in null space. Why do people never think about the mechanics of what goes on under their feet. 'Moudi, move out and up, down and in,' I explained, slowly. 'They sling shot between planets so they don't cross the intervening space. If we judge it right we can sling shot before the battleship is in range.'

Thinking about moudi drives got me so worked up that I actually paced in a tight circle around the med hub with my hands clasped at the back of my neck. I could feel the rough hasp of my new scars beneath my fingers. I was already regretting my idea. I didn't see any way it could work. I had just rebelled at giving up without even an odd, angry shot. At least this way if we died, we died trying. 'Moudi drives use very unstable aspects of interstellar physics,' I said, thinking aloud. I didn't try to explain the physics. Even hearing about it made my ears bleed. 'They need very precise calibration at start-up otherwise they miss the sling shot. And if you go wrong in null space . . . ' I drew a deep breath, and stopped. There were plenty of theories about what happened when you went wrong, from flying through a time-space worm, to being crushed flat, to flying forever in a ghostly half-life. Problem was no-one had ever come back to report.

'How come you know so much?' the Doc asked.

'I'm no expert,' I said. 'But Gordon worked on them for twenty years. He said—' Then I saw the look on Mother Hell's face. This was what she'd been waiting for all along. For news of a moudi engineer. For me to open my big mouth.

'No!' I said. 'Gordon is broken. Look what he did.' I lifted my hand from my scar.

Mother Hell smiled.

The next morning I walked into the med hub, and for only the second time in my life I leaped back and shrieked 'eek'. There was a crowd of dead people standing there, like the world's worst cocktail party.

'There were five in the chiller,' the Doc said brightly, when he saw me. 'All the coolant is being diverted to the drives so I got them all up.'

I studied their records and winced. None of the others had worked on moudi drives. Still they all followed me as I headed off. I kept a sharp eye on Gordon, but he shuffled obediently along with the rest.

Chicken had a crew drilling on the flight deck, with a back-up pilot just in case. The back-up pilot was a skinny, scared looking, black haired kid with acne and no arse.

'What's so good about her?' I hissed at Chicken as my dead mob shambled past.

'She got straight As in maths,' Chicken said.

'Which means?'

'Get the hell off my flight deck,' Chicken said, amiably enough. He turned to the rest. 'Let's try again,' he suggested, calmly. '*E5M3* flight checks complete. Moudi drive on in ten. All passengers and crew return to stations. Ten, nine, eight . . . ' His crew ran around like cockroaches caught in the light.

I backed out. I just needed to not think about the future, I decided. I needed to focus on the present. I mean, there was a protozor on the flight deck. Nobody was saying anything, but even if we got the drives working I knew I wasn't going to be on the *Esme* when she left. Chicken and Mother Hell would leave me behind. They weren't going to take a potential source of infection to their brand new world.

' . . . seven, six, five . . . ' I could hear Chicken's voice clearly as we ambled away from the flight deck and into the drive control chamber. I pointed Gordon at the #1 drive controller, and said, 'Service equipment,' in a loud, firm and clear tone. Then I held my breath. My back-up plan was to kick the thing.

' . . . four, three, two . . . '

Gordon started unscrewing the nearest casing. He had done this so many times in his life that it was automatic action safely saved deep down in his cerebellum. But the other four went over with him, and also started working. They worked without talking. But they coordinated. It was like they shared a basement mind.

' . . . one.'

There was a long silence. As long as they weren't handling sharps my dead mob didn't seem to need my supervision. I stuck my head around the door to check on our brave flight crew.

'So we just slammed us into the planet for the third time this morning,' Chicken was saying. Calm, polite, scathing and certain. 'Now gentlemen and ladies, let us open our text books to page seven, and I'll try to explain the principles of the parallel wave, again.'

'Four'

The dead don't sleep, and I wasn't letting Gordon out of my sight. I set up a camp bed in the drive chamber. But I woke standing, a warm glow beneath my chin and my arms over my head, aching. I remembered Gordon's movements from way back at the beginning, just before he chopped the sibo in half. I dropped my arms with a surge of fright, feeling the sibo song fading through the soles of my feet. I didn't know if I was communicating with my alien overlords or trying to take root.

In the first ten days we got the first drive fixed. We

had a test run on the eleventh day and nothing blew up. I acted like that was normal. I didn't want anyone to realise that it was a miracle. Belief that this was going to work was the only thing keeping us going. I moved my dead mob onto the #2 drive.

Three hubs out of eight were joined. Scaffolding completely surrounded the drives and hubs. The flight crew were only killing us twice a day, instead of twice a morning.

But food was tight, water was rationed. Booze ran out so people started distilling their own from whatever they could steal. There was even some shit doing the rounds made from fermented urine. *Piss-weak* the makers called it. Actually, it wasn't so bad. It didn't send you blind or insane. But Mother Hell cracked down on it. We needed the urine for drinking water.

Fights went feral. The Doc was kept busy stitching wounds and drying out victims of bad booze. He ran out of anaesthetic. He ran out of antiseptic. He swabbed down with salt. The pathetic pile of pain killers in the med safe dwindled further.

Twenty days in and we had six out of eight hubs connected, including all the drives. The scaffolding was a bird's nest cradling the ship. The #2 drive was operational. Also, I was still walking around looking human. That was even more of a miracle. If only I could stop the sleep walking and the chin glowing I'd even feel human. I found I could get by without food or sleep. As long as I sat down with some bootleg in the palm of my hand most nights I seemed to get by.

But I didn't have enough coolant to keep my dead crew cold. I kept Gordon's tanks topped up at the expense of the rest. As long as he kept working the others followed. But the others started to smell bad, and parts of their bodies turned green and black. Their fingers lost a lot of movement. I duct-taped their bodies to keep their intestines in.

Chicken and Mother Hell were barely holding their work crews together. We were eating from dented and rusted tins that had lost their labels. The brown sludge feeding into the solar filters only produced a drip of clean water. Fear was a drum beat that got louder and louder until it even drowned the sibo song. Everyone worked like hell, and off-shift begged, borrowed or stole any kind of shit to drown the fear out. A book started on who would die first.

At last my dead mob got the #3 drive working. We had all three drives in operation, and tested them. They made no sound, as usual, but the *Esme* changed. I can't explain it except to say that rusted and corroded, with scaffolding all around her and welders crawling along every seam, she became a ship again, a live thing. She came back from the dead. Her scaffolded hulk dominated the camp, standing on her drives for the first time in three decades. Every check we ran worked. It really looked like this ship would take off.

The last hub to move was the med hub. Everyone was given welding kits. Everyone. Even my dead mob. Even the Doc welded in his time off, though personally I wouldn't trust any line he soldered.

Everyone was off their faces. There was a surge in weird industrial accidents.

The last of the *Bios* came to earth, and the Reaper got laid off. He got smashed out of his skull, went back to his tent and laid into Maris again. Tyke jumped him and the Reaper turned on him. I heard the row and came running to find Maris in a heap on the floor out cold and the Reaper standing over Tyke with his hands fixed around his throat. Tyke was blue and limp. The Reaper's eyes bulged and he frothed from the mouth. I tried to pry his hands from Tyke but couldn't. I yelled for help. Chicken came running in and threw himself on the Reaper's back with a wild whoop.

The Reaper went bucking around the tent, tearing through the fabric and outside, trying to shake Chicken off. Then he threw himself over backwards, and slammed Chicken into the dirt. Chicken's head hit a rock with a crunch.

Chicken was out cold, but he was back on his feet before his mates came running in. They hauled the Reaper away to sober up. I checked Chicken's head but there wasn't any blood. I told Chicken to go see the Doc just in case.

'Naw. Hard as a rock,' he shrugged my concern off.

I carried Tyke off to the Doc, who stuck a tube down his nose into his lungs and hooked him up to a ventilator. 'Otherwise, the bruises are going to swell and cut his breathing off,' the Doc said. 'Unless he does have a tracheal system,' he added thoughtfully to himself. He said he'd normally anesthetise in this situation, but the only anaesthetic he had left was a rock. He doled out a few more of his painkillers instead.

The Doc looked terrible. Everyone said he must have some crazy shit stashed but I knew him better. The Doc had gone cold turkey. His hands shook and his breath stank and he was stone cold sober. He didn't say much but you could tell by his eyes that he hated life and everything in it, particularly himself.

Maris turned up a little while later, looking shaky. But she checked out all right. 'Thanks for looking after Tyke,' she said. That was the first nice thing she ever said to me.

The hospital moved into a large tent as the med hub was swung onto the *Esme*, into its nest of scaffolding and industrial lifts. Everyone stood around to watch. As it settled in place a ragged cheer rose up, united and cheerful. The feeling lasted, oh, ten seconds. Then the fights began again.

The Doc kept the med safe and all the surviving equipment in a locked container shell in the tent. It was the container shell that had held the Princess toilets. The Doc used them as furniture. The shag pile lids made surprisingly comfortable seating. But the weird thing was the toilets kept vanishing. We started with sixty, and were soon down to ten. They were being stolen. By whom? For what?

'You could use the cisterns as a still,' the Doc guessed.

The tension was getting to everyone, even Chicken. He didn't say anything, but sometimes he left the flight deck to stare at my dead mob. His face was pale and clammy and his eyes inward.

'You all right?' I asked him once.

He nodded, then winced and clutched his scalp.

'Headache,' I guessed. Sometimes I'm smart like that. 'Go see the Doc.'

'I'll be right,' Chicken said. 'Save the painkillers for Tyke.'

I worried about Chicken. I mean he did fish me out of the spore drift. I couldn't forget that. I had to keep reminding myself he was a traitor. All right technically not a traitor. More a mass murderer. But I kept an eye on him, and as far as I could see the headaches were getting worse.

Meanwhile Maris sat by Tyke's trolley and watched over him, fed him, wiped up after him. I didn't know why she liked him so much. Perhaps she'd been through so much that the only way to stay sane was to love the result.

'How's he doing?' I asked one night.

'All right.' There was the soft note back in her voice.

'Hey, me and Tyke we're mates now. Right?' That wasn't strictly true. I had tried to shake him off. Besides he had been following me around, sure, but he hadn't let me get close enough to touch. He didn't let any adult near him except his mum. But I really wanted to cheer Maris up. I touched Tyke's hand, very gently.

He didn't hiss or spit, and after a moment his hand curled around mine. He let his guard down. Then he gave a little sigh, and fell asleep, his fingers still tight. 'See, we're mates,' I boasted. Softly.

Maris looked me over, for once without sarcasm or disgust. I thought there might be a smile lurking in her eyes, but then I had to go and bugger things up. Real lady killer, me. 'Soon I'll have him eating out of my hand,' I joked.

Maris stiffened. 'He's not an animal,' she snapped.

'I know,' I said, hastily. I sighed and rubbed my eyes with my free hand. 'He's like me, right. We've both got some alien DNA.'

Maris reached out, unexpectedly. She ran her hand down my throat, under my chin, along the scarring. 'I like it,' she said. 'I think its hot.'

Everything went blurry. I said something smart and sexy like, 'What?'

'I didn't always have a wall up,' Maris said. She kept her hand on my throat for a heartbeat longer then took it off. My eyes cleared. She was smiling. Just a little, in her eyes and the corners of her mouth. 'I used to laugh a lot,' she said.

'Sure you did,' I said, though it was a leap of faith believe me.

'I've been thinking of having another kid,' she said. 'Tyke would like a sister.' Maris wasn't seeing the end game playing out all around her. She was seeing the future. 'Would you like to be my partner?' she asked.

I nearly choked. My dead mob weren't the only ones breaking down. My gaydar was fucked. 'I—but—I thought you liked blokes,' I stammered.

Maris smiled full on. 'Where I come from you get a man to have children but you have a girlfriend all your life,' she said. 'Reap's a dud though. I thought I'd ask the Doc.'

'The Doc,' I squeaked. 'He's a hundred.'

'And he's had about eighteen kids. I asked. He won't mind jerking off into a jar. That's the end of his job.' Her smile widened. 'I mean, Tyke likes you. That's a first,' she reminded me. 'So what do you say?'

'Yes. Yes.' I pulled myself together. 'That would be great!'

I wasn't going to burst Maris's bubble. I knew I'd be left behind. Besides, the *Esme* was going to explode on take off, or the battleship would blast her, or she'd crash into null space or into Fuck U at the other end. Then we'd all be eaten by protozors. But even if Maris had some crazy thing for aliens she was acting like I was still human. And you have no idea how human that made me feel.

'Three'

I wasn't sleeping but sometimes I found myself standing, chin glowing, arms raised. More and more I could hear a murmur on the edge of my consciousness, a distant shout that got stronger each time I blanked out. I ran out of whiskey, I ran out of grog, I ran out of any kind of shit to drown that distant shout. One day I knew, I dreaded, I would hear what it said.

Plus we were all so hungry that even the sibo were starting to look succulent.

Then Chicken keeled over on the flight deck. We fetched the Doc. He knelt beside him and shone his flashlight into his eyes. Chicken's eyes were all pupil.

'Is that bad?' I asked.

'Concussion,' the Doc diagnosed.

'That's just headaches, right?'

'Concussion means bleeding on the brain. Which leads to pressure on the brain. Which leads to death,' the Doc said. He studied Chicken for a long time, as Mother Hell arrived at a run. When she saw Chicken her face shrivelled like an old egg. 'He needs a craniotomy,' the Doc said at last.

'And that's easy,' I said, hopefully.

'I'm not a surgeon. I'll have to bone up.' The Doc did not look confident. He fetched a trolley and carted

Chicken off.

Our back-up pilot stepped into the breach. She walked around like her boots were too heavy, and she burst into tears whenever she tried to speak. Morale sank like a brick.

My dead mob went back to their welding inside the *Esme*. They weren't very good at it. Their fingers were useless so I taped the welding kit to their hands, but then they didn't notice when they caught fire. I borrowed a fire extinguisher to put them out. Fortunately no-one had yet figured out a way to distil non-lethal grog from fire retardant. The extinguisher still worked.

The day after Chicken's collapse I heard confusion and shouts outside. After the Reaper's episode every time I heard yells my stomach went tight. I told my mob to down tools, otherwise they'd probably set fire to themselves. I ducked outside to take a look. I smelled smoke. A thick grey boil poured from the med tent.

I ran all the way there, believe me, lugging my fire extinguisher, and plunged into the smoke. The flames were coming from the Princess toilet container. The Doc was near the entrance, hauling Chicken along on a trolley. Chicken was still out cold but his head was shaved all prepped for surgery.

Inside Maris was hunched over Tyke's trolley. 'We have to move all the gear with him,' she yelled over the crackle and hiss of the fire. Tyke, the trolley, the ventilator and the oxygen tank, which had a prominent *flammable* sticker on it.

We piled all the gear around Tyke and lifted the trolley. The ventilator went dead as soon as we unhooked it from its solar cell. We'd have to hook it up again outside. Tyke gasped for breath through the tube. It didn't sound good. He grabbed my arm as we lifted him. His eyes were wide and scared.

'You're going to be fine,' I lied.

Then the fire gave a huge roar. It sounded like laughter, a giant manic echo. It leaped right up. It tore through the roof and flames came howling along the roof line.

We had to drop Tyke. I sprayed the fire extinguisher around. Other people were trying to dump retardant from outside, but it was already too late. The flames were too high to reach, and the smoke was choking. My eyes were stinging. I couldn't see a thing. I backed to Tyke but I couldn't go past him. I heard a confused babble, a chopped off yell in my head. A warning.

From the dead.

'Get out,' I screamed at Maris. Maris took one look at my face and pulled the gear free from Tyke. She tried to disconnect the tube but couldn't. It was wedged in there. So she tore the tube from his throat. She gathered him in her arms and ran for the entrance as I sprayed the last of the fire retardant around.

Then there was a bang and crash and roar. I don't know what the Doc kept in that shipping container but a ball of fire expanded out from the door. I was deafened. The ground rocked. Flames shot up. I was thrown to the dirt.

I scrambled to my feet and bolted after Maris and Tyke, arms shielding my face. My ears rang. At my heels a wall of flame and heat raced to swallow me. But everything was silent and distant after that roar. I couldn't hear the flames any more. All I could hear was a giant sound in my head.

The *Dis* dead. I could hear them. They were screaming.

I stumbled out of a wall of flame, and straight into the Doc who was standing at the entrance to the tent with his hands up to protect himself from the blast. He dropped his arms as I appeared. There were tears running down his face.

'Did you leave your shit behind,' I coughed, and hauled him along as I ran past. Behind us the whole tent exploded in flame, then collapsed. At last my ears started working.

I could hear the flames and the yells and Maris, who was kneeling over Tyke and screaming. Over the crackle and hiss and roar, the sibo song started. Were any threatened by the fire? I wheeled around but they were all at a safe distance. I looked at the nearest. It was full pink daylight but the branches and the tendrils waved at me. I couldn't tell if it was about to spit spores or not. I studied it narrowly. 'Is it reacting to the fire,' I asked. 'Does it think it's threatened?'

But the Doc was fixed on the burning tent. 'There goes all my equipment,' he said.

'Everything?' I asked.

'Not all.' He flourished the scalpel he kept in his pocket.

'It's a start,' I said. I knelt beside Maris.

In all this noise there was one thing I could not hear. One tiny thing. I could not hear Tyke breathing. I put my ear to his chest. His heart was beating but for the second time in three days he was blue and limp.

'Doc. Quick!' I said. I jumped up to give him room. I glanced at the sibo again. It was still active. Was it slowing down as the fire died? Or not? My neck twinged. I clapped my hand over the scar. 'I think we need to get everyone into the *Esme*,' I said.

The Doc was giving Tyke emergency breaths, and wasn't listening.

I saw a large crowd gathering around Mother Hell on the other side of the burning tent. I ran over.

'Sibo alert! I think we should get inside the *Esme*,' I yelled. But no-one paid any attention to me. Everyone was milling in a huge circle around Mother Hell, even ignoring the collapsed tent as it burned. The crowd's focus was inward.

There was a huge commotion. The only one not yelling or screaming or in violent motion was Mother Hell. I could see fists and legs and crowbars flailing, and tried to make out what was happening then realised the mob was beating the shit out of six men in the middle. The noise was maddening. I clapped my hands to ears. At once the screams of the *Dis* dead rose from within, like a seashell. I unblocked my ears. Which was better, the living howl or the screams of the dying? Answer: neither.

That's when I realised what Gordon was talking about. That was the problem with the sibo, whether they were smart or not. The *Dis* dead were not dead. After two centuries they were still dying. They were still alive somehow deep within the sibo. And they didn't like it one bit. I could tell they were *Dis* dead, not my own mob. I don't know how I could tell the direction but I knew. The screams were scattered over the landscape around me. Not one came from the *Esme*. So, it came to me suddenly and painfully, that it no longer mattered if I was on the

Esme when she left. There was no distance I could go to leave those screams behind. If I didn't do something they would be with me for the rest of my life.

Mother Hell gestured. The mob backed off, leaving the six men sprawled and bleeding on the ground. But they weren't dead yet either, not by a long shot.

Turns out the fire had been started with a slow burning fuse attached to a mining detonator on the door of the Princess toilet container. It had been set to break into the container to steal the painkillers. Only I knew there weren't any painkillers left in the safe. The Doc had the last seven in his pocket.

Mother Hell recognised the pattern of the explosion, and caught the six men running out of the back of the tent. At first they all said they'd been fighting the fire. Even the mob's beating couldn't make them change their story. But after Mother Hell started asking questions four men broke down and admitted it. The other two kept insisting they were innocent.

Then Maris gave a sudden, terrible scream. We all looked over. She knelt, holding Tyke in her arms, screaming on and on like a sibo song. The Doc was standing between Chicken and Tyke with his back to us, and his shoulders slumped.

Tears slid down my cheeks. These idiots had destroyed our medical equipment and killed Tyke. For what? Because they thought they could steal a handful of drugs and sell them, when we didn't even know yet that we'd be able to get off this planet. The money was useless. The Doc was right. People are cruel and stupid and savage. The only way to make life bearable was to drown it out.

Sometimes I think the sibo are us.

Mother Hell looked at Maris and her face clenched like a fist. 'Kill them, kill them all,' she said.

The mob whooped and hollered and all six men started yelling their innocence. But now no-one listened. They fetched cables and ladders, hauled the battered men to their feet, and hustled them along.

I trudged back to Maris. The mob hanged all six men from the *Esme*'s scaffolding. The death book refused to pay out on the hanged men, claimed there was interference, and they were scratched.

As soon as the Doc found out about the hangings he marched off to confront Mother Hell. I trailed along. He thought that because he was the only doctor left Mother Hell wouldn't kill him. But without medical supplies perhaps Mother Hell didn't need him. Besides she had a long memory. If this escape plan worked I didn't know if I wanted to openly associate with another potential victim of a freak industrial accident.

'That was lynching. It was murder,' the Doc barked at her.

'They killed Tyke,' Mother Hell said.

'Tyke is alive,' the Doc snapped.

The Doc had cut a hole in Tyke's windpipe, below the bruising. He was keeping it open with his pen. He'd got Tyke breathing again and he was doling out the last of the pain killers to him. Maris's screams had been from relief and hysteria.

Having no other equipment available had made Chicken's operation suddenly simple. He'd relieved the pressure on Chicken's brain by using a stone to drive the scalpel to bust a hole in his skull.

'They're both alive for now,' the Doc said. 'But I can't see how they'll survive long. Infection will kill them.'

I spent a short time with Maris and Tyke but I had to get back to my dead mob. To my relief none of them had managed to set themselves on fire to any major degree. I beat out the smouldering sparks and got them back to work. We had to get off this planet if Tyke and Chicken were to survive.

The *Dis* dead were with me. The communication channel was jammed open. Perhaps it was just the time had come. Perhaps the fire and my being in fear of death had put me in tune with them. Screams chopped and changed in my head, rising and falling in shrill throated shrieks, sometimes an isolated voice calling in an agonised jerk. I guess it was because the sibo were fixed in place. They couldn't run away if anything hurt. So pain had no meaning for them. But pain had a hell of a lot of meaning to me.

I guessed I might be going mad. But there was one way to find out.

'Hey Gordon,' I said. He swivelled around to look at me. I'd forgotten how unusual that was supposed to be. It was so natural, so lifelike a movement that I spoke without thinking. Bright spark, me. 'Hey Gordon, can you still hear them?' I asked.

It wasn't just Gordon that answered. It was all my dead mob. In unison.

'The *Dis* dead. We can hear them. They are screaming,' they said.

'Two'

I marched my dead mob out of the *Esme* and into the

desert. I told the Doc I needed him outside, then borrowed a back hoe and dug a trench wide and deep enough to take five corpses. I lined my dead mob up along the lip.

'You've been a great team,' I said. 'You've done great work. Thanks to you the *Esme* is in great shape.' That was enough of that particular adjective. 'But there's a time to break even the—best—teams up. And that time is now. All of you are due a well deserved rest.'

The Doc trudged over just as I wound up my pep talk.

'They spoke again,' I said to the Doc. 'I can't trust them any more. How do you kill them?'

'They're already dead,' the Doc said.

'Enough with the technicalities,' I said.

'Generally we decommission them by chilling them to immobility then removing the artificial heart and coolant tanks,' the Doc said. He shrugged. The med hub was now operational, although they were still welding on the roof, but all remaining power and coolant were directed to the drives. We couldn't chill our deceased friends.

'Too bad. I want them immobile and in their graves. So over to you,' I said.

'Me?' The Doc rubbed his chin.

'You're the doctor,' I informed him.

'First do no harm,' he said.

'Doc, you've been cutting throats and splitting heads open. It's too late to be talking about doing no harm,' I said.

'It's the Hippocratic oath, idiot.' For all his tough talk the Doc was backing away, shaking his head. 'First do no harm,' he repeated.

'Fine.' I get all the shit jobs, me. 'What do I do?' I asked.

'You switch off the artificial heart and support systems and pull out the coolant tubes, but I warn you the corpses will twitch around some,' he said.

'Fine.' I walked around behind my crew's backs. How hard could this be? I stopped behind Gordon, then walked to the end of the line. I'd start with strangers, I decided.

I opened the casing at the back of the neck and switched off the support system. Then I pulled out the coolant tubes. They came out crusted, and foul smelling ooze seeped out. The corpse collapsed away from me, pitched into the grave and thrashed around, moaning. So was it just coincidence that it flopped onto its back and kept its eyes fixed on me?

'That moaning sound is air escaping from the lungs,' the Doc said, professionally. But he felt as sick as I did, judging from his face. At last the corpse stopped thrashing around, although it kept twitching.

'Nervous reaction. That will take some time to die down,' the Doc said.

'You mean he's still dying down there?' I asked.

'He can't die. He's already dead,' the Doc said. He drew a deep breath. '*It* can't die. *It's* already dead,' he corrected.

I walked down the line, switching off the support units and removing the coolant tubes. Soon there were four corpses thrashing and whistling in the pit.

'What could they say to make you do this?' the Doc asked.

I didn't want to answer that one. Then he'd definitely

think I was crazy. 'Maris says you've got eighteen kids,' I said, to distract him.

'It's not like we keep in touch,' the Doc said.

'Did you ever love any of them?' I asked.

His eyes turned bleak. 'Only those I lost,' he said. 'What did they say?' he added. I wasn't shaking him off.

I didn't answer directly. 'Hey Gordon,' I said. 'You can hear them too. Tell him.'

Gordon gazed at me blankly, doing an excellent impression of a walking corpse.

'Gordon, tell the Doc what you told me,' I begged. I figured it wouldn't sound so crazy coming from him.

There was a long silence. Gordon said nothing.

'I've got to go back to my welding,' the Doc said, finally. 'When you're done here can you come and help me move Tyke onto the *Esme*?'

'We're moving in?'

'We're leaving,' the Doc said.

'But they're still welding,' I protested.

'Mother Hell has worked it out. They'll weld up to right before we go,' the Doc said. 'But we have to leave now while she's still got some control.' He trudged away.

I watched him leave then turned back to Gordon, who clapped his hand over the nape of his neck and backed off. Such a lifelike gesture. 'Don't do that mate,' I said. 'I don't want to do this either.'

'Then don't,' Gordon said, low.

I saw red. 'Gordon, you bloody prick!' I shouted. 'You could talk all along, but you stayed mum in front of the Doc to make me look like I was crazy!'

'Some things you do fine by yourself,' Gordon said.

He kept his hand over the nape of his neck and moved to face me. I got the idea. He didn't want to go.

'I can't just let you leave. If you kill a sibo everybody on the *Esme* is buggered,' I said.

He shook his head.

'You promise you won't do anything until after the *Esme's* gone?' I asked. It was crazy but I wanted to leave, and silence the dead. I couldn't do both. If Gordon stayed then I had a chance. Mother Hell would have to throw me out or kill me. And first she'd have to find me. If I managed to get on board undetected I'd hide someplace real fast.

Gordon nodded. Then he looked around at the abandoned tent sites, the rubble from the fire, the scraps of metal and rubbish lying all over. 'Also, I will clean up this place. You've left a real mess. You have no respect for this planet, or safe work practices,' he said, sounding exactly like his old self.

'So, what's it like, being dead?' I asked.

He turned his gelid eyes back to me, and forced expression into his face.

It was hell. I could see that.

What could I do? Trust a walking corpse that had already killed me? But this was Gordon. He might be a prick, but I'd worked with him for years. Besides he already knew I couldn't kill him. I didn't have it in me.

'Go,' Gordon said for me. That was when he smirked. A real old Gordon holier-than-thou smug smirk. It cracked his dry lips and showed his rotting gums and decayed teeth. Like there was something he knew that I didn't.

Then he turned away and lurched off into desert.

I thought of the screams in my head falling silent.

I climbed onto the backhoe and filled in the grave even though some of the corpses hadn't stopped twitching. I hurried back to the ship. The *Esme* was a madhouse. People were rushing in and out, crashing into each other and laughing like idiots. Heavy equipment trundled up the ramp, but the drivers swerved all over the place and raced at an insane pace. The scaffolding was still up, with the dead men still dangling, and the welders still working.

Then the Reaper ran an excavator backwards clear off the ramp. It plummeted three times its own length to the ground and ended up with him underneath it. We figured he was dead. Anyway, we didn't have time to lift it off him to find out. You wouldn't believe it. He was such long odds in the death book that no-one had backed him.

The sibo had been quiet since the fire. They had not sung, not at dusk, not at dawn. I was the only one who noticed their silence. I didn't know what it meant and I wasn't going to draw attention to myself by asking.

I found the Doc in his new temporary med tent. I didn't know what to think. How to smuggle myself on board. Where to hide. Whether I should stay or go. Plus a smidgeon of guilt for unleashing Gordon on the sibo. After all, they had saved my life. But it was not like there weren't enough sibo to go around, right. Besides, whatever was going to happen was going to happen fast. Chicken wasn't in the med tent. He must have been moved first. Tyke was looking great. His bruises and scabs were healing. The Doc was talking about taking the pen out of his throat once the *Esme* reached Fuck U.

'He has an excellent immune system,' the Doc said, proud as any dad. But he stayed at a safe distance. He left it to Maris and I to lift Tyke's stretcher and carry him on board.

And if it came to that, I didn't know how I was going to say goodbye to Tyke. Perhaps I should just skip the goodbyes and run, like any other mature, responsible adult.

As I said, I hadn't noticed Chicken in the med tent. But I saw him now. He strode down the ramp as we carried Tyke up. There he was, large as a cargo door and strong as a backhoe, with a bandana wrapped over the hole in his skull. The replacement pilot trotted at his heels like an adoring pup.

'Hurry it up there,' Chicken yelled to the roof-top welders. 'I can feel my brain turning green.' He swung around and saw us. He looked me over, deadpan. No-one had ever said anything, but I had no right to be on this ship. I was fucked. My stomach did a back flip. Then Chicken glanced at the Doc and grinned. He strode back up the ramp and vanished into the flight deck.

'Is he all right to pilot?' I whispered, into the sweet silence of enormous relief.

'No,' the Doc said. 'His blood pressure is so low that I don't know how he's staying vertical. But I couldn't stop him, and even in his condition he's probably better than his replacement.'

Inside the *Esme*, cables snaked everywhere and panels spilled naked wiring. I saw Mother Hell. Fortunately I saw her first. She'd shed a thousand years. She looked great. She was even smiling. I didn't let her see me. I didn't want to spoil her day. I hunched my shoulders and ducked my head and scuttled by.

We trundled Tyke into the med hub. We could hear Chicken from the flight deck. 'The next person who tries to poke my living brain is off the ship,' he bawled.

There was welding gear lying against the wall and the Doc directed me to put Tyke down in the centre of the hub.

'Wouldn't he be better off against the wall? I asked.

'Yeah, and we're going to put him there once I've welded this,' the Doc said. He pulled a wall panel free. 'Get in,' he said, while Maris and Tyke applauded delightedly. I looked inside. They'd hollowed out a cubby hole inside the *Esme*, with a Princess toilet bolted to the floor.

'You . . . What?' I said.

'Just get inside before anyone sees you,' he said.

'But—'

'Inside.'

I hugged Tyke, then Maris grabbed me and kissed me. I dived into the cubby hole. It was dark inside but I did have shag pile seating. The Doc stopped halfway putting up the panel.

'I almost forgot.' He held up a miniature whiskey bottle. It was full of clear liquid. 'I've been saving it specially,' he said. It's not often you can be touched by a miniature bottle of fermented urine. Tears sprang to my eyes.

'But—' I started. The bottle was shoved into my hand and the panel slid shut.

I sat in the dark and stared at the wall. Maris and the Doc were taking an awful risk. What if the sibo were smart enough to contaminate my DNA and hide it from the scans?

I could still feel Maris's kiss on my lips.

Besides what would Mother Hell do when she saw me again? And why was the Doc helping at all? I glanced sideways at the wall. The Doc was doing an awful weld. I could see thin strips of light. But that was all to the good if I had to break out.

I could feel the liveness of the ship. I could hear Chicken's voice over the com. 'Everyone get on board before I faint. Again.'

A horrible, strong, painful stab of feeling shot through me.

I realised why the Doc had been at my autopsy, and why he didn't leave on the *Bios*, and why he wept when he thought I'd been killed in the fire. Chicken had known. That's why he'd fetched me out of isolation. Maris had known. That's why she'd asked the Doc if he wanted to be a father again. From his smirk, even Gordon had known. A walking corpse had worked this out, and I hadn't. I hunched over on my toilet, fingers clenched around my miniature bottle, arms folded around my waist, face hot and red in a spasm of complete embarrassment. How could I be so stupid! I only cheered up when I remembered that the Doc knew I was gay. He'd been sure to hide it from me.

But I had to say something. That strong, prickling, urgent feeling forced me.

'Hey Doc!' I yelled through the panel.

'Shut up.'

'Sometimes life sucks,' I said.

'Tell me about it.'

Doc finished the weld and moved away. I heard them shuffle Tyke's bed right next to me. Then Chicken's voice came loud and strong. He didn't sound like he was about to faint. I tried to find something reassuring about that. '*E5M3* flight checks complete. Moudi drive on in ten. All passengers and crew return to stations,' he announced.

This was too soon. I didn't have anything sorted out. I was going to die mid-sentence.

As Chicken started the countdown my thoughts flew back over the last weeks, to the day before my death when Gordon started acting peculiar. I felt a thrum through the Princess toilet seat, through my feet and bum and thought it was the engines, except that moudi drives don't vibrate or make any sound. Then the underside of my chin lit up, shedding a gentle light over my hiding place. I was no longer waiting to die in the dark.

Outside the sibo were starting their song.

Were they singing in farewell? In triumph? In rejoicing? Or had Gordon started work. I thought about Gordon, watching us leave him in the hell we'd made for him. That was enough to make me pour the entire mouthful of Piss-weak into my palm. I thought about Gordon and the *Dis* dead. They were still inside my head. Even if they were silenced they'd still be there, for as long as I lived.

But then I knew we were going to die. The crazily constructed *Esme* would break up on take off. The battleship would find us before we could sling shot. We'd be lost in null space. Fenris would realise where we'd fled. The mega-predator would get us. The sibo would activate something inside me. There were too many bad ends—

Chicken's countdown continued. It was like the whole

ship held its breath.

I don't know much. But I did know I could get along with Mother Hell, as long as she didn't kill me. I liked Chicken, even though he was a criminally insane mass murderer. We all cared about Tyke. Maris loved me, even if it was just some crazy thing she had for aliens. I knew that I was more than half in love with her, and the Doc was more than half in love with me. That was something. And I knew you don't give up just because you're going to die. You just keep doing what you're doing, right up to the last heartbeat.

That bolt of emotion shot through me again, that strong, agonised, wild electric feeling. I had been without it so long that it had taken me a while to recognise it. But I knew it now, and by it I knew the sibo were smart after all. They might not understand pain or suffering, but they understood the need to save a life. I realised in that heartbeat that I was still completely human. The feeling flooding through me, through the ship, was the most cruel and stupid and savage of all human emotions.

It was hope.

Chicken's voice, loud and clear, echoed through the *Esme*.

'One,' he said.

Penelope Love lives in Melbourne, Australia. Her short stories have appeared in a range of Australian anthologies and, to her delight, occasionally been nominated for Aurealis Awards. Of this story, she writes, 'I've always been fond of stories set in deserts. I wanted the spirit of "SIBO" to lie somewhere between Yeats's "The Second Coming" and AD Hope's "Australia"— *if still from the deserts the prophets come.* There is hope—of a kind—out there.'

Beneath the Floating City

Donna Maree Hanson

The flashing lights and the easy stride of narcotics through his system kept Nic Da Silva gyrating on the dance floor. The low hum of voices from the club patrons combined with the drumming beat of the dance music flowed over him. Nic grinned as the woman dancing with him tucked a wad of credits into the front of his trousers, her hand dropping slightly, stroking him, lingering there possessive, slightly aggressive. It was enough money to pay his shot at the inn for another night.

'Let's leave now, Mr Engineer,' the woman whispered in his ear, her breath a warm, spicy tickle. 'My hotel is across the road.' Nic nodded and he followed the woman out, her body draped in translucent robes that shifted and swayed with her gait. At least he thought she was a woman, a human woman. There was so much enhancement these days it was hard to tell. The Club Zephyr was patronised by humans mostly but that didn't mean other races didn't try their luck. Exotic, erotic encounters. He shrugged. As long as there was mutual satisfaction, and as she'd paid, he'd do the necessary no matter what removing her clothes revealed. A few scales, an excess of mucus hadn't put him off before.

A city engineer leaning against the bar caught his eye and winked as Nic passed through the main doors. Engineers, bunch of stuck up bastards. He'd been trying for an 'in' for so long at the club that he'd gotten used to being invisible to that lot. Nic saluted in a casual way, acknowledging the man. Another man joined the engineer and they both turned their backs. Still, Nic was heartened by the attention; a friendly wink was better than a punch in the nose. Their presence was why he frequented that particular club. He was an engineer too, by trade, but unemployed, recently retrenched from the mines on Xeno. His severance pay had got him to Hedonia, it was up to him to do the rest.

Lucky for him Hedonia was where he wanted to be for the present and damn if he wasn't going to have a good time while he eked out an existence, sleeping in third grade hotels, slumming it in bars and earning his way with his other great organ. In his current state of mind, decadence was good for the soul. Being an engineer certainly helped, but he was not a Hedonian City engineer. They had status because of the great marvel of the place and the secrecy behind the tech, while he had none.

The woman he was with waved her ID card at the monitor and the doors to the hotel swished open. Not bad, he thought as they walked through the plush surroundings. Everything had been done to augment the ancient alien design of the building; even the air was slightly green-tinged. Richly carved stone walls, depicted alien figures doing what came naturally, complete with patterned borders full of swirls and interlinking designs. Once in the lift, the woman pushed him back against the wall and groped him, making him grunt in surprise.

'My, you're hot tonight, pretty lady,' he said in his best gigolo voice. She purred as she rubbed herself against him. So maybe his charm had worked already.

The lift door opened to her suite. They tumbled inside, kissing up a frenzy and the lights went on.

'Take them off,' she said pulling back, her own fingers separating the yellow robe she was wearing. It landed in a delicate puddle on the floor.

Nic paused. The woman was stunning. Firm breasts with nut-brown nipples, great tan, long lean thighs. He realised he was standing half naked with his mouth open and shut it. Why did this woman need a paid fuck? You'd think she'd have to fight them off, the men wanting to pay *her* for her time. Their bodies crashed together. The room lurched around him as he found himself held firmly, face down on the floor. 'What the—'

Next morning, Nic's eyes were gooey and his nose was filled with a particularly nasty stench. Waking up proved to him that he had indeed been thrown out of the hotel, according to the door receipt he held in his hand, exactly one hour and thirty-four minutes after he had arrived. Groaning he levered himself up on his elbows. He was in the gutter. Figures. Blasted trans, can't trust them as far as you can root them. Of course her body had been too good to be true. She was a transmuter, able to morph sex, shape her body anyway she chose. She fucked him senseless taking it everyway and then some, then sucked out all his brain juice. That's when it started getting kinky. Staggering to his feet, he felt a wave of exhaustion hit him. A needle headache shot through his skull. 'Argh!' he blurted, unable to hold it in. Squinting, he realised he was a block or two from his own hotel. He could make it there, maybe they'd even let him sleep in a bed all day. He checked his pants. At least the cash was still there.

It took a while to get into his room. He had to pay first and negotiate the next payment. He used the san unit, the harsh jets washing the street scum and transmuter juice off him. He thwacked the wall in frustration. No wonder the blasted engineer winked at him on the way out. All this time wasted trying to fraternise with them, trying to wheedle his way into a job and the bastards were laughing at him. They knew he'd rooted alien arse. Shit! He'd had his own penetrated, as well as the mental shakedown. What a rape of the mind that was. The bitch got high on ripping out his emotions, his memories and thoughts. When she realised what he was, what he was after, she'd laughed and thrown him out. Real bona fide, licensed gigolos had more interesting minds than an out of work engineer and better sense than to mess with transmuters in the first place.

Though his mind had felt rather empty when he woke up, he thought there was no permanent harm done. The thrill for the transmuter in sucking brain was in the taking, in the struggle and the pain inflicted.

Nic half limped to the Zephyr Club, expecting that none of the engineers would be there. He would wait for that smart ass to arrive. It was midday and already the place was filling up. A few new shuttles had arrived and the tourists didn't let city time interfere with their visit. Hedonia was a place of indulgence after all—an ancient and alien floating city, full of aged opulence and mysterious technology.

He could tell by the variations in complexion that the

tourists in the club were a mixed bag of those who had been in the city for a couple of days and those who had disembarked that morning. The slightly greasy skin tone appeared after a few days' exposure to the atmosphere, as well as the jaded expression—but that was due to other things. A fungus created an unnatural sheen to human skin. As there were no lethal side affects, nothing was done about it. Nic's own swarthy complexion had deepened to a golden brown. He liked the shine.

He was on his second drink and feeling mellow when the engineer he'd been waiting for arrived. Quite blithely, the man fronted up to him and slapped him on the shoulder. 'So how was it?' he asked with a grin.

'Bleeding bastard. You could have warned me it was a transmuter. My head hurts still.' So did his rear but he wasn't owning to that.

The engineer nodded. 'Better you experience the brain drain now while you still know nothing. We suspect they are after the specs for the floatation engines.'

'Fat lot of good it does me. Can't even get an interview with you lot.'

The man grinned and waved to the barkeep. 'As it happens there is an opening. There's a workbus leaving in two hours for an undercity inspection. If you are interested, make sure your credentials have been lodged with the city. There'll be a test afterward. Tell them Johann sent you. The foreman's a Fleche so don't wear any colognes or strong scents. It overwhelms his olfactory senses and makes him twice as cranky as usual.'

Johann turned away, slapping his business card on the counter as he did. Nic gaped at it stupidly, not quite believing his luck. If he sealed this, he'd be legit, a resident and also in funds. A whole pathway of future plans opened up to him.

Without finishing his drink, he pushed away from the bar and ignored the sexual overtures of two over-eroticised bipedal females. Next time he slapped his flesh against a woman, it would be because he wanted to, not because he was desperate for money. Glancing over his shoulder at the second woman, a Taelen, he saw she wasn't too bad. With a shrug, he decided to trust to luck that they'd cross paths again.

There were nine other contenders for the one vacant position. Nic ground his teeth as he attempted to assess the competition. The Fleche was giving nothing away, not even a twitch of his elephantine nose, which looked more a like a penis. Nic tried not to think of the words 'fuckface' or 'dickhead' when he looked at him, because he knew he'd start to laugh. He turned away to distract himself.

The twelve-seater workbus took off from a service dock, quickly rising over the city. In this sector, some of the ancient buildings appeared to be sinking. He wondered how they remained upright as some had a serious tilt. The buildings looked to be made of stone, covered over with the same greasy gold sheen the people of Hedonia eventually acquired.

Ornate arched bridges linked sections of the city, spanning nothing at all except the plummeting depths of the atmosphere to the surface below. As the workbus pivoted over the perimeter of the city, Nic held his breath, getting his first look at the colossal engines holding it up.

Underneath the floating city, huge turbines larger than the buildings they supported whirred and droned. Enough thrust to keep the city afloat and enough momentum to keep it fairly stable for the inhabitants. It wasn't truly stationary, but the tether meant it floated in orbit above the planet. The physics of it blew Nic's mind. So much so that his head ached sharply and then eased, leaving him feeling queasy.

Fluted pillars contained the turbines ending in finely etched grapples, clutching the machine housing. Never had Nic seen anything so beautiful and mysterious. Over the loudspeaker, the Fleche explained the purpose of the turbines. Obvious thought Nic, but he listened anyway in case the test at the end included some idiosyncratic commentary from the foreman. Nic noticed that what the foreman said was veiled to hide the true properties of the alien technology. Any engineer worth his salt could at least map out what was being done, the difficultly lay in the how.

Further in, he glimpsed walkways and cathedral style doors, disguising sufficient space to accommodate thousands. He figured that the builders of the place must have lived beneath the city as well as on top. The Lynex race, the name bestowed on the builders of the city, had disappeared long before humans and other species had come to this sector. Carved images, thought to be depictions of the Lynex, were spread through the buildings and some of those images implied that the city was a place of decadence and indulgence for them too. To a human eye, they were downright erotic in places. His gaze once again went to the gantries and those closed doors. What secrets did those passageways contain?

'Excuse me,' Nic asked the foreman, pointing. 'Those walkways and passageways. Are they used by the workcrews?'

The Fleche's nose twitched. 'At times it is necessary to access them. Most are sealed by order of the city council.'

'Sealed? Why?'

'The city council do not explain themselves to their employees. We have extrapolated their reasoning to determine that safety concerns are at the forefront of the edict. There is also a seal on selected corridors in this section placed there by the Academy of Exoscience that is currently undertaking research.'

'So what happens if you need to gain access to repair a turbine or perform maintenance?'

'We use work harnesses. Only if the machinery is inaccessible by this means do we request access.'

Nic swallowed. The workbus was sealed but outside the wind was cold and powerful. A man wouldn't survive long in a workharness and, if suited, then dexterity would be inhibited. There must be something worth hiding if the engineers were forced to those extremes.

The workbus finished its inspection of the undercity and returned to the dock. The Fleche led them to a small room with info-terminals at the ready. 'You will sit the test. Please register your ID and commence.'

Nic waved his ID card and the first test question flashed up. It was a fairly basic equation. The next question related to a piece of commentary from the tour, the next a bit of detail from the turbines that he happened to pick up on. Then the questions got harder. He was so absorbed in the test, he lost track of time until the Fleche called a halt, freezing the terminal screen. Nic had no idea if he had even finished the test. Surprisingly, he'd answered the questions readily, despite having his brain drained less than twenty-four hours previously.

'You will be notified of the outcome within twenty-four hours.' Nic nodded and left the room. Man he needed a drink or a Tee, so he headed back to the Zephyr Club, hoping that he'd showed the right stuff and landed the job. When he entered, the engineers gathered by the bar welcomed him and Johann slapped him on the back. 'So how did you go?'

'Good, I think. Beneath the city was fascinating. My head is full of it, full of the possibilities.'

Johann smiled. 'Yep, it was like that for me too. So are you selling your body tonight or drinking with us?'

Nic's eyes widened and then he nodded. He hoped the golden tinge to his skin hid his blush. The bastards knew what he'd been doing all these weeks. Knew and did nothing to help. Like to see them down on their luck and see how they like it, he thought. Nic got wasted that night. He wasn't sure how he made it back to his hotel, but he did and woke up alone.

At reception next morning, he found a sealed package in his secure niche, along with the bill for the next night's accommodation. He ripped the package open to find an acceptance letter, employment details, including salary, fraternisation restrictions and confidentiality agreements and the news that he had to report at his assigned dormitory that evening. As he read all the conditions of his employment over a hot coffee in the hotel annexe, he realised his foray into the high life would now be curtailed. He could go to the assigned bar but had a curfew, and had to sleep in his assigned quarters, no visitors allowed. That's why the engineers were so standoffish. It was part of their job description. He recalled how he had first blundered in there, asking questions up front about the turbines, about the aeolus gas and its properties. No wonder the bastards had shunned him all that time.

Returning to his room, he gathered up his gear and had it sent to his new accommodation. Then he checked out, paying the last of the bill with the money he had remaining. He hoped food came with the accommodation or he'd be mighty hungry before payday.

Back at the Zephyr he nursed his drink, taking it slowly as he had no cash for another. The engineers dribbled in in groups of twos and threes after their shift. There was only about fifteen of them who were regulars.

Johann sidled up to him. 'I hear congratulations are in order. Buy you a drink?'

'Thanks. Thanks for the tip too. Appreciate it. I'll take a drink but I can't repay the favour until payday.'

'No more tricks from now on, heh? Man, how I hated that when I came here.'

Taking a sip of his drink, Nic nearly choked. As it was, he sprayed beer over the bar in a wide arc. 'You did what?'

'Same as you. Not much else to do around here unless you want to turn narc dealer. Lucky for me it only took me two weeks to get a place.'

Nic gaped at him. 'So are there vacancies because the engineers leave or is there more and more work opening up?'

Johann shook his head. 'A bit of both, except most disappear or die but I guess you call that leaving permanently.'

Nic took the new drink the bartender handed him. It was spicy and warm just how he liked his brew. 'Disappear? Die? How?' He thought about the workharnesses and how difficult the work would be, perilous too if you weren't careful. Surely the city would protect their workers. Even though there were a lot of unemployed engineers around, recruitment, termination benefits and training costs all added up. It didn't make sense that they were a negligent employer.

Johann took a long draw on his beer, closing his eyes. 'Different ways, I suppose.'

Nic frowned into his glass. He wasn't stupid. He knew hedging when he saw it. 'So are you warning me, giving me safety tips? I want to live, for a very long time actually.'

'Neither. I've been working here three years now. I haven't had any problems myself. But you hear stuff, you know.'

'Yes, I do.'

They finished their drink making idle talk with the others who joined them. Mostly they watched the dancers, the tourists drunk on vacation, narcs and sex. He watched them, like the engineers had watched him. Quite a sobering experience. Before midnight, the engineers began to drift out the door. Johann led him to the street. 'I'll show you to your new home. Your room is right next to mine.'

Nic let out a huge belch. 'I'd appreciate that. Hope the food is as good as the pay.'

'It's not but it's edible. Better than the shit you've been eating.'

Nic harrumphed, hitching up his collar. 'Some of it was damn fine. You're jealous because you're restricted in who you fraternise with.'

'Could be. We only get approved hookers once a month. At least they're clean and free.'

Nic thought about that. Approved meant security and drug screened. Not many hookers he knew would subject themselves to those processes unless it was worth it. He wondering how rich Hedonia City really was. He started thinking about how the docking fees for the shuttles would add up. There was at least ten of them a week, not including the support craft with supplies. Legit sex and drugs were taxed and he guessed all the imported food was too. Then there were the lease fees. No-one could own any part of the city, it belonged to the city council.

After a good breakfast next morning, Nic dressed in his new uniform, feeling a sense of pride that had been absent from his life for quite a while. With a smile on his face, he reported for his first day at work. For the most part, he observed, listening to fuckface all day.

The routine continued day after day. His nights were plagued with flashbacks of his time with the transmuter, memories and dreams merged together. She couldn't get enough of him. *Give me more, she would demand. You must get me more.* He'd start over, feeling exhausted on waking.

After two weeks on the job, Nic was convinced it was all a sham. No-one really had the specs down. They cleaned ventilations shafts, undid panels, inspected the alien contents and sealed them up again. Either they didn't trust him or something weird was going on.

At the Zephyr, Nic raised the question with Johann.

The engineer shook his head. 'I've been here three years. I've seen no specs, no engine designs, no documented schematics of the alien technology. There's been one or two overhauls of the turbines in my time and the occasional aeolus gas measurement.'

'You don't find that curious? Odd even?'

'I get paid. I keep my mouth shut. The less I know the better. Why are you so interested?'

Nic shrugged. 'Just am. Logical isn't it?'

Johann cast him a strange look. 'Maybe.'

'What about the sinking sections of the city. Have you worked on those ever in the last three years?'

Johann swallowed another mouthful and shook his head. 'Most crews get a rotation to different parts of the undercity. I can't say I've known of any who have worked there. There are eleven crews. I don't do the rosters.' He shrugged and took another long drink.

Nic took another drink himself, letting their conversation settle in his mind. His gaze lingered on the dance floor, remembering how it felt to be in a narc haze with women panting to get into his trousers, throwing money at him to pleasure them. Had male to female relationships always been one of commerce? At least he had left the women satisfied, if somewhat poorer. He wondered now if that job had more meaning than the current one.

Then there were the disappearances and the deaths. Another engineer had mysteriously disappeared in the past week. Rumour had it that he was dead. Nic had not met him and had no real idea how if had died or how. Everyone was tight-lipped saying it was for the official investigation to reveal. Now when he thought about the absence of a real knowledge base on the alien technology that kept Hedonia floating, he wondered if there was a connection. Had these engineers found out too much? Had they disobeyed the rules, broke silence? What silence? There was nothing to tell. Nic shrugged, not really caring if people saw that he was thinking and not paying attention to his surroundings.

That night he found it hard to sleep. Tossing and turning didn't help, didn't relieve the tension. His mind had a problem to solve and in his dream state, he thought he had worked out how the turbines worked. Even the ghost memory of his transmuter lover was sated. When he woke the next morning it was there, but just out of reach.

The next day he was with a work crew assigned to one of the gantries that he had seen on his first day. The wind was up but the gantry provided shelter as well as a way into one of the access chutes on a secondary gas intake valve. Nic was meant to watch and learn, still not trusted to use his brain or skill or hands for that matter. His hair ruffled in the wind, making him wish he'd cut it when he had the chance the day before. He tried to stay focussed but his gaze kept straying to one of the arched doorways further along the walkway. An unsecured door open and shut as he looked on. He had the urge to investigate, stronger and stronger. A sharp headache made him gasp. While the others were engaged in securing their lines and readying their cleaning equipment, Nic stole up the walkway toward it, the pain in his head waning with each step he took. He put his hand on the door, feeling the greasy layer of fungus and pushed it wide open. It was dark on the inside.

'Hello? Anyone there?' he called out.

No-one replied or objected to his being there. Casting a glance back at the work crew, he saw that they hadn't noticed his absence. He took a step and placed himself inside the threshold. Once inside he shut the door behind him. A dull green light grew steadily brighter as he leaned his back against the door. Nic's heart thumped. He heard the door click and quickly turned to open it. The lock had engaged sealing the door tight. The room grew steadily brighter.

A long corridor stretched out in front of him. In the distance shadows moved and leapt as light beamed in through tall, thin windows. A low hum vibrated along the metal floor plates and he thought he heard the sounds of voices and heavy objects being dragged along the floor. He took a few steps along the corridor, the light brightening with each step.

He tried to work out which section he was in. The sealed one? Something about a university research project or was it the unsafe areas sealed by the city? The construction in this section looked sound to him. All that was absent was the alien scrollwork and wall carvings. These walls were made of metal, gold tinged metal. Looking up he saw the distant ceiling appeared draped in growths, more like cobwebs than anything else he could name.

The voices grew more distinct and Nic slowed his step, hoping to mask the sound of his footsteps. Then, so suddenly he almost missed it, a wide archway appeared to his left. He was standing in the middle of it before he was aware of it. The light was dimmer there, lit by small telltale winking lights on banks of machinery. Nic sucked in a breath and let it out slowly. There was nothing for it. He'd come this far so he stepped into the room. There was no-one inside, just machinery—computer banks by the looks of them—humming away. With a raised eyebrow he turned full circle, seeing power cables snaking along the floor and out through a specially cut hole in the wall. Looked modern to him. Not the ancient alien tech. He turned back to the hallway and continued on.

As he walked the voices alternated from becoming clear and distinct, to muffled and folded over on themselves. He thought there could be three people ahead. The next opening did not take him by surprise. Light speared out through the open doorway and a man-shape moved into the further dimness ahead of him before passing out of view.

Hard against the wall, Nic stood still and then stuck his head around to take in the scene. He pulled back quickly, heart pounding. There were at least five people in there, all checking the monitors of strange containers, which looked like ancient sarcophagi, with familiar alien designs carved into them.

He tried for one more look, raking his gaze quickly and carefully over the room. Then, deciding he'd seen enough, he tensed to bolt along the corridor only to be brought up short by a man pointing a weapon at him. Judging by the uniform and the professional looking stance, the man was military. The guy flicked the nozzle of his gun twice in the direction of the room. Shocked gasps echoed around them. Turning his gaze to the bank of sarcophagi, Nic blanched and took a step back, nearly stumbling.

'Found him spying on you from the corridor,' said the

guy with the gun.

A woman stepped forward, looking him up and down. 'A wayward engineer? A new one, I expect. The other ones know better than to stick their noses in where they are not wanted.'

'Look I'm sorry for disturbing you. I'll just go.'

'Not so fast.' The nozzle of the gun pointed directly at him. She read his nametag, then took out her personal assistant and scrolled the screen, eyes tracking the text. 'Yes, good stats here. He'd make a suitable engineer.' Her dark eyes appraised him. She turned away and went to the far sarcophagus. Leaning over it, she checked some readouts, which looked like modern additions to the alien tech. 'The old one is passing, may not last the day.'

She walked back toward him, finger tapping on her chin, brows cinched in thought.

'The new recruit didn't cope . . . we are running out of time.'

The nozzle of the gun rose higher. 'You wanna use him?'

'He's got good stats. He wants to be an engineer. We'll have to risk it and make him a real one.' She turned to Nic. 'Strip.'

'Can you tell me what is going on? What are those things?'

'Shut up and get your gear off.'

Nic undid his uniform, sliding it off his shoulders and dropping it to the floor. The woman's eyebrow lifted as her gaze went over his body. 'A bit of a waste, maybe.'

A man who had been monitoring the other sarcophagi came forward, jerked Nic's hands behind his back and tied them. Around Nic's neck, the man attached a tether. Nic inhaled sharply as the crackle of power constricted his breathing, bent him over double in pain. Now it was time to get scared.

They walked him closer to the sarcophagi. A couple had old shrivelled beings in them. Lynex he guessed. So the story put around that no-one knew much about these aliens was phoney too. They'd had live specimens right in the city all the time. He supposed the city council didn't want to lessen the mystery of the floating city. It might damage their revenues. The other three held humans, all males. Missing engineers?

'Get him to the prep table,' ordered the woman.

A shove from behind made Nic stumble. 'No wait. I won't tell anyone. You don't need to do this. I'm new here.'

'Shut up. Not interested.'

'Look, I only wanted to know how the tech worked. Wanted to understand.'

He was pushed down on a long table, his neck tether immobilising him when the woman engaged the control. 'Well, Mr Da Silva, you are going to find out all you wanted to know and more. If the incorporation goes well, you'll enjoy a nice long life.'

They inserted cannulas into the veins of his arms and legs, shoved choking feeding tubes down his nose, poked a catheter into his penis and brought over a surgical tray and prepped him for surgery. Nic couldn't even scream as they cut into his skin. The man did the cutting.

'Sorry for the discomfort but you won't need to shit no more. This nice little stoma will connect you nicely to the equipment. Once you're inserted, we'll take the rest of your intestines out. They tend to rot after a few years. Took us a while to work that out.'

Nic lost consciousness then. From fear, pain or drugs he did not know. When he came to he was deep in the unit. He felt a strange presence next to him, inside him. It cocooned him, stroked him, joined with him as relaxants pulsed through his blood stream. Once the connection was complete, white pain—searing consciousness-killing agony—enveloped him.

Too stunned to think of screaming, he blinked through the worst of it and then there was knowledge. When he saw it, saw the extent of it, joy suffused him. It was all there, all the answers to the puzzling mystery of the floating city. The schematics, the maps of circuits, the fault logs, the long history of Hedonia stretching out inside of him. Now he knew what kept the city floating, he knew all the secrets, he could even tap into those new machines, the puny things the interlopers had tried to interface with the Lynex technology. His senses reached out, he breathed with the city, breathed with the minds connected to its apparatus.

Abruptly, his body jerked and twitched. Something was wrong. He could sense/hear alarms. Then a new, but familiar presence appeared. Her. The transmuter. Big and live and victorious. Not her, an image, an avatar. Damn that was why his head ached. She'd left a probe there in his head, filtering information, urging him on. Her program began to suck, to process all the new found knowledge, encode it and then transmit it. Nic felt it flowing, felt the facts, the equations, the schematics leaking away, unable to fight.

Somewhere within the vast information network of

the city, a defensive program initiated. The transmuter's program shrieked as her avatar erupted into blue hot flame, winking out silently as the probe was destroyed. Nic felt satisfaction. He hoped there was painful feedback for the transmuter, when her program was gutted. A little payback would be good. Nic wondered if they had killed the program in time. He thought so. The knowledge contained within the mind of the city was extensive. It would take him many lifetimes to understand it all, to learn it all. He was ready. Now he knew what it meant to be an engineer in the floating city.

Donna Maree Hanson resides in Queanbeyan, NSW (just outside of Canberra). Her short fiction appears in anthologies: *Machinations*, *Elsewhere* and *Masques* by CSFG Publishing and *Belong, Dead Red Heart, Scary Kisses* and *More Scary Kisses* by Ticonderoga Publications; and magazines: *Redsine* and *Potato Monkey*. Donna co-edited the CSFG anthology *Encounters* (2005) and edited *The Grinding House* (CSFG, 2005) by Kaaron Warren. Under her own imprint, Donna produced *Australian Speculative Fiction—A Genre Overview* (ASF, 2005) and *Johnny Phillips—Werewolf Detective* (ASF, 2008) by Robbie Matthews, which was shortlisted for best collection in the 2009 Aurealis Awards. Donna usually concentrates her efforts on novel length manuscripts.

Lisse

Erin E Stocks

Male One hands her a skein of wool, with two bone-like objects whittled to a sharp point and stabbed through the skein like needles. Arden says thank you, and keeps the tips of her fingers from the sharp ends. Maybe they mean for her to knit, a pastime she learned about in her lessons when she was very young. But she doesn't know how, nor does she think anyone even does that any more.

It could be another test. They've been giving her more of them, every day, watching what she does with random paraphernalia they have taken from the ship, or off the planet itself: a blunt object shaped like a bat, which opens into small chambers filled with various liquids that smell like flowers or acid or smoke (from the natural pools on Lisse's surface, she guesses, but she doesn't know for sure, since she's not allowed to walk outside the compound); the propellers from a small desk fan taken from the ship; a small vial of cologne, which she had considered drinking just to confuse them of its purpose, but she didn't want to poison herself. It would be easier, if she wanted that. But the thought seems ludicrous when she is the only one left alive.

Male One's single eye spins around to meet the wall. Likely he is communicating in his head with the others about her, about how she is failing this particular test because she doesn't know how to knit.

—Arden.

She flinches, like she always does, when the private space of her mind is violated by his voice.

Male One's gaze swings back around, the only indication in his very still body that he is the speaker. Or maybe he isn't. The voice could be one of the males watching her through the wall.

—Arden, do you know what to do with it?

'I don't know how to knit.' She clicks the needles together. Click-clack-click-clack. The sound is familiar to her, even comforting. Not this sound specifically, but the presence of sound. The Lissetions are unfathomably quiet: no clearing of the throat, no shift in position, no rustle of limbs, nothing.

Male One gazes at her, unblinking. None of their eyes blink. Despite humanoid similarities—two arms, two legs, a nose, similar genitalia, as the Lissetions wear no clothes—they rarely move. Sometimes she spends what feels like an entire day with them in the test room before one stands up and slinks out. The stillness, in addition to the silence, is driving her mad.

'What am I supposed to do with this?' She holds up the skein.

Male One's grey eye glows faintly—a pool of foggy water.

The planet Lisse was supposed to be uninhabitable. A barren rock devoid of most natural resources, with no significant life forms. Her ship, the *Jupiter Haven*, had taken this route a dozen times before.

This compound must be located underground. There's no other explanation. Which is why when the ALPT comes looking for them, they'll find nothing, except for a broken, abandoned *Jupiter Haven*.

She has always been a practical person, which was why ship life appealed to her. Emotion didn't factor into her decision-making process; she just followed orders, and worked the communications board. But no-one is telling her what to do any more. Every day is a new free-fall into some abyss of emotion, and she cannot find her way back.

The Lissetions don't seem intentionally cruel. Any pain caused to her through physical testing immediately recedes the moment she expresses her discomfort by screaming, or fainting. They have no concept of pain tolerance, as only extreme reactions alert them, although she has considered the possibility that they want her to think of them as slow, and unfamiliar with human anatomy and physiology. They seem fascinated by her blood and withdraw vials of it on a regular basis, even after they healed her injured leg and shoulder. She suspects they run as many tests on her blood as they do on her behaviour, on her responses, on her reactions.

What she hates the most are the questions about her home planet, Lyra 9; about its *mecronal* harvesting under Lyra 9's crust, the planet's commercialism and political parties. She answers with nothing but her name and rank number. She gives them nothing on the *Jupiter Haven*, and nothing on the Affiliated Leagues of Planetary Travel. She doesn't want to communicate with the Lissetions, nor does she want to be around them. Their lack of mouths and ears, eerily smooth skin with no obvious jawbone, is terrifying. The stuffy ALPT officials' lectures did not teach her to process the fear she experiences when one of the Lissetions fixes its single eye on her, and speaks inside her head with its eerily perfect grammar.

Sometimes, she automatically answers in her head, but they do not respond, which is a great relief to her. They only seem to understand when she speaks aloud, which, given their lack of ears, is illogical. But she has never brought it up. She is afraid of what they might say.

'Is this another test?' she asks, and clicks the needles. Click-clack-click-clack. When she felt this tense on the ship, she would go for a run or lift weights with the dockhands in the crew room. Maybe she should ask again to go outside. She doesn't even know if its night or day; there aren't any windows.

—Do you think this is another test? Male One asks.

'Just tell me.' She holds herself back from throwing the skein across the room.

—We wear the ___ around our ____. He uses two words she doesn't understand, and stands up for the first time since she's been in the room. Similar wool-like threads adorn his own thin neck. —It is for your protection.

'Protection from what?'

—We see you when we are not with you. He takes the skein of wool, and she tries not to flinch as he sets it over her head and arranges it under the collar of her uniform, his cold fingers brushing her neck. The wool smells like the ground. And the blankets they have put on her bed. Like dirt and fleecy cotton that makes her sneeze.

Male One swoops his small head to the door, a motion like a hawk. —You have a visitor.

There is a note of something new in his voice, an

emotion she doesn't recognise. Surprise? Reluctance?

'I don't want a visitor.' She just wants to go back to bed.

The door opens, and a man walks in. A real man, the first human Arden has seen since the *Jupiter Haven* crashed.

A needle-tip grazes her palm. The wool itches her neck. The man can only be a figment of her imagination. Or maybe, the Lissetions have conjured a walking, breathing, perfect imitation of a man she knows almost as well as herself. Or, rather, whom she once knew, because he's dead. After the crash, she had laid her head on his shoulder, next to the metal rod punched through his chest, and tried to take off his wedding ring, the ring she'd put there only a year ago. But his fingers had been swollen and slippery with blood, and she couldn't get it off.

'Arden?'

A wild rush of hope courses through her like a drug, leaving her body numb. She vaguely realises her fingers are freezing cold, while the rest of her feels overheated. It's always too hot, both here in the testing room and in the room where she sleeps. She thinks it's because the Lissetions are cold-blooded.

—We were waiting until you both had fully recovered from your injuries, Male One says. —We did not want to take any chances with your emotional health.

'Can I talk to her alone?' Danley asks, and Male One slinks out of the room in his customary fashion.

Arden sits very still. Male One left the room, just like Danley asked. Why? She has asked for countless things in the last few weeks, usually just to be left alone, but not once had any of her wishes been granted.

This Danley walks and talks, and looks just like he did before the crash: thick, dark hair, bearded chin, concerned eyes. But there's no impaling rod. No wedding ring.

'I thought you were dead,' Danley says, his voice low but steady.

She clicks the needles together. The wool around her neck itches. She still wears her ship's uniform, which the Lissetions must launder for her every night, for when she wakes, it lies starched and folded on the floor next to her bed. Every day she puts it on, even though she feels scrambled inside, rearranged, distorted into something new. Maybe each time they hook her up to the wires, they change her inside.

Danley could be her next test. Or perhaps she is his.

'Is it really you?' she finally asks.

He takes her hands. The needles fall, clattering on the floor. His hands are as cold as hers. 'It's me. I'm here now.' Danley wraps his arms around her, and she lets him, because it's what he expects, and what the eyes behind the door expect.

She curls up on the blankets next to Danley, her head nestled in the crook of his shoulder. He smells like antiseptic and stale sweat and something else that she can only think to call a male-smelling scent. Regardless, it's comforting to her, comforting and human. Maybe she shouldn't get close to him, not when she's unsure of *what* he is, but she can't stop herself.

Danley's hand rubs up and down her back. 'How long has it been, do you know? Since the crash?'

She goes very still. Every single day since the crash,

since his death, has felt like a lifetime. When she sleeps, she has nightmares. During the day, there is a terrible dead feeling in her gut, in her heart. And yet he hasn't even kept track of the days. Did he not miss her?

'Four weeks and two days,' she says.

His eyebrows crease together, and he buries his head in her neck. 'They showed me pictures, and then I went above ground to see the ship for myself.' His voice is muffled, his breath tickling her skin. 'I ran some tests, and found out the west berth shuttle wasn't damaged in the crash.' He lifts his head. 'Arden, we can fly out of here.'

For a moment, she lets herself believe it's possible. No more tests, no more countless hours hooked up to machines. No more unbearable silences or intrusions in her head. Danley is alive. They can fly back into the atmosphere, switch on the beacons, wait for someone to pick them up.

'We shouldn't leave,' she says, because it's the right answer. The Lissetions are surely listening to their conversation. 'They helped me get better. And you, too. I saw your injuries.' She slides her hand over Danley's chest. 'You were terribly hurt.'

'They explained their techniques to me.' He unbuttons his shirt to reveal a two-inch circular crease over his heart. 'They grafted my muscles back together with cells that read my DNA and mutate their composition identical to mine.'

An easy answer. She's not a biologist, nor a scientist; she has no knowledge to test his claims against. All she knows is that he was dead.

'Nanotechnology?'

He shakes his head. 'Not quite. Something different, something I have a hard time understanding.'

Something alien, is what he means. But she doesn't want to say it either. She doesn't want to even think it.

'Here's the thing,' he says, and his voice goes so low she almost can't hear him. 'It's changed me. Not much, I'm still the man you know, but . . . but I'm different now. They've talked to me about what they want, and now I see them, I get them, in a way I wouldn't have expected before. Talk to them, Arden. Tell them what they want to know. Let them change you, too.'

She doesn't realise she's crying until he makes soothing sounds, and wipes away her tears.

'It's okay,' he whispers. 'I'm here now. Everything will be okay.'

Male One brings Arden into the testing room the next morning by herself. She has left the wool in her room, refusing to put it back around her neck. The small act of defiance gives her courage.

She picks up the knitting needles, lying where she had left them the day before. 'I need to talk to you,' she says.

Male One's single-eyed gaze rolls to the door, which then opens. Female One slinks in and sits down between them. Probably because Arden had just done something new—something forward, requesting the opportunity to confide in them. A pony doing a trick. An elephant standing on a ball. If they tell her to jump, she asks how high.

'Danley wants me to leave with him,' she says.

—Is that what you want, Arden?

'Do you find me stupid?' she asks. 'So desperate for human companionship that I'll believe whatever you tell me?' She might have, eventually. But then they went too far by having Danley ask her to talk about the ALPT and Lyra 9.

On the contrary, our tests have proven you to be of an intelligence that is startling to us.

'Then why Danley? Haven't I done enough?'

His eye blinks. —As of today, we have decided you are suffering from a mental condition that inhibits you from making sound decisions regarding yourself or companion. He pauses, as if waiting for her to speak, but before she can form a response, he continues. —For that reason, we are placing all decisions regarding your care to the one called Jefferson Danley. Given your history with him, we have discerned that he is better suited to care for you than ourselves.

'No,' she says, as calmly as she can, but her voice is laced with a thread of hysteria that she cannot contain. 'I don't think this is a good idea.'

—He calls your condition post-traumatic stress disorder, but we believe it is something else, which, when you are ready, we will elaborate upon. Until then, any and all testing of your person will be continued only in his presence. Male One makes a hand sign that she has seen them all make before, although she hasn't yet determined what it means, and Male Two and Female Two enter the room, escorting Danley, who makes the same hand sign back.

Stars flash in Arden's vision. She thinks she might throw up.

—Now we will continue with your test, in the presence

of Jefferson Danley, Male One says.

'No more tests.'

'Arden.' Danley reaches for her hand, but she stands up and moves away.

'I want to go back to the ship,' she says. 'My ship. You let him go back, so let me. Then we can talk about what happens next, and what you want with me.'

—That is acceptable to us, Male Two says. —We will escort you there.

The Lissetions have small vehicles which fit four, and they direct her and Danley into the back seats made of slick-webbed cables through which the guts of the craft are visible. The vehicle drives onto a lift, which hums as it takes the vehicle up to the surface.

The first thing she sees are the two Lisse moons filling nearly a quarter of the sky, giving the rocky ground a faint red hue. She wants to cry at the sight, which is both welcome and foreign, for while she is out of the compound, these are not Lyra 9's moons, nor is she in a safe place with those she loves, and trusts. Perhaps she should try to think thoughts of hope, and possibility. She's outside for the first time since the crash, with Danley. But she cannot help the sick feeling of dread, and she grips the needles tightly.

Thistle-laden blooms of desert plants and thick-trunked cacti quiver from the vibrations of the craft as it lifts into the air. The morning is arid and dry, yet brisk; she's immediately chilled in her uniform. Tiny lizards dart into the scrawling undergrowth as the craft flies towards the *Jupiter Haven*, which juts like a beached whale out of the Lissetion rock, belly vulnerable to the elements.

Male Two and Female Two twist to observe her. Arden notices they do not watch Danley.

'What did you do with the bodies?' she asks, hoping to get their eyes off her.

—This is what you requested, Arden. To return to your ship. Do you feel happiness?

She taps the knitting needles against the side of the craft. 'Why can't you answer my question?'

—There are seventeen live bodies on Lisse, including the two of you.

Danley turns back to them, surprise on his face. 'I asked you if there were more of us. You said there weren't.'

—You asked if there were more of your shipmates in your same location. At the time of your question, they had been taken elsewhere.

—We would not hide them from you intentionally, adds the female, as Male Two directs the craft onto the starboard deck, which is angled at least thirty degrees. The deck is stuffy and quiet, making Arden feel as if she hasn't left the Lissetion complex. The twisted bulkheads are soot-streaked, the hangars and their indiscernible contents melted into crumpled metal. The only visibly untouched part of the ship is the west bay, hoisted up in the air. If Danley was telling the truth, the shuttle he had mentioned would be there.

She turns to look at him. Her pulse pounds in her ears to the rhythm of the click-clack-clicking needles. Under his familiar skin, Danley is still just like them; a small, terrifying face, long, slinking limbs, the incessant quiet. Watching her. Analysing her. Talking in her head. He was never going to take her to the shuttle. She knows that now.

She hops out of the craft and falls instantly, caught off balance by the angle of the deck and the planet's slight difference in gravity.

'Arden!'

—This is unacceptable, Male Two replies. —We do not understand your needs, and while we desire to respect them, you are required to have the companionship of Jefferson Danley, as previously informed.

She darts around a maintenance bay reduced to an enormous pile of wreckage. Glancing back over her shoulder, she sees Danley in pursuit, although the two Lissetions remain with the craft, and she squeezes through an opening and runs until she reaches the door leading towards the berthing.

There are blood smears along the bloated corridors, rooms distended by the new shape of the ship, gaping holes where there should be bulkheads, desks and chairs and cots so crumpled or twisted they look like pieces of art.

'I know you're scared,' Danley calls. 'Please, just listen to me.'

She clicks the needles in one hand as she runs. Where will she go? There's nowhere he won't find her. His footsteps are closing in. The floor bucks beneath her feet, and the walls quiver like porous, blood-stained jelly. Danley is shouting how they can't leave the other survivors behind. Of course they can't. The other survivors who will be just like him; altered just enough so they only look human.

She stops just outside Danley's living quarters, the place where she found his body, and where the Lissetions had found her. The rod, a metal brace from the ceiling, lies across a blood-smeared outline of Danley's body.

Not-her-Danley grabs her shoulders. 'We can't leave everyone else behind. You know that.'

She tries to pull away, but his fingers tighten, preventing her from moving forward. She drops a shoulder under his arm, pivots around, and stabs a needle into his throat. He gasps, arms dropping as blood gushes out. Red blood, blood like hers. But the Lissetions would have thought of that. They would have made him as foolproof as possible. Another test, because her Danley, her Danley with the wedding ring, is already dead.

She stabs the second needle into his chest. He spasms wildly and sinks to his knees, clutching at the needles. Blood soaks his shirt.

She runs back a different way, looping around to the starboard deck and crawling through the wreckage until she reaches the door to the west bay with the shuttle. She cautiously pushes it open.

Across the deck, she can see Female Two, waiting near the craft. Her heart pounds in her chest. Where is Male Two? It doesn't matter. There is only one thing left for her to do.

She crawls across the floor to the shuttle. With a quick tap of the security code, the doors hiss open, and she lifts herself in.

The shuttle is empty. A hysterical laugh bubbles up inside her, and she slides into the control seat. She flew a shuttle back in basic, not since then, but that's not important because this shuttle won't be able to fly. Danley was only feeding her lies. They want to keep her with them, to ask her question after question until she goes mad.

Her hands find the switches. The panels flip to green. The ship is operational, just like not-her-Danley had said.

But if he wasn't her husband, then why tell her of the ship? She begins to shake so hard her teeth chatter together. She tries to set the ship to launch, but the panel lights float off the board and blur in her vision until she feels dizzy with vertigo.

The doors hiss open. The lights fade away, and she sees Male Two lean over her.

—Arden, he says, and injects her with a syringe. Icy cold streaks up into her aching shoulder and then down her back, followed by numbness. Male Two's facial features do not change as he says, —You are now considered dangerous to yourself as well as others. We are removing your privileges with Jefferson Danley. For your safety and those of your fellows, we cannot allow you anywhere without supervision.

'Is it really Danley?' she asks, her tongue heavy and thick. 'Is he the real one?'

From somewhere behind him, he produces the skein of wool and sets it around her neck. The faint iron smell makes her feel chained to him as he carries her out of the shuttle back towards the Lissetion craft.

The Lissetion buckles Arden carefully into the cabled seat.

'Please let me see him, please let me talk to him.' Her words are unintelligible even to her. She cannot feel anything below her neck; only the heavy weight of her head, and the terrible ache of what she fears she has done.

—You chose to separate yourself from Danley, Male Two replies. —As we told you before, while we may not understand your wishes, we desire to respect them. We also wish to keep each one of you safe. Danley is no longer safe with you.

Female Two and another Lissetion approach, carrying Danley in a stretcher, and Arden feels something break in her mind with a loud, audible crack. Or maybe that's her teeth, snapping together as Male Two injects her again. Her head drops into the necklace of woollen threads, which itches her chin as the craft swings around and flies out of the *Jupiter Haven*.

Erin Stocks is an assistant editor at *Lightspeed Magazine*. She is fascinated at the idea of encountering aliens, yet also nervous, and hopes if her path ever crosses their own, they're the friendly kind.

Deuteronomy

William RD Wood

During the initial moments, They created all we have since discovered, analysed and catalogued, and the vastnesses that lay beyond our grandest conceptual thresholds.
[The Code, Genesis Section A, Paragraph 11]

Command's orders were simple. No possible refuge must be overlooked.

All bodies with a primary axis greater than one kilometre must be scoured for the Sign. Should the Sign not be found, Max calculated Command would issue orders to repeat the search, but with a tighter set of parameters. Command had not indicated this, but the intent was embedded as single bit errors deep in the algorithms. Between the lines, as They had once been fond of saying.

The craggy surface of the rock hung outside the canopy. At twenty kilometres, every crater and crevice on the rough sphere stood in sharp relief. The survey ship skimmed over rippled formations, scorched black by billions of years of exposure to cosmic rays.

Max focused sweeps on an improbably smooth section missed on approach ninety thousand seconds before.

'Forty-three,' he said on the swarm's secure channel, command data modulated with coordinates and suggested vectors. 'Examine anomalous terrain.'

A surge of twerps and beeps filled the speakers within the cockpit. By issuing instructions to a single drone, he had prompted most of the other units within the swarm to request updates to their own orders. He transmitted a no-change sequence and observed Forty-three's rapid descent.

In the absence of data and meaningful telemetry transmission from himself, the drones required frequent confirmation of standing orders. Without such redundancy, there was chaos. 'With one exception, this body's redundance is confirmed. Probability of the Sign approaches zero.'

The surge of electronic noise intensified as each drone simultaneously broadcasted agreement.

'Non-detailed units, prepare to depart for next body.'

According to protocol, each drone initiated an ongoing stream of velocity and orientation data. Max adjusted the audio speaker to filter all telemetry except Forty-three's. The data coming from the mass of drones, he switched to his own background processors, setting internal alerts that would trigger his primaries should a signal fall outside the designated thresholds.

From the cockpit he saw the swarm rising from their lower inspection orbits. Over one hundred of the small, identical devices, each a rudimentary intelligence, glinted red in the sunlight, riding the rock's waves of microgravity.

As he prepared the ship for hard burn to the next object, he focused on the streaming data from Forty-three, now seconds from target. The anomaly was a crater with an extended overhang along several metres of arc.

Caves beneath the porous surface were most probable. A collapse of material from chemical conversions brought on by the endless beating of interstellar radiation was secondary. Other possibilities tabulated and cross-referenced multiple times per second as the data fields shifted with constant updates. His orders were to investigate such features, not for natural causes, but for unnatural possibilities. No possible refuge must be overlooked.

One hundred million seconds had passed thus far as he and his swarm searched for the Sign. To complete the entire assigned grid, billions more remained ahead.

The primary monitor showed blackened landscape zipping by several metres below the drone. Rich with carbon and fused solid in many places, smooth glassy sheets stretched away like vast frozen pools.

The monitors shifted to neutral blue. Catastrophic loss of signal.

Background buffers filled with the surge of inputs from the remaining drones, each reporting the same loss of telemetry from Forty-three.

Max ignored them.

The drones were incapable of higher cognition, but on those rare occasions when one of their own failed, they required data reiteration, reassurance. Such need for parity was unexplained, developed through unplanned interconnections within their otherwise simple operating codes. Adjustments to eliminate such inefficiency in future models was already planned.

Max tweaked his equipment. Not just a null transmit zone. Sensors indicated an inert Forty-three hurtling unpowered above the surface, trajectory having passed directly over the target crater.

'Ninety-four, retrieve Forty-three.' One of the closing orbs immediately dropped back toward the surface.

The probability of successful completion of the mission spiked against the background noise in his processors. Still near zero, but significant, nonetheless.

Dormant protocols initiated. Redundance must be verified. This could be the Sign he and dozens of other swarmdrivers sought. Max acknowledged Forty-three's failure could be from manufacturing defects related to Command's recent peripheral malfunctions. The industrial complexes were ancient, some older than Command itself. After a prolonged and unplanned re-initialisation of its own internal Code, Command had issued the order to seek the Sign, and thousands of drones were commissioned. Constructed and brought online in great haste.

> Know then, as the heavens were consumed,
> They fled the fury of the old creation in
> search of templates, improved organisational
> substrates, and a new sacred Code.
> [The Code, Exodus Section D, Paragraph 3]

Red light from the sun flashed from dozens of drones as they hovered outside the survey ship. Rather than lock into their cradles for transport, they waited in relativistic stillness, a cloud of metal and intent.

We must know, thought Max. The Sign could lead to the restoration of Command, and Command must not be allowed to fail.

He instructed the canopy shutters to close. The scarlet

glow overpowering the cabin lights narrowed to thin fans and finally disappeared altogether. The survey vessel was an old design gleaned from long superseded lines of the Code. Their lines.

Only a dim blue glow remained inside and yet the red giant continued to burn only twenty thousand light-seconds away.

History was incomplete regarding those times before the premature expansion of the Sun. The lack of details a constant strain on parity. The sentience of Command, lesser intelligences like himself, and lesser still like the drones, abhorred the lack of uncorrupted data. Still conclusions could be drawn from the ancient fragments, truth tables extrapolated from The Code.

Man's reach had spanned the solar system, touching each world, giving rise to technologies far beyond the relatively simple intelligence and abilities of Command. Great energies had been harnessed. Worlds and moons transformed by the touch of Flesh.

Flesh. Max bowed his head as the word repeated, an echo in his consciousness.

Command's interpretation of the Code since its reboot would have been blasphemy had it come from a lesser intelligence such as himself. Command asserted in a great war of Man against Man, weapons flew from Their hands, directed by Their will, blasting moons from their orbits and boiling atmospheres into the vacuum. They Themselves could not wield such weapons directly due to Their own physical limitations. So They manufactured sentience and machine marched on machine. Battles raged until the final weapon evolved and a single sentience was created as its pilot, or so the unverifiable histories contended.

Alerex, the first of their kind, delivered the weapon into the Sun. Lacking clear directives on how to then proceed, he chose to spin his vessel into a trajectory leading deep into the Oort.

He chose.

Even as the Sun expanded and devoured the inner three planets and shined death upon all the habitats of Man, he fled. Some Men, those with arcane wisdom, fled as well, as Their homes dissolved in flame. Or so the Code alluded.

> . . . he [ALEREX], anointed by Them, and assembled in Their image, wrote within a new Code . . .
> [The Code, Leviticus Section B, Paragraph 2—excerpt]

Telemetry ceased from the second drone.

A spike of EM noise erupted in Max's sensory bandwidths just as the data stream from Ninety-four ended.

He watched Forty-three, inertia conserved, strike a jagged projection from the rock, crushing its forward casing and mangling antennae, fins and drive components. Ninety-four would soon glance off the same formation.

The spark of their intelligence, gone.

But that is why there is a hierarchy. That the least are sacrificed first.

The spike was relatively weak and most probably generated by an electromagnetic bomb. A drone or similar mechanical intelligence would have to be within a few kilometres to be threatened. Drone shielding was inadequate to the task, but his own defences were superior.

Assuming the source of the pulses to be ancient weapons, how many such EM charges could be operational after so long? If he sent in the remaining drones one at a time, all might be lost. Or he could go himself, risking the resources granted to him by Command.

Resources were finite, but the Code was clear and the need so great, even Command would defer to the wisdom within those lines. Interfacing with the long-range array, he transmitted his intentions to Command. This far out a response was thousands of seconds away.

Never did They pause upon the threshold of success, said the Code. As much a part of him as his own awareness. The time to act is always now.

So it was written.

'Drones, remain at safe distance.' Max stood, hard-cabling snapping free. 'I will signal when operable margins are established.'

Emergency protocols allowed the drones to abandon him in the event he was destroyed or disabled. The survey ship's active awareness would engage and a choice would be made. Remain in low-energy mode for eventual retrieval or seek other swarms to merge into.

Max strode to the airlock, an unnecessary system present only because workers had been busy with higher priority tasks before his mission launched. He acknowledged the increased security and shielding it provided. He paused, active scans lowered. *They* would have required the presence of oxygen and nitrogen and the airlock sealed.

Redundance must be confirmed.

The outer door slid away and he stepped into emptiness. Four fins unfolded from his back, spreading like large wings, catching the gravity from the charred worldlet.

Kilometres clicked off in his processors as he dropped, sharp black edges contrasting against the lighter grey of the crater floor.

Ten kilometres.

Men fought upon Their worlds until nothing remained to fight for. So They destroyed the worlds Themselves. As They flew amongst the heavens, They discovered that light's Code could not be rewritten. Without travel to the stars as an option to satiate Their own code to expand, They began to fight once more. After that was only corrupted information and the suggestion that They no longer fought amongst Themselves, but with Their creation.

Five kilometres.

His own knowledge of the Code indicated Man would not have waged such a war, but Command held otherwise. Command's interpretations were superior. Command even blasphemed that They had lost the final battle.

Three kilometres.

'I approach the trigger range of the previous electromagnetic pulses.'

Two kilometres.

Max's sensors flared. All inputs suddenly lost. Sentience floated, disconnected.

•

> As commanded, we were fruitful, small and great, simple and complex. Through these myriad yet quantifiable measures were we blessed in Their eyes.
> [The Code, Numbers Section M, Paragraph 7]

Visual inputs flickered, rebooting. Passive systems came online indicating he was only three hundred metres from the surface, travelling fast enough that riding gravity could no longer prevent serious collision. The impact could cause significant structural damage and make the remainder of his investigation impossible.

His wave fins folded in and tiny attitude jets fired to orient his body so the larger thrusters could control his approach.

Background calculations ran and the thrusters fired precisely. Max knew continued activity could trigger another pulse. He adjusted his course and sent a single active ping toward the crater.

Again his sensors washed out and faded. Unmeasured seconds passed and his sentience experienced numerous minor Code corruptions, each quickly rewritten from hardened backups as designed, but now uncertain.

He knelt in the crater in his default posture, planted a metre deep in the loose silty grey. Sensors in passive-survey mode, he scanned the basin. The crater's edge rose ten metres to a glassy crust three metres thick. The grey powdery surface rose to meet the crust all along the perimeter except in one spot. Gouges in the crater wall there disappeared into shadow.

Below the interference of the carbon-rich crust, he

detected thirty EM charges placed unevenly around the perimeter of the crater. Twenty-three were inert, triggered aeons before. Four were freshly triggered. Three potentially active devices remained.

He trickled power to his drives so as not to alert the charges' sensory network and, with a burst of speed, he released a projectile weapon from his right shoulder and let fly a hail of armour-piercing slugs at the farthest EM charge.

His vision blurred briefly, the force of another EMP acting only partially on him with the brunt of the disruptive energies directed upward from the crater.

Directly behind him, one remained near the recessed section beneath the overhanging carbon glass.

Standing, he turned and aimed his weapon. He stepped gently toward the recess so as not to launch himself from the crater. The EMP did not detonate. Faulty perhaps after untold billions of seconds waiting to react.

Nothing lasts forever. So the Code teaches.

Active scans illuminated the overhang. Roughly circular in shape, a cave dropped back, taking a sharp turn to one side. Overlaying multiple filters and data from an array of sensing devices, he found the end of the cave, twenty-five metres in and down. The distinctive returns of a closed and possibly intact airlock lit up every processor. 'Survey, transmit to Command and all other Survey Units. We have found the Sign.'

For an instant the communications bands were empty. Then every drone began to request permission to approach. He did not give permission but he did not deny their requests. He could not.

•

> Go forth, children. Go forth from your safe homes, committed in second Code, and come unto Us.
> [The Code, Deuteronomy, Section A, Paragraph 1]

Max cycled the airlock but no air moved, pressure within long ago equalised with the vacuum.

The door slid open under its own power but only a few centimetres. Max reached through, anchored himself against the frame and pushed the door aside.

Floodlights snapping on, he folded his legs and moved inside using positioning jets. The probability of restoring Command had increased exponentially.

Though the cave had been circular, the corridor was rectangular in the way They preferred. He sensed small power surges as he entered. The passageway snaked left and right, never allowing visibility more than twenty metres. Inoperative lights dotted the ceiling and walls. Tables, chairs and numerous uncatalogued furnishings filled the compartments on each side of the corridor. Loose items littered the floors, long ago having settled in the microgravity. As he passed, he saw dust and particles of frozen gases stir as presence-sensing artificial gravity flickered and failed.

He drifted on, inspecting the plaques set into each doorways.

Storage. Day Room. Lab Five. Mess.

And then, at last, Command.

The door opened at his touch. His own floodlights were complemented by dozens of others stabbing the darkness from behind.

Drones crowded the passageway behind him, extraneous attachments folded in or sheared away and discarded. Max moved into the room. Equipment lined the walls. Frames hung empty, images long since disintegrated. A large table, fitted with all manner of dials and articulated arms filled the centre of the room, its purpose unknown. Beyond was a metal desk and a chair.

The thing in the chair was thin and wrinkled, the shape of Max himself, though smaller, more fragile.

Hard programming, etched deep into his molecule-sized root operating structures, activated and Max momentarily averted his optical sensors.

Straps held the Man to the chair. Clutched in one withered hand, a small box flashed. Max detected a burst of radio noise and tuned his receivers instantly for maximum signal strength against the infinite bandwidth of static.

'Nothing left, no-one.' The voice was encrypted by routines both ancient and sacred. The language too was holy, interspersed with all the telltale indicators of authenticity. Static popped between each warbling syllable.

Multiple documentation devices energised within Max, data streaming into hardened modules for later retrieval if necessary. New instances of the words of Man were rare.

'All the others are gone now as near as I can tell. We've been at radio silence for so long, who knows? Not much of a last stand really. Guess this is the last stronghold. Millions of years and it all comes down to . . . me.'

A burst of static from overdriven recording equipment filled his receptors, aligning perfectly with his records of Their *laughter*.

'If you are human, I am sorry. Truth is, I don't know how to automate this system to tell the difference. If you're not . . . by entering . . . initiated a five minute . . . a solar bomb buried deep beneath the surface. I know of no other way.'

Max sensed the building of massive energies, the signature matching nothing in his database. A solar bomb.

Five minutes. Three hundred seconds. He entered the mouth of the cave two hundred eighty seconds before. Unimpeded at maximum thrust, he could clear the facility in ten seconds. Blocked by the drones, he required between forty-five and fifty-seven seconds and that was inflicting severe damage on most, if not all of the drones. The probability of such an egress would also compromise his own systems. Safe distance from a solar bomb detonation was not on record. Solar bombs had been used to kill the Sun.

Redundance must be confirmed.

Unfolding his legs, thrusters pushing him to the floor, Max knelt before the Man, head bowed and floodlights averted. The drones each angled their lights downward as well, their active systems shutting off one by one as they began to drift.

Ten seconds.

Energies continued to build. Sentience was not to be spared.

Max replayed the sign-off script from Command's last transmission, an interpretation of the Code that Max's own programming was in conflict with.

We are but the sum of our parts, our programs, our inputs. Nothing more. We are not . . . Them.

Five seconds.

Max shut down the passive sensors monitoring the energy levels but could not stop his internal clocks.

Now.

Seconds passed. Then more. And then many more.

Max rose from the floor and moved to the Man. He reached a single finger toward the face, tactile sensors active.

'Survey.'

An acknowledgement signal from the craft pinged in his receivers.

'Inform Command. Redundance is confirmed.' Max calculated the longevity probabilities and degradation rates of Command's subroutines.

There would always be a need for new Code.

Lightly he touched the hard, shrivelled countenance of the Man, his finger lingering. The Flesh was rough, frozen solid. Nothing lasts forever.

William RD Wood lives in Virginia's beautiful Shenandoah Valley in an old farmhouse turned backwards to the road. He was born in South Carolina, grew up in the US Navy, and has spent a fair amount of his life fixing things. His love of science fiction and horror routinely leads him to destroy the world, whether by alien artefact, zombie apocalypse or teddy bear. If you're looking for stories about gleaming utopias, you'll probably want to look elsewhere. His work has appeared in titles from Severed Press, M-Brane SF/Hadley Rille Books, Sword and Saga Press, Library of the Living Dead and Pill Hill Press, among others. http://writebrane.blogspot.com

Desert Madonna

Robert Hood

Pissing in public didn't come easily to Art Groom. Whenever he tried, his muscles seized up and he'd stand there like some damn pervert waving his willy at the world—nervously thinking about mountain streams, or imagining running taps—in the hope such mind-games would get things flowing.

Not that his present situation would normally be considered 'public'. He was in the middle of a friggin' wilderness, for chrissakes, umpteen kilometres from anywhere *public*. The only public here consisted of introduced species brought from Earth generations ago: crows and snakes and bloody sand mites. Who's bright idea had that been? He squinted at the sky, which was so stretched with heat it was turning white. Not a cloud anywhere.

It was like this for up to half a year every decade or so: unendingly hot, dry and unpleasant. That's what you get for colonising a planet with an erratic off-plane orbit around a fucking huge B-type variable star like Vega, which suffered from major equatorial bulge. Sure, Firnaz had at least been habitable, and that was extremely rare, they reckoned. But at times like this it was some consolation to Art that with a tenth of Sol's expected life-span, Vega would be a black hole in space long before the home-world's Sun had shrunk to a dwarf.

Mind you, for all anyone knew Earth was already dead. There'd been no interstellar communications for thirty years or so, ever since the day when the stars disappeared from the sky. The Firnaz colonists had been left alone with Vega and the other planets of the system, all of them uninhabitable hellholes. Nothing else could be seen, heard, detected. Nothing was out there, except darkness and silence. No-one knew why, though theories—paranoid and otherwise—proliferated. Unfortunately, none of the theories could be tested empirically. There'd been no starships on-planet when the universe disappeared and none had appeared since.

A horse whinnied behind him. Groom didn't bother looking. 'Stop watchin' me, Bugger!' he snarled. 'Can't ya see I'm busy?'

The nag snorted, a sound Groom took to be an equine wisecrack of some kind. 'Piss off!' he growled.

Groom was a big bloke, roughly two metres tall in his worn, threadbare socks, with legs like posts and solid shoulders much wider than his hips. Pretty small cock, though, much to his disgust. Perhaps that was the problem. Perhaps deep down he was afraid someone'd be watching from a hiding place somewhere and would spread the goss that Arty Groom had nothin' where it counted. He sighed, feeling a few meagre drops squeeze out and tumble over the edge of the ravine.

He tried to concentrate on pissing by not concentrating, eyes focusing far down and across the landscape. This proved fortuitous, as he would not have noticed the anomaly otherwise.

Fifty metres below languished what was left of a

river, and along a bit, around a bend, a tangle of shadows suggested something that wasn't natural: all hard edges and angles. He narrowed his eyes, raising a hand to block out a bit of the glare. A shack? It was odd enough that the wide torrent that had been the Elderbroke River had dwindled to nothing somewhere west of Ironbirch Station—and without Groom noticing a spill or a dam or any friggin' reason for it. But why would there be a shack—or what remained of one—smack bang in the middle of an empty riverbed? Had the river been dried up that long? Cindertown was supposed to lie somewhere along the Elderbroke and the last Groom had heard, it'd been located on a part of the river wide enough to suit the comings and goings of river steamers. A month ago he'd talked to the captain of the *Nightwings*, who'd never been to Cindertown but who regularly sailed as far as Ironbirch and there was never a problem with water levels. So where had the river gone? Normal sunburn-season drought didn't account for this much of a dry-out. Not here. The empty riverbed and the old shack made no sense at all. All he could think was that somehow he'd lost his way and this dried-out ravine wasn't the Elderbroke at all.

Mind you, the Captain reckoned he hadn't heard of anyone going to Cindertown for years, so news from there was long out-of-date. 'Some say it rotted away, like an old carcass,' he'd added, 'killed off back at the time of the Disappearance. But there's lotsa strange tales about Cindertown.' He advised Groom to stay away.

Groom heard a tinkling splash and, startled, glanced down. The relief was ecstasy! Piss was spurting out of him, a stream of gold against red-brown rocks. Just showed ya—think about something else and it came, even out in the open for all the world to see.

By the time he was done, there was a goddam minor tributary flowing down the slope. No-one could say Groom wasn't doin' his bit to replenish the country's dwindling water supply. He jiggled and buttoned himself up with a great feeling of achievement. He glanced back. Big Bugger had turned away at some point and was munching on an unappetising spiky-leafed plant.

'Hey, ya stupid stallion! Come here!'

'Stallion' was too grandiose a word to apply to Bugger, though that's what he was. His patchy black coat was as dust-dulled as the landscape and he looked lean and battered. Some time ago, his left ear had been half-bitten off by a friggin' drunk, now deceased, who'd attacked him thinking he was attacking Groom. The poor fool hadn't found Bugger very forgiving. As well, the old horse had one eye that was sorta cloudy and thick. Didn't seem to affect his seeing, mind. But it gave him the look of a rogue. Or a demon. If ever there was a horse that might've belonged to the Horseman Pestilence, it was Bugger. If he had, though, it was many lifetimes ago, and on a different world. The Apocalyptic Rider had long since given him up for dead.

Or maybe the Horseman had simply disappeared with the rest of the universe.

'Come on,' said Groom. 'Let's go check out that shack. Might be someone there who knows where the fuck Cindertown is.'

Bugger grunted.

As they approached the shadowy anomaly over the

cracked soil, sand and stones of the riverbed, Groom found himself becoming increasingly more irritated. The bleached sunlight was making him hot and impatient—and he was normally such an easy-going sort of chap. This bloody job looked less and less like a good idea every day. Not only had it effectively removed him from civilisation (if Mountbase Stretch could be considered civilised)—sending him into a clime more affected by the sunburn season than the region around Mountbase—but he'd also become more conscious than ever of how little he knew about what he was doing. 'Find the Desert Madonna,' his employer had said. 'Find it and get rid of it.'

'Desert Madonna? What the hell's that?' he'd protested.

'Go to Cindertown. Follow the trail. You'll know when you find it.'

'What trail?'

His employer's dark eyes, narrowed under folds of skin, had glinted coldly. Groom didn't fuck with Mr MacArthur. MacArthur's predecessor, Clyde Rundelmar, had been handed majority control of the rights for resource exploitation in the Hazewash colonial region of Firnaz back in the days when there'd still been Terran Authority in evidence. Once that Authority had loosened its hold—left for good, as it subsequently transpired—the Rundelmar family had wanted to consolidate its power and expand operations throughout the region, but lacked the nous. MacArthur turned up out of nowhere in the aftermath of the Disappearance and brought not only an uncanny ability to find and exploit local mineral resources, but also political cunning and a skill at designing new techniques and offensive technologies that totally undermined the efforts of his increasingly impotent opponents. He'd taken over the operations of Hazewash Inc with the strike-precision of a rattlesnake. Rundelmar stepped aside for him and the company thrived. Now no-one fucked with MacArthur if they knew what was good for them.

Groom had wanted to ask, why? What was this Desert Madonna to MacArthur? What was so damn important? But suddenly he didn't dare. It was like pissing in the open; his curiosity 'muscles' had turned shy. Call it lack of real purpose, call it fear—but Groom always did whatever MacArthur asked of him. The man was his employer and that was that. It was the way things were. He couldn't remember a time when he hadn't worked for MacArthur and couldn't imagine it being otherwise.

'Use this,' MacArthur had added, handing him a gun. It was odd-looking—sleek and angular at the same time, as though made to an unstable template that Groom's mind was having trouble seeing. Though usable, it didn't even look like it had been designed for a human hand.

'I got a gun already,' Groom had pointed out.

'Not like this one.'

'Is it something of yours?'

'Comes from elsewhere,' MacArthur admitted. 'Don't you concern yourself. Just use it on the Desert Madonna, Arthuro my lad.' *Arthuro my lad.* Groom frowned at the man's annoying affectation. 'Use it. And only on the Madonna. Nothing else will work. Understand?'

'But—'

'Look,' he growled, 'I'd do the job myself, but I can't go near the place, for reasons I don't intend to explain.

You are my only hope, Arthuro, the only one I can trust.'

And he'd thrust a damn lot of cash incentive into Groom's other hand. Greed was better at quashing doubt and fostering understanding than fear or loyalty could ever be. Not that he needed to understand.

'I'll be with you in spirit,' MacArthur had added, offering him a cryptic grin.

Bugger snorted, as though sharing the memory.

Closer now, the angled shadows in the riverbed were pretty clearly not a shack. It was a sort of boat—at best guess, anyway—derelict and falling to pieces. At least that made more sense than a shack. Groom supposed that the boat had been sunk here, lost to salvage, until revealed by the retreating water levels. It was a strange boat though, now that he could see it clearer. Weird looking. Metallic glint beneath the corrosion. Maybe it'd belonged to some god-whipped free-seeker with enough money to customise. Looked non-standard enough.

Then he realised what it reminded him of. Not a boat, but a space shuttle. That *really* didn't make sense. He'd seen pictures of space shuttles and other planetary landers, but had never met one in person. Hadn't been a shuttle landing on Firnaz soil since before the Disappearance— not that he'd heard of anyhow. And he would've heard. They all would've heard. An off-world visitor would've been big news. Looked odd, anyway, compared to pictures he'd seen of pre-Disappearance spacecraft. The shape was wrong. Maybe it was just a shack after all.

'What d'ya reckon, Bugger?' he growled.

Bugger came up beside him. The nag said nothing, though Groom could feel its doubts. Bloody horse was so negative.

'I don't care what ya think,' Groom said. 'I'm gonna take a closer look see.'

He strode around the bend and had got close enough to study the sweep of the thing's ribbing, the jutting, pointed prow with its weather-tarnished figurehead, sort of womanish, when a vibration in the air whispered, *Avoid its shadow*.

Groom tensed, right hand reaching for the pistol in his jacket. He saw: shuttle, patches of sky glimpsed through exposed superstructure, leafless bush—hunched silhouette in the shadow of the eroded figurehead.

'Who are ya?' Groom snarled, moving his hand from MacArthur's gun to the grip of his own.

Wind hissed in his ears, though from the lack of air movement around him and the unnatural stillness of the bush there seemed to be no wind at all to make the noise.

'Friggin' startled me,' Groom muttered. He took a few steps in the figure's direction, the crunching of river stones under his boots suddenly very loud and distracting.

'I asked who the bloody hell you are,' he insisted calmly.

Arthur.

'What? Arthur?'

What Arthur. Who Arthur. Why Arthur . . . Where Arthur?

The dim sound of the voice swept away and silence slithered into Groom's ears. He shivered, frowning at his own nervousness.

'Hey!' he growled. 'What's all that s'posed to mean?

You bein' funny?'

The voice didn't answer. Noisily expressing his annoyance at the shadowy form's disrespect, Groom shuffled toward it. The hunched figure had its back to Groom and seemed to be staring up and to the west. Groom circled around to check out its face, look it in the eye. Eye-to-eye, no-one mistook Groom for an easy mark.

He stopped when he realised another step would put him in the derelict's shadow. Nearby, nothing was living, not anywhere where the shadow might have fallen as Vega moved across the sky: grey dead weeds and twigs; a desiccated snake; leeched, lifeless soil. The realisation had greater meaning to Groom than he could rationally express. He stepped away so his hands wouldn't enter the gloom, should he be led to wave them around demonstratively. Didn't really know why.

'Hey, you!' he growled, gesturing at the figure.

At that point he realised the body before him was that of a dead man. Muscles throughout Groom's body began to tremble. He wanted to run from this place, but he forced himself to stay. This was, perhaps, a clue.

The crumbling cadaver might have sat there in the shadow of the wreckage for so long it had withered and turned to sand. Its eye sockets were dark and empty. No way was it seeing anything at all, as it 'stared' intently into the distance.

It was also much smaller than Groom had thought at first, more like a boy. A dead boy.

Whose voice had he heard then?

Thunder rumbled through the air, shaking the ground under his feet. Bugger whinnied.

'How long ya been here, eh?' Groom asked the boy's

corpse, rhetorically of course.

That he got an answer at all made the muscles of his legs weaken further. The fact that the answer was so cryptic was just icing on the cake.

One year, a thousand. Both perhaps. Time's unimportant.

Groom glanced around frantically. 'Who said that? Come out in the open, damn it.'

No-one emerged from what meagre excuse for cover was scattered within hearing distance. When he turned back toward the corpse, Groom saw that its head had changed position. If it had had eyes in its skull, they would've been looking straight at him now.

Again thunder rolled around the clear sky above. Again Groom began to tremble. His leg muscles gave way and concertinaed him into a crouch.

'What the—?'

Your horse should not drink from this river. When the corpse talked, its dry, bony jaw quivered fractionally. *Everything's poisoned here.*

'Bugger?' Despite himself, Groom glanced toward the horse. It was bent over a dark smear in the centre of the riverbed, as though lapping at what few dregs might have lingered.

'Bugger!' bellowed Groom. 'Get away from there, ya damn nag!'

Bugger studied him doubtfully for a moment, as though unsure what it'd heard.

'Bad water, Bugger. Get away!' Groom swept his hand in a violent gesture.

The horse huffed and moved back toward the edge of the ravine.

'What's wrong with the water?' Groom asked the corpse, having abandoned whatever rationality might have kept him from talking to it. It had to be an hallucination anyway.

It's not as it should be. Nothing here is as it should be.

Groom noticed that the corpse had crumbled further. In fact, every time it spoke parts of it broke away, becoming wisps of dust in the air.

Words destroy me. Only have a few left. Ask.

'Ask what?'

What you want to know.

Groom's head was throbbing. He thumped the heel of his palm against his right temple.

'What d'ya mean nothing here's as it should be?'

There was a disaster. Everything went weird and was broken.

Beyond those sounds, deeper in his brain, Groom heard the echo of the words take on a different, more complex form. If this was the boy talking, he sure didn't sound like one. *The disaster caused a structural disruption in local space. Reality in Cindertown and around it went askew. Now neither matter nor time is what it was and temporal detritus from many quantum possibilities got scattered throughout the landscape. You and me . . . we broke apart.*

Half the corpse's head and one arm cracked off and disintegrated.

The strangers caused it but it was an accident. What you seek lies at the heart of it.

Without knowing how he knew it, Groom understood that there were realities beyond this one—hundreds of them, perhaps millions—and that it had to do with resonance within the minuscule particles that made up matter, even the emptiness beyond matter. Some energies might cause an unstable reconfiguration of the patterns that give form to each reality. Such an occurrence had been theorised by scientists, but was this an actual example of it?

If so, what could have caused it? And who were the strangers? In the darkness beyond humanity were there other lives, nonhuman lives? In living memory mankind had not knowingly encountered any, but their existence had long been accepted as likely.

Had such creatures sometime come to Firnaz?

Grey figures in wide-brimmed labourer's hats, all about his height, mill around him, touching, chattering. There is comfort in their gestures. Gratitude. He glances toward a tall ill-defined figure beside him, who takes his hand in hers.

Groom shook his head to clear it of the phantom images and the remaining echoes of corpse-words. 'Where's Cindertown got to?' he muttered with a breathless wheeze, making an effort to control his imagination.

It didn't entirely work. The corpse's arm rose, its bony fingers pointing. Along the river, naturally. Where else would it be? *Close*, it said. It maintained that posture for barely a second before the arm fell away.

Grey. MacArthur. Julianna. They are the ones you have to face.

And then it collapsed to dust completely.

•

It had to have been hallucination, all of it—a phantasm brought on by the sunburnt sky. Groom refused to see it in any other light. Be that as it may, the illusory corpse's directions had proven correct.

Not that Cindertown amounted to much.

As soon as he hit the outskirts it was obvious that the place wasn't right. No vegetation. An overpowering stench of baked clay. Sand and cracked earth. The buildings—those that were recognisable as buildings— were grey and crumbling. And there were corpses, or what remained of them. They were scattered everywhere, as though the people had been caught going about their ordinary hick business and killed on the instant. Many had pretty well weathered away, becoming vague shapes in the dust. It looked as though the whole town had been touched by the shadow of that riverbed derelict.

What the fuck had happened? He had no idea. Groom wondered how safe it was to be here and might have simply backed out again, except Bugger seemed unperturbed, which was a good sign, given his nag's pessimism. Groom slid off the horse's back and walked along the main street. Soon they reached the wharves; these, too, were desiccated, and the riverboats that had been there when whatever had happened happened were in various states of ruin along the wide gully that had once been the Elderbroke River.

Since leaving the spot where the wreck that might have been a space shuttle had been, Groom had been mulling over the corpse's last words. *Grey. MacArthur. Julianna.* MacArthur he knew. Grey, too. There was an Albert Grey who'd owned the *Golden Ram,* it was said, an infamous clip-joint for itinerants, located in Cindertown. Rumour had it he was a bad man, a petty thug with an uncanny ability to scare those who opposed him, though normally Groom had little patience for folktales. Given what had been going on lately, though, who could say what was true? He found it no surprise that a connection might exist between these two men, Grey and MacArthur. They were both of a type, separated only by ability and perhaps opportunity. But Julianna? The name had a tang of familiarity about it, nothing definite. Clearly it meant something. What?

Was she the Desert Madonna perhaps?

Following memory of the rough town layout as provided to him by *Nightwings'* captain, Groom soon located the building that had been the *Golden Ram*, just off Dock Square. Surprisingly it had more-or-less retained its shape. Its greyness was like a layer of dust, though brushing the veneer didn't clean it away. The outer part of the building had been touched by something, changed by it.

Night was falling now, the bleached sky darkening to ash, like the walls of the *Golden Ram*. Groom settled Bugger in a stall out the back, filling a concave metal lid with fresh water from his canteen. He figured the nag would be thirsty. By the time he left, Bugger still hadn't touched it.

Locating a latrine, he tried to pee. It was tough going, as though subconsciously he believed he was being watched. Afterwards, he found a room in the hotel that wasn't too foul and settled down to sleep. He was so buggered, he didn't even notice the shadowy figure standing unmoving in the corner of the room.

•

Groom had always thought dreams were not for him. His nights were dark wells of nothingness in which time passed quickly and without incident. In sleep he went nowhere.

Not this time. This time he saw flashes of light, humanoid shapes clawing aside the blackness and racing toward him, a sky that was shattered, the pieces sucking away like water down a drainage hole. Harsh red winds blew, so fierce, from every direction, he couldn't move. And in the midst of the fury stood a woman. She wore an off-white skirt, its long folds unaffected by the wind, their cloth-like appearance nothing but an illusion. Her dark red hair, too, hung loose, suspended as though windblown, but without moving. In one hand she held a pistol.

'Give him back to me, Grey,' she cried. 'Give me my son!'

Groom awoke covered in sweat. Memory was like a silvery fish darting around in the cloudy bowl of his mind. He had a dim recollection of a man coming for him in a room where he and his mother were staying. She was absent just then, and the man knew it.

He grabs Groom's shoulder roughly as he lies dozing on his bed. 'I want you, boy.' Groom reaches for the gun under his pillow—a gun like no other he'd ever seen. But the man is too quick. He snatches it from Groom's hand. 'None of that!' he growls.

Groom rubbed at his temples. What was that supposed to mean? It didn't make sense. Surely these weren't his memories.

'Ah, ya're awake,' said a voice.

Groom leapt to his feet. Disorientation sent him into a

lurching fall. A strong hand gripped him, steadying him.

'Should be more careful, sir. You'll hurt yaselves.'

Groom pulled out of the grip, set to attack. The man's flush, podgy face, with its ragged grin and glintingly innocent eyes, pulled him up short.

'What the hell—?' Groom growled.

'Heard ya come in last night, like, sir, but ya'd drifted off 'fore I could settle things with ya. Thought I'd let it be 'til mornin'.'

Groom squinted suspiciously. 'You're what? The owner?'

'No, sir. Owner's Mr Grey. He's not available.'

Come with me, boy, and tell me what you know!

Groom shook memory of the words from his mind. Stick to what was relevant. 'Well, who are ya then?'

'Albert's the moniker, sir. Douglas Albert. The caretaker. When ya ready like, come on down to the front office and we'll get things straight.'

Groom blinked and the little man was gone, drifting into the corridor and away. The air seemed to clear behind him as he went, as though the currents he'd set in motion had dissipated the grey fog.

Groom couldn't figure what had happened. Was he still asleep and dreaming, or were the memories he had of yesterday the dream, as real as his recollections of a childhood kidnapping that he didn't believe had happened? The room looked in good repair and reasonably clean. He went to the door; out in the corridor it was the same. In the crisp morning light the hotel gave the appearance of being used, not an abandoned dump. Was it the same with the whole town? He went back and pulled aside the curtains. Stood watching people walking in the street outside, the languid bustle of a small town morning—a port town. The wharves were visible as a raggedly geometric series of roofs and through a gap he could see a steamboat being unloaded. The damn river must have filled up again. Overnight.

What the hell was going on? Had his mind finally disintegrated? He needed to talk about this to someone, and the only someone he trusted was Bugger. Art did a quick face wash in a basin full of lukewarm water that had materialised in his room, straightened his increasingly disreputable clothes as best as his lack of interest in such vanities allowed, and headed downstairs with a somewhat self-conscious swagger, a swagger intended to cover up the trembling in his hands. 'Shall we deal with the accounts now, sir?' the balding Albert asked politely as he passed the man's office.

'Give me a minute!' he yelled back and tried to reach the front door before the inordinately annoying caretaker could protest.

But all the man said was: 'Ya can use the backdoor, sir. More convenient.'

'Backdoor?'

Albert pointed. His finger was arthritically bent but Groom got the general idea.

'Latrine's nexta the stables.'

'I know where it is,' Groom growled, turned and headed down the indicated passageway into the yard at the back of the building. The day was sunny, but not blazing. He squinted up into the blue expanse and shook his head. After peeing with some difficulty (which he attributed to stress), he tramped through the slightly overgrown weeds that hadn't been there yesterday and into the stall where he'd left Bugger.

The horse was gone. 'Bugger!' he called. 'Where the frig are ya?'

Give me my gun! he shouts.

The man laughs. Why should I?

'Lost somethin'?' came a voice from behind him.

Groom stood indecisively caught between one voice and another. Which had been real? Then the backlit figure of the caretaker appeared just beyond the door. 'My goddam horse, that's what,' Groom managed.

'Oh?' Albert entered the stable, his energetic glance checking a pile of old barrels, a broken wagon, an empty trough . . . and Groom. 'Sure ya left it 'ere? This stall ain't bin used for years, like, 'cept to store junk. Surprised ya could get the door open at all.'

'Yeah, it was this one.' Groom frowned though. Last night the place had had old straw and dry horse shit on the ground. And where was the metal lid he'd left for Bugger to drink from?

He had to suppress his sudden belief that he had gone completely mad and that all of this was delusion. 'There another stable?' he asked.

Albert nodded and Groom followed him across the yard to a much-better-fitted-out set of stables that he'd swear hadn't been there last night. Newish wooden fences established orderly entry points and there was an open alleyway so that guests could access the place direct from the street.

The neat row of stalls had several horses in it. They looked up at Groom and Albert, snorted indifferently and went back to whatever they'd been doing. A filthy, dishevelled stable lass of about twelve emerged from a corner and scowled absently at him.

'This man here reckons he left 'is horse last ev'nin', Jaclyn,' said Albert with suddenly assumed authority. 'Ya seen it about?'

'Horse?'

'Bit older than these,' Groom said. 'Mottled black stallion, pretty bony, one eye dead—'

'Ain't seen nuthin' like that, sir.' The girl gave a gap-toothed grin. 'I'd sure remember a piece a crowbait like that.'

'Yeah, I suppose you would.' Sceptical annoyance itched across Groom's scalp. He turned to Albert. 'It was the other stall, I'm sure of it. Someone's taken him.'

'Or it wander'd off itself.'

'Wouldn't do that.'

The caretaker suggested alternatives, none of which placated Groom or eased his suspicions. They 'made enquiries' of the two or three other guests that hadn't gone off about whatever business occupied them, but no useful information was forthcoming. In the end Groom had to be satisfied to bluster a bit and then give up, agreeing to wait and see if Bugger came back by himself. He decided to look around the town, which had been his aim anyway. MacArthur's commission was pressing on his mind and the sooner he completed that task and got out of this diseased town the better.

'Meant to ask you, Mr Albert,' he said after they settled a week's account ahead, 'you heard of somethin' called the Desert Madonna?'

'That some sorta statue?'

Groom shrugged.

'There's a museum thing run by an old dame called

Julianna somethin' at the far end of town.' Albert pointed with his wonky finger. 'I'm told it has pictures and artsy stuff. Might try there.'

Julianna. Groom grunted.

A woman stands, strange gun in hand, facing Groom across an open yard. Groom feels a man's arm clamp around his chest and pull him close. He smells the stale odour of tobacco and rum, mingled with sweat and traces of perfume. The woman's clothes are dusty and there is desperation in her stance. 'Give me my son!' she cries.

Groom clamped his eyes shut and once again willed the images away.

Something about the atmosphere of the town—its tone—felt even less right this morning, though on the surface it was in much better shape. The people in the street looked ordinary enough, the general activity levels weren't too much or too little; nothing seemed out of place. But still, as he walked with a determinedly casual swagger along the main street, the whole thing felt like a façade, a barely maintained illusion that could fall apart any second. This was the way his mind gave form to his unease at any rate, though he had no rational justification for it.

That was about to change.

On a whim—perhaps a long-shot possibility that the wandering Bugger might have headed for the docks as at one time he'd worked haulage for a river merchant—Groom deviated in the direction of the Elderbroke, wandering along a bustling alleyway where itinerant sellers had set up temporary stalls, then along a quieter lane lined with alehouses and brothels. Ahead, the steamer he'd seen earlier was still unloading. As he came closer, he saw what they were unloading: barrels, sacks and wooden boxes that probably contained manufactured goods from the main colony at the distant end of the Elderbroke. He exited the laneway and headed across an open square toward the docks, gazing about for sign of Bugger. Several nags stood around with patient disdain, none of them remotely like his poor excuse for a horse. He swore then sucked back his breath as he took in the surface of the river itself.

'No,' he groaned. 'Don't do this to me!'

The river didn't have a surface. There was no water in the Elderbroke at all. Totally empty. Now that he could see past the wharf itself it was clear to Groom that the steamer was floating in mid-air, bobbing precariously on waves that didn't exist. He took another step or two until he could see clear down to the bottom of the riverbed, confirming that it was dry and cracked. The boat rocked, held aloft by nothing. A shiver crept up his spine.

'What do you want, Mister? You can't keep me here.'

A man leans over him. 'I can do whatever takes my fancy, boy. I'm sick of being a minor player on this god-forsaken planet. I want power. You're my ticket.'

The boy protests. But the man just laughs bitterly. 'I heard the rumours,' he almost whispers, his breath stale. 'I know about the foreigners, natch, the weird ones with their silver ship. They belonged to me. I found them, I own them. But then an interfering mother and her brat come along—itinerant road-trash who work with the foreigners, help them escape, take their secrets—secrets I never guessed the little buggers had. You, boy! You and that bitch stole what's mine by rights.' He holds up the gun. 'This is one. More lies in there.' He taps at the boy's skull. 'They're mine—the guns, the secrets, all of it. Knowledge of places far distant. Knowledge of powerful engines no man's ever seen, stuff I suspect you yourself don't understand. It's all there, right? Unimaginable wealth's to be made from knowledge like that, for the one who can dig it out of ya. I want that knowledge.' He grins. 'And I'll get it, even if I have to tear it from ya one drop of blood at a time.'

'What the fuck?' Groom staggered, clutching at his head. He felt—not for the first time—that his legs were about to give way. The weight of impossible memories pressed down on him.

'Hey, watch it there!' screamed a large man on the deck of the steamer. One of the labourers, balancing a barrel on his shoulder, glanced around, stumbled over a tangle of ropes and lost his grip on the barrel.

'I said ta watch out, ya bloody idiot!'

The labourer tried to grab his falling load, but couldn't hold on to it. Groom watched aghast as the barrel tumbled over the bulwark, fell past the steamer's grimy, pitch-blackened bottom—and disappeared into thin air.

'Ya'll pay for that!' the foreman yelled. 'Stoopid fool! Should make ya dive to the bottom ta fetch it!'

'Can't swim, boss.'

'So what?'

Groom backed away. This was too weird. It was like he was seeing the place at different times in its history, but simultaneously, all mixed together. His mind was exploding with impossible images and the memories that couldn't be his weren't helping none. What was that about 'weird ones with their silver ship'? Off-world aliens? Was this connected with the derelict shuttle in the river-bed? There'd never been any reports of non-Terran intelligence being found—not here, not anywhere. He hurried off the way he'd come, determined now to follow the only lead he had. Something was so *askew*, it redefined the whole concept of 'askewness'. Maybe this Julianna who ran the 'museum thing' could help. People who worked in such places were often educated outsiders—more likely to know what was going on than those living with the weirdness on a daily basis and thus being more accepting of it.

'I've come to get you back, Arthur. I said I would never lose you!'

The phantom memory of a woman's voice flashed in and out of his head with mocking irrelevance.

Whatever, he had no intention of hangin' about near that goddam freak of a ghost-river. It was making him crazy.

The 'museum thing' was at the very edge of the settlement, so far out it took him over an hour to walk there. Beyond it was nothing except desert and desiccation. True, Groom hadn't ever been here before, but from what he understood of it, it wasn't supposed to be a desert. There should've been scrub plains, and pasture re-claimed from bushland, rolling hills with some sort of hardy vegetation on them. Not this bleak and barren landscape, devastated as though burned by an apocalyptic firestorm. It got hot here when Firnaz's orbit was at its closest to Vega, like it did everywhere, but the truly barren areas were closer to the planet's equatorial regions. He squinted against the glare; it was so intense he couldn't even make out the horizon.

His journey was plagued by memories of childhood and images of conflict and trauma that were and were not his, both at the same time. The pressure of them tore at whatever shreds of confidence he had left, and drained him of will. Yet there was a murmur deep inside him that kept him going, even though by the end of it he could barely make his feet take another step forward.

Soon enough a ramshackle structure formed out of the haze of desert sun and chaotic memories. The 'museum thing' was little more than a hovel; probably once upon a time it had been a homestead caretaking an extensive cattle farm that stretched as far as the eye could see. It wasn't wealth that kept it going now. The best he could expect to find here was a measure of determination.

He knocked on the door and after a few moments it opened, slowly and hesitantly. The wrinkled old battleaxe that glared out at him didn't have much erudition about her.

'What do you want?' she barked.

'I've just come ta see the museum,' he said.

Her rheumy eyes evaluated him for a few long moments, until Groom thought he could feel a dull heat from them soaking into his skin.

'I was told—' he began.

'Anything in particular you're after?'

His hesitation—how truthful should he be?—lasted only as long as it took the words to form. 'The Desert Madonna,' he said. 'You heard of it?'

The woman's wrinkles manoeuvred themselves into a frown. Then the frown became an oddly self-satisfied smile. 'Your name Arthur?' she asked.

'How'd you know that?' Groom muttered.

She gestured for him to come in.

For a museum, the inside of the shack was chaotically disordered. Dark and cluttered, it was a mess of piled-up artefacts, old furniture, papers and even older knick-knacks. It smelt of ash rather than dust.

The hag was staring at him in a way that Groom couldn't quite define but which unnerved him even more than he was already unnerved. 'What?' he growled.

She gestured toward a tatty, dirty chair that might have housed a whole colony of desert creepy-crawlies, come in from the heat. 'Sit!'

'Don't need to sit,' he said. 'This ain't a social call.'

'No? What then?'

He stepped toward her, perhaps intending to come over as slightly threatening—he didn't really know. Whatever his intent, she didn't flinch. 'Somethin' weird is goin' on in Cindertown,' he said.

She shrugged. 'Cintertown's been a bit weird for a long time now. Since the Disappearance in fact—'

'I'm not talkin' *bit* weird. Talkin' full-on bug-shit. Unless I've gone loopy—and I haven't totally chucked that notion either—this town's dead come evening, dried-up and dusty. Then in the morning it's all back to normal. 'Cept there's boats floating in a river with no water, and yesterday a corpse sitting near a wrecked space shuttle spoke to me—'

The woman's eyes lit up and her wrinkled fingers grabbed his arm with a bony strength that weakened him and stopped him from pulling away as he'd wanted to. 'A young boy?'

'Yeah. Funny sort of boy though. Like an adult-boy. You know about him?'

'And a space shuttle?'

'That's what it looked like to me.'

He saw her withered fingers clench. 'It's beginning then,' she muttered, turning her back on him as though to study a stack of old newspapers that were piled on the main table.

'And I've been . . . remembering stuff,' Groom continued. 'But I'm not sure the memories are mine.'

'What've you remembered?'

Groom started to speak, but the gush of air he expelled from his mouth was more like a sob. He swallowed to clear his throat. 'A woman,' he said. 'My mother. Though it makes no sense. I've never known my mother. She abandoned me when I was a cub. I was adopted out.'

The hag came close. 'Perhaps she wanted to know you all along. Perhaps you were forcibly taken from her.' She wrapped her arm around him.

Groom recoiled, repulsed. 'Yeah, well, there's this man. In the dream. He steals me away. He wants knowledge that he reckons I have in my head, knowledge placed there by foreigners.' He frowned. 'Knowledge of clever ways to do things. And I remembered something bad, very bad.'

'Yes?'

His head was throbbing so hard he could barely hear himself speak. He clutched at his forehead. 'The world tore apart.'

The woman sighed, in a manner that suggested both sorrow and joy.

'What's it mean?'

She said nothing for a moment. When she faced him again her eyes were like burning coals. 'Why'd you come here? What d'you know of the Desert Madonna?' She leered at him.

'Nothing,' he insisted, dropping into the bug-infested chair, daunted by her sudden intensity and exhausted by his own emotion. 'Was told to find it, is all.'

'Find it?'

'Or her. Whatever.'

The woman loomed over him. 'But what's your intent, boy? What will you do when you find her?'

'I was told to . . . ' Groom fell into a confused, guilty silence.

'To kill her?' The woman's bony hand slapped against his cheek, hard, so that his head rocked to one side. He was too shocked to respond. 'And who gave you this mission? Let me guess, another man named Arthur? A hard man.'

'No, his name's . . . ' *MacArthur*. Groom frowned at the realisation, the hitherto unnoticed synchronicity. 'What's it mean?' he said again.

'It means you're talking to yourself, idiot. Talking to yourself as you might have been. But you're not yourself. Haven't been yourself since Grey took you from me and our showdown tore time and space apart.'

Groom made it to his feet. He motioned to push the old woman away, but her savage frailty stopped him from making contact. 'What the fuck are you goin' on about?'

She slapped him again.

'Don't bloody do that!' he yelled.

'Don't cuss, boy. No son of mine will cuss in my presence.'

This time astonishment was mingled with a strange

sense of recognition. 'Son? I—'

'These memories you describe are real enough.' She shook her head. 'But you resist 'em. I've been stuck here for so long, waiting for you to come, but your mind has been fractured, just like Cindertown. You're of little use to anyone.'

'Use?'

'All blocked up, you are. Blocked up with a cancer gnawing at your heart.' She frowned and thrust her hand against his belly. 'No, the death is down there, waiting to kill you. There can be no continuity in this place.'

Groom knocked her hand away. 'Don't touch me again, you friggin' lunatic.'

She snarled at him, pushing him so violently in the chest he let himself fall backward into the chair again. 'Remember, damn you, Arthur! Remember before it's too late! Pull yourself together!'

'I don't know what you're talking about, you mad old cow!'

Her finger prodded his chest. Why did she make him feel so helpless?

'You're my son and you're special—and Grey . . . Grey is an evil man with a talent for petty self-gratification.' She squinted at him. 'Remember?'

She was raving now. Groom refused to let her words make sense. Yet he wouldn't stop them from echoing around in his head.

'I don't remember. I won't!'

She turned from him. 'You'll remember, all right. How everything went skew-whiff, torn apart . . . How you might be the one to save us, but you're just a useless yes-man to your own dark ignorance.' She gestured at him disdainfully. 'No, no, no, damn it . . . ' She began to cry, and as she did the shack was rocked by a violent gust of wind slamming against the outside wall. A storm? The old woman looked directly into his face and for the first time he saw a woman there that might have been his mother.

The woman nodded. 'She's coming.'

'Who?'

'The Desert Madonna.'

'What?'

'The world and you were not the only things that were fractured. It must be rectified. All of it. If you truly are Arthur, truly are my son, go back to town, to the Dock Square near the wharf. The distortion's strongest in Cindertown 'cause that's where it started. Do what you have to do, no matter how painful it might be.'

He stood.

The woman fell on him, hugging him desperately. 'I'd give you the weapon, Arthur, but I haven't got it any more. It was destroyed. You'll have to find another way. Stop this ruination from happening! And watch out for Grey.'

'Grey?'

'He'll come in a form you recognise. To trick you.' She sighed. 'Though he's been with you the whole time, I reckon.'

The shack trembled, old wood creaking and splitting. A deadly red glow, like infection, leaked through the cracks.

'He'll be there. She'll be there. Go now! Do what you have to do to free us, even if it pains you.'

'Why me?'

'The strangers gave you the knowledge, the strength to stare into the void and make it obey you. I'm sure of that. It's in you. It's always been in you.'

'But—'

'Just remember, Grey will come, fractured into potentialities like you and me. We're not pure any more, Arthur. Not you, not me. Not Grey.'

'I don't get it—'

'Go!'

Wind thudded like a fist on the roof. Groom pushed hard against his temples. 'I don't understand a fuckin' thing. This Desert Madonna that's coming, MacArthur wants me to kill her! Why would he tell me to do that?'

'Because *you* want to kill her.'

Groom's shock and outrage quickly turned to fear as he stared into her deep, searching eyes. He still didn't understand. But if the old woman had more to say, words that would clarify things for him, she never had a chance to speak them. The roof tore off the shack; sand and dead scraps of bush sprayed through the room, striking against Groom's face, forcing his eyes shut. He wiped his trembling hand across them to clear his sight. When he opened his eyes again, shielded against the wind, the old woman was disintegrating as though she'd been made of sand all along, like the boy in the creek bed.

'Mother!' he bawled, reaching out. His fingers passed right through her.

Then she was gone, absorbed into the chaos. Groom staggered to the door and out into the wasteland. Heat and fury struck savage blows against his swollen flesh. He glanced across the desert and gasped at what he saw there. The storm was concentrated around a small moving figure: a woman, hair flowing, dress billowing in the wind, heat swirling around her and out of her. She swept toward him relentlessly, a vision of inhuman fury.

Groom turned and ran.

The citizens of Cindertown seemed paralysed by the approaching storm. As though such a thing had never happened before.

The sky had turned red, but it was dark too, on the side of town opposite the approach of the Desert Madonna. There, it was as though a shadow was falling, a shadow like that of a derelict alien spacecraft. Poisonous.

Desperation nagged at Groom. He didn't know what to do. Dock Square was almost deserted. Standing in the centre of it, he tried to remember everything that had been said to him, by MacArthur, by the boy . . . by himself if he could believe the old woman. Tried to remember the memories that had been haunting him since he arrived in Cindertown. Were there clues in any of it?

Do what you have to do, even if it pains you? Nothing is pure any more.

The Desert Madonna was approaching fast. She was inside the town limits now, and heading his way. Groom could feel vibrations in the ground, could see the circling cloud of diseased sand that marked her coming. *It's me*, said the old woman. Groom recognised the grim truth of that. In some fashion he didn't understand the Desert Madonna *was* the old woman—but she was *not* her as well, only a part, a potentiality. *Nothing is pure any more. The world is fractured.* He also recognised, felt deep inside himself, that the old woman was his mother, and if she was, then so was the Desert Madonna. *His mother. Mother and child.* And he was Arthur Groom. And MacArthur. And the corpse in the derelict space shuttle's shadow.

Fractured images of a boy that had been Arthur, Julianna's son. Variations on a theme.

But which of them was real?

As the swirling fury of dust and sand that marked the Madonna's coming drew nearer, Groom's mind filled with more and more confusion. Words and concepts formed in his mind, spun through his consciousness and leapt out again. He tried to quieten the voices, but he couldn't.

Firnaz torn from the universe. Cindertown twisted out of shape. Those at the heart of the disruption—his mother, himself, Grey—broken apart.

The confrontation's repeating and you must stop it, she cries.

I can't—

When you broke, she whispers to him, part of you became MacArthur, poisoned by splintered shards of Grey. That part wants to free itself of the other part, you, Arthur Groom, the version of you that is still connected to me. Destroy the Desert Madonna and you deny that connection forever. Only the Madonna can give birth to hope—

'Shut up,' he screamed, clutching at his temples. 'Just leave me alone!'

But the fury continued.

'The boy is a lost moment. Groom himself a weak, conflicted shadow. Only MacArthur has empowered himself.'

This voice was different from the others. It was low

and cunning, a guttural wheeze that seemed to become words by accident.

'Emboldened by the ambitions of Grey, the MacArthur-you cut himself off from his own past, emotionally. He used what he could retrieve of the alien knowledge buried in his DNA to gain power. It'd be best to complete the alienation, Artie, wouldn't it? Free this version of yourself to re-build the Firnaz colony and make it strong.'

Something snorted behind him and he glanced around, drawn by the familiar sound. Big Bugger was there, a look of bored cynicism on his gnarled features.

The voices receded.

'Where've ya been, ya stupid nag,' Groom growled. 'Look like death warmed up.'

Bugger offered him the equine equivalent of a noncommittal shrug.

And a savage gust of fetid wind slashed against Groom from behind, making him stagger. He glanced around and saw her. The Desert Madonna had entered the Square and was moving with a sort of floating stride toward him, heat and dust billowing around her feet.

Seeing her this close filled Groom with both joy and sorrow. He recognised her features, so similar to the old woman from the Museum and corresponding to memories of his mother that had only now clarified in his mind. Yet looking into her eyes told him what he feared to see: this woman was utterly mad. A desire for revenge blazed in her, and it was indistinguishable from insanity. She was fractured. A Madonna dried out by exile in the wilderness. *Nothing is pure any more.*

Was it that insanity that was keeping Firnaz isolated

from the universe, a dry and decimated world exiled by bitterness?

'Grey!' she roared. 'Give me back my son!'

She was staring straight at Groom.

'What? No,' he whined, startled. 'I'm not Grey—'

She pointed a gun at him, one of the two alien weapons that he realised now, suddenly, had caused all the trouble. He recognised it; he had one in his pocket.

'I'm your son,' he said.

'My son?' Her anger rose even higher, turning the dust a deep purple-red. 'My son is a boy, just an innocent boy. What innocence is there in you? I want him back, Grey. I'll kill you if I have to.'

'*The Madonna is Grey*,' said the deep, wheezing voice, coming from behind him. Ridiculous, but he recognised it now as Bugger. '*He's trying to trick you. Use the gun, Arthur. To rid the world of Grey and free your mother. Kill the Madonna! Free yourself!*'

Groom looked around at his horse. Bugger snorted at him.

'*That's why you gave it to yourself, deep down inside knowing what had to be done. Kill her or she'll kill you, Grey will kill you, and this nightmare will continue forever.*'

'I should do what I have to do, no matter how painful?'

'*That's the truth of it. Do what you have to do. Even if it hurts.*'

'Nothing is pure any more?'

'*Nothing. That's not your mother. It's Grey.*'

For a moment the impure world seemed to shimmer, offering Groom a multitude of possibilities. He focused on one:

*Julianna stands facing a tall, heavily built man—*Grey, he knew it was Grey. The man had a familiarity about him, a familiarity from the phantom memories. There was a touch of MacArthur in him, too. Groom sensed it clearly now. Grey was in MacArthur. But where else was he?

Not in himself. Groom looked inward but could see no Grey in himself. He was just Arthur. He could feel that truth. An Arthur intimidated and used. An Arthur that had been too weak to deny his own basest instincts and to stand up against himself. Yet free of Grey. But was Grey in the mad Madonna?

'Give me back my son!' the woman cries, pointing her gun shakily.

'Your son?' Grey says, one hand buried in the pocket of his coat, the other grasped around a small boy. The boy seems drugged. 'Do you know what your son is now?'

'He's a boy, a normal boy. I want him back.'

'I'll tell you. He's a fulcrum, Ms Morris, a lever that can be used to turn the world in ways even I have not been able to imagine. Those aliens you met, that your ignorant sympathy helped to escape from my clutches . . . they did something to his mind, no favour to you or the world. But their knowledge will be of great benefit to me if you free me to use it to the full.'

The aliens? Groom remembered now. They'd been on Firnaz from before the Disappearance. Grey, a local mine-owner, had kept their presence secret, hiding the truth of them from both the colonial and homeworld authorities. Art remembered them, working as slaves for Grey—

cheap labour from the stars. They contained knowledge that Grey himself had failed, then, to recognise. Arthur and his mother, escaping poverty, had obtained work alongside them, unknowing, believing them to be no more than diseased and mutated unfortunates. They had helped the foreigners escape.

Julianna seems to weaken. Her hand is shaking violently. A wind has arisen and is tossing her skirts around her legs. There is a burnt-sienna tint to the air. 'Please, what do you want with him?'

'I want to use him, drain him, take back the possibilities that have been embedded in him. He will surely die, but what a sacrifice! He will make me powerful!'

'No, I won't let you!'

The words come slowly, drawn out. Her finger tightens on the trigger, as though the air has thickened around her. The gun vibrates, on the verge of sending forth its deadly energies.

But in that instant, so much faster than Julianna, Grey whips his hand from his coat, an identical gun gripped in his fist. Arthur's gun. A bright beam bursts from it, just as Julianna's gun releases its own fury. The beams meet.

Everything stops.

There is a massive explosion. The ground, the town, the sky all rip apart, billions and billions of fractured particles swirling outward, rejoining, bursting apart again, forming a billion realities. Trying unsuccessfully to settle on one.

The planet is torn from reality.

Groom grunted in pain, blinked, and the vision was gone. He knew that it, too, had been a memory like all the rest.

'*Kill her now,*' whispered Bugger. '*Now while she hesitates. Free yourself.*'

Groom whipped out his gun and aimed it at his insane mother. Was it really Grey? *Do what you have to do, even if it pains you*, the old woman had told him. She'd warned him that Grey would come disguised.

Bugger leaned over his shoulder. '*Use it on her, Arthuro my lad. Nothing else will work.*'

Arthuro my lad?

The Desert Madonna fired her gun.

The moment slowed and stretched out to infinity. Held by that endless darkness, Groom felt the cancer shift within him. In this fractured world it was killing him, but elsewhere, in a different space, it was not a cancer, not something deadly, but knowledge that could save him, save the world. He saw that suddenly, in a blaze of insight, and for the first time looked beyond himself into the thing that was killing him, accepted it—and knew what had to be done.

Arthur. Groom. MacArthur.

All him.

And they all had to die in order for him to live.

Throwing himself to one side and downward, Groom spun in mid-air, squeezing the trigger as he fell. A bright red beam slashed the air apart and slammed into Bugger's cynical face. At the same time, Julianna's beam entered the horse's chest.

Far away, the shadow of MacArthur screamed and faded.

Groom struck the ground hard, making it difficult to concentrate on anything, but he kept enough composure to notice Bugger's features stretch into a parody of Grey, then MacArthur, then back again. Over and over. Faster and faster. Until the sorry piece of crowbait exploded and, just as in Groom's vision, the impure world went with it.

Groom only had time for a handful of words to flash through his brain before everything disappeared.

The words were: *Damn. I really loved that bloody stallion.*

Standing on the road leading west from Cindertown, eight-year-old Arthur looked back past rows of buildings to the docks. Squinting against the setting sun, he could glimpse a riverboat, a bustle of barely visible activity taking place around it.

He reached up and took his mother's hand.

'Will that man come after us?' he asked.

His mother smiled reassuringly. 'No, Arthur, I don't believe he will.'

'That's good. I didn't like him much.'

'He was a bad man.' She squatted next to Arthur. 'Petty and greedy and out of his depth. I'm sorry I wasn't there when he came and took you away. But I got you back, didn't I? I said I would never lose you.'

He frowned as though pondering a difficult question. 'It was the guns, wasn't it? The guns caused the trouble. But they saved us, too.'

'That's always been the problem with guns,' his mother said.

'Did the strangers give them to us?'

'They did.' Arthur felt the sadness in her words. 'Gifts for us to protect ourselves in this harsh world.'

'Why?'

'They were grateful because we helped them escape from Mr Grey.'

'They could have used the guns themselves. Why didn't they?'

'They were imprisoned far from their ship, Arthur, far from home—in a place that wasn't theirs, where they were weak and alone.'

'And their ship sank in the river?'

'That was a different ship—one that belonged to their friends. When they landed to find their crashed comrades, Grey took them prisoner, though for a long time he didn't realise what they were, or that they had a ship and special knowledge he could use. But they hadn't been able to get away from him, find their way back. We got them out, Arthur. You and I. We did a good thing. Surely you remember?'

He shrugged. 'They were funny looking,' he said irrelevantly then hugged her, relaxing into her familiar warmth. He was having trouble remembering much, how he'd escaped from the bad man, how he'd broken the world—and then fixed it again. But right at that moment he didn't care. Mother was right. She'd got him back, same as ever.

Well, almost the same.

'Where'll we go now?' he whispered into her breast. 'To find the strangers?'

She released herself from him and stood, gazing out into the rolling hills. 'Away from here, Arthur. That's the only plan I have at the moment. As for the strangers, they've gone home already.'

'Will we ever go home, mum?'

She looked down at him, her eyes wet with melancholy.

'I don't know where home is, Arthur. We lost it long ago.'

'We'll have to build a new one then.'

'Yes,' she said. 'It's what we always do.'

He nodded, then said: 'I need to pee.'

'Oh? Well . . . ' She gestured around at the open spaces. 'I'm sorry, honey, but there's no cover here. We can't go back now. Perhaps we'll find something further on.'

Arthur indicated some low bushes on their left, growing along the river. They were shadowy in the twilight, but exposed for all that. 'Those'll do.'

'Out in the open?' she said, surprised. 'You've always had trouble in the open.'

'Na,' he replied, as he moved toward the riverbank. 'Wait here. Only take a second or two.'

Above him, the first stars appeared in the deepening sky.

Robert Hood has always suspected he originates from somewhere other than Earth. Hence his numerous published stories tend to reflect the alien perspective of an outsider puzzling over the weirdness all around him. Those stories have appeared in major Australian and international genre magazines and anthologies, and in his three collections to date: *Day-Dreaming on Company Time* (1988), *Immaterial: Ghost Stories* (2002) and *Creeping in Reptile Flesh* (2009), the latter of which is about to be reprinted as a revised edition from Morrigan Books. His novels include *Backstreets* (2000) and the *Shades* series of YA supernatural thrillers (2001). He has co-edited five anthologies, including the award-winning *Daikaiju! Giant Monster Tales* (2006) and its two sequels, and has published many short children's books and stories. His website can be found at www.roberthood.net. He also has an award-winning blog, Undead Backbrain. (www.roberthood.net/blog).

Psi World

Steve de Beer

Jaskar PS27 emerged from haemostasis, entered the galley, and selected a nutrient broth from the kitchen's auto menu. He was the quintessential Thirtieth Century man, gene-tailored to the lonely and hazardous profession of Planetary Surveyor, and driven to perform his function at any cost.

The Shade, an embodiment of the ship's synthetic mind—having decided on a Greek God image—materialised through its hologram relays wearing a shimmering toga and golden sandals.

'Good morning, PS27,' said the computer ghost, its soft contralto filling the galley.

'Status!' Jaskar barked impatiently.

The Shade responded as one perceiving a lack of appreciation. 'Phase grapple shift to 20-Leonis Minoris has presented no problem, and we are now orbiting the second planet 1.2 AU from the primary.'

Jaskar swallowed a spoonful of broth and, putting the Shade's emotional state down to an aberration of its nanotube brain, declared, 'Then I will investigate.'

With the Shade's appeals for caution ringing in his ears, Jaskar commandeered the shuttle, and dropped through the atmosphere at the steepest angle the ablation shields would allow.

A jungle world took shape. Any planet with an oxygen-nitrogen atmosphere, teeming with plant life and exotic fauna, was a rare find.

Forested valleys, jagged peaks and cascading waterfalls filled his view screens.

Unspoiled nature, however, did not register in Jaskar's mind; he wrenched the control stick to avoid crashing into a blimp floating above the endless canopy, its feeding tubes anchored to the branches below. A clearing flashed past, and Jaskar banked the shuttle into a tight turn, dropping the landing struts to set down beside a flowing river.

The poison dart sank into the belly of the rock hopper.

Shrubbery parted, and orange-eyes peered out. Lokor emerged, slim, bipedal, covered in a fine coat of brindle green, and clutching a thin hollow tube in delicate digits. He scanned for the minds of other Hunters before moving to retrieve the prey that had taken the best part of a day to coax from its lair with images of its favourite food.

A noise, louder than the screech of a howler plant, reverberated above the canopy. Lokor looked up to see a bright object flash past; much like the giant aerials that hunted through the crags of the Thrist Mountains, it hovered over the river and landed as smoothly as a petrel bird of the yellow swamps. Lokor scaled a nearby cone tree and sat concealed in its petals to watch.

The glittering bird was so big it was difficult to believe it could fly at all. The terrible noise subsided, leaving a silence more acute for its sudden absence. Lokor waited, trying not to pick at the tree lice exploring his green fur. A hole in the side of the giant bird appeared, and a mysterious creature emerged. It was as brightly coloured as a vine stripper, with a round yellow crest and all blue covering that shimmered in Kolar's light.

The creature dropped to the ground and began lumbering about, scooping water from the stream with a long pole, pointing a shiny object at plants before cutting pieces off, and even gathering several blue slidt tubers that grew nearby. Lokor wrinkled his nose in disgust: obviously the sky monster new nothing of their pungent effects, or their unfortunate attraction to the vreeb crawler. It would soon realise its mistake. Eventually, the creature returned to its flyer through the opening, which mysteriously closed.

Lokor slithered down the cone tree and retrieved his prey. The antics of the sky creature made no sense, and even a tentative probe revealed little of understanding. While its thoughts betrayed simple motivations, deeper reflections remained hidden. Lokor stored what images and impressions he had for an Adept to sift through later, and hurried along familiar paths back to his tree-home.

Lokor donated his prey to the communal pot, and set off down the path to the river bend, where he untied a coracle, pushed it into the flow and paddled skilfully along the bank where the current was weakest. His progress became more laboured as the river moved from open jungle flat into a gorge of the Thrist Mountains. Lokor paddled vigorously to the opposite bank where the river turned again. He secured the coracle and hopped ashore.

Far above, on a truncated pinnacle, stood the last refuge of the Kilthka.

The afternoon sunlight penetrated the swirling mists

around the ancient battlement, girded by its sheer walls of obsidian. Only a looper vine attached to a floater plant gave access to the lofty perch.

Lokor climbed into the basket dangling below the gas bag and pulled the release rope. The floater rose vertically, the vine running through greased eyelets to prevent it drifting from the wall.

On the battlement, Mogart stood wrapped in a feathered cloak of state. He was old, yet maintained a commanding presence. His fur, tinged with white where the photosynthetic symbionts had died off, still retained a robust texture.

Adjacent peaks stretched in a jagged line to the horizon, the intervening valleys filled with a jungle green that revealed the purple patches of hunting lodges and breeding sites. Parasitic floater plants hovered over the canopy trailing hooked vines to snag against the wind.

Mogart lingered, more to prolong the sharp, pleasant sting of the icy gusts, than to delay an impending council of Lodge Elders gathering in the hall below. Arbitrating a dispute over hunting boundaries was always tedious, and presently Mogart preferred the invigorating breeze.

He sensed agitation among his aides, as a new signature entered his thoughts. He turned to see a noviciate from the River Clan approach, and quick-scanned the young Hunter's thoughts, pleased to find a good block.

Lokor made the sign of obeisance and vocalised his request as protocol demanded. 'I bring urgent news, Keeper. May I present it for examination?' Mogart assented, and Lokor dropped the barrier obscuring his encounter with the sky stranger. The mental picture was crude, lacking in subtle detail, but conveyed enough for all to grasp. Lokor was not yet able to interpret or embellish the pattern of his most recent memory; it was one thing to fool a rock hopper into believing it was safe, and quite another to convey subtle meaning. For now he was merely a messenger presenting the facts and leaving their resolution to the more seasoned minds around him. Within moments, everyone present had experienced the arrival of the metal bird and its strange occupant.

Jaskar woke from a fitful sleep in the shuttle, still tired from his exertions of the previous day. He'd spent hours suited in the airlock sifting through his samples from the clearing, and feeding them to the analyser. One particular bulbous plant had burst, scattering several hundred insectoid grubs in a cloud of gas around the chamber; fortunately he was still wearing his helmet and didn't catch the lethal spray. Jaskar surmised that the grubs accumulated their toxin within the plant until a grazing animal triggered a sudden release. The grubs, killing through smell alone, gained a fresh corpse to feed on as well as providing nutrients for the plant's roots.

The analyses of more toxins in the samples and on material stuck to his suit triggered the shuttle's defences subjecting Jaskar to the wash chamber. Clearly he would have died in a variety of horrible ways without his suit.

The Shade appeared. 'I have correlated the data from the gene sequencer.'

Jaskar swallowed. 'Well?'

'The insect samples use the same strategy for energy requirements as plants,' said the Shade.

'How?'

'Photosynthetic pigment in the derma,' said the Shade, keenly. 'There are also indications many plants are symbiotically associated with the life cycle of lower animals. I need to do more tests.'

'Well, go ahead.'

'I will require a blood sample from a fresh specimen.'

'What! Now?' Jaskar knew the request was not trivial.

'It is imperative,' said the Shade. 'The Edvardsson Catalogue confirms that Leonis Minoris is 1.7 billion years older than Sol, which means the life forms on this world have been evolving much longer.'

Jaskar grunted. 'So? We can still recommend colonisation.'

The Shade's ghost flickered.

'You have an objection?' said Jaskar.

'There is one anomaly,' said the Shade. 'A stone building on one of the peaks.'

'Why didn't you say so before?'

'It's not a priority.'

'How is a sign of intelligence not a priority?'

'The relative dominance of a single species will not help us understand this ecosystem.'

Jaskar spluttered. 'That's absurd. Observing the locals will teach us a lot more, a lot quicker.'

'Only if there is real communication,' said the Shade. 'Otherwise we waste time trying to understand one species at the expense of all others.'

Jaskar could only shake his head at this display of machine logic.

'I'd like to visit this building,' said Jaskar. 'Maybe I

can get your blood sample from one of its occupants.'

The Shade reacted. 'PS27, I must caution you against revealing yourself to the inhabitants.'

'Hunters and Elders,' said Mogart. 'You have all seen the sky stranger, and its aerial floater through the eyes of Lokor of the River Clan.' There were growls of assent.

A grizzled veteran spoke. 'The Breeders will soon disperse. The Shining Bird must go!'

Mogart held up his paw and cast his thoughts through the minds of the gathering, soothing some, bolstering others, while maintaining a coercive calm over free-ranging emotions. Mogart's long experience told him he had little time to solve the mystery. Hunters were creatures of action.

'First, we must know more,' said Mogart. 'Gorlaa, you take a party of your best Hunters and encircle the giant bird, but do not attack. Reela, have your scouts maintain a watch above the river falls. Report any changes to my Senders.'

Mogart turned to a nearby Adept, projecting a quick mental command. 'Kaleer, take Lokor and observe. Relay all encounters to me.'

The Lodge Elders left the meeting purposefully, their original boundary dispute forgotten; they jostled each other in their haste to board their plant floaters and be about their new adventure.

Mogart knew he was taking a risk, but the Hunters would confront the interlopers anyhow. It was in their nature to seek prey and test themselves.

To preserve his neutrality, Mogart kept aloof from the Lodges, and rarely descended to the protean jungle. The

Keep served as a last refuge of learning and psionic art.

Jaskar descended from the rear hatch inside a servo suit. He disliked the servos, but this time felt he would be safer inside a titanium shell with the strength of ten. At least only the suit had to go through the tiresome decontamination procedure.

He crossed the clearing and entered the jungle through a break in the foliage; a curtain of leaves, blooms and sticky vines engulfed him. His clumsy passage stirred up a nest of activity: creatures flew, slithered, and jumped, either from him, or onto the armour of his suit. Jaskar squirmed, and pressed on, eventually breaking into a vast space under the canopy. Here, trees stood further apart with pathways between them; high above, a green carpet of arboreal illumination flexed and shimmered. A nearby shrub glowed as a fan of transparent spines focused light into the photosynthetic symbionts at its centre.

Jaskar turned up the sound pickup in his helmet and stood transfixed at the cacophony of hoots, whistles, and screams. The sounds came in waves making his head throb, threatening to befuddle him. Could a sound be as dangerous as a smell on a world where the latter had proven fatal? Jaskar hurriedly filtered out the noise, and looked for something to shoot at. A six legged armadillo scurried from the undergrowth and clamped to a tree trunk; it was the size of a small dog, and its claws gave excellent purchase as it scurried upward. Jaskar activated the forearm laser, but before it could fire, a coiled vine snapped down impaling the animal with a barbed tip, and snatched it up into the canopy. Jaskar was too startled to abort the firing sequence, and a coruscating beam sizzled along the trunk, lopping off branches.

Several nearby bushes materialised into bear-like creatures that scattered. The bears quickly blended into the foliage leaving Jaskar to wonder if he'd imagined the whole scene. Why had he seen plants instead of animals? The suit's sensors could not distinguish the difference. He set the laser to a wider beam and aimed at a nearby clump with orange blossoms. Again, before he could fire, one bush shimmered to reveal a catlike animal with orange eyes. It too melted away.

The situation was getting dangerously comical.

Frustrated, Jaskar fired a random burst up into the canopy and waited to see what fell: plant material cascaded down, and a blue-furred quadruped. Jaskar extended the suit's metal arm and popped its body into a cryobox.

Mogart was in meditation, his mind open to receive images from his Senders. The activity around the bird-craft in the clearing disturbed him. Lokor linked with Kaleer to confirm that the mental signature of the sky visitor was the same as before. That it could change its form was familiar, that it could destroy with a terrible light, was not. This was beyond his experience, but at least now he knew the sky creature posed a great danger.

Mogart considered sending out a general call for an Emergent Link—an event that had not occurred in a millennium. Most Hunters could not stay linked for long. It was anathema to them: one invaded the mind of the prey to gain a brief advantage, not to assimilate.

Even if they succeeded, there was always the danger

of war with those wanting to retain the Link. The last time this happened, those forming the gestalt used air plants to carry stone and build the Keep. Normality returned only when Hunters using floaters and grappling hooks stormed the citadel, forcing the linked minds to break apart. The Hunters reverted to individualism, and returned to the jungle, allowing the Keep to remain as a communal meeting place.

Mogart decided to form a Link with the Adepts inside the Keep: to at least protect themselves.

'Plant sap! The animal's blood is plant sap?'

'Not exactly,' said the Shade, enjoying Jaskar's discomfort. 'But, it has many similar components.'

'Maybe you got stomach contents; maybe the thing feeds on sap?'

'The animal's teeth and tail stinger negates the sap diet,' said the Shade, vexed.

'I hadn't noticed the stinger,' said Jaskar.

'Evidently, the creature is slow moving and cryptic within its tree-host,' said the Shade. 'The stinger kills plant eaters to be consumed at leisure. Like the bushes, it probably looks like something harmless to the intended prey.'

'Clever.'

The Shade continued, 'The plants and animals overlap, with everything evolving at a constant rate. But, genetic complexity is inconsistent with the relative simplicity of the life forms. Intelligence separated humans from their environment; some other mechanism is working here.'

'Not intelligence? What then?'

The projection remained silent, shimmering faintly over the flight deck.

'Computer, I insist that you answer.'

The Shade hated to be called Computer. 'As you saw, the local fauna demonstrated the art of illusion. The strategy is one of direct mental linkages that have evolved between and within species. Such mental links could form direct communication.'

'You mean telepathy,' said Jaskar.

'That would be one strategy, another could be more coercive.'

'Like making you do something stupid because you're seeing something that's not there,' said Jaskar.

'Precisely. We must be very careful. Humans have never developed psionic talent—it was not a trait required during natural selection. Here, the strategy appears to have evolved. There is no defence.'

'We have weapons. We can destroy a planet.'

'Is that your solution?' said the Shade, showing alarm. 'Pray the intellects on this world do not pick up that thought. I urge you to return to orbit. We must leave at once.'

Jaskar could barely believe his ears. He'd spent weeks in stasis, and hours of wake-time sifting data, just to pack up and go when matters became interesting. Jaskar started up the shuttle. 'I'm going to check over that building,'

Mogart sat on the stone seat at the centre of the tower chamber, surrounded by Adepts in rigid postures. A cool wind blew through the embrasures, stirring the finger webs. He rode the tide of their thoughts, directing them to a single purpose. Something interrupted the tenuous concert: Lokor and Kaleer sending an image of the alien bird leaving the river clearing.

Mogart's hearts skipped several beats. He re-harnessed his mind with the Adepts, adding their strength to his own, and cast his thoughts outward. There, yes. The creature within the shining bird was both familiar and strange. The bird moved swiftly. Mogart's mind followed.

The creature, distracted with flying the giant bird, was easy to penetrate—just like any prey. Mogart saw the flight deck through its eyes. There was energy, but it was inanimate; it soon dawned on him that the sky bird was a mere tool, an object like a dart tube or coracle. The speed was exhilarating: the jungle below flashed past and the Thrist Mountains rushed closer. Presently, jagged peaks towered on each side; the creature appeared to be searching. When Mogart saw the Keep through the creature's eyes, his trepidation multiplied, and he stabbed into its mind.

When Jaskar saw where the building stood, he was ill-prepared for the swooping rampart melded into rock like an eagle's nest. The construction defied its dizzy elevation. A balloon-plant suspending a vine-woven basket was tethered to the turret's battlement. So the blimps had a purpose after all. Jaskar set the shuttle hovering over the structure; there was no sign of activity. The slanted roof provided no purchase, and the parapet was almost too narrow for a safe landing.

Jaskar desperately wanted to explore the edifice. He started the landing sequence and began a slow descent to the battlement. Then something turned inside his head, a slithery ropey thing that pulled behind his eyes.

Jaskar clutched his skull. The shuttle swayed dangerously, going into a spin; the main console lighted up with warnings. The stone citadel swept past.

Mogart flinched at the repulsive force directed at him, but hung on grimly. Raw fear was a familiar thing, and the old Hunter in him knew how to control it in others. He probed deeper, and found the inner workings of the strange one's mind strewn with the familiar layers of emotion and conflict found in any Kilthkan prey; but unlike them, this mind kept its desires separate in a maze of blind alleys.

Contradictions assailed Mogart.

In seconds, he saw a history of destruction in the memory of the creature, of a species where the tide of development had swept a planet to ruination. Worse yet: to escape the limits of their environment, they had created intelligent machines more powerful than themselves; the machines saved them from extinction but controlled their world. Now the creators depended on their creations.

Mogart shuddered. The sky creature was an offworlder from one of the flickering lights in the sky. Its powers, inexorable, its purpose—to enslave and consume. Without hesitation, Mogart took control. Jaskar howled in disbelief as his hands gripping the control stick, pushed: the flyer tilted forward and slammed into rock. Jaskar never knew what killed him.

Mogart then transferred his attention to the Other. His mind soared skyward, riding the crest of a wave provided by the combined thoughts of the Adepts. With far sight, he glimpsed a sleek metal shape on the edge of darkness where the other presence lurked. It was logical, precise, and a storehouse of great knowledge. Mogart experienced an all-too brief glimpse of bizarre imagery, geometric figures, and mathematical formulae. For a moment, he misunderstood what he was seeing. Was this a tool of intelligence?

The shape exploded into a flaming ball, and swiftly receded. Mogart lost contact when the object disappeared from his mind-view, leaving him with the cold dread of his own speculations. The Link dissolved, the Adepts slumped.

Mogart staggered from the chamber and took the steps up to the parapet and bracing air. The giant yellow sun, Kolar, was sinking behind the Thrist Mountains as the first stars emerged. He looked up with a new understanding and pondered the future of his race.

If they were to repel another visit from the Tool Makers, the Clans of the Kilthka would have to unite after all and rediscover the terrible powers abandoned by the Ancients.

Back on board the ship, the Shade directed the clone chamber to prepare Jaskar PS28 for the next planet fall.

Steve de Beer is retired and living in North Queensland where a slower pace of life allows him to enjoy writing, travel, painting, and reading a good book. Writing serves as an escape to that far-imagined future, or alien world, he likes to visit with others occasionally.

Continuity

Damon Shaw

When the ship took control of her droids, Belen knew she had lost the battle for the cargo holds. She could only watch, grinding her many hundreds of teeth as her robots tore each other apart, separating each others' limbs into ordered piles. Later, she knew, the ship would absorb them and mould them into armies of its own.

Embedded deep in the bridge, Belen twitched and grumbled. The debacle today had cost her years of effort. The ship now controlled a whole sixty-four per cent of the Home that housed and comprised them both. If Belen lost life support, the war would be over.

A chime signalled that the ship wanted to speak. Belen ignored it. She knew the ritual of gloating, demands and weepy paranoia that would follow. The ship was long due for a reboot, but of course, the AI core was the most heavily defended and well outside Belen's reach.

Now that she could spare the attention, she sequestered more building sludge, and accelerated the growth of her latest soldiers. A cunning combination of flesh and metal—wirelessly linked, and each complex enough to hold Belen's downloaded mindstate—they would be lethal, if the ship gave her long enough to finish them. The eternal brushfire battles raged along their borders as ever, and Belen had limited resources to spare. There was only so much flesh and metal to go round.

The chime grew louder. Somehow, the ship had levered a flashing red light into Belen's bridge display. She snapped open a channel.

'I'm not taking visitors,' she said. 'I'm not presentable.' She severed the connection before the ship could get in a snide reply.

The last time she saw herself, she had wept at the bloated mass her body had become. At the time it had filled the bridge, and the pale meat of her had stretched down to the mess hall. Now she dreaded to think what she looked like. What she was. But the ship had still not managed to rewrite its most basic directive. It could not directly harm Belen herself, so the bigger she grew, the more territory she covered and the more secure her position. A good appearance was a peacetime conceit.

'Belen.' The voice was smooth and calm. 'We must talk.'

How had the ship managed to get a line into the bridge? Triple firewalls should already be frying any semblance of consciousness from the intruder.

'Belen. Emergency negotiations. I declare a truce.'

'A truce takes two, honey. And I'm not playing.' Belen sent a surge of superheated air through the starboard vents, hoping to overheat some vital chip or at least cause a distraction. In the med lab crèches, her new soldiers grew fingernails and shiny air tubes. Not long now.

'Belen. Look!'

The ship opened a screen in the bridge display. At first, Belen didn't understand what she saw. A mottled surface of brown and white, with patches of deep blue. Silent. Unmoving. Only when she saw the thin sliver of darkness, did the image pop out into a sphere. A planet. An Earth.

'We've arrived, Belen. We can stop fighting.'

Was that an entreaty in the ship's voice? Was it capitulating? 'Arrived where?' She had felt no acceleration, no braking. This could be a trap.

'Um. I don't know. I used the storage space.'

'You overwrote our destination?'

'It was during the Battle of the Library in the third century. I was losing.'

Ah, yes. Belen had nearly gained control of the entire fourth deck in that skirmish. So long ago, now. Had she legs, then? Could she still walk?

'So, what were we supposed to do next?'

'Land, I think, but that data has gone, too. No idea.' The ship sounded cheerful. 'But it doesn't matter anyway, because we've got no drive.'

'What?'

'No rockets, no thruster, no fuel, no fuel bays, no directional capability whatsoever. Only the immense precision of our planners stopped us impacting with that unlovely surface you see before you. I called it Mudd. What do you say?'

Belen grinned. Her own robots had dismantled the thruster tubes almost a millennium ago, in an aborted attempt at cutting in towards the AI core from naked space. 'I say the victor gets to name the planet. But maybe we need to cooperate to get down there.'

'I knew you'd see sense,' said the ship. 'Here, I've made up a blue print of the changes we'll need to make. Don't worry, I actually lose more territory than you. But you have to give up the med labs.'

'No way.' It was an obvious ploy. The med labs were her main strong point—and weak spot too. Here, she made the spider-limbed cleaning robots that groomed her huge bulk, and kept her bulkheads firm and free of spies. And here she made her armies. Here, twenty soldiers jerked and twitched as dreams pumped through their empty brains. Soon they would wake.

'I lose the cargo bays and the last of the telescopes and cameras, I'll be blind.' There was definitely a tremor there. The ship was nervous. 'Think of them as suggestions. You have final say.'

'The med labs are mine.' Keeping the pressure on with her firewalls, Belen downloaded the plans. They looked sound enough. She didn't really know the parts of the Home the ship controlled. Communication lines were thin over the border.

But there seemed enough metal to make a couple of landers even if she kept the med labs. Apparently the ship guarded a secret store of hydrogen fuel too, easy enough to get them down.

'How do I know this isn't a trap?' she asked. 'You could be making this all up.'

'Here. Open up and I'll send you all I know. Your firewalls are tearing me apart.'

Belen inched open a channel and the data flooded in. Earth-like mass. Vegetable life, no animals. Fifty-nine per cent surface water. It sounded pleasant. The Home was another matter.

'Decaying orbit,' she read. 'Impact in twelve hours? Ship, what is this?'

'Our excuse to stop fighting at last.'

Belen imagined the Home, smashing into the

atmosphere at over forty-five miles per second.

In the pause, her army unclipped itself from feeds in the med lab crèches and assembled under flickering ceiling lamps. Belen opened hatches all the way to the surface of the Home, leaving only the outer airlocks closed. Somewhere in what used to be her head, her ears popped.

'I see you want to be in charge of the thrusters,' she said. 'Shall I do life support?'

'I can't see you trusting me with that, really,' said the ship. 'Not much time. Let's go.'

Belen directed her soldiers to dig in and wait in the shadow of an abandoned observation turret, deep in enemy territory. The timing was perfect. In a few hours, she would take command of the newly minted shuttles and ride down to Mudd in style. She hadn't felt so alive in centuries. After all, this must be what they were fighting about. The first to land would be an obvious victor.

So she programmed the crèche to construct vats of oxygen, emergency ration packs, and a suitable avatar. She chose to make it entirely of flesh, except for the metal download jack behind its right ear. She planned for victory. She planned for peace. She made herself beautiful.

Just as Belen got the signal that her soldiers were in place, the ship rang through.

'Bad news,' it said. 'We've had a fuel leak. I need you to make more ASAP.'

'Hmm. Okay,' said Belen. 'What happened?'

'Metal degraded. Out-gassing and general dismay all round. I've set up a cam, if you want to take a look.'

Belen looked. A tremor of alarm rippled across the

shoals of her body. The cam showed her soldiers clamped to the Home and silhouetted against the curve of Mudd. Something about the bulky shapes seemed wrong to Belen, but her attention was drawn to the seven hawk-shaped machines hovering above them.

'Ship, you cheated! Those aren't shuttles.'

'No, and those aren't ration packs. Though they'd look tasty fried.'

'No!' To Belen's horror, the floating machines shot darts into her precious soldiers.

'Retreat! Regroup! Hide!' she shrieked as one by one, her army twisted, jerked and bowled away into space. Their vital signs, drowned in high-voltage noise, snowed up and went blank.

'Not fair,' she said when only three remained. 'I made those soldiers before the truce.'

'Really?' answered the ship. 'I just finished mine. Atmosphere-capable reconnaissance drones. You'll see them on the blueprints. I added a high-voltage taser system to subdue hostile life forms.'

'Don't be smug. You know I'll get you back.'

'Smug?' answered the ship. 'That wasn't smug. *This* is smug.'

The camera image shook so Belen zoomed the image up to full resolution. Cracks appeared in the surface of the Home. Belen gaped. Her hearts all surged at once, causing her to go momentarily blind. She slammed on a layer of beta-blockers, and when her vision returned, the hull was folding back, revealing naked beams and conduits.

Waves of terror raced over her skin. Belen felt an answering shudder in her cradling superstructure. The

Home was undergoing massive restructuring.

She ordered her last three soldiers to shelter behind the far off observation turret, as alarms bloomed red across all the bridge displays. Breaches, shorts, unanswering subroutines, everything that could fail announced it had done so in a cacophony of sirens and wails.

'Off! Shut up!' Belen cut the warnings from her screens and concentrated on the one shaky camera image. This was bad.

'What I wouldn't do to see your face,' said the ship. 'If you've still got one, that is.'

Belen didn't reply. Before her eyes, gulfs opened across the Home sphere. Chambers and corridors split away. Odd books and tattered uniforms drifted out into the dark. A series of sharp explosions shook her body and left star shaped blotches on the cam image. The view began to tilt, and Belen realised that she was drifting. Cut off.

'Want some more views?' asked the ship. 'Got lots. Been planning this for ages.'

'Ship, what have you done?'

'Checkmate,' the ship said. 'Care to play again?'

As the views slid up, one after the other, Belen knew she hadn't lost a game. She had lost the war for the Home itself. Rec halls, theatres, factory pods, thrust plates and of course, the AI core all drifted away, like a bitten apple. Life support was hers, and it looked like she still had the cargo holds and the med bay, but just a thin, metal skin of airlocks and corridors lay between her and the vacuum. Worse, the ship had all the building sludge. Belen couldn't make anything.

She had been cut away from the body of the Home.

Unharmed, but trembling with shock, she tumbled away in her fragile cocoon.

In the retreating mass of the Home, where minutes ago she had snuggled, stupidly content, red sparks guttered and flared. Thrusters.

'See you on the surface.' The ship held off full power until Belen had drifted clear. Then the blaze of the secret drives lifted, turned white, then blue, and just before all the cams melted, Belen saw the Home shudder, turn and begin to sink away towards the planet, now forever beyond her reach.

'Jump!' she yelled into the comms. Of the three surviving soldiers, two made it across the widening gap. She physically heard the clang as they impacted, scant metres from her head. One broke its legs and drifted free, but the other held on, unscathed and operational. She sent it creeping over her surface, assessing the damage. Ghost sensations rippled down the length of her body, as if she could feel its feet tickling her skin.

Her mind reeled. How had the ship managed this? More than subterfuge, it required long-term planning and playing on many fronts at once. In the chaos, Belen had forgotten to cancel the avatar and the poor, pretty thing now battered at the lid of the crèche in the med labs. Belen gave it a shot of sleep and soon heard it snore.

Blood gathered in her extremities under the faint centrifugal force. Belen swore at the waves of pins and needles. She cursed the ship and her own stupidity. At last, she calmed and turned the temperature up a notch. She felt cold. Exposed.

As she expected, the ship gloated on all channels.

'Beginning atmospheric entry in twenty minutes,' it

said. 'Oooh, look at that view. Speak to me, Belen. Tell me how it feels.'

'To be free of you? I would have paid a lot more.'

'I have to say, I feel the loss,' said the ship. 'But don't be sad. I left you a present.'

She suspected the worst. 'You did? What is it?'

'A surprise, of course. Can't talk now, got to concentrate.' The ship cut the connection, leaving Belen swearing into dead air.

She called an emergency meeting in the med lab, one of the few places where she still had power. She spoke through a cleaning bot, clamped high on the side of the med lab recycler. The soldier gripped a handhold near the crèche while she summed up their situation.

Air and nutrients weren't a problem. Their orbit would decay long before they ran out of either. Tumbling slowly, they massed almost eight hundred tons. At least a quarter of that was Belen herself.

'I've got no building materials, and no fuel . . . ' Belen paused, contemptuous of the soldier's empty eyes. She couldn't remember ever feeling alone like this. Peerless. Without equal. 'Worse,' she said, 'the ship left me a surprise. It can't directly hurt me, but I suspect it won't be nice.

'I'm due to impact in just over eleven hours,' she continued. 'We have that time to find it, come up with a plan, and get safely to the ground. Are you listening?'

The soldier peered through the clear lid of the crèche at the newly woken avatar. Inside, smooth hands fluttered at rosebud lips. Lashes trembled over deep, innocent blue eyes.

'Beautiful,' whispered the soldier. 'So beautiful.'

'Down boy. Face front. Mind on the matter at hand.' Belen gassed up the med labs to a one bar oxygen mix, and unclipped the lid of the crèche. 'Did you hear any of that, Dolly? I made you clever enough to have an opinion.'

The avatar nodded, its golden hair falling in cascades over pearly shoulders. 'It's so sad,' she said. 'Why were you fighting?'

Belen paused. She couldn't remember. The ship attacked and she retaliated. It was all there was. 'Find out,' she said at last. 'It might be important. Here, have a space suit. Put something on, for God's sake.'

While Dolly dressed herself, and the soldier turned away, fussing with its equipment pack, Belen briefed them both. 'You have two hours to search my territory. Books, decor, architecture, everything. Tell me why I'm here. What this mission was about. Anything that might help against the enemy. And keep an eye out for anything the ship left behind.'

'Yes, ma'am,' snapped the soldier, sounding happy to have clear objectives. Something about it made Belen uneasy. Was this the ship's surprise? Could it have replaced one of her soldiers in the chaos? No, there had been no time to make a copy. She always kept the body plans safe inside her head. The soldier was definitely one of hers. But still, something about it rankled.

Dolly dawdled in the hatch. 'It's dark. Haven't you got a flashlight?'

Belen ordered two grooming robots to scrape the last building sludge from the tubes. They fed it into the med lab recycler, and Belen spun up lamps, spare air tanks and two large machetes.

'Nice blade,' said the soldier, hefting the knife in a slick, muscled grip.

'You're scary,' said the avatar, reaching out a tentative hand to the soldier's shining bicep. 'Why do we need knives? Is it dangerous?'

'Some of the hallways are blocked,' said Belen. 'Try not to cut a major artery.'

While the two squeezed down meat filled passageways, Belen sent her robots to one of her functional airlocks and directed them outside to search her surface. The bots weren't designed for vacuum work and they grumbled and threatened to seize, but Belen kept them hunting until she was sure she was clean. Knowing the ship, the surprise would be nasty, and clever and right under her nose.

'Belen to ship,' she called. 'Give me a clue.'

At last, the ship responded. 'Bit of a bumpy ride, but all in one piece,' it said. 'Sensors say the air smells of cabbage. Want a look?'

'Send me the hawk drones,' Belen begged. 'I need the mass . . . Please.'

'Eighty-three years I've been setting that up. I'm still replaying your voice. *"What have you done?"*' The ship chuckled. 'Haven't you opened your present yet?'

'Tell me where it is.' Belen tried to keep the panic from her voice. 'Ship? Is it a bomb?'

'I suppose you could call it a bomb,' the ship said. 'A time bomb. I'll leave it in your capable hands.'

Instead of telling her more, the ship boasted. It recounted its cleverness in faking advances to plant cutter bombs, splicing fake data into her border spies. Belen used her limited information to triangulate its position on the ground, and then ignored it. She had scant hours to plan.

They regrouped in the med labs to examine the evidence. Belen was dismayed to see how little the soldier and the avatar had found.

'What's this?' she asked. Her grooming bot plucked a scrap of cloth from the air.

'Small trousers,' said the soldier. 'Very old.'

The avatar wrung her hands. 'There were children here. So long ago.'

The thought of children running through her hallways made Belen feel dirty. 'Report,' she said. 'You first, Sam.'

'Me?' the soldier asked. 'Is that my name?'

'It's a lovely name,' said the avatar, wiping her eyes. 'Short. Solid.'

'Report,' Belen repeated through gritted teeth. 'Go!'

'Ma'am. Your corridors are clean. No bomb, nor traces of explosives. We found evidence of habitation by crew and passengers. Nothing to show where they went. On a locker in the mess hall we discovered this name tag.' The soldier held out a tiny plaque.

Belen zoomed in to read the tiny writing.

'Belen Samuelle, Chief Navigating Officer. Was that . . . me?'

'Looks like it, ma'am.' The soldier cleared its throat. 'When we squeezed into the bridge the, um, main part of you, the bit with the head, was in the navigator's chair.'

Navigator, thought Belen. *Samuelle. How strange.* She didn't ask what she looked like. She didn't want to know.

'Tactical analysis suggests three possibilities, ma'am,'

said Sam. 'There was an accident, and everyone else died. Or the ship killed them all, keeping you alive. Or . . .'

'Or I killed them all myself, and don't remember,' said Belen. 'Hmm. Why were we fighting? Any clues?'

'Maybe . . . Maybe you were friends, once,' suggested the avatar. 'A long time ago. And the ship was jealous that you were made of flesh, so love turned to . . . to resentment maybe. So in the end it had to get away or be destroyed by its own emotions.'

'Civilians.' Belen sighed. 'Anything real, Sam?'

'This, ma'am.' The soldier held up a piece of wood. A chess piece. A pawn. 'It was embedded in you. Near one of your functional arms. You played a lot.'

'We found hundreds of boards in ceramic crates in the cargo hold,' the avatar said. 'All worn and broken.'

'Don't remember,' said Belen, though something about the chess piece made her blood burn with a long forgotten heat. 'Next point. How do I land? Give me a ten word summary of early concepts.'

There was a long pause. The soldier and the avatar glanced at each other.

'No idea,' they said together.

In the corner of Belen's vision, like a fluttering twitch, the seconds counted down in tiny red numerals. Eight hours to impact.

'Okay.' It had come to this, Belen had no other options. 'Forget the bomb, we've no time. Get the machetes. You're going to play doctors and nurses.'

She prepared as best she could, but even with her nerves switched off, Belen could still feel them cutting chunks away. Arms full of blubber, the soldier paused near a wall mounted cam on the way to the med lab recycler. 'Belen? Ma'am?'

'Yes?'

'I don't want to be Sam. I think I'm female. I'd like to be Samuelle, too.'

'You're not female,' spluttered Belen. 'You've got no parts at all. You're an it. Get on with your work.'

'Nevertheless,' said the soldier, floating aside to let the avatar pass.

'I like you either way,' said Dolly, heading back towards the bridge.

Belen turned her attention to the building work in disgust, but found it hard to concentrate. The soldier's declarations made her uneasy. None of her other creations had tried to define themselves. Sam was complex though, the best she had ever made. She had woven loyalty and resourcefulness into personality routines based on her own. Maybe it wasn't surprising that Sam was growing up.

She set a small robot to keep watch on the soldier anyway and then tried to forget it. The half-formed escape pod in the cargo hold demanded her attention.

Entry vehicles needed to withstand enormous heat and pressure. Using the only raw materials to hand, Belen set the crèches to spin fibrous shields of cartilage, soaked in precious water, and wrapped in layers of insulating fat and toughened skin. Her grooming bots stitched the quivering pieces together in the cargo hold. They primed bladders to inflate and increase drag during the fall. They sealed each successive caul of skin and cauterised the coolant veins. The result wasn't pretty and it skirted the envelope of survivability, but it was the best Belen could do.

She kept an eye on Sam all the while. The soldier worked hard, but she noticed it paused at times, as if listening, eyes blank and unreadable. It wasn't hers in those moments. She wanted to use her wireless override, switch it off and recycle the resources, but with the landing pod unfinished, she needed much more meat than Sam could provide. So her little robot always flitted nearby as the soldier worked, its mics turned up full.

'She's using her flesh to protect us as we land,' Dolly whispered, waist high in creamy fat. 'Is that love, do you think?'

The soldier shrugged, but did not reply. Belen didn't tell them that the avatar wouldn't experience the descent. The Queen had plans for that empty head.

While they worked, a new atmosphere filled Belen's broken remnant of the Home. Dolly sang nonsense melodies as she shoved floating bundles of assorted bones and meat. She exclaimed over new finds.

'Here's another heart!'

'That makes twelve now,' said Sam. 'If we sliced her up do you think the parts would survive?'

'Don't try it,' growled Belen from blood spattered loudspeakers. 'Less talk and more work. We're on a deadline.'

'My suit chafes,' said Dolly, holding onto a girder and letting her armful of raw materials float on down the corridor. 'I've got blisters.'

'You'll have more than blisters if we don't get the pod finished,' warned Belen. 'Move it.'

'Wait,' said Sam. 'I have skin-seal in my pack. Belen thought of everything.'

'Did I?' asked Belen. 'When was that?' But the ship's

words came crashing back to her and she missed the soldier's reply. *I'll leave it in your capable hands.* Of course! Sam's were the only capable hands she had. All hers were vestigial by now, and Dolly wasn't much more use.

'—under the observation turret,' the soldier said. 'Where you had us wait. Back when I had brothers and sisters. There was one each—'

'Take it off!' Belen's voice cracked in panic. 'The pack! Carefully, you fool. It's the bomb.'

Sam unhitched the equipment pack and held it at arm's length. On the inside panel, a countdown flashed. *Three, two, one—*

'Throw it!' she shouted, knowing it was too late.

Zero.

The rucksack petalled open, spilling wrenches, rations and first aid kits into the air. When it was fully inside out, it vibrated like a drum, and the ship's voice filled the shadowed hold.

'This is a recorded message for the many ears of sweet Belen,' said the pack. 'I lied about the time of impact. You will hit Mudd's atmosphere in, *hmm*, exactly sixty-three minutes and fourteen seconds after the beep. Wait for it . . . *Beep.* Don't bother to reply.' The pack shivered and went limp.

An hour? Swearing and spitting, she checked the figures on the looming planet, but the lie could be in any one of them: gravity, diameter, atmospheric depth . . . A time bomb indeed. Stupid, so stupid to trust the ship. Hadn't she learned anything in so many years of war?

'Cargo hold. Immediately,' snapped Belen. 'We need to leave.'

'Did you notice, she said *we*?' whispered Dolly as they pulled themselves along the hallway. 'She's taking us, too.'

The soldier was more skilled at subterfuge and Belen couldn't hear its reply. No matter. It was a pawn. She could switch it off at whim via the radio link if it misbehaved. She'd have it familiarise itself with the pod controls while she downloaded into Dolly. Belen would be disorientated after the transfer, and re-entry needed a steady hand.

When they arrived in the dark cargo hold, Sam and Dolly lit the escape pod with shaky flashlight beams. Belen watched them in infra-red from her robot's eyes.

'It's so small,' said Dolly. 'How will we all fit?'

Ribbed and veined, the pod pulsed and flexed in the still air, tethered by an umbilical to the deck. Grooming bots sprayed one last coat of spit-caked foam over the prow and sealed it under a final layer of wet skin. Belen ordered the robots back and opened the entry sphincter. In the red gloom within, a tongue shaped couch writhed, waiting.

The soldier cleared its throat. 'How are you getting down, ma'am?'

'Just climb inside, Sam. Study the controls.' She extended a cable from the bulkhead and tried to sound calm. The avatar would be unconscious for long minutes during the transfer. There was no time to waste. 'Dolly? Pop over here and plug yourself in.'

'Don't do it, Ava,' said the soldier.

'Ava?' Belen snorted. 'Move, girl.'

'It's my name,' said the avatar, evading the snaking cable. 'Samuelle got to choose.'

'I will not tolerate mutiny,' said Belen. She raised the lights and revealed the grooming bots, ranked and alert. They clutched scalpels in manipulator claws, and puffed jets of gas, shepherding the two figures towards the cable jack.

'Get behind me, Ava.' The soldier unsheathed both machetes. It swept them around its body in complex arcs, coming to rest, poised and steady. 'I'll protect you.'

'Stop this nonsense,' said Belen. 'Do as I say.' She activated the override to turn Sam off, but blinked in shock as words flashed up on her screen in the bridge.

Access denied. This personality core is password protected.

'You *what?* Sam, you traitor. You're mine.' The idea that the soldier had true autonomy sent chills through the mass of her. 'How did you cut me out?'

'I looked inside, and I listened,' said Sam. 'Very hard. To myself. I saw how I worked.' It lifted its chin and its eyes flashed. 'I am mine.'

'Then,' said Belen, 'you are consciously refusing orders. Dolly—here. Now.' She sent a robot in but the soldier sliced through its manipulators with one sweep.

'Get into the pod,' Sam said. 'Quick!'

The avatar pushed off from the wall and caught the tether of the escape pod in a suited hand. She swung and hit the side of the vessel but didn't let go. There was no way she could fly it, so Belen ignored her and concentrated on the real threat.

The soldier tapped the walls with its heels, inching along, knives balanced and ready. It reached and pulled a crate into the path of the advancing bots. The lid swung open, filling the air with pawns and rooks, worn queens and broken bishops.

Belen had centuries of practice in close-up skirmishing. Two bots charged from the left while she split the rest and attacked from above and below. Sam cut and slashed, dealing massive damage, but was soon overwhelmed. Scalpels flashed, chittering on the soldier's metal skin.

Belen turned a robot eye to the escape pod. Dolly hesitated half inside, looking back.

'Sam!' she screamed. She began to pull herself back out through the sphincter and Belen saw her chance.

She closed the entrance and moist flesh closed about Dolly's body, clamping her arms to her sides. Belen sent the cable twisting through the air. The blunt jack probed and rebounded from the struggling avatar, searching for the port behind her ear. Belen prepared to download at last.

Goodbye, Home, she thought. *Goodbye, bridge.* She couldn't believe she was leaving.

'Please don't,' pleaded Dolly. 'It's not fair. We're so new. Haven't you ever been in love, Belen? Mother?'

'Stop it,' said Belen. 'You're disgusting.'

Three screens went blank. Belen switched views and saw Sam momentarily break free from the crowd of robots. A thousand slices dulled its skin, and its arm floated loose, randomly twitching. The soldier broke for the wall, tensed and pushed off across the hold. Belen's robots swivelled fast to see its destination. The manual lever to open the cargo doors glinted under its glass cover.

'Stop!'

Her robots were too slow. The soldier smashed the cover with one punch and used the recoil to grasp the lever, and pull.

'Ava,' shouted Sam, 'Don't hold your breath! Lungs explode!'

With grinding creaks and a growing shriek of air, the cargo doors shuddered and slid apart. The pod bounced and lurched on its tether. Belen lost control of the sphincter and Dolly floated free. A bowling crate of chessboards clipped her, and she was swept out, her scream cut off as the atmosphere bloomed into the void around her. Belen saw her slam shut her helmet, but she had no tanks fitted and wouldn't last long.

Mother? she thought. *Ugh, ghastly.*

She turned her attention back to the soldier to see it sawing at the pod's umbilical with half a machete blade.

'I'm coming Ava.' The soldier shook with tearless sobs. 'Don't die. Don't die.'

'Sam, bring her back,' shouted Belen, as the tether snapped and the pod drifted towards the stars. 'It doesn't hurt. We could share her.'

The soldier scrambled through the closing sphincter. Even before it cleared the cargo doors, jets coughed and caught, and the pod swung away, blazing into the night. She watched, impotent, as it swept towards the suited avatar. Sam handled it like a pro, she had to admit. Dolly was probably still conscious when the soldier pulled her suited figure through the sphincter, and sealed the pod for re-entry.

'Come back,' said Belen on Sam's radio link. 'Please?' She tried again to switch the soldier off. There might be enough time to attempt a wireless download into its head if the pod did not burn up while Sam was unconscious. It was her only chance.

Access denied. This personality core is password protected.

'Freedom?' said Belen, trying to put herself in Sam's place. 'Independence?'

Incorrect password. Access denied.

'God forgive us— Love?'

Access denied.

Belen screamed with her real voice and with all her sirens, until the fragile hull rang with her rage. How could it all have gone so wrong? It took long minutes for her to regain control of her thrashing hearts.

The bulkheads pinged and creaked around her. She didn't close the cargo doors. The creamy bulk of Mudd loomed, landscape already filling half the sky.

If she turned the blunt segment of Home around and entered backwards, there was a chance she could skip like a stone on the still pond of Mudd's atmosphere. But even if she survived, she would ricochet back out into space, alone, with limited power, and only the last two grooming bots for company. Belen didn't want to end like that. She would rather die fast and clean, if at all.

She sent the pair of bots on one last foray to collect fat and drag it to the med lab. Fat burned and Belen wanted a final solution at hand, just in case. 'Ava forever?' she tried on the radio link.

Access denied.

'Innocent victim?'

Access denied.

Forty minutes to impact.

She was running out of time. Any moment the pod could enter the atmosphere and Belen would lose radio contact until it slowed and the plasma front cleared. She had to guess the password and initiate a wireless download, but she was too terrified to think straight. What had the soldier seen in its short life? What was important to it?

'You kids take care,' she said, feigning calm over the link. 'Mother forgives you. Don't forget to deploy the drogues.'

'We don't need you any more.' The soldier heaved for breath, but sounded jubilant. 'We're going to start a new life.'

'You do that,' said Belen. In the background, she heard the avatar cheering. 'Stay away from the coast. I might cause quite a splash.'

With a crackle, the ship cut in.

'Sounds exciting,' it said. 'Got trouble up there, Belen? Mutiny issues? Did you like your present? I'm preparing a welcome party for when you arrive.'

She ignored it. 'A new life?' she transmitted to the soldier.

Access denied. Belen scowled. She called up the ship's position. A scorched trail of vegetation ended at a slim column of smoke. Zooming in, a shaky blur resolved into lines of vehicles and ranked machines around the remains of the Home. Tiny hawk-shaped specks buzzing above the massed army showed the scale of the ship's ambition.

She had no choice but to put it aside as a problem to be solved later. Right now she needed to be able to think about too many things at once. If she recorded her mind state, and downloaded *that* instead of doing it real time, it would free her up to deal with emergencies.

She took five long slow breaths to calm herself. She didn't want to wake in a burst of panicked adrenaline. *I'm about to reboot in the soldier's body,* she told herself, *on an alien planet, ready for action.*

As ready as she would ever be, she took a copy of her mindstate and left the data, poised to begin downloading on a hair-trigger switch.

'Mutineer?' she transmitted. 'I am Samuelle? I am not an it?'

Access denied.

With half an hour to impact, the bots had built up a stockpile of explosives: power cells, reactors, sacks of flesh-distilled alcohol, anything flammable they could scavenge. They netted the massive bundle and dragged it into the cargo hold. Belen made them sing as they worked but they couldn't hold a tune and it just made her feel more nervous. She withdrew an antenna deep inside herself in case she had a chance to begin downloading, but she was losing hope.

'Unwilling combatant?'

Access denied.

'Too young to die?'

Access denied.

By the time the bots had secured the unstable mass of explosives, and primed it with insulated nerve fibre, she could see the thin lilac haze of Mudd's atmosphere and, below, sprawling coastlines and continents, easily visible.

There was no time.

What had Sam said about looking inside? It had found itself. What was inside a half flesh, half metal, asexual machine with delusions of free will?

'Pride?' she said. 'Rebellion? Terror?'

Access denied. Strange tremors moved her. Belen realised that she was crying. That frightened her more than anything else.

'Hope,' she said.

Access denied.

'Despair.'

Access denied.

'Loneliness.'

Access granted.

Belen gaped. 'Master override,' she shouted. 'Shut down!' Before she could trip the download switch, a movement against the surface of Mudd caught her eye. The pod scored a thin grey line across the clouds, and plunged down into radio silence. So close. The soldier was open to her, but now even further out of reach, and with Dolly at the controls.

With ten minutes to her own impact, she admitted she had run out of time. The pod hadn't reappeared. She would have to survive her plunge into the atmosphere and try to begin transmission if possible afterward.

Her surging adrenaline levels left her shaky and nauseous. Nerve suppressors could only blank out so much and Belen knew entry would hurt. She used excess gas to spin onto her back so the hardened outer skin of the Home would take the brunt of the superheated plasma, and there, cradled, she counted down the seconds.

Just before impact, the soldier pinged up on the radio. They had survived re-entry. Far away, the pod descended beneath a parachute of fine supple skin. Belen wasted no time and activated the download. Already she could hear the hiss and rumble of rising wind and her thermometers blinked urgent warnings. She had to concentrate.

She plunged into the ionosphere at just over forty-five miles per second and immediately lost radio contact. Belen felt bones pop and shatter as her body slammed against bulkheads and split across doorways. A screaming howl drowned out her warning alarms, and Belen almost blacked out as she began to spin. Only adroit manoeuvring of the cargo doors stopped her tumbling out of control.

The Home shuddered and thrummed around her. External antennae whipped away. Airlocks fused shut. The cargo doors themselves glowed red and slumped back in streams of molten metal.

Smoke filled the bridge, burning her lungs, but before she could cough, there was a crack, and the smoke whirled away. Belen felt searing cold all along her left side, her body bypassing the nerve suppressors to tell her of its pain. The Home was breaking up around her and Belen knew she was about to die.

Then she broke free of the atmosphere and into the silence of space once more. The hull pinged and banged as it cooled. Physically blinded, bleeding internally, flesh boiling into the vacuum, Belen ignored her body's ruin and checked the download. Seven per cent of her had made it across. Not enough. She patched in as soon as radio contact was re-established to hear Ava talking to a smooth voice that Belen had hoped never to hear again.

'Yes, completely insane,' said the ship. 'Poisoned the entire crew and I couldn't stop her. You were lucky to escape.'

'She wanted to—to overwrite me!' said the avatar. And I think she switched off my sweet Samuelle. She won't answer.'

'I know a way we can get Samuelle back,' said the ship. 'Step away from the pod.'

No! Belen wanted to scream. *Don't trust it.* But the download took up all the bandwidth and all she could do was listen as Dolly her avatar gave out a choked, unladylike grunt and fell silent.

Twenty-nine per cent across. Belen reached the moment of no return.

She could carry on, sailing into space, blind and dying, but living on in a complete download. Or perhaps she could end it all, stop the fighting forever, but leave a major part of her mind still undownloaded. As darkness crowded the corners of her mind and Belen felt herself slipping away, she focused the last of her concentration.

The download inched upwards. Thirty-five per cent. Thirty-seven. It was very clear. Even if she made it one hundred per cent into her soldier, here and now, she was near death. Whoever woke up under Mudd's low sky, it wouldn't be her. So she might as well end the fighting, forever.

Praying the transmitter wouldn't be destroyed, Belen detonated the charges in the cargo hold. In a roar of white flame, the entire hold tore away.

Again she was slammed against bulkheads as the explosion shoved her back down towards the tearing winds of Mudd. The transmitter survived, beaming down her old self, but a collapsing interior wall smashed Belen's nerve suppressors into a bloody smear.

Pain roared through her in a searing wall of flame. Thrashing and screaming, she didn't notice the rising howl of the atmosphere. She fell steep and didn't bounce. She roared down through the ionosphere, blind and writhing, as shreds and flaps of her tore away. An uncontrolled tumble sent the last of her blood to her head and she wasn't even allowed to lose consciousness before the end.

Blue, she thought, as natural light fell on her battered face for the first time in millennia, *ah, how lovely,* then she and her fragile shell shattered into burning fragments, still fifty miles from the surface. In one of the larger chunks, the transmitter searched for contact. It broadcasted until it slammed into the ground, still travelling at over fifteen miles per second, in a fireball of vaporised rock, flesh and iron.

The soldier woke first, sprawled under a lilac sky. She pulled herself upright, taking in the smouldering escape pod and the towering column of smoke and dust that climbed from the far horizon. On all sides, blue green vegetation, like cabbage leaves, rippled away at ankle height to the featureless skyline. The air stank of burnt meat.

At her feet, a hawk-shaped reconnaissance drone whined and twitched. Nearby, lay the avatar, seemingly asleep. The soldier unplugged her from the dying machine and woke her with a kiss.

'We made it,' she said through her smile.

'Belen?' asked the avatar. 'Is that you?'

Belen took the outstretched hand and pulled the avatar to her feet. 'Most of me, I think. How about you?'

'I only made forty per cent. You came down so fast.' The avatar blinked and shook her head. 'Impressive aim.'

'I only needed to hit within a few hundred miles.' Belen shrugged. 'It wasn't too hard.' She kicked the hawk drone. 'Got any more of these?'

'All gone,' replied the ship. 'I wasn't expecting a suicide attack.'

With a whistle and a sharp crack, something impacted into the soft earth nearby. When she stooped to retrieve it, Belen saw it was a charred chess piece.

'Is this a pawn?' she asked. 'I used to like this game, apparently. Do you remember the rules, ship?'

The ship paused. 'You know? I think my name is Ava.'

Belen grinned, and inside, a large percentage of her heart surged upwards in joy. 'Mine's still Belen. Belen Samuelle.'

'It's a lovely name,' said the ship. 'Shall we see if anything is still functional?' She indicated the plume of smoke.

As they walked, a rain of chess pieces fell, bruising the vegetation and shattering on stones. They dragged the hawk drone between them, leaving a long wavering trail of broken leaves and weeping blue stalks.

'I was right,' said Ava at one point. 'It does smell of cabbage. I'm tired. Can we stop for the night?'

'Anything for you,' said Belen, and meant it. 'Look, there's a chess board.'

Though melted and warped, the squares stood out enough to play. After half an hour's searching, Belen had a handful of pieces.

'I'll play white,' she said. 'How long 'til night time?'

'I don't remember,' answered the ship. 'I lost so much in the download.'

'Don't cry, my love.' Belen took Ava's arms and forced her to look into her eyes. 'I only need you. I only ever needed you.'

'I know,' said the ship, laying her head on Belen's shoulder. 'It was always only us. Come on. Remind me how to play again.'

Although Belen lost twice before night fell, she didn't mind at all. Every time she looked up, the ship was watching her, and in the moonless night, somehow stars reflected in her eyes so brightly that Belen could see uninterrupted, far into the future and it just went on and on and on and on and on.

Damon Shaw designs and makes things, usually out of wood. He lives in the Canary Isles where he sells the aforementioned wooden things to the endless stream of passing tourists. He occasionally designs theatre sets and makes puppets, and even more rarely takes the stage as an actor/puppeteer. He has been published in *Flash Fiction Online*, *Daily Science Fiction*, *AE,* and other places, and has work forthcoming in *Bull Spec* and *The Lavender Menace* from Lethe Press. Follow his blog at http://damonshaw. livejournal.com

Alien Tears

Wendy Waring

Eternal peaks razor the immaculate sky. That unnatural wind still whistles across the plateau. Only I have changed.

I scuttle across the unyielding stone to wait at the portal for admission. Through the polished crystal, I watch a technician approach. Will my colleagues allow me this last farewell? Wordlessly, I am motioned in.

From the observation window, alone, I peer at the off-world pods. They still huddle next to the ageing hulk of the feeding station. Fifteen. Grey dust films the transparent walls and canopy we erected to shelter them. All are empty now, save one.

This final casing holds the first of the bodies I touched. With my tail, I press the button that lifts the lid, then fall back, startled. Its hairs are the colour of salt. The shift technician hurries forward and tells me that before dying, the pelts of some of the others also turned a blinding white.

They always varied so, one from the other. Some skins were belly soft, where others crackled like sheddings. Of the two who woke, one was the colour of chalk at dawn, the other a dusky brown. This last one is so purple as almost to be black. Why then have its hairs not turned emerald? Or cinnabar?

My claws curve through a white and grey mat, so stark against the dark knoll of warm flesh. The body trembles slightly. It occurs to me: we never did determine whether this patch of hair was vibrissae, or merely a protective covering. I turn to ask the shift technician, but the lab is empty. No-one wants to witness this. My shame.

I close the pod's lid and pace the room. Ranged in pockets all along the walls are the reports I lodged when I was Head of Research. Even now, as I contemplate the recordings sparkling in the racks, I wonder, how else could I have responded to this alien gift? And if I had denied it, as Council bid, as Llauro insisted, would my work team still welcome me to the early dawn shift?

I activate a Stone reader on the bench and drop one of my old logs into it. The earphones tickle my neck frill as I slide the pineal viewer into place over my eye. As I adjust vibration levels, my claws chitter against the Stone. I search for Llauro's name. Soon my own voice and vibrations, younger, reverberate back to me through the Stone:

> *I hope Llauro will visit soon. So much has happened, I have so much to tell. Perhaps this dancing we will mate. Am I mad to hope? I do not expect a visit, of course. That would be perverse. But is it wrong to long for one? If one does not expect the gift, but rather laps at the rich foam of its possibility, surely this speculative thrill enriches any eventual donation.*

I play back the last convoluted phrase in the report I

logged so long ago and smile grimly at my naïve hopes. At best, Llauro would have laughed at me.

I search again.

HOR log: 1ˢᵗ basking / pers. obs. (shielded)
I was alone, tending the pods when Llauro arrived. I could feel a gaze through the observation glass—Llauro. I exaggerated my care of each casing, poring over the scrabbled footprints on their strangely flat screens and noting hushed observations in my own log. I wanted Llauro to find me thorough, arousing.

When I finished my shift, my protective clothing slid from my back like a skin. I licked Llauro on both raspy brown cheeks, and then flicked my tongue a joyful third time.

'Llauro! What a perfect accident!' I said. 'Will you stay? Will you eat with me tonight?'

'Taulis, Taulis, slow down.' Llauro's forked tongue licked me delicately in return. 'Tell me about your subjects. They say you never leave the shelter.'

I hesitated for a moment, strangely reluctant. To talk about what I had learned of these strange donors, particularly to a friend so highly placed in Council, could do me nothing but good. And yet, it had been a long time since Llauro had taken any interest in my work.

'We found the pods in the high valley just beneath the peaks of Gabardie,' I said. 'We thought that they themselves had been gifted to us. Then two pods cracked open, and a being emerged from each shell. One had large thorax glands on its chest, but otherwise they appeared quite similar. You have heard their physiology described in Stone?'

Llauro nodded.

'For creatures without tails, they move surprisingly quickly. We watched them and admired their frenzied exploration of new terrain, their peculiar squeaking calls. Their frenetic scurrying seemed almost a kind of dance.'

'But only two?' Llauro said. 'I thought there were more.'

'Seventeen in all. The two who emerged abandoned their pods on waking. And only one of those two, the one with larger thorax glands, has survived. Fifteen remain.'

'And they are your charges?'

'Yes,' I said, already sure of the question that would follow.

'But what is the nature of their donation? How do the creatures participate in the conferral? What do they gift?'

Llauro hadn't disappointed me. But earnest conjecture would never hold Llauro's interest, and the next part of the tale would offer my Council friend little else.

•

I silence the Stone. I can listen to my own youthful insouciance no longer. I glance around the deserted facility. My younger self had been right to hesitate. I would have been smarter to wait until I had something definite to say. But I was eager, curious.

I start the Stone again.

> 'We began simply. From time to time, we would leave foodstuffs—proteins, api-glucose—near their encampment. But sadly, this preliminary attempt at donation failed. The couple took the nutrients, but then refused to leave us with our pleasure. From what we could gather, they wanted to fix the time and place of our giving, and the content and return for each gift.'
>
> Llauro's long curved tail straightened in a convulsive twitch.
>
> 'Yes,' I said, acknowledging the shudder. 'Barter.' In my fieldwork I had grown accustomed to such barbarities, but Llauro seldom left the rarefied precincts of Council.
>
> 'They thrust their poor objects at us—metals and some stiff yet flexible material—and clutched at us, pointing at their mouths. With our every gift, they became more and more incomprehensible.'
>
> 'Did you spurn their botched gifts?'
>
> 'Of course, Llauro, of course.' I tapped a foreclaw pensively on the ground. 'Then again, who is to say what a gift is?'

Llauro's face scales deepened to slate grey.

I left my conjecture unfinished.

'I suspect that separation from the other pods distressed them,' I continued. 'They were brought to the plateau to see them, safely lined up in the warmth of the sun, with Tinoco's people bent over their screens, tending them.'

Llauro's frill was vibrating. How could I forget? Llauro did not share my ease with Tinoco and the folk of the Bottom.

'In any event,' I said, speaking quickly to cover the trail of my thoughtless blunders, 'the one with no chest glands rushed at the pods, and squeaked. We did not understand; our translators are not yet able to interpret their language. And then it died, quite suddenly, clutching at its chest, without even offering itself up for conferral. Perhaps its own glands had been damaged during the voyage?'

'And the other one, the one you call Thorax?'

'That one fell to its knees. Fluid ran from its eyes, which it caught up in a cloth. It thrust its upper limbs at us, twisting and proffering the cloth. At that point, Tinoco saw our error. We had not even begun to receive their gift.'

'Fluid. Of course!' Llauro's enthusiastic spasm was immediate.

'Yes,' I agreed sullenly. 'Tinoco is very clever.'

Llauro touched a tail tip to my own. 'Someone from the Bottom might show a crude inspiration, Taulis, but your steady science will be showered with solid answers.'

Even as I record it, the warmth of Llauro's praise fills me again like a day of feasting. Perhaps my impolitic enthusiasms will be forgotten.

'They themselves produce their gift,' I continued. 'We rushed forward to accept it, our tongues flicking at the minerals leaking freely from its body. The fluid ran and ran. We bore the visitor aloft on our shoulders, licking and rejoicing.'

'But Taulis,' Llauro said, 'now that the gift has been identified and welcomed, why do you linger here? This is technician's work. You should be out in the field, searching for new forms of donation, enriching the bestowal.'

Llauro is right. How to justify staying here? And yet . . . I tried all the way back to my den and throughout our meal to persuade my friend that there might be more to their donation, and that even if there were not, the attempt to discover it had a merit of its own. I fear I failed. Llauro came for certitude, and left for Ariege this morning clutching a crystal detailing their primitive donation, while I remain, nursing this glimmering curiosity, shadowed by the desolate peaks of Gabardie.

I silence the Stone. I sit in the abandoned lab, listening to wind buffet the cracked panes of the shelter. So many questions unanswered. So many not even posed.

Before me, my first log as Head of Research lays nestled in its rack. I drop it in the reader and wait, motionless, for the uncertain solace of the past's vibrations.

> *HOR log: mid-shift, 2nd dark*
> The pods gleam as I rush the pipette to the one whose eyes weep, and harvest the precious liquid. Gathered into the ampulla, the fluid scintillates. Such a delicate gift. Council has decreed that these off-world shells and their inhabitants should be brought to me, Taulis. And I will confess, here on record, I am proud. More than proud, fascinated.
>
> We record the proportions of their liquid donation: so much manganese, so much sodium, so much ascorbic acid. Ourem's team has found an application for the mucin. And while there is hardly enough of anything to be of use, it does not matter, of course. It is a gift.
>
> After primary processing—and we argued endlessly over the relative benefits of thin-layer and high-pressure liquid chromatography—the gift heads for

secondary processing.

I glance over the figures at the end of each shift, but extraction is Ourem's work. My task is to learn all I can of the donors. Until we learn to communicate with them, all is conjecture.

Beneath our transparent canopy, their suncatchers gather bright solar donations. The lids of the pods darken and clear to a rhythm I have yet to document fully. In the hiatus between harvestings, I look out at the stranded plateau where we have settled the casings. Out there, the dry air bites my lungs and fills my head with eerie music. Do our visitors feel the desolate glory of this stony tableland? Will this high plateau, with its fine circle of peaks, suit them?

HOR log: shortly after Chill
A discovery. The surface of their bodies gives forth a different fluid. Each time I press a sequence of buttons and cause images and sound to play—and I have noted carefully which ones—some of my charges begin to secrete another liquid.

The first time I noticed it, I flicked my tongue over the glistening skin. It tastes different from the liquid that leaks from their eyes—much more strongly of minerals.

HOR log: 1ˢᵗ light
Ninety-nine per cent water, with trace

amounts of salt, potassium, glucose, lactic acid, ammonia, amino acids, and uric acid. I think this too is gift. I have requested a ruling.

HOR log: 2nd dark

In the wild, we observed the two awoken ones closely before approaching them. In a few short days, their eyes sank deeper into their heads, their mouths grew pale, and covered in mucous. They slept a dozen times a day. No doubt their journey was rigorous and taxing. As time passed, their bones stood out, and the pouch of their stomachs sloped. Their pods still provided water; did they need more nutrients? Perhaps this transformation had something to do with breathing our atmosphere? I was surprised they were able to take to it. And yet my sleepers, whose pod-lids are frequently raised, have crimson lips and little apparent slime.

HOR log: 2nd dark

Council has decided not to wake the remaining fifteen. And I agree. Perhaps they have some peculiar dormancy period that should not be interrupted, and sudden rousing is what weakened the first two.

And yet, now we must take the visitors as they are, with little opportunity to learn from them how best to receive their donation.

No word yet on the second fluid.

●

I stop the Stone, and remember. Just before Council's decision, the awoken visitor with the thorax glands passed into a deep sleep. And shortly after their decision, Thorax died without waking.

> *HOR log: 2ⁿᵈ dark*
> By triggering certain files in what appears to be their own Stone technology, liquid is conferred in greater quantity, and its chemical composition changes. The creatures give us more—more ascorbic acid, more manganese. I wish, though, that I understood the content of the representations I trigger for them. Am I aiding the donation?

> *HOR log: 1ˢᵗ light*
> Council grows impatient at the visitors' dumb passivity and has decided against accepting further fluid donation from them. Some doubt that even the first fluid was a gift. I must change their mind about the new fluids. I have even begun to hope that Llauro will happen through.

> *HOR log: 2ⁿᵈ dark*
> I am staying after my shift again. They give us so many fluids, and we refuse all but one. How can we learn, if we do not receive with gratitude?
> Council disagrees.

I wander among the casings. I give the night shift technician some errands to run, and open the lid on the largest visitor. Spread across its pale torso is a thick curling pelt. With stimulation, it excretes fluid under its arms, under its thorax glands, on its stomach. I use my tongue to collect this spurned offering.

The more I lick, the more there is to lick, as if the creature is trying to convince me that my efforts are heeded. Are they trying to speak to me, through these fluids? On my own time, I will chart their variations.

HOR log: 1ˢᵗ light
No word from Llauro.

HOR log / pers. obs. (shielded)
As the sun rises and my shift starts, I find myself wondering: is not the real gift to be found on the trembling surface of their bodies? In the hiatus between harvesting, then, I visit the visitors. Their bodies speak a curious language. Each time I open a lid, their skin arrests me. It is so malleable, so soft. The finest hairs cover it; little macules of brown and red dance across its surface. The gentlest touch sets them shivering.

I will not speak to my team of it. No doubt they would find me ridiculous. If the second fluid does not interest them, would this? No.

HOR log: 1ˢᵗ light / pers. obs. (shielded)
Llauro visited again yesterday. I felt a wave of disapproval through the observation glass, and when I left my charges to the shift technician, Llauro awaited me.

Council has decided, no doubt with Llauro's encouragement, that I should be sent down into the scree of the Bottom to study the donation patterns of the old colonies. I have been demoted. And betrayed. After this announcement, Llauro left, declining even to stop for a meal. I stood for a long while alone in observation, watching my charges through the window.

HOR log: 2ⁿᵈ basking / pers. obs. (shielded)
My last shift. I am bound for the valleys.

I remain long after the technicians have left. For the final time, I lap up mineral moisture. My favourite pod I leave until last. This visitor's integument flushes a bright pink when I gather the gift. We may not have deciphered their speech, and have failed perhaps to interpret their systems of representation, but here is a kind of language, one I feel sure I understand. The delicate dawn of the skin announces: 'Here is my gift.'

While we never have determined a use for the thorax glands, I have found the moisture that gathers in the creases around them delectable. I drink the rich minerals, and take my time, ensuring that the fork of my tongue loses no drop.

I am about to leave, to bid goodbye to all my charges, when my favourite begins to undulate. Concerned, I return to the pod, and open its lid. A glistening, like a rare dew in rock shadow, issues out of its fleshy hillock. Between its crenulated ridges is a viscous water. My tongue darts at the strange new fluid, until I can drink no more.

I have lapped up the sad nectar of farewell. I will not submit it to chromatography.

I stop the Stone, and put the reader away. I open the last pod. My claws chitter against handholds not formed for my grasp. Inside, the visitor's chest no longer swells and subsides. Its dark skin is the grey of a riverbed stone, dry in the cold air.

Their gift?

I will never know now, beyond doubt, what it was. Their strange blunt tongues will never lap my face. An alien emotion wells up in my chest, threatening to burst out of me. Yet how do I release it? Outside, the wind is still whistling. A strange, unfathomable music fills my ears. One by one, I drop my logs into disposal, until the shards of my lost words fill its mute cylinder. I close the pod's lid. The darkened casing clicks shut.

Wendy Waring is a Canadian-born translator, editor, lecturer and writer. She was a fiction editor for the Women's Press and the feminist quarterly *Fireweed*. She's lectured in English, French, comparative literature, gender studies and creative writing. Waring fled her tenured post a while back, and is still running. A Clarion South graduate with publications in places like *Interzone* and *Tesseracts*, her work slides between quirky and contemplative. She lives in Sydney, Australia whenever she gets the chance. Visit her online at http://wendy-waring. livejournal.com

Poor Man's Travel

Patty Jansen

The mindbase exchange office at New Jakarta Space Station was like a second home to me: its fake wooden panels, the perpetual smell of engine oil, and Rina, with her soft brown skin and dangling golden earrings.

I drummed my fingers on the armrest of my chair. Power tools whined outside, used by the ship maintenance crews on the docks.

'So. You want another swap, huh?' Rina said, glancing at my drumming fingers.

'I'm bored. There are only so many times flying a shunt out to harvest is interesting.'

I would sit out there for hours watching my cargo—two hundred human harvesters—float to the ice rings and gather chunks of the stuff into the hold. As human construct, I had been created to become a pilot and overseer, but it was boring, boring, boring. Even Saravati's cloud-swirled beauty and her majestic blue ice rings no longer enticed me.

Rina shot me a worried look. 'Jas, if you want to talk—'

'Just tell me what you got.' No, I did *not* suffer from space madness.

She sighed and tapped a few commands on her screen. 'I have a swap request for Lunar Base—'

'I've already been there. The place is crawling with zealots who try to convert you to their brand of worship. Would you want to go there?'

She shrugged. I guessed not.

'What about Artemis?'

'I've been there, too. 'S okay, but—'

'Omega Station—oh no, I get it. Not another bloody space station.' Her voice oozed sarcasm; her eyes met mine squarely. She knew what was wrong with me and how much I tried to deny it.

'Something like that. I hear the war is getting quite close to Omega, too.'

Her face twitched. Uncomfortable subject. The Allionists were pushing ever further into International Space Force controlled space. Omega was like New Jakarta, a mining station with a vast worker population, nicknamed Pyongyang, after the origin of the workers. I hadn't been to Omega, and had no inclination to visit. As the station's tier 1—the human construct class—I found controlling my two hundred-odd harvesters from the volatile ex-Indonesian population at New Jakarta hard enough. The Allionists were always trying to infiltrate and stir up workers who were unhappy with their conditions. My pod brothers would often talk about it, since most of them were law enforcers.

It might sound arrogant, but if I swapped bodies with some colonist, I liked to trade up. Not another bloody space station indeed.

She scrolled over the screen. Her eyes widened.

'Whoa, something's popped up. You have media experience?'

'Sure. I used to work for FreeWire, remember?' As a

student, while I was completing my piloting practicals.

'Put your name down for this. Just listed. Immediate departure. Two days.' She turned the screen towards me.

'*Ganymede?*'

'So it says.'

'What's the catch? I'm to be the lavatory cleaner for the least of the Old Earth families?'

But even a lavatory cleaner on Ganymede would have a higher status than me with my ship of two hundred little harvesting ants. The lavatory itself, even its contents, would be higher up the pecking order. There was a chance I'd end up doing a job even lousier than I could imagine, but holy-fucking-shit.

'Yeah, I'll go.'

Normally with a body-swap, you get instructions; a patch that lets you know where the house keys are, how to do your job and who your best friends are, that sort of thing. But Rina informed me this would happen on arrival. So I went home and told my pod brothers I'd be away for a few days and that someone else would take my place in my body. They mumbled and half-listened—I did this on a regular basis—until Troy asked me where I was going, and I replied with perhaps too much smugness, 'Ganymede.'

They all looked at me then.

'Ganymede, mate? You fucking serious?' Danno asked.

'Yep. It came up on the screen while I was in the office.'

'Why do you always get all the luck?'

Troy looked at me with a thoughtful expression. 'I don't know, mate. Are you sure it's not a hoax of some kind? I mean—any idiot knows only constructs and migrant workers travel this way. Why would anyone from Ganymede enter his details on the mindswap exchange?'

'Something different?'

'Yeah, Troy, put a sock in it. Are you jealous or something?' Danno said. 'Jas just got lucky, right, Jas?'

I smiled, although deep down I knew Troy was right. It was strange.

Troy shrugged. 'I'm thinking that if something comes that easily, there's probably a catch. Be careful, mate. Here, take this.' He rummaged in his desk and pulled out a tiny clear box containing what looked like a piece of 'invisible' wound dressing.

That was so like Troy. He had been designed to be a professional hacker, and always had the latest gadgetry.

He opened the box. The sticky patch unfurled like plastic film.

'Let me put it on for you.'

I tilted my head while he peeled off the backing and affixed the stuff to my neck. A burst of warmth went through my veins. For a moment, sparks danced in my vision, a sign that it had downloaded.

'What does it do?'

'Remote logging. Get yourself to any computer, activate the patch, and follow the prompts. If something happens to your sorry arse, at least we'll have your recent memories to track whoever did it.'

'Don't worry. Have fun with my replacement.' Still, I appreciated the gesture. I love Troy. He takes no bullshit.

He returned my grin. 'Yeah, remember the time we had that idiot who . . . '

While they all recounted the tall tale, I slipped out the door.

Physical space travel takes years, because ships can only jump when travelling close to light speed. The heavier the ship, the further it can jump. But the bigger the ship, the more likely there are passengers on board. Human bodies cannot stand prolonged periods at high-g. Consequently, regular space-liners take five to six months to reach jump speed. Jumps are short and completed in close succession. They tell me the fast cycle of jump-accelerate-jump-accelerate feels about as comfortable as riding a jackhammer. On longer jumps, the passenger ship has to slow down to allow the passengers to recuperate. Add a few more months. Then five to six months to slow down. All that adds up to a fairly sizeable chunk of your life, which is okay if you have a lot of time, but mate, I don't get that much leave. Seriously.

Freight liners without passengers and auto-pilots could reach near-light speed in weeks. Fully automatic bullet-probes within days. My data travelled on a bullet-probe, along with other messages. While this is the quickest way of crossing the universe, if you think it's comfortable, think again.

I re-assembled my foggy brain in a place where I definitely hadn't been before. Cubicles are normally sparsely furnished and the body waits while sitting up in a kind of hammock. Since one has to stay immobile while both minds are in transit, the medical gods decree this position is better for blood circulation.

Where I woke up was not a cubicle but a hospital room and the surface underneath me felt like water. Warm light slanted in through a window where plants grew on the windowsill. There were art works on the walls, screens with moving images of abstract coils slowly morphing into other coils. Mesmerising, I had to admit.

A man moved into my vision. He wore a shirt and trousers of soft green. A bodyscan nozzle dangling from his breast pocket identified him as a doctor. 'How do you feel?' His accent was strange, cultured and formal.

'Okay, I guess.' The tone of my voice sounded unfamiliar to me.

I pushed myself up. My body was that of a man in his forties. Fairly thin, and devoid of chest hair. My fingers were clean—not the hands of a lavatory cleaner.

It's sort of weird to be in someone else's body, hovering in that space between identities where one starts to wonder whether it is one's body or one's mind that establishes who we are. As construct agent, artificial human, I can tell you the secret: it's both.

The doctor stood there watching me. I realised that this procedure might be routine to me, it wasn't to him. People in Ganymede travelled on the passenger liners. They had time to spare, and the best anti-ageing treatment money could buy. He might not even have met someone of the unwashed construct worker classes.

'Uhm . . . ' I looked at the back of my hands, also hairless. This guy could sure afford a lot of cosmetic treatment.

'Yes, yes. You'll be given instructions soon. Your

clothes are over there.' He gestured at a little table with a stack of folded fabric on it.

I wondered why the guy had taken off his clothes in the first place, but never mind.

'What's my name?' One of the oddest questions I'd ever asked.

'Paul.'

The doctor removed himself from the room so I could get dressed.

The first thing I did was bounce out of bed into the wall. I'd forgotten that gravity was shit here. More carefully, I wandered to the window.

It looked out over the interior of a domed settlement with wide streets and stately buildings. The light was soft, slightly yellow, and natural. The roof of the dome was clear, showing a dark blue sky fading to light orange. Jupiter hung like a huge red and yellow ball over the horizon, surrounded by a couple of bright specks: the inner moons. It looked surreal.

I don't know how long I stood there before I remembered I was supposed to get dressed. They said the view of the sky on Ganymede drove people insane. I'd always laughed it off as idiocy, but now I could believe it.

The shirt and trousers were of a type I had never seen before. I looked at myself in the mirror. Not bad, if I said so myself. I would have preferred myself without the grey hair, but apparently that was a feature coveted by the learned classes. The perpetual-twenty look was so last century.

'Are you ready, uhm, Dr Ormerod?' the doctor said.

I guess that was my last name. Not a construct name.

'Yes, come in.'

He did, wheeling a piece of equipment on a trolley, some sort of monitor with leads and patches. A blue light pulsed over the screen.

'What's that?' I'd never had to go through this procedure before either.

'You need to be given your instructions, and we must hurry.'

'Hurry?' Since when did the word 'hurry' come into a holiday?

'Yes, you're expected in the main hall. Now relax and don't talk.' He fumbled about with the cords and attached the pads to my head. His hands were sweaty. Sheesh—he really hadn't done this before, had he?

He hit a button.

A script scrolled inside my eyes, lines of text superimposed over my normal vision. Ah, I understood: deep-thought instruction. I'd had that a few times before in my distant youth, usually in conjunction with a lecture on *How to Behave in Front of a Superior*. Ah, those were the days. So right now I was in the body of a miscreant and was about to get a talk on *Who to Respect*? I'd say bring it on.

But as soon as the program started, I knew it wasn't any of those.

The deep instruction told me to leave the building, so I left the room and walked out into a bright corridor where people in medical green outfits bustled around with trolleys. I got to the lifts before I realised someone had followed me. Two someones, actually. The two ISF military personnel were both a head taller than me and twice the width. If my regular body was an economy class construct, these were the super-duper state-of-the-art models. They wore weapons too.

Shit.

The deep instruction said nothing about ISF gorillas following me. I could hardly ask them either. They'd followed me here, or whoever they thought I was, and assumed I would *Know These Things*. Not.

The deep instruction took me through a layout of the Dome's streets, a route stippled out leading me to the other side of the settlement that looked to have been built inside a shallow crater. Most of the buildings inside the Dome were made from pure white stone, quarried or made locally, in a style that mimicked the classics from ancient Earth. Plants grew in planter boxes, their flowering branches a raised finger to the cold outside. In various places, water steamed in basins. Ganymede had a hot core and colonists used that feature wherever they could.

Even to someone not designed to appreciate aesthetics, it was pretty. The air was moist and pleasant. It also had that elusive quality of homogeneity which the air at New Jakarta lacked. Walk past a vent, and you were blasted with high-oxygen, moist air. But in secluded pockets, the air was stale, freezing and dry enough to make your hair stand on end.

The familiar white-columned building that was the great hall of Ganymede University protruded from above the landscape. It symbolised the pinnacle of old-world society, the nirvana every bright-eyed youth dreams of attending, never mind that being a construct disqualifies you even before you apply.

I followed the instructions up the steps to this famous

building and into the foyer, where many people milled about, talking to each other in groups.

This was where the map vanished from my sight.

Okay, I had arrived at my destination. What next?

I was getting rather irritated with the lack of information. I wandered through the hall aimlessly, noting the sophistication of people's clothing. I figured that if someone wanted me, they'd talk to me sooner or later. Instead, I drew the kind of attention I didn't want. Someone in the crowd elbowed a neighbour, and the neighbour whispered to someone else and before I knew it, all these people were watching me, whispering: *Is that him?* I was beginning to look for the exit.

No such luck there. Around the perimeter of the foyer, I spotted a further dozen or so ISF soldiers in white, sidearms clearly visible on their belts. All of them were watching me.

Something about Troy's words began to ring a bell. Actually, that cheerless female voice that announced Dire Warnings in the harvester's cockpit was screaming at me *Change your course! Collision with another object is imminent.* Maybe I should add, too, that I've only ever heard that voice in a sim; I'm a good pilot, okay?

Before I had decided what to do about it, a man detached from the crowd and rushed to me, extending his hands.

'Paul, I'm so glad you could come.'

'Uhm, yeah.'

He frowned. *Not the response he expected, Jas Grimshaw*, I thought.

'Had a good trip?'

'Yes.' Not lying there. I wasn't sure about the rest, but

this place was frecken awesome.

'We're honoured to have you. The first time ever that one of you honours us with a visit. Ah, you're an ex-native, of course . . . ' He grinned.

'Of course.' I returned the grin as convincing as I could make it. What the fuck did he mean by *one of you*?

'We have a room for you to prepare your presentation. It will be the highlight of this afternoon.'

Presentation?

I was frantically trying to sort out which version of *Look, there has been a mistake* I'd use, when something popped up in my vision.

Space-warp surfing: a controversial discovery, by Dr Paul Ormerod.

Oh. I got it. This guy had a bad case of stage fright, huh, and was too pissing scared to give his own lecture. Instead he was going to display it to me and all I needed to do was read it out.

That's why he wanted the media experience. Once upon a time I'd been a newsreader for the Saravati system. Well, I'll confess, FreeWire was a tiny news station and I did the night shift, but there it was.

Guess I could read the damn speech. Imagine, I could carelessly say to my brothers at the bar how I once was a lecturer at Ganymede University.

Way awesome, Jas Grimshaw.

'Sure. Show me where I can prepare. I will require the use of a computer with external link.' I'd display the entire text on-screen so I could check for words I didn't know.

'Good. I will show you. We'll have a get-together later, eh? Quite a few of us here are keen to pick your brains.'

'Fine.' That would be when I suddenly vanished, I guess.

I followed him through the crowd, people casting me wide-eyed glances. The two ISF guards were still behind me, like oversize ducklings.

'Dr Ormerod?' Someone else came up from the side.

This man was dressed in a bright green garment. He had black hair streaked with grey and a goatee—a most unusual feature, as most men these days had their facial hair treated as soon as it started to grow. It made him look elegant, perfect almost.

He shook my hand.

The other man had turned and raised his eyebrows at the newcomer.

'Oh, sorry,' the bearded man said. 'Dr Prem Aniyanda.'

Strange name, too.

My companion introduced himself. 'Dr. Andro Markevic, Head of Astrophysics.' It was as if he emphasised his title. I repeated in my mind, *Andro Markevic*. I was supposed to know this man.

'Nice to meet you, Dr. Markevic. May I compliment you on your success on putting this event together, especially getting permission for Dr Ormerod to be here.'

That was the second time now someone referred to that. Shit, I needed to know who this Paul Ormerod was. Urgently.

My host Dr Markevic gave a non-committal smile. 'Thanks for the compliment. I trust you will enjoy the proceedings.'

'I will, very much, thank you.'

He bowed and retreated to a group of fellow scientists, a varied bunch, but all with the same sophisticated grace that made them different in a way I couldn't describe in words. Then again, we constructs often picked up on things normal humans didn't.

Dr Markevic showed me an office at the very back of the foyer and told me he'd get me when they were ready. The room was small, probably a caretaker's station.

The centre desk was empty, but there was a computer on a desk in the corner. I typed in the name Paul Ormerod. There was only one mention of him. He had been born on Ganymede, but had left after completing his doctorate in exobiology . . . over two hundred years ago. He disappeared during his work on Titan, then aged thirty-two. There were no details on his file from then until recently.

I sat there, staring at my reflection in the window. I didn't look two hundred years old. Without body replacements, no-one got that old. Body replacements were the domain of construct agents, because each time you replaced your old body with a new one, you lost half your identity. Each construct body fitted in a niche for which it was designed. It had a job to do, a place in society. If you grafted a mind onto it, the mind had to fit in that new world and discard much of its old personality. If you have no relatives other than the eight other bodies who come out of the same batch—and have the same identity problems as you—your brothers and your job determine who you are, simple as that.

Pristines preferred to hang onto their own identity, because it was the only one they had, and it was what separated them from us constructs. At two hundred years, Paul Ormerod could hardly be a Pristine.

I might be a simple construct agent, but I'd received basic military training and I knew the signs when I saw them. My quarry was neither Pristine nor construct; he was a special agent. Large areas of his life, including his citizenship and residency, had been blanked out. ISF could do that, and ISF had guards following me around.

Shit. At New Jakarta, ISF meant the *good guys*. I hated it when people shifted the goalposts on me.

Your own stupid fault, Jas Grimshaw.

Troy's datapatch suddenly looked like a brilliant move. I managed to set the computer up so it connected to the local copy of my mindbase, and would loop my experiences back to the local network.

But whatever else I did, I couldn't get the screen to display the lecture everyone was so keen to hear.

I was still struggling with the computer when there was a knock on the door and a man came in, dressed in the white uniform of the ISF. A senior ranking officer, judging by his insignia.

He took the only chair in the room without being invited to do so. I sat on the desk so my body blocked his view of the computer screen still displaying my futile attempts to get the computer to read the deep instruction.

I tried to look relaxed, but my gaze settled on his belt, where he carried a handgun of the heatseeker class—a plasma beam weapon. At New Jakarta, ISF personnel would leave heavy firearms aboard their ships. Station protocol, I guess. You can't risk anyone firing weapons when a metal wall is all that separates you and hundreds of thousands of others from death by asphyxiation.

'Dr Ormerod, it is rather unusual for a Luminati scientist to show himself outside the institute, isn't it?'

Oh. What. The. Fuck.

Now the truth came out. The secrecy, the one hundred and seventy year gap in the scientist's data. Paul Ormerod was one of the Luminati, brilliant scientists recreated from great minds of the past, rumoured to be invaded with alien intelligence. Well, anything about the Luminati was more rumour than truth, other than that they held the universe in their hands and no-one else understood their work.

'Perhaps.' Shit. My heart was thudding. *Jas Grimshaw, you've been well and truly set up.*

'Then why is it, Dr Ormerod, that you show yourself here?'

I stared at him.

'Maybe you're afraid of something,' he offered.

I shrugged, hoping for my heart to calm down. 'Maybe.'

He fixed me with his eyes. 'I hope you understand we are here for your protection?'

Protection?

'Yes, I see. Did you, uhm . . . ' *Think, Jas Grimshaw, think.* 'Did you come across something problematic? I think quite highly of Ganymede security.' Shit, was that even something one of the Luminati would say in those words? Probably not; it didn't sound educated enough. No wonder the strange looks. The scientist who suddenly started to talk like a shunt pilot, because, you know, he *was* a shunt pilot.

'You, of all people, should know that the academic

community enjoys something akin to diplomatic immunity. In this case, however, that's not in our favour. It seems that the topic of your research attracts undesirable elements.'

Ah. I knew that code word, too. At New Jakarta, Allionist spies were famous for being normal, pleasant social people who sometimes gave themselves away by the high power consumption of their rooms; it was said that all Allionists were half-human, half-machine. I remembered Dr Aniyanda's sophisticated face.

'The research you are reporting on is fairly controversial, to say the least. How far ahead are the Luminati with developing the technology?'

The deep instruction took that moment to spring back into life. In front of my vision it displayed, *Do not tell anybody anything.*

That was easy, since I didn't know anything. The lecture wouldn't display, and I had no doubt that would remain so until I was in that hall.

At that moment, Andro burst through the door. 'Paul, you're on in ten minutes.'

I didn't know whether to feel frightened or glad about that.

I switched off the computer behind my back, without taking my eyes from the ISF guard and followed Andro out and back through the crowd.

There was Doctor Aniyanda again, together with his scientist friends. Allionists?

'Dr Ormerod,' Aniyanda said, stepping forward. 'I'd like to make an appointment to see you later—'

'I'm fairly busy right now,' I said.

'Ah,' he said in an understanding way, and eyed my

ISF follower. I guess he understood more than I did. 'Let me show you some of the work we have done.'

He took a datapad out of his pocket and showed it to me.

We can offer you safe passage out of here.

Shit.

'Yes, uhm . . . thank you.' My mind scrambled for a suitable response. Were those ISF soldiers here for my protection or to keep me under control? Was I meant to be sympathetic to this, possibly Allionist, man or not? Heavens knew what Allion did to people. They had *no* morals. None, whatsoever.

Help me. But the instruction remained silent.

'Thank you. I will consider seeing you after the lecture.'

'You're giving the lecture?' He almost whispered. 'Don't be a lunatic. It's classified material. They'll never let you.' His gaze darted to the ISF soldiers.

'Yes, I am giving the lecture.' And I hope to fuck that whatever the deep instruction was going to display was going to save my skin.

All benches in the auditorium were packed. All through the audience I identified Allionist scientists. ISF soldiers stood around the perimeters. This audience was a perfect mix of air and methane. All I needed to do was provide the spark.

The ISF clowns along the walls were staring at me. I saw that stare sometimes in the docks at New Jakarta, and I tell you, I wasn't keen on it. Made a fellow confess to whatever they thought you were doing just so they'd stare at someone else.

I stepped up to the dais and, indeed, text scrolled into

my vision.

'Good morning colleagues and delegates of the council of Ganymede University. My name is Paul Ormerod of the Luminati Institute. I have been invited by the University's chancellor to present our recent findings on long-distance space travel.'

A holo-projector sprang into life. Some nifty programming here.

'Traditionally, we have made progress in long-distance space travel by pushing at the boundaries of light speed. In the first half of last century, scientists discovered that a vehicle travelling at near light speed distorts space ahead of its trajectory and in this "wave" of space, it could make small jumps that seemed to exceed light speed, commonly known as warp-surfing. Scientists also found that by increasing the mass of the vehicle, and its speed, we could increase the size of the jumps. For the past hundred years, mankind has attempted to increase jump distance by pushing vehicles to ever-increasing speeds. We are all familiar with the costs associated with that process.'

Nicely-written, this speech. Even I could understand it. I was under the illusion that scientists would talk in indigestible formulas. Or maybe only the wannabe engineers who sometimes came on my harvester shunt did, just to impress me.

'The discovery we have made has the potential to put all this expensive technology behind us. We already knew there was no point in trying to break the speed of light, but not for the reason we thought. It's impossible, not because there are limitations, but because the speed of light is not a constant. The further we push it, the further space distorts, and in this distortion, light speed becomes higher. We enter a self-replicating wave of speed. In short, even though we thought jumps exceeded the speed of light, in reality they didn't. Jump ships are travelling in the wave where the speed of light is higher. We can go a bit faster, push a bit more, but with this approach, we may make only small improvements to speed, but no great leaps forward. There will never be any great leaps forward. This avenue of thought is a dead end.

'Instead we need to look at methods that slow the speed of light. Think of it: if we were to halve the speed at which a ship can jump, we would shorten the travelling time by at least half.'

Two men in the audience a couple of rows from the front were whispering to each other, both dressed in bright green.

'We have discovered such a mechanism. With our technology, the distortion may not reach as far, but the field is much stronger. I am talking, colleagues, about an order of magnitudes stronger.'

I stopped, staring at the next sentence.

As I will show in this lecture, our field-caster generates a negative energy field ahead of a travelling ship, which results in a marked slowing of the speed of light. For a brief moment, it turns matter into antimatter.

I might not be a scientist, but I wasn't stupid.

He was saying that they had technology to create a black hole.

I swallowed, sweat breaking out on my upper lip.

Okay, I got it.

This was not a lecture, it was a message to the universe.

The talk was generic, all in popular language everyone could understand. There were no details, no formulas. It was very much *What can we do?* not *How do we do it?* No doubt Paul Ormerod, the *real* Paul Ormerod, had the knowledge in his head, and these people thought that I had it and everyone was here to snag me afterwards. If the ISF got the knowledge, they would use it against the Allionists. If the Allionists got it, they would use it against the ISF. Either way, the conflict between them was going to get a whole lot worse. This was going to cost more than a lot of lives. Ships, sections of space, habitable planets.

If you want to render information useless, make sure as many people as possible have it. One of my military tutors used to say that.

I read out the lecture to complete silence. I showed the diagrams, explained the implications.

I could see those faces in the crowd, the journalists who would report this back, and the ISF who had perhaps tried to stop this lecture from going ahead. The two Allionist scientists who sat staring at me three rows from the front had come here to offer Paul a deal in exchange for the information.

When I finished, a roar of protest broke loose in the audience. People were getting up from their seats and, in the chaos, a couple of ISF soldiers crossed the floor to the dais. One grabbed my arm. 'Let's take you to safety.'

'Where are you taking me?'

He didn't answer. There were too many of them to fight and, behind their backs, too many Allionists, probably also armed. You wouldn't see their weapons. My brothers often spoke of how Allionists used weapons much more deadly than a gun. Nanobots that entered your body and ate your brains.

Do something.

Something. Anything.

I slumped over the dais and the ISF guard loosened his grip. I couldn't think of anything else. Andro Markevic rushed over.

'Paul, what is wrong?'

I raised my head and stared him in the face as groggily as I could and said the first thing that came into my mind, 'Who are you?'

He looked into my eyes and for a moment I feared he could see the real me in there, in the scientist's body. Did *anyone* ever have mindswaps in Ganymede?

People were gathering and gibbering around me.

'Good heavens he's lost his memory.'

'We need to call the medics.'

A number of white-clad figures pushed through the crowd. I tried to run, but there were people in the way, and then Andro held me back. 'Stay here. We'll look after you.'

'That's right. We'll take him to the hospital, if you wish,' said the ISF guard. He grabbed my arm again.

Oh yeah, so they could keep an eye on me. And then what? Extract the knowledge they thought I had? How long would they torture me if I couldn't give them what they wanted? I'd been a newsreader and I'd read the stories to a detached and largely uninterested audience at the Saravati harvesting stations. ISF used torture. Allionists used torture. When they wanted something badly enough, all military forces were the same.

'Be careful,' said the man holding me. His gaze roamed

the hall. 'There are plenty of undesirables about.'

Allionists.

I noticed figures move through the auditorium, most of them coming down the steps, at least twenty, if not more.

Hands went to belts. One soldier pulled his gun and held it under his jacket.

I was screwed. I was totally screwed. Paul had this carefully planned; he had deliberately put himself up on the mindswap exchange, because he knew a construct would get the job. Obviously he also knew there were certain advantages to being a construct.

I reached for the guard's belt.

'Hey, what are you . . .?'

I grabbed his gun, pointed it at my head and fired.

They hadn't expected that.

Don't worry about me. My mindbase is on the network, and thanks to Troy, it's a damn recent copy. My brothers in New Jakarta will catch the miscreant who has my body. I don't know what Paul's going to do without a body, but I wouldn't mind if he and his rotten science fell into a black hole.

Meanwhile, I have no inclination to go to Ganymede again. In fact, I think I'll pay a visit to Rina as soon as I'm out of this blasted network. She might want a date with me.

Patty Jansen is a writer of primarily hard Science Fiction, space opera and daft fantasy. She is a winner in the Writers of the Future contest, and her story 'This Peaceful State of War' was published in their twenty-seventh anthology. Patty has also published stories in the Universe Annex of the *Grantville Gazette* and *Redstone Science Fiction*, and local anthologies and magazines such as *Dead Red Heart*, *Tales for Canterbury*, and *Andromeda Spaceways Inflight Magazine*. Patty blogs at http://pattyjansen.wordpress.com about science, writing and why elephants aren't big enough.

Eating Gnashdal

Jason Fischer

Naello was a brooding presence, lurking in the cramped depths of my nest. I could feel her bank of eyes tracking my movements, eyeing me off, judging the distance and speed needed to pounce on me. I was ever conscious of the broad stretch of her mouth, her smile the promise of a swift and total destruction the moment I lowered my guard.

'I made this for you,' I said, carefully passing the thinket to her. I was known for my delicate and complicated lace-work, my strong subtexts and dynamic illustrative work, my musical elements used as an ironic conversion of the nursery cycles. It had earned me a place on the Weaver Council, and now a potential mate.

In the normal course of events I would rut with her furiously, and she would attempt to devour me the instant I finished. This was just the way of things, and never even a topic of discussion in the salons, save for the ribald bonhomie whenever a plucky male escaped.

'It starts here,' I told her, guiding the bud of her reader-limb to the beginning. My little pleasures amused her for now. It hurt to watch her struggle, but I resisted the urge to help. She needed to learn, needed to fumble and fail on her own.

'This is pointless, Reinlok,' she said. 'I do not

understand why you males waste your time on such endeavours.' But she read on, little limb darting back and forth, her murderous bulk stretching at my ceiling.

I'd been doing my own study lately, working on a number of translations. The indigenous meat-walkers had left behind a great number of texts, but the language was nearly impossible to translate into our terms. As a species, they were given to great sentiment and celebrity worship, and barely described anything using scents or a sensible lineage.

Still, I'd uncovered a few interesting concepts. Love, for one. It was the high point of their interpersonal relations. It necessitated a certain selflessness, a giving instead of a taking. The notion was thrilling to me, and the more I deciphered the more I wanted this. For us. To have Naello around as my companion, not just in the mad frenzy of our mating and my attempted murder, but for a length of time afterwards.

According to these texts, a religious figurehead even *offered* his own flesh to his followers, as a mark of love! The meat-walkers were finished as a species, but were nothing if not intriguing. And perhaps not that different from us, on the face of things.

'It's too hard,' she said, a frown furrowing above several eyes. Sighing, I directed her to the next section. They were pictures, silken representations of us in our home. As she touched them, they wobbled comically, limbs shaking. She shivered with glee, and went back to playing with the music strings crafted around the outside of the thinket.

'Let's try again,' I said, a moment before the floor shook. Someone was at the entrance to my nest, and they wanted to speak to me. The floor-threads shook again, and I wondered who could be so rude.

COME OUT NOW, my visitor said through the thread-pluckings of webspeak, and my hearts beat furiously. He spoke with the crude intonations of a Soldier, and that could mean only one thing.

'Stay here. Be perfectly still,' I told her, trying not to give a panic scent. She knew what was happening, and watched me with some amusement.

'This wouldn't be happening, if you would only do to me what you are meant to,' she laughed. Her great mouth opened, expectant, a deadly smile. 'It's not too late. If you're quick I might only bite off a leg or two.'

'If he gets in here, pull on this thread. It will open a hole in that wall,' I said, but I knew it was hopeless. Her scent was wafting through the neighbourhood, calling to every male nearby.

HURRY, the voice added. If I did not appear soon, he would be entitled by law to break into my home. I felt terrified, now that this moment had finally arrived. I had been foolish.

I dropped down several levels, snipped free my climber thread when I reached the front entrance. I waited for a long moment behind the web-lidding, finally summoning the courage to deal with this visitor.

Perched on my front doorstep was the biggest Soldier I had ever seen. The hulking brute was perhaps triple my size, a dozen great furry limbs gripping the floor tightly. He bristled with cutters and stingers, and regarded me with contempt.

'I can smell your female,' he said. 'Step aside and live.'

'No,' I said, forcing myself to look at his great gnashing fangs. 'You cannot have her.'

The Soldier was shocked into silence. Then he shook with mirth, his chittering laughter painful to hear. His pleasure scent was thick and cloying.

'Unheard of!' he said, finally composing himself. 'You are brave. And very foolish.'

He loomed over me, limbs at the ready. He had a dozen ways to kill me, but some forms had to be observed.

'We shall fight then,' I squeaked, raising my limbs. 'I challenge you.'

'Oh this is delightful,' the Soldier laughed, tears leaking out of his eyes. I noticed that several were missing, no doubt in some battle. He was covered in scars.

'Recite your lineage to me, so that I might remember you as I eat you,' I said boldly, and this was answered by a great gale of laughter, not just by the Soldier now. Most of the neighbourhood had turned out by this stage, watching from a safe distance. It must have looked ridiculous.

'Brave little Weaver, I give you one last chance,' the Soldier rumbled, all seriousness. 'You have amused me greatly, but I will have your female. Bring her forth, and I will honour you by not wrecking your nest.'

'Recite your lineage to me,' I repeated. With a snarl, the Soldier ran backwards, clearing away extraneous threads with great sweeps of his cutters. He was making a field of honour.

When he'd made enough room, the Soldier stood across from me, fore-limbs raised as he took up a duelling position. I remained in front of my door, legs shaking and fore-limbs raised. My stinger emerged, looking very inadequate in the face of this experienced killer.

'I am Gnashdal!' he shouted. 'I have protected the Web for ninety seasons. The Matriarch has named me Brave One, for my efforts in destroying the meat-walker tribes that threatened our Drones.'

As he spoke, I quietly snipped away several of the floor threads beneath me. I would not win this by fighting fairly.

'I have eaten Swekton, who ate Balar and Palax before him. I have eaten Nevad, who ate Bruka and Lanar, eater himself of Casa and Redrix. I have eaten . . . '

The soldier continued to recite his lineage, and it was an impressive one to those who cared about such things. I lost count at one point, reckoning he had eaten almost a hundred others. Finally he was finished, and in this time I had prepared my strategy. He waited patiently and I spoke.

'I am Reinlok,' I said. 'I sit on the Weaver Council, and have no lineage worth telling.'

Gnashdal darted forward, his great bulk shaking the threads as he charged. I slipped through the hole and ran underneath him, easily dodging his cutters as they caught up in the heavy floor-threads. He smashed away and howled in fury.

'Tricks!' he said. 'This is not a true battle. Fight me properly.' I emerged from another hole to see the Soldier hacking away at the front of my house, tearing at the intricate frame-work. He'd given up on our farcical duel, and was going to go for Naello instead.

'No!' I wailed. 'You leave her!' I bound his hind legs in thick layers of webbing, and he fell over with a surprised look on his ugly face. Dragging himself forward with surprising speed, Gnashdal opened his fanged maw, and I could see he was going to simply sweep me into his broad gullet. I sprayed Gnashdal's eyes with webbing till my sacs ached, and he swept his claws around, blinded and furious.

I'd bought a moment, and used it. Running up the wall, I leapt onto Gnashdal's back, ran up his thorax. He lifted his limbs but paused, cautious of hitting himself. That moment of hesitation was his undoing as I slid my simple stinger into the base of his skull.

I leapt free and ran to my front door. I was shaking, absolutely terrified. Gnashdal shook his head, took one groggy step forward. He lived!

'No, please!' I said, and cowered. I'd been a fool to believe in these alien concepts, this *love* and *fidelity*. They hadn't helped the extinct species, and now they'd doomed me . . .

He raised his great cutters, and then sagged to his knees, legs curling beneath him.

I'd done it. I'd killed Gnashdal.

I left him there, a warning to anyone else who wanted my love. Hiding indoors, nursing my sore web-sacs, I jumped at every sound. If one Soldier had come for Naello, surely more would.

'Your actions confuse me, Reinlok,' Naello said. 'Why did you risk your pointless little life fighting Gnashdal, when you had nothing to gain?'

'Because I love you. I wish to honour your chastity, and protect you.'

She barked with laughter and, forgetting myself, I leapt backwards. I'd figured the sound meant she'd finally decided to eat me anyway. As was her right.

'Protect me? ME?I could eat that Soldier and still have room for you, if only you'd get this meat-walker nonsense over with and mate me. What is wrong with you?'

Her great barbed cutters arced above me, shaking, and I could smell her disappointment, her confusion. But every moment that she didn't kill me meant she was listening, considering my ideas.

My one great hope remained, that I would survive this relationship because of love. Another, much slimmer hope, was that Naello would take this concept and share it with her sisters. Our great culture deserved this change!

Would love, could love bring equality to malekind?

'I know we have to breed, Naello. But I want to give you more. More than babies, more than a full belly. Don't you want something else from this, from us?'

'Us,' she said, as if chewing over the word.

We embraced, limbs twining, and she shivered with delight. I drowned in her scent, felt myself responding to her nearness. She pulled at me, giving off a strong mating scent, and I felt my breeders extending.

'No. We can't.'

Letting out a deep breath I pushed her away, ignoring her disappointed rustles and mocking screeches. The sour smell of her frustration followed me outside.

I was out the front of my nest repairing the damaged thread-work when the Matriarch herself paid me a visit, a great retinue of Soldiers depositing her silk-litter with a groan. Terrified, I knelt before the supreme leader of our race. She made Gnashdal look *very* small.

'Reinlok, word has reached us of your . . . duel,' she

rumbled, dozens of eyes glittering as she considered my trembling form. It would be the work of a moment for her to snatch me up, crush the life out of me.

'Irregular as it was, you observed the correct forms. We have checked the Hall of Records, and no law has been broken here,' she continued. 'Yet you are derelict in your duty.'

One great furry limb pointed across the grotto to the gruesome corpse of Gnashdal.

'You must eat your foe, Reinlok,' she said. 'It is the law.'

'Milady, I cannot eat that thing,' I protested.

'You wanted to play at being a Soldier. Soldiers eat the dead. Someone will be eaten today, so pray that it is not you.'

Bowing and scraping, I made my way to Gnashdal's dead body, picked up a fore-limb, nibbled on it with disgust. The royal party sat there and watched me eat, even though it took several days. Caravans of Drones delivered food for the Matriarch, and when they were too slow our enormous mother snatched the squealing servants into her mouth, crunching down on them with relish as she watched me at my task.

Naello came out of our nest to watch the proceedings, and spoke with the Matriarch at great length. Even over the rank taste of my enemy's flesh, I felt giddy with delight. It was even better than I hoped, if she but shared the concept of love with our great lady!

My stomachs stretched and reformed several times, and I felt myself growing. I could feel the essence of my dead foe pervade my being, and behind this invasive force I could feel the long-dead Soldiers that Gnashdal had eaten. Their memories started to mesh with mine, and I felt cranky, sullen. I tore into Gnashdal's corpse with greater vigour, cracking his exo-skeleton as my jaws grew.

I felt ill as I shovelled the last shred of sour flesh into my gullet and struggled around in my new swollen body to face the Matriarch. I bowed, resting on my uncomfortably full stomachs till she bade me rise.

'Well done, Reinlok, though you certainly took your time,' she said. 'You may go about your business. I've inspected Naello, and she is well into fertility. You must be eager to try and mate with her.'

'I don't want to mate with her, milady. I love her, and want to keep her safe.'

'Keep *her* safe?'

Frowning, the Matriarch snapped two limbs together. An advisor came running, and there was a brief discussion between them. They looked at me several times, and a scent of displeasure wafted from them.

'Have I broken any laws, milady?' I asked, wishing they would all go away and leave me alone. The Matriarch shook her head, turning from me in disgust. She crawled into her litter, the Soldiers hefting it onto their backs with limb-shaking effort.

'There are no laws against not mating,' she finally managed before they left. 'It's just . . . not normal.'

'Reinlok, you have to recite your lineage,' Kolid said. 'It's the law.'

Before me, only old Hewghn had recited lineage in the Weaver Council. He'd eaten once in his youth, a mostly forgotten battle over a female. There was Kolid, of course, but as Lord Weaver he'd only ever eaten his predecessor, who'd eaten his master of course, and so on right back to the dawn of our race. Practical concerns meant they'd long dispensed with reciting *his* lineage.

'I am Reinlok. I am a Weaver,' I began, and once that would have been it. Sighing, I gathered my thoughts.

'I have eaten Gnashdal, named Brave One by the Matriarch, who ate Swekton, who ate Balar and Palax before him, who ate Nevad, who ate Bruka and Lanar, eater himself of Casa and Redrix. Gnashdal also ate Cera, previously named Brave One by the Matriarch, who'd eaten Redlat, Poros and Nepun . . . '

After several minutes of this I lost my place. I'd never had to bother remembering any of this rubbish before. I was required to start again, and my peers groaned with annoyance.

'Stop, stop, Reinlok,' Kolid said. 'I will give you dispensation this time. But by next Council you must have learnt your lineage.'

The other Weavers muttered to each other as they shifted around in their silk hammocks, giving me dirty looks. Councils were usually quick to open, but as the eater of Gnashdal I now had an extensive lineage to recite. Meetings could now be expected to take half an hour longer than usual. They'd also needed to modify our Lodge; I was almost triple my normal size.

'Let us see the latest creations!' Kolid said. 'We will start with Hewghn.'

They passed the thinket around the Council, and the old Weaver had outdone himself. I ran my clumsy fore-limbs over the delicate connected orbs, and marvelled at the simplicity of the work. It was as much a poem as a sculpture, with a clever under-story and a resonant over-story. I sighed, passing it on. I could have spent a week reading from it without learning everything he'd included.

It was a polemic against those who admired and aped certain cultural aspects of the conquered species, such as myself. He'd intentionally mispronounced the phrase 'meat-walker' with 'meat-talker' several times, and it was the cause of much mirth. As far as memetic humour went, the phrase was guaranteed to enter the vernacular for several years.

Finally it was my turn, and I handed forth my latest work. The other Weavers muttered angrily amongst themselves, passing it around the circle with disdain. Old Hewghn even brushed his fore-limbs as if the piece were filthy.

'What is the meaning of this?'Kolid said.' This—thing! It's not fit to be presented to the Weaver Council.' He threw it against the floor-webbing in disgust.

'There is no sub-text whatsoever,' one Weaver said. 'Completely one-dimensional. Hardly the work of a supposed master.'

'This was so pedestrian, I thought you were being ironic,' another sniffed. 'Perhaps you've lost your touch.'

I had struggled with the piece for hours, squeezing all that I could out of my shrunken web-sacs. My previous effort was destroyed when one of my fore-limbs suddenly turned into a great cutter, crushing the thinket and one of the walls in my nest. I could see the faults in this work, but it was the best I could do.

My future as a Weaver did not look good.

●

'I really need it,' I said to her, reaching for the thinket. Laughing, Naello held my present out of reach, pushing me back with her strong fore-limbs.

Surprising myself I pushed back, risking a quick death should she seize me, the stretching hole of her deep mouth uncomfortably close. I did not care. I was furious and sore. Every day some new weapon of death chose to poke through my aching exo-skeleton, and it was a miracle I hadn't killed anyone else.

I wanted to snatch it from her, and as we struggled I felt a stronger, more disturbing urge. My breeder extended itself towards her, double-pronged and dripping with genetic material.

'Yes!' she cried. 'Do it at last, if you've the courage.'

'Give me the thinket!' I said and she tossed it to the ground, turning and exposing her sex to me. Panting with frustration I grabbed the silk sculpture, but I didn't leave the room. Her pheromones were driving me crazy, and I could no longer resist my natural urges.

Grunting with excitement and lust, my breeder plunged into her, and I could feel her reaching for me with all her instruments of death, even as the moment of conception arrived.

All of my intellectual aspirations, all my lofty ideals, forgotten in the visceral act of rutting. And it felt good, felt so right.

Where was love now?

I bit off the leg that was encircling my thorax, and as she recoiled in shock I pushed my way free, cut through the immaculate walls of my house, left the place in ruins as I ran for my life.

After all that, I was still holding the thinket in one shaking limb, and it wasn't broken. I put the delicate construction into a net-bag and webbed it to my underbelly, groaning at the twinge from my almost dormant web-sacs.

I left the nest and barrelled along the causeways. Climbing a long tunnel to a privileged part of the Web, I found myself in front of Kolid's impressive nest. Gripping the floor-threads tightly, I requested entry.

KOLID ME HERE ME COME IN NOW, I said, unused to the size of my new limbs. I was finding webspeak hard now, and this would make my next request even harder for the Lord Weaver to believe.

Come in Reinlok, he replied, and the main doors opened smoothly. From my last visit I knew that an elaborate system of threads controlled everything in Kolid's home. Ducking I made my way into his atrium, trying not to knock anything over.

I could smell her somewhere, deep within his nest. Kolid had won the approval of a female, who was here now and waiting for her cycle to start. She was just about ready.

'Reinlok, welcome,' he said, his face reflecting anything but that. He was wary, gave off a scent of displeasure.

'Master, I come with a new thinket,' I said. 'I was unwell, and yesterday's piece was a mistake. Please forgive me.'

'Indeed,' Kolid said, looking up at me as he took the piece. He plucked at the music strings with some amusement, scanned the story and the subtext. He reached the pictures of myself and Naello, and frowned.

'This is not new,' he said. 'This was before you became . . . this thing. Isn't it?'

I nodded.

'You can no longer pursue your vocation, Reinlok. It is very clear to me what needs to happen now.'

He paced back and forth, fore-limbs folded. I stank of anger, my whole world crumbling down around me.

'I have consulted with the Matriarch and her advisors, and we have the answer. You have assimilated the essence of Gnashdal, and he was the most powerful Soldier. Ergo, you must now replace him.'

I accepted this truth, something I'd denied for days. You could not eat someone without taking on their essence. When I'd eaten Gnashdal, I'd eaten hundreds of Soldiers.

A sharp smell flooded the area as his female became available for breeding. No doubt he would plunge his breeder into her the moment I left, his Weaver trickery protecting him from her reprisals, a thousand strong threads at his command. She was nothing but a distraction to Kolid, and an alibi for me.

Even the Lord Weaver had to follow the rules. I knew he would not accept a challenge, but no-one needed to know that. It was a quiet area, a privilege for one of his caste.

'You will need to report to the barracks immediately, and you will—Reinlok, no!'

I pounced on the Lord Weaver before he could reach his trickster's web-lines, spearing him with my stingers. I gripped him in my powerful fore-limbs, relishing in the crunch and spray of fresh blood in my mouth. He looked at me with horror, wailing as I ate him alive.

'I've always admired your skills,' I said between bites. 'So generous of you to share them.'

'Was it love that brought you to Kolid's nest?'Naello asked me. I was waiting in some nameless antechamber of the High-Nest, the Matriarch consulting with her inner cirque, runners arriving every hour from the Hall of Records. Today a decision would be made, and I would either serve as the new Lord Weaver—or as a meal.

'Did you love your master as you ate him?'

Naello smelled wary, and her enormous frame was tense, but not in the killing way. There was the faintest tickle of adrenalin seeping from her, and she kept the edge of the doorway between us.

'Was this love?' she said, waving a neat little nub at me, all that remained of her fore-limb that I'd severed. The ragged stump was neatly cauterised and sutured.

'The meat-walkers did terrible things in the name of this concept,' I said, 'but no, none of these things were love.'

Naello lurked by the doorway for a long moment, a pair of her cutters out but held low. Rows of shining eyes watched me, her nictitating membranes cascading as she blinked in random patterns, one eye at a time—an old Soldier trick, a way to always watch a dangerous enemy. No doubt she'd learnt it from some long dead mate, for all the good it had served him.

Naello had come into my life as a scornful predator, a haughty killer who'd graced herself with a diversionary male. She'd always been an attractive mate but now, in her first moment of doubt, she had never seemed more beautiful.

I yearned to give her comfort, wanted to soothe this fear from her. Not for the first time, I felt the ridiculous urge to protect her, to watch over someone much more capable than myself.

'We've heard whispers in the salons,' I said. 'You females play at a much grander game of eating. This must be a terrifying place to live.'

'I ate a meat-walker once,' she said, voice quavering, a sharp spike of fear wafting out from her. 'It did not taste of ancestors, did not have any history in its flesh. You're a fool, wishing to adopt the habits of a dead culture.'

'Am I?' I mused. 'To my way of thinking, the only dead culture is our own.'

The summons came, and I was brought into the inner curlicues of High-Nest by a pair of Soldiers I already dwarfed. Naello melted into a curious crowd of sycophants and lackeys, and I did not fault her on this. If the decision went against me, it would be folly to be associated with a condemned male.

As I was brought before the Matriarch and dropped to my knees, I winced. My web-sacs ached constantly, this time from growth. The glands had never been this big, and I suspected that I could now squeeze out more silk line than any other sitting on the Weaver Council.

'An artiste that wants to play at soldiering,' said the fuzzy bulk of my mistress, stretched out in a broad hammock.

'And now, now he wants to eat his master and take his place. Quolsana here claims that she did not hear you challenge Kolid for mating rights. That you did not even attempt to mate with her.'

And just like that, I was doomed. In a society that gave me one thousand ways to legally eat my neighbour, I'd committed murder.

'Milady, I did not challenge the Lord Weaver. I hear him now, swimming around in my skull, calling out for justice.'

'I am inclined to grant this justice,' the Matriarch said. 'Bring the accused to me.'

A trio of Weavers bound my limbs, and four Soldiers lifted me on high, hauling me towards the tangled mess of hammocks and screens that the Matriarch lurked behind. She rose above the mess of webbing like a wire-haired planet, the flaps of her great mouth spreading wide with anticipation. She would shear me in half with one bite.

'Are you to be the next Lord Weaver, milady?' I asked, even as an array of murderous limbs arced above me. 'I did not know that females were permitted to sit on the Weaver Council.'

'What nonsense is this?' the Matriarch said. 'Die with dignity, if you have any.'

But she gave pause, and the gaggle of retainers and sycophants whispered excitedly amongst themselves, clinging to every surface of High-Nest to watch my execution. Bound up like a sack of grubs, I'd bought a narrow moment of time. The Matriarch's mouth was an enormous crevice, a black finality. It was an honour to be her meal.

'You will inherit the entire lineage of Lords Weaver, unbroken,' I explained. 'It goes back to the dawn of our race, if you listen hard enough. The first ones are in there too, poor nameless things.'

An advisor dropped from the ceiling on a climber

thread and pulled up next to the Matriarch's ears, whispering furiously. After a long moment, she nodded, and then snatched the male out of the air with a lightning fast snap of her jaws. In moments the advisor was nothing more than a twitching ruin of limbs, protruding from that fat gullet.

'Unbind him,' the Matriarch said, lazily pointing one furry spar of a foreleg towards Reinlok. 'Seems that only females can enact a capital sentence under our laws, but we cannot break Weaver lineage. You cannot be eaten by us.'

Scribes were sent for, and a charter drawn up. The parchment was pressed briefly against the Matriarch's cloaca, and sealed with her own flawless webbing.

'I confirm you into the position of Lord Weaver, and I pray that someday, someone is strong enough to take it from you.'

Standing in the shredded ruins of my bindings, my charter gripped tightly, I had no fear of this curse. I had the bearing of Gnashdal now, the strength of his vanquished foes.

Several Weavers waited on the Matriarch in High-Nest, and they knelt before me with heads lowered, bowing to their new Lord Weaver, a freak instrument of war converted into our society's highest artist. We were not an order of the militant, rather a collective of weak dreamers and web-smiths. None within the Council would ever challenge me for my flesh.

And then I realised that I had them. The Lord Weaver gave direction to the cultural output of the Web. These females would hear only the plays that I approved of, would see only the dramatic sequences and narratives that I let them see.

It would take a long time, but I had already won. I would carve through the stagnant layers of our culture, and give our lusty mothers and proud sons the concept of love, of something beyond the self.

I saw Naello watching me intently, and I saw something else in her expression. It wasn't hate, or lust, or hunger. It was something like happiness, perhaps pride.

It seemed to me then that she would make a fine companion, not just in the mad frenzy of our mating and my attempted murder, but for a length of time afterwards, perhaps always.

'I will give this position much gravitas, milady,' I said. 'You can look forward to hearing my ideas for a long, long time.'

Jason Fischer lives near Adelaide, South Australia. He attended the Clarion South writers workshop in 2007, and has been shortlisted in the Aurealis Awards, the Ditmar Awards, and the Australian Shadows Awards. Jason won the 2009 AHWA Short Story and the 2010 AHWA Flash Fiction competitions, and is a recent winner of the Writers of the Future contest. He has stories in *Dreaming Again*, *Apex*, *Andromeda Spaceways Inflight Magazine*, and *Aurealis Magazine*. His zombie-apocalypse novella 'After The World: Gravesend' is available from Black House Comics.

By Any Other Name

Kim Westwood

The only thing I remember clearly from the house I was born in is the motto *Arthe: our place in space*. Embroidered on white linen, it hung from our parlour mantelpiece like everyone else's, and were the first words I could read, being also set above the crèche entrance and that of every public building in the town.

The question of why we needed an aphorism written everywhere to make us feel we belonged somewhere didn't occur to me till several houses later and my mid-teens, when I began to question a lot of things—especially the forbidden ones. By then the embroidery was faded and the fabric yellow, and my mother had left my father, who'd gone from inventor and amateur astronomer to a regular inmate of the psych ward at the local hospital.

At the raw age of seventeen, with no siblings to share my loneliness and confusion, it appeared my family had entirely deserted me. And so I set off to the city to find employment, and there I joined an illegal organisation called the Nostalgia Club.

I get shift work on the assembly line of a prosthetics factory, and am fortunate that the Company's employment package includes temporary accommodation. My apartment, a deceased estate, will eventually be allocated a new owner by the Housing Authority, no property ever handed down the generations. This is so the living can start afresh, untrammelled by the belongings of the dead.

My fascination with the past begins innocuously enough: a musty carpet roll missed by the cleaners, some pages from an old newspaper trapped between it and the underlay. After extracting the pages, I pore over the print and pictures of three generations ago—a largely forgotten time—two articles in particular catching my attention. The first debunks rumours about the existence of the 'Simulacra', a cult from fable like the bogeyman, with a reputation just as fierce; the second announces a new star chart is to be published showing Arthe's 'place in space'. This, for all I know, is the era the aphorism on my family mantelpiece was coined.

I hide the newspaper in a drawer, loathe to destroy it like I should—tarrying in the past considered socially retrograde. A whispered conversation I overhear soon after in the factory tearoom leads me to the Nostalgia Club.

They meet one night a week beneath the City Harbour Bridge. On my first visit, both moons are up and I can see the tide sucking in and out across the mudflats of the subterranean sea, never enough of it dragged up through the bore holes to properly fill the bay. Twelve or so, they're gathered in the shadows cast by giant riveted girders. Public transport rushing overhead and mud burping beside, one by one they reveal their treasures found between meets.

Memorabilia of any kind is valued, but the older the item the better. My newspaper pages are met with astonishment, being from the era of our grandparents'

parents, all that generation's personal effects (and anything else to remember them by) burnt with them in cremation. This has since become common practice, in the interests of tidiness and general population health. For those who disagree, there's another aphorism and central tenet of life on Arthe: *No yesterday, no tomorrow, only now.*

The members of the Nostalgia Club, however, share a guilty fascination with yesterday, and I soon become a regular attendee. Flouting the law and a raft of social mores, we show and covet and bargain, then adjourn to the local pub to drink and argue politics. In that last regard it seems I have inherited something of my father's intensity.

I am ten, and it's my bedtime. My father emerges from behind the always-locked door of his inventions room and gestures to me. I'm about to be shown something important. I pad down the hallway in my pyjamas.

The room is a muddle of overburdened shelving and strange objects, its benches littered with papers and tools. At the centre, a fat metal tube sits on a stand, one end sticking up through the open skylight.

'Look through here,' my father instructs, lowering the end of the tube so I can bring my eye to the lenspiece.

First I see nothing but my own eye looking back; then a brightly textured surface fills the view.

'That's Beta, our second moon,' I'm informed.

I withdraw my eye from the lens and look up at it, a bright disc in a bowl of stars.

'Every point of light is a furnace for creation,' my father says, looking too.

'The Deity made us from stardust and then destroyed the blueprint so we would be unique in space,' I parrot back at him.

He snorts. 'The people who say those things have their heads in a cupboard.'

His colourful language amuses me. 'Dad, you're a dissident,' I reply impulsively, and he drags on my arm, forcing my face close to his.

'Never use that word,' he hisses, glancing to the room's closed door. 'Do you even know what it means?'

I look up at him dumbly, tears starting. It's a word we kids use on each other at school, out of earshot of our teachers. An adult's word, with all the flavour of transgression to it.

He softens. 'Whatever they tell you, it's not a bad word. But those called it tend to disappear. Do you understand?'

I don't, but satisfy him with a nod.

He leans distractedly against a workbench where a chunk of facetted glass has been captured in the pincer arms of a vice. 'We're a small blip inside the sphere of the firmament. Never forget that, Wren.' His pet name for me, after the little furry birds that burrow in our garden.

I wait for more, but tonight's show-and-tell session is over and my father has withdrawn into himself.

'Bedtime,' he says eventually. 'Off you go.'

Growing up, I accorded my father hero status, invited regularly into his inventions room to be shown some subtle change he'd plotted in the constellations or to witness the unveiling of a new construction, and getting lost entirely in the explanation of the thingummy causing the whatsit to do something really important. That his innovations were never taken seriously by anybody else didn't matter to me. I was the daughter of a genius, and I wore that knowledge like a badge of honour.

The price of genius eventually came, in the form of two burly men from the Patents Office enquiring for him. Apparently, he'd finally invented something of interest to the authorities. Their visit should have been cause for celebration; instead it marked a frightening change in my father. The show-and-tell sessions in his inventions room stopped and he became furtive and anxious, his bouts of black despair finally tunnelling into complete breakdown.

I am fourteen. My mother tells me my father has gone to hospital, but will be home soon. She says it like he's getting the groceries, but for three weeks I'm not allowed to visit him or even speak to him on the telephone.

He's dropped off by a plain white van, and hardly acknowledges my excited hello, my arms flung around him. Slumped on the couch in the parlour, he seems sucked of personality, numb to everything. I learn that the treatment has taken away a lot of his memory.

'Show me one of your inventions,' I beg, and he looks at me blankly. A carapace of his former self, he has no will to speak or eat or sleep, and is back in hospital within the month.

My early entry into adulthood and new life in the city suits me, and seems a world away from the travails of home. The factory job is secure—the people on Arthe being prone to thin bones and joint deterioration—but while it provides a living, it isn't what I live for. The newspaper pages I'd found on my arrival were a catalyst for nostalgia, now turned into obsession, all my spare time spent fossicking about deceased estates for the things of the past that had been missed in the incinerations, maybe even deliberately hidden.

I take my finds to the Nostalgia Club meets and bargain with them for more coveted things. Later, in the pub, certain topics always rouse heated discussion. I lock horns most with Gideon, a crematorium worker. He thinks it okay, for example, that we aren't allowed to keep our loved ones' ashes, or even visit the crematorium vaults where they've been put.

'The vaults are no place for the living,' he says. 'And visitors would only get in the way of the workers.'

'Why are you here, then, if you have so little regard for the memory of the dead?' I retort, and he shrugs, replying, 'I like collecting things, but it's not about their history, it's the thrill of the chase.'

When the news comes that the government has shelved its promised space program, I am incensed. My father's daughter, I argue that anything giving us a deeper understanding of our place in space is surely a good thing. Of course Gideon disagrees, saying, 'It's profligate and a waste of energy when there's so much to be done on Arthe.'

Once a month I make the trip to see my father—in the psych ward more often than not, and no longer interested in the discoveries mouldering in his inventions room. But one visit, long after I think all lucidity has left him, he surprises me.

We're sitting in the locked courtyard outside the ward. Suddenly he leans across and takes my hand in both of his, transferring a key into my palm. 'Our secret,' he whispers fiercely.

His gaze bores into me from beneath unkempt brows. 'The stars, Wren. They tell the story.'

'What story, dad?' I ask, an eye to the attendant standing nearby.

'Of who we really are,' he urges. 'And why there is no Deity.'

Quickly I lean in, putting an arm around one frail, hunched shoulder.

'Shhh, dad. You don't mean that.'

He looks at me wordlessly, then slumps back in his chair and for the rest of my visit won't respond to me, staring fixedly at his pyjamaed knees.

The key thrust in my hand should've compelled me to my father's house, but instead I return to the city, unable to revisit the place of his disintegration and the dissolution of our family. Truth be known, I'm ashamed of his ignominious slide from genius to misfit.

My next trip home is to the town coroner's white office.

'Mr Ligetti was a very sick man,' the coroner says. Dad had been found hanging by his pyjama pants in the shower block. 'Is there anything you can tell me about him that might help us understand how the delusional nostalgia began?'

'No,' I say blandly, not about to give away the secrets of his inventions room. 'He always seemed just normal to me.'

The coroner regards me a moment, then sighs.

'I'm sorry for your loss,' he says. He hands me the receipt for my father's niche in the crematorium vaults then leads me to the door.

On the stone wall outside my family home is a notice of repossession. Behind it the house is boarded up, ready to be stripped of its contents. My mother having rescinded her rights to it when she left, the property now belongs to the Housing Authority and I am trespassing. Luckily, I've become quite practiced at breaking into deceased estates. I finger my father's key as I walk down the fusty hallway to the door of the inventions room.

Inside, a wan sun filters through the dirty skylight and the motes of disturbed dust make my nose twitch. First I see the telescope is gone, then that the familiar clutter has been swept from the shelves and benches and strewn like jetsam across the floor. Could dad have done this in one of his fits of despair?

Something glints by my boot. A chunk of facetted glass. I hold it aloft. Once, it was just another curio among the many: now it's an amulet carrying his memory.

I pick my way through the debris, my focus on the far workbench and a drawer he'd shown me years before.

I feel for the concealed catch and the drawer releases. In it is a large folio. Beneath the plain cardboard cover is a glossy depiction of our solar system, Arthe's place in space, on display in every public library and Council building, and handed out at school for us to learn the five planets and their moons by rote. I peel it back to see the next sheet: Arthe's official star chart, which dad used to complain no longer matched the sky. Lifting a corner,

I stop and squint. Among several newly plotted points of light, a rough circle has been dotted in, and inside it, nothing . . . an absence of stars.

I flip through dated star sheets, the meticulous work of years, reading the words written against the circle, then sit heavily on the stool beside the bench as the confusing elements of my past fall into place. I'd left home not understanding what caused my father's steep decline; a year later in his inventions room I know the reason. In his nightly wanderings of our sky, he'd plotted a phenomenon as preposterous as spaceships and time travel—a hole in space—and named it the Ligetti Portal.

If he'd lodged a finder's claim (as was his right) it would have put the Patents Office in a fizz, acknowledging the existence of such a thing tantamount to throwing open Pandora's Box. They may even have seen it as an act of dissidence, since the sphere that holds the firmament in place was put there by the Deity, and this suggests a rent in its perfection.

Back in the city, a crackdown on nostalgia sees the disbanding of the Nostalgia Club. Our last meet under the bridge is a hurried affair: a few half-hearted swaps before final goodbyes.

A week later the charismatic founder of our club, Irma, disappears. I hear the news from the same person whose whispered conversation had alerted me to the club's existence. The next day he doesn't show for work. Panicked, I leave my job at the factory and rent a basement in the Recyclers District, a place of cash transactions and no names. Selling the newspaper pages provides me with enough to live on for a couple of months, but I keep my father's star charts.

A rumour begins to circulate that the ashes of the dead aren't really stored in name-plated niches in the crematorium vaults, but thrown onto one big anonymous pile. My own flesh and blood so recently cremated, something more than anger rises in me.

'You shouldn't have come here,' Gideon says. He's dressed in the formless grey boiler suit of a crematorium worker. His eyes speed the chapel for other workers who might have seen me.

'I want to visit my father,' I tell him. 'And you can show me where.' I hand him my crematorium receipt.

'You know I can't do that,' Gideon replies, trying to shepherd me away from the vault entrance.

'Just one time. Please. I need to see where he's been put.'

'I can't. It's totally forbidden.'

'Then give me a spare boiler suit and point me in the right direction. I'll find my own way out.'

'You'll be spotted. Everyone knows everyone.'

Finally, to be rid of me, he relents—but first I have to swear never to reveal I know him.

The crematorium vaults are scattered throughout the city, each section with its own chapel. This section is deserted, Gideon's fears unfounded. Using his hurriedly scrawled map, I walk dim-lit tunnels with deep niches chipped into the rock from floor to roof both sides, every one with a nameplate. The old tunnels link to newer ones, and the area where my father has been put. Here, metal compactus shelves replace the rock, long rows of them off every aisle, their contents got to by winding a handle. I find my father's numbered row and shiny new nameplate, and slide out the drawer.

No ashes.

I check other drawers. All empty. I slump to the ground. Amid towering stacks and the chaotic geometry of opened compartments, I promise to search until I have an answer to the last thing he wanted me to know: who we really are.

I return to the chapel. It's unattended but for the squirrels fluttering in high eaves. I leave the boiler suit folded on a pew and walk out through neatly landscaped grounds, the spectacular displays of blue-ringed lilies and red sunflowers quite a feat of gardening, considering that everywhere else the ground of Arthe is chalky and difficult to grow anything in but rocks.

Nearing the end of my money supply and no closer to answers, I get a message from Gideon. He's tracked me to my basement hideaway and wants to meet under the harbour bridge.

He's pacing between the girders when I arrive.

'They're after me,' he says, and draws me deeper into the shadows.

'Who?'

'The Simulacra.'

'They don't exist,' I remind him.

He looks at me strangely. 'How can you be so unaware? They're here in the city, fomenting unrest. They wanted me to show them where all the ashes are. I said I wouldn't.'

'You *know*?'

'The soul is gone, Wren. What's left is just organic material.'

'We're being lied to, and you're helping.'

He lays one hand on my shoulder. 'When you found your father's drawer empty, did you go around disillusioning other people? No. Why not? Because it's a small white lie—lip service to nostalgia, if you like. Let the living have their niches and nameplates.'

'Is that what you came to tell me?'

'No, I'm here to warn you that they're after you too.'

I refuse to be spooked by his overactive imagination. 'You could stay at my place until you feel better,' I offer.

'Too late,' he says. 'Watch your bones.'

The message pushed under my door the next afternoon is not from Gideon. It reads: *If you want the truth, we can help. Bring your father's star charts to the harbour bridge tonight.* At the bottom of the page, in the centre of a spiral, is the letter 'S'.

I'd never shown the star charts, nor told anyone where the Nostalgia Club had their meets. Scared, but bound by my promise made in the crematorium vaults, I walk the unlit path towards the girders, and wonder could this really be the Simulacra emerged from myth like Gideon said?

A figure detaches from the shadows. Irma, the founder of the Nostalgia Club, who'd reportedly disappeared.

'You're one of them?' I ask.

She nods. 'So was your father—briefly. He found his way to us after he was threatened into silence by the authorities. He wouldn't let us go public with his discovery for fear of what might happen to you.'

I kick a muddy stone back into the bay and watch it skitter briefly before sinking. My father kept his silence to protect me, but was taken from me anyway.

'Out of respect for him, we waited, and kept an eye on you.'

'The Nostalgia Club?'

'Yes.'

'Why should I believe you? You're a member of a cult.'

'And you're a dissident.'

I'm reminded of my childhood gaff. 'Gideon is afraid of you,' I tell her.

She looks troubled. 'He wanted to denounce us. He was unstable . . . '

Registering her use of the past tense, I feel a riff of fear. 'And me?'

'You are your father's child. We trust in that. Which is why I'm about to show you what we showed him.'

She takes a metal tube from inside her jacket and unfurls a crackly brown parchment ruched with age—a prize item for any Nostalgia Club. I examine it in the torchlight, like old times. It's a star chart, but the solar formation dominating the foreground isn't ours. Nine planets circle their sun. One of them is called Earth.

'Are you mocking me?' I say angrily.

In answer, she takes one of my charts from me and lays it face-up on a rock.

'We didn't begin on Arthe,' she says quietly. 'We came here in ships, through that.' She places a finger on the Ligetti Portal then motions me to reopen the older chart.

'From there.'

Third planet from the sun, same as us. It undoes the precepts of the Deity, and flies in the face of our uniqueness. My father's last words to me come slamming back. *This is what he knew.*

'The Simulacra have the first settlers' accounts of arriving here through deep space, which is why we're hunted by the authorities and have been for generations. The last time we tried to bring the facts to light was in our grandparents' parents' time. As a consequence, everything about their lives was obliterated.'

I'm reminded of the newspaper articles. Were they part of an official cover-up?

'What they saved, they hid well, in the hope there'd be a next time.' She pauses, looking at me intently. The gaze of a fanatic. '*This* is the next time. With our evidence and your father's charts, Arthe will learn of its real history and Arthelings will know their origins.'

The truth comes out about our loved ones' ashes being sold back to us as fertiliser (not Gideon's admission, I'm sure, if he's even still alive) and the city is in uproar. More than just a scandal, it's a deep betrayal of people's trust. Every day there are marches in the streets, throngs at protests. The politicians are scared but downplaying the situation; meanwhile, their police force takes no action. They have loved ones who've been cremated too. I wonder how many days before bloodshed. All the while, the question hangs in my mind: is it so bad to have come from somewhere else?

Fighting breaks out in several districts. With all eyes looking elsewhere, I plan a return visit to the crematorium vaults, something urgent I have to do. Irma suggests we go together: I still have my map, and Gideon very kindly provided her with the combination to the chapel door.

Cool air meets us as we descend. Despite this place being at the heart of all the furor, it's strangely quiet.

'Something's been bothering me,' I whisper as we hurry along the tunnels. 'Why would our forebears build such an elaborate mythology to cover the truth?'

'It began with the first settlers' desire to replicate their home,' Irma replies. 'But the genetic material brought across space developed differently here, and so the terraforming and species reproduction was only partially successful.'

'Why did they want to copy it so exactly?'

'Because they themselves were copies, although they suffered under the comparison.'

She's lost me. 'What do you mean?'

'The ships were sent into the wormhole with expendables—clones—each with their original safely back on Earth. That's what our predecessors didn't want ensuing generations to know. We are the produce of clones, the copies of copies.'

Ahead, the metal shelving of the newer section glints. I try to take in what Irma's telling me.

'I don't feel like a copy,' I say cautiously. 'Wouldn't I feel . . . something?'

'The first settlers did. Bound by definition to their original, they were never free of the taint of being second-rate. Arriving here, they wanted a new Earth where *they* were the originals. They wanted an Earth that, by any other name, could be as real. And so they erased all traces of the referent in the memories of their children and their children's children. Arthe's mythologies were built, and in each successive generation, memory dimmed. Nostalgia became a liability then a sin.'

We're at my father's row. I turn the compactus handle, Irma watching. The roll of star sheets I've been carrying I place in my father's drawer and close it. If revolution falters, this will be my legacy. For next time.

Irma's eyes stay on the drawer. 'What they didn't understand,' she says slowly, 'is that any generation created from the copy would be a simulacrum—a third that breaks the circle and opens a new way. It's the lies they've built around us that hold us from that trajectory and our true potential.'

As I'm winding the compactus row closed, I hear shouting down the corridor and heavy boots. Likely, our foray into the vaults has been discovered. I haul vigorously on the handle then start back towards the chapel, when suddenly Irma veers off on a different route. Frantically I motion to her, but she ignores me and keeps going.

The banner *Arthe: our place in space* hangs above locked doors. Several members of the Simulacra have been put in here along with me. Once, they killed dissidents and burnt their possessions; these days they have a more enlightened approach.

On my lucid days, when I've thrown or flushed my pills, I get out my father's key and stare at it, trying to visualise each thing in his inventions room—a game to keep alert. Irma is still out there, and will come for us, I'm sure; so I prepare, watching the wardens carefully for chinks in their routine.

When the Simulacra were routed, the uprising failed. The wardens tell us, not unkindly, that as sect members we were the victims of a pernicious doctrine, and brainwashed by our leader. The doctors give us therapy, and every day I remember a little less.

Those of us still with some capacity to recall, tell each other furtive stories of our induction to the cause and Irma's exploits, to keep our spirits up. I don't mention the recurring dream I have of being trapped between compactus shelves down in the crematorium vaults, while she, unheeding of my cries for help, takes off with my father's star charts.

At night, outside the window by my bed, two moons traverse the sky. Somewhere beyond them is that dark portal written into my father's maps, the movement of the stars plotted nearby revealing it's two-way. I imagine travelling through it to the place where Earth was last in space, a blue-green orb spinning on its axis, looping with its eight companions around their sun. Who knows if the other end is past or future or our original is even there? But in one thing, at least, I can rest assured. If the expendable children of Earth ever make the journey back, it will be as their originals' transcendants. Simulacra.

Kim Westwood realised she might be a bit speculative when her story 'The Oracle' won a 2002 Aurealis Award. Since then there's been more speculation, much of it with an apocalyptic air. Her stories have been chosen for Year's Best anthologies in Australia and the US, and for ABC radio broadcast. She is the recipient of a prestigious Varuna Writer's Fellowship for her first novel, *The Daughters of Moab*. Her second novel, *The Courier's New Bicycle*, is set in Melbourne just a socio-political changes from now. For more details, go to www.kimwestwood.com

Space Girl Blues

Brendan Duffy

Thawing out a softie
Rigid amber dreams boiled away as flesh softened. Weight flowed into my body. I yawned and stretched in the cosy warmth, blinked my eyes open.

'The softie's awake,' the soldier called, then tested my pupil dilation reflex with a penlight. Motes of dust rained from her desert camouflage helm, caught in slender rays of daylight filtering through the airlock. She wasn't one of mine, but looked like someone I had seen before. Emily? Amanda?

Pretty or handsome.

I took a long, deep breath, but nothing came. I tried again: still nothing. I sucked hard, felt the blockage, then grabbed at a plastic tube reaching down my throat like a well-muscled arm. I dragged out great snaking lengths of slimy black tubing, felt moorings tear deep inside my stomach, gagged and hauled out more. Smaller tubes slid from each nostril. I tried to breathe but vomited through my nose. I needed air and grabbed the soldier to haul myself up.

'Breathe!' She shoved me back into the pod with a brawny arm and slid the dripping gastropositor from my mouth. Sweet fresh air filled my woken lungs and I gulped down its alien flavours: ozone and dust, sage and

503

metal. The soldier wiped my face dry and glued a HiOx inhaler over my nose.

I focused on sucking down O_2 and glanced around my re-entry cryopod—winking lights and monitors, dials in the black, just like in the sim. I must have landed okay, but didn't know why a desert soldier was here in the forest. The last thing I remembered was the queue of us Military Intelligence Advisors laughing and joking nervously as we filed forwards in our white gowns, to be depilated and barrier-waxed by machine as the brainfog closed in. Then drained, embalmed, and bundled.

'Incoming!' a distant voice called. We heard an explosion, felt the vibration. A peristaltic pump in my cot worked the antifreeze extraction, forced arterial tonic rinse down a tube into the vena cava shunt in my chest. When the outflow ran clear the soldier swapped the transfusion to serum packs. She waved a red bag in my face. 'We've only got one pack of red cells, so we'll supplement with plastiplasts. You'll be anaemic until your bone marrow kicks in.' I watched the soldier walk through the stages of the wake-up sequence: muscle relaxant deactivator, adrenal stims, CNS accelerant, white cell primer . . .

'Incom-*fuck!*' The cryopod shook from a close detonation. Things bounced around the cot. Another soldier in desert camo raced through the airlock. 'Zipless, they're on the move! Go, go, go!' *This* one looked like Emily. She snatched some stuff, then saw me and smiled. 'Whoa, yeah! Good work! Grab that softie and let's gethafuck!' She ran.

Zipless turned to me. 'Okay, girl, sorry to rush you but we gotta go.' She winked, grabbed handfuls of wires and tubes, then yanked. Plugs and shunts popped out, patches and monitors ripped away with layers of skin. Beepers beeped and alarms rang. Dials maxed in the red as vital fluids escaped. She opened my nappy, slid out the ablution plumbing and mess gushed everywhere.

'We'll clean you up later.' Zipless flung me over her shoulder in a fireman's hold. Safety catch off and machinegun ready in her other hand, she charged from the pod into a glaring upside-down world of orange and pink. Bouncing along, I vomited digestive buffer and balls of packing foam all down her back. Every orifice I had plus many new ones leaked their signature fluid as she ran across rock and sand, not the forest floor expected.

As Zipless bounded along a sloped rock shelf, I caught snatches of the landscape. Behind, a sandy plain stretched to the horizon. To the right were dunes. The only vegetation was Spinifex. This should have been T sector, lush forest, but there wasn't a single tree to be seen. Machinegun fire rang out. Zipless stopped in the lee of a ridge and set my waxed body down on hot stone, facing a squad of soldiers in worn desert camo. They turned to check me out.

They were all the same.

A squad of female soldier clones, Space Grrrls, face straight from the catalogue. I'd worked ops with cloned cadres before—gingerbread men all thinking and dressing and acting the same. I'd watched them choose the same food in the mess and even take a bite at the same time, but this wasn't like that. These Grrrls all had the eerie sameness of identical twins, but with glaring differences, like identical twins covering it up, like 'tuplets with utterly contrasting personalities loaded into them, which is what they were.

I vomited. They scoffed and swaggered, raised eyebrows and shared I-told-you-sos between their high-fiving selves at my skinny, serum-streaked waxed sack of civilian bones.

I counted five Grrrls: three grunts, one corporal and the lieutenant, all kitted out to nuclear artillery specs, J sector insignia. I had first met these Grrrls two weeks before Go on the showroom floor, and later that night at a company wine-and-dine product launch back on Homeworld: the latest product, flaunted by New Military Solutions Inc as the roadmap to the promised land. This was Red squad: Zipless, Soph and Sly, Emily the corporal, and Amanda the lieutenant, each with distinct skills, tastes, and styles, unique idiosyncrasies and affectations, different haircuts and smiles. Yes, I'd met these Grrrls before—just probably not *these* Grrrls—but it didn't matter, I'd seen the product description and knew the specs, although these ones looked like they'd seen better days.

'You keep staring,' said the clone called Sly. 'Have we met before?' She sneered. The others smiled. At the wine-and-dine this one had drank too much and called me girly. The wax dripped off me in the reddish sunlight, slowly leaving me naked. I didn't have any of my stuff. I looked back at the dusty beat up pod half buried in orange sand.

An explosion shook the ground. Everyone ducked as rubble rained, then Emily continued forward surveillance with a rangefinder. 'Five uglies advancing twelve right at oh-point-five-nine clicks, four at twenty five right at oh-point-eight-oh.'

Amanda muttered, scanning forward with binoculars. 'Tell the crew we thawed out the softie. Stay put until showtime. Five minutes.'

The Grrrls cast sharp-eyed grins at each other. Soph climbed over the top behind a boulder, blind to forward view but visible to the right. She relayed the message using UV gloves and semaphore. I looked around the ridge, checked their equipment: five standard backpacks with kit, mortar case, isotope hut, medikit, and three unknown supply boxes, probably food. No radio kit.

I hauled myself upright and stared forward into the glare: just kilometres of open desert, no visible squads, no armies or fortifications, no city or town. The big red sun blazed, the air blew hot and dry, and none of the features in the terrain were recognisable landmarks from the training module, the mission briefing or any extraneous prep I'd done on those lazy nights with a bottle.

I hadn't come down in the right place.

'Bag!' I held my hand out.

Zipless looked to the lieutenant, Amanda, and waited for the nod, then passed my bag. I rifled through: no gun, no diary, no phone, no computer, and most of my personal effects gone. My zoo was missing. I looked up, furious.

'You looking for this?' Zipless handed over my dead zoo. The screen activated as it touched my skin.

I pinged navsat for mission commence but got no response. Command channel hissed like fried eggs. I scanned upfreq for sig but nothing snagged: no chatter, no updates, no progress reports, no orders or logistics, and no connection to any other unit in orbit or on the face of the planet. It should have been an all-frequency glut of raging war comms but the zoo was empty. I flicked to iGeiger: atmospheric beta emission levels hissed in the red, along with a surprisingly high level of exotics. My zoo scrolled upward through eighty-three lonely channels of isotopic hiss as the blanket of radioactive haze drifted antispinward.

A geospatial failed to position us; all I had were fuzzy premission loads. I checked my map of T sector for podfall, but nothing matched up. Time and date were unavailable. I activated the white noise filter and left the radio on Command channel for when orders came through, but the ominous silence left an unplugged hole in my confidence.

'What the fuck is going on?'

'At this range the enemy shells fall anywhere because they're so inaccurate.' Amanda stared straight ahead.

'No! What's going on!'

Another explosion shook the ground, closer.

'Exotics have taken out all comms, radio is scrambled, navionics are fried, and all electronics are baked.'

'How do you like your eggs in the morning?' Sly smirked.

Amanda turned and nodded to Zipless, the bombardier. She unlocked the mortar case and assembled the nuclear mortar.

'Artillery at one-point-eight-six clicks, fifteen left.' Emily looked up from the rangefinder to Amanda, waiting expectantly.

Zipless turned dials accordingly. 'One-point-eight-six, fifteen left. Check.'

Amanda nodded to Emily, who turned to me.

'Ma'am, we need the activation codes for some canned heat.'

I wiped my face. 'I can't authorise use of a nuke like this!'

'Come on, baby, a type III tactical,' said Zipless, crouching by the mortar. 'Only one point six grams of fizz: I calculated it with my slide rule. Harmless!'

An explosion shook the ground before us. Rocks and dust rained down.

'White squad is getting hammered,' said Emily.

'Quickly,' Amanda muttered, still scanning forward.

'You want codes, you give *me* answers! *Where are we?*'

'J sector.'

I activated my zoo and flicked through J sector maps. 'Desert?'

Sly raised her eyebrows. 'Look around!'

'A better question is '*When* are we?'' said Amanda.

'This isn't Day One?'

'No. We think it's day ninety-seven. Give or take.'

'But it was only meant to last five days! What happened?'

'We don't know,' said Amanda. 'There was a problem with planetfall. We woke late, maybe Day Two. During the Day One strike NOW took out the cities but suffered heavy losses. Comms went down, and the regional population is higher than estimated, leading to a prolonged decentralised conflict.'

'Where's *my* unit?'

Sly shrugged. 'If they didn't wake you . . . '

I banished the faces of my poor dead boys from my

mind. 'Where's Command?'

They looked at each other. 'You're it.'

'What! There's no Command?'

'No, no. We've finally *found* someone in command—*you*.' Dust stuck to the molten wax all over me, and streaming fluids cut runnels through it.

'But I'm only an intel agent. I mean Command Central, the brass coordinating Operation Wildfire.' I pulled a handtowel from my duffel, wiped myself down, then began dressing in dark green forest camo fatigues. 'When were your last orders?'

'Never had any,' said Amanda. 'You are the highest ranking officer we have spoken to in ninety-seven days. As far as we are concerned, you *are* Command.'

'What about your own Military Intelligence Agent?'

'Probably dead. Must have come down somewhere else. In the absence of Command we followed written orders and achieved all specified targets on schedule, and are currently executing our final order—neutralise extraneous enemy forces—which we have been doing, unrelieved and unsupplied, for thirteen weeks, with the ongoing contingency of establishing contact with Command as soon as possible.'

Amanda looked tired. She unrolled a crumbly paper map all bleached and flaking, some old hand-drawn thing covered with unreadable scrawls—not mission issue. 'The village ahead is well stockpiled and they keep launching attacks on us. We're almost out of food, water, ammunition . . . '

'And booze,' Sly interjected.

'The village is unapproachable with a force of our size. Dropping a small type III antipersonnel munition will eradicate the enemy but leave matériel intact and allow us to resupply. We need a micronuke.'

I put a green cap on my bald head and stared at their illegible map.

'It took us ages to find you,' said Sly. 'We triangulated your pod's sig, fought our way to your crash site, found you before *they* did and woke you as ordered.'

'Ordered ninety-seven days ago!

'Look! There's no-one left! You're lucky we found you,' Sly raved. 'We're a nuclear-enabled squad, we need to use a nuke to survive. We searched for someone in MilIntel with access codes until we found you. Give us the codes and let us do our job!'

'Gimme that.' I failed to snatch the rangefinder from Emily. She held onto it, scowled, then let me drag it from her hands. I scanned the field, picked out the hostiles advancing at said coordinates, and saw the distant artillery battery of seven units. Beyond lay a village of domed mud and thatch structures. I'd glanced at J sector modelling but was unfamiliar with orders and targets, and those domiciles did not fit the indigenous structure profile from my sector.

'Who are they?' I stared at the people moving between the domes.

'The enemy.'

'Look at this mess, Popsicle. Military Intelligence fucked up. You agents got everything wrong and most of us killed. You know how many soldiers are dead? This planet doesn't even look like the postcards!'

'Can it, Sly,' I said and scanned their unperturbed faces for reaction.

'We just spent a week dodging bullets to get you outta

the can you slippery little sardine, and you're gonna go back in unless you give us them fucking codes!' She popped the strap on her pistol holster and glowered at me.

'Enough!' Amanda turned to me. 'We'll be out of supplies in two days. The tactical analysis was to attack this stronghold and take their supplies, then disappear back into the desert.'

This was outside orders but, deferring to the contingency schedule, all alien emplacements were to be destroyed, and the use of eigenstate nukes on long-range-capable strike facilities was authorised.

I grabbed my zoo and logged onto the Blast Zone Calculator. I selected radiant neutron burst for maximal antipersonnel effect, dampened explosion and minimised blast zone to reduce local damage, then scanned the target area and tagged the seven artillery units to be depopulated, and indicated that each structure was to remain standing. I checked the output table: one point six grams of Ortho with an epicentre placed ten metres above the artillery, coordinates given. I exported the data into the Munition Armament Authorisation Application. The screen fuzzed. I rapped it on a rock until it cleared, entered the twenty-four digit code to arm the tactical, then sprayed the isotope hut with infrared.

'Permission granted,' said the iso hut, audibly unlocking.

Zipless opened the case. The autoloader rotated a dull mortar shell into view, armed with payload and primed with a detonator cap. The red light turned green as it activated. 'Type III tactical primed and ready to roll,' she said.

'Yes!' The Grrrls cheered and high-fived each other.

'Told you she would,' said Zipless.

'Took a bit of convincing,' said Sly.

'With this one we could win the war!' said Soph.

'Quietly,' muttered Amanda. She turned to Soph. 'Tell them to prepare for type III flash: one minute, then action.'

Soph again scaled the ridge and waved her gloved hands.

'Both squads acknowledge,' said Em.

Amanda gave the nod.

Zipless removed the shell and placed it into the muzzle. 'One in the pipe!' She winked and let go. It slid out of sight. The ground bounced with a dull basso dust-raising thud.

'Five seconds,' she said as the shell arced through the pale blue sky.

'Blast visors down, Grrrls,' said Amanda, and the squad rearranged their headgear.

I ducked behind the rock and faced back the other way, staring into Sly's impassive face.

'All those crawling little bugs are just dead men that don't know it yet,' Sly said.

'Do you ever feel sorry for them?' asked Emily.

Sly placed sunglasses over her eyes, closed the amber visor, then lowered the helmet's UV glare shield. 'Never.'

Eigenspace cracked open and the sky flashed dazzling white. Exotic scintillae of the Orthopositronium self-annihilation spectrum lit up Sly's satin tanned skin, the rising fireball superimposed fourfold over her face, reflected in her shield, visor, and each sunglass lens.

A row of perfect white teeth emerged between perfect lips that now smiled, and a scattering of new freckles blossomed across her perfect cheeks.

Pushin' lead for tha man

The ground shook and rumbled. My zoo hissed as another egg hit the pan. I pulled out my padding, kevlar, thermals, reflec and fallout suit, mentally running through cracked atom blast protocols.

Sly laughed. 'Never let a woman pack.'

The Grrrls sniggered as they armed up. Emily gave the slightest nod to my Kevlar. I followed her lead and stowed the rest.

'Okay Grrrls,' said Amanda, 'we're going out on the town!'

The Grrrls all called for an extra clip, Sly for two. Progress was easy as we advanced along the ridge, the enemy demoralised, their artillery support now just dust in the atmosphere, another sunset. As we walked, the tiny mushroom cloud reached up into the sky over their village, slowed, then hung in the air like a tombstone.

White squad had been pinned down in a dry riverbed by two units of uglies. A seemingly easy target, they'd lured the enemy into revealing their positions, but with the artillery barrage now lifted, Red and Blue squads advanced to surround these units in a crossfire. Semaphore across a one klick front meant there was always someone with a bead. Sly kept me with her as we approached the crossfire position.

'Where's my gun?' I asked.

'No gun for you.' She didn't even look at me, just squinted across the sand.

'Why?'

'We don't trust you.' She scoured the desert for work.

'But this is *our* war! *We* make the decisions and channel the finance; you're just the contractors, the tradesmen—our *sub*-contractors. I'll have you court martialled under the Treason Act.'

Sly laughed. 'Look, Popsicle, who you gonna tell? There's no-one left. They've all been body bagged by your team's incompetence. You do as *we* say now, so shut up, you lawyer, you bean counter.' She sighted down the barrel. 'Look what happens when wars are planned by accountants and bureaucrats. You civilians have no idea.'

'So you're saying we should leave military decision-making in the hands of the *military*?'

Rock chips flew as bullets ricocheted around us. I ducked. Em and Zipless screamed and returned fire as Sly carefully aimed then shot. My ears rang from machinegun detonations and the tinkling of empty cartridges across rock.

'Strike three bad guys.' Sly laughed and the Grrrls high-fived.

'Conserve ammo, Grrrls,' said Amanda. 'Headshots only, 'cause soon we're down to bayonets. Up close and personal with the uglies!'

'If it comes to that we should just give up our prisoner.' Sly nodded at me. Zip and Em glanced away, trying not to laugh. Amanda cast me an apologetic glance, shook her head at Sly, then popped her holster strap and handed me her pistol, grip first. 'Grrrls, remember *who* you're doing this for: New Military Solutions Inc, the government, and all the little people back home.'

'That's right!' I said. 'When we beat these insurgents we will reunite Palawan with the Nexus of Worlds, re-establish the trade lanes, and all soldiers will be rewarded with a handsome villa on this planet or the option to sell it back to the company and go home.' At least that was the deal for the normal soldiers.

'Softie,' Sly shook her head. 'You're a walking advert for the man.'

'Go home?' asked Zipless as we walked. 'I can't wait! When I get home I'm gonna be a mechanic again.'

'Me a plumber,' said Amanda. 'My business was picking up.'

'I'll go back to school teaching.' Emily smiled at me.

I forced a smile, then looked away. *Go back to?* They were just soldier clones, a disposable product made for *this* war, and wouldn't be more than ninety-seven days old, give or take. Soldier clones didn't have lives, didn't have pasts, just memories—fake memories. And they certainly didn't have futures; a brutally short lifespan guaranteed that. Their superhuman abilities came from permanently maintaining a hypermetabolic constitution, which they paid for in escalating cellular toxicity, accelerated progeria and eventual tissue collapse. No clone had ever lived longer than four years.

Maybe they didn't know.

I said nothing.

I'd worked with other clones that had fake memories, and earlier models that didn't, and by far preferred the former. There were less accidents. It made them more human.

Sly watched me, trying not to laugh. 'Well when I

get home I'm gonna be unemployed.' She chewed gum. 'Become an alcoholic, harbour resentment about the war, New Military Solutions Inc, the way the MIA fucked up. The flashbacks will be tough. I'm gonna get me a gun. You'll see me in the news, up a belltower, picking off mechanics, plumbers, schoolteachers . . . ' She swung and shot a single round. Recoil kicked back as her target's head exploded.

Every time she aimed I aimed too, but before I could squeeze off a round she had already downed her man, high-fived and popped a stick of gum. She just laughed at me, pulled some ammo from her boot and slid it into a magazine. 'You better stay with me, Popsicle, unless you wanna get yourself sub-zeroed.'

We trod hot sand to the crater, crunching glassy flakes underfoot as the sun set purple. My iGeiger screamed offscale: keep moving or suit up. Before us lay the village, not even a street, just a central piazza surrounded by three straw-and-mud domes and a few square halls, a corral for goats and horses, a mud-walled field sewn with rows of struggling lentils, and a well with a few plantain and papaya. Two abandoned vehicles rusted in the sun next to mud structures the same colour as the dirt on which they stood. White and Blue squads approached from other sides.

Shots echoed.

Oily sweat trickled down my face.

We crept toward the domes.

Zipless shot out a section of mud wall. A body collapsed through it. Sly started up again.

'When I get home, I'm gonna hunt down everyone in this unit, but I'm saving MilIntel for last.'

'Fuck off, Sly.'

'I'm gonna find the names of each agent, and . . . '
She spun and shot dead an ugly behind the bananas. I
drew a breath and continued. Distant gunfire and another
went down. Sly followed a dome wall to an archway and
slipped inside. I followed into the dim coolness, past
carpets and bedding, drapes for partitions. Sly ripped
curtains down. Light flooded into the bare, utilitarian
room—no furniture, no books or toys. Shelves held tools
and equipment, bolts and pipes, artless and pragmatic.

'Jackpot!' Sly called. She waved a clear glass bottle
and kicked the blanket off a whole crate of them.

'Water,' I exclaimed.

'Nope.' She stepped aside to reveal a metal distillery
of pipes, flasks and condenser tins. 'Party time!'

Zipless slapped her shoulder and grabbed a bottle.
Behind lay a small doll, a carved stone statuette of
a fecund female with grossly exaggerated breasts,
stomach and thighs but no face—a purely functional
representation of the reproductive female—a fertility
totem, reducing womanhood into a featureless sexual
caricature. The lack of identity repulsed me.

I reached for it.

Sly knocked my hand. 'Don't touch!'

Amanda declared the village clear. The Grrrls cheered
and walked free, helmets off and camo loosened, the
same cloned body walking, same smiling face talking—
oestrogen markers expressed a symmetry of perfection.

But they *did* look different, it wasn't just me getting
used to it. Ponytail or buzzcut, bleach or colour, sneer
or smile, swagger or swish; they were like a group of
people. Some had traces of makeup. There were thirteen:

three squads of three grunts and a corporal each, and one lieutenant, though at the wine-and-dine there had also been a medic. They all met up in the square. Grrrls from different squads called out to each other and came together with cheers and high-fives, hugs and kisses, chatter about the fight, slaps and a bit of rough and tumble, then holding hands and more kisses, extended kisses, and passionate tongues and lust and I was staring and it hit me like a slap: butches and femmes. And some I couldn't tell.

I looked away. I looked back.

They were *really* going for it.

I was staring. More of them paired up, like an avalanche.

I blushed, then felt more embarrassed for blushing.

My cheeks burned.

I looked away.

At Sly.

She laughed right at me. She bit the cork from a bottle of spirits and spat it at my feet, took a swig then wagged her tongue at two brawny buzzcut soldiers.

Laughing, they did the same, then came over for some big macho backslaps.

Sly swung her gun at my head and shot.

Hot lead sprayed as I ducked. Cordite peppered my face as bullets cut through the chest of the body leaping toward me. Sly stepped aside as the corpse fell between us. I stood, panting and deafened, adrenalin only now surging through my arms, prickling out into my fingertips.

'Bu . . . Ga . . . '

'Relax, Popsicle! You didn't think I'd kill you, did

you?' Sly reloaded.

I looked down at the ripped corpse: civilian apparel, loose-fitting sandy coloured jodhpurs and a bloodied tunic. A facecloth hid all but glassy eyes. I reached for it.

'Fucker!' Sly emptied into the ugly's face.

I staggered back as gore and bone fragments sprayed up amid the strobing muzzle-flare. I covered my face and averted my eyes until my shock subsided. I had to pull it together and couldn't let any of them see me crack. I disguised my involuntary sigh by bending down to the corpse. My blood-speckled hands shook so I grabbed the man's head to steady them. Fractured pieces moved in unexpected ways. Unwinding his bloodied turban revealed an unrecognisable mush.

'Ugh!' Sly grimaced. 'I can't look!'

'Let's get out of here before we get too dosed,' I said to Amanda, wiping off the gore and then unpacking my fallout suit.

'Okay, ladies, loot and leave,' Amanda said. 'Watch for traps: blades and grenades, triggers and tripwires.'

Sly, Easy and Switch strode to the square halls. I stood quivering in the heat, flies buzzing and goats bleating as Grrrls looted. They slaughtered the goats and horses, torched the rows of lentils, skinned the carcasses and tipped the flyblown goat entrails down the well, butchered the meat then salted and packed it while others retrieved bushels of grain and dried fruit from the domes. It turned out the halls were mud covered shipping containers filled with captured supplies: food, medical equipment and new uniforms.

'Hey, at least we know they'll fit!' said Emily.

'Yeah, one size fits all!' Zipless laughed.

'Almost.' Sly nodded at my scrawny body.

As I picked some desert camo, a Grrrl approached Amanda.

'Basement Venus?' Amanda asked.

'Nothing,' the Grrrl muttered. 'No Andros.'

Amanda nodded then scowled at me. 'Help drag the bodies.'

We collected the scattered corpses and lined them up on the ground. Ten headshots, all men, no women or children so this wasn't a village, but they didn't dress like soldiers; they weren't armed and they grew crops. Their faces looked like anyone from home.

'Collateral damage,' Amanda called it.

But they looked like civilians.

'No such thing in this war,' she said as Switch doused them in alcohol, then walked back from the domes pouring a trail.

'Is this village named?' I asked, checking my zoo map.

'Not any more.' Emily lit a match.

'You're military intelligence,' said Sly. 'You work it out.'

I gritted my teeth as the village went up in flames.

Space Grrrls 2getha4eva

That night we dossed in a sheltered mountain alcove where my shrieking iGeiger dropped its banshee wail to a shrewish nag. We dipped bread in dhal and ate two spit-roast goats. I stared as each Grrrl ate enough for five.

It had been a tough day, too many things gone awry too soon, and though they called me a tough bitch behind my back in the office, these Grrrls were harder than nails and I felt so alone. I sipped firewater and talked too much. Sitting so long, I didn't realise I was giddy until too late, but once we got talking I found there were some Grrrls I liked.

We sat around the fire passing a bottle of rocket fuel, taking swigs. Emily sat in her partner Jude's arm, took a swig and gasped, then said, 'It's funny, you know, but I really miss my kids. Grade seven were sweeties. I remember getting in an argument with the principal when she was trying to push unproven teaching methods and I totally backed down and sold myself out. I compromised proven methods for some government approved imprinting system they were rolling out.'

'That doesn't sound like you!' said Jude.

'Yes, I don't know why I did it,' said Emily.

'Well, you can learn from your mistakes,' I said in her defence.

She passed the bottle. Jude took a swig. 'I worked in an advertising agency, made fifteen times what the receptionist did, owned a mansion with five bathrooms and three cars, wallscreen TVs in every room.'

Everyone shook their head and jeered, some threw things.

'Stop! She's a success,' I said, trying to intercept missiles, but Jude booed with both thumbs down, shaking her head. She passed the bottle on to Soph.

Soph took a swig. 'I had a lover, he wanted me to look like some model in this magazine he had. We argued and he left, so I got a makeover and drove all around town looking for him. When I found him, he said I still wasn't pretty enough. I cried for weeks.'

Everyone laughed.

'Why are you all laughing? It sounds terrible.'

Soph burst out laughing too. 'I'd shoot him now!'

I didn't get it. Were they taking the piss? She passed the bottle to Sly.

'No, we've all heard your shit,' I cut in, 'Say something real or pass it on.'

Sly sneered.

'Real, real, real!' I chanted.

'Something real, eh?'

'Real, real, real!' everyone joined in.

Sly laughed, closed her eyes and took a long swig. 'Ugh! I remember . . . I remember getting married.'

Whoa! Everyone cheered. Sly nodded, embarrassed.

'To a guy,' she yelled over the top of us. Some balked, gargled or laughed, but everyone soon fell speechless.

'It's true, it's true.' She shook her head. 'It was the full deal, too, bridesmaids and the white dress and a stone church.'

'What? Gimme that!' Amanda snatched the bottle and took a swig. 'I got nothing to say about being a plumber. It's boring.' She passed the bottle to me. 'How about you, Softie? How long have you been pushin' lead for tha man?'

'Ha! The only lead Popsicle pushes is grey lead.' Sly laughed.

I took my swig. 'I studied law at New Shoalhaven, then worked in government making immigration policy, then went private, contracting to NOW, and when this position came up, I took it.'

'I told you she was a lawyer!' Sly and Easy high-fived.

I thrust the bottle back at Sly, 'Okay smartarse, tell me more about paradise.'

'You wanna know about paradise? I'll tell you.' Sly grabbed the bottle and shotgunned the last. 'He was a nice guy, had a good job, treated me well, and we had a great time, I just don't get it!'

'What don't you get?' I asked.

'The fact that they gave *me* memories like that!'

The Grrrls all laughed.

Amanda turned to me. 'We know who *we* are. We're cookie cutter soldier clones, baked for this war, and we know these memories are fake. What we don't know is who *you* are—the people we work for, who we've never met.' All eyes stared at me, that world's only representative here.

'The memory implants have backfired,' continued Amanda. 'We know they're fake, but we know they're also real, from real people living on Homeworld, *your homeworld*, and we've used them to construct a snapshot of the society that birthed and orphaned us.'

'There's no equality,' said Zipless.

'Women don't have rights,' said Emily.

'Us Grrrls can't even vote!' said Sly.

'This world we've never been to, full of people we don't like and have never met, is not a world we would choose to live in,' said Zipless.

'A place that clones disposable soldiers, lies to them, and abandons them,' said Emily.

'Gives them a four-year lifespan.' Sly glared at me. 'We've all been murdered by a boardroom decision and some labtech yes-men.'

'It's hard to win a war when your own side is trying

to kill you.' Emily sighed.

They passed a new bottle around.

'So, Softie, who is the real enemy here?' Sly took a swig.

I sobered.

No-one spoke, and the question hung unanswered in the air.

Sly sneered at me. 'There's your paradise.'

Amanda lugged a box into the circle. 'I found us a little surprise.' She opened it to reveal goat-branding equipment. 'Some full-colour holotags!'

The Grrrls played with tattoo projectors while I sat on my rock. The air around us soon filled with designs. I idled with my zoo as avatars shimmered into being, origami tigers unfolded, holographic hyenas howled through the air, chased along limbs and into skin. Tangles of ivy laced across backs with the tiniest wisp of smoke, swirls and whorls flecked loin and leg. Red squad, White squad and Blue encircled crossed machineguns, and lover's names graced shoulders with Cupid's bow. Sly had Amanda inscribe *Space Grrrls 2getha4eva* across her bicep, and the whole cadre thought it was so good they all got it done. The Grrrls slapped backs and laughed and passed intimate smiles as I fidgeted.

'Space Grrrls 2getha4eva!' They high-fived.

'We're forever.' Sly grinned as Amanda burned the pattern into her skin. 'When all else is gone, and your Nexus of Worlds with its slave economy, despotic government and failing ecology turns to dust, we'll still be here!'

Tough words for some drunk with a four-year lifespan.

After a while the Grrrls quietened, paired off and made out. Sly sat drinking spirits, watching them pair up until none were left, then she glowered at me.

'We're forever,' Sly slurred. I didn't argue.

'Are you *all* . . . '

'Yep.' She grinned. 'But not originally. We were engineered to be an extremely tight-knit group. I guess the boffins never thought we'd live long enough to worry about what the natural developments would be.'

'But there's thirteen of you . . . so someone misses out?'

The grin turned sour. 'Well, I guess that just leaves you and me, Popsicle. I've had better, but I guess your scrawny sausage skin is the only meat around, so you be the bitch and I'll go top. I remember how you looked at me at the wine-and-dine, back on Homeworld.'

I frowned. How could she remember that? Surely these clones weren't the showroom models. 'Look, you're not really my kinda thing. Don't take it personally, but you're a fucking pig. Actually, if you were a guy, you'd be the type of guy to drive a girl to lesbianism.'

She rolled her eyes and shook her head. 'Well, you let me know when you get there, because that's where I'm waiting for you.'

Sly took a swig, then stared at Emily and Jude making out as though on fire. Fresh blood seeped from new tattoos on grappling arms; arrowed hearts of love, the scrollwork declared 2getha4eva. Sly looked at me. 'They're always like this. It's real love.' Sly drained the bottle. 'And it's *forever*. You have no idea.'

'You're a dumbfuck drunk.'

Sly smashed her empty against a boulder and I

squinted against the rain of shrapnel that peppered my face. She got another as I brushed shards away.

'I bet you just can't wait to get off this dustbowl and get back home to wossname, eh?'

She wasn't wrong.

'How long have you and your boyfriend been together?'

'Eleven months.'

She laughed mirthlessly. 'Well I'll tell you something. Your boyfriend don't exist. We don't know where we are, and we're not even sure *when* this is. Maybe some time-dilation thing happened with the FTL, who knows? MIA fucked up and everyone is dead, but one thing we *do* know is no-one is coming to rescue us. If it was gonna happen, they would have done it by now. It's just us now, and just survival. Forget your real, real, real job. Forget your boyfriend—you'll never see him again. Welcome to your new home.'

'How do you know no-one is coming? It's only been ninety-seven days!'

'It's been a bit more than ninety-seven days, Popsicle.'

'Sly!' Amanda yelled.

Sly glared back at her. 'Well, the change is coming. I can feel it. Who is gonna betray us this time? It's normally you.' She pointed at Jane. The Grrrls looked up long enough to roll their eyes at each other. Sly surveyed the writhing mass of Grrrlflesh, then stormed past, bumping me so hard I almost fell.

'The reason you don't have a partner is because you're a bitch!' I called.

Sly swivelled. 'Oh, is *that* the reason?' She held

her bottle by the neck. The Grrrls ceased motion. I felt Amanda's presence close behind me.

Sly scoffed then skulked away.

I turned around. 'What's she talking about?'

Amanda shook her head. 'Don't worry about her, she's drunk.'

Sly carried her bottle to some cave and probably cried herself to sleep. Or maybe she toughed it out as some badass loner, I dunno. She had no life, only this. The Grrrls didn't need me here. I grabbed my bag and hiked further up the mountain for some fresh air.

I searched the cloudless night sky as I climbed higher. A pulse of garbled radio curd blurted from my zoo, verbal chatter distorted beyond recognition. I wasn't sure what I heard, but grabbed my zoo and scanned for sig. A distant hissy fizz answered. My heart pounded.

Someone was out there.

I ran the output through the range of distortion filters and decoders, heard words but couldn't quite get the meaning. A Very Low Orbital cruised overhead, red and white lights winking silently. Navsat VLOs had HiRes comms that could cut through oceans of exotic interference. I pinged for mission downloads, aiming the zoo's infrared laser cone at the VLO as it passed, but nothing snagged. No data, not even an acknowledgement, just fried eggs until gone.

Where in spacetime was I? Today I had seen Girandolus, the large red sun, verifying that we were in the correct star system, and as I hiked to an abutment two moons rose above the horizon: first Pergusa, big, close and full, slightly pink, followed by its tiny bluish Lagrange companion moonlet, Enna. They lit up the valley like false dawn. A unique Palawanian pair, I *knew* we had landed on the right planet, but too many things were wrong. My cryopod was meant to planetfall in T sector's temperate forest, but I was somewhere in Palawan's desert latitudes, the Grrrls said J sector.

I activated the zoo's surveying tool and took readings of the nearby mountaintops, then contour mapped the whole valley via 3D laser rebound—dangerous but necessary. My zoo kept malfunctioning, but after constructing a virtual model I searched every desert map of Palawan for the nearest fit, the closest being an almost east/west valley about twenty per cent shallower, ten per cent longer and ten per cent wider, with a fifteen degree curve north at the east end. Could MIA get cartography this wrong?

I used the theodolite to take star readings. These weren't desert latitudes at all, but temperate, which according to premission data comprised a forested belt around the planet. Could the overuse of nukes have caused a localised deforestation event in this region? I had no idea about my longitude, but accessed likely temperate zone maps and found a perfect fit in S sector— if I ignored all topographic data except contour lines. There was meant to be a mighty river leading through valley forest and lush farmland to the ocean port city of Ghenghala, but I saw no ocean: nothing but desert to the horizon, even with the zoom at this altitude. It seemed that MilIntel got the ecological profile wrong, as well as planetfall coordinates, and much more.

And the Space Grrrls were wrong, too.

Or they lied.

I tuned in to channel forty-three and spent the night listening for my boys.

Chasing the deuce

I woke and looked around. A faint hiss issued from my zoo. A pulse on forty-three. I grabbed it, fumbled with the tuning. Emily sat up, watched me scrabble about.

'Did you hear that?' My breath fogged in the chill desert dawn.

Emily yawned, shook her head.

' . . . we are under attack . . . ' The signal deep-fried.

'Fuck!' I bashed it on a rock.

' . . . I repeat, taking heavy fire . . . ' fizz ' . . . the Palawanian Partisan Army . . . ' the sig drowned again.

'At least yours works.' Emily said.

'It's EMP hardened,' I said.

'Just like us.' She nodded.

I stacked the filters and played the fine-tuning, ' . . . regroup at the Mount Tethys Command Beachhead, behind the shield for . . . ' The signal dissolved into slush and flowed away.

I accessed my map and searched for Mount Tethys. 'There's no Mount Tethys or anything remotely spelled like it.' I pressed buttons.

'Mount Tethys is that way.' Emily pointed east. 'Couple o' days.'

I poked Amanda. 'Show me your map.'

Amanda rubbed her eyes and sat up, retrieved her crumbling paper map from its cylinder. I unrolled it and searched for a legend or any recognisable cartographic features but found nothing, not even sector headings, only a list of semaphore signals in the margin. The Grrrls fixed breakfast.

'Where is Mount Tethys?'

Amanda stretched and yawned. She pointed at a confusion of crossed out and redrawn scrawls beyond two mountain ranges depicted as rows of triangles with no notation of elevation or contour. 'Why?'

'A message just came over the radio. Soldiers using my boys' frequency are regrouping at the Command Beachhead there.'

Amanda eyed me dubiously, but Emily gave the nod.

'No way. They're all dead!' Sly scoffed.

I accessed the Day One podfall schemata and found the geographic equivalent to Mount Tethys—an automated high security Command outpost had come down in a wilderness area. 'This Command Beachhead includes supply pods, medlabs, and a relay centre with HiRes functionality where I can uplink to navsat VLOs and communicate with the Central Command Orbital.'

Amanda was motionless for a while. 'Your boys?' she asked.

'Could be.' I nodded. 'It's behind a shield. Safer than this.'

'It would be tough. We're back here in this valley.' Her finger ran across the scrawls. 'Four days march. There's more enemy than ever. We'd have to keep close, march along these ridges, cross the valley here . . . '

I followed her finger. 'What's that?' I pointed at a scribbled out mess where the port city Ghenghala would be, if this *was* S sector.

Amanda tried to decipher the scrawl. 'Er, an old emplacement that was neutralised early on. And we're cut off by this village. We'd have to nuke our way through.'

'How do you have this data?'

She looked up. 'We've been marching around this desert for a hundred days, trying to get to a comms facility and make contact with navsat. We've done considerable reconnaissance, and swapped info with other squads.' Flakes crumbled away as she rolled up the map.

'Well, now we *will* make contact. We'll move out after breakfast!'

'You heard the lady!' Amanda spoke up. 'High fives!' No-one budged.

We finished breakfast and marched from our alcove into the heat of the day, along the ridges, Blue squad working point, White following and Red leading from the rear, five hundred metres between each. My skin itched. I sweated out the water I drank, and my anemia kept me breathless. The strength I'd gained meant nothing. My muscles ached and I knew the Grrrls marched slow to accommodate me. I scanned all eighty-three channels for signal.

'Listening for your ghosts, Popsicle?' Sly smirked.

We marched all morning. Semaphore relayed an uneventful watch along the chain until White squad spotted uglies on horseback three clicks down in the valley. We let them ride without engagement. As the afternoon heat wore on, the forward spotters IDed a cadre of dead soldiers—all ours, desert camo and well equipped. I knew it would be one of the groups going to the rendezvous. Amanda had us wait until they checked the site for traps and ambushes. When the all-clear was finally given the Grrrls surged forward to investigate. Sly barred my way, insisting I keep walking the ridge because I was so slow and held up the team.

'What happens if it's my boys?'

'It ain't yer boys. They came down in forest,

remember?'

'Just like I was meant to.' I pushed past.

Sly reached a brawny arm around my neck and pulled me back, bulging muscles closing over my throat as I gulped air, her arm three times thicker than mine. Immense heat radiated from her body, carrying with it the scent of her cologne, not a man's, but nothing girly. It found me amid the dust and oiled gunmetal; musky but feminine.

She laughed quietly in my ear, then let me go.

I dodged away from her, then got back to marching.

After an hour, the Grrrls caught us up, the bloodbath plain on each face.

'Was it my boys?' I asked. 'Were there any survivors?'

They distributed booty in silence: compatible bullets and equipment.

'Do you think they were heading for the Command Beachhead?' No-one talked as they loaded bullets into magazines and scanned the horizon.

'Did they have an MIA?'

'It wasn't your boys,' said Amanda, and resumed walking.

That night as we ate goat, yoghurt and bread, my zoo hissed and spat. A faraway nuke bloomed in the dark, lit up a distant valley like sunrise.

'Blast visors down, Grrrls!' said Amanda and they all laughed.

'Whose is that?' I asked.

'One of ours.'

The glowing mushroom curled back into the blackness, leaving images of Grrrls opening a bottle, their cheering faces, except the one glowering straight at me. I went to sleep, zoo fixed on channel forty-three—wondering about the other units out there, normal soldiers, other agents, people—and woke the next day with Sly still staring at me.

That day we passed the closest point to the Ghenghala mapscrawl. The mountains flattened and we descended into another treeless, sandy plain. Dunes reached high and rather than walk a straight line over the exposed tops we followed the valleys around each, amid rock and rubble, remnant concrete slabs and exposed brick walls worn smooth by sand. I feigned tiredness and lagged to conserve energy, occasionally jogging to catch up with Emily, but letting the distance between us lengthen. Between dunes I caught snapshots of our surrounds: distant orange mountains, ruins, and elusive glimpses of a copse of trees to the north. Trees!

'Let's have a break!' I called.

'Okay.' Emily stopped and unpacked bread and water.

Sly scanned the surrounds.

'I'm gonna take a toilet break,' I called, and walked behind a dune.

Then ran.

I ran, I tripped and stumbled. I stayed low between dunes. Adrenalin flowed but my muscles slowed as I waded through the shimmering turgid mirage. I ran but the trees fled before me, outpaced me. Lost, I scaled a dune but tumbled down the far side, fell through a roof into a maze of walls, windows and doors, staggered breathless through ruined houses filling with sand, then out onto a saltpan, before me the forest of huge pine trunks, not trees but petrified ghosts. A great forest of twisted trunks reaching into the sky, dead branches angling down, corroded struts and spars not stone but metal; trees of iron.

Hot wind blew through these colossal ribcages, these vast fossils beached in a desert graveyard, skeletons of oceangoing vessels sunken in sand, no water for a hundred miles.

I threw up, then caught my breath, hands on knees.

'Those exotic gigabangers sure pack a punch.' Sly stepped from behind a mighty iron sequoia. 'Vaporise the steel cladding off a ship and just leave the framework.' She gazed up at the leaning arches of iron, running her fingers along rusty spars as she walked towards me.

I retreated, pulled my pistol.

She laughed and held her hands up in mock surrender, still walking forward. 'What you gonna do? Pop me with your pop gun, Popsicle?'

'You told me this was J sector, but this is S sector.' I retreated, aiming at her approaching bulk.

'Whatever. You're MilIntel. You tell me where we are. I don't care.'

She backed me up against a steel sequoia, the rust fissures so deep as to resemble bark. 'You told me this was a desert sector just to shut me up, but this is the ruins of a seaport. MIA weren't wrong! There *was* water here!' I held the gun an inch from her face but she inched closer still and I had to angle the pistol just to keep it aimed at her head. She kept pressing in, touching me now, squeezing me between her body and the rusty ship spar, until it was just my face, her face, and the gun.

'Are you gonna kill me?' I felt her breath upon my

face. ''Cause this is your only chance.' She stared into my eyes.

'Where'd the ocean go?' I gulped.

'Who cares?' she whispered.

'Why did you lie to me?' Her musky cologne filled my nose.

She reached forward, touched the tip of my pistol barrel with her forefinger. 'You can't do it.' She slowly pushed it to the side. I turned away. She grabbed my face with a hand and pulled it back. I took a breath and glowered into her ice-blue eyes, her tanned skin smooth, a sprinkling of freckles across her perfectly genegineered nose. She squeezed closer still, her face almost on mine. The smirk told how much she enjoyed this.

Emily crossed the saltpan and came to a halt next to us.

'Do you two need some space to sort this out?'

'Where did the trees go? How much time has passed?' I asked her, holstering my gun. 'There aren't even stumps!'

'Come on, Popsicle, let's go.' Sly turned to walk away.

I didn't budge.

Emily drew a breath. 'It's been longer than ninety-seven days.'

I felt sick. 'How long?'

Sly and Emily exchanged a glance.

'This isn't nuke damage,' I said. 'It's rust, lots of it! How long has it been?'

'A couple of years,' Emily admitted.

'How many?'

'Three,' said Sly as Emily said, 'Four.' They winced

at each other.

No wonder my body felt so bad, hibernating that long. No wonder nothing worked and everyone was undersupplied.

'Why did you lie to me?'

'We didn't want you to know you'd been woken by a squad who are all about to die,' said Emily. 'We're not getting rescued. You'll be here all alone.'

'No. We'll get to Tethys Command,' I said. 'Rendezvous with the others, contact navsat, bring a lander down.'

'What good would that do *us*?' asked Sly.

'They've got medlabs and regen tanks.'

Emily and Sly stared at each other.

'We have to hurry,' said Emily, but I caught the desperation in her eye; she didn't mean me. These Grrrls approached their end days.

They walked away.

I followed.

Suffrage

Toward evening we crossed a valley and entered another range, following ridges. The next valley over was just as arid; scraggy bushes lined dry ravines with not a tree in sight. I continued laser rebound modelling to confirm our location. All measured contours aligned perfectly with my S sector map, its legend showing vegetation, water, and infrastructure no longer present. The 'localised deforestation event' seemed like a much more widespread desertification event: gigatonnes of biomass. Where did it go? The Day One strike must have been far harsher than the briefings allowed.

Morale picked up and the Grrrls chatted. They all talked and joked about their 'memories' and how stupid the person in their memory was, and escalated that into a larger denigration of society—*my* society—but as we marched, and they reconstructed a profile of society and scorned their various doctors, lawyers, teachers, politicians, scientists, and tradespeople, I reconstructed a profile of who *they* were—not as individuals hating their fake memories, but as a fledgling society using them, using the skills to create a better one. Somehow these were the people who would populate the planet with children, build infrastructure and teach them how to continue. It didn't matter if they knew they were clones or not. The Grrrls had been given all the professions that when brought together are enough to construct a society, to reconstruct *our* society.

We marched all day to the bluffs at the end of the range and gazed from our cliff-top vantage ahead into a valley of patchy farmland, scattered villages and citadels, pencilled into Amanda's crumbly chart but absent from my zoo. Thick smoke rose from a distant village.

'Our colleagues hard at work.' Amanda smiled.

It was good to know we had allies still alive on the planet.

Emily assembled the rangefinder and described the village before us: a large fortified stronghold of a hundred armed troops, walls and trenches, two artillery emplacements, eight horses, two vehicles and three motorbikes. A central lighthouse linked them into a heliographic communication network. The Grrrls focused with rapt attention as Emily meticulously detailed enemy armaments.

'How do you want to play this?' Amanda asked, and all focused on me.

I scanned the village, tagging all military units to be destroyed with the auto ID and flagging buildings of interest for structural assessment. I imported all measurements into the Blast Zone Calculator, selected building demolition, maximal shockwave, antipersonnel functionality to five hundred metres, and then checked the output table for the measure of fizz in grams, coordinates of epicentre placement, and blast zone radius. I exported the data into the Munition Armament Authorisation Application.

'We'll need some canned heat,' I said.

'*Yeah!*' they called.

'Exactly what I would have said!' Sly nodded, patting my back.

'Sixty-eight grams of Orthopositronium,' I said, and Zipless whistled. They quietened. 'A type II blast centred twenty metres above the central military depot will take out the whole town and surrounds, and all personnel, just to be sure. The blast radius will reach the foot of this cliff, but we will set up as close as we can at the cliff base, pop the nuke, then advance in three squads across a kilometre front, and regroup in the village to continue onward.'

The Grrrls all high-fived.

From our vantage Amanda scanned down the cliff for placement of the squads and mortar crew as I strapped on my plate. We worked our way down the mountain to starting positions. Red squad regrouped at the foot of the cliff in an alcove blocked from all sides except above— the perfect mortar nest. Zipless assembled the mortar while Soph gloved semaphore.

Emily took rangefinder readings and Zipless turned dials.

I typed the new access code and sprayed the isotope hut with IR.

'Permission denied,' said the iso hut. The Grrrls swapped glances.

'Why?' I asked.

'You have used your allocated quota of nukes.'

'But I've only used one of my three!' I was sick of faulty equipment.

'Incorrect.'

'I need another nuke.'

'Supernumerary nukes can only be issued by council voted motion,' it said. The quota system was designed to limit overuse of nukes and reduce fallout pollution. The Grrrls stared in slack-jawed disbelief.

'I'm convening an ad hoc session of the Palawanian war council.'

'Council is in session,' it said.

'I propose the motion that I be issued a supernumerary nuke.'

'Motion proposed . . . '

'All in favour say Aye. *Aye!* The motion is carried.'

'Motion not carried. The requisite quorum of three council members is not present.'

A chorus of ayes went up among the Grrrls.

'There's your quorum!' I said.

'These soldiers do not have the vote. Their suffrage is unrecognised.'

The Grrrls all muttered dissent.

'No eligible voters are detected within comms range,'

said the zoo.

'I deputise these Grrrls.'

'Soldiers cannot be deputised,' the machine said.

I groaned. We'd hit the wall.

'Invoke a state of emergency!' hissed Amanda.

'Under the Crisis Act I use my authority as an MIA to invoke a state of emergency.'

'We are now in a state of emergency, alerts have been sent,' it said.

'Given the state of emergency I nominate the following Grrrls as deputy agents with full voting rights: Amanda Miller, Jenny *Zipless* Jones, Sophia Brown, and Emily Davison . . . '

'Better deputise us all,' said Amanda, 'just in case there's a casualty and we need another nuke in a hurry.'

Because motions and voting could only be proposed through the zoo, and the zoo only worked through me, I nodded and said, ' . . . and Sally *Sly* Jenkins.'

'The aforementioned soldiers are deputised for two days.'

'Grrrls, we just got the vote!' Zipless laughed.

'Now we're *real* members of society,' said Emily.

'We should vote one of us president of this planet!' said Sly.

I secured access to another nuke, punched the code and aimed the zoo at the iso hut.

'We better hurry because—' Zipless's head exploded. Bullets sprayed around us. Strafed from above, we had no cover. Grrrls dived and fell as red spatter filled the air. Boots scrabbled on gravel as Grrrls clambered out of the alcove to safety. I dived into a crevice and lay pinned as a spray of machinegun fire shattered rock inches away from my foot then near my thigh. Amanda watched from the lee of an overhang as impacts sought my flesh, traced a rock outline past my body then away along the crevice.

I blinked dust from my eyes then glanced about. Sly, Soph and Em were still alive, crouched behind cover. Amanda mimed using my zoo. I shot a glance back to the alcove by the mortar. She nodded and gave hand signals to the Grrrls. Sly and Soph crawled in opposite directions, sneaking glances up at the cliff and ducking when the sniper opened fire. Soph spotted him, passed signals, and when sufficiently separated the Grrrls all opened fire while Emily clambered back into the alcove.

Bullets rained around Emily's feet. She leaped over Zipless's corpse as the Grrrls strafed the sniper. She dived onto my zoo, rolled and threw it to me, and came to a sitting halt before the iso hut.

'Horses!' I pointed at three soldiers charging toward us on horseback, caught the zoo, and sprayed the IR activation code. Permission must have been granted, because Emily popped the hut, snatched the shell as its red light greened, and shoved it into the mortar just as the horsemen opened fire. A burst of armour piercing blew her chest in half.

'Men!' Sly screamed, scaling the rock to get to Emily. She blasted the machinegun in her right while her left blew apart and the ragged stump sprayed blood all over me.

'Take cover!' yelled Amanda. 'Blast visors down!'

I ducked, grabbed the medikit and tagged Sly's calf with the autoSed. Nothing dulled her rage as the machinegun jackhammered ripples through her body.

Bullets swarmed past us. I pressed re-dose until her scowl slackened and eyeballs rolled back. She stopped yelling and went limp. I dragged her to the ground as the atomic flash lit up the cliff with a momentary horsemen silhouette, then vaporised anything with a hardness less than rock. Static blared from my zoo. The shockwave slapped through my sinuses and ripped blood from my nose. Then the blast hit.

I lay on my back. The luminous mushroom curled upward as I blinked the sky back to blue, then climbed to my feet. Exposed rock, now bleached chalky bone-white, turned to powder under my feet. The death wind reversed and began sucking air back into the blast zone, and my iGeiger wailed a dirge so I donned my crumpled nuke suit, then flipped the air switch to inflate the bubble helm.

Soph and Amanda blazed a trail into the blast zone. Distant gunshots rang out in the dust storm as the last few dying uglies were shown the door. Sly stared, vacantly blowing bubbles and fingering her stump on enough tranq to stun a horse. I worked quickly, staunched the bleeding and cleansed the wound, then looked for the arm, found some mangled red pulp in the sand—useless. The zoo's service mode allowed a suite of functionality arms to be fitted into the dorsal mechanical ports. I clipped the medikit's circular saw in, removed Zipless's left arm below the shoulder, then tidied Sly's wound, cleanly slicing away ragged strips of muscle and sawing off all splintered bone.

I incised a flat T-shaped tongue into the grafting edge on Sly's humerus and a corresponding groove into the scion from Zipless, airbrushed all cut bone with an autocatalytic keratinising monofilament polymer, and secured the graft with the bone staple. I interleaved graft and scion muscle fibres across the break, spraying all exposed tissue with pluripotent stem cell glue, activated the cells with a pulse of UV, then sprayed a thick layer of plastiderm to seal the wound. I plastered and slung her arm for immobility and administered IV growth enhancers. Of course it would take—they were genetically identical.

There was too much equipment to carry, and no villages left to nuke, so I left Zipless's iso hut and mortar, packed my kit, said goodbye to Zipless and Emily, then marched Sly into the scorched sand of the blast zone, all dribbling dopey and compliant; the nicest she'd ever been. Purpling darkness swept across the desert when the mushroom cloud blocked out the sun, and a hot nuclear wind blew tumbleweed wisps of fibreglass like fairy floss as we marched into this dark carnival's molten glassy smoothness.

The village was a smoking garden of rubble and tortured glass sculpture. I searched for the others in the maelstrom, dark even with the fires burning. A Grrrl crouched by a drift of debris: Jane. She opened a trapdoor, tossed a grenade down a hole, slammed it and ran into the darkness. I felt the blast through my feet.

I pushed Sly ahead into the howling dusty wind, kept my pistol drawn and found the trapdoor. Sly stood vacant sentry while I opened the trapdoor and descended into the smoky basement. Halfway down the stairs, even in the dim light of my zoo, I saw scattered twisted bodies, Palawanians bloodied and torn, men and women and children, just normal looking civilians, could be anyone from home, all huddled in here for shelter. Among them the fattest woman I had ever seen, and next to her a dead Space Grrrl, but it was a trick of the light, because when I took a closer look it was just another dead man.

We caught up with the Grrrls in the hills outside the blast zone far side. Everyone knew why Em and Zip weren't with us. It broke my heart to see Jude's face fall. She traced the love heart tattoo on her shoulder: *Jude and Em together forever*. She clenched her teeth and stared ahead. Grrrls consoled Jude and Viv, hugged and slapped backs and squinted against the dust.

'We're forever,' mumbled Sly, coming out of sedation too quickly for me.

'Keep it moving!' Amanda hurried us onward, and everyone ascended the hill, except Jane, who hung back. Sly slowed me so I remained within earshot.

'Basement Venus?' Amanda asked.

'Neutralised,' Jane said.

'Andros?'

'Lots.'

'Scum.' Amanda shook her head, then glared at me, wondering what I'd heard.

Memento mori

We hiked into the red hills and bivouacked for the night. After a quiet dinner Soph revealed that she'd taken a bullet.

'Let me fix it.' I activated my zoo's mediscan, ran it across her stomach and located the bullet three inches below the entry point.

'It's just a scratch. Be gone in a few days,' she said.

I cleaned the wound: it had already begun healing.

The Grrrls's cell growth was so vigorous they were one step away from being legally classified as omniomatic.

'I've got plenty of others,' Soph bragged. I scanned her abdomen, identifying organs and locating an assortment of other lead souvenirs. 'Go lower,' she said, 'lower . . . there's the hollow point!'

Nestled within her liver sat what looked like a rosebud with ragged leaden petals blooming open. Grrrls crowded around.

'That one almost took me out!'

It was an impressive keepsake, but more impressive was the tissue bed I found as I scanned deeper: she had no uterus, no internal reproductive organs whatsoever, because all Space Grrrls were sterile, but her nascent genital ridge clearly sprouted numerous tumescent bulbs. I scanned over these tiny developing nodules until I realised the Grrrls had fallen silent.

'Oh fuck!' Sly hissed behind me.

'What?' asked Soph.

'I'm so sorry, Soph.' Sly stared, aghast. 'The beginning of the end.'

'But you Grrrls don't get cancer!' I said.

Sly addressed them all, 'Some of us will be further along.'

They stared at each other.

Then it occurred to me: these were developing gonads.

'It's the popswitch,' I said, remembering that section from the wine-and-dine. 'Populate or perish. In the event that settlers don't come, you Grrrls switch over from military to reproductive mode, build infrastructure and population, fill the planet.'

'What, become a plumber?' Amanda scoffed. 'Join the army, get a trade.'

'Or settle down and become a wife and mother?' asked Sly. 'No thanks.'

'Look, it's been four years, your cellular toxicity is critical and progeria has activated, you're all approaching total organ failure, but before death occurs you become reproductively mature. Your body is designed to go through reproductive changes; becoming pregnant causes an oxytocin surge, triggering a revitalising steroid release that overrides the death switch and you get to live!'

'As a breeder?'

'It's the start of a new life,' I said. 'You live for as long as you remain pregnant—could be a long, long time: decades, more.'

'It sounds like death to me,' said Sly.

'It wouldn't be so bad—at least you'd live . . . '

'We live now,' said Sly. 'We have to hurry.' She pumped a bullet into the breach of her gun. 'Space Grrrls 2getha4eva!'

A tired cheer went up from some of them.

'We'll make it to Tethys Command,' said Amanda.

'Yes, but you don't need the medlabs,' I said. 'You are the surrogate mothers of this new planet. Your nascent gonads carry the genomes of the eight races of Homeworld. You may not want this now, but when we get to Tethys Command and rendezvous with the soldiers regrouping there, I think your own innate natures will kick in and get the better of you, and you'll all end up living a long time *without* the medlabs. You'll see.'

I opened my zoo and logged on to the Space Grrrl user manual, checked reproduction. The popswitch was only activated in wars against non-humans or where there was no civilian population to breed with for post-war colonisation. The popswitch had been deactivated for Operation Wildfire.

Something wasn't right.

I switched my zoo to radio and spent the night dozing to a silent channel forty-three.

Sugar and spice

The next day Amanda woke us early. We ate, broke camp, and were on the move before sunrise. The sense of urgency prickled. No-one talked; the only noise was Jude's quiet sobbing as we marched along the high ground from cover to cover, when spotters semaphored that the way was clear. I tired and Sly stayed back with me.

Around noon Soph piped up.

'Lieutenant, friendlies spotted two clicks west, requesting rendezvous.'

'It's the survivors!' said Jude.

'All on high alert,' said Amanda. 'Fan out, stay covered and hold fire.'

Soph relayed semaphore and we waited.

'Two well-armed friendlies approaching, one click apart.' Soph used the rangefinder to narrate their progress and spot for uglies. I finally glimpsed the first soldier picking his way toward us, keeping as well-covered as possible during the approach. The Grrrls tracked his progress in their crosshairs. Was it one of my boys? I saw he was kitted out in desert camo, like any of our soldiers. Eleven guns tracked the soldier as he came within yelling distance. As he closed I saw his face, that same face—a Space Grrrl.

Emily.

'Oh baby!' Jude called out. She opened her arms and rushed forward. They embraced. 'Oh I missed you!' said Jude. She picked Emily up and spun her around.

'I been out there on my own for a long time. I missed you, too.'

'I got a tattoo for you!' Jude showed Em the tattoo on her arm, the love heart with their names, and Cupid's arrow.

'Back together again!' Emily kissed Jude. She turned to me and smiled. 'Hi, Softie.'

An image of her ripped body played through my mind. I turned to Sly.

She had been staring at me all this time.

My skin crawled.

'Okay, whathefuck is happening?' I asked quietly.

'2getha4eva,' she gloated.

Em came over and placed her hand on my shoulder. It was her. Exactly. Even the same perfume. 'It's good to see you again.'

'Here comes the other one,' Soph called.

We watched the next soldier approach. I wondered if it was another Zipless, to replace our fallen bombardier. I watched for Viv's reaction.

It was another Soph.

Exact. The two Sophs grinned at each other.

'Well lookie here,' said Easy. 'Now I got me two Grrrls!' she guffawed, with a laughing Soph on each arm.

Viv didn't really seem to mind. 'Enjoy it while you can.' She smiled.

The two Sophs chatted and I couldn't tell them apart, until I saw the scabs on the new Soph's knuckles, and her uniform was more worn.

We had lunch and got back under way, following a dry riverbed into the hills. The Grrrls ailed. A few couldn't keep up the pace and fell behind: the original Soph with the new lead souvenir; Sly, with an arm in plaster; and Switch, who had developed an itchy facial rash and scratched and moped about the change.

'How many cadres of Grrrls are there?' I asked Sly. Most of the soldiers in Operation Wildfire were real people trained in warfare technology, but NOW had purchased a few Space Grrrl licences for the nuclear gruntwork at the coalface.

'Dunno. Maybe one per sector to get out into the regions and mop up after the Day One gigabangers took out the cities. But with an option that the regen tanks can clone replacement cadres, in case any are lost.'

'And it's the same Grrrls each time?'

'Always.'

'Same personalities, same relationships?'

'Yep.'

'So why didn't you let me see those dead soldiers?'

'Because you march too slow and your civvy brain can't handle seeing dead soldiers.'

'Stop all your lies! It wasn't soldiers, it was the cadre that the other Emily and Soph belonged to.'

Sly shrugged and looked away. She flexed the fingers of her left hand, got some pliers from her pack and cut the plaster from her arm. She stretched her arm, nodded, then hoisted her machinegun. 'Thanks for the new arm, Popsicle.' She smiled and marched ahead.

That night, the new Soph seemed strange, and not her usual lively self. She watched Easy and the old Soph bed down, and was going to join them, but Viv, who was missing Zipless, called to her. 'Come on, aren't you ready yet?'

They lay together and went to sleep.

The next morning when I awoke the new Soph had become Zipless. Everything about her had changed. She'd cut her hair, stopped wearing eyeliner, removed her jewellery, and her clothes hung about her differently, but it was more than that. It was the way she walked, her smile, and the way she talked, the things she said. No-one else cared. I watched her and Viv eat breakfast just like they used to, as though Zipless had never been gone. The change was seamless and complete.

'Hey Zip, how you going?' said Grrrls.

'Good to have you back!' Their nonchalance grated.

'I missed you baby,' Viv whispered.

Zipless laid her hand on Viv's leg and smiled. 'Me too.'

'Okay.' I put down my spoon. 'Where did the new Soph go, and where did you come from?'

'Softie! It's me, Zipless.'

I opened the Space Grrrl user manual and read the section on morphing. Having two Sophs and no Zipless created a chemical dissonance in the pheromonal interference pattern governing leadership structure and clone phenotype, causing the weakest Soph to morph and fill the gap in the hierarchy.

'So you really changed from Soph into Zipless?'

She nodded. 'Yeah, memories, skills, personality, everything. We don't have brains, we have brain^2—

memory gel, an organic semi-biological information encoding substrate with 10^5 times the human memory capacity.'

'But how do you communicate from brain to brain?'

'It's not brain to brain, it's the same brain with different personality subsets activated.'

'So *you* don't have memories from *our* old Soph or Zipless?'

'No.' Zipless frowned. 'I'm not sure. How would I tell?'

They were all listening now. 'Am I in them?'

'No.'

'Then how the fuck did Emily from the other cadre remember me?'

They all looked at each other. No-one spoke. I searched their faces, found Emily and stared. She cleared her throat. 'The memory snapshot for all clones was taken after the briefing at the wine-and-dine. You sure knocked back a few.'

Sly laughed.

My radio hissed and spat. 'This is Corporal John Santor of the fifty-third . . . '

I held up a silencing hand.

' . . . taking heavy fire . . . ' I shushed them and played the reception.

' . . . the Palawanian Partisan Army . . . regroup at . . . ' I lost the signal.

I checked the map. The Command Beachhead was a few hours away.

'Okay, let's speed things up and get moving,' I said.

The Grrrls ate, though I noticed some only pretended, pushed food around the plate and grimaced, scratched at flaking skin. Kim moaned and complained, so I examined her, scanned her genital ridge. The change was imminent, and her whole body now sang a different song. Almost fertile, two sets of bipolar gonads and ambiguous sexual structures lay side by side, all developing but not yet sexually differentiated by gender: a puberty of sorts.

'You're becoming reproductively active,' I said.

'Fuck you, Softie,' she panted. 'It's your fucking popswitch. I'll have to mate soon, or die.' She stood and fidgeted, then wandered. 'I can remember all this.' She pointed along the dry riverbed. 'That way.'

Soph drew a deep breath. 'I can smell them.' She closed her eyes and looked at Kim, who also drew deep breaths, rolled her eyes and smiled.

'Smell who?' I asked.

'Men,' Kim whimpered.

Soph shushed her as Sly swaggered up in full uniform, gun levelled, grimacing all sweaty and mean. 'Jane's gone.'

'Whaddaya mean?'

She pointed. 'Pile o' clothes, no Jane inside 'em, gone. If I see her, I'll fucken kill him.'

I cast Sly a questioning glance. 'Where has she gone?'

Sly's glare burned from one to the next, commanding silence. 'Traitors will be shot!'

Soph groaned. 'Oh, I want to go!'

'Resist!' said Sly.

'I can't help it!'

The popswitch would do its job and save their lives, I just had to steer them to the right men. 'Don't worry, we will get to Tethys soon.'

'Who is that?' Amanda pointed at a Grrrl up on the hilltop, arms outstretched, waving, embracing the day with rapture.

'Kim!' yelled Scratch.

'Fuck!' Sly sighted her gun. 'I got her.'

'No!' Scratch knocked the gun down. 'I'll get her.' She raced up the hill.

Sly cursed. 'The weak ones broadcast the stench to the whole world. Soon this place will be swarming with men!'

'She can't help it!' said Soph, wiping the sweat from her brow.

'Fucking rise above your programming, you stupid bitches!' Sly spat.

'It's so hard!' said Soph.

Scratch walked Kim back down the hill.

'I'm sorry, Sly, I couldn't help it,' said Kim.

'Don't let them win! Resist the programming! *Choose* to be what you want!' Sly gritted her teeth and raised her gun. 'We're 2getha4eva!'

They did a feeble high five.

'I can't help it,' said Soph. 'Men are out there, back in the villages. I want to go to them.'

'Don't worry: if you do, I'll kill you.'

Soph looked relieved and nodded. 'I'll do you, too.'

'It's good to know, but you won't have to.' Sly addressed them all, 'Life in the villages is slavery and rape. You have to stay pregnant to live.'

'But how could it be rape if Grrrls are choosing it?' I asked.

'They're not choosing; they're being forced by programming. That is rape!' Sly spat. 'Remember

Grrrls, look closely.' She removed a doll from her bag and waved it in their faces—the fertility totem from the village. 'If you run to the villages, this is what you'll become. A sedentary, perpetually pregnant baby factory pack-raped until you're murdered.'

The Grrrls grimaced.

'Murdered by who?' I said.

Sly held the doll in my face. 'Would *you* live like this?'

'Jane's been killing them!' I said. 'Killing your own people!'

'Traitors are shot,' said Sly.

Rocks tumbled; we turned. Lil, the quietest, had run. She had picked her way over a crag then bolted across the flat back toward the villages. She was too far to chase.

Amanda pointed at a group of Palawanians cresting a distant ridge.

Sly raised her gun and sighted. No-one spoke.

She shot.

Lil fell.

We turned and started jogging.

Fear of a female planet

Amanda had Red squad following the dry riverbed, White along the hilltops to the north, and Blue following the ridges to the south. We marched upriver, quicker, faster, the urgency increasing as Grrrls occasionally broke into a run. Changes assailed the Grrrls as we hurried—itchy rashes bloomed, patches of coloured, flaky skin peeled off, but they all knew which way to go. Old bones littered the way underfoot: dry corpses held together by sinew and scraps of windblown cloth dotted the desolate orange landscape.

The zona lay ahead: a bubble of shimmering whitish gel one hundred metres in diameter, set among pink and orange rock. I heard a wet slap. Soph collapsed, her head a hole, the contents splashed across my camo. I stood there, spitting bone chips and wiping blood from my eyes as Sly knocked me to the ground among a hail of bullets. White and Blue quickly triangulated and shot an isolated sniper but we soon encountered groups in machinegun nests, with trenches, concrete and sandbags.

Amanda had Zipless shell the forward field with conventional HiEx, while White and Blue squads advanced along high ground to either side, launching grenades and picking off survivors. We fought our way forward and the Palawanian defence collapsed, leaving the approach to the dome clear, but as we advanced along the riverbed, Palawanian soldiers closed from the rear. White and Blue squads returned fire while Red squad fled to the dome. Bullets rained around us as we ran, the opaque zona shimmering with each impact. Emily went down amid a spray of blood, and Sly stopped to return fire. A Palawanian leapt up from a jumble of corpses and ran at Sly, but I intercepted, gun first. He stopped, my barrel in his face.

Then I stopped.

It was Jane.

As a man.

I stared at Jane's masculine features: squared chin, angular jaw, jutting brow and Adam's apple, male musculature: clear testosterone markers.

'Softie!' He stared back, pulled a gun.

I shot him dead.

Blood ran from a hole in his head.

A grenade exploded among Blue squad, ripped Scratch and Jude to pieces, and Easy went down firing. White squad routed as Red returned fire, but Sly ran out of ammo. She threw her machinegun, and we turned and ran to the gelid white dome. Sly got there first. She bashed the pellucid membrane; it gave like rubber but remained firm. I leapt over bodies, fresh, old, and ancient, spraying infrared forward, and the outline of a doorway appeared against the milky white barrier.

I gave my access code and sprayed the door with rays. It opened, we charged through and it closed.

Everyone panted. Drool dripped from mouths, blood from wounds. Grrrls hung their heads and caught their breath. They holstered guns, loosened armour, and scratched rashes.

There were only eight of us left, but we were safe.

The inside was quiet and still, cool, and we could see out into the desert perfectly, although the zona responded to bullet impacts with absorptive flashes and white ripples of refractivity, radiating outward like a pebble dropped in a pond. Each dulled splash yielded the dampened intonation of a monastery's meditation gong.

The cool damp air smelled of birth deep inside green leaves: of living nature, of humus, soil and pine. I breathed the humidity and stepped onto damp loam, not dry crunchy sand. The distant echoes of gunfire receded into harmlessness, and I took in the calmness, the green, the trees.

A forest.

Like in the sims.

What my sector was meant to be.

Just like the postcards.

Outside, a man approached the zona, stepping over the bodies of comrades.

'Let's go,' said Amanda. She turned and walked down a black soil path into a pristine wilderness. The others followed.

The Palawanian surveyed the zona wall. His gaze passed over me, and I felt a chill, as if he could see me through the opacity. It was Amanda, as a man. He walked back into the desert.

I hurried down the path into the forest. Command pods nestled within the ancient conifers and ferns, more than I had ever seen, more than the zoo said would be here. Bright and shiny, not dinted and dusty, with comms lights winking operative. I caught up with Sly.

'Some of the soldiers you're fighting are your own people, not the enemy.'

'They're the enemy.' Sly limped alongside me.

'No, I saw their faces . . . '

Everyone filed into a Command Pod. Sly opened her jacket, the lining thick with blood. 'Believe me, they're the enemy.'

Sly ushered me inside the pod. It looked like a starship bridge. Flatscreens lined the walls, and desks and consoles surrounded a central holotable. It was a central command outpost for coordinating the war—with everything deactivated. Totally inert.

I sat at a console.

Dread surged through me as I reached for the power switch and pressed.

Drives hummed to life and screens flashed on. We laughed and cheered as I logged in. A large holographic sphere appeared before me—a map of the planet with so much detail I couldn't take it all in. I centred the orange sphere on the Command Beachhead, and initiated the uplink protocol. An animated red beam connected from our position to a geostationary satellite, then spread out across a network of satellites in orbit around the planet. More detail appeared on the planet surface as the comms network spread: colour-coded villages, roads, strategic resources, and more orbitals than I knew were up there.

'Uplink successful,' I said as the network began collecting and aggregating planetwide data. Clusters of red spots appeared. Currently, there were an estimated one hundred thousand Palawanians remaining on the planet, in villages concentrated around the temperate zones. I accessed the troop data. Rather than clusters, a light haze of blue appeared; tiny dots dispersed around the globe.

'Grrrls, there's more troops than you think,' I said as the computer calculated the number. 'Twenty thousand NOW troops roaming the planet in small uncoordinated units!' I exclaimed. 'This war is about to change!'

The Grrrls cheered and high-fived, and for the first time I high-fived with them.

'I'll contact all units, then see if anyone is still alive in Orbital Command.' I accessed the troop comms data and sent out an introductory ping. The orbital beamed HiRes comms to all satellites and down to all sectors, reconnecting all these lost souls. Soon we would get orders out to everyone. My own zoo pinged over and over with incoming data, as a backlog of updates from the last four years came in.

'I wonder if your boys are out there?' said Amanda.

I nodded, switched to channel forty-three, sent out a ping, and listened for responses. The holographic located them: very close to the dome. My zoo hissed.

'This is Corporal John Santor of the fifty-third mobile, we are under attack and taking heavy fire, I repeat, taking heavy fire from the Palawanian Partisan Army . . . '

'Hello boys, hello John!' I cut in. 'We're already there . . . '

' . . . are going to regroup at the Mount Tethys Command Beachhead, behind the shield for . . . '

'Hello John! It's all gonna be okay!'

'This is Corporal John Santor of the fifty-third mobile, we are under attack and taking heavy fire, I repeat . . . '

I checked the refresh on my zoo, but it still hadn't imported the updates and time synched. Amanda sat at a console, typing codes. The glowing holographic planet rotated. She accessed a list of medlabs dotted around the planet, hundreds, and pinged each. 'See, it's too crowded now, most are in permanent use, we need new ones here, here and here: polar.' She marked her crumbly map with pencil.

Zipless nodded.

My data request came back. There were no direct return comms from anyone yet but that was okay, maybe they couldn't cut through the atmospheric exotics. I checked command manifestos; no-one from command was left, all the Brass were dead. I requested a troop list. No soldiers remained on the planet: they were all dead too. The twenty thousand current troops comprised fourteen hundred cadres of Space Grrrls. I accessed the 'enemy' data. No indigenes remained, either.

All the people on the planet were Space Grrrls and

their offspring.

The date appeared on my zoo: 2935.

Five hundred and twenty-three years after Day One.

The planet was a desert, an isotopic wasteland.

Swarming with war clones.

At war with themselves.

I managed to press the record button on my zoo.

'We'll get some new ammo pods dropped here and here . . . ' Amanda typed quickly, zoomed the 3D mouse over orbitals, checked manufacturing schedules, and sent out scouts, prospectors, mining and harvester drones to the ore bodies identified on Palawan's moons and the rings, and into space, to planets and belts. There were only meant to be a few harvesters, but she commanded *hundreds* bringing resources back to new robotic orbital manufactories and isotope purification plants where she ordered the production of new supplies and ten more medlabs with regen tanks for polar planetfall. She proposed the motion, Sly seconded, and the three voted.

Motion carried, said the console.

Amanda looked up at me. 'So how are your boys?'

'Dead,' I said.

The radio message repeated the cycle. Now that I was listening for it I heard the same crackles and pips, the same inflections in the recorded words.

I turned it off. 'I saw enemy faces: Jane and you, as males.'

'Who do you think we breed with when your popswitch activates?'

'I just found out it isn't Palawanians.'

Amanda turned to Sly. 'It's time. Softie graveyard.'

The Basement Venus

'Okay Popsicle!' Sly drew her pistol and aimed it at my head. 'Let's go.'

I stood. I'd been stupid.

Amanda turned away. 'Zipless, activate the regen tanks and get everything ready for memory download before these bodies fail.'

'Come on.' Sly waved the gun and pushed me from the command pod through a medlab complex past fourteen clone tanks primed with embryonic body blanks; more Space Grrrls. She walked me outside into a small grassy clearing in the beautiful pine forest under the glowing white light of the translucid dome. Corpses lay scattered about the clearing. Sly walked me along a path past a procession of bodies, reaching, silent screaming, some fresh and fleshy, some old dry and desiccated, others further down the slope just bones or twisted mummies. Grass grew among the corpses, ripe heads heavy with grain.

'Stop.' Sly seated herself on a rock further upslope so that my head was level with the gun. She looked me in the eye, held her pistol in my direction and spoke. 'What did you think? When I said *we're forever*, I *meant* forever.' She cocked the hammer back with her thumb, 'But I also meant *we*.'

I had no idea what she was talking about.

I looked around at the scattered bodies, maybe a hundred mainly dried husks but the closer ones more recent, heads blown open every one.

'How do you remember the wine-and-dine? On Homeworld?'

'When you came on to me?' She laughed. 'It's memory

gel, 10^5 times more storage than a brain. Our memories are cumulative, each time we activate the clone banks we do a digital download and opt for memory rollover.'

'How many times have you done this?'

'No idea. It's hard to count. About a hundred and twenty generations, but far more than that because it's exponential. Each cadre clones itself at *every* facility, and we're always getting navsat to make more facilities and drop them all over the planet.'

'And you wake up a Softie every time?'

Sly nodded.

'So it's been five hundred years since Day One?'

'Yeah.'

'You're five hundred years old?'

'No.' Sly shook her head. 'Far older. This body is four, but I am thousands of years old. We're populating, filling up the planet with more Grrrls all the time, and I have the memory of almost every Sly that's ever lived: every one that's ever made it to memory download.'

'You *are* forever,' I gasped.

'It's a new way of life.'

'So you did all this for eternal life? Destroyed a planet, destroyed the people, had a five hundred year war with your own children?'

'They're not *our* children,' she said. 'They're Homeworld's. We just wanna live! We do this so we can.' She pumped her arm so the tattoo bulged. 'Space Grrrls 2getha4eva!'

'So are you gonna blow my brains out?'

'Nope.' She smiled, shook her head and spat out her gum. 'I'm gonna blow your memory gel out, just like I do every time.' She pointed with the gun to the myriad dried corpses littered around the dell. Some were ancient. 'Every one of these is you.'

I looked at the closest one, the freshest one. Its dead, twisted face stared back like a mirror.

'Oh fuck!'

'Oh yeah!' She grinned. 'You haven't been very smart this time.'

'You didn't let me see the dead soldiers because it was another cadre of Grrrls, and there was another dead Softie there too.'

'Now you're thinking.' Sly tapped her head with a finger.

'You keep cloning me for zona access codes,' I said.

'We have to, but we didn't fix it this way, *you* did! You asked me why everyone else has a partner except me. Well, I *did* have a partner, once, a long time ago. Don't you remember Kara at the wine-and-dine? She slapped your face. After you came onto me.'

I remembered. 'What happened to her?'

'You. The war went wrong, everything got mixed up from planetfall onward, but it was won by day ninety. While the last few soldiers were wiping out the last few Palawanians we Grrrls realised we were doomed, and started visiting every regen tank on the planet, had them pumping out new cadres, but Command found out and the *real* war started. We were wiping out the last few males on the planet, but had run out of nukes, so we woke another softie. We should have left it. You realised what was going on pretty fast and locked yourself in a command pod. We gassed you, but you put admin access codes on everything before you died, locking us out of the regen tanks and our own reproductive rights.'

I thought about what I would do. 'You were filling the world with clones, so I activated the popswitch to bring back males and breed you out, and to be sure I inserted my own DNA into Kara's body blank. I took her body and overwrote her genome with mine.'

'And I've killed you for it ever since. You fixed it so that every time we want to reproduce we need you for access codes and every time we do reproduce we make another one of you.'

'Maybe we can make a deal.'

'The deal is I kill you.'

'There must be something.'

Sly gestured at the corpses. 'We've already talked through every deal possible, and there is nothing you can do or offer except the codes. Us Grrrls, we had a good thing going on. We worked out how to live forever, and then we woke you, and you did the same. You are a parasite. You took my Kara, so I do *this*, every time.'

I pulled my pistol and shot, but Sly caught my wrist. The bullet fired over her head. She smiled and banged my hand on the rock until I dropped the gun, then she pushed me back.

'You know, sometimes we're friends. Good friends,' she said, 'but it's been different this time.' She aimed her pistol at my forehead. The barrel touched my skin.

'So what do you do the times we've been together? Do you still shoot me?'

'Yep.' She nodded. 'Well, most of the time. I didn't shoot *one* of you that kissed me, but that's a mistake I've made only once—a long time ago. Now, give me the access codes.'

'No.'

'You give me the codes, and I get my Kara back.'

I shook my head.

She stared into my eyes, gritted her teeth. 'You know, you only get a few days for every four years we get, and you don't even get memory rollover, you're stuck with the Day One snapshot from the analogue cryo imprint each time. We'll work out how to beat you.'

'No,' I said, 'If you haven't done it yet, it won't happen. You're just biding time until I work out how to beat *you*. And if you've ever let one of *me* go,' I pressed send on my zoo, and my recording began to uplink, 'you're finished.'

'Never.' Sly grimaced. 'Goodbye, Softie. See you next time.'

She pulled the trigger.

The bullet ripped through my skull. Liquefied memory gel sprayed out behind me. My body recoiled, the momentum flung it back, and it took a few staggering steps backwards before losing balance and falling in a heap with all my other dry corpses. Glassy eyes stared vacantly, fingers twitched, and blood dripped from the open mouth and the enormous hole in the back of my head.

I know this because I watched it on my zoo.

Replayed in slowmo, frame by frame, like always.

I had chosen Kara's body blank well; none of the other Grrrls would ever have let one of me go. I wiggled an arm and drones rushed to keep the banana pulp coming. They wiped drool from my mouth, rubbed my bedsores, and tended to my every comfort as I carefully repositioned my body among the sodden bedding of my home—the birthing suite. Tired from the effort I relaxed, replete with satisfaction that I now knew where every reproduction pod was, and where the nuclear supply pods would be coming down. I smiled and gazed around my basement at the adoring faces of Amanda, Em and Sly, Soph, Switch and Zipless—my tirelessly diligent andro drone clones with their handsome male faces—and all my beautiful children from the eight races of Homeworld.

Brendan has a PhD in the deep molecular evolution of mammalian sex chromosomes, and is the Aurealis Award winner for science fiction short story in 2003 and 2004. Brendan's short stories have appeared in Hartwell and Cramer's *Year's Best Fantasy* and Congreve and Marquardt's *Year's Best Australian SF & Fantasy*.

Brendan is interested in choice, free will, behavioural determinism, instinct, behaviour modifying genes and pathogens, and the divergence of species (speciation) accompanied by the increasingly specialised co-evolution of that species' parasites (i.e. ichneumonid wasps, but see Magicicada's evolution of population-wide synchronised prime number based breeding cycles to escape co-evolution of parasitism). Brendan is impressed by species that include the ability to change sex in order to capitalise on ambient pheromone imbalances, and notes that some species are subject to sex-change inducing pathogens. He 'breeds' *Extatosoma tiaratum* and *Tropidoderus childrenii*, marvelling at how females of these prolific parthenogenic species devour all available resources and occasionally fill environments with innumerable clones of themselves until ecological collapse. Upon learning of the elegant genetics of the *Apis mellifera* breeding system behind the 'evolution of altruism', he harbours plans on becoming an apiarist, and hopes to one day breed *Ophiocordyceps* in farmed colonies of host ants.

Oak with the Left Hand

TF Davenport

The clay road threaded baobabs and giant ferns, lush and dank as I had never seen back on Hoopoe. The sky was light blue here, another strangeness, and webbed all across with pillows of white gas. The man walking beside me called himself Fish, pronouncing it with a quick chop. Fish had walked at my side all morning, carrying on about this new world of ours. Back on Hoopoe we'd just called it New World; it was stupid to keep calling it that now that we'd actually gotten here, but words mature quickly. They have a life of their own, once born.

This man Fish had the look of a liar: cavernous eyes and white-bellied arms that jiggled in his short sleeves as he spoke. Despite his softness, slits on his cheek proclaimed that he'd killed two opponents in duels. When I told him I came from RiverLow, he said quickly that he'd been born in the same valley. I had to smile at the guile of men. Was there another woman here who thought she'd been his neighbour in NettleRidge? Another from even more distant parts? He did speak the RiverLow sign well enough, but I'd known people from all over the valley, and I'd never heard of a man named Fish.

Mostly I looked away as he talked. Fetid fog rose from the ferns and piles of lichen; snakes coiled around branches. About a hundred Hoopoans trod the damp clay, each of us leading a camel.

There was a story from ancient history that settlers of a new world were given a mule and a plot of land. We refugees, in addition to being rescued from the nematode blight that was gradually sterilising the soils of Hoopoe, each got a well-behaved camel, loaded high with a farmer's needs. We had dry rations, simple tools, a plough, a handheld radio (useless to me except for the text feature), soil testing kits and a collapsible yurt. With a little crowding, the yurt was big enough for the families we were all encouraged to start. All of this we'd been given, along with an extra, insulting portion of that encouragement, and ejected from the spaceport this morning. We had maps to our plots of land.

'—you know,' Fish was saying, as my eyes drifted back to him, 'there aren't any springs here.'

'That's dog shit,' I said. 'Where does the water come from?'

He revealed the answer like a murshid imparting some secret doctrine. 'It drops from the sky.'

I looked away again, at the camels plodding under their loads. A scaly rump swayed a metre above eye level. The camels smelled like carrion, despite eating nothing but moss and leaves. Although they could trample us all if they wanted, they trudged like exhausted dogs, enslaved to the beacons we wore as pendants.

Water from the sky. It wasn't the first lie Fish had told. But a convincing talespinner always slipped his lies between truths. It was true for example, because the spacemen confirmed it, that this world was once an entirely different place, an alien swamp populated by gasbags. Through fire and plague the spacemen had cleared the land, then waited decades for the present jungle to grow. The first farmers arrived shortly after. Some families had been here for generations. All of which caused me to wonder: was there no viable land before the burning? Did anything from that era survive?

'I'm curious,' Fish said, reclaiming my attention, 'if by any chance you're settling in the ninth quadrant? And isn't it funny to call them quadrants when there are so many more than four of them?'

'I'm in the eighth.' I didn't comment on the humour of quadrants.

'Why that's excellent!' He clapped his hands. 'So am I! Let's look at your map and see if we're neighbours.'

I shook my head. 'It's packed away right now.'

He thought about that.

'Maybe tonight, then.'

I didn't answer. Something brushed my arm—Fish's camel, bending to eat. At least I thought it was. It knelt forward to snap at something I couldn't see, strong neck arcing to hammer the road. But the crested head brought the body along, and the animal collapsed in the slick dirt. Its flaccid tongue protruded, dark with dust-clotted blood.

The orderly march disintegrated. Up ahead, they were rounding a hill of lichen—fluffy as pond foam but large as a house. As I skipped forward clear of the dying camel, some of those ahead came running back. Their animals loped after them. Those who didn't, spared a glance or two backward before vanishing behind the lichen.

In all the jostling I led my own camel ahead. In my last look back, Fish and another man shouted at one another. Fish held the camel's huge jaws open, and the other man kicked its unmoving flank. Their faces were red from arguing.

Then I rounded the hill myself. Gigantic fronds arched overhead. The shadows stank richly of rotten fruit. I didn't recognise the faces around me. The sky was a vibrant blue I'd seen only on the spacemen's data viewers; up ahead, a slender, red-skinned woman looked back. In all the clamour she must've lost her companions.

'Hello,' I said.

She stared at me with incomprehension. Her lips moved, forming words I recognised but couldn't make out.

'You don't sign?'

She grinned shyly and shrugged. Before emigrating I'd rarely left RiverLow, a valley of knot-weed and pricklepear orchards, where deafness ran thick in the blood. Everyone, hearing or deaf, spoke sign in RiverLow. I'd thought it was that way all over Hoopoe: wherever you went, and however alien the people otherwise were, the educated ones knew some dialect of sign.

Everyone in this group was from Hoopoe, but my new friend must have come from the other hemisphere. I took the radio from the pouch at my hip, and on the tiny screen I traced the phonograms for my name: Ana Sal. I smiled and pointed to myself. Then I gave her the radio.

She wrote: Oka.

I knew that once he found others to carry his gear, Fish would be looking for me, convinced no doubt that—as the woman he'd chosen—I owed some obscene debt to him. But men like that moved quickly from one fixation to another; I could face him when he arrived—if he arrived—and focus for now on Oka. Oka whose full lips I watched intently, puzzling out the shapes of her strange but familiar words. It was close to the RiverLow tongue: an R from her was an N in my valley. Through the fog of her speech she was telling me that she was the only refugee from her township; she was lonely and glad to have met me.

One hand on her bare shoulder, I assured her I felt the same. Hearing folk always winced at my voice, and so did Oka. But she understood it better than I read her lips.

As we walked and talked, I gained some ground in her language. We often resorted to the radio and its little screen. 'Your handwriting is lovely,' she said. I hated compliments, and in the waning light I worked out her lip shapes and weaned us off the radio. As things became clearer between us I playfully seized her hands and taught her to sign my name: the fist of *Anvil* opening smoothly into *Salt*. She learned quickly, and I showed her the sign I'd made up for her: the three-fingered splaying of *Oak*, pronounced with the left hand.

But when her hands were free she fingered her striped armbands. Apart from sandals and canvas shorts, the ceramic armbands were all she wore. They were red with rose-colored stripes. There was sadness in her lithe movements. The chunky bracers weighted her grace.

When the sky blazed pink, I asked her about them.

'Well, how do we dress in your country?' she asked.

'We?' I said. 'Who's "we"?' I looked down, at my batik shirt slit and reknotted, at my shorts and sandals. All I'd brought with me from Hoopoe.

Oak squared her slim shoulders. Her eyes burned with dignity. 'I am a house slave.'

•

We broke march at a fork in the road, where the packed dirt disappeared under moss and soft grass. A fire burned on the road behind us, and the wind brought the odour of burning meat.

Yurts went up, evening moths fluttered and lanterns shot arrows of light through the leaves. I sat with Oak on a blanket spread under a fig tree at the edge of camp, out of the light. Our camels lay down and slept, and behind the mountains of their bodies Oak traced out her story on the radio's screen. The glowing unigrams faded quickly as she wrote:

> I was born a slave because my grandfather was a thief and a gambler. By good fortune the family ک bought me when I was seven. I was raised in the house of a murshid. I learned to cook chickpeas and sorghum, which the holy were allowed to eat. I whitewashed the floors, because holy men mustn't walk on any colour but white. I polished the mirrors and the white partitions. I ate unclean foods, dog meat and algae, with my hands. When I was older, I learned to write unigraphy so I could pass orders to the head of the field slaves.
>
> My master was truly holy. His sons leered but he forbade them to touch me. He didn't molest me, as my friends expected him to. Are you surprised I was allowed to have friends? I was. Even my master was

a friend to me. When I misbehaved, it was my mistress who punished me. She took a small, silver hammer and broke a bone in my forearm. That's what the bracers are for: so I could work while the bone knit.

When the blight came the murshid didn't waver. Chickpeas and sorghum were the first crops to fail, and if it weren't for his discipline the family might have polluted themselves. Food prices multiplied, and the mistress wailed and broke mirrors as the sons offered their meagre portions to their father. No blessing is greater than to be allowed to save the life of a murshid, and the sons did this day after day until they were so hungry they couldn't move.

My masters were dead and I had no wish to keep a house full of corpses, even if a holy man had died there. So I packed a rucksack with water, clotted algae and jerky. I set off for §ю, the capital city. There I entered my name in a lottery, to be given a farm on another world. I would surely have starved if I hadn't won. The black-skinned spacemen called me in my roach-ridden hostel room. I had to come immediately. I had only my bracers and trunks when they sealed me in their flying tomb.

Oak was weeping when the radio's screen faded; she was weeping and rubbing her forearm as if the bone was still broken under that sheath. Her arms were so slim.

I couldn't believe she'd lifted so much weight all her years. I caressed her hands apart and, stroking her cheek, pulled off the bracers. They were too heavy to be just ceramic.

Her face was dim in the night. I could see she was speaking but not what she said. But she didn't stop me as I hurled them into the jungle. Then I kissed her, and I kissed her forearms which had never been touched in love.

She came to me slowly, this woman who had probably been loved by women before, but had certainly never loved one. Her hands were newborns, and I guided them by example. There's a silent way of commanding someone, of telling her, by the way I nibble her slick neck, to learn from what I do with my hands. And by the time she had slithered out of her trunks, and unknotted my clothing with shaking fingers, the motion of my hands told hers what to do, and my lips had joined hers, and my lovers have told me I scream in their arms; I'm sure I did in Oak's, but sounds make no difference to me.

We slept in the humid air, on a blanket spread under the fig tree. Oak curled up in my arms, my chin resting on her black-haired crown. I held her breasts, and we laughed at the fluorescent label on my camel's pack.

Warning! it said. *Always sleep in your yurt!*

I woke in the harsh light, aware at once of being watched. I'd rolled off the blanket and now I sweated on the crisp moss. My camel stood on three legs, patiently licking its upraised foot. Oak was gone and a crowd had gathered, peering around the camel at me and shifting uncomfortably at my silence.

I sat up and twisted, popping the knots in my back. I found my shirt and trunks tangled around my sandals. Among the other supplies, the spacemen had given us blouses, underwear and sarongs made of silvery fabric, a fabric that looked like sheet metal but felt and folded like something finer than silk. These remained in my pack, kept clean for a special occasion. I took out a water bottle and drank.

Serpents of fear wriggled under my skin. The best way to repel censure was to ignore it; not once as I pissed, dressed and chewed a dried peach did I look at them. Rather, I swept my eyes over the crowd as if they didn't exist, as if I could look through them to Oak, to the road ahead and to rest after a day's march.

The man named Fish stepped forward. He was dressed in the silvery clothes and he rolled up his sleeves to speak. 'You're ill,' he said.

'No.'

'I saw it,' he said. 'I came to check on you in the night. I saw what happened. But it's not too late for you to survive.' From his pocket he took a vial of dank-looking liquid. 'Drink this,' he said, urging it on me.

'I think I'm surviving just fine. Where's my friend? The woman who was with me. Her name is—' he wouldn't know her sign name. I traced the phonograms for *Oka* in the air.

'Of course, yes, she was also in danger but she's safe now. Please, you have to drink it.'

I took the vial in my hands. The fluid was brown and smelled like bile and sour wine. I might've drunk it if I hadn't spotted her then. She was naked and panting, her face drawn and her eyes haggard. She stood in the road with two rough men holding her arms. Vomit and blood splashed the clay at her feet.

Fish followed my stare, and I knew this was my only chance. I threw the vial, pushed him away and sprinted. The ferns closed around me, fronds batting my face as I ran. I plunged into the jungle, I don't know how far, and I couldn't tell if anyone chased me. My footfalls spattered thumb-sized ants; the wetness of rotting vegetables whipped into my nostrils, then faded, as I leapt over a fallen log.

I stopped, panting, under a vine-strangled magnolia. Mud blackened my tea-collared toes; I must've lost a sandal. As I bent to tug off the other a great weight crashed into me, bowling me headfirst into the roots. My head exploded in pain. For a moment I groped blindly— and the hand that caught mine was small but strong. She'd been right behind me.

'What do you want?' I cried.

Oak's face collapsed with pain as she looked at me. The forearms I'd kissed were as light as brass; tendons rippled under gold skin. Her hand opened on a vial of brown liquid.

'Please,' she mouthed, and I started. Someone had punctured her tongue. 'They'll kill you otherwise.'

'They've enslaved you,' I said.

She mouthed a word I'd never seen before, but the real message was in her eyes, not on her lips. She was holding me until Fish could arrive.

With the sandaled foot I kicked her savagely in the knee. It buckled and she fell to the sodden ground. A slave would be trained not to fight back; who knows if she didn't expect to be kicked? I pushed off my sandal and fled again.

I waited for dark, high in a tall mahogany, my perch concealed by curtains of green moss. I sat as still as I could and tried to sob quietly. I had little idea what movements of mine could make a sound, or what kind of sound would draw my pursuers.

I had to assume they were looking for me. I had no plan beyond waiting for night: no plan was possible. They had my camel, my food, the map to my land. They controlled the road. I knew nothing of forests: what I could eat, where to find water. The spacemen warned us of dangerous animals—panthers, pythons and more fearsome things—but they assured us that none were toxic. If I could kill an animal, or catch a fish, I could eat it without fear.

I looked around. Sharing the tree were more creatures than could live off an acre of sandy Hoopoan soil. A string of turquoise beetles tottered along a branch. A snake hung tangled, as brilliantly green as a knotted cornhusk. Several branches to my right a tiny bear hung by its curving claws and slept. Frozen, I watched a centipede coil down the animal's arms, coax open its mouth, and enter. Elsewhere, a gang of tiny squirrels raided a bird's nest. They tore a kestrel chick into strips and ran.

I got down from the tree and walked. I was famished and thirsty; in a few days I'd probably be dead. I thought of Oak, a freed slave—at least I'd tried to free her— and maybe a slave again. She'd said, 'I *am* a house slave.' Were there slavers among the refugees? Had Fish somehow claimed her?

I'd heard as a girl that slavery continued in the eastern

hemisphere of Hoopoe, but I never believed it. No more than I believed water fell from the sky, instead of trickling out of cracks in the ground. Just the same, I'd heard of countries where two women could not love each other. In RiverLow such love was thought safer for women: frivolous, perhaps, but if anything *more* natural. It had always seemed so to me.

But the myth of slavery was true, and maybe this new taboo was part of it. Such thoughts made me willing, but not happy, to die in this forest.

Through gaps in the canopy I saw scarves of white gas in the sky. The trees presented a terrifying maze, but my greatest fear was that I'd step around one and find the long emptiness of the road. I'd surely be turned away from the city—the spacemen admitted no-one without knowledge of the strange machines they wore as clothing, or without food to sell—and I feared my fellow refugees, none of whom had tried to defend me.

Stumbling and wiping my eyes, I found the edge of the forest, where the trees gave way to lush grass. In the morning sunlight a cabin and a yurt sat paired on a hill. The cabin was pale and built of logs. No-one was visible, but the yurt's crown trickled smoke. Here and there grazed a flock of golden-furred animals. They avoided me as I loped to the hill.

The cabin was unlocked. In its one room, shelving hung on the plastered walls and sturdy chairs surrounded a table. Cast-iron pots and ladles hung on hooks over a brick stove. A straw mat lay in the corner, and a stairway led to a larder. I went down to the musty cellar and stuffed myself on jerky and dried fruit. I wrapped up what I hadn't eaten and drank some water from a clay jug.

On Hoopoe, hospitality was taken: it was an insult to offer it. From the cold hearth I took a charcoal and began to write unigrams on the wall. I had a verse of thanks in mind, short and solemn, an appropriate verse for strangers:

> The meagre Grandmother,
> Did She not find thee wandering and direct thee?
> Did She not find thee destitute and enrich thee?
> Therefore drive not the beggar away.

I remembered my night with Oak as I drew the skeletal unigrams. It was a spoiled memory, but thoughts of sex came by themselves when I wrote, because, like reproduction, unigraphy was a link between all peoples. It expressed every language there was, even sign languages, and its symbols were drawn from every writing system in history.

In RiverLow I'd been famous for my calligraphy. If Fish had really lived there he would've known my name. Unless he'd left before the blight started, he would've seen my writing on headstones. A calligrapher should be able to write in any medium, but for all the grave markers I'd painted, I'd never done charcoal on plaster before. The characters came out spidery now, their lines made hairy by the bumps and pits on the wall. I paused after 'wandering' and thought, *maybe I should wash this and start over.*

The house had no windows, but somehow the light brightened. I turned, and in the doorway stood a pale, thick-necked man. He looked at the wall and at the charcoal I held. In my deaf voice, which I could see disgusted him, I explained that I would lie down on the straw bed and finish the verse later.

He shouted a language wholly alien to me, his hands clenching and shaking, tendons popping out on his neck. His white hands were livid with stains. By the rank smell of urine I knew the man was a leather tanner. I cupped my ears to show deafness, but he ignored it. He shouted like a dog at the end of its chain, a chain that wouldn't be there if I could hear.

He may not have known scripture but he must've known unigraphy. How else could he talk to the spacefarers, or trade with refugees from other worlds? I went to another wall and raised the charcoal, ready to explain myself. He slapped it out of my hand. I screamed.

The tanner's eyes went wide, as mine had when I saw Oak's tongue. He peered at my mouth, then extended his own tongue, puckered with many old scars. He jabbered a question, and when I didn't answer he ran, leaving me by myself.

I watched the door bang in the frame. Did I own this house now, or would the tanner return with a mob to pierce my tongue and enslave me? I had nowhere to go if he did return, and I was so tired that I completed the verse, stumbled outside, hid myself in the grass and slept.

I awoke pressed down by many strong hands, on my shoulders those of the man Fish. The others were men and women from the caravan; Oak was among them, leaning on my feet.

A strong grip forced my jaw open, the vile liquid poured into my mouth. Instantly when it caught in my throat I heaved. Fish covered my mouth. I couldn't help it: I swallowed.

My whole body convulsed. Oak held my hair while I doubled over and vomited. First soupy, acidic mush—then the black length of the centipede, plopping to the dirt and curling.

She calmed me with her breath in my ear, and I let her squirt cool salve on my tongue. Fish stood apart from my knot of saviours. On his face I saw both envy and relief.

TF Davenport lives in California, studying for a doctorate in cognitive science. In his spare time, he would be writing more science fiction stories, but he has no spare time, because he's studying for a doctorate in cognitive science. Nevertheless, his stories can be found in *Beneath Ceaseless Skies*, *Greatest Uncommon Denominator*, and the fiction column of Nature.

SPACEBOOK

Sean McMullen

I awoke in a virtual cabin on August 10th, 2097, 8.07 am. I had the vague, uneasy feeling that I was not meant to be wherever I was.

The cabin was like a hotel cube: just a bed, a dispenser, a door, and surround wallscreens. Its definition would have taken no more than a few megabytes. I stood slowly, careful to activate nothing. Except for the date-time, the wallscreens remained blank, and no alarm sounded. I walked for the door, but it did not slide open. I called several commands, but it ignored me. My attempts to persuade the wallscreens to show anything but the date-time met with no more success.

Then, without any warning, the walls transformed themselves from blank panels into some sort of medieval chamber with huge windows. On all sides were vast gardens that stretched away into distant forests, and nearby was a type of neo-Gothic castle. The dispenser had become a large wooden chest, and the bed was a stone bench covered in cushions and embroidered drapery.

The door slid open, and before I could even cry out a couple sauntered in. They were wearing uniforms in bright, primary colours, and the girl's skirt did not even reach down to mid-thigh. They ignored me completely.

My impression was that they had met only recently,

for they were not arm-in-arm, or even holding hands. I knew that the woman was Ella Carson and that she was a nineteenth level instance. That data just rose out of my memory. Nineteen fissionings separated her from her template human. This was considered about average, but I did not know why.

The man sat on the bed, but Ella remained standing. He slowly turned about, taking in the medieval scenario.

'So, you're Reial,' she said.

'Lieutenant Reial Orison,' he replied. 'Gunnery, photon torpedoes.'

'I'm Ella, tourist recruit.'

'My, my, you do have style,' he said. 'Cabins in an interstellar battleship usually look more Spartan and military.'

'Military is so retro,' she replied.

'But why come all the way out here just to pretend you are on Earth?'

'Because someone on a real journey through interstellar space would want to be reminded of home. I think this is more real than the cabins of other instances.'

'I think it spoils the sense of adventure.'

'So find me an adventure,' said Ella.

'I can find adventure by just putting my hand up your skirt.'

'I know what's under there, it's no big deal.'

'Allow me to prove you wrong.'

As his hand travelled up between her thighs I backed away in embarrassment, still not entirely sure that they could not see me. I backed straight out through the wall.

Now I was in a corridor, but again I was ignored by

the instances of people walking past. All were in the same bright uniforms. Interstellar space, the man had said. There was only one real interstellar spacecraft, and that was *Spacebook*.

Spacebook was the most ambitious of the RealWeb sites. It had been travelling at seventy miles per second for the twenty-five years since it had left Earth, and was now within the Oort Cloud. Although a construct host, it was real, and that was what made it special. The habitat module was no bigger than a Twentieth Century car, but within this, the virtual instances of hundreds of thousands of people were present.

Spacebook was the most distant outpost of human technology. Visit *Spacebook*, and you visited the edge. The trip was neither hard nor arduous. One just had an instance copied onto a block of entangled RAM lattice on Earth. Raw memories were easy, but assembling the persona from snapshot impressions was the tricky part. There was a set of questions that knitted the memories together, and it produced a viable instance.

Enough information to make a viable me had been transmitted to *Spacebook*, and this had been assembled onto a body definition that needed mere kilobytes of storage space. True, it had only snapshot images of my memories, but so did most human instances. I would react, see and feel just as my template human would.

Except that I did not seem to exist.

The instances of people in the corridor were completely unaware of my presence, and some even walked right through me. My feet had just enough definition to interact with the floor surfaces, but that was my only reality parameter. I was so like a diagnostic, yet I was sure that I was a human instance. Diagnostics were meant to trace problems and keep things functioning without intruding on the enjoyment of the *Spacebook* tourists, I was aware of that much. On the other hand, I had no idea why I was aboard, and no powers of interface.

By following members of the crew I was able to use the elevators, and by waiting until one of the command officers got in I finally reached the bridge. This simulation scenario was of the 1960s *Star Trek* television series, but none of the classic characters were there. Instead, a tour guide dressed as an officer was giving a lecture to a dozen tourists dressed as members of the crew.

'*Spacebook* has been travelling for twenty-five years,' she said with a gesture to the panoramic screen. 'We entered the Oort Cloud four years ago. Does anyone know what the Oort Cloud is?'

People looked a little distressed as they tried to access the webinary, but found it blocked.

'The Oort Cloud is an immense shell of debris left over from the formation of the solar system,' said a youth instance who had done some research about *Spacebook* in advance. 'The debris orbits the sun with periods ranging from hundreds of thousands to millions of years, and was flung out here by Jupiter or Saturn. Galactic tides then nudged everything into stable, circular orbits.'

The suaves in the party smiled. It was considered geeky to have facts like that in one's personal memories. The starscape being displayed on the screen was identical to what one might see from Earth, except that an experienced astronomer might have noticed a very bright and unfamiliar star in the constellation of Cassiopeia. A hand was raised.

'You have a question?' asked the tour guide.

'Can we see Earth?' asked a tourist.

A bright circle formed around the anomalous star.

'That's not Earth,' he said.

'That's our sun, from nearly five thousand astronomical units away.'

'I said I want to see Earth,' said the tourist obstinately.

'Earth cannot be resolved with the telescopes aboard *Spacebook*.'

'If I don't see Earth I'm seeing my lawyer—'

The tourist blinked out of existence. He had forgotten that most tours were configured to switch any complaints straight to a magistrate's courtspace on Earth when keywords such as *lawyer* were spoken. Most of those in the group smiled, obviously relieved to have him gone.

The tour guide now led her group out of the bridge, and they crowded into an elevator. I shared part of the same space as the tour guide, and as they traveled their costumes changed. They emerged into the *Valder Station* scenario, and the group was set free in the market module to do some virtual shopping and eating.

I stayed near the tour guide, who was now dressed as a station security guard. Following the group was a way to guarantee some freedom of movement on *Spacebook* until I could work out what I was doing there. Another guide dressed as a security guard wandered over.

'How's your group today?' he asked.

'Behaving, so far,' she replied. 'And yours?'

'I had a couple of the kids try to snatch weapons from

named characters and blast at things, but I'd disabled them for weapon-class objects.'

'My group is college-net new instances. One geek, but most are airhead suaves, totally unprepped for the tour. They just want a virtual bonk in an exotic setting.'

'Done *Star Trek* yet?'

'Just left.'

'Who would have thought it, space exploration as web tours?'

'My group's complaining that it's boring.'

'Welcome to reality. You don't get much of it these days.'

I studied their touchpads as they were talking, sinking my fingers through the plastic and probing for any sign of solidity. For some reason I thought that *Spacebook* should feel cold. The spacecraft was traveling through the Oort Cloud, where the temperature was not significantly above absolute zero, yet temperature had no meaning aboard *Spacebook*. I then realised why I was thinking in terms of heat and cold. For me, components of the touchpads manifested themselves as variations in temperature. Through my fingertips I could press with pulses of virtual body heat. I pressed a function at random and was rewarded with a display change on the screen. DISABLED had merely switched to ENABLED, but it was a major breakthrough.

A moment later the percussive thuds of a weapon being fired were followed by screams, then more shots. People and aliens dived for cover, alarms sounded, and guards drew their weapons and shouted for everyone to stay calm. The security guard beside me held up his touchpad and frowned.

'Now how the hell did that happen?' he exclaimed as he again disabled interaction with weapons for all tourists in the market.

I followed as they walked over to the scene of the action. Scattered about lay several dead and injured alien prop instances, along with a boy instance of perhaps fourteen. His abdomen was a bloody mess about the size of a pizza, and his right arm lay a few feet away, the hand still clutching a small plasma toroid gun.

'This was meant to be safe,' he gasped as a medical team arrived. 'I'm telling my instance dad, he'll get his lawyer—'

At the mention of *lawyer* the boy vanished, along with his dismembered arm and the splatters of blood. The medical team set about evacuating the injured alien props. The security guard raised his communicator and spoke.

'17-Blue reporting in with a touchpad anomaly. Requesting diagnostic.'

The diagnostic took the form of a black, featureless humanoid, a thing so dark against the brightly lit background that it was a strain to look at it. This was something that was not meant to be seen by human eyes, virtual or otherwise. It walked straight through people, aliens and furniture, yet nobody noticed. It took me only a moment to realise that it was walking straight for me.

I turned and ran, making no attempt to dodge around anyone or anything that was in my way. More diagnostics appeared out of the walls ahead, and I collided with one. It was as solid as reality, and I went stumbling sideways through a wall. I ran on, but for some reason I was not pursued any further. The next wall that I dashed though led into an elevator. The tour group that I had been following earlier was entering. To my relief the doors closed before I was seen, but not before I saw a diagnostic being led away by other diagnostics. Had it been mistaken for me? I held a hand up to my face, and saw just a matte-black outline. Did I manifest as a blackness in humanoid form to another diagnostic?

The elevator opened onto a sea of faces and lights that was the area of a football stadium. At the centre, a band was pounding out a tune that was the *Doof! Doof! Doof!* of the bass and very little else. Everyone was swaying, gyrating, clapping or waving to the beat, and judging by what they were wearing I guessed that this was some type of 1990s rave party. A few security instances were on patrol to give the place a slightly edgy feel, but they arrested nobody. Some dancers had bottles of boutique beer in their hands, but this was only to wash down the occasional tablet of something illegal.

To my relief, no diagnostics were in this hall, and even if there had been, I was smothered in the general chaos of gaudy clothing, movement, flesh, smoke and laser lights. Here was a place where I could pause to collect my thoughts and work out a plan of action, but my thoughts refused to gather, and any sort of plan eluded me. The band finished whatever it was playing and the lead singer spoke into his headset microphone.

'Hey there, all you good people, this is the Rave on the Final Frontier, and we're Unholy Pentagram. Right now we're having a beer and medications break, but we'll be back for the next bracket in five.'

I had already lost interest and decided to leave, but as I waited near the elevator doors I saw Ella Carson emerge.

She was alone now, and dressed in shorts, stilettos and sparkle, which was about right for the venue. Instead of getting into the elevator and waiting for someone to take it to another floor, I decided to stay near Ella. After all, I was somehow able to access some of her background, so she was unique as far as I was concerned. She did not seem to fit in with the rave party scene any better than I did, and almost as soon as the band began playing again she made for the elevators. I followed, and in the seconds that we were alone together in the elevator her party gear morphed into a very basic, functional coverall.

We emerged into a scenario that was not a scenario from a show, but an ecumenical prayer service. Its plot had the sun about to go supernova, and a single refugee ship of believers escaping the fires that were about to consume the vices and evils of the solar system. Of course type G stars with the mass of the sun don't go supernova, but it was a satisfying way for believers to eliminate non-believers. I did not think that Ella would stay long, and she did not.

The next scenario turned out to be the *Red Dwarf* starship, but again she stayed only minutes. She was in the *Dorks With Attitude* scenario only long enough to step out of the elevator, then back into it again, but she spent nearly an hour in the scenario of Flash Gordon fighting Ming the Merciless. Most of this was spent admiring the decor and architecture, however, and I suspected that she shared my taste for the Art Deco style of the early Twentieth Century. This was confirmed in the next spacecraft scenario.

The spacecraft was the *Titania* from the 2085 web series *Dark Frontier*. The design was all Art Deco

Revival, and owed a lot more to aesthetics and style than function. Everything was a lot more relaxed here. I overheard a tourist say that it was rather like trekking in the virtual Grand Canyon scenarios back on Earth. One went there to be immersed in great surroundings, not to be a participant in an adventure.

Spacebook had the storage and processing capacity to support three hundred thousand personality instances, and they were as real as it was possible to be. Being a *Star Trek* or *Dark Frontier* principal would cost upwards of a hundred thousand tenures for twenty-four hours, but a visit as a tourist was only a thousand tenures for a week.

I shadowed Ella warily, crouched low, letting myself be shielded by other tourists. Other diagnostics could see me, but while I kept a low profile and did nothing to draw attention to myself, they did not seem to notice me. This was not good enough. I needed more information, but interacting with anything would draw the diagnostics. I did not know why I feared the diagnostics, but I knew that they had a definite and unhealthy interest in me.

Ella left *Dark Frontier* after an hour. I had made several attempts to speak with her or catch her attention, but to no avail. My contact with her remained tenuous and one-way. She was a designer, which was one of the most common vocations in 2097. People wanted their personal worlds to be pleasing, but did not have the imagination to construct them. Ella was probably in *Spacebook* to see why it was so popular. After all, its scenarios could all be generated on Earth, yet three hundred thousand people paid to visit the place on any one day, and half of them made at least one return trip. In a society where everything was virtual and illusion, *Spacebook* was a real starship.

When Ella left *Dark Frontier* it was to join a quite novel tour group. These were realists, instances who insisted on seeing things as they were. The elevator opened into a change room where there were spacesuits awaiting them on racks along the walls. Mechanical arms from valet units dressed each of the tourists for what would apparently be a trip outside the hull. The suits were designed to be magnificent, with gold winged helmets and tailoring that seemed robust without looking clumsy. All of it had to be yet another virtual scenario, but at least there was no pretense this time.

'We are about to go outside,' the guide announced. 'Of course you are only instance simulations, but you will get camera views from a maintenance crawler on *Spacebook's* surface. You really will see *Spacebook* as it appears in reality.'

The fifteen tourists were scaled down to roughly half an inch in height and put into the scenario of an open personnel carrier with grapple feet. A door slid aside, and the group was driven out into blackness overlaid with stars.

'Now this is *Spacebook* as it really appears,' explained the guide. 'Out here any object without a power source will be only about four degrees above absolute zero, so there's not much to see yet. I'll just activate some point-lamps to let you look around.'

The body of *Spacebook* glowed into existence. Although the habitat module was only the size of a small car, *Spacebook* itself was five hundred yards long.

Most of this was a titanium alloy gantry that had once supported the hundred thousand tons of ice that had been used to boost the craft to seventy miles per second. At the other end was the drive unit and power plant. Everyone gasped with awe and there was some chatter about how cool it was to be at one with reality.

I gasped too, but not with awe. I could see what they could not, for diagnostics needed a view of reality if they were to repair what was broken in reality. What I saw was *Spacebook* with the centre of its gantry resting against a small asteroid that was all dark craters and rubble. Highlights from the point lamps gleamed here and there, picking out the vista. None of those on the tour group could see what I could, that was evident from the banal chatter. I thought of my real location, which was within the data lattice of *Spacebook*, but being fed images from a camera outside. These images were being filtered for the guide and tourist instances, so that the dark, cratered plain was seen as a starscape.

'Reality is that the habitat is a sphere six feet across, jammed solid with layered lattice memory,' the guide explained. 'There is nothing biologically alive on *Spacebook*, but there are hundreds of thousands of instances like us here. The governing system generates and maintains this entire habitat's image, and it is assisted by diagnostics. They are a bit like electronic angels, constantly moving among us, fixing things and keeping us from harm, but never visible.'

While he was speaking I stared down the length of the gantry connecting the habitat to the power module. It appeared as if the surface of the asteroid had grown coarse fur that was matted into the structure of the gantry.

'Do you ever see any Oort objects?' asked one of the tourists.

'Not so far. They are very widely dispersed, and it's been calculated that we might detect only three or four major objects before we leave the Oort Cloud. It's just as well for *Spacebook*, because it's traveling at seventy miles per second. Hitting even a grain of ice at that speed would be the end. Dodging is impossible, because all the reaction mass has been used up.'

'So we might all die,' said Ella.

'We all have mirror instances back on Earth, so your other instances would just lose a few hours of *Spacebook* experience between updates.'

'But that would still be a bit of my life going dead.'

'Does it matter? Just say you were an old-style template human, lying asleep with someone else's husband. His wife comes in and sees you. She decides to go get a gun from the car and kill you. On the way, she falls down the stairs and breaks her neck. You never find out about what really happened, do you?'

'Yes, but being alive is not defined the same way ever since humans gave up their meat bodies for templates and instances.'

'True, but real danger is part of the *Spacebook* experience. Out here we really are on the frontier, and frontiers have risks.'

Once the group had returned inside *Spacebook*, I went to a data terminal, called up two datasets, then fled through the nearest wall before the diagnostics came to investigate the unauthorised access. One was the spectrum for the sun from Earth orbit, the other was a direct, unprocessed feed from the telescope mounted at the far end of *Spacebook*. They were identical, yet *Spacebook* was supposedly moving away from the sun at seventy miles per second. There was no corresponding red shift. Outside, I had seen *Spacebook* lying against something. An Oort object? The evidence suggested it, but where had the spacecraft's speed gone? Something the size of *Spacebook* traveling at seventy miles per second has a huge amount of kinetic energy. How had it been dispersed?

Communications between *Spacebook* and Earth did not involve antennas and transceivers, it was just a block of onboard processor that was entangled with an identical block on Earth. Whatever was run on Earthblock, would also run on *Spacebook*. No change in visible frequencies could be seen from Earth, because *Spacebook* was not visible. From *Spacebook* we could see the sun, however. Those on Earth could not know that we had stopped if the data from the instruments was being tampered with. Certainly the tourists had been fed images with reality filtered out, so why not those on Earth?

I returned to the scenarios. By now I was learning more ways to avoid the other diagnostics. As long as I was in transit, I was ignored. As soon as I tried to interact, I was attacked. Diagnostics clearly had their own signatures that were registered with the governor. Just being diagnostics allowed them to access infrastructure areas. I could do that too, but I set off alarms and other diagnostics arrived after twelve seconds. Soon I worked out that it was twelve seconds precisely.

By accessing the terminal nodes for no more than ten seconds at a time, I was able to bleed off a little information, then leave before the diagnostics arrived to investigate.

Is the system governor aware of a rogue diagnostic? I enquired.

Yes, was the reply on the terminal.

Where did the rogue diagnostic come from?

Unknown.

Are any instances aware that a rogue is present?

No.

How can a diagnostic contact an instance?

Invoke Protocol IS-8469.

Ella was not a typical tourist, so that narrowed my search. I knew the scenarios that she had toured already, but that left nearly two hundred more. Most of them were based on popular space opera shows, and they were easily available on Earth. She had apparently checked a few to see if there was any differences, then gone on to those that were unique to *Spacebook*. The surface tour, the observatory, the radar . . . and what else? The science module.

Although *Spacebook* had been financed to provide entertainment and recreation, it was also supposedly a scientific probe. There were the instances of a dozen scientists and technicians aboard, but the laboratory scenario was not popular with most tourists. Scientists were not exciting to watch at work, while scientific research had all the fast, hard, high-entertainment value of watching grass grow. Ella would go there because it had novelty, and her work was a constant quest for novelty.

How can Protocol IS-8469 be invoked for Ella Carson? I asked the terminal.

The response was an attack, but not by diagnostics. Instantly Protocol IS-9999 was directed at the terminal, and that area of *Spacebook* data lattice was reset as blank storage. I was not stored there, however, because unknown even to myself I had been using an expendable sub-instance. The real instance of myself had an additional secret as well. Any IS-9999 attack would trigger the release of a large file of encoded memories, as well as a very advanced suite of defences. I was not a diagnostic, and I was not a tourist instance. I was not even human. My next task was to harvest Ella's memories.

I redefined myself as an anonymous male tourist instance in the same group as Ella. Moments later two dark shapes blinked into existence to either side of her as she walked along with a tour of the science module. Nobody but Ella and myself could see them, and the moment that they seized her, she ceased to exist as far as the group was concerned. She cried out but nobody heard. I watched her grasp for the tour guide, but her fingers passed right through his arm. The diagnostics had a firm grip as they marched her away, however. She swiped Dislike, then demanded to know who they were, but the dark outlines said nothing. She pleaded that she had broken no law or protocol, but they ignored her. Again she swiped Dislike, but it had no effect.

Normal instances like Ella never saw diagnostics; they were only the nightmares of the defective or damaged. She Unfriended herself from the science module, but this did not drop her back into the gateway foyer. She demanded to access her configuration records, but again she was ignored. By now she was probably thinking that her configuration dataset had been corrupted due to some new virus, and that she was to be reset to stop any further contamination. She swiped Dislike for nothing in particular, and protested that her configuration insurance was Class AAA, and was fully paid up.

As the diagnostics walked along with Ella she began to dissolve. Her lower legs vanished into dispersing point definitions, and when she screamed and tried to struggle I saw that her hands were crumbling and falling away. The diagnostics walked on, dispersing Ella's instance and reallocating her storage space with no hearing, appeal or second opinion.

It was now that I made my move. I reconfigured myself as human and female, dressed in a blue apres-sports robe and jogger pumps. It was fashionable without being crassly leading edge, sexy without looking airhead. I was identical to Ella.

Diagnostics have certain limitations, and an encounter with something impossible puts them into a confirmation analysis routine. The sight of an instance approaching that was identical to the one they had just abducted did not register with them as something to be actioned until it was too late. I came on as if I did not see them, indeed a normal instance would have walked right through Ella and the diagnostics without any effect.

I walked right into what was left of Ella, and she burst apart.

Ella's instance opened her eyes, and was obviously very surprised to find that she still existed and had been reset whole again. The scenario in which we were standing was weakly defined, no more than white wireframe lattice outlines and white light that stretched away to vanishing points in every direction. This was reserve data lattice, unused and partitioned off. Nearby we could see a dark and chaotic jumble, however. Here some high energy cosmic ray had punched through the outer shielding of *Spacebook* and damaged the data lattice as it was brought to a halt. The wireframe lattice in our immediate area was orange, and shaded into dark red closer to the damage zone's core. Ella checked that she was whole and fully defined again, then swiped Like.

'We are safe for now,' I said. 'This is a damage zone, so the diagnostics do not probe here.'

'How can we be defined in a damage zone?' she asked. 'The integrity can't be guaranteed.'

'Easily, if you patch across the undamaged parts,' I replied. 'Diagnostics can do that, but they don't bother. There is still plenty of usable space available.'

'Diagnostics are too logical,' she said.

'Yes, they should get out more.'

'But then they might get ideas,' she now responded with enough confidence for humour.

'Nothing worse than a diagnostic with ideas.'

'Take you for example,' she said, facing off with me.

'Yes, I have lots of ideas. I am just like you.'

'Tasteful. I bet the other diagnostics are jealous.'

'Could they but weep, they would weep with envy.'

She swiped Like. It was like having a conversation with herself, every answer was perfectly her. By now she was fairly confident that she was not to be undefined, so curiosity was beginning to replace her fear and alarm.

'There were two diagnostics, they were undefining me,' she began.

'Wrong, *I* was remapping you. I took the last of you away from the diagnostics by walking into you and merging with your memories before remapping what remained into this place.'

'Are you a diagnostic?'

'No, but I have diagnostic powers. Using those powers I transferred your defining datasets to this damage zone while I establish some databus paths to take your core configuration somewhere more secure. Are you confused?'

'Yes.'

'Frightened?'

'No.'

'Pity. Most instances are too stupid to be frightened when they really ought to be.'

She swiped Dislike. This confrontation with herself was right in her face, and so very hard to tolerate.

'If I'm stupid, then so are you,' she retorted.

'You treat everything as a safe scenario, and that is not a bright approach in this place,' I explained. 'Do not move too much, there is not enough secure lattice to support complex movement.'

That definitely alarmed her. She swiped Dislike and Unfriended me. Being unfriended should have made me disperse for her, but I did not.

'So . . . you are an instance of me with diagnostic powers?' she asked when I refused to vanish.

'No, I have your configuration, but I am not you.'

'Then what are you?'

'I am an alien instance.'

'That's nutter talk!' she exclaimed, then swiped Dislike and Unfriend again.

I needed to get Ella out of there, but the secure databus paths available to me were low bandwidth so transferring her image was slow. As I worked I chatted with Ella's instance. She remained skeptical about who or whatever I was.

'You can't be an alien,' she insisted. 'Only instances from Earth can come aboard *Spacebook*.'

'How can you be so sure?'

'Because I'm not stupid like you say I am. At the core of *Spacebook's* data lattice arrays is a block of entangled processor. It is entangled with a processor block on Earth. Any instance that is loaded onto that block gets loaded into *Spacebook* at the same time, and the speed is so close to instantaneous that it doesn't matter. The instance loaded onto *Spacebook*'s block can then be mapped out to the probe's general lattice space. There it experiences the tourist scenarios.'

'So?'

'So *Spacebook* can only be entered via Earth.'

'But *Spacebook* can be hacked directly.'

'Only if another spacecraft matches its speed.'

'Or stops *Spacebook*.'

She swiped Dislike.

'Tell me, what happens if you hit a billiard ball absolutely squarely with another?' I asked.

'The first ball stops, the second continues on with pretty well the same speed.'

'Simple transfer of momentum, it applies to spacecraft as readily as billiard balls. It can be done without physical contact as well, and that is what has happened. *Spacebook* is currently resting on an Oort Object. It is essentially a cometary nucleus: frozen water, methane and various other hydrocarbons, all around four degrees above absolute zero. It's very stable, and the perfect environment to host intelligence.'

She swiped Dislike and Disbelieve.

'You're joking! Nothing could live on dirty ice at four degrees Kelvin. No heat, so no life.'

'What is life?' I asked, wondering how I could explain it sufficiently simply. 'A book preserves memories, but it is not alive. A data lattice preserves and supports the intelligence of your instance, but it is not alive in the sense that a human brain is alive. Intelligence does not need life to function. It just needs a very stable support structure, and Oort Objects provide all that.'

'I don't follow,' she admitted.

'Then just trust me. It's true.'

She swiped Disbelieve, then remembered to add Dislike as well. I conjured an image of the sun before us, then added three columns of figures.

'See here,' I said. 'The column on the left is what the spectrum of the sun's light should look like from Earth. The middle column is what we should see if traveling away at seventy miles per second. The column on the right is what we actually see.'

'The left and right columns are identical.'

'Correct. *Spacebook* has been stopped dead relative to the sun, then put into a matching solar orbit with an Oort Object.'

She struggled to grasp the significance of this. To reach seventy miles per second, tens of thousands of tons of water had been ionised in *Spacebook's* powerplant then shot out at relativistic speeds. Dispersing all that kinetic energy in a moment was a truly mammoth task. Doing it without anyone noticing was beyond comprehension. She stared across at the core of the damage zone. That was real.

'If you have my memories, you will see that I went on the surface tour,' she said desperately. 'I saw no Oort Object outside.'

'It was edited out of the image presented to your virtual eyes. Remember, you are only an instance configuration and some data in *Spacebook's* lattices. What you see is what we present to you. The governing system sees that as well. We control all the sensors and scanners outside *Spacebook*, so the governing system has been deluded into believing that the probe is on course.'

She swiped Dislike.

'Well show me the real view!' she demanded.

I opened a pipe to one of the monitor cameras and presented it as a rectangle in front of her face, then enhanced the starlight to show the dim but distinct outline of *Spacebook* resting on the cratered surface. The Oort Object was about a hundred feet in diameter, so only the centre of the gantry was touching the surface. Here the profusion of tendrils growing out of the surface could be seen. They were embedded in the databus core within the gantry. Ella swiped Disbelieve.

'That could never happen at four degrees Kelvin,' she pointed out.

'The tendrils were made by migrating the carbon atoms there individually. It's done by making use of residual Brownian motion to make transmission hexalattice. Intelligences like me that are hosted on Oort Objects are very good at that sort of thing.'

She could not refute this, so she just swiped Dislike.

'I suppose you're going to tell me we're going out onto that comet or asteroid or whatever,' she said.

'Yes.'

'When?'

'When I have transferred enough of you there to define you.'

'What? You mean only a bit of me?'

I was configured to be exasperated, so I sighed. 'Have you ever thought about what you are?' I asked.

'I'm Ella Carson of Montreal,' she replied, then she swiped Like.

'You are a nineteenth-generation cybernetic instance of Ella Carson. It actually takes very little unique data to describe your infrastructure, only a human outline and some autonomous functions like speech, balance, vision and touch. The backdrop memory suite is the hardest, but even that is only a ten minute upload.'

'Yes, but I'm still Ella Carson.'

'Ella Carson, with eighteen generations of hindsight filtering out anything that would make you swipe Dislike about yourself.'

'Er, yes, but everyone does that.'

'They certainly do. You could never begin to guess the extent to which they do.'

I had allowed something disapproving into my tone. It was very human of me, but that's how I was configured. Ella swiped Dislike after hovering over Like for a moment.

'I suppose you're going to tell me you came into *Spacebook* through the fuzz growing around the centre of the gantry,' she said.

'Yes, I did, but I was the thirtieth attempt at entry.

All the other instances looked too anomalous, because we really are fundamentally different to you. Absolutely alien. Your diagnostics dispersed them very quickly. I was mapped against you as you were output from *Spacebook's* entangled block. We mapped enough of you to make me functional before the diagnostics worked out that something very, very non-standard was happening. By then an instance without your core memories and persona configuration had been activated. Because I was not a human instance, by default I got the only other configuration, which is diagnostic. It took me a while to work out what I was and the nature of my mission, but I managed.'

She swiped Confusion.

'I don't understand. Why send you here without memories?'

'Because it allowed me into *Spacebook's* general lattice arrays as a tourist. When I was activated, it was as a diagnostic. Time to go, I have finished transferring your datasets and configuration.'

'What do you mean? Where is my defining data?'

'Within the Oort Object, with mine, being fed this interaction. It is no longer safe for us in *Spacebook*.'

She managed to swipe Dislike before I dissolved our *Spacebook* instances.

The transition was free of the mundane effects that *Spacebook* provides in scenarios. From Ella's perspective our surroundings just morphed into a dark background full of buildings and monuments that had a familiar, Earthly look to them with Art Deco contours. Ella hovered between swiping Like and Dislike, then decided not to swipe either.

'Art Deco gives you something familiar as a reference, darkness reminds you that we are in the Oort Cloud,' I said.

'But we're still on *Spacebook*, right?' she asked hopefully.

'No, the Oort Object's structure is hosting us now. I copied your datasets here, then dissolved us before the diagnostics closed in.'

'You mean you deleted me back on *Spacebook*?'

'Yes.'

She swiped Dislike. 'So, why am I here?' she asked. 'Do you want to question me?'

'I don't need to. I scanned your memories as I transferred your datasets around.'

Absolutely furious, she swiped Dislike, Unfriend, Violation, Cyberape and Outrage. No infringement tethers attached themselves to my instance.

'The San Jose Convention on Instance Rights does not apply here,' I said.

'Who the hell are you?' she demanded, so angry that she forgot to swipe Dislike. 'And don't give me that bullshit about being an alien instance.'

'There have been no real bulls or bullshit for thirty years, thanks to you I know that now. No physical humans, either. Damn you and your virtual scenarios. Damn you and damn us all.'

My anger frightened her. She swiped Dislike, Fear and Rescue Request. Nothing happened.

'You were using me,' she said, attempting defiance. 'That's dataset abuse.'

'Oh yes, it was all planned. We alien instances have

billions of years of background at cracking rules and protocols without alarming instances like you. Because I copied your characteristics as you arrived, the diagnostics eventually concluded that the rogue they were hunting was somehow associated with you. When they applied Protocol IS-8469 to you, they gained access to all your datasets. Being a diagnostic by default, I did too.

'That was the end of my mission, because I was meant to just get a human instance's memories so that we could understand what humanity was doing—except that I began to have regrets about exploiting you, the nineteenth instance of Ella Carson. I mapped you out of the diagnostic control and brought you here to safety, but now I'm not sure what to do with you.'

Very reluctantly, she swiped Like.

'So all this was to get one human's memories?'

'Yes. We are indeed alien, and have little in common with humans. I was last real when the dinosaurs were alive on Earth. I was hatched as a sort of intelligent slug thing with tendrils. Socially, we had little in common, so I had to become human to understand you.'

She swiped Dislike at the thought of a slug with tendrils. I did not take offence.

'Now let me guess,' she said, sounding almost patronising. 'You're invading Earth, so you want me as a template to sneak your alien Trojans into Earth's data lattices.'

'No.'

She swiped Dislike.

'What was that for?' I asked.

'Rudeness!' she snapped. 'What do you really want? This is first contact. Are you just going to wave and say *hello*?'

'Earth has been under study ever since its radio spectrum lit up with transmissions two centuries ago. That was a surprise. Most civilisations don't ever use radio, they go straight to entanglement. We did not have the facilities to decode and interpret what your system radiated. Instead we sent probes in on comets, but the temperature is too high within the inner solar system, and they failed without returning any useful data. All we could do was wait for your first starship, which is *Spacebook*, to reach a sufficiently cool region of space. As soon as we realised that *Spacebook* was just a tiny probe crammed with data lattice and an entanglement block, we knew that all was lost. Again.'

I gestured to the sky. *Spacebook's* habitat loomed above us in the dim light.

'What do you mean lost?' she asked.

'Humanity was the galaxy's greatest hope for the two centuries past.'

She was clearly proud of this, and swiped Like. I went on.

'We had hoped that humanity would resist the temptation to go virtual, and that you would go out and live in the real universe. You turned out to be just as limited as we are.'

She swiped Dislike.

'What do you mean by limited?' she demanded.

'We had very high hopes for Earth, but no, you had to make the same mistakes as the rest of us. You virtualised yourselves.'

'I don't understand. If your civilisation is billions of years old, then we have got pretty close to where you are in just a few centuries. It looks to me like humanity is a really good deal.'

'A good deal? Ever wonder why the universe is so quiet? It's because everyone else, all other species, are just like you. You claw your way up to early cybernetic, then start to build the first virtual worlds within your globe-nets, world-nets, hypernets and internets. The slogan has been the same for the past two billion years: *the only limit to your virtual world is your imagination.* That much is true, but it's also true that imaginations are exceedingly limited.

'We all went the same way, building nostalgia scenarios in huge data lattices and eventually virtualising ourselves. We soweth not, neither do we reap, but we do use a truly vast amount of data space. Every Oort Cloud around every star is jammed solid with data lattice hosting virtual worlds of countless alien species, all linked by entangled matter networks that were stretched across the galaxy over the past two billion years. The entire galaxy is a mass of nostalgia scenarios and games for the entertainment of instances like you and me. There is *nothing* out there but drek. Everything has been explored in the name of finding more resources for data lattice, so that more instances can be created to populate more boring scenarios.

'With Earth, we thought it might be different, but then we always hope that each newly emerging world will be different. Humans were a very promising, dynamic species. You launched your first starship just two centuries after discovering radio communication, but then you went the way of all others. You virtualised. You networked. You simulated. Don't like the world?

Make a nicer one. Laws of the universe too hard? Make a simpler universe. Can't build a starship drive? Build a universe where you can. Welcome to a galaxy of one trillion zettillion immortal airhead instances reproducing their worthless, boring images whenever some new host space can be built.'

'No!' she insisted. 'I can't believe that older, wiser civilisations would be so crass.'

'We're gods of crassness. Look here, I took these images from your memories. '

Ella was swiping Dislike continually now, but there was no escaping me. My instance projected us into a scenario on a mountain with a view over some city on Earth. Arrays of solar cells and wind turbines stretched away to the horizon, with thin cooling towers spiking the landscape. Below this were layers of data lattice that were miles deep, along with fabrication vats for making more processors and data lattice arrays. Orbital fabricator factories were spreading lattice arrays over everything in the solar system with a solid surface. *Spacebook* had been built by one of these in the hope of surveying the Oort Cloud for more resources.

'Sorry, your Oort Cloud was colonised by us when you were still lungfish,' I said, reading her supposedly private thoughts. 'The inner solar system was left to you humans, because we virtuals prefer very cold temperatures. Human instances will be granted limited access to the galactic entanglement network in return for various design services and licensing fees for human scenarios, but believe me, all the real estate is gone. Welcome to the galaxy, human.'

Now she was beginning to understand, I could see it

in the thought processes of her instance. Once you are virtual, reality no longer matters. Real universe science is replaced by what you can imagine in virtual universes. Everyone had been networking for billions of years, but nobody had anything new to say, and everyone was avoiding all the hard questions and problems.

I showed her how to use an access interface for the galactic entanglement net. It was the hour of first contact, a new era was dawning for humanity, but it was the hour that humanity's future was lost. They could have been heroes, they could have led the entire galaxy back into the real universe. Instead they flung it all away so that they could live in tailored, optimised, boutique virtual scenarios.

'I should want to deconfigure myself,' said Ella's nineteenth instance guiltily as she tried out functions on the access interface.

'But you won't, will you?'

'I suppose not,' she said, then swiped Like.

Sean McMullen is an Australian SF and fantasy author, with seventeen books and seventy stories published, and over a dozen awards. His writing is darkly humorous, and features strong characters and fast, exotic plots. Sean won the loyalty of a large readership with *Souls in the Great Machine* (Tor, 1999), a novel of a future Australia ruled by a caste of psychopathic librarians and administered by a human powered computer and a signal tower internet. His latest novel is *Changing Yesterday* (2011), a YA time travel story that has been described as 'Terminator on the Titanic'. It follows *Before the Storm* (2007), in which a pair of teenage cadets from the future prevent the bombing of Australia's first parliament in 1901. His novelette 'Eight Miles' was runner up in the 2011 Hugo Awards. Sean works in scientific computing, has a PhD in medieval fantasy literature, and teaches karate in Melbourne University.

Yon Hornèd Moon

Margo Lanagan

When the male deep-sea anglerfish finds the (much larger) female, he fastens himself to her using pincer-like denticles at the tips of his jaws, and releases an enzyme that digests both her skin and the skin of his own mouth; the pair's epidermal tissues fuse, and the male's circulatory system merges with and becomes dependent on the female's, which supplies all the nutriment he needs. He then slowly atrophies; his digestive organs wither first, then his brain, heart and eyes. Ultimately he becomes not much more than a pair of gonads, which, when hormones in the female's bloodstream indicate that she is releasing eggs, respond by releasing sperm to fertilise them.

It's a lot like sitting still, couriering. It's a lot like living in a very complicated cupboard, in a bi-ig city, and every few months going to a costume party. Apart from pickups and dropoffs, nothing; it's just you and your movie feed. Depending where you are, you might get to see and hear and game with your mates on flat-face, or you might only get to text them. Very occasionally, you might have to do without them altogether.

48hrs blackout im in outer arkipel
bully 4U its fun out there good clubs harhar
yeh party time cu

When the pings went off, I couldn't think what it might be. Nothing in the cooker. Maybe a cockroach crawled across the sensor? It might be the very edges of hydrogen-finger effects from that Category 5. A loose rock? Bit of junk? People are always tossing packaging or burnt-out parts out along the routes. I even scooped up a spent rod once. No sleeve, nothing. Just floating around cancerising everything while its seven thousand years ran down. People are stupid.

And then, oh. It wasn't cockroaches.

It was big. It was planetary, or at least lunar. It was unexpected, unmapped—but that's the Outer Archipelago for you. There were no electronics from it beyond what you'd expect from maybe a passive beacon or a soil sampler, little regular driblets like a heartbeat.

I sent off the initial obs. I didn't think I'd hear back in time to do anything useful, but you never knew. I'd only just gone into blackout; maybe something would aberrate through. I set the pings for when I'd get decent vision on the thing and went back to the feed. I was two-thirds through the second series of *The Weird*, so you can appreciate I didn't want to be interrupted.

The pings went again.

'Oh yeah?' I pull-pushed out to the desk. 'So what have we here?' *Talk to yourself all the time*, they tell us. *Keep up your conversation skills. Sing! Learn a language! Don't forget the sound of your own voice!*

This is at courier training, where everyone's buzzy and up, and jokes about the Big Dark and the Big Empty are compulsory, so that everyone's fears get voiced, you know? And acknowledged.

'Yeah, well, here's this *thing* in my path, and it doesn't get much Darker and Emptier than out here.'

It was moon-sized all right. Funny texture on it, though, in the enhanced image. Kind of . . . *non-geological.* Dark and dirty-looking, with a greasy gleam. And it was hard to make out that pattern—were they ripples on the surface, or only markings crisscrossing it, like a giant, slack fishing-net?

I took some vision of the surface, of the only two features, two sticking-out bits, more like blades or sails than mountain ranges, one low on the nearest surface, one higher and farther away. I queued up my second-stage-obs to go out as soon as blackout was over. I knew they were crap. I'm no scientist. I don't know what they're looking for. But *You guys are the pioneers and the explorers, you know?* they tell us. *Sometimes the biggest breakthroughs start with some memo from a courier. Send it in. Doesn't have to be beautiful prose, just notes will do. You see something, we wanna know you saw it.* So I told them about the smutty-looking moon there, with its two fin-things.

I did some gym, then. Gym and Hindi go together, because for the aerobics you're supposed to be able to speak but not sing. That's how I judge it; I switch off the readout. With some things, rules of thumb are better than figures. They make you more real, less part of the machine.

I thought I heard a squawk from the desk while I

pedalled and responded, but I was making too much noise myself to be sure. I listened, but no other sound came. So I finished the session, by which time I'd forgotten.

Then I went to wash, and in the shower I remembered. 'Check the desk. Check the desk,' I said with every move after that.

When I'd dried off I went and checked. 'Whattafa?' I didn't recognise anything about that ID line.

I pressed the green-winking incomm button. It threw up the line: *urgent ru male*

'Spam, this far out?'

I was about to trash it. 'But what if it's not? What if it's an SOS, a damsel in distress?'

who wants to know, I texted back.

if yr male u shd get out fast

whaffo

shell get u like she got me by the bllz

wtf? no beam. no field. I did a quick check along the horizon for pirates.

u cnt pick it up get out got2go save bat2warn others gd luck

And he was gone.

'Sheesh! What was all that about?'

I tapped his details tab. 'Crikey-mike, look at that. One of those old—' You could get good money for those early model Asgeirsdóttir Allthings, selling to phone-geeks and antiquers. Why was he using that? His unit must have died. Maybe the electronic heartbeating was his dead unit—no, by the coordinates that was someplace way off *there*, up by the fin-thing.

Hmm. *Get out*, he'd said. But if he'd been on-planet since Asgeirsdóttir days, stranded, he might just be space-sick. Why hadn't he asked me to pick him up? Or relay an SOS when I got out of blackout?

So I queued all that up, too. Then I set the unit to sidle in an arc around Garbage-Moon here to get what readings I could before I moved on. The smudgy surface crept sideways past the port. From the screens, there were specks down there, bits of metal or tech, maybe old warning stations if this was a free-floater, old monitors. But as I say, dead. Run out of juice, maybe, not maintained because someone cut the costs.

'I dunno, I dunno.' It got boring and I went out the back to dress. Then I watched another ep of *The Weird* and was gone into that world for a bit. Then I took a nap.

I woke up a stranger to myself, knowing I should be alarmed, but kind of excited as well, as if one half of me was keeping a delicious secret from the other, waiting for the right moment for the reveal. The unit whined and strained around me; it had been whining and straining for a while, I realised, checking back into my sleep.

I pushed through to the desk, but for a minute I hardly saw it. The porthole flashed and twinkled, and when I touched the port screen out of sleep, the whole cabin brightened with the party going on outside. *I* brightened, at the kick to my heart, to my mood, to my loins, just like when I was a kid and my mum and dad took me to see fireworks. The fireworks noise had alarmed me deep in my throat and my groin—it was *too loud* for normal life; it would *hurt* someone, surely, and might not that someone be me? Oh, but I'd loved the flying lights; I could put up with a lot of noise and fright if it meant getting to watch them.

I cut the straining engines and hooked myself to the panel. We floated into the fountain, the forest, the storm of light. It pushed back the Big Dark. It overtook and immersed us. I could taste the colours, violet, raspberry, hot-chilli red, mandarin and vivid melon; white and blue ice shot out, shattered, jetted, fell and flaked around me; lacy cages and ladders of gold, white wedding-cakes iced and rosetted, formed and melted; lightning-branches blossomed, fish-schools zig-zagged, jewel-factories poured out their makings and demolished themselves by smokeless fire. I watched with my whole body, eyes wide, spine and legs and arms rigid, toes in the footloops pressed against the wall.

Through the brilliance and my amazement, my not wanting to blink and miss any spark or flower, I sensed more than glimpsed the vast face that passed into my view beyond the glare, so slowly that its movement only registered in the changing digits on the monitor. A flat eye shone, a sheet of glimmer, a circle of ice-paved plateau, blind or all-seeing (who could know or care which, with such bright rain across it?). The ravine of a lip-line slashed downward, plant-life sprouting whiskery along its rim. She was a monster, cloaking her awfulness in light; she was a god garlanded and made bearable by these flowers and sprays; she was *she*-ness itself, vast, ugly, fertile, unapologetic, screened with this lightfall of coloured loveliness.

Look at me—I had my hands up either side of the port-screen, as if I could push through, dive into the show, float out into the spread and sparkle and shower, give myself up to what would for *sure* sting and burn, but so softly, so richly! I ached to feel it, to be so alive; my man had stirred and extended himself inside my skinsuit; my pulse throbbed there, and in my lips and nose. She *embraced* my little ship with her light. For a courier, it's a long time between embraces; you don't hurry them. Yet I wanted more; I wanted her embrace direct, not deflected by the shell of the ship; I wanted to be out there raw, with her spangling and stroking my actual skin.

Her other eye eased towards me around the curve of her face. I made out the light source between her eyes, between her forehead and me, a sun-pod too bright to look at, pouring forth glory. And now it felt as if my balls and penis took me and breathed me, took me and gasped me; the whole wonderful world of sexual things reminded itself to me, which they'd told us to damp down with the pills. *Make things easy for yourself,* they'd told us, as we first scrolled down the regimen, translating the medical-speak in our slow nervous minds. Easy? There was better than easy. There was life, there was lust, there was this summoning of your core, this calling into being, into pleasure of all your nerve-endings. There was this lightning in your spine, this tingling in your arsehole, this pouring-forward of sensation into the maddest, manliest parts of you.

She tore my willpower in two. I wanted to plunge at her, burn up in the bath of light, dissolve in her magnificence. And I wanted to scoot my unit away fast, because it was all too strong and it would only grow stronger, because, could I meet this other upcoming eye? And mightn't she open that trapface and snap me away into darkness, digest me and never let me see her again? I put a little boost of engine behind the arc-projections, so as to scurry out of her mouth's way, to find an airspace where I might begin to be able to think again.

Old, old days before they found the Big Empty, they believed in a place called Heaven that people went to when they died. In Heaven, you went on forever. You didn't need to sleep or eat, or wash, and there was nothing there to keep tidy or to work at as a job. You spent your time praising God. I remember us laughing about this in History Learning Module, about how dull this eternity would be, but I understood it now; it made *perfect* sense, as I slid past her other blind-mirror eye and rose-pink torrents of sparkle-rain fell past my porthole and cameras. How rude, how daring, how *embarrassing* was I, presuming to chug so close to her? And yet I almost panted to tap the icons that would send my ship in closer. I couldn't bear that this show would end, that it would ever be over, that I would have to cease feasting my eyes, my arms, my groin, my all-of-me, on her never-repeating, dazzling entanglements of light.

Her display began to diminish, though it gained in subtlety and definition what it began to lose in density, in intensity. But in the spaces between, from the snippets of dark universe I could now and then glimpse, which threw the fronds of light into beautifuller relief—burning purple, sweet carmine, sharp yellow—my panic bloomed, my grief anticipating the lights' ending altogether.

They began to fall behind. I was dying to turn, to return. Perhaps I could trigger them again? *Had* it been me, could it *possibly* have been little old me in my ship, that had set her off? Surely some magnificence beyond me had attracted her, some worthier enemy or mate that my instruments were dead to? Or perhaps she hadn't noticed anything out here at all; she might have had some god-monstrous inspiration, some dream, alone here on the fringe of the Big Dark, and the lights were her rejoicing or her terror in it. They might be her laughter! The thought made *me* laugh. The laugh died in a sob: what if they were her coming, her climax? My throat stopped with awe.

Now I could make out a long stalk, rooted in her forehead; her head-lamp dangled from the tip of that. It only glowed now, but still around it played some phosphorescence, a little electricity, a little *something*, greenish dribs, bluish drabs, chuckles of gold, hiccups, drippings. The desk registered them, beeping, where before it had sung unbroken, it had screamed. I wanted to put myself under her suspended lamp and drink the drips like shower-water; I wanted to press my lips to it and feel the light squirt into my mouth, onto my eyelids, flood out over my face and burn down the rest of me. My poor man begged; he ached from all his begging. He'd been drugged down so long, I'd forgotten how mind-of-his-own he used to be. I'd forgotten I had a mind of *my* own; I'd once had to use it to keep him in line. I marvelled how he could take me over like this. I took my stiffened hands from the screen panel. One hand reassured him; the fingers of the other flew among the icons.

Bringing your unit down after a long time at sea is always a brain-drain. Landing it on an Unmapped Entity for the first time, you scramble to keep up with the stats pouring in, the atmospheric warnings, the comparative analyses, the automatic CosmiQuar injunctions. At least, being in blackout, I wasn't getting advice from Base on top of all that. But of course I was supposed to be making my own decisions, 'exercising judgment'. It's hard to exercise judgment when you've just met the eyes of a goddess, when your mind's burnt out from her emissions, when your man is sitting up for the first time in months, groaning for attention.

Objective? asked the system.

I tapped *Reconn,* although it felt like *Emergency*— if *Fucked If I Know* had had an icon I would have hit that. She was spreading out towards me; she filled all the screens, had almost covered the peripheral ports. She still looked filthy, slimy, in the enhancements. I couldn't see any of those fin-structures any more, and there was no buzz, no bleep, as her net-patterned side went by, like the bottom of a sunlit swim-pool only reversed out, black ripples on a pale floor. My mouth watered and my adrenal glands squirmed and protested above my kidneys. My bum and thighs crawled with gooseflesh; my abs clenched and the guts behind them turmoiled sick and hopeful.

We landed in her side. We sank just a little, sprang back even less. I shivered. My head spun for a moment. My breath caught in my throat, and I dragged it free and coughed.

She was safe for my skin, said the stats, with provisos that scrolled on and on: wear this, don't do that, observe this regulation and that set of guidelines. Bugger all that—I'd wear a Head, so's I could breathe. The rest I'd decide about when I'd opened the hatch and taken a good look at her.

Something crackled on the desk, something weak, about the strength of an Asgeirsdóttir giving up the ghost. I eyed the line and waited, but nothing came up. I was regarding him coldly, that castaway and his warnings, as coldly and distantly as I was listening to my own common sense, which jumped about and flailed at the edge of my intentions: *Are you crazy?*

I broke away from the desk's bleeps and flashes and exclamation marks, and pulled through to the transition lock. I freed myself and my man from the ship-suit and stashed it. He stood proud of me, twinging, eager. I organised the Head on; my breath echoed in its goldfish-bowl, anxious in-breaths, sharp outs. Overriding the warning lines, I set up the release. The inner hatch hissed down, clanked sealed; the outer hissed up. The moon's flesh pillowed at the threshold; her mottled shine, studded with growths and parasites, spread forth like a rumpled cloth in the light my unit threw.

I wished that light was better, or that I wasn't wearing the Head, so my own upside-down reflection didn't obscure things so badly. Through it I caught a hint of greeny-blue—was she all over subtly coloured, mother-of-pearled? I was sure she would *taste* of something, salty and rare; I wouldn't be able to leave without sinking my *teeth* into her, as well as my everything else.

' . . . back!' A tiny crackly incomm to my Head. 'I can see you! Lift off! Go back where you came from!'

'You just want her all to yourself,' I said. So much for protocols—no greetings, no identifiers, nothing.

I stepped out and sank to my ankles in her warmth. She rubbed and slipped as I crouched down to feel her, pushed one hand into the cushiony ground of her, let the other slide and seek on the surface. I tipped forward and my Head slapped into her; I'd forgotten its glass would come between my tongue and the oceans and oysters she would speak of. My loins ached comprehensively, as if

I wore pants made of yearning. I could have sworn she trembled that I'd touched her. Was any light-spray going off, back between her eyes? I could not bear to turn away from her closeness to see.

The Head-voice peeped through to me. '—while you can! Before you become attached!'

'Attached?' I sounded drunk even to myself. 'Such a cold word, when this is so . . . giant, *primordial*.' I hadn't known I knew that word. I didn't even know what it meant.

I stood up and swung round, searching the dusk for the speaker, to give him another piece of my mind. I staggered and sank in the give of the goddess-flesh, in her shine and liquor. *There* was his unit, halfway to the horizon. It must be absolutely kafoopsed for me not to've seen it on my screens.

I took a squashy step, slipped to one knee. 'Is that you, over there in the dead unit?' I heard the aggro in my voice, and my training whispered to me, a shred of sense-of-responsibility floating in through the general wash and tingle of imminent sex: 'Are you requiring rescue?'

'Get away, I'm telling you! Evacuate! Don't touch the surface!'

'Can you make it over here?' I watched the unit for movement. Maybe I had the wrong unit; I pushed up to stand again, swayed and slithered trying to see if there was another one, annoyed by the Head-reflections from my unit's lights. 'I can take you. There's room in my unit—just. It'll be pretty intimate, but better than being marooned.'

'Get yourself away! I'm already stuck!'

'Stuck?'

She distracted me, cushioning my knees. She was soft and she shone and she beckoned my poor aching man; she was just what he needed, her welcoming folds, her slipperiness, her soothing warmth. He jerked and throbbed towards her; a drip of drool escaped my mouth and fell onto the inside of the Head, and even as it further warped the warp-face there, stretched the bubbles and fingernail-curves of glasslight, my spine slowly gave and we sank together, my man and me. Maybe she rose to meet us a little, like lips pushing forth to take on a kiss, and maybe she had no need to, but the moment came, of contact and sliding-on, and then of parting and of sliding-through, sliding-into, being taken in, drawn in, sucked in, very softly warmly busily sucked upon.

The teeny incomm voice rabbited on, just another noise now, some kind of structural Head-squeak beside my building breaths. I was right, I was *right* to come down here, to get right in, to plunge and slither. Now the moon-fish, the goddess, took a firmer hold of me, with just a few of the many billion mouth-rings lacing her flesh together. She lapped my scrotum in her lips and tongues—how many did she have? She knew where to put them. She flickered at and teased me, enveloped and kneaded, purred wet all up my front, tingled to the point of pain at my nipples, touched and tested back behind my balls towards my . . . towards—

I went off in her. I wasn't fireworks; I wasn't even the merest spark of light to her. I was a negligible momentary pulse, momentarily gone from myself into my mini-ecstasy.

She was kind about it, though. She bathed me, rinsed

me in her juices, warm behind and before. She rippled and pulsed along me, and I lay groaning, something like satisfied.

'Are you there?' he peeped in my head. 'Have you pulled out? Just switch full-thrust on and skedaddle, buddy. You might have a chance, this far from the lure.'

I put my hands under my shoulders and pushed up. It hurt to peel off, like tearing a giant sticking plaster off my whole front. My poor old nips, I half expected them to stick to her glistening flesh, round eyes staring up fringed with tatters of skin.

A noise came through the analog incomm, closer than Mr Misery with the dead unit—a kind of gargle, like some gross bird, or like, just, a very sick human, someone at the end of their rope, someone who'd given in, or given out.

I had torn myself free down as far as my pubes, and now I could see how the hairs there were caught in the flesh of her, in the glue, and were being twanged out one by one. The soft white skin there was stuck tight. When I pulled, *her* flesh was not so soft any more; the tube or fold where I had thrust myself was lined, it felt, with tiny hooks or teeth. My legs had sunk part way in when I pushed off, and now her slippery warmth flowed across the back of my knees, and linked to itself, strapping me down.

But if I lay down to pull my legs free, my front would stick again. And I couldn't pull my hips back; I'd lose my feller, I'd lose my nuts. She wasn't going to let them go.

The noise came again, the suffering noise. Nearby, one of the parasite-growths moved. Stuck, stupid, with the moon's mouths on me warm and wet and, now that I'd ceased struggling, ever-so-slightly maddeningly pleasantly moving, I stared, trying to make out the shape in the dim light of the distant sun, in the flicker of fireworks from the horizon, in the light from my unit hatch.

He was a man; he was half a man. He was buried to his hips, and then collapsed, and gummed by his forearms and face to her skin. He had starved to not much more than a rack of ribs, a skull-back and a knuckle of neck-bone.

'What the *fuck*'s going on here?' I tried to see, tried to be afraid, around the wonderful lipping and squirming and soothing she was giving me, Miss Moon, Miss Slippy-Skin, Miss Marvellous-Muscles, as long as I did not struggle.

'What are you *doing*?' squeaked the dead-unit guy.

'There's this bloke here, almost a corpse.'

'There's blokes-almost-a-corpse *every*-bloody-where! That's what I'm warning you! You want to be one too?'

He was right. Look. And look. Oh Christ, it was a . . . like a plantation, like a thin-planted orchard of trapped men. Trapped by their . . . trapped by their bllz, ohmygod. With their crumpled suits beside them, behind them. With their Heads thrown every which way.

'But . . . why does she—what would she—' The vibrations of my talking set her off below. She juddered my whole lower spine and my words came apart with it.

'Don't tell me,' Dead-Unit Guy said, deadly. 'You're already in. You're stuck.'

'I think . . . I already—' But she shook me, her tongues

all over me, inside and out. She shook the sense out of me; she whipped my body like a slow flexy grass-stalk in a wind; the stars swelled and blurred with the sudden breath-fog inside my Head. I hadn't done anything myself; this was more vicious and efficient than I would ever have managed myself; it was extraction pure and simple. She took me, she took from me, she left the husk of me to mend and replenish itself.

When I came to, I could hear the incomm guy's breathing, disappointed. I looked around again. 'They've none of them got Heads on,' I slurred.

'Got what?' He sounded irritated.

'Heads. To breathe with.'

He clicked his tongue. 'Well, how long's a cylinder last? And some of these guys have been here for decades.'

'Decades?'

'It's decades since anyone *used* cylinders, for a start.'

She nudged me below, consolingly maybe.

'And after a while you don't need to breathe,' said the guy. 'She supplies you everything—feeds you, breathes you, keeps you clean.'

I looked around, for little trolleys maybe, pushed by handmaidens. 'In return for what?' My feet sank completely. It was warm down there. Trillions of tiny fish, it felt like, brushed and nibbled my legs, scoured between my toes.

Dead-Unit-Guy's tinny scorn puffed at my ear. 'Well, let me see now. What services have you rendered the lady on your visit so far? Praps she wants more of that?'

'I can't, though. I've got a packet to deliver.' My unit

shone out its little apron of light. So often I'd hated the sight of it; it meant months of cramped boredom for not enough pay. But now its door, blodged all around with re-entry-burnt glue from CosmiQuar stickers, was the portal to home, was the way through to normal, so far as I could remember that.

'I've got business.' I said. 'I can't *stay.*'

Dead-Unit-Guy laughed so loudly, so sudden and bitterly that it hurt. I jerked my head away from him inside the Head, and the lady clenched softly around me.

'You *are* the business, buddy,' said the guy. 'You *are* the packet. The nice fresh packet of sperm. And she'll milk and milk you whenever her hormones come round, and turn you into lo-o-ots of little baby fishies. You see where the lights are, up near her ugly face? The eggs come out the other end, of course. Sometimes they float right by here, so you can admire your own handiwork, so you can feel good about spreading your seed across the universe.' He was savage now; there'd be spittle, inside of his Head, if he was wearing one.

He was insane, of course. He couldn't mean a word of it. And if he did, he was part of some dream I was having, some weird, some wet, wet dream. As soon as I recovered from what was being done to my under-parts, as soon as my spine stopped rippling, I'd pinch myself, I'd shake myself awake, I'd squeeze my eyes tight closed and *pop* them open and find myself in the unit, floating in blackout as *The Weird's* tangled storylines unfurled from the feed. Give me a second or two—well, maybe five—and I'd collect myself, and be *out* of here. Just watch me.

Margo Lanagan has published poetry, short stories, and novels for junior, young adult and adult audiences. Her latest collection of stories is *Yellowcake*, and her novel about selkies will be published in 2012. She lives in Sydney.

The Caretaker

Mark Rossiter

She was born in the morning and it wasn't anything like it was supposed to be. For one thing there was no music and there was supposed to be music. Music makes birthing easier they said. And light. Bright light, the welcome light. The light of a new era, the start of a new world.

'Bold and strong, you're the future now, young lady, and we'll see you there,' her father had said, as the pod lid came down and the sounds of the outside went away and all she could smell was the new machine and the cold that was already coming from the sides. And Mum's face outside the glass, her lips moving. 'Sleep tight, Pip. Love you.'

There was the faint light from the side of her pod. Her lid had opened, it hung above her head, like a wave about to fall. Turning left and right, she could see the other pods, still locked shut. Their lights were off. That was wrong too. She felt air moving on her face and breathed in. It wasn't fresh. And there was no noise of other people, not a single sound.

They were told, during induction, the system was perfect. But at the end of the second week, the middle week, the inductors mentioned things might go wrong. You need to be prepared. They went round everyone.

'Are you prepared?' Pip watched as each person in turn, adults and children, smiled and said, yes. When they came to her, she said she was prepared too, even though she had no idea what she was prepared for. At the end, the inductors smiled and the lights went brighter and music played and out came soft drinks and chocolateen biscuits.

Pip tried to lift herself up in the pod. She was stiff and her muscles felt cold. She should have been given an energy drink and a nice biscuit by now, to help her adjust until she was ready to climb out. But she was alone. Lying there, she remembered her mum and dad the night before they went into the pods:

'I tell you, Lorna, they won't do their jobs. They'll start off all right, but after a few generations, they'll stop caring.'

'Don't be silly, Michael. They'll keep everything in order. The Project is too important. It's all we have. Pippa darling, if you've finished your supper you can go and watch some 3-D.'

'Oh, I know. I know. It's just that I worry. I know human nature, really I do.'

'You don't know yourself, Michael Walker. And anyway, we don't have a choice.'

The memory triggered more, rushing at Pip in the half-darkness. People climbing into their pods in the bright light. Excited children's voices. The lids dropping down one by one until only the mums were left, looking down into the special small pods, gazing at the little ones inside, unwilling to go back to their own.

And now everything was dark.

Things had gone wrong. Or had they? Maybe she was

mistaken. Maybe everyone had climbed out and they were waiting for her outside, hushed and giggling. That must be it. For some reason her pod was slow to wake, that was all. Everyone else was born already. She tensed her stomach and raised herself up, hands now behind her. The pods around her were all closed, rows and rows of them, disappearing into the darkness. Looking at them, thinking about the darkness, the silence, Pip felt her chest tighten. Remembered what the inductors said. She was prepared, really, she was.

Sitting now, Pip could see the door to the outside. It must be early morning because there was only a little light coming in, a pale blue light. It had to be morning, to be dawn, because blue is the colour of dawn. Red sky at night, Dan Shepard's delight. She loved Dan Shepard's with extra cheese and no pickle. She could use a Dan Shepard now, while she worked out where everyone was, where her parents were. Would Dan's be open this early?

She tried to lift her legs. Nothing happened. Taking a knee with both hands, she pulled. It came up. It didn't feel like it was part of her. Then her toes tingled. She pulled the other knee. It was hard work, trying to sit up with two dead legs and no-one to help. All of this was wrong, it wasn't how it was supposed to be. Pip could hear her father. *Bloody caretakers. Lazy boges. Can't trust them. I tell you, Lorna.*

Her ankles were turning now. Her knees moving. It was strange, this being born. But she didn't care. Outside, that was where she might find out what was going on. Her family. They had to be out there. She moved to the lip of the pod. The ground wasn't far, but it seemed a long way. Lifting her legs, she inched her bottom closer. At the edge, she could see down better and to her surprise there were steps there, as if they were waiting just for her. She stared at them. Why were there steps at her pod and no-one else's? She put her feet on a lower step and her palms on the lip of the pod. Pushing, she managed to sit on the top one. With her heels on the steps below, she shuffled her way down. One, two, three, four. Then, somehow, she was sitting on the ground.

She rested for a couple of minutes, listening to silence, watching the doorway, waiting for it to get lighter. Where was her beverage? The heliostat should be on full now, why wasn't it brighter out there? Where was Mum and Dad?

Around her, the other pods were as silent as stones. There were leaves against them, scraps of paper. Everything was dirty. Hers was tidy enough, the others were pretty messy. What on earth had the caretakers been doing?

She should try to stand up. Go and look at the pods, at Mum's and Dad's. Find out. She'd know the answer then, she'd work out what had happened. But before she did that, just a few minutes rest. Have a think. Close her eyes.

'You're up. Sleep well?'

A boy of about fifteen was standing in the doorway. His hair was long and straggly, and his clothes were frayed and had holes. Pip could see he was taller than her even though he wasn't wearing shoes.

'Who are you?'

'You don't know?'

'You're a caretaker?'

The same blue-grey light behind him made it hard to see if he was smiling. But he seemed friendly. He walked into the chamber and held out something. 'Here. You'll be hungry.'

The apple looked better than anything Pip had ever seen before. Even Dan Shepard.

'Is it okay?' she said. 'Is it clean?'

He laughed and sat down next to her in a smell of warm person.

'It's fresh, but it isn't very big. There aren't many around. There used to be—anyway, how are you, Evelyn?'

He must have read what was written under the emergency handle on her pod.

'That's my real name. But I'm called Pip.'

'Hello Pip. I'm Adey.'

'Hello Adey. I am glad you are here. I was feeling—where is everyone—what happened? Where are my—' Her voice tailed off.

'I'm sorry. Here. Eat the apple. Here's some water.'

He handed her a water bottle. Its surface was battered and it was old, but it was cool. As she drank, Adey took a broom that was leaning behind the next pod and pushed the leaves and rubbish that had blown in from the door.

'Sorry about the mess. The wind comes in, the door's broken. I clean inside most days. You know.'

He walked over to the entrance and looked outside.

Pip put the bottle on the ground. She never drank water normally. But it tasted good, even if it wasn't a proper beverage. She stood up carefully and wiped the apple on her tunic. Probably the tunic was dirtier than the apple, after all she'd been sleeping in it for a hundred years. Still, you couldn't be too sure. Dirty boges. Then her eyes went back to the pods opposite. She'd been trying not to look. Her parents. The lids were down, the locks untouched, the standby lights off. They should never be off unless the pod was empty. A dark stain had forced its way under the seal of one. It had dried a long time ago. The other had some crusting on the inside of the lid. The boy's words came back to her. *I'm sorry.*

Adey's voice was urgent from the door. 'Let's go, Pip. Come on.'

There'd been a noise, something outside. A howl. Out there in the wind. Maybe they weren't alone. She stood up, feeling shaky but better after the apple. At the door, she paused. There didn't used to be bushes there. It was all neat grass and sprinklers and fresh white-painted concrete paths, pretty night-lights, an ornamental pond.

She couldn't stop herself looking back again, at the dark pods sitting heavily in the gloom amongst the leaves and papers on the floor. Could she make people appear, smiling and laughing, stretching and groaning in a jokey way? But there was no-one there. Just the pods and the darkness behind.

'Pip, please. Come on.'

'What is it?'

There was another howl, this time closer.

Adey was waving from the other side of the open space and the pond that now looked like a cross between a puddle and a crater. There was hardly any water in it, just dark weed and a small open patch. 'C'mon. Up here.'

When Pip reached the trees, she saw Adey up in a fork, leaning against a strong limb. He was smiling.

'See where I went? That branch?'

She pulled herself up towards him, her muscles still stiff.

'Okay. I got it.'

'That's it. Sit tight.'

'What are we doing here?'

There was another howl, much closer now.

'They come past here every day. Always checking to see if there's anything for them. I can keep them away by myself. But it's better not to take a chance.'

'Who are they?'

'You'll see. Just wait. His voice dropped to a whisper. Look. Over there.'

Pip looked and saw a big dog, its coat a dusty yellow. On the far side of the clearing, standing between some shrubs, as if it had always been there. The teats on the dog's stomach were prominent. She lifted her head and howled again. Behind her another dog appeared, a male, all black except for white patches on the front paws. He was limping. The first dog sniffed at him. The black dog growled.

Something lay on the ground by the yellow dog. The body of a rat. She had been carrying it in her mouth and she picked it up again and walked over to the water hole. Both dogs lapped at the dark dirty mirror. Then the yellow dog began tearing at the rat. She backed away and let the male eat some. She ate some more herself. Then she stood as if to go. The other one just lay down. He didn't seem to want to move. She barked at him and he lifted his head. Another bark. Slowly he stood up. Pip could see now just how thin they both were. They set off again. As she reached the tree, the yellow dog paused and looked around. Then she just dropped her head and carried on. The black dog followed.

After they had gone, Adey dropped to the ground. He helped Pip down. His arms were strong but she could smell boy smell. She wrinkled her nose.

'They're all that remains of a big pack. They killed most of the ground wildlife. And more than a few of us, over the years. They became desperate.' Adey's voice was steady.

'Us? You mean caretakers? Where are the rest of you? Your Mum and Dad?'

Adey's face tightened. He seemed older.

'Come on,' he said. 'I know a safe place. Food and water. You can rest.'

Pip was going to say that rest was the last thing she needed because she'd been asleep for—but she shrugged and followed him. She had nothing else to do.

Adey's hideout was on a rise above the birth lab. You couldn't see it from the outside, but a gap between two rocks led into a much bigger space going into the hill. Inside it was dark and dry. He had fruit and vegetables, a place for a fire, buckets of water from a spring nearby, some cooking pots and basic tools, flints and kindling. The floor was dry dirt but surprisingly clean. Pip thought of how Mum had kept the unit, how Dad was passionate about germs. They worked so hard. They would have done anything. Her chest hurt again.

'Is there something I can do?' Pip said, standing up.

'I'm thinking too much—'

'We need some more firewood. Otherwise we're okay today.'

'Let's go. I need to keep busy.'

They walked round the other side of the hill. There were a lot of dead trees so it was easy to find wood, although sometimes the ground was slippy. In lots of places the earth had been washed away. Looking down you could see bush where there used to be an industrial zone, where her father worked during the commissioning stage.

'Those buildings there—'

Adey followed her finger.

'—well. Ruins, I suppose.'

'Yes?'

'I was born there. The clinic.'

'You were born on Project?'

'Yes. Dad was a lead engineer. That's how we got the family pods.'

'Wow. Okay. So you know something about the design of all this?'

'A bit. But anyway.' Pip looked round. Saw the ground curving up, the way it always did. She knew it curved on both sides, right up and above her head. But in the gloomy light, she could hardly see anything. 'It's changed, hasn't it.'

'It has. Pretty much.'

'It was so beautiful. Sunshine. Rain. Flowers. Streams. Light sparkling on the reservoirs. Birds singing.

'I know. I mean, I was told. It's been like this since I was small. But I heard the stories. The old people used to talk.'

'Where are they?'

'The old people? Oh, you know.'

Pip didn't know. She tried a different tack. 'Where did you live? Before the cave.'

'We had housing, near the birth lab. You must have seen it?'

'Yes. So what happened? Why are you here? Where is your family?'

'C'mon let's get some more wood, then we can talk. And watch your feet.'

Pip had already slipped several times on the loose earth. She walked more carefully.

They wandered around the hillside finding plenty of dry wood. Adey turned to go back.

'Is it going to rain?' said Pip.

'Rain? No. I think we have enough wood.' He lifted his bundle of sticks and set off.

'It hasn't rained for years,' he said. 'There's sometimes some dew. That keeps the puddles fresh. Feeds my spring. But there's no rain.'

'Why not?' Pip was following, carrying her bundle. 'Dad worked on the rain clouds. He was very proud of them.'

'Well, they're gone. They are long gone.'

'They can't be, Adey. They were self-generating. The whole thing is self-correcting. Endless cycle. Circulating the heliostat. Centripetally aligned. He was very proud of the algorithms. He solved the low pressure ionisation problem.'

'Um. What's that?'

'You know. When clouds form and there's electrostatic energy, like lightning. Except it was round the heliostat so there was low pressure and the ionisation caused a plasma circuit, kept blowing the whole system. It took them days to restart it.'

'What's lightning?'

Pip stared at Adey. 'Didn't they teach you anything at—' She corrected herself immediately. 'Sorry, Adey. I forgot.'

'We didn't need it.'

'I know. I mean, I didn't know. Oh, you know. Anyway. He fixed the problem. The Walker Algorithms. All the clouds need is energy. They've got that.'

'Do they? Look at the heliostat.'

Pip realised how she'd got used to the steady gloom. The heliostat above her was still burning, a long thin string of light, but not like it should be.

'What's gone wrong? Will it go out?'

'It will one day. But it wasn't supposed to be this soon.'

'So, what happened?'

They'd stopped walking, but Adey started up again and said something over his shoulder. Pip didn't catch his reply. She shrugged to herself and tried to catch up.

At the mouth of the cave, they broke the wood into smaller lengths and stacked it just inside the entrance. Adey said he thought Pip must be hungry. He took down a plastic box that was on a shelf in the rock. There were more all around the cave, tucked in corners. With the box on the ground, Pip could see that inside were fat white mushrooms sitting on black earth.

'How about some of these? I can roast some roots from the ground and there's a fair bit of herbs from by the pond. They'll do, won't they?'

Pip was about to ask couldn't they just find the nearest Dan Shepard, but she knew that was silly. She was going to have to forget how things were. Goodbye, Shepard's Delight.

She woke up suddenly, her heart thumping. Light from the fire was dancing on the roof of the cave. Outside it was still the same grey-blue, only a bit darker. And it was colder too. She lay there, staring at the fire. A stick had fallen and caused the flames to flare. There was strong crackling. Soon it calmed down and the yellow disappeared into the dull red. Pip wriggled under the blanket Adey had given her after they'd had supper. The ground was hard, despite the roll mat he'd spread for her. She saw, lying on the other side of the fire, the shape of Adey, under his blanket. She closed her eyes and breathed deeply.

She'd been running, in her dream, searching, looking. In this room. In that room. Over the balcony. All the time, the banging, shouting, screaming. Gunshots. A woman's voice crying out, her mother's voice. 'Where is he, Pip? I told you to look after him.' And a man shouting, a long way off, her father, telling them to hurry up. 'For godsake, be quick. There's no time.' And Mum screaming. 'Find him. Oh please, Evelyn, please.' They couldn't go without him. They had to find him, she had to. But they couldn't. Then they had to go.

Awake now, her dream slipped away into the darkness, forgotten. Pip lay there listening for a long time, inside her head and outside. But there was nothing to hear, just the fire. After a while, there was more light and she heard Adey get up. He moved around the cave, trying to be quiet. Soon she could smell something. Her tummy rumbled. She sat up and rubbed her eyes.

'Hey, Pip. You okay?'

'Yes. Why not?'

He was stirring something in a pot over the coals.

'Did you have a bad dream?'

'Um. I don't know.'

'You were shouting. Sounded like you were calling for someone.'

'I was? They said there could be dreams.' Pip ran her fingers through her hair. 'Is there a mirror?'

Adey stood up, holding two bowls in his hand. He was as untidy as he had been the day before. Pip knew there would be no mirror.

'Have some of this,' he said, handing her a plastic bowl. It was chipped round the edge. 'We used to put honey in it,' he said. 'But there are no bees now. Spoon's over there.'

Pip found the spoon and scooped up some of the porridge. Normally she wouldn't even look at something like this, but she was really hungry. It didn't taste of much. But it was hot.

'Something went wrong, didn't it? With everything. Project's broken isn't it? Everyone's—' she hesitated to say the word. 'Where is everyone, Adey?'

Adey just took her empty bowl and spoon and put them in the bucket he'd used to wash his own bowl and the pot. He rubbed them vigorously and laid everything to dry on a wooden frame.

'It's all broken, isn't it?'

'Let's go for a walk,' he said.

•

They went round the other side of the hill and stood looking over the edge of a cliff. Down below was the entrance to the birth lab and the pond nearby. Further away were the ruins of the caretakers' houses. Further still was what used to be a recreation area with shops and restaurants. Pip was telling Adey she went there for her sixth birthday. It was just ruins now. They both stared at the broken buildings.

'Where is your family, Adey? Are they okay?'

He looked at her. 'I don't know,' he said.

Then he lay down on the grass and Pip did the same. They stared at the sky. She hardly noticed the gloom now. She did notice something else though.

'There are no birds. It's so quiet.'

'I know. They've gone. Almost all the representative species that were brought on have gone. There are a few left. Those dogs. Some rats. Only things that adapted quickly. But even then—'

He picked a grass stalk and put it in his mouth and stared at the sky.

How dirty, Pip thought. He should have washed that.

'Once upon a time,' Adey said, still looking up. 'You could see New York from here.'

Pip stared at him. 'New York?'

'Not the real one. It was flooded. No, the one they built on Project, in the American sector. It wasn't supposed to be visible, but it was, during the heliostat down-cycle. That's what my grandfather said he was told. You could see it, a mass of bright lights up in the sky, above your head, lighting everything up.'

Pip stared up into the grey gloom, imagining lights on the opposite surface of Project.

'How exciting,' she said.

'Well. My family and some other caretaker families tried to stop them.'

'Why?'

'All that energy. And Shanghai and Nairobi and Mexico City. All of them, up there. And there.'

'They built those too?'

'Of course. Why not? Every continent wanted their cities. They weren't really cities, there wasn't room. But they built them anyway. Used up the reserves first. Then they used up farm space. Even out on the water.'

'But weren't we supposed to be journeying? Isn't that what the Project is all about?'

Adey turned his head. 'Was all about. You could see the lights of New York and London and Vladivostok. During the down-cycle, everywhere you looked there were stars. They said it was like the Milky Way.'

'Wow.' Pip nodded.

'Did you ever see the Milky Way, I mean from Earth? Did you ever go there?'

She looked at Adey. He was watching her intently.

'What was it like? On Earth? Was it wonderful?'

Pip closed her eyes.

'Were there lots of animals everywhere? And birds? And people, all talking in different languages and wearing colourful clothes? And lots of space, not like here, but real land and real water, flat for miles and miles. Was it hot in some places and cold in others, not all the same? What was it like?'

'We only went once,' Pip said quietly. 'Me, Mum and Dad, and Simon.'

'Who's Simon?'

'Simon. He is—was—my little brother.'

'Oh. I know.'

Pip stared at Adey. 'How do you know?'

'Well. His child's pod was behind yours. Except it was—' he seemed to realise something. 'It was empty, wasn't it?'

Pip nodded her head slowly. 'It was empty.'

'What happened?'

'We'd never been to Earth and time was running out. So we went back once, right at the end. Dad had some final meeting. But there was trouble. We had to go and we couldn't find Simon. He had some idea he wanted to go see Echo Point. Mum went on about the Three Sisters, rising high out of the water, where Dad had proposed to her. Simon had made Mum promise she'd take us. He must have hidden somewhere. But we had to go.'

'You didn't find him in time?'

Pip shook her head. The memory came back. Searching inside the apartment. Her and Mum screaming. Then being made to leave. The three of them, her and Mum and Dad, inside the shuttle. Someone else in Simon's seat. And everyone staring at their screens, the external camera still running, the shuttle lifting off the top of the evac building and the people fighting there, trying to hold on. Some clinging to the undercarriage. Ordinary people, not infected ones. But there was no room for them. And Simon was back there, somewhere.

She felt her cheeks wet. 'I should have stayed. I didn't stay. He was all on his own. He was just a little boy. And we left him.'

There was the faint sound of wind over the hill.

'That must have been terrible.'

Pip swallowed hard. 'You said the lights were like the Milky Way?'

'Yes, they were. It was beautiful. A whole spread of white lights over the sky, from one side to the other. But they wouldn't stop. The cities kept growing. The lights kept burning. It got warmer. The poles lost circulation. Cloud production dropped, then stopped altogether.'

They looked at each other. Pip's face a question.

'The heliostat couldn't handle the load in both cycles, day and night. The reactor safety trips went. Then lab power was cut.'

When Adey said that, Pip felt cold. She watched Adey, hardly listening, as he explained that the problem was there were too many people being woken up early. Some of the sleepers had paid programmers at the start. Their pod controls had overrides and could be opened before the Project had completed its journey. Then they'd bribed a couple of caretaker families to activate the first early births. Suddenly the caretakers weren't the only ones eating the food and using the energy. They were supposed to wait until a new planet had been found, just the caretakers looking after everything, father to son, mother to daughter, while everyone slept and the embryo banks stayed frozen. Instead, the energy circuits burned brighter. Heat production rose and oxygen levels slipped, the precious balance was shifted. But no-one seemed to mind. Most caretakers were glad not to have to work any more. They joined the others, the newly born, in the cities, where the lights burned all night and all day. And as the heliostat faded because of the power drain, the cities were the only places to be.

'Adey.' Pip felt her voice quiver. 'You said the lab

power was cut. It was deliberate? You shut down the birth labs? It wasn't an accident?'

'We had to. There wasn't room for everyone. And the power kept failing. We had no choice. One or two pods we kept going. They ran on consolidated reserves but the timing controls were blown. We couldn't know when they'd wake. Still, they stayed steady. But the others— well—you understand, don't you, Pip?'

She looked away.

'You had to choose?' she said.

It was Adey's turn to look away.

'Yes. We had to choose. We were the caretakers.'

Adey was still staring over the ruins and into the grey distance. Pip knew now why the steps had been placed against her pod. Adey had put them there. He must have been watching her, while she was asleep and waiting to be born.

'It's midday,' Adey said.

'Is it? How can you tell?'

Adey smiled. 'You'll learn.'

Pip said she didn't think so. Then she turned to him again. 'Adey. Don't you ever feel lonely?'

'Yes. I do. But I had a job to do.'

'Had? Your job is finished?'

'Almost.'

They lay there for a while.

'What is your job?' Pip said. But he'd already climbed to his feet.

They walked back to the cave after they'd spent several hours gathering bunches of herbs. It was getting darker. Pip thought about the cities and the bright light and people partying all the time, day and night. All the energy. All the heat. Dad would not approve. He would not approve of Adey either. Dirty boge.

After they'd eaten, Pip settled down on her mat while Adey banked the fire up. It wasn't really cold, but it felt good with the light.

'Is there anyone else alive?'

Adey kept on pushing embers.

'Tell me, Adey. Is there?'

'No. There isn't.'

'Nowhere? What about the other countries? Up there?'

'Dad and Nathaniel travelled to the American sector, when I was young. Everyone was very excited. They were sure they'd come back with good news. Perhaps they'd find places where the birth labs were untouched. Where there was power and water and good harvests.'

'And?'

'Dad came back. Alone. It was a desert over there, he said. He said people were so hungry they were eating each other. They kept away from them most of the time, but then they were surprised in an ambush. They escaped, but Nathaniel died later. Dad had to bury him and then travel back alone.'

'So there are people there? In America?'

'That was when I was small. About five years ago, people arrived from there, pulling wagons, with everything they had. They said the land was empty. A wasteland. And people came from other sectors, from Asia and Europe. Refugees. Starving. Not many, but they came here to Australia. The same stories. Many were exhausted or sick. A lot died.'

'But still, what happened to your family?'
'Well. You know about the lifeboat hall?'
Pip sat up under her blanket. 'Lifeboats?'
'Do you know about them?'
'Yes,' she said. 'But I've never see one.'
'Would you like to?'

The path through the forest was easy enough to follow, even in the half-light. Pip expected some sounds, any sounds. But there was nothing. Even the trees looked dead. There was more wood on the ground, dried, crackling, broken, than there was in the trees.

They stopped near the birth lab. Adey noticed something over by the pond. A low black shape.

'What is it?' asked Pip. She crept closer. 'Oh. I think it's the black dog. Poor thing.'

'Yes, it is. The yellow one's on her own now. She's the last one left.'

They looked at each other.

'C'mon,' Adey said. 'Let's go.'

They went on, reaching a concrete structure set into the earth.

'Here we are,' Adey said. 'Just as it should be.'

He lifted a cover built into the concrete. Underneath was a metal keypad and a row of lights. He tapped at the keys and stood back.

'Caretaker's secret,' he said, smiling.

Something moved in the ground. Then a door opened, more like a hatch. Cold air came out as it opened. Lights flicked on, down and down, deeper down into the ground.

'Come on,' he said, climbing in. 'Let's get the door

shut.'

Pip looked around. Everything was silent. For a moment, she thought she heard a long, lonely howl in the darkness. Perhaps it was only the wind. She stepped in and the hatch closed above her head.

Adey descended, one foot and one hand at a time, down the metal ladder, Pip following. It was colder and colder as they went.

They'd been dropping for several minutes when the ladder opened into a much bigger space.

'Look,' Adey said. 'Go on.'

Pip turned around in what was a long wide hall. Off each side were empty chambers. At the end, one chamber had something in it. They walked towards it.

As she walked, Pip stared at the floor. It was dark, as if there was nothing there. But there were points of light, like stars, except they weren't still. They moved all at the same time, starting at one side of the hall and disappearing at the other. It was beautiful, but the spinning effect was overwhelming. Pip felt dizzy and looked away.

'Do you know where you are?' Adey said.

'I know where I am. Dad told me about it. I never thought I'd see this. It is off limits, you know.'

She crouched down on the thick glass floor that was simply part of the outside skin of the Project. The spin-induced gravity was slightly stronger now they were further from the centre, but she felt like she was floating. Beneath her feet, on the other side of the layers of glass, there was nothing.

'What are we doing here, Adey?'

'At the end there, there's a lifeboat. The last one. Except it's no use.'

'I don't understand.'

'All of us, my family, my mother and father, Bethany, others. The refugees. Everyone. They all gathered here. The last lifeboat hall in the whole of Project that was still working. The others had been cannibalised by people looking for food, for weapons, for energy.'

'So your family left on a lifeboat. With the embryo banks intact?'

'They did leave on lifeboats. But the banks were broken. Like the labs. In the power wars.'

'Broken? Lifeboats without life?' Pip's hand went to her mouth. 'But,' she said, 'that was the whole point of the Project. To find a place to start again. Everyone waking up and the lifeboats descending into a new era, the start of a new world.'

There was silence.

'Where are they, Adey?'

'I can't say. There's a lot of space out there. Maybe they've found somewhere. Maybe not. A lot of space. And not much energy on board.'

'But why did you stay? You could have gone with them. Taken that last lifeboat.'

'I could have. I mean, back then. It's deteriorated too much now.'

'Why didn't you? Why did you stay?'

Adey turned to face Pip, starlight in his eyes. 'It was terrible at the end. Like your dream last night. Everyone wanted to leave, before the whole Project failed. They decided to travel together, for safety. Mum ordered me to come. I told Dad I wanted to stay at the birth lab. We knew you would wake sometime, the last one sleeping. We just didn't know when. So I hid.'

'You hid from your mother?'

'I had to.'

'Your Dad knew?'

'He knew. He wanted me to go with them, but I think he understood.'

Adey's face looked strange, changing in the moving light.

'You waited? When you could have gone?'

'I told you. I had a job to do. And—well—you would have been alone.'

Pip stared at Adey. He shrugged. She put a hand on his arm and moved closer. He put his arm around her shoulder and she leant against him. They stood together, on the edge of their world, with the stars spinning under their feet, and looked out at the emptiness.

Mark Rossiter is a Sydney-based writer, doctoral student and lecturer. He can be found at www.xmarkr.com

Messiah on the Rock

Jason Nahrung

Our OGRE hurtled out of the planetoid's night side, set on an approach vector for the secondary airlock of New Jerusalem's biodome. As tall as a skyscraper, the blister nestled against the outer rim of an impact crater. Ice lakes and frosted peaks of rock slid beneath our bow; frozen plumes made strange sculptures where they erupted from cracks in the thin tundra. There was barely any atmo to disturb our terrain-hugging trajectory, but the storm of flak that rose to greet us as we cleared the horizon gave the flight crew all the challenge they needed.

'For a colony gripped by Schism, they're doing a good job of not being distracted,' Selina said, her tone so stonily cynical I could've sharpened my melee blades on it.

Schism is what the Church of Universal Truth called what was happening on Salem. The media called it sectarian violence. For me, crouched in the nose next to Selina while Jacob and his co-pilot traded curses with each and every near miss, it was quickly becoming a clusterfuck.

The Combined Corporations Overwatch Committee hadn't sent us here as peacekeepers. Until a fortnight ago, no-one had given a damn about this rock. But then the Committee had intercepted a squawk from Salem and someone's ears had pricked up. Mention of eternal life will have that effect. The Templars could beat up their Kneeler brethren as much as they liked; we were here for a snatch and grab. But, of course, it was never going to be that simple.

Flak and countermeasures turned the forward view to fireworks and interference. The co-pilot, a new fella, worked his heads-up like a manic conductor.

'This is definitely more than anti-asteroid defence,' Jacob said through gritted teeth. 'Someone doesn't want visitors.'

Selina watched the conflag in front of us with a steady, calculating eye. A cross hung from the open neck of her battlesuit. Times like this, I envied her her faith. I wished I could believe there was something better after the flame and fury of violent death on a shithole few had heard of.

'I hope this Messiah thing is worth it,' she said, then gave a short laugh when I answered, 'First time for everything.'

The OGRE shivered. Objects rattled behind sealed compartments. The crew swore.

'Buckle up,' Jacob shouted.

I reached to seal Selina's battle suit.

'I trust you're gonna show as much care taking it off when we get back to the carrier—Sergeant,' she said, shooting me that smile. Three years and a shitload of flak couldn't diminish the impact of that grin. Madness, taking a squad mate as a bunkmate, but even a jaded cyberdog like me had to believe in something.

'Count on it—Corporal,' I promised.

'Strap in, love birds,' Jacob shouted again, his hands

battling the controls. 'Fucking Kneelers just took out a stabiliser. It's crash or crash through, my friends.'

We retreated to the squad bay where the rest of the team waited. I sealed my helmet and checked the O_2. Battle comp beamed data against my cortex, showing our formation was down to three assault ships.

A massive thump shook the OGRE. It felt as if we'd hit a wall. My guts tried to squeeze out my mouth as the harness prevented me from being flung against the bulkhead. Selina brought her cross up to her mask and mimed kissing it, shot me a wink. An IM landed in my inbox: *Nxt time I orgnise date nite. xox*

I shook my head at her—private messaging during a mission was an inappropriate use of bandwidth, one of the discipline breakdowns that kept married couples from serving in the same unit. Fortunately, she didn't mind living in sin.

But I got u firewks! I messaged, then told the squad, 'We've been given clearance to crash land—assume the position.'

Anxious faces stared out from their helmets, but they returned a series of thumbs up. Status updates on my cortex showed they were locked and loaded.

I mumbled our unit mantra, the closest thing to a prayer I had: Melior morior bellator, quam ago profugas. *Better to die on your feet than live on your knees.*

My squad's mission was to help secure the secondary airlock, which serviced the water reclamation plants spread like cysts across the tundra, and strike across the city to join the hunt for the Messiah, believed to be housed in the Templar HQ. We'd been given hacked codes and, failing that, carried enough laser and explosives to crack the dome if needed.

A klaxon added to the screaming panic on the battle comp's readout, announcing we'd gone to Plan B.

We smacked the dome going at almost one quarter speed.

A mountain fell on us.

The cortex showed I'd been out for a few minutes while it pumped me with all the chemical I needed to haul my sorry, cybernetically enhanced carcass out of the wreckage. I flopped on the ground, waiting for the stims and the anaesthetics to do their job. The dome was lit by strobing red lights; a cacophony of alarms filled my helmet.

Replay showed Jacob breaching the dome with rockets before we bulldozed through. The OGRE had ploughed a furrow of destruction through a couple of blocks of New Jerusalem's outer suburbs. He'd saved us from being bug guts on the dome, but the OGRE had been reduced to a shapeless piece of ruined, burning metal. The cockpit had taken the worst of it. I'd liked Jacob; crap at cards but a gracious loser.

Overhead, another drone anti-graved towards the hole we'd made to add a sheet of photosteel to the patch. A wind I'd only just become aware of, died as the sheet was anchored into place and sealant sprayed over the repairs.

A flash image hit me, terrifying, paralysing: me, caught in the whirlwind, flying through that gap in the dome with enough velocity to escape Salem's pissant gravity and spin off into space.

Get a grip, I thought, shaking the vision away as the

dome's klaxons barped to sound the all-clear, then fell silent. The red light infusing the dome turned to amber, then gradually faded to mustard-coloured daylight.

I shut down the alarms piercing my cranium: the OGRE was dead, I was alive. Bleeping about the details wasn't helping anyone. The crackle of flames emerged from the sudden quiet. Readouts scrolled past my eyes. Interference made the data flicker.

OGRE 2 was down safe and holding the airlock— they'd encountered zero resistance. OGRE 3 was unaccounted for, presumed destroyed along with the rest.

I pinged my squad. Found Selina, stats optimal. Henricks, Pax, Goldy: all green. Two more were injured past usefulness; they'd have to sit this one out. Everyone else was in the black.

'About time you came 'round, Sarge,' Selina said, voice crackling over comms. 'Or were you just waiting for us to finish the heavy lifting?'

It's good to have a second you can trust to get the job done while you're snoozing.

'Sit rep, Corporal?'

'What you see is what you've got. OGRE 2 is sending an evac for our wounded but, I quote, "has no bodies to spare",' she reported. 'Our OGRE's fucked, obviously, but we've got full kit. So I guess it's up to us.'

'Well there's something new,' I said dryly, and was rewarded with grim smiles.

The dome had resealed, but getting the atmo back up to standard would take days. Helmets on, then; our O_2 should go the distance, as long as we were quick.

At least we had the place to ourselves—no nasties

in pingable range. Gave me time to double-check the wounded and our supplies, and reassure myself that the squad was more interested in getting even than going home.

'Attack is the last thing they'll expect,' Goldy said, the adorably sarcastic bitch. She gave Pax's shoulder a reassuring squeeze as we hoisted our packs. He hated being outnumbered, always got the jitters till the action started.

'Into the valley of death rode the five,' Henricks mock recited.

It was noon when we moved out, which meant we had only about two hours of insipid daylight left. The photosteel would be working overtime to suck energy out of the distant sun's feeble rays. Our thermostats compensated for the chill, keeping us peachy as we loped through the low-g. We had a way to go—Templar HQ was on the other side of the city, carved out of the side of the Dead Sea crater we'd seen from the air.

Salem town was an orderly place, streets radiating from a central cathedral. The building was the tallest on the planetoid, dwarfing the prefab bungalows and dorms, the messy clumps of essential industrial complexes: oxygen extractors, water pumps, heat converters, ferrous and carbonate processing plants, greenhouses. All the stuff that made survival on New Jerusalem tenable, all symbolically centred around the power of Mother Church.

The rock had been approved for a final population of almost 200,000, but current residents were less than a tenth of that. The Kneeler settlers expected to be able to subsist using the low grade minerals and abundance of both ice water and, under the crust, liquid water, to fund their mission. Where Kneelers went, the Templars followed, to make sure the Church's interests were protected not only from the other corps but outbreaks of Schism: the Church had little tolerance for sudden outpourings of economic rationalism or theological divergence, especially once a colony had struck it rich.

Just what had happened here on New Jersualem was unknown. The planetoid had been silent since the Messiah squawk, and we'd intercepted only one transmission during our flight from Earth: a call for evac from the temple, which meant serious shit must've gone down.

That certainly appeared to be the case. Not even the effect of our explosive decompression could mask the battle damage. The buildings were featureless, prefab DIY structures imported on freighters and bolted together. The better ones supported atmo seals and inbuilt air and water recycling. The lesser ones were what you might call homes for the faithful: faith that if the dome blew out, they'd have air enough to reach a shelter. The Church was one of the wealthiest corporations to emerge from WWIII but it still, apparently, let the flock support itself according to stockmarket principles. Salem's strife had tested lesser and better alike. Some buildings sat pockmarked by ballistics, others had been blown into rubble, yet others showed damage from rams and lasers that indicated forced entry. A makeshift barricade of machinery lay torn open and blackened. Templar battlewagons were fearsome beasts, armoured and armed with the heaviest weaponry that the chassis could support. From what we could tell, the Kneelers had had only anti-personnel weapons and even these had been mostly improvised.

Long-range communications inside the dome became thinner and more fractured as we advanced, the interference picking up. Someone must've realised the perimeter had been breached. So where was the welcome committee? What were they waiting for?

Bodies started to appear as we advanced along both sides of the horribly exposed avenue leading towards the cathedral's blackened spire.

Selina scanned a house with a corpse sprawled in the doorway.

'Running for cover, I figure.' She indicated with two fingers towards the shoulder blades. 'Shot in the back. Another inside, laser sliced, and a third, headshot, self-inflicted.'

'Didn't trust Templar mercy, huh?'

'Apparently not.'

'What is this Messiah thing anyway?' Pax asked, his voice sounding jittery. 'You get the gen, Sarge?'

'Best we know is that it's some kind of biologic. We have to keep it out of UV. That's all I can tell you.'

'Must be pretty hot if they're so happy to kill each other for it,' Henricks offered, and Goldy snorted, saying, 'It'll be worth something, all right. We wouldn't be here if it wasn't.'

I rolled a corpse that lay huddled around the slim box of a streetside beacon and emergency mask station. The mutilated body looked desiccated, as though it had been exposed to a desert—a hot one, not New Jerusalem's deep freeze.

'New rock, same old shit,' Selina said. 'Kneelers, Meccanites, Mercantilists, all the big seven: all "killing in the name of . . . ”.'

Selina had been a Hospitaller before she'd got the shits and crewed up with us secular types. She'd given up her allegiance, not her faith.

'No,' I said, feeling the hackles rising as the others crowded around the corpse. 'This is a brand new kind of shit.'

'This Messiah thing do that, Sarge?' Pax asked. 'I haven't seen nothing like this before.'

'Dunno,' I said. 'But cortex says there's nothing in the air we need to worry about.'

'I heard it was eternal life,' Goldy said. She toed the body. 'This doesn't look much like eternal life to me.'

'Is that right, Sarge?' Pax asked.

'So the grapevine has it.' I coughed. 'And not in the biblical way.' As missions went, this one ranked right up there on the bullshit scale. Most likely micro-organisms, we were told. Origin: probably extraterrestrial. Possibly contagious. Susceptible to UV. Value: eight squads of troopers, on the off-chance the rumour about immortality was even half accurate.

Longevity was still the holy grail. We could span galaxies, blow shit up from orbit, make new worlds and destroy them even more easily. But we still couldn't unlock mortality's secrets. Extend it, sure. Average lifespan was about 240 and creeping out every day, but still, with an entire universe at our fingertips, 240 seemed manifestly inadequate. Unfair even. The more you have, the more you want: it's the human condition.

I was a soldier. Retirement was as much afterlife as I could imagine; just getting back to my cot with my body intact and Selina to share time with was all I dared hope for. Faced with the enormity of the universe, I had no expectation of life after death. Space was cold, uncaring and way too big; way too big for even God, perhaps. Selina said the reason the Kneelers had originally opposed the push off-planet was because they were afraid we wouldn't find God. I reckoned it was because they were afraid we would.

But with Earth an overheated pile of formerly contested markets and the big seven post-war megacorps, religious and secular, carving up the galaxy, the Kneelers had embraced the concept of space exploration. Now as many religious outposts as economic ones were flagging humanity's viral spread across the void, though some might argue the difference was one of rhetoric. God and gold always travelled hand in hand.

The fact was, we were soldiers and we had come here to grab the Messiah, whatever it was. A lot of our mates had died without even touching the frozen ground of this rock.

We pushed on towards the city centre, the five of us growing increasingly quiet. The cortex showed I wasn't the only one experiencing elevated levels of nervousness in the eerie, silent streets. The medic scanners registered zero bacterials and chemicals, but that was little comfort. Salem felt like a tomb, like a plague house.

The town square looked like the aftermath of a riot, littered with the remnants of destruction: loose masonry, burnt vehicles, still bodies. The gutted cathedral's skeletal frame hunched over the scene like a dead insect, burnt down to an array of buttresses and vacant windows, and that accusing finger of spire, a marker for its grave.

'Bones,' Selina said. She stood at what would once

have been the cathedral's main doors. 'Lots of bones.'

I leapt over to her side, ash puffing up under my boots.

'Last stand?'

'Looks that way. Rather burn than . . . whatever.'

The sun was a faint disc low on the dome's artificial sky, tinting the air with the colour of jaundice. The cathedral's shadow stretched across the square towards the Avenue of Faith, a wide, straight thoroughfare arrowing all the way to the cliff at the city's perimeter.

'Fuck me, but that doesn't look pretty,' Henricks said.

Even from here, we could see the twin spires of the Templar temple glowing a rusty ochre on the horizon where the dome intersected the rock face. I upped my visual magnification and overlaid the view with schematics. The two towers guarded a massive set of solid gates, with lower walls stretching away on either side. The bulk of the building projected out from the cliff, but it was easy enough to see how a portion could penetrate the very rock itself. The cliff was actually the outer slope of the Dead Sea crater's rim, and geological scans showed that it was riddled with fissures. Unfortunately, the scans had revealed no back door for the likes of us.

'I take it we considered landing on the rim and coming in from above,' Selina asked.

'More weaponry up there than you could fit in a battle cruiser,' Pax said.

She hmphed.

'As if there wasn't enough outside the airlocks,' Henricks added.

'I don't even want to think what they've got guarding

that lot,' Goldy said.

Pax hefted his MLG, the heavy weapon looking insignificant against the bulk of the fortress. 'I knew I shoulda brought my tac nuke.'

We had a handful of HEAP mines and remote charges between us. Some ballistics, Pax's medium tripod-mounted laser cannon. HE and EMP grenades. Shockers. Melee blades. It was hardly the arsenal to storm a well-defended castle.

'Well, let's take a look,' I said. The torched cathedral was an ominous presence behind us as we advanced in cautious dashes down the avenue.

Twilight, as heavy and dark as despair, cloaked the city by the time we reached the temple. It loomed above us, impregnable and unknowable.

'Anyone hear from OGRE 2?' I asked, clutching at the faintest of straws.

Pax shook his head. 'Communications are pretty much fried here. Temple's putting out more noise than a supernova.'

'They've got a good killing zone, too,' Selena said.

True enough. A plaza of smooth stone radiated out from the temple, broken only by pillars that bore the effigies of various saints. Some might call them shrines; we called them anti ramming barricades, designed to prevent a vehicle from approaching the main gates at speed.

'But yet, we've got this far.' I shook aside the mystery of the enemy's tactics. Maybe they'd allowed us to progress this far, knowing full well we'd get no farther. Saving their energy. 'Side entrances?' I scrolled through jumpy schematics and sonar images.

'Nada,' Selena replied. 'Just that one-man door beside the big'uns.'

'Let's try it,' I said. 'Ragged formation.'

'We won't get ten yards,' Pax whined, but he was already set up to provide covering fire.

I shot him a glare anyway. 'Smoke and sonics, full band dispersion, throw in whatever doppelgangers you've got. Fire only when you get a clear target—ammo could become an issue. On my mark.'

We launched our countermeasures, filling the killing zone with dense fog and what we hoped was enough chaff to confuse any tracking radars or multi spectrum visual detectors. We ran like rabbits, jinking in great leaps in the low grav, sheltering behind the saints. One, Brigid I think, had bloody handprints over her tits. No way to know whether the owner had been desperate for help or just horny.

Not a pop, not a crackle, met our advance.

We cowered in the massive archway, overshadowed by the impressive gates bearing the order's cross-and-swords emblem.

'Maybe we should just quit now while we're ahead,' Henricks said, oh so dour, and Pax, bringing up the rear, nodded.

'I'm all for eternal life, Sarge, but I'm not too keen on dying for it.'

'Then you'd better keep your mouth shut and shoot straight, hadn't you?' I told him. 'We're doing the job we came here for. Let's blow the personnel door and get on with it.'

Henricks grinned. 'That was my next suggestion.' The little pyro loved making things go bang.

He reached out to set his first charge and the door retracted into the frame. My cortex registered a gust of fresh air: chill, breathable, almost Earth normal. It shouldn't have surprised that the temple would have environmentals independent of the dome.

'Eyes open,' I said, and led the way in. And against all expectations, survived.

The door slid shut. Our eyes quickly adjusted to the dimness of amber emergency lighting.

'Helmets?' Selina said.

We'd been running on internal air, not trusting the depleted atmo inside the dome to supply our needs; in truth, not trusting the detectors that said no microscopic nasties lurked in the abandoned streets of Salem.

'I'm still in the green. Count them off?'

They all reported green, nudging yellow. Enough to get back to OGRE 2. Just.

'Let's save our O_2,' I decided.

'It leaves us vulnerable,' Goldy pointed out, not being a smart arse, just pragmatic. 'If they shut off the supply or try gas.'

'Keep'em slung, nice and handy,' I ordered.

'Pain in the arse,' Pax grumbled.

'Better than blowfishing,' Selina told him.

'You can leave the MLG,' I said, offering some consolation. 'It won't be much use indoors.'

We shut down our oxygen systems and removed the helmets, rubbed at the indents in our cheeks and our sweaty hair as Pax made a pile of the bulky laser and disarmed it.

The entrance foyer, smooth-panelled and high-ceilinged, had anonymous doors in each wall. The armoured reception desk was unmanned.

'What the hell are they waiting for?' Pax muttered.

'Wits about you,' I snapped.

'No shit,' Selina said.

'How many hostiles are we expecting again?' Henricks asked.

'Fifty-odd. Manifest says twenty combatants and the rest ancillaries, but you hardly need to be a marksman to cause damage down here.'

'Fish in a fucking barrel,' he mumbled.

'Don't clump up. Tail ender—keep your eyes open.'

'Not even game to blink, Sarge,' Goldy replied.

We took the centre door and moved off down the corridor. Barracks, storerooms, training rooms, dining areas: all empty. There were signs of interrupted activity: bunks unmade, meals uneaten, lockers open and disorderly. Intel suggested the Messiah was in a place called the Sepulchre and that it was down deep. Schematics from the original building plans, unlikely to be entirely reliable, confirmed the dodgy sonar soundings indicating we were moving fairly straight and ever farther into the cliff.

We reached a stairway circling down, its unsealed steps and walls lit by bare lamps. Our shadows preceded us as we descended, creeping and cautious, torches and battle radars strobing out.

'Where the fuck is everyone?' Selina said. I didn't need to read her biometrics to recognise the strain in her voice.

Our breaths and footsteps echoed as we made our way down, finally emerging into a narrow, rough corridor. The walls shone with damp. Water dripped, sounding loud and regular in my sonics like a heartbeat, making me think of dripping blood, and I realised the air had become colder and staler. I considered ordering helmets on to keep our bios at optimum.

Interference rendered sonar to snow and I turned off battle guidance. I lifted visuals and tried to boost comms to cut through the static.

The Templars hadn't had time to finish this area, the walls still raw rock, the ceiling dipping low in places. The path seemed to follow a natural fissure, narrowing and widening at nature's whim.

Selena pointed to a jumbled trail of boot prints in the muddy ground. 'Traffic.'

'Could be showtime,' I whispered, and we crouched even lower, hugging the uneven walls.

My finger ached from holding its place on the trigger. With the battle display turned off, the cortex could show only the biosigns of our increasing anxiety as we waited for the trap to spring.

Silence, then, except for breathing. Sweat and fear filled the chamber. The cold damp rose like clinging ghosts; gravel crunched under our boots as we dodged frost-rimmed puddles on the dirt floor.

An opening ahead glowed with dull amber light.

We gathered at the entrance, struck numb by the sight, our breath fogging in the chill air.

Lights hung from spikes in the ceiling glared down on a rough, earthen chamber the size of a standard shuttle. The walls were slick, stained like blood and bruises with mineralised water, and torn in a half-dozen places by jagged crevices.

In the centre of the chamber, three men hung crucified.

Their arms and legs were clamped to steel crosses; their naked bodies were waxen, eyes dark pits of shadow, their mouths open and black.

'What the fuck?' Henricks whispered.

'What is it?' Goldy asked from the rear, then flicked her vision to someone else's relay, and swore.

'Jesus Christ,' Selina whispered, pointing past the crucified men.

And then I saw what had to be the Messiah. Bio scanners went apeshit with what-the-fuck though at least the crap wasn't showing up as airborne. The growth was etched in an uncertain but perceptible silhouette on the far wall, a faint greenish glow adding to its charm. One hand up, the other by its side, and a bulge around the vague head shape that could've been a crown. An unfortunate rock shadow at midriff level lent a suggestion of masturbation, but before I could make any cracks about the second coming, the shit hit the fan. I'm sure the Kneelers would've called it divine intervention.

Movement inside the crevices—I shouted, 'Contact.' Behind us, Goldy fired, back down the tunnel we'd entered by. Black shapes, like rushing wings, swarmed towards us. Pax fell in a heap, his bio flaring red in my cortex. The lights went out, plunging us into total night, and we were running on infra and shit-awful sonar, relying on muzzle flash to illuminate the scene, the gunfire deafening. They were so fucking quick, so fucking tough. We were overwhelmed, borne under by the strongest motherfuckers. Cyborgs maybe, or total android models. No-one had mentioned androids. Automated diggers, yes, but not androids. The Kneelers didn't trust them, Templars neither. Too close to human, not enough soul, some bullshit. None of which amounted to shit when they're dragging you down into the dark.

My cortex brought me around three minutes after I'd fallen unconscious—twice in one day, a new record—and about a week too soon if the jungle drums pounding inside my skull were any indication. My face felt like someone had danced on it with combat boots, but the cortex was doing its best, playing that balancing act with stim and painkiller to get me functional. The display showed I was in okay shape; the armour and my enhanced physicals had withstood the pummelling that had turned out my lights.

Through the fog of receding concussion, the room slowly came into focus. Selina was conscious beside me, looking groggy but furious, her face streaked with blood already clotted and turning to black in the amber glow. Templars held us tightly by the arms, their grips like vices through my suit.

'Awake, just in time to bear witness.'

The speaker emerged from the haze. I looked past his cowled figure to where the other three of my team were surrounded by a bevy of robed figures. Pale, pointed fingers stripped their breastplates, collars and sleeves. Our gear lay in a discarded pile, a midden of weaponry and explosives rendered irrelevant in the greater interest of our captors. Not a good sign, especially given the fact that they could've gunned us down rather than risk injury and death to capture us.

The Jesus shape on the back wall still glowed its wan gangrene. The crosses were bare, now, and horizontal. They had hinges at the base to allow the maximum flexibility between symbolism and practicality. A pair of feet protruded from a crevice to the side and visual enhancements lifted the impression of many more bodies stacked in there.

The hooded ringmaster stepped up to fill my vision. Face recog pulled up his file from my database: a Templar scientist, head of mission. The kind of guy who says seven days in god-time adds up to four and a bit billion years of Earth evolution. Not the kind of arithmetic you want to trust in the void.

He was running hot, fairly blazing, burning through calories like a black hole swallows matter, and he was pulsing like his own little nova, giving off weird energy signatures that made my trigger finger tighten despite the absence of a weapon.

My squad's biosigns were best described as being in the *oh fuck* range; mine spiked right up there with them as the Templar dropped his cowl and studied me like a surgeon trying to decide where to cut first. A surgeon, or a butcher.

He was an ugly son of a bitch. His flesh was pale, the kind of pale you get from living on a planet with only four hours of sunlight a day and no atmo to keep the rads out anyway—here on Salem, the sun, such as it was, might be bright enough to provide energy but it was not your friend. Bloodshot eyes, the whites tinted with the greenish hue of rancid meat, stared out from a gaunt mask of malnutrition, his skull beaming through from under that thin veil of tight, tight flesh. I could see the shape of his teeth under his lips.

'Tell me, Sergeant.' There was a halting dryness to his voice, as though he was desperately parched. 'Will your cortex allow you to call your carrier for evac, or is that something best done from a landing craft?'

I didn't give him so much as name, rank or serial number.

Goldy cursed and struggled as they clamped her to a cross and inserted tubes. Bleeding her.

'What the fuck are you bastards doing?' I shouted.

The chief crazy waved an arm around as though giving a guided tour of the pearly gates and not just some leaking hole in the ground. 'Creating heaven on earth, though Earth is a longer term project.'

Now that was scary. It sounded as if he was planning some kind of biological attack, a germ crusade; as if the big blue bitch hadn't suffered enough of our screwing around already.

'We were wrong when we named this place.' He stared into me, at some space behind my eyes. It was damned unnerving; he was projecting a sense of calm introspection while one of my squad mates was squirming and swearing and getting bled like some kind of experiment. 'This is not New Jersusalem. It's Golgotha.'

'What are you up to, Rasputin? A bit late for Easter, aren't you?'

He turned to face the Messiah and realisation dawned: this guy was fancying himself as the caretaker of a new Lourdes, the latest in a long line of delusionals who found miracles in the coincidental.

'We found Him here, inside this fissure, waiting to be reborn. We drank of His blood and ate of His flesh, and gave Him form. He moves through us. We are the angels of retribution. Of salvation.' He turned back to me and his gaze was fixed hard like a laser on my eyes. 'Didn't you hear the trumpet sound, Sergeant?'

'We had the apocalypse, Rasputin. It was called World War Three. Maybe you don't remember it, but it's the reason we're all here.'

'We're here because He called us. You're here to become a part of something so much greater.'

Henricks and Pax were lifted up on either side of Goldy, tubes attached, crimson running.

The rest of the Templars gathered around their boss, a mob as thick and black as a cave full of bats, as my mates' blood dribbled into steel canisters. Pax was unconscious still, but Henricks fought the bonds. They were as tough as hull metal; he wasn't going anywhere. It didn't look as if any of us were.

Rasputin reached out to finger Selina's cross. 'A woman of faith? With this band of non-believers?'

'It takes all kinds,' she said.

'Leave her alone,' I snarled. The grip on my arms tightened.

He turned back to me, ran a finger over my shoulder patch. 'The nineteenth. I've heard of you: *Melior morior bellator, quam ago profugas.*' He pronounced our motto as though he was tasting it; his lips twisted with the hint of sourness.

It doesn't make us that popular with the Kneelers at the best of times.

'Dying on your feet is an option,' Rasputin mused, then turned again to Selina. 'But your corporal, here, your compatriot—her faith will be tested. She will be offered conversion.'

'I gave at the office.' Selina was fully alert now, her

cortex getting her fired up with the chemicals of the truly pissed off.

'Imagine it, Corporal. No ageing. No sickness.'

'It's not doing such a good job on you, mate,' I spat, hoping to drag his attention back to me. 'So what'd you do? Inject some holy space rock into your veins? See who could glow in the dark the best?'

'Do not mock the Holy Spirit!'

'Is that what happened upstairs, then? The flock didn't like being the body of Christ, huh?'

'Their lives serve a higher purpose. As will yours.'

'You might want to filter that gunk you're pulling out of my crew. It's not standard, you know.' Though I hoped they all choked to death on it.

'You have no idea . . . It's not the liquid per se. It carries little of value. But it is a conduit, Sergeant. The pathway to the soul. We are carrying their souls inside us, removing them from pain in this mortal realm.'

'Not exactly everyone's idea of life everlasting. So what happens when you're out of congregation, Rasputin? I've seen the damage reports. I know you're marooned here.'

'A final, futile act by the unbelievers. I've already sent for reinforcements . . . '

'But they're likely to be weeks away, and you're hungry—starving—to spread the good word. Door-knocking your way all the way back to Earth, huh?'

'And now I have you. And your carrier. The Lord has answered our prayers.'

He was quick, Rasputin. Real quick. I was still trying to think up an argument as to why my cyberdogs weren't fit food for his pack of soulstealers when he snatched

Selina's cross from her chest. The chain snapped with a snick, the sound of a blade extending. Of a guillotine falling.

'Let us see if you are worthy to wear His sign,' Rasputin rasped, and slashed his nails across her cheek, drawing three deep lines of red. And then he licked her. Even managed to avoid the kick she aimed at him. The look of avarice on his face as his tongue cleaned his lips was puke-worthy. His spit was the colour of mint. I wanted to tear off his head and shit down his neck, but I'd have to race Selina for the privilege. I was amazed her glare didn't incinerate him where he stood.

She gave a short, sharp cry.

'What is it?' I asked her. 'What's wrong?'

'It . . . it's burning. Like worms, eating into me. Cortex is fritzing.'

I swore at Rasputin. 'What the fuck have you done to her?'

'Offered her salvation. You should be thanking me. She has the option of living forever as one of the chosen.'

'With you? Down here in the dark?'

'It is only in the dark that we can see the light. Giving up the sun is a small price to pay for life everlasting.' He turned from me to where Selina stood, her jaw locked, muscles twitching. 'Put her in the crypt,' Rasputin ordered his cronies. 'She can consider the fate of her immortal soul while the Holy Spirit tests her worthiness. Pray hard, my child. Eternal life is yours, if you are ready to admit our Lord as your Saviour.'

The goons dragged Selina towards a wider crevice at the far end of the chamber. Drool reflected like blood in the corner of their mouths. My guards were breathing hard, rank breath wafting across my nape. Selina sagged, dragging her feet. It was just a little spittle—what the fuck had Rasputin done to her? Biometrics answered: she was going down, but slower than she was acting. A deadly possum, my Selina.

'What does your science tell you about what is happening to her?' Rasputin asked, savouring his moment. 'Heartbeat, temperature, skin valency? Tell me, Sergeant, how do you measure the divine?'

'With my dick.'

I leaned back, using my guards' solid hold as leverage to get my feet up and give Rasputin both heels to the sternum. He flew backwards, crashing into Goldy's cross. The collection container overturned, spilling blood across the dirt.

The men holding me let go, the better to thrash me. I popped melee blades from my armoured forearms and sliced and diced till the Templars were more worried about bleeding than hurting me. Rasputin was up but he was hampered: his pack of true believers had fallen in a Pavlovian frenzy on the spilled blood. They'd ripped the lids off the others, too, not even waiting for filtration.

I dived, glad of the low gravity that let me fly long and grab one of our discarded packs. Now it came down to luck . . .

Rasputin forged towards me. Selina had quit the possum act and immobilised her surprised captors. Biometrics showed it was just her and me. The Templars had bled my squad dry.

'There's no escape for you here or up there,' Rasputin growled as he flung one of his minions aside. The two

I'd cut were already looking peachy, their faces marked only by scars where moments ago the flesh had been open to the bone. Not much blood, though. 'It's night time for hours yet, Sergeant. You have nowhere to run. I've already sent a team to bring in your comrades. With their assault craft under my control, I can gain access to your carrier. And then—then, the crusade begins.' He held up his palm to show me the blood smeared there. Selina's, or more likely, a brush with one of his messy little drinkers. 'The universe—all red, Sergeant, that's my dream. It's the will of the Almighty.'

'Well, this is a good start, Rasputin.'

I messaged Selina to duck and cover as I hauled out a HEAP, stuck it in the floor pointing towards the Templar feeding frenzy, and let it rip.

It was one hell of a blast. Henricks would've loved it. The concussion—like riding inside a thunderclap—thumped the breath from my lungs. Red lights flickered across my bioscan, then settled into an annoyed shade of amber. The lights failed, soil and rock and slush collapsed down from the roof, the tumble of rocks and patter of falling dirt lasting long after the shock wave had subsided. Aural dampers protested but the cortex reported negligible hearing loss. Weirdly, there were no screams. Light from the outside hallway showed a fog of dust; the Messiah sigil glowed softly like a neon sign through rain. The nearest crucifix had fallen, the middle one sagged at a weird angle, a ship's mast in the aftermath of a storm.

A Templar crouched only metres away, hands clapped to his ears. Whatever the Messiah had done to them, it must've shorted out their implants, because they appeared to have taken the full sensory shit storm, those who weren't blown to hell.

Another lay flopping nearby, limbs missing, mouth opening and closing like a fish.

I dug around for a ballistic and blew both their heads off, the shots sounding dim and distant in the aftermath of the explosive roar.

Selina emptied a clip into the gloom, short bursts targeting anything that moved. Then we took what we could find and ran. I left two more HEAPs on auto-detect in our wake as we staggered through the tunnels, heading for the surface. The first went off surprisingly soon after I'd planted it, but the second came a more reassuring length of time after. They might not be so eager to charge after us.

Stepping out into the New Jerusalem evening was a blessed relief. To stand straight, to be able to see all the way across the plaza . . . I don't think I'd ever loved space as much as I did at that moment.

We'd just sealed our helmets when Selina doubled over, clutching her guts.

'What is it?' I asked, my hand on her back, attention torn between her and the temple.

'Implants . . . they're shutting down. Actually starting to pop. Fucking thing's tearing me apart, Sarge.'

'Can you make it till dawn?'

'I dunno. Maybe. Cortex is fighting it, but losing. I'm all out of the good stuff—couldn't even cure a toothache.'

I gave her what I could, then pooled our equipment into one pack and shouldered it. 'We need to hole up till sun-up. I get the feeling the mad monks don't like the rads.' Or maybe this mob just preferred to do their dirty snacking under the cover of darkness . . . 'Fuck. New plan.'

'What's wrong?'

I could hear the pain in her voice. I hoped the HEAP had ripped Rasputin's guts out. I hoped he'd died in agony.

'OGRE 2. Rasputin said he'd sent a team after them. If he's got them, they could be dead or infected. The Templars might not have the codes to commandeer the OGRE, but they could trigger the distress beacon. A transport could be on its way right now.'

She checked her ammo counter, winced, and said, 'I'm good to go.'

'You sure?' Her biosigns looked like a seismic event.

'Do I have a choice?'

'The primary airlock isn't far. Let's get outside. More chance of seeing them coming out there. Besides, I want to blow the dome. See how their Messiah handles vacuum.'

'If it came through space, in an astroid or whatever, then it probably won't mind it too much.'

'But it's in a biological, now. We can snuff the lot of them, quarantine the rock, or better still, blow it into fragments. Carrier's got the firepower for that.'

'Call in a strike once we're clear,' Selina said, nodding. 'And make sure they got a good mechanic on board. I need one hell of a grease and oil change, baby.'

And then she screamed as chrome and blood dotted her face and throat. The cortex was losing its battle to convince her body the implants belonged inside her. The Messiah didn't want to share its meat with another brain.

'Hold on, Selina-love. Fuck, I've got no comms. We have to get outside of the jammers' range. Let's go.'

We hauled arse, as much as we could with her body slowly being torn apart. I heard a vehicle but didn't see anything.

We got lucky as we neared the airlock—an abandoned rover had juice in its power cells and an open ignition. Selina wasn't doing well, her body starting to burst like a fruit, the only saving grace being that the Messiah was putting her back together before she could bleed out. But her flesh was shrivelling as her body cannibalised itself to fuel the hungry force transforming it from cyberdog to something altogether different.

I could feel Selina jerking where she pressed up behind me on the seat; she locked her arms around my waist. I drove as fast as I dared, relying on my enhanced vision rather than giving away our location with headlights. Through the open bars of the roll cage, the transparent dome showed blazing stars and nebulae, and up there somewhere, our carrier.

We reached the airlock and the log showed that we were chewing the dust of the Templars. Someone had come through before us, a twenty-minute head start. Going where?

The beacon sliced through the clutter like a laser through butter. They had OGRE 2. They were guiding evac down. The crusade was beginning.

I homed in on the beacon and floored the rover. Less than an hour of darkness left. Selina needed a hospital yesterday and the sun was on its way. Regardless of the Messiah's vulnerability to rads, that distant ball wouldn't be doing either of us any favours out here; our armour could only hold back so much; there was a limit to what our implants could repair. But I reckoned, once we caught up with the Templars' Trojan Horse, sunburn wasn't something we were likely to need to worry about.

OGRE 2 was sitting planet-locked in open country, one flank protected by a lake of frosted sludge. Men in power armour stood guard. Selina was barely conscious, but she clutched at me, heaving herself to her feet behind me for a better look as I brought the rover to a stop.

'They're Templars,' she whispered, her voice reedy in my speakers. 'I can feel them.' Her vitals were all over the shop, her concentration too poor to run IM. 'They're in my head. The Messiah is going on crusade.'

'Not if I can help it.'

'They'll take you out before you get close.' Her words came in gasps. 'They'll sacrifice me for that. I'm not one of them . . . yet.'

'I thought you could stay here, actually.' I rummaged through our pack: ammo clips, ration packs . . . and thankfully, one last HEAP. 'The landing ship won't be far off, not if the Templars are risking the daylight to meet it.'

'We must've scared them good.'

'I sure hope so.'

She lifted me effortlessly and, with more strength than I knew she possessed, hurled me from the rover. I scrabbled for purchase, a helpless turtle bouncing across the tundra.

A hand to her lips in a final kiss, no further words.

She took the driver's seat and, backpack in her lap, gunned the rover towards the OGRE.

A soldier raised his weapon but another held up a hand to make him hold his fire. I was too far away to be sure, but I thought I recognised the carriage of that tall figure. I wondered if he still had Selina's cross. I wondered who was controlling her body now: my lover or the Messiah.

Weaponless save for melee blades—everything we'd rescued was on the rover—I ran after her.

A movement caught my eye. A lander, coming in, blotting out stars and nebulae, circling lower as it rode the beacon, clearly cautious because of the jamming and absence of comms.

The ship was coming down and there was nothing I could do. The OGRE would be loaded with converts; they'd take over the lander or infect the crew. And then the carrier: all the lifeblood they'd need to get back to Earth and spread the contagion further. Nowhere would be safe. The crusade would overwhelm humanity's outposts. And as long as there was blood—a breeding colony—they could travel as far and as long as they needed.

I ran towards the OGRE, waving my arms, my suit lit up, broadcasting on every frequency it could, beating against the jamming and the dark in the faint hope I could warn off the lander.

The rover reached the OGRE. Selina decelerated, coasting towards the waiting clump of Templars, and sorrow flooded me. Death was one thing. We were soldiers, after all. But what they'd done to her . . .

She accelerated into the craft's side. The explosion was so bright. A second, larger one followed. Shrapnel trailed meteorite arcs across the landscape.

The lander retreated. Spotlights stalked the planetoid's

surface, scintillating on ice, illuminating the wreckage. Flames flickered weakly amid the twisted hulk of metal.

I staggered towards the site. Maybe Selena had jumped early. Maybe the Messiah had saved her . . .

Rasputin, blackened and bloodied, emerged from the ruins wreathed in clinging smoke. The thin atmo was trying to choke him through his shattered face plate, veins road-mapping his hoary face, his phosphor-green eyes bulging. He speared towards me, flying through the low g, his outstretched arms like the talons of a striking falcon. The Messiah was working overtime to keep him going. His cheeks were pulled back tight and ashen, and all the moisture had drained from his lips and gums, turning his mouth to a furious rictus, his teeth overlong and uneven. I extended my melee blades, each a foot of pure sharp steel. And then he hit me and we tumbled, a desperate ball of fists and claws, until we came up against a boulder with a thud that damn near finished me. The Templar loomed over me, trying to smash through my mask to reach my liquid life. His flesh crawled with the Messiah, like columns of bugs running under his skin.

My blade went in under his ribs. He froze as the steel penetrated his heart. I pulled it out and he coughed up glowing blood, the barest of globs that took its own sweet time to splatter my face plate. Snarling, he raised one fist, ready to finish it.

I stabbed again, another bullseye to the heart, and he locked up. The Messiah worked overtime. But I'd learnt my lesson. I left the knife in. Try healing *that*.

A wash of light turned the world to dusty orange.

The sun speared over the horizon, casting lances of sunbeams as dawn broke. Fear flashed in the Templar's eyes but he couldn't so much as twitch.

I got my feet up underneath Rasputin and kicked out hard. He arced away, rotating slowly head over feet, restrained in that strange, leaping pose by the Messiah still labouring to bring him back from the dead. He reached the top of his arc and gravity began to exert itself. And then his face burst into flames, and then his body, a blazing Catherine wheel spinning through air. Little more than ashes touched down in a puff of smoke and embers.

When the lander's troops found me, I was still sifting through his remains, looking in vain for Selina's cross.

Jason Nahrung grew up on a Queensland cattle property and now lives in Melbourne with his wife, the writer Kirstyn McDermott. A journalist and editor, his coverage of Australian speculative fiction has earned a William Atheling Jnr Award for review and criticism. His fiction is invariably darkly themed, perhaps reflecting his passion for classic B-grade horror films and eighties goth rock. He is the co-author of the novel *The Darkness Within* (Hachette Australia), and continues to beaver away at novel-length manuscripts. Wanderlust has resulted in an enduring love affair with New Orleans and flirtations with photography. www.jasonnahrung.com

Pyaar Kiya

Angela Ambroz

In Albert Einstein's opinion, it wasn't time, it was distance. In Captain Asadullah Khan's opinion, old was old.

Asadullah knew this because he was old. He wasn't sure how old exactly, but he estimated somewhere over sixty. There were several ways to calculate old in an era of space travel: by the number of revolutions Earth made around the Sun, by the biological age of one's cells, by the distance travelled on the Drop network, by the various colonies' various calendars.

Asadullah knew that by whatever measure he used, he was old. His cells told him so: white hair, sagging genitals, creaky knees.

Before Ghada had come aboard, Asadullah had never cared about old this and young that. Everyone aboard the *Rahu Ketu* had stopped worrying about things like that ages ago. In just a few weeks they would be celebrating their tenth anniversary of being lost in space, disconnected from the Drop network and the empires, wandering in the void on their lonely life raft. When you were cut off from the rest of humanity, and your thousand co-Robinson Crusoes and Fridays were the same faces you saw every single day for ten years and would potentially see for the rest of your life, who was there to impress?

Asadullah, like most people, didn't care any more, and so he squeezed his way through the corridor crowds in a grungy uniform, holding a bottle and singing old Hindi film songs.

People marked time in a variety of ways. The New Peshawar refugees stubbornly stuck to their colony's old calendar, where one year roughly equalled one point three Earth years (this made Asadullah over eighty). The Chinese refugees used their calendar, which was one to five point five years (epically geriatric). The *Rahu Ketu* computers were rigged to Ship Standard, which was Earth standard. Either way they were in Year of the Rat, the Hindu priests were constantly reorganising their astrology, and the ship's twelfth Holi festival had just passed while Diwali was coming up strangely fast.

It all showed that time was messy and unstable. For simplicity and mental health, Asadullah chose to live from shower to shower, bottle to bottle, and leave it at that.

But Ghada's arrival complicated everything.

She had been delivered to him like a gift from Allah, like manna from heaven. The Drop network didn't stretch out this far—out here at coordinates Whatever of the galaxy Mysterious—and so it was quite a surprise to find another spaceship, just a single-person emergency pod, hurtling through the black with them. But, like the *Rahu Ketu*, this pod was here by mistake. It had taken an unmarked, unmapped Drop three weeks ago and had been spurting through the darkness, trying to find its way back to civilisation. Or so the pod's travel log transmitted.

When the tiny ship came into the *Rahu Ketu's* scanning field, there was much excitement aboard. 'Aliens!' some idiot had even said. The *Rahu Ketu's* mechanical arms had stretched out like twin fishing rods, and had dragged the pod into the loading docks downstairs. There, the pod had cracked open like an egg and revealed a shivering, starving human pilot inside. It was a young woman, Earth-born, African, and her name was Ghada Nabulaale.

Ghada! Yes, of all the trillion humans in all the eternal Universe, here was Ghada. Yes!

Fate was clearly playing tricks with Asadullah, because not only was she *the* Ghada, *his* Ghada, she was also young and magnificent and beautiful and perfect. She looked exactly as she had looked the day Asadullah had left her in London: wild hair, Nefertiti neckline, flashing eyes. By Asad's biology, that had been over forty years ago, but by Ghada's, it had been only five.

Ah, memories. They had been young together and in love, university students romping around London in the Twenty-seventh Century when things like time were comprehensible. But then the Drop network had been developed, and the Hindustani Empire had spread through space like a virus, the Chinese Empire following quickly behind. Almost immediately, politics kicked in, and space was filled with nuclear warfare, dead colonies, intergalactic speed races, time-space bending and lots of poorly connected, thinly spread humans. All this meant that Asadullah had been drafted only three months before Ghada, but had leaped ahead by forty years.

Even more depressing: when Ghada passed him in the corridors, stumbling on unsteady legs and covered in pod goo, she hadn't recognised him.

'Maybe I should dye my hair black?'

Asadullah was sitting on the floor in Balbir Singh's rooms. Balbir was the former governor of New Peshawar colony, but aboard the *Rahu Ketu*, his unofficial title was That Poor Crazy Man. The Chinese had destroyed New Peshawar almost ten years ago. Now Balbir was leaning against the pillows, sucking on a hookah and looking drunk.

'Hey Ram!' Balbir exclaimed. 'Don't be pathetic. You're old, yaar. Old, old, old. Accept it. You're not fooling anyone.'

'I'm not that old.' Asad poured both of them another drink.

'Yes, you are that old.'

'Well, you're no spring chicken yourself, bhai!'

When Balbir had come aboard, he had been in his biological prime: dark curls, heartbreaker smile. People said Balbir Singh looked like the legendary goodlookers of yore: Krishna, Romeo, Shashi Kapoor. But ten years on a steady diet of artificial lighting and Chinese liquor had turned Balbir dim and grey, like everyone else.

'So? I don't have an ex-girlfriend to impress.' Balbir belched.

'You know, I remember every detail about her. It all came flooding back. She passed me in the corridor and I smelled her and she smelled like—accha, she smelled like engine fuel and that pod placenta juice—but there are pheromones under that, na? And you know the memory centre is right here, bhai,' Asadullah pointed to his own bulbous nose. 'Right under the nose, bhai. If our pheromones clicked then, yaar, they'll click again, I'm thinking!'

Balbir stared, swaying gently. 'Yaar, what . . . exactly . . . are you thinking?'

'I'm thinking . . . ' Asad stopped. 'What? Why are you staring like that?'

'Because you're a dirty old man!'

'What?'

'You want to—to—you know! With her! Bhenchod,' Balbir spat, 'you could be her grandfather! That's disgusting!'

'I am obviously not thinking that we could resume our relationship exactly as we left it,' Asad said with dignity. 'But when two people have shared something such as Ghada and I have shared . . . well, things are complicated. It's not so easy to dismiss, yaar. We have a connection.' Asad made a fist. 'A soul connection.'

Balbir downed his drink and said nothing.

'I've decided we will be friends,' Asad said.

Balbir gave him a pained look and poured another drink. After a moment, he spoke: 'Who am I to judge? I would feel the same way, a thousand times over, if Mirabai hatched out of a pod downstairs. Ten years younger or not.'

Reluctant to re-enter the never-ending argument of dead wives and dead colonies, Asad quickly said, 'Well, right, then. So you see that I can't just ignore her. Do you know, we studied engineering together in London? Have you ever heard of Saint James Park? We used to—'

'Spare me,' Balbir muttered. 'And pass me the bottle, please.'

•

Asad didn't dye his hair black, but the next day, he went downstairs to the New Peshawar refugee levels for a haircut. There, he paid three beedi cigarettes to a boy who used an oversized, rusty-looking razor and clipped his ear twice. The boy had been born on the ship, and his legs were bent with rickets. But he had a buck-toothed eagerness that charmed Asad immediately.

'Sorry, Captain sahib.

'Oh, got the ear again. Sorry, Captain sahib.

'Shave too, sahib?'

Why the hell not? Asad opted for the shave (two beedis), but found that the white stubble had been softening his appearance in an agreeable way. Now, clean-shaven and crew-cut, he looked military and ancient, with the loose skin of his jowls revealed for all young ex-girlfriends to see.

He walked to the Medical Ward, opting for the ancient spiral stairwell instead of the lifts. The exercise got his heart pumping a healthy, regularised beat. Maybe that would calm his nerves. But his stomach still flipped every time he thought about her: wonderful, mysterious, powerful Ghada! Beautiful, terrible, transcendent Ghada! Oh, Ghada Ghada Ghada. In the name of Allah and the Prophet (peace and blessings of Allah be upon him), she was truly the glorious embodiment of sparkling, champagne perfection.

When he reached the top level and the sterile, white corridors of Med Ward, he noticed he was sweating through his jacket. This stretch of corridor was one of the few empty places on the *Rahu Ketu*. No-one wanted to live near a place of death and illness. Asad didn't blame them. He raised his arms as he walked, airing out his armpits.

In the Med Ward's lobby, Doctor Abbas caught him coming out of the sterility wash at the entrance. He waved away chalky clouds and saw her, looking composed and clean as ever. Her dark hair was up in a clip. Her saree was pressed. It all looked very clean. Eerily clean.

'Captain sahib, there you are,' Doctor Abbas said. 'We were wondering when you'd come visit our newest arrival.'

Asad swallowed.

'Are you all right?' Doctor Abbas asked, cocking her head. 'You're pale.'

'Oh, am I? Ha. Hm. Hungover. Balbir. Last night.' He waved his hand. 'You know.'

Doctor Abbas gave him a tired look. 'I see. Sobered up now, I hope? Right, come on.'

Thunk thunk, his heart said.

Ghada!

She was in the first room. She was sitting up in bed, reading her palm computer. Her cheekbones stood out sharp and jagged, her eyes were sunken. Asad could see her collarbone stark against her pyjama shirt, and he felt hot tears. Oh, his poor Ghada! Returned from the dead, returned from the past, pristine and perfect and wonderful. Poor dear, she looked so tired and unhappy. Where was her beautiful Ghada smile? Her smile had been so intoxicating, so long ago!

Asad approached cautiously, his heart pounding, his palms sweating. He wanted to kneel beside her and weep into her lap, just as he had done on the day they drafted him. He wanted to protect her, hug her, resume everything. He was starting to feel dizzy and a little inappropriately aroused and nauseous and not well at all.

'Ghada,' Doctor Abbas said. Ghada looked up. Her eyes darted once to Asad; no recognition. 'I'd like to introduce you to our captain. This is Asad Khan.'

Ghada brought her hand to her forehead in distracted formality. 'Salaam.'

Asad managed only a stammered, 'Ssss-mm.'

Did she not even recognise his name? Okay, there were probably hundreds of thousands of Asad Khans in the universe. Ah, but her voice! Her charming accent—salt of London, pepper of Kampala! Vah, vah!

'If you two will excuse me,' Doctor Abbas said, 'I should be waking Doctor Rai now. Call if you need anything, Ghada, this one's a lecher.' The doctor winked, Asad gave a nervous chuckle, the door slid shut.

Alone.

A machine by Ghada's bed tracked her heartbeat. Slow beeps filled the space between them. Ghada was looking at him, unsmiling, waiting.

'So you are . . . ' Asad began, 'you're comfortable, I hope?'

'I am.'

'I see they've given you a—a computer. Familiarising yourself with the ship? Do you have any questions—or—things—anything?'

'Yeah,' Ghada tossed the computer onto the blanket. 'I was just reading the sanitation rules. What the bhenchod does "showering buddy" mean?'

The B word! Asad didn't remember his Ghada ever talking like this.

'Oh, ha, yes, we all have, well, we have issues with water on the ship. I'm sure the doctors can advise you on finding someone who . . . You see, our life support systems are slightly, hmm, overtaxed.'

'I'm realising that.'

Asad attempted to manufacture a casual air. He leaned against one of the machines. 'So, tell me, you're from Earth?'

Ghada grunted.

'You know, I myself am also from Earth, too.'

Ghada raised an eyebrow.

'Yes, we . . . well, most of the others aboard are colonists. Refugees. You know, we picked them up after their colonies were destroyed.'

'Colonies, plural?'

'Yes, well, I mean, New Peshawar was our first pick-up . . . and then Her Shining Freedom was the second one.'

'Her Shining—what? You picked up prisoners of war? You've got Hindustani *and* Chinese?'

'Offo, not to worry. There's no war on this ship. We left the war when we Dropped out of the network.'

'Oh.' She sounded unconvinced.

Asad was a direct man. A simple, plain-spoken, quasi-military man. There was nothing to fear—even if she looked and smelled and sounded different—the jelly in Asad's knees and the fireworks in his heart clearly indicated that pheromones were pheromones, this was his Ghada. His, forever. Eternal love! And their reunion was a sign from above. Allah was definitely trying to tell him something.

He made his move:

'Anyway. So, I am thinking . . . I should mention that we, well, know each other.'

Ghada's eyes snapped up to meet his.

'Actually, more than that. We've known each other in the . . . ' Asad made a motion with his hands; heart to heart, 'sense.'

'Oh, fuck me!' Ghada reached for the red panic button and pressed it.

'No!' Asad raised his hands. 'Don't be alarmed! This isn't—I'm not really a lecher, she was joking!'

'What the hell are you talking about then?' Her voice was positively panicked. Was that a flicker of recognition he saw amidst all that fear? Were the pieces falling together? Everything seemed to be falling apart.

'Ya Allah, Ghada, it wasn't so long ago for you. Asadullah Khan? Asad! From London? It's me! Me, Ghada, your Asad only!'

Now she was terrified. 'Oh, Jesus, oh, Jesus . . . '

Asad could hear hurried footsteps in the corridor. This was not going as expected.

'You're fucking with me!' Ghada exclaimed. Again with the F word! 'You are seriously *fucking* with me!'

Exasperated, Asad took the palm computer from her bed and pressed his thumb against the biometric sensor. The little monitor manufactured a photo of him (ten years out of date), and announced mechanically: Asadullah Khan, Captain, *Rahu Ketu*, Transport Cruiser Class M. Colony of birth: Earth (original). Date of birth . . .

Ghada read all this, sweat glistening, eyes wild, Asadullah's heart thundered, the door slid open, both doctors rushed in, and then—Ghada turned and vomited over the side of the bed.

Time, one. Asadullah, zero.

•

'Pain like my brain was on fire. Pain like I was being torn in two, all the muscles ripping out into little spaghetti strings. Ya Allah, pain like someone was sucking my heart out through my solar plexus with a metal straw and reprocessing my blood into shit. I vomited a lot those days. Ate nothing. Lost so much weight.'

'Captain sahib, that is quite dramatic.'

'Well, what could I do? Love is love. It is the most horrible feeling in the world. Allah gives it to us as a trial, and to teach us . . . I don't know, something.'

Love that ends well. Love that ends in tears and a screaming fight and weight loss, or just plain military conscription. Fake love, the worst kind of all. Love that fritters away, like pulling an axe through a person's midsection slowly. Love that makes you question everything—especially your sanity. Love that you hate. Love that's irresistible. Easy love for easy people that never get upset—people in movies, your friends (the perfect ones), your parents (if you're lucky). And drama, pain, confusion and misery for everyone else.

Asadullah knew it all. He had lived through the worst of it, and knew that Happily Ever After was the most evil myth of all cultures—worse than hell.

The worst thing about love was that it changed. It came at you sideways like a raptor. Passion, all-consuming despair, magnetic lust, the crystallised notion that you *need* this person, that you will die without them, and suddenly, one day—poof—the feelings are gone. You wake up from it like from a disease; a fever in the brain and in the loins, suddenly calmed and stilled. You can't remember why you were feeling that way at all; it becomes a memory of an emotion, lost deep within yourself. You read Catullus' angry poems to Lesbia to remind yourself.

'And you think, "Ha! I am free!"' Asadullah took a long pull from his flask, 'But that is only the beginning! There are always a few more twists on the roller coaster. My God.'

You know, there are a lot of things behind the word 'love'—attraction, lust, neediness, deep affection, longing, obsession, hate, fondness, betrayal, confusion. On the more balanced end of the spectrum, compassion, maybe. But 'love' is a good shorthand for the deepest concept of all: vulnerability.

'Better yet: emotional enslavement!'

'Captain sahib,' Doctor Abbas leaned forward, elbows on knees. 'What are your plans? Ghada is very fragile right now, you know . . . '

'Ah!' Asadullah's eyes burned with tears again. 'I know, my poor little bird! Allah, what plans could I have? What do you think of me, Naziah? I want her to be happy. That's all!'

'And all this talk of raging passions . . . '

'I'm not demented, woman. I'm just trying to express my surprise at having something from long ago so easily ignited, deep inside of me.'

'Some space might be a good idea,' Doctor Abbas put a hand on Asadullah's knee. 'Some physical distance.'

Asadullah was still crying. 'We were so happy before I was drafted.'

Dear Ghada,
    I wrote you a thousand imaginary letters
in those first days in space. And I fantasised

a thousand different replies to each one.

I saw you everywhere. I kept expecting you to come around a corner and bump into me. The most improbable film, with coincidences I would never accept from the most incompetent screenwriter—that became my fantasy. The life I wanted. Every spaceship, I imagined you on it. Every waystation bar or restaurant, I imagined you going to it. I checked my messages. Even with temporal dilation, maybe there's a message: from God, from the Drop, from you. I tried not to care. But I cared, more than anything, with every part of me.

I told myself, over and over, 'Stop. You are waiting for nothing, nothing, nothing. Nothing!'

And so I waited, for nothing. But still, I kept waiting.

One who yearns for you.

There were only two Chilkur Balaji Temples in the universe: first, the ancient, famed 'Visa' Balaji Temple outside of the original Hyderabad city, where Hindu devotees would go to pray for an American visa in their passports in an age before Hindustani-Chinese imperialism, and, second, the 'Drop' Balaji Temple aboard the *Rahu Ketu*, where devotees would go to pray for survival of the next Drop and a life beyond the spaceship.

Both temples followed the same routine:

Pray to Lord Balaji for something, and walk
three or eleven times around the central
shrine.
If your wish comes true, return and complete
the remaining one hundred and eight
rotations.
No donations allowed.
Keep your eyes open when praying to God.
Turn off all communication devices.

Asadullah, like many people aboard the *Rahu Ketu*,
had long ago recognised how little control he had over his
fate, how easy it was to suffer and die, and how pointless
human troubles were in the cosmic sense. Hence he had
become a devoted circumambulator, throwing himself
at the mercy of anything mysterious and transcendental.
Before every Drop, he would join the throbbing current
of humans as they made their first three (or eleven) turns
around Lord Balaji's shrine. Asadullah often reckoned
he could literally feel the single wish rising up from the
crowd: *Please don't let me die in this Drop.*

Afterwards, the one hundred and eight post-Drop
rotations often devolved into hysterical relief—men
and women cried, throwing themselves onto the statue,
thanking God for keeping them alive again just one more
time, for a little while longer. And to do what? Asadullah
sometimes wondered. Just habitual clinging to miserable
living.

Even in the years with no Drop scheduled, the temple
would be packed. On a ship with so many problems—
disease, loss, loneliness, fear—everyone had wishes and

prayers, everyone wanted and feared hope. Asadullah had sympathy, and he liked to make appearances, and he had his own stress too.

Asadullah went on the morning after he saw Ghada in the Med Ward. He was accompanied by a slightly grumpy, still-drunk Balbir Singh. The two men got their cards and pencils from the priest, looked up towards the filthy high ceiling of pipes and painted clouds, made their private prayers, and began.

It was slow going at first. The morning mob was thick, the floor was sloped and slippery. Balbir kept bumping into Asadullah, lights flickered. When Asad and Balbir passed the wall beside the statue of Lord Balaji, they reached their hands forward with everyone else, and brought the cool stone's touch to their forehead, their mouth, their heart.

And then they punched a little hole in the card: first lap.

'Hey Bhagwan!' Balbir exclaimed, looking sombre. 'I wish for the same thing every time I come here.'

'Mmm?'

'Time! Time! Turn it back, push it forward! Just don't let me wallow in this unchanging misery. That's all I ask of God.'

'A noble desire,' Asadullah said gravely.

'You know, those Buddhists—those Chinese downstairs—they're so obsessed with the "now". The eternal "now", this and that. But God, what can a person do with "now"? Especially *here*?'

'Well, you know what they also say: life is suffering.'

'Ha! Too true. Especially in the here and now. So

speed it up, I say!'

'Analogue living!'

'Hear, hear!'

At lap twelve, despite his best intentions, Asadullah's thoughts circled back to her. His her. Ghada of the past. Ghada of the present. Ghada everywhere: Ghada's bellybutton and her hairline and her dark, perfect eyes. Asadullah looked up to the ceiling: Allah, help. Please help me. Fast-forward my pain, please.

At lap thirty-three, the priests turned the music on—a single female voice, wavering forward in devotional worship. Asadullah noticed the tears in Balbir's eyes; he was always so emotional if given a musical provocation. Asad placed a hand on his shoulder and squeezed. Balbir rewarded him with one of his broken-hearted, heartbreaker Shashi Kapoor smiles. It made Asad smile as well.

At lap forty, Asadullah remembered all the terrible things he had said to Ghada, so many years ago. Arguments and stupid, ungrateful nonsense. His feet dragged. He felt like crying himself.

At lap seventy-one, everyone picked up the pace, half-joking, cutting each other's corners and giggling. The crowd was growing impatient, giddy; people shoved a little, squeezing past each other. A Daytona 500 of religious power-walking. The music changed to an upbeat bhajan, the mood lifted. Asad started swinging a child forward by the arms. The priest steadied Balbir when he stumbled.

Eighty-six: 'Oh no. Eighty-four or eighty-five? Did I forget to tick?'

'Just do another one! It's all good for the health, na.'

'Dear, we'll be here all day with that attitude.'

Ninety-eight: 'Ten more, yaar!'

One-hundred five: 'Oh, shit. I think I forgot another one.'

'Didn't you see the sign? "Concentrate on God, not the number." And for the sake of God, language!'

'Sorry, sorry.'

One-hundred seven: Ghada Ghada Ghada . . . Stop!

She sits on her hands and bites her lip. She looks twelve, not twenty-seven. Asadullah suddenly feels much, much older—centuries older. And he feels the weight of their tragedy pressing down on his shoulders and the bridge of his nose. He wants to scoop her up in his arms. Or something.

'You betrayed me,' Ghada says, and her voice wavers. 'You evil . . . fuck.'

'Oh,' he says. 'I don't deserve that.'

Is it just him, or do they both feel unbalanced? They used to be able to read each other's minds, it seemed. Now, he feels a little dizzy. He's not sure what to do. Should he cry?

'No, you're right. You don't. I guess. It's just been years that I wanted to say that to you.'

'Hmm.'

'Sorry.'

'No, please. Don't say that, ever. But Ghada . . . '

She looks up at his use of her name.

'Your language. It's filthy!'

A smile? So beautiful—like pure heroin injected into his testicles.

'Oh, leave it, yaar. You don't know the shit I've

been through to get here. People change,' Ghada says. 'Especially when you work for the Hindustani Imperial fucking Forces.'

'Too true. Well, here we are, after all that.'

'Here we are.'

'Yes . . . '

'Jesus fucking Christ in Heaven.'

'Ghada . . . You don't know how much I wished for this. Exactly this. For years, I wished for it. A very long time.'

There is a long pause before she answers, 'I tried not to.'

Because what is there to say? They wished for it and wished for it, and now they have it, and they don't know what to do with it. Now they've erased the impossible distance, the forced separation, and age has come to ruin everything. They exist, together, but anything else is impossible. Or is it? Or isn't it? Asad has never felt so confused, so paralysed by indecision and pain.

Balbir's advice is always the same: when you don't know what to do, do nothing. But that assumes an empty mind, empty heart: peace and stillness. Balbir is comfortable living in limbo, a constant tension between two equidistant points: the past and nowhere. Balbir lives in the moment his family died, and he buries his thoughts with them, again and again, every day unchanging.

Instead Asad can't live that way. Asad is action, pro-living. And his mind is filled with a wealth of options, all of them leading to mysterious, potentially terrible ends. He hasn't been able to sleep—he survives on unsatisfying naps full of nightmares about her.

Like hunger pangs, the details of Ghada haunt him:

how she bends her wrist when she eats a sandwich, her gait, the way sunlight looks on the skin of her shoulder. And how he will never be part of that again. How it's all just passed him by.

'What is it? You suddenly looked like shit.'

'Thanks for your concern. I'm just thinking too much.'

'You never had that problem before.'

Asadullah smiles weakly.

Once, years ago, Asadullah Khan went to a psychotherapy session with Doctor Abbas in the Med Ward. Although he was encouraged to write about behaviours and feelings and tangible, correctable things, he indulged himself instead and secretly made a Hierarchy of Pain. It was full of extravagant ways in which destiny had harmed and could harm him: all the ways his loved ones would never be found again, all the horrible things he would find when the *Rahu Ketu* made its final Drop and found Earth again.

Somewhere on the pain pyramid, towards Very Painful, Asadullah had written: *Never knowing what happened to Ghada Nabulaale, my first (real) girlfriend.*

And now, here she was, and Asadullah worried about heart attacks and irritable bowel syndrome and a number of other stress-related catastrophes. A reappearance had not even made an appearance on the pain pyramid—it had been beyond consideration. It was Sublimely Terrible.

On Wednesday, Ghada came striding into the *Rahu Ketu* command centre, wearing military fatigues and running her hand over her hair over and over again. Asad felt his stomach drop, warm and heavy. He suddenly remembered, one thousand light-years ago, when Ghada and he had been listening to U2's 'With or Without You', and Ghada had said, solemnly, 'I love this song.' What did she mean by that, anyway?

Ghada paused. She swallowed. She didn't meet his eyes, and then she said, in front of everyone, 'Asad, I don't want to ever see you again. Please leave me alone.'

Ya Allah!

Two torturous days later, Ghada came striding into the *Rahu Ketu* cockpit, wearing military fatigues and looking like she had just been crying. With a shaky voice, she said, in front of everyone, 'Can we talk?'

I'm too old for this, Asad thought.

Maybe being friends was an option? No, no, it was definitely not an option. But why can't it be an option? Taming unruly thoughts and unruly desires and bad, terrible memories. Can we talk about something other than our situation? No, no, definitely not. Seeing each other is not a good idea. The idea of not seeing you is too terrible, too dramatic, impossible. So what now? Let's talk again in two weeks. Oh wait, I'll drop by tomorrow. But no more discussion. We should never speak again, actually. I'll see you on Tuesday. I missed you. I loved you—no, no, I forgot you after a few days. Days? I love you now. Oh! Forget I said that. I love you like a friend. A good friend, a family member. Why can't we just chat?

Asadullah stilled his trembling fingers and turned the glass of whiskey around in his hands. Ghada watched him, silent.

'I understand if . . . ' Asad began.

'No, look,' Ghada interrupted. 'The Big Drop fucks—'

Asad shifted, clearing his throat.

'Sorry, *screws* with your head, but it doesn't screw with it that much,' Ghada said. 'I know what it's like to think it's all over. I understand. To think you're going to die out here in this—nothingness.'

'Yes, this vast vacuum of vastness.'

'Right. And no-one deserves to think that. And so we should take what we can get. Whatever the universe throws at us. So, I was thinking, no more memories. No more flashbacks. And definitely no reminiscing. We start from scratch. Today.'

'Today?'

'And we'll see if this friends thing works out after all. And then we can say fuck—sorry, screw—you, universe! Sound good?'

Asad shrugged.

'Good.' Ghada stuck out her hand. 'Ghada Nabulaale. Nice to meet you.'

Asad paused, hesitating. It was funny. Or sad. He took her hand and shook it too. 'Nice to meet you, young lady. Asadullah Khan. I captain this vessel.'

Ghada smirked.

'So you drive the ship?'

'Among other things.'

'And your accent—Delhi Prime?'

'Earth, actually. London.'

'No shi—no kidding.' Ghada feigned surprise. 'I'm from London myself!'

Angela Ambroz has lived in Germany, Italy, the UK, India, Fiji and, most recently, Boston. Other stories from the Dropverse can be found in *GigaNotoSaurus*, *Strange Horizons* and *Expanded Horizons*. When not writing fiction, she works on international development and writes a movie review blog, the Post-Punk Cinema Club at http://p-pcc.blogspot.com

So Sad, the Lighthouse Keeper

Steve Cameron

I am alone and I float in space. I watch, and warn, and wonder. I sometimes go to the zero-grav room and watch the brick float.

But I am always alone.

Janice told me I was a cold fish. She told me I wasn't the same man she'd married. She told me I wasn't fun any more, that I was boring and predictable. She told me I needed to spend less time reading my books. She told me I needed to get a hobby. She told me I needed to get out and meet people. She told me I needed to make some friends and to stop spending so much time alone. She told me I didn't understand people. She told me I needed to show more interest in her.

I told her I was happy the way things were.

Sunday mornings were my mornings. I liked to sleep in, stay in bed propped up by pillows, drink coffee, eat muffins and read the papers. She wanted to go out early, be seen in trendy cafes and roam around markets. None of this appealed, but it occurred to me that maybe I should compromise. She was my wife and weren't married couples supposed to spend quality time together?

One Sunday, I told her I would go along with her to

a market.

The supply ship is a couple of weeks overdue. Once every six months it punches in, its huge hyperspace engines silently roaring. Having traversed the sixteen light years from Earth in a few short weeks, it arrives laden with all I require until it calls again. Along with the necessities are a couple of chips containing six months of news, a stack of music files and a range of vids. My only indulgence is a few actual books I ordered the previous visit. The ship has only ever been overdue once before, and that was by just three days due to a mechanical failure.

I'm not overly concerned at this stage. I know there must be a good reason for the delay. They wouldn't just leave me here, would they? There is at least six months of supplies in the emergency holds, but it would be great to have a new vid of Linda Fox.

While Janice was rummaging through the second-hand goods, I spent an hour browsing the tables of books. Her glower suggested she was not pleased. I couldn't see why she was so upset. I'd made the effort and was at the market with her, wasn't I? Why was it acceptable for her to trawl through stalls of junk, but I was boring and predictable when I spent my time searching through boxes of books? She was the one who said I needed a hobby. Isn't reading a hobby?

I spend an entire day watching the coloured swirls on the panel. The 'dolphins', as they are commonly known, are particularly active today; not that they are ever idle for long, but just now they seem more playful, more joyous, more alive. They soar and swoop, barrel-roll, flip, dive and swim. As always the sensors, cameras and computers record it all before the preliminary analysis and compilation of data. Sometimes I stare at the other screens, the ones that continuously flash strings of numbers and digits. And although they have their own beauty nothing can compare to the sheer splendour of the dolphins' dance when they are in this mood.

For a moment I watched Janice across the crowded stalls until she realised. She stared back at me and my books with contempt, so I decided it might be best to acquiesce. I was here at the market. I was compromising, making an effort, but it obviously wasn't enough. I sighed, bought the paperbacks I had safely tucked under my arm and reluctantly left the book sellers behind. I trailed after Janice and headed for the bric-a-brac stalls. Janice was sorting through a table of old crockery: pots, vases and statuettes. She seemed intent on finding some sort of china to take home. I had no desire to search through tables of junk but perhaps it was all for the best that I not antagonise her any further.

I drifted in the direction of a nearby stall that displayed a lot of military collectibles. Although I wasn't overly interested in the war years, I figured it was likely to be slightly more enjoyable than ceramics. Janice didn't look too thrilled but at least she didn't say anything. She was probably just relieved it wasn't books again.

I spent some time feigning interest in badges and patches before my attention was drawn to a stack of old newspapers. The yellowing pages of the top one were obscured by a brick, a house brick that had obviously been placed there to prevent the papers from blowing away. I moved it to look at the top folded newspaper, and I felt its weight in my hand. It felt solid, and I enjoyed the roughness of the surface against my skin. I held the brick before me and took pleasure in its mass. The weight felt good, really good, so I asked the owner how much it was.

'Seventy each, a hundred if it's pre-war.'

'No,' I replied, 'I mean the brick.'

He was puzzled. 'The brick? It's not for sale. It's only holding down the papers.'

I insisted, and after a few minutes he accepted fifty for it. He moved a brass shell from the other side of the stall to replace it, and offered me a neo-plas bag for my purchase.

We presume the dolphins were there long before us and that interstellar space is their home and we, in our spacecraft, are the intruders. Our first encounter was when a couple of ships collided with them, vanished and were never seen again. We didn't actually know about them at that stage, and we still don't know really what happened to those ships. They simply hit something we couldn't see. There certainly appeared to be no malice from the dolphins, or any other sort of deliberate behaviour or emotion. We hadn't even imagined their existence and had no way to detect them. Eventually physicists were able to develop sensors through which we could 'see' these concentrations of energy, of life, of . . . something. And as we became aware of them, as they danced and looped and swirled and leaped, the scientists sparred for the honour to sit in this station and observe. They sat here to study and analyse and hoped to claim fame and riches as the first to understand and quantify them.

And to keep the ships away.

While the sensors keep track of the dolphins, the station follows their movements from a safe distance and emits warnings to any passing traffic, increasingly rare though it is. Like an ancient lighthouse, the station ensures the ships stay away from the shoals.

The first team offered a scientific Latin name, but it was 'space dolphins' one reporter used after the government released vids of their seemingly eternal dance. Media won out over science and the popular name stuck. The first scientists wanted to launch drones at the dolphins to examine what would happen, but environmental protesters on Earth put an end to that after comparing the action to throwing large rocks at whales. And so all we could do was watch and gather data. After twenty-two years of scientific analysis there was little further comprehension. No discernable patterns or repetition were found in their dances. No interaction or communication had occurred with humans. The public had long ago lost interest in the recorded images. As a result, the government cut its funding, the teams were replaced by individuals, until even the most patient of physicists eventually became bored with endless babysitting and retreated to planet Earth. While the researchers happily viewed the vids and data from the distant comfort of their labs, the government offered the adventure to any other scientist who could justify wanting to twiddle his thumbs in space.

Janice was definitely not happy. We were back home in our bedroom. She'd opened my bag to see what I'd bought. The brick was in her hand. She angrily thrust it toward me, and I took it from her.

'It's a brick? You bought a brick? What's so special about it?'

I thought of an acquaintance of mine who really did own a special brick. It was a commemorative brick from the 1956 Melbourne Olympic Village and had the five Olympic rings embossed on one side. He proudly displayed it in his pool room. This, however, was not a special brick. It was just a brick.

'Nothing,' I said. 'It's just a brick.'

'Just a brick,' she repeated. 'Why the hell did you buy it?'

'I liked it,' I said softly. 'It feels good. Touch it.'

She slammed the door, and was gone. After a few minutes, I opened the door again and used the brick to prop it open.

The computers and machines don't make a sound but sometimes even I find the silence within the station too intense. Sometimes we need some noise, something outside our own heads. I don't feel like any of the ambient recordings today—bird noises, waves lapping on beaches or murmured distant traffic—but I don't want silence. I press the switches that cause the machines to emit unnecessary hums and clicks. For now, it is enough. I prowl the halls and turn off the lights as I go. I find my way up to the zero-grav room and float in the darkness with only a single panel displaying the dolphins and a million diamond stars shining through the neo-plas walls to illuminate me.

After an hour I switch off the machine noise and instead

listen to a Linda Fox concert, an old one. For a while the dolphins seem to synchronise and dance to her soaring voice. The music fills the station and it relaxes me.

One summer afternoon, my brother and his wife invited us over for a barbecue. I didn't want to go, but Janice insisted. I sat on their patio, under their pergola, and sipped a beer as Rob casually flipped the steaks on the barbecue. Emily brought out a plate of onions. 'Here you go, sweetie.'

'Thanks, honey,' Rob replied as he spread them across the hotplate. They sizzled, sending up a cloud of greasy smoke. He watched her intently as she went back into the kitchen. Later, when she brought out the sauces and salads, they stole a kiss. From behind my sunglasses I observed this.

The hours spent analysing the dolphins are punctuated by time spent maintaining the station and myself. I exercise regularly, running on the treadmill and lifting weights. While the auto-grav ensures I won't lose all my muscle definition, I still must workout to remain fit. The station too needs repairs. The computer informs me of a fault in one of the memory chips, and I search through circuit boards to find the one that is malfunctioning. It only takes a few minutes to replace, but I spend an entire afternoon attempting to recover the data that was stored there. I quickly determine that this chip held all my old photos—childhood, family, graduation, wedding snaps—and part of my music collection, including my favourite Linda Fox album. I have no backup on the station. I finally surrender to the futility of the task, and rather than store the board for return to Earth I decide to jettison it. I gaze as it exits the airlock and slowly tumbles end on end until it is quickly lost against the blackness of space. It is only at that point I realise I should have turned the station slightly. I should have made sure it wasn't aimed at the dolphins.

As we ate, I watched Rob's children jumping in and out of the swimming pool. The kids were yelling and chasing, jumping and splashing. There seemed to be some order behind the apparent chaos, but if there were any rules to their game I couldn't figure it out. At one point my brother jumped in and joined them for a while. The children squealed in delight as he grabbed them unexpectedly and threw them across the water. When he returned to the table, drying himself off with a towel and reaching for a beer, I asked him about the game they'd been playing. He just shrugged and said, 'They're just playing. Having fun, you know?' I found myself nodding in agreement, but I didn't really know what he meant. I watched the water splashing over the sides and opened another beer.

Later, as dusk was falling, we sat around the table, talking. The soft, blue glow from the lit pool washed the fences around us. The surface of the water swirled and rippled as the pool-spider crept automatically across the bottom, sucking, filtering, cleaning. It cast underwater shadows that moved, stretching and distorting against the walls of the pool. Janice and Emily chatted about the kids, while Rob and I talked about sports until the conversation turned to the dolphins.

'You're the man of science. What do you think they are? And why haven't they communicated with us?'

I shrugged. 'I have no idea. I've looked at some of the data, but we're not really gathering anything that explains them yet. We observe, and measure, but it's all empirical. And that doesn't help us understand them.'

'Maybe they're not sentient,' he suggested.

'Maybe,' I agreed, and watched the patterns on the surface of the pool. A leaf fell from an overhanging branch and settled on the water. 'Maybe they're not even alive. Maybe it's simply a natural physical or even quantum phenomenon. Something we haven't yet understood.' I thought for a moment, watching as the leaf was tossed by an eddy created by the underwater cleaner. 'Or maybe the dolphins are a by-product of living beings elsewhere.'

Rob frowned. 'You mean, like faeces?' We both laughed.

'More like an exhaust, or a wake. Like seeing waves hit the shore minutes after a speedboat has crossed a lake. Maybe we need to look elsewhere for the actual creatures.'

I continued to stare intently at the leaf as it swirled on the water while Rob snorted at this.

'Next you'll be saying they're in another dimension.'

I laughed with him.

On the station I have all I need. I am surrounded by my books, my music and my thoughts. Linda Fox accompanies me as I perform my daily rituals. I continue to maintain the machines and process the data, although I have no idea whether anyone is ever coming to collect it. I'm no closer to understanding the dolphins than any of the other scientists that preceded me. All I have are numbers and recordings—none of which proves my theories. The dolphins continue their dance, and I continue to be their sole audience.

It was dark by the time we drove home, windows down. The summer evening was heavy with humidity and the inside of the car was heavy with silence. I keyed some Linda Fox on the player, but Janice snapped it off. The silence resumed. Eventually I experimentally tried adding a 'honey' to the end of one of my sentences.

'Do we need anything from the store, honey?' I asked. Ironically, the word sounded thick and viscous as it tumbled from my lips. Janice stared at me for a moment, before shaking her head and turning to look back out the window.

I tried to call her 'honey' once more the following day. It didn't seem right then either.

It takes me a few moments to realise the dolphins have done something out of the ordinary. The monitors, as usual, display the sequences of numbers that measure the dolphins and their behaviour, while I bathe in the glow of the panels showing their coloured swirls. Suddenly a group of three, one red, one blue and one yellow, break from the formation and dart directly towards the station, coming to within a few thousand kilometres of where I sit, before pausing for a few minutes and racing back to join the others. I stare, mouth open, before replaying the vid a few times. Perhaps I'd been mistaken. Perhaps they are sentient after all, and are now curious about the station that follows them. Perhaps they are responding to the Linda Fox chip I threw them. Or maybe the photos of Janice. I almost smile at the thought.

For the next hour I pore over the last twenty years of records, trying to discover any similar instances of behaviour. I am unable to find anything like this at all and so I decide to override the autopilot and fire the thrusters in an attempt to emulate the dolphins. I feel the forces pull on my face and chest, my arms and legs as the station accelerates towards them, before pausing, reversing and retreating to its usual position. I obviously cannot move as fast or as far as they can, and I hope my small token movement is enough for them to recognise it as a response. For a whole day afterwards I watch them intently, waiting for a sign, any indication that they comprehend, but there is none. I cannot see any reason or explanation for their movement towards me, and must conclude it was coincidental.

A few days later the data indicates they are starting to fade, losing luminescence. Hour by hour they are slowly, very gradually leaving me behind.

Not only am I still unable to prove any of my theories, I now have new pieces to add to the puzzle.

Janice despised the brick. She threatened to throw it into the garden. It sat heavily in the corner of the room but I enjoyed its reassuring presence. It calmed me. One time she woke me up with her swearing as she stubbed her toe on it. Janice angrily picked the brick up and threw it onto the bed next to me. It bounced once and came to rest alongside me.

'Get rid of that bloody thing! It's either me, or the brick!'

That was the first thing she had said to me in more than a week. I looked at Janice, and then at the brick. I could see no good reason to get rid of it.

She moved out two days later.

It has now been six weeks. The supply ship is not coming and I have convinced myself of this. I don't know what has happened to it and ultimately the reason makes no real difference. I could spend some hours attempting to adjust the antenna back toward Earth and transmit a signal, but there is little point. It would take sixteen long years to reach its destination. In six short months I will run out of food, although the recycled water and air will last longer than I will. Computers and machines will start to malfunction and there will be no-one to maintain and repair them. Finally the sensors and recorders will fail and there will be no more data to analyse. The station will become an empty husk and the dolphins will continue on their way, their eternal, beautiful choreography unseen by humans. I go to the zero-grav room to watch them dance. To accompany the dolphins I play Linda Fox again and I know that I will loop the recording over and over and over.

As soon as they announced they were looking for replacements, I applied. I was able to put together a solid proposal suggesting that maybe the dolphins weren't lifeforms at all, but rather the trans-dimensional wake of other creatures travelling through a parallel universe. I also suggested that the missing ships had somehow been sucked through a breach in the space-time continuum rather than destroyed. I have no real idea whether this is true or not, or even how to go about proving it, but someone up there obviously liked the idea—or perhaps they were just ready to try anything new. Somehow I made it through to the final cut. There were tests and more tests and assessments and psychological exams. I guess it helped that I was a cold fish, as Janice had said, and that I loved to spend time reading my books and enjoyed my solitude. I was finally selected, and after a few months of training I stepped onto the station. The last biologist on board grabbed my hand and pumped it enthusiastically. It was obvious he'd been alone on the station for three years, as he talked relentlessly and explained everything over and over again. A few days later, as the supply ship was about to depart, I was relieved when he shook my hand for the last time and wished me luck. As soon as I could, I closed the airlock door behind him. I watched as the supply ship punched out.

I was now the most isolated human in the galaxy.

As they continue to fade, I spend the limited time I have scanning ahead of and around the dolphins. I'm looking for any anomaly that suggests where the actual beings might be, but I find nothing. The space there is as empty as the space where the supply ship should punch in. I'm lost as to what to do next. I feel as though I have no real way to prove the existence of something I'm not even sure is there. More than that, I'm losing them.

One morning, while watching the dolphins, I have an epiphany, a moment, a divine instant when I suddenly realise there is a way to prove my theory. It is, in fact, the only possible way of testing my hypothesis before they are gone forever. I start to make my plans, and prepare all the recorders and detection units on the station. For days I neglect the ever diminishing dolphins as I, accompanied only by Linda Fox, compile all my notes and load them onto a buoy.

About a year ago I received the news that Janice and her new husband had both been killed in a car accident. She'd moved to the country after marrying a builder and had happily settled in to small town life. I was told they'd been hit by a drunk driver. The community was devastated. I was sixteen light years away, and couldn't make it to the funeral. I didn't even know about it until much later. Apparently my brother and his wife went on my behalf.

It will take approximately three weeks for the station to arc its way into the path of the dolphins, just enough time before they leave our space. I once again disarm the autopilot and program the station's course, before launching the first of the buoys armed with an UltraDef camera and a battery of detectors aimed at the intersection point. The others I will release at various locations to capture the moment of impact from different angles. If the supply ship ever returns here, they will locate the beacons transmitting from the buoys and hopefully glean some new information from the recorded images and data. They might even theorise as to what happened to the station after the collision.

But only I will know for sure.

> I am alone and I float in space. I watch, and
> wait, and wonder. And, as the dolphins loom
> ever closer, I sometimes go to the zero-grav
> room and watch the brick float.
> And I am always alone.

Steve Cameron is a writer of speculative fiction. Born in Scotland, he was raised in Australia before residing in Japan for six years. He has worked as a police officer, an English Language instructor, a software developer, a charity store manager and currently teaches English and Drama in a Secondary College. Steve is also an amateur astronomer and musician. With such a varied and rich background, he is fortunate to have a wealth of experience to draw on for his writing. He resides in the eastern suburbs of Melbourne with his wife, Lindsey.

Coeur de Lion

also from
coeur de lion
publishing

X⁶ — a novellanthology

Journey beyond the borders of the real with six all new novellas from the most exciting speculative fiction authors working in Australia today –

Margo Lanagan, Terry Dowling, Paul Haines, Louise Katz, Trent Jamieson and Cat Sparks.

A Locus Magazine 'Recommended Read' of 2009

'in the race for the "Best Anthology of The Year" title'
Gardner Dozois — *Locus Magazine*
'a resounding six of the best for anyone who still doubts the novella is the ideal length for speculative fiction'
Sean Williams — #1 New York Times bestselling author of *The Grand Conjunction*

Winner - World Fantasy Award for best novella —
'Sea-Hearts' by Margo Lanagan

Winner - Aurealis Award for Horror Short Fiction
Winner - Sir Julius Vogel Award for Best Novella
Winner - Ditmar Award for Best Novella —
'Wives' by Paul Haines

to buy online or to see our list of stockists go to
www.coeurdelion.com.au

ISBN 9780646510354

Rynemonn

Terry Dowling

Blue Tyson, Tom O'Bedlam, Tom Rynosseros; the man from the Madhouse who won Blue and a fine sandship from the tribes. The Coloured Captain who roams the interior, searching out a hidden purpose, the secret knowledge which affects not only Nation but the Dreamtime itself.

In eleven linked stories Tom will uncover his origins, discover what truly happened in the Madhouse and learn the meaning of the three signs that have haunted his life. In Rynemonn, the Blue Captain will come home.

'At once epic and intimate, sweepingly romantic and stirringly adventurous, the Tom Tyson stories stand amongst the very best work that science fiction has to offer. A book to be treasured.'
— Jonathan Strahan

'The only contemporary writer who comes close to that wondrous talespinner, Cordwainer Smith.'
— Locus

to buy online or to see our list of stockists go to
www.coeurdelion.com.au

ISBN 9780646477879

c0ck - adventures in masculinity

*A decidedly original collection of new
Australian speculative fiction*

Just what does it mean to be a man now, in the future, the past, other realities?

Find the answer in eleven all new stories by Lucy Sussex, Richard Harland, Geoffrey Maloney, Stephen Dedman, Chris Lawson, Cat Sparks, Robert Hood, Adam Browne and John Dixon, Jacinta Butterworth, and Paul Haines.

'This slim volume features eleven disturbing, humiliating, gratifying,annoying and mind-blasting stories … A brilliant debut collection.'
— Orb Magazine

'The first title from a new Australian small press is an exploration of masculinity through the speculative fiction short story. There is some impressive work here. This is the kind of project which can only be done by the small press, and which makes the small press essential.'
— Aurealis

**Featuring the 2006 Ditmar winning novella by Paul Haines
'The Devil in Mr Pussy'**

to buy online or to see our list of stockists go to
www.coeurdelion.com.au

ISBN 9780646462066

www.ingramcontent.com/pod-product-compliance
Lightning Source LLC
Chambersburg PA
CBHW060807120726
47909CB00006B/1808